HARP SONG

Vivienne Maxwell

Cover design by Claire Barker

ISBN 978-0-9569207-9-9

THORNS OF TRUTH

HARP SONG

THORNS OF TRUTH

DEDICATION

To Richard

Who was there at the beginning,
and the end,
and every step in between.

With love and thanks

THANKS

As always, go to Claire Barker, who has created all five book covers, and whose skill in taking my vague ideas and transforming them gives a glimpse into that other, sometimes fey, realm that lives inside my head.

Also to Rick Deveau-Maxwell,
who kindly allowed me to take his original verse
and adapt it to suit my harper's needs.

Finally to all my family - Richard, Rick, Jamie and Alex -
for their love, patience and support,
which has allowed me to see this saga through to the end.

Dramatis Personae

ROYAL FAMILY OF THE REALM OF MITHLONDIA
Prince Raymund*
Prince Marcus II* – born 1145, the only legitimate son of Prince Raymund, died 1194
Prince Linnius IV   succeeded 1194
Linette – his sister, bound to Prince Kaslander of Kaerellios

DE CHARTREUX
Annette (Anne)* – Gilles de Valenne's natural daughter by Aneta de Lacey, briefly Lady of Chartreux, sent back to Valéntien after the birth of the son sired by Prince Raymund on the eve of her binding to Arnaud de Chartreux, now living in Lasceynes Forest
Lucius Raymund (Louis)* – former Lord of Chartreux, arrested on a charge of high treason and executed as a traitor in 1194
Lucius Valéri (Luc) – his only legitimate son, now an outlaw living in Lasceynes Forest
Rowène – Luc's sister, believed to have died in childbirth in 1195, now living in Lasceynes Forest as an outlaw known as Jacques of Chartre. Also known as Sister Fayla, by the healers at Vézière
Alysiène Annette (Lissie) – Rowène's daughter by Guyard de Martine, but acknowledged by Joscelin de Veraux as his child at her birth in the Palace of Princes in 1195
Valéri Lucius (Val) – the son of Juliène de Chartreux and Ranulf de Rogé, conceived during the sack of Chartre castle in 1194

DE LACEY
Justin – Lord of Lasceynes and the Rathen Fells
Nerice – Lady of Lasceynes, daughter of Robert and Marguerite de Vitré

DE LYEYNE
Isabelle – Dowager Lady of Lyeyne, widow of Henri, mother of Hervé, elder daughter of Guillaume de Veraux
Hervé – Henri and Isabelle's eldest son, now Lord of Lyeyne
Juliène – Hervé's second wife, Rowène de Chartreux's twin sister

Herluin – Hervé's son from his first binding
Léon – Hervé's younger brother

DE MARILLEC
Jean – Lord of Marillec
Gabriel – heir to the lordship of Marillec, currently Second of the Guardians, friend and foster-brother to Luc de Chartreux
Bayard – Jean de Marillec's younger son, born of his second wife

DE MARTINE
Alys* – the only daughter of Armand de Martine, companion to Rosalynde de Rogé, died in the Beggars' House in Montfaucon in 1161 soon after the birth of her son
Guyard – the illegitimate son of Alys de Martine and Jacques de Rogé, formerly Governor of Rogé, Chartreux and Valenne, a slave at the royal Kardolandian court since 1197
Mathilde – Guyard's estranged wife, tire-maid to Ariène de Rogé
Gaston – castellan of Montfaucon, brother to Alys de Martine
Mariette – Gaston's ambitious wife
Adèle – daughter to Gaston and Mariette, betrothed (not by choice) to Gabriel de Marillec

DE ROGÉ
Jacques* – previous Lord of Rogé, died at the hands of Lucius de Chartreux in 1176
Rosalynde* – his lady, sister to Henri de Lyeyne, died in 1169
Joffroi – Lord of Rogé, Chartreux and Valenne, Chief Counsellor to Prince Linnius
Ariène – formerly Lucius de Chartreux's lady until his attainder and execution, now bound to Joffroi, mother of Luc, Rowène, Juliène and Raoul
Ranulf – Joffroi's younger brother, the rightful Lord of Valenne by his grandsire's will, assumed to have died by Taneth-Rath Tarn in 1196, now serving as a royal guardian under the name of Rafe of Oakenleigh
Raoul – Joffroi and Ariène's only son and heir to all Joffroi's vast, ill-gotten wealth and land

DE VALENNE
Gilles* – Lord of Valenne, ambushed and killed by Taneth-Rath Tarn by Joffroi de Rogé in 1196
Justinian* – Eldest of the Brothers of Peace of Falconsford, Gilles' younger brother, died peacefully at Falconsford in 1199

DE VERAUX
Guillaume – former Lord of Veraux, father of Isabelle and Céline
Joscelin – present Lord of Veraux and High Commander of Mithlondia's Guardians, commonly believed to be the illegitimate son of Prince Marcus II
Céline – Joscelin's mother, once Lucius de Chartreux's mistress, the mother of his unacknowledged son, now the Eldest of the healers of Vézière, known variously as Sister Héloise or Sister Herluva

DE VÉZIÈRE
Nicholas – Lord of Vézière
Hal – his only son and heir

COMMONERS
Aedde – a fisherman of the Star Isles
Aedwald – an old fisherman, Aedde's father's father
Aelflin – Aedde's young daughter
Aedgyth – a kitchen maid working the Healing House in Vézière
Aelric of Anjélais – one of the outlaws of Lasceynes Forest, a runaway from a village in Chartreux
Jarec of Anjélais – his younger brother, groom to Ranulf de Rogé
Aelfraed, Beorn, Halfiren and Maury – Nicholas de Vézière's household musicians
Alfgar and Eadric – respectively steward at Vézière castle and Nicholas de Vézière's body-servant
Hilarion of Valéntien* – Gilles de Valenne's eldest natural son, garrison commander at Valéntien, hanged, drawn and quartered at Joffroi de Rogé's orders on a false charge of treason in 1196
Ancalion of Valéntien* – Gilles de Valenne's younger natural son, died shortly after being attacked by Joffroi de Rogé's men at Taneth-Rath Tarn in 1196

Gwynhere of Valéntien – Ancalion's sister and Hilarion's beloved, now living in Lasceynes Forest

Beowulf of Mallowleigh – once headman of a village in Rogé, he became Rowène de Chartreux's bodyguard in 1195

Melangel – Beowulf's woman, once Joffroi de Rogé's mistress, mother of Linnet, Wulfric, Benet and Merula

Linnet and Wulfric – Joffroi de Rogé's two surviving by-blows

Benet and Merula – Beowulf's son and daughter

Beric, Siward and Ulric – soldiers in the Mithlondian army

Birch, Cherry and Willow – prostitutes working at the Crowing Cockerel in Vézière

Brec – a boy in the Vézière household, son to Brett

Brett and Dickon – soldiers of the Vézière garrison

Bryce – Justin de Lacey's chief huntsman

Dominic Fitzjoscelin – Joscelin de Veraux's illegitimate son

Caitlyn – a whore, originally from Marillec, rescued from the Black Lily in Lamortaine and brought back to Lasceynes Forest by Luc de Chartreux

Edwy of Rogérinac – formerly the garrison commander at Rogérinac, then Guyard de Martine's body-servant, now bodyguard to Guy's daughter and Ranulf's son

Geryth – formerly groom to Guyard de Martine, now known as Gryff, a groom in the Vézière household

Gerde* - Geryth's sister, once Ranulf de Rogé's mistress, she died in childbirth and his illegitimate son with her

Gilraen – a seller of musical instruments in Lamortaine

Guthlaf* – Jacques de Rogé's right-hand man, died at Joffroi's hand in 1196 at Taneth-Rath Tarn

Ulf* – a man of Rath-na-Cael, hanged by the Black Hunt

Nessa – his woman

Nick – formerly Luc de Chartreux's squire, now his bodyguard

Oswin One-Eye – Joffroi de Rogé's chief torturer and captain of the Black Hunt

Siflaed – Juliène de Lyeyne's tire-maid

Mildrith (Millie) – her sister

Sister Winfreda – senior healer after the Eldest at the Healing House in Vézière

CATS
Amber and Jade – Princess Linette's pampered, if unpredictable, pets
Lyra – a wild cat living at the Healing House in Vézière
Mist – also known as Pearl, a very special cat indeed, beloved
companion to the Moon Goddess of the Faennari herself

* deceased – for the most part in unpleasant, unnatural or suspicious
circumstances

HARP SONG

Rain falls upon my face,
And stars reveal our fate.
I know, if I look towards the sky,
I will see, my family long gone,
Stars, show yourself to me,
Send to me a sign.
I will raise a horn for you,
A blade for you will shine.

Stars, never fear for us,
Those you left behind.
For we will make you proud.
Harper, healer, warriors we,
Fey and mortal both,
We honour you and await,
The day when you will welcome us
Onto those gilded golden shores.

PROLOGUE

LATE SUMMER/EARLY AUTUMN

1202

GUYARD

Gods, but I never thought I would see this day!

Guyard de Martine took one last step against the tugging current as the fierce undertow tried to drag him back to sea, the foaming white waves splashing with a nasty chill against bare legs accustomed to the silken warm waters of the southern ocean.

Taking three paces up the beach, he dropped to his knees, just as the dawn light drew the first blush of pale pink colour from the cool sands, so different to the grey and white pebbles and stark black granite cliffs he remembered, and yet... this was still Mithlondia, the land of his birth.

Gods help him, he was *home*!

One of the sailors who had accompanied him from the small boat presently rocking on the waves just off the shore laid his pack on the sand beside him, and with a brief farewell in Kardolandian – a language with which he had perforce become all too familiar – waded back into the sea.

Left alone, Guy stumbled to his feet, his legs not yet accustomed to the unmoving land, and then stood still and watched, shading his eyes against the dazzling glitter of the rising sun, as the smaller boat returned to the sleek vessel anchored out in deeper waters.

Feeling some obscure sense of obligation, he remained there unmoving until finally the huge white sail of the *Royal Xandra* was raised, filling with the morning breeze to belly out beneath the flickering golden streamers of the Kardolandian banner.

Only when the ship was no more than a speck on the southern horizon did he breathe a sigh, turning his back on the sea and the last reminder of his former life.

Bending, he picked up the pack that contained all he now owned, checking it over in his mind.

One pair of sandals of Kardolandian workmanship.

A spare linen tunic similar to the one he was wearing, and a light wool mantle – neither of which would provide much by way of warmth or protection from the Mithlondian elements.

The silver slave ring that had become so much a part of him that almost he missed the weight of it now that it was no longer about his neck.

And finally, a small pouch of Mithlondian coins, bronze marks for the most part, and a couple of silver half-nobles.

Little enough in all truth but still considerably more than he had possessed when he had first arrived at the slave market in Kaerellios – half out of his mind with fever, lacking sword, harp and even his name, naked save for a ragged loin cloth – this having been stripped from him before he had been put on the auction block – and the filthy bandage that had been wrapped about the swollen flesh and broken bones of his right hand.

Now flexing that same hand – mended not by a Kardolandian physician but by the peculiar healing skills of the Mithlondian outlaw who had, most unexpectedly, turned up in Kaerellios soon after his own arrival – Guy reminded himself that while it was undoubtedly asking for another death sentence to reclaim either his given or his family name, let alone make any rash attempt to regain his sword or harp from the man who had callously condemned both his brothers to death, he did once more have the means of earning a living for himself.

For his pack, surprisingly heavy for all it contained so little, held something far more precious than clothes or coins, and with the weight of it singing softly against his shoulder, he set off across the sandy beach, heading westwards for the mainland.

A land he would never have seen save for the hard bargain driven on his behalf by that same Mithlondian outlaw with the Kardolandian queen, and while there had been many times when Guy had thought he would never be able to endure the terms set on his eventual release, he *had* fulfilled his side of the agreement, and somewhat to his surprise the queen had in her turn kept her word.

And so, five long years after he had been forcibly exiled, here he stood on the shores of Mithlondia's Star Isles.

The harper, it would seem, had finally returned.

JULIÈNE

Goddess, no! It cannot be so!

With a startled cry, Juliène de Lyeyne recoiled from the calm, lily-studded water of the palace fish pond, the raised rim of which she had been seated upon, idly watching the great golden carp as they swam lazily through the darker depths.

Glancing about her to make sure that no-one had witnessed her odd behaviour, she bent forwards to peer, with no little trepidation, into the darkly gleaming water.

As the goddess must surely know, scrying had been the last thing on her mind when she had chosen to pause by the pond, seeking only a few moments of peace away from her mother's watchful green gaze and her wearisome questioning as to whether her daughter had managed to "see" or sense anything of Guyard de Martine's present whereabouts.

Lady Ariène was so determined that Guyard would return – and that Juliène would seduce and destroy him when he did – that she rarely allowed her daughter out of her sight, and Juliène was beginning to feel the strain of this constant surveillance in every corner of her mind.

So much so that now she feared she was seeing things that did not exist!

The fishpond, she told herself firmly, was just that. A fishpond. Filled with dark water, lily pads and... fish. Nothing more. Nothing less.

And yet, when she forced herself to look again she *did* see something that was neither golden carp nor green lily leaf... something that was not the flashing silver shards of reflected sunlight... something that was beyond all doubt the shadowy image of a man.

A man clad in Kardolandian fashion, kneeling on a pink sandy shore, head bent as if giving thanks to the gods for safe passage over the treacherous seas.

She could not see his face, hidden as it was by a swathe of hair the colour of sunlit wheat.

She could, however, see quite clearly the shape of the musical instrument in the leather bag lying at his side.

Panic rising in her, she fought to keep his name from her lips, his very presence from her mind, knowing that for her own sanity she must keep Guyard de Martine's return a secret from her mother...

And then, sensing eyes upon her, she jerked back with a gasp, to find herself the subject of an intense, enigmatic green stare.

Her heart almost bursting in her throat, her breath blocked behind it, one slender white hand rose to clutch at the constriction in her neck even as she realised that the unblinking jade-green gaze was set amidst dark fur and surmounted a pair of long, dark whiskers.

Sitting back with a shaky laugh, she watched as the cat opened its mouth in a dismissive yawn, showing an array of dainty but very sharp teeth, before settling back to watch the fish, her white-pawed sibling curled neatly at her side.

Only Princess Linette's pet cats, Juliène assured herself, as she hunted in her sleeve for a handkerchief, and clearly missing their royal mistress since they had taken to following Juliène around almost as closely as her mother did.

"You did not see anything, did you?" she whispered, feeling a fool for talking to a pair of cats, both of whom were now watching her, ears twitching slightly at the sound of her voice.

"Or hear anything? Goddess forbid I spoke his name!"

Not truly expecting an answer, she was still sufficiently on edge to start when they both bristled and leapt down from the pond, disappearing with a distinct hiss into the tangle of honeysuckle growing over the nearby wall...

Then she heard a cool voice insinuate itself into her mind and she knew why the cats had abandoned her so abruptly.

So, Daughter, this is where you have hidden yourself! But what is this pallor in your cheeks? Have you perchance seen something in the water? Something that will tell me whether Guyard de Martine has returned.

Then when Juliène said nothing, the cool voice became burning ice.

Well, have those pestilential cats run away with your tongue? A shame if so, for I am sure you are eager to find your harper and begin his seduction. For your son's sake if not for your own – since you have made it very clear how distasteful you find the thought of sharing any man's bed, even de Martine's. Well... I suppose I cannot blame you for your reluctance, Mathilde has never made any great claim as to his skills as a lover.

Taking a deep breath to steady her nerves, and swallow the sudden hot flare of anger at Mathilde de Martine, Juliène allowed her hand to trail casually in the water, the resultant ripples distorting any image that might yet remain, hidden just beneath the surface.

"No, Mother, there is nothing here."

Unfortunately the Winter Lady was too sharp to be taken in by such simple prevarication, too alert to the subtlest nuances of her daughter's mind.

"Not now, maybe."

She spoke now, in actual words rather than the silent invasion of Juliène's mind, her voice only one shade warmer than a dripping icicle.

"But you saw something earlier, did you not, Daughter?"

"I do not know... perhaps."

Her heart still beating like a bird trapped in a net, Juliène risked a hesitant frown.

"I thought I saw something... a glimpse of sunlight on fair hair... or it may just have been one of Kardolandia's golden sea mews wheeling in the sun... it was difficult to tell it was gone so quickly. I... I will try again later when my head has ceased to ache."

"If you practised more diligently your head would not hurt so much," Lady Ariène said, her tone coldly unsympathetic. "And just remember, my dear, your son's life depends on your successful seduction of my lord's bastard brother."

A flicker of frustration thinned the otherwise lovely mouth.

"If only I could sense the wretch myself, I would not have to place so much reliance upon your feeble skills."

"I am sorry, Mother."

Juliène kept her head down, as if embarrassed, studying the silver lilies embroidered on the spring green silk of her gown, beneath which her heart pounded so powerfully she felt quite sick.

"It is no secret between us, Mother, that I do not want to... to lie with... with Messire de Martine, but I *will* try harder to find him. For you."

And for Val.

If only because her son's life hung from the thinning thread of her mother's patience, and the ever present threat of violence should Joffroi lose control over his notorious temper.

Feeling the weight of her mother's penetrating green stare, Juliène forced herself to meet it, shivering uncontrollably as she did so, despite her best efforts not to betray the chill biting at her flesh... gnawing at her bones... freezing her heart's blood... and eviscerating her very soul.

Even as she thought she must yield to the Winter Lady's will and spill *all* her secrets, she felt something brush against the skin of her leg, a caress of soft fur, a whisper of living warmth... *almost* as if a cat were twining affectionately about her ankles.

Looking down, she half expected to see one or other of Princess Linette's felines, except there was nothing there... unless it be the merest hint of a silvery-grey shadow?

No, whatever it was, it was not even as solid as a shadow. More like a flicker of moonlit mist before her eyes... and then nothing.

Nothing at all, save that her heart now beat steadily within her breast and her blood ran warm once more.

Blinking, she looked up to find that her mother had gone and she was alone in the autumn sunshine with the desperately unwanted yet unavoidable conviction that Guyard de Martine had indeed returned to the land of his birth.

Where in all the vast realm of Mithlondia he might be, she had not the slightest idea. Nor did she want to know, and yet...

For her son's sake she must discover it, and quickly.

PART I

LATE SUMMER - MIDWINTER

1202

Verse 1

The Harper

"Kelpies abroad! Who be thee then?"

The old fisherman dropped the mackerel he had been gutting and, squinting against the glare of the rising sun, stared up at the man who had appeared so unexpectedly before him on the narrow strip of beach. Surprised but fatalistic, he braced his gnarled hands, coated in shiny scales and pungent fish guts, on his knees, before remarking with a certain amount of tranquil curiosity,

"En't seen the likes o' thee 'round here afore."

"I am no pirate, if that is what you are thinking," the man replied equally mildly, his common speech slow and careful as if he were unpractised in its usage.

He lifted strong, sun-browned arms away from his body as if to prove his lack of violent intent and indeed, save for a small eating knife at his belt, he had no obvious weapons about his finely-clad, well-built person. Unless, of course, he carried them in the bulky bag that hung at his back.

"Pirate, kelpie, selkie, makes no odds. Thee'll be wantin' something," the fisherman retorted, a hint of dry humour in his voice. "Though we've nowt ter give save what thee can see fer thysel'."

"I need only your help, if it be given freely," the man replied. "I wish to get to the next isle and thence westwards again. Or better yet, straight to the mainland if you know a man who can spare the time to take me so far."

The old man sucked his near toothless gums for a moment or two, his weathered face wrinkling into even deeper creases as his gaze settled thoughtfully on the waves gently splashing against the shingly sands, before lifting to stare in unfocused fashion at the closest of the myriad tiny islands tiptoeing between the open sea and the distant coast of Mithlondia.

An earthbound echo of the silver-white jewels scattered by the gods across the endless night sky, on formal maps they were shown as the Astran Archipelago. Men knew them simply as the Star Isles.

Finally the fathomless eyes, the greenish-brown of wet kelp, lifted to study the wisps of pale cloud woven across the arching shimmer of blue that stretched from horizon to horizon, against which indistinct line a ship was just visible, running before the wind, white sails flashing bright in the sun, a flicker of purple and gold showing at the masthead.

"Thee came off yon trading ship?" the fisherman asked, his eyes narrowed against the reflected silver glare of sun on sea.

"I did," the man confirmed, his voice quiet and composed. "I told you I was no pirate."

His firm mouth quirked in the faintest of wry smiles.

"And certainly I am no kelpie, nor selkie either."

The old fisherman's eyes took on a muted twinkle as he carefully observed the younger man's broad, powerful, very solid and unseal-like build, but all he said was,

"Thee may have come off a Kardolandian ship, but I'm thinkin' thee'll not be born under a southern sun, fer all thy skin be burned as brown as a cobnut. In truth, I doesn't rightly know what to make o' thee. Only man I e'er seen in these parts wi' hair so driftwood fair were one o' them soldiers the Prince an' his Counsel in far-off Lamortaine sent last time pirates came reivin' an' burnin' up the coast. He had something o' the look o' thee too, as I recall, though his eyes were darker and colder, a winter sea to thy summer sky."

The open curiosity in dark orbs beneath wild, salt-white brows was reflected in the old man's tone, and brought forth a carefully emotionless reply,

"I have no kin amongst the royal guardians that I know of. Or indeed anywhere else in Mithlondia as would care to acknowledge me. So... will you help me? Or must I try and swim?"

"Oh, thee can swim, can thee?" the old man asked. "An' where did a soft-spoken stranger such as thyself learn such a skill?"

Stranger, was it?

It was a shock to hear the word, though in all truth he could not argue with that assessment.

Not when he *felt* himself a stranger! In this, gods help him, his own land!

For a long moment Guy was silent, a slight tightness that was almost a flinch marring the hard-won calm of his features, at the memory of what had made him a stranger...

Until another, far more welcome reflection pushed through the pain and shame.

A much older memory. A song of white water rushing over grey pebbles, of grey-green waves crashing and breaking under a grey rain sky... of himself, his brother and, as often as not another boy, all three of them wet and naked, splashing and laughing, their hair dark with rain water, sea water clinging to cheeks not yet roughened by a grown man's stubble...

Voice unnaturally hoarse, he said,

"If you must know, I grew up within sight and sound of the sea."

"Not 'round here though, I'll be bound," the old man commented, his tone disparaging.

"No," Guy agreed. "The place I speak of is many long leagues south of here."

A crumbling castle on a black crag.

Then he allowed his mouth to relax into a smile as humorous as it was honest.

"But while I *can* swim, I confess I have no wish to chance my life in these unfamiliar currents."

"Aye, they're treacherous all right to those as don't understand their ways," the ancient agreed.

Then, obviously having come to a decision.

"My son's son'll take thee to Malvra when he comes back wi' the boat. 'Til then, seat thyself. My lass'll bring thee food to fill thy belly, an' fresh water to ease thy thirst."

Gratified by this sign of acceptance, Guy allowed much of the tension that had overcome him on his first sight of one of his own countrymen to slip away, like water through sand.

Dropping down onto his haunches in front of the old fisherman he said formally,

"For your hospitality and your help, I thank you. I have been a long time from my homeland and your welcome gives me hope that the gods will look more favourably on my return than they did on... the manner of my departure."

Seeing the old man's gaze touch briefly on the mark on his throat, he knew that it was the first of many such looks as he must bear, for it was not the sort of scar he could hide.

"Thee were a slave?" his host said, no condemnation but a certain amount of curiosity in the creaking voice. "In Kardolandia? Or the Eastern Isles?"

"Kardolandia."

"Thee escaped?"

"I was... released, my agreed term of servitude being done."

He had no intention of explaining that situation any further or of discussing the man – youth really – who had been responsible for that unlooked for mercy.

Not when it had been the same grey-eyed outlaw lad who had by some mysterious power of healing given Guy back the use of the hand his older brother had crushed beneath his ruthless boot in one of his mad fits of murderous rage.

Instead he said,

"And now I am come home."

He stared into the endless blue sky beyond the old man's sinewy shoulder.

"The gods only know what changes have taken place during the years of my absence."

"Hmph. Well, nay point askin' me, lad. The only thing we hear out here on the outermost isles is the sound o' the sea, an' sometimes when the moon is bright, my lass reckons she can hear the selkies sing."

When Guy made no reply, only cocked his head as if to listen to the music of the sea, the old man clearly felt the subject closed, and turned his thoughts in a more practical direction, a whistling call bringing his lass out from the hut.

Not, as Guy had unconsciously expected, a young woman worn by the hard life on the lonely isles, but a little lass in truth, no more than eight or nine summers, with the luminous eyes of a seal pup and brown hair falling about her thin shoulders like tangled skeins of seaweed.

Perhaps, Guy thought as he looked at the slight form and shining eyes, it was not beyond the bounds of belief that this child did indeed possess the ability to hear the fey song of the seal people.

By no means as reticent as her... great grandsire, as Guy guessed the old fisherman to be, the girl regarded him with wide, wondering eyes, from his wind-tangled fair hair – lightened still further by sun and salt water – to his bare feet, both ankles marked with a similar scar to that about his throat.

"Aelflin, cease yer starin' an' bring bread an' water, there's a good lass."

"Aye, Granda."

Aelflin divided a glowing smile impartially between both men and disappeared back into the hut, leaving them smiling after her.

"My son's son's only bairn," the old man explained. "Like sunlight she be, bringing joy where'er she goes."

"Indeed she must," Guy agreed.

Wincing at a thought he did not intend to share with the old man, he pulled the leather bag from his back, untying the tightly-knotted cord to reveal a small harp – Queen Xandra's parting gift to him.

This he settled against his shoulder, and after a moment's thought began to pluck a light, lilting series of notes from the copper strings.

And when the lass had brought a wooden bowl of bread and smoked fish, and a cup of water, and set them on the sandy ground beside him, this time favouring him with a shyer smile, he looked up with an answering grin,

"I thank thee, Mistress Aelflin," he said carefully.

"Pretty music," the child said in halting common speech. "I like. Not hear before."

"I shall call it Aelflin's Song," Guy said gently. "And it is for thee. And thy granda, in thanks for the food and your kindness to someone like me, a mere stranger washed to shore by the tide."

Feeling barely more in control of his destiny than a piece of driftwood cast up by the waves – a sensation he had become all too familiar with during five years as a slave to his royal owners' whims – Guy had left the outermost of the Star Isles, heading west, in the shimmering calm of a summer's dawn, the only sound the soft lap of wave on shore, the almost silent dip of paddle into water as Aelflin's father, Aedde, steered the small fishing coracle between the low-lying islands.

Aedde had returned to the hut in the silvery quiet of the previous evening's lavender dusk with his catch of mackerel and crabs, and as Guy had looked up from stringing the shells he and Aelflin had collected into a necklace, it was quite obvious that the child had not inherited her slight, but still tangible, sense of feyness from her father, Aedde proving to be a dour, eel-thin man of some thirty summers, clad in a pair of seal-skin breeches, carved fish bones piercing his ears and strung about his neck.

Taking a seat by the flickering fire, the younger man had listened in silence as his grandsire spoke in their own soft dialect, the narrowed black eyes never leaving the outlandish looking stranger with his shoulder-length fair hair and foreign clothing.

Finally Aedde had spoken in rusty common speech,

"We leave with dawn's light. Be ready, harper."

Taking the man at his word, Guy had risen before the dawn was even a glimmer of green flame below the eastern horizon.

Whispering a near silent farewell to Aelflin, who he found seated cross-legged outside the hut singing softly to herself, Guy walked down the beach to the place where Aedde had drawn his coracle up onto the sand the night before. Settling onto his haunches, he had prepared to wait, watching the sun rise, the sound of the sea mingling seamlessly with Aelflin's haunting song.

Aedde's surprise when he discovered Guy there before him had found expression in a single, sullen grunt.

Other than that, he made no acknowledgement of the man he was to convey to the mainland, and Guy likewise held his own silence, his eyes, and indeed all his senses, alert and alive to every shade and shadow as he scanned the slowly passing scenery.

Thus he saw the sea eagle hovering over the shining waters... the plummeting dive... the slow, flapping rise skywards, a silver fish clasped in its talons...

Thus he marked each low isle as it passed... pink granite cliffs, glittering pink shores, clumps of waving pink thrift...

Thus he heard the chiming of goat bells as the hardy animals climbed upon the crags...

Thus he observed the women working at their looms outside stone and driftwood huts in the late summer sunlight...

And finally spared a moment to consider his own appearance, his body no longer garbed in the finely woven linen tunic such as he had worn for the past five years, but rather a rough homespun shirt and sealskin breeches, his long hair tied back off his shoulders with a bit of braided wool Aelflin had given him for that purpose.

The breeches were far from comfortable, being a poor fit and stinking of fish, while the cloth of his shirt was lumpy, the spinning and weaving that of an inexpert hand, yet Guy wore the garment with a gentle pride, thinking that if he had a daughter he would wish her to be as tenacious and generous as Aelflin.

If...

Thrusting aside the thought that he dared not pursue, Guy returned his attention to safer waters, if such a state existed.

And he rather thought it did not, since he was obliged to admit to more than a momentary qualm on behalf of those who had aided him so freely, the quiet joy he had felt in the first heady days of his freedom swamped by his sudden fear that such innocents as Aelflin and her grandsire should suffer for helping him.

Before reassuring himself that, if he continued to be careful, those who sought his destruction would never know that he had returned to Mithlondia. Indeed, was this not the very reason behind his decision to be put ashore at the Star Isles, rather than the bustling port of Chartre, where it was not inconceivable that something about his appearance would be familiar, even after such a lengthy absence, to those he had governed for two years?

Here, this far north, his identity was known to none. His name untold. His arrival – or so he prayed – soon to be forgotten.

For if it turned out that his presence here brought the daemons of death down on the old man and the child, he knew he would never forgive himself. Even Aedde, silent and little short of hostile though he was, did not deserve such a fate.

As the sun rose higher into the clear northern sky, Guy saw other men out upon the waters, some close enough to call greeting or question in the odd speech of the isles, Aedde returning both briefly, and without pausing in his rhythmical paddling, his face remaining closed and tight throughout the long day.

Nor did this change with the onset of night, which the two men passed on one of the smaller, uninhabited isles, wrapped in goats' wool blankets, curled upon the soft sand of a tiny cove, the sound of the lapping waters gradually lulling Guy into a state that was as close to sleep as he ever came these days.

He woke in the pale dawn and finding Aedde still snoring, walked on bare feet – no hardship when he had spent most of the past five years without footwear of any kind – down to the water's edge. Having relieved himself, he began to walk along the shoreline, looking at nothing and everything, when something specific caught his eye among the drifts and tufts of mermaid's hair and sea fern.

Dropping to his heels he picked up a tiny, perfectly shaped pink shell, his gut knotting into a dull ache compounded of recognition, recollection, and regret. He made to cast the shell aside, then with a grimace at his own folly, dropped it into the pouch at his belt.

After all, even if he did throw the shell away he knew he would never escape his memories of a certain ethereal beauty, with eyes as green as the dawn sea, dainty feet with toenails no bigger than the shell he had just secreted in his purse, and a heart as fragile as spun glass.

Never mind that she also had a soul of ice, and that he had spent every day and night of the last five years trying to forget her, both hating her for condemning him to the life he had lived – and loathed for every day of those hellish years of slavery – and pitying her for her own enslavement to her witch of a mother.

That being so, was it likely he would be able to put aside all thought of her now, simply because he no longer bore the weight of the thrall rings about his neck and ankles.

He was, for the moment at least, free.

He doubted that Juliène ever would be.

Returning to the place where he had slept, Guy found Aedde awake and already eating.

Taking up his own share of the gritty bread and dried fish, Guy found his gaze drawn back to the smooth sea rippling between the isles, the water glimmering now blue, now green, shimmering pink and grey with the reflection of cloud and the rising rocks, the gentle swell of the waves broken here and there by a flock of white sea birds or the dark heads of a family of seals.

Even the sky here was different from anywhere he had been before, the unbroken blue seeming to entice him into eternity rather than smothering him with its sensual allure as it had in Kaerellios, and he felt he was finally beginning to feel like the man he had been before he had become Queen Xandra of Kardolandia's personal pet.

Yet even then, Guy reflected, he had never walked beneath a sky such as this – a harder, cooler blue, remote as the gods themselves, the dreaming silence it guarded the realm of sea eagles and otters and majestic red deer with their burnished hides and antlered crowns, lords of forest and fell.

The water here was different too – as clear as any he had seen in the south but made darker, more mysterious, by kelp strands and cloud shadows, the shoals of fish mere silver shimmers darting through the depths...

"Come, harper. We go now."

Aedde's dry voice broke into his far-flighting thoughts, bringing him from poetry to practicalities, and moments later the two men were seated in the coracle, once more paddling steadily westwards.

Continuing in this manner throughout the day they reached their destination just as the sun was sliding behind a bank of fiery cloud, and slipped quietly into the shelter of a small, stone-built harbour on the Malvraine coast.

Barely had Guy stepped into the shallows of the inner shoreline before Aedde was turning the coracle to paddle back the way he had come, seeming to have no regard for the night's shadows lying long across the dully-gleaming water.

Guy watched him go, the silver coin he had meant to offer in payment folded in his fingers, then with a small shake of his head he turned towards the houses, taverns and tradesmen's workshops that spread out around the horse-shoe shaped harbour and sprawled across the slopes above him. A place where windows glowed with candlelight, and raucous noise spilled out onto the cobbled quay and alleyways ankle-deep in the filth and detritus of folk living crowded together.

It was a crude homecoming for a man grown accustomed to the simple music of water and sky, or the creak and splash of a ship under sail, and for five long years before that, the privileged quiet of the queen's apartments of the royal palace, the hush broken only by the screech of peacocks and other exotic birds, garishly-bright and noisily-bold, and as foreign to the cooler air of Mithlondia as Guy felt himself to be at this precise moment, though for vastly different reasons.

Stranger, old Aedwald had called him, and the description was fitting.

Even with his bare feet set firmly on the land that had seen his birth Guy was as much a stranger as he had ever been, first in the eyes of the Kardolandians amongst whom he had so unwillingly found himself, then again when he had come to a halt before Aedwald's hut and seen his strangeness reflected in the old fisherman's eyes. And, gods help him, he was a stranger still, only the harp at his back giving him any solid sense of himself.

Harper, Aedde had called him in unknowing irony, and indeed he had deliberately allowed his name to be lost for the last five years, only the faintest echo of it remaining obstinately in some hidden place in his mind where he still thought of himself as Guyard de Martinc.

Pride had forbidden him from claiming his family name from the moment the silver ring that marked him as a palace slave had been hammered closed about his neck, and his given name he had abandoned when he stood at the great pillared entrance to the marble palace of the kings of Kardolandia, knowing that soon he would take those first shameful steps into the sultry warm waters of the infamous, flower-hung pools of Kaerellios.

Then, with his honour in shreds, his heart still weeping for his brother's needless death, and his swollen hand throbbing with all the screaming agony of broken bones and inflamed flesh, he had stripped off the one ragged garment remaining to him and walked into the water.

He had wanted nothing more than to allow the warm peace of the gently rippling waves to close over his head, to avoid the indignities and the final dishonour of the life that now awaited him. But he had not.

Instead, in the nauseating moment when he first felt the questing touch of another's body against his own, he had swallowed down his disgust and done what had to be done.

He could puke his guts up later, he had told himself grimly, turning into the embrace of a stranger. For now, he would do what he must to survive, for he would be damned before he gave the marble maiden who had sent him there the satisfaction of suicide, and one day he swore he would return to Mithlondia and see Juliène de Lyeyne damned in turn.

If the little witch thought he could so easily be broken, then by the gods she would learn her mistake!

If the successive deaths of her sister and his own brother had not destroyed him – though the gods knew their loss had left a great gaping hole in his life – *she* was not likely to.

Not now that he was wise to the bitter darkness that twisted through her, from her coldly manipulative mind to her icy, uncaring heart.

True to that vow, he had not allowed himself to be broken, and now he was finally back in Mithlondia. But whither now?

Commons sense told him he would achieve nothing skulking about the Malvraine coast, and so he was determined to go right to the heart of the realm... and then take stock anew.

It took the better part of half a month but Guy came at last to Rath-na-Cael, the village just north of Lamortaine where the four great highways of the realm met and merged.

Limping slightly, for it had been no easy journey on foot from Malvra harbour, he paused to survey the noisy, bustling scene, the first thing he saw being the grisly gallows and set of stocks, the latter at least unoccupied.

For the rest of it, four muddy roads bordered by more or less well-kept thatched cottages opened onto the village common ground with its reed-rimmed duck pond, across which a prosperous-looking half-timbered tavern faced him. Clearly full to overflowing with mid-day custom, the Three Hares sat square on the corner of the southern and western highways, the harsh ring of iron on iron proclaiming the presence of a blacksmith's forge further along the road that wound its narrow way towards the rising peaks of the Rathen Fells, the grey heights of which were still lost within the sullen remnants of the previous night's storm.

Yet even without the storm Guy would have felt the season's change, not only in the aching bones of his sword hand but in the bright crisp edge to the air he breathed, bitingly unfamiliar after five years away, and which he could not help but revel in as a further reminder, if he had needed one, that for all the imperfections and dangers this was Mithlondia, not Kardolandia.

No more would he swim in warm, pellucid water or tread through lush growths of flamboyant kylinia vines, laden with petals of purple or magenta or vermillion. Instead, on his trek from Malvra to Rath-na-Cael he had passed woods where bramble and bough were laden with berries and nuts. He had walked between hedgerows where meadowsweet and pale blue harebells lingered amongst the dying grass. Where the butterflies that could yet be seen fluttering amongst the fading petals were tiny things of brown or pale blue, beautiful to him despite their muted colours, and not for anything would he exchange them for the bright-winged creatures, some disconcertingly as big as his spread hand, that had flitted casually about him wherever he went in the palace in Kaerellios.

And while he was fully aware that it would be unwise to be wandering the highways once winter swept down from the north, for now the day was once again deceptively gentle and in spite of the storm's warning, swallows still swooped and soared above him, not yet flown south to Kardolandia's warmer skies.

Yet even as he watched their graceful flight, he became aware of something familiar and much less pleasurable to his stretched senses. A cloud of tiny, whining, winged things – would that he could have left them behind in Kardolandia too – clung about his ears, a constant irritant to one and all.

Reacting to a sudden, stinging bite, he swore and swatted a voracious, and much larger, brown fly off his arm, feeling considerable sympathy with those horses he could see through the tavern's arch, their discomfort obvious in their twitching skin, tossed and shaken heads and constantly swishing tails.

Barely detectable over the pungent aroma of fresh horse dung, he caught the briefest waft of fresh-baked bread, before it was submerged once more by the less pleasant but ever-present stench of daily life, the sweet-sour tang of decaying cabbage, and the stale-sweat reek of those folk who passed directly in front of him, many of them with that peculiar sidelong look of curiosity for someone who was clearly not Mortaine born or bred.

Having given his fine linen tunic to Aelflin – indecently short by Mithlondian standards on him, it would be sufficient to make a fairly respectable kirtle for her – he still wore the seal-skin garments of the folk of the Star Isles, which made his appearance odd enough in this particular setting, even without taking into account the fact that his skin was burned browner by the fierce southern sun than the most weathered local would be, in contrast to which his fair hair must seem far paler than it truly was.

So much for how he looked.

As for the rest... well, he was all too keenly aware that he smelt no sweeter than any villager, and quite possibly far worse, since even though he had bathed in a stream a few days before, the fading odour of fish remained ingrained in his borrowed clothing.

Thus being in no position to pass judgement on anyone, Guy was therefore grateful for the occasional muttered greeting he received and which he returned in like fashion, even as he fingered the few coins in the pouch at his belt, and wondered whether he dared spend one of them on a loaf of that very tempting bread of which he had just caught another delightful whiff.

His belly, empty since his scant morning meal the day before, growled a loud affirmative, and with sudden decision he turned his feet in the direction in which his nose told him the baker's shop was situated.

In the end, it was the crowd of village women gossiping amongst themselves as they waited their turn outside, as much as his nose or the wooden sign above the doorway, that told him he had reached the right place and with salivating mouth and cramping gut he joined the queue, his thoughts tumbling into something of a tangle.

His once unthinking mastery of Mithlondian common speech had been just one more thing lost over the past five years and though his grasp had been growing stronger over the previous days he still did not feel at ease using it. He had been surrounded by Court Kardolandian for far too long to slough it off in a score of days, his thoughts and tongue still unwillingly trapped in that language to the exclusion of the one that should have given him some sense of familiarity, some sense of home-coming, and welcome.

As for the harsh dialect he had grown up with, that still remained lost to him. And would do, he supposed, until he heard it spoken by someone else whose roots, like his, were buried deep in the mysterious moors and black craggy coastline of Rogé.

Unfortunately of the two men he had grown up alongside, Ranulf was dead and far from resting in Rogé soil alongside their father and Lady Rosalynde, had been left to rot in Taneth-Rath Forest, his bones picked clean by carrion creatures. As for Edwy, he knew the man had survived the cull on his retainers carried out by Joffroi and Lady Ariène, but that was all the outlaw lad, Jacques, had told him.

For all intents and purposes Guy was alone. And, for all his joy in his return, still the stranger Aedde had called him.

One moreover who knew dangerously little of the politics and power alliances of present-day Mithlondia. An ignorance Guy needed to address with some urgency if he wanted to survive.

The splattering sound of approaching hooves, though far from unusual, had him glancing over his shoulder to see who was coming.

Too many horses and these being ridden too fast, he thought, instinctively assessing the sound, for it to be something as simple or harmless as a merchant convoy. A group of noblemen out hunting or hawking was a possibility, with the village situated on the edge of the Rathen Fells and Lamortaine an easy day's ride away. Or even a troop of guardians heading north towards the far distant border with Atarkarna...

The sight of a man spitting onto the dusty roadway, taken in conjunction with a series of obscure curses and the way the women fell silent and huddled together, told him that whoever the riders were, they were not welcome here in Rath-na-Cael.

Turning as casually as he might, Guy frowned as he studied the approaching group of dark horses with their black-clad, heavily armed riders, the sombreness of their attire relieved only the silver outline of a boar's head on each man's breast, the ugly brutality of their faces unrelieved in any way.

It was the first such patrol he had seen since his return.

Some small, grim voice inside him told him that it would not be the last.

Told him too that Joffroi de Rogé – the man he had once called brother, and sworn his allegiance to – had clearly grown in standing with Prince Linnius and the High Counsel to an unprecedented extent for him to be able to maintain a personal retinue of men-at-arms which, if these were but a sample, must amount to some considerable strength.

Evidently, far from being curbed, Joffroi's ambition and grip on power had increased ten-fold during the years of Guy's enforced exile.

Unconsciously flexing his fingers, he watched the boisterous, boastful bullies as they dismounted in front of the tavern, tossing their reins to a couple of the bolder village boys, before swaggering their way inside.

Reminding himself yet again to tread cautiously until he had a more complete knowledge of what had taken place during his absence, Guy hunched his shoulders and deliberately turned his back on the tavern, handing over a copper coin to the baker's formerly cheery good-wife in exchange for a small loaf of warm, dark bread, which he ate in the street, forcing himself to chew slowly, wary of grindstone grits and of overburdening his empty belly, tossing his last crust to the spotted pig foraging in the road nearby, just as the soldiers spewed noisily back out of the tavern, wiping ale from their bearded mouths.

Warily Guy watched them as they mounted up and took the western arm of the crossroads, careful to keep his face set in a bland mask that lacked even the smallest trace of emotion or expression of thought. It was a mask he had moulded to perfection during his five years as Queen Xandra of Kardolandia's personal slave...

His dry throat suddenly craving the raw relief of honest Mithlondian ale rather than the sensual smoothness of the Kardolandian wine he could still taste whenever he thought of that time, he was about to slog through the ankle-deep, hoof-rutted mud of the highway to the tavern when he heard the sound of another cavalcade coming up the road from Lamortaine.

Even as he paused, the coiffed and capped heads around him were turning almost as one, a collective sigh easing through tradesmen and good-wives alike as they realised it was not another of Black Joffroi's patrols, and with a ripple of movement, as of wind through a field of flowering fax, women dipped into curtsies and men dragged their rough caps from their heads... and as Guy narrowed his eyes against the sudden glare of sunlight piercing the grey clouds that yet clung to the underbelly of the sky, he finally saw a face he recognised, and who might well recognise him.

As much to avoid that possibility as to conform with the behaviour of the villagers around him, Guy lowered his head, only glancing up briefly through the strands of hair that had straggled loose from the knotted wool, his curiosity and... yes, yearning, to see a familiar face – for if not exactly a friend, neither was Joscelin de Veraux his enemy, or at least he had not been five years ago – shouldering aside his caution.

A lean, strongly-defined face, the mouth set in stern, unsmiling lines, the watchful grey eyes beneath straight dark brows reminiscent of cool autumnal rain. Riding a big grey stallion with a black mane and tail, the young nobleman appeared little changed from the last time Guy had seen him, the lines carved a little deeper between his brows perhaps, the feathery hint of white threading a little further through the thin braids at his temples.

Behind Mithlondia's High Commander, almost at his right

shoulder, rode a man in guardians' gear. Not so tall as de Veraux –
few were, after all – and considerably broader through the shoulder,
his face was hidden behind his helm, all save for the close-trimmed
flax-pale beard several shades lighter than Guy's own thick straw-
gold stubble. A distant pain touched his heart at this reminder of his
dead brother... and was gone as his gaze flicked over the rest of the
entourage.

This comprised an ornate litter harnessed to a pair of sturdy
horses fore and aft, together with its attendant escort. The leather
curtains that would normally have provided privacy for the occupants
of the litter had been drawn back, and within could be seen the
figures of two women, one of whom Guy saw with no real surprise,
given de Veraux's presence, was Princess Linette. The other he
recognised with an abrupt release of the tightness in his chest, as
Lady Isabelle de Lyeyne. Not, as he had first feared, her daughter-by-
binding.

There were two other women in the party. Sisters of Mercy by
their pale grey robes and white linen headrails, one mounted on a
grey donkey, the other on a black mare with a small white star
between its deep brown eyes. Neither of these women being Juliène
de Lyeyne – Guy almost choked at the sheer improbability of the
luxury-loving noblewoman taking up the humble life of a healer – he
turned his attention to the remaining members of the cavalcade,
these being fairly much as he expected them to be.

Frowning at the nagging sense that he had missed something he
should have noticed, Guy watched until the princess and her retinue
were out of sight, crossed the road, avoiding the pig, and finally made
it to the tavern.

Carrying his ale to a table, he took a seat and a deep, appreciative
swallow, deciding then and there that he would remain in Rath-na-
Cael for the rest of the day, during which time he hoped to be able to
earn enough by entertaining the villagers with his music to pay for a
meal and a pallet on which to sleep for the night.

Then with the benefit of a night's rest he would decide which of
the roads to take out of Rath-na-Cael in the morning.

Lying on a hard straw pallet on the floor of the tavern's sleeping loft
under the eaves, listening to the assorted snoring and snuffling of
others who, like him, could not afford the price of the bedchambers

below, Guy rolled over so that he lay on his back, staring up at the cobwebby ceiling beams and the dusty underside of the thatch, just visible in the murky moonlight filtering through the rough shutters covering the tiny window opening.

He had expected to sleep well with a roof over his head, especially with his belly full of coney stew and ale, a reward for his skill at drawing music from the copper strings of the small harp that had been Queen Xandra's last gift to the man who had – or so she had told him, with a pout and purr – given her so much pleasure over the past five years.

Gods help him, even now he flinched at the memory of how that pleasure had been given.

But that was behind him, he reminded himself firmly, and if all that remained was the life of a wandering harper, he had at least proved during his journey from Malvra to Rath-na-Cael that he would not starve.

It was not the life he had been born to as Lord Jacques de Rogé's son, a life that was now lost to him forever. Nor would it bring him any of the discreet luxuries that came the way of a favoured slave at the royal Kardolandian court.

On the other hand it was a life he might live with some measure of self respect, with the freedom to make his own choices and mistakes, to love again if he dared...

He cut that thought off sharply, love having brought him nothing so far save the pain of betrayal and knowing that the woman he loved had lied to him.

So... what to do next?

There was always revenge, he thought – albeit he much preferred to call it justice – but while he had not forgotten the oath he had sworn to Ranulf's wraith that one day he would see their older brother stand trial before the High Counsel of Mithlondia for fratricide, Guy was also very well aware that now was not the time to make such an attempt.

For who would take note of anything an impoverished, itinerant and nameless harper had to say? And if he dared to raise his voice in accusation in his own name against the man who was so obviously high in royal favour, all that would come to him this time would be a swift and certain demise rather than the living death he had been sentenced to before.

Not, if he were honest with himself, that it was the thought of facing Joffroi again that caused him to break out in a sweat whenever he was stupid enough to consider the possibility of returning to Lamortaine.

Rather it was the memory of the dream that had licked at the edge of his mind every night since setting foot on Mithlondian soil, depriving him of the rest his weary body craved and disturbing the sleep from which he had woken too many times already.

Always the same, it was a shockingly vivid dream of such dark desire as had him hard and aching, even though he would have sworn that he had no wish to plunge back into the all-encompassing carnality he had finally managed to escape.

Nor could he pretend that it had been the dark-eyed queen of Kardolandia – whose luscious body he had reluctantly come to know as well as he did his own – who had cast such a spell into his blood. And, in spite of his determination never again to allow himself to be manipulated into cold-bloodedly warming *anyone's* bed, neither could he disavow the subtle tug of this other woman's will as she attempted to draw him to her, like some hapless carp in the palace fishpond caught upon her barbed hook.

Indeed, such was the strength of her skill that he could almost see her in the moonlight, standing in the shadows before him, her long hair lifting in the night's cool breeze, the mantle she had been wearing falling to pool around her dainty feet, leaving only a gossamer shift to conceal her exquisite body. Surely no mortal man could resist the enchantment she offered and yet he knew that to succumb to her fey allure meant disaster for them both.

For this was the woman who was responsible for his long years of slavery, the woman who had sentenced him to the life of a whore in the bathing pools of Kaerellios. For no other reason than he had rejected that which she had offered him one morning in the rose arbour of the palace gardens. Oh, she had been subtle enough in her offering, but he was not such a fool as to have mistaken her meaning. And when he had declined – out of honour rather than any lack on the part of his body to rouse to hers – she had taken her revenge.

For five years now he had hated Juliène de Lyeyne, and despised her with a cold contempt he had never felt towards any woman in his life. Certainly not his faithless wife, Mathilde, who had made a cuckold of him more times than he had ever bothered to count.

Not even Juliène's sister, Rowène – whom he had been guilty of loving when he was not free to do so – had managed to cause him such torment. Neither when he had learned of her death, nor when he had first begun to question whether she had lied to him about the identity of the man who had sired the babe she had borne six years earlier.

Although even now all he had were suspicions, rather than firm conclusions, and this based on the most flimsy of evidence in that Joscelin de Veraux, High Commander of Mithlondia, was the man who had publicly acknowledged paternity for Rowène's child, yet oddly enough to Guy's way of thinking – for in all other ways de Veraux had seemed an honourable man – he had not taken the binding oath with her, as honour dictated that he must, but had instead given her over into her outlawed brother's care.

Luc had taken his sister and her new-born infant away from Lamortaine, disappearing like morning mist into the Rathen Fells, never to be seen again, and eventually word had come back to Guy through her grieving lover that though Rowène had died, her child survived.

The same child Guy had held just moments after she had been born, not knowing then whether the babe in his arms was a boy or a girl. Well, he knew now, even knew her name. Knew too – though it had taken him overlong to admit the possibility – that if not de Veraux's, there was every chance that Lissie was *his* daughter.

And if it were so, that made her not only illegitimate but also the result of an unlawful, adulterous liaison. In which case, it was scarcely to be wondered at that Rowène had not wanted to make her daughter's paternity public knowledge.

As for what she might have confessed in private to her brothers, Guy had not seen Luc de Chartreux since to demand the truth, always supposing the outlaw leader could be persuaded to give it, and Jacques had simply refused to discuss it, damn him.

Whatever animus Guy felt towards Luc and Jacques, however, was but a mild emotion compared to that which he felt for their surviving sister.

Gods knew, Guy would never have believed himself capable of hating a woman as he did Juliène de Lyeyne, yet he did. Not merely for what she had done to him by sentencing him to whoredom in Kardolandia but even more for the humiliating fact that his body still answered to hers in the darkness of his dreams – as doubtless it would do if ever he saw her in the flesh.

Which, if he were clever, sensible and careful, would be never.

Restless and aching, he rose to his feet, and edging around the pallets where the other travellers lay, he knelt to push open the shutter of the small, unglazed window, the cool of the autumn night a welcome relief after the close warmth of the room behind him, stuffy with the odours of unwashed bodies and the sharp reek from the piss-pot in the corner.

By contrast, the breeze coming off the fells brought with it the cleaner tang of pine, together with something sweeter, perhaps the last of the summer's honeysuckle.

And as simply as that his thoughts were back with Juliène de Lyeyne...

Just as something white drifted past the window with a low, haunting call, the soft whisper of feathers close enough to brush his cheek.

Starting back, a chill shiver rippled over his skin, raising the hairs on his forearms, even as his mind cursed his folly, belatedly identifying the apparition as a wraith-owl – which, for all the eerie appositeness of its name and appearance, was merely a nocturnal hunter seeking a meal, not an omen or a messenger sent by the fey woman who still haunted his mind in spite of his rigorous determination to keep her out.

The owl was calling again, and he caught another glimpse of white wings in the moonlight, and then with a terrifying sense of illusion made real, heard the echo of a distraught voice pleading in the startled silence of his mind,

I will do anything, just do not hurt him further...

His hands lifted to lock about his head, fingers digging into his skull, as if by so doing he could drag that dramatically vivid memory free... whereupon he might slice it asunder, silencing it forever, or failing that, thrust it at sword-point back into the darkness, there to suppress it, bind it in iron chains, never to escape again.

I will do anything...

No, damn it, he would not yield to the enchantment of honeysuckle-scented night air!

Would not follow her voice into the same madness that had robbed Joffroi of his soul, Ranulf of his honour.

Would not wonder what those frantic words might have meant for her!

Would not question what *she* – he would not name her, would not give her that power over him – might have been forced to do for his sake, to save him from further hurt.

Obviously when it had come to the point she had not meant anything by that frantic plea, had not held to her promise...

Yet what if she had?

What if those words proved to be more than mere sounds strung together, words easily spoken in a terrifying moment filled with the horror of watching a man writhe at her pretty, green-slippered feet... then just as easily forgotten when he was gone.

For if those words had been truly meant... God of Light, it did not bear thinking about.

Morning came at last – a brisk, blowy, autumn dawning bearing the scents of damp bracken, heather and rain-wet earth down from the fells to the village – and saw Guy once more standing in line to purchase bread, and a small round of the goat's cheese from the shop next to the baker's busy establishment.

Stowing his provisions in his pack, he pulled the length of grey and blue woven cloth that served him as both mantle and blanket about his shoulders against the chill damp of the morning, and then stood regarding the crossroads in consideration of the choices before him.

There was no sign of yesterday's pig so presumably it had been captured and returned to its pen, but a pair of raffish-looking goats and several enterprising chickens had taken its place.

Though the highway did not appear to have been further travelled since yesterday's horsemen had passed along it, the muddy strip looked distinctly unappealing to a man accustomed to the dry, well-maintained trade routes of the southern kingdom. One moreover whose only footwear was a pair of sandals of Kardolandian workmanship – suitable for treading the marble halls of the royal palace, worse than useless on Mithlondia's rough roads.

Guy acknowledged a moment's regret for his old chestnut stallion, Fireflame, and a wish for a pair of sturdy riding boots but there was no possible way he could afford the latter and as for the former... well, given that Joffroi had disposed of his bastard half-brother so pitilessly, he would surely have had no compunction whatsoever about ordering the slaughter of the horse Guy had had from a foal.

Of course, none of these reflections, either wishful or pragmatic, made it any easier for Guy to decide which road he should take from here, the night having brought more questions than counsel.

To return the way he had come was quite clearly pointless.

South was sheer folly, for more reasons than he cared to think about.

West would take him to the Rathen Fells, the outlaws, his brother's son and the little girl who might – or might not – be his own child.

Or he could go north towards Vézière, where he knew no-one, and no-one knew him. Thus obviating the risk of anyone recognising an itinerant harper as the former governor of Chartreux and Valenne, and where if the gods favoured him he might have a breathing space in which to decide just what he should do now that he had returned to Mithlondia and discovered Joffroi's hold on Prince Linnius and the High Counsel to be even more powerful than before.

For there was no doubt in his mind that something had to be done.

Standing there, contemplating the problems and possibilities of each road, a cry from the sky above him made him look up to see a red kite soaring above the fells. A high and lonely sound, he had always found it desolate, even in the long-gone days when he had ridden the dark moors of his own land and had known the warmth of his brother's companionship.

Now, when he had lost both brothers – Joffroi to a witch's manipulation, Ranulf to death – he felt that desolation more keenly than ever.

Though perhaps, that was a loneliness that could be assuaged if Luc and Jacques permitted him to join their ranks and play a kinsman's part in Val and Lissie's lives?

In all honesty, though, he had to admit that he had no idea how the outlaws would greet him, even if he did succeed in finding them.

What he did know was that he could not stand all day in the centre of Rath-na-Cael as if he were an oak tree rooted there for the past two hundred years.

His gaze drawn inexorably south again, he narrowed his eyes until he could just make out something that might have been the flicker of banners atop a tall tower of golden-grey stone, though given the distance between Rath-na-Cael and the royal palace, what he saw was in all probability nothing more than a fleeting glimmer of sunlit blue through the breeze-blown grey cloud.

Folly, he reminded himself tersely, determinedly turning his back to the Lamortaine road. A dangerous folly which would put neither food in his belly nor coins in his purse, and could quite possibly cost him his life.

The sudden squelch and splatter of rapid hoof beats had him glancing back warily over his shoulder, only to snap forwards again as the sound was answered from the road leading towards the Rathen Fells.

Echoing off the cob and plaster walls of the cottages to either side of the road, the noise provided warning aplenty for the villagers to step out of the way, leaving the heedless chickens to be sent squawking and fluttering as the two groups of horsemen met in a tangle of tossed manes, stamping hooves, chinking bridle bits, shouted oaths and raucous greetings.

Guy saw immediately that both sets of men wore his half-brother's black boar badge, saw too that save for the western patrol being noticeably muddier there appeared little to choose between the two packs. Until, that is, he observed that the incoming patrol had with them a captive, a young man – barely a youth really, of slender build – bound at the wrists and forced to run behind them. From the state of his torn and filthy attire, bruised face and matted brown hair, he had lost his footing more than once, being dragged along after the horses with no more care than if he had been a fallen log.

With his ear finally attuned to Mithlondian common speech, and with his recollection of the Rogé dialect he had grown up with returning in a rush, Guy had little difficulty in understanding the conversation between the captains of the two patrols or the order that the prisoner be taken to Lamortaine to be *questioned* by Lord Joffroi before being returned here to Rath-na-Cael, if he survived, to be hanged as a warning to any of the villagers who might feel sympathy with the outlaws who still roamed the Mortaine fells and the moors to the west of Vézière.

As to the prisoner's identity, Guy's initial fear had been laid to rest in those first few frozen heartbeats, it being obvious that beneath the daubing of mud, pine needles and dung that partially obscured the prisoner's features, the underlying broad bones and muddy eyes bore no resemblance to the sharply-chiselled lineaments and clear grey eyes of either of the de Chartreux brothers, both Luc and Jacques sharing a definite and dangerous likeness, not only to each other but also to their dead father.

Nor could the starvling, stoop-shouldered prisoner be the burly Beowulf of Mallowleigh, whom Guy had once accounted his friend and who was the only other member of the outlaw band he knew well enough to recognise.

Thanking the gods for these small mercies, Guy reminded himself that whoever the captive was, he was still a young man on a course to a terrible fate. And probably, to judge from the hopeless despair on his battered face, an innocent one too. Or at least innocent of any knowledge of Luc de Chartreux and his followers. Moreover, as Guy knew to his frustration that there was not a single damned thing he could do to prevent the other man's torture and eventual death.

Training was stronger, however, and regardless of the truth that it had been five years since he had worn a sword at his hip, his hand still moved to grasp the hilt that was not there, the mended fingers of his sword hand clenching painfully when he remembered the reality of his situation, and unarmed though he was, instinct had him taking a step towards the black-clad soldiers...

"Oh don't, master, please don't!"

"What?"

Feeling a trembling hand clasp about his arm, he halted and looked down at the woman holding onto him. A respectable good-wife of the village to judge by her neat, carefully mended kirtle and apron, her hair bundled up beneath a linen headrail, an abandoned basket at her feet containing a round loaf of bread and a gleaming jumble of blackberries. Not so young as to be heedless of the consequences of accosting a stranger, yet not so old either, he thought, perhaps his own age.

None of which explained why she would concern herself about a stranger's doings. And concerned she undoubtedly was, her brown eyes pleading, the worn lines of her face tightly drawn by her obvious anxiety.

"Please do not do what, mistress?" he asked, ingrained courtesy not quite concealing his impatience.

"Don't go up agin' those blackguards. 'Tis not worth it. Ye'll not save the lad an' ye'll end up payin' the same price."

"You know him?" he asked, nodding his head at the mud-splattered prisoner who was now breathing in deep racking gasps that were little short of sobs.

A quick shake of the coiffed head answered him.

"Nay, poor lad. But I do know *him!*"

And she jerked her chin at the leader of the patrols, her brown eyes burning with hatred.

"That one there, he took my man back in the spring, said he'd been caught out in the fells north o' the road where he'd no reason ter be, save he were either poachin' or in league with them outlaws the High Counsel wants so bad ter catch, an' either way he'd end up on the gallows."

"Since when has Rogé's lord held the hunting rights over the Rathen Fells," Guy enquired, his voice quick, low and simmering with anger. "Those are Justin de Lacey's lands surely?"

The woman shrugged, either not knowing or not caring about the complexities of which nobleman held authority over such a barren, empty wilderness.

"'Tis royal hunting grounds, that's what that blackguard said. My man he were lost whiche'er way he jumped. He'd gone out fer ter see if he could maybe snare a coney or two. He'd naught ter do wi' outlaws, I swear. I tried ter tell them bastards that, begged that piece of scum there ter spare him. Said I'd do whate'er it took ter see my man free. I'd ha' done *anything!*" she finished, her fingers clenched so tight about Guy's arm it was all he could do not to wince.

Or perhaps it was the emotion trembling in that last word, reminding him of another distraught woman, that caused him to flinch inside.

Forcing himself not to think of Juliène de Lyeyne, he asked instead,

"What happened?"

"That black-hearted scum hanged my man anyway. Right there..."

Her head jerked in the direction of the gruesome gibbet standing stark in the middle of the village hard by the place the four roads met.

"An' then he had his men hold me down while he took what he wanted o' me, then an' there, even afore my man had finished chokin' on his last breath."

"Gods above!"

33

Guy stood appalled, seeing the woman's mouth twist in remembered anguish, her eyes blazing in her bone-white face. He wanted desperately to offer her some comfort but nothing he said would bring back her man.

There was one horror more, he realised, as the breeze flattened her apron against her body.

It had been spring, she had said, when she lost her man.

Two seasons had gone by since then and the child in her belly would be born before winter fell.

"Aye," she said bitterly, evidently seeing the direction of his gaze and catching the thread of his thought. "It's that one-eyed bastard's babe I'm carryin'."

A shudder shook her frame but her voice was as dry as tinder just before the spark sets it alight.

"I tried ter be rid o' his get an' nigh on killed mesel' in the tryin', but as ye can see the babe was stronger'n my will an' the herb-woman's potions. All I can do now is bring it up ter hate the man what put it in my belly, an' maybe if the gods are kind an' 'tis a boy, he'll put an arrow through that Oswin's remaining eye when he's grown."

"Oswin! Oswin One-Eye?"

Forgetting all caution, Guy whipped around to face the soldiers, his own eyes narrowing as he stared at the brute who was clearly in command, cursing himself for failing to recognise the man before now.

"That bloody cur always did have a taste for torture, murder and rape," he muttered, more to himself than his companion. "And one day I will see him pay, I swear to the gods I will."

"Ye know him then?" the woman whispered, eyes widening in curiosity.

"He helped his black lord torture and murder my brother," Guy told the woman grimly, watching as the two patrols separated and went their different ways, Oswin leading his men along the road towards the Rathen Fells, the others heading back south to Lamortaine, the prisoner stumbling and sobbing in their wake.

When all sight of them was gone Guy turned back to the woman.

"Tell me your name, mistress, and that of your man and I will add your need for justice to mine own, though the gods know it may take years to accomplish. And if there is aught I can do for you now, you have but to name it."

Some faint colour came back into her pallid cheeks as he turned to look at her again and her gaze settled on his face, seeking what he did not know.

Or rather he did know, but chose to ignore the mingled wariness and interest he saw in brown eyes the colour of fallen oak leaves.

"Nay, then."

She dropped both her gaze and her hand from his arm, and stepped away from him.

"My brother keeps the tavern here an' he do let me help him in the kitchen, fer all his good-wife frowns on him fer his kindness ter me. 'Tis not much but enough ter keep me from starvin' or sellin' mesel'."

"Then I have you to thank for the stew last night," he said, hoping to ease the tension he still saw brightening the colour in her cheeks. "It is a long time since I ate so well."

"Aye, well... 'twas none so bad, though I say so mesel'. 'Twas arter I were done in the kitchen as I heard ye playin'."

She nodded at the bulky bag slung over his shoulder.

"Yer music were so sweet an'... shinin' somehow, it took me away from this place an' all that's happened. After that, I couldn't let ye go up agin' the Black Hunt."

She hesitated, then added diffidently,

"Where'll ye go now, master?"

"I did think west..."

He nodded towards the slopes and shoulders of the grey fells, mantled and dappled with purple and green and gold, sliding down into darker shadows at their feet, then smiled a little grimly.

"But perhaps not. I doubt Lord Joffroi's men, the ... Black Hunt, did you call them?" Gods knew, it was a fitting title. "Have much use for music, and there are few enough folk otherwise along that road."

Or at least not until one came to the far end of the fells and the village of Taneth-Rath, beyond which the highway continued on to Valéntien. It was a road he had ridden many times before when he had been Governor of Valenne. In between Rath-na-Cael and Taneth-Rath lay neither homestead nor hostelry, croft nor castle, and even if he continued as far as Valéntien he would scarcely be safe there. As for Montfaucon, fireflowers would bloom in the frozen depths of hell before he sought refuge with his mother's brother.

Memory of Gaston de Martine inevitably brought his cousin Adèle to mind. The last he had heard, she had been living with the Sisters of Mercy at Vézière. By now though she was probably bound to some nobleman and the mistress of her own household.

So long as it was not Gabriel de Marillec's binding band she wore...

He severed that line of thinking sharply, reminding himself that there were far worse men to whom Adèle could be bound. At least, Guy considered, in light of the oath de Marillec had sworn, he would treat her with indifference rather than cruelty.

Unlike that hell-spawned scum Hervé de Lyeyne!

Banishing the inevitable recollection of Juliène's white face and pleading gaze – he *would not* be swayed to pity for her, damn it! – he returned his attention to the woman at his side. A woman, gods knew, who *did* deserve his compassion.

"You never did tell me your name, mistress? Or that of your man. If I am to seek justice for you both, I would like to know."

"Nessa," she said with a rush. "I am called Nessa, an' my man was Ulf. And your name, master? If you do not consider it an impertinence to ask."

Guy hesitated and then shrugged,

"If I had a name fit to own to, I would give it you, Mistress Nessa. But the name my father gave me at birth has long-since been lost. Now..."

He allowed a rueful smile to grace his mouth as he gestured back along the road towards the Malvraine coast.

"Now I seem to be known merely as the harper from the Star Isles."

The next day saw Guy several leagues distant from Rath-na-Cael, following the highway through a gentle, green countryside, in what his head told him was the only sensible direction. North towards Vézière, and away from any possible entanglements with Joffroi's Black Hunt or Lady Ariène's beautiful daughter, the memory of Juliène's tear-stained face and the last words he had heard her speak locked securely away again.

And while he knew that those words, and her tears, would return to taunt him in the darkness of his dreams, for now it was daylight and he was safe – from her at least. The Black Hunt was another matter entirely, but at least it was a tangible menace.

Regardless of the chill that took him whenever he thought of Juliène de Lyeyne, or his brother's hounds, the day was a warm one, and he felt no need of the mantle slung over his shoulder. As he walked, he kept one ear out for the sounds of horsemen, the other part of him that did not wish to feel like a fugitive concentrating on the cheerful sound of birdsong, so different to the harsh calls of the Kardolandian krokers, and with a small sigh of quiet pleasure, he paused to watch the graceful swoop of a score of swallows, the fluster as a flock of fieldfares and redwings rose from the fallow earth of a nearby meadow, a cluster of lively finches flashing their colours before him in a confusion of green and red and gold.

Absently, he recalled the expression on Mistress Nessa's face the day before when he had confessed to his lack of a respectable name. Curiosity. Alarm. Tempered perhaps by a touch of pity. No doubt she thought him at worst an outlaw, at best a man fleeing some nobleman's vengeance.

As, in a sense, he was.

Even so, he should have a name by which he could call himself.

No part of his own name, certainly, but something that held some significance for him.

Hearing the cry of distant hawk, he bethought himself of Montfaucon, the place where he had been born, remembering also that his grandsire's device was a silver falcon. Faucon, or even Hawk, however, were far too lofty and suggestive for a humble harper to lay claim to.

But what about Finch?

He eyed the small flock of gold-winged birds searching after seeds in the hedgerow... and the decision was made.

Finch the Harper, he would be from now on, and the name his high-born father had given him when he had picked his bastard son out of the obscurity of the Beggars' House in Montfaucon would be lost forever.

Or at least until the day Guy carved it on his half-brother's black heart, the day he would reclaim his name as well as his honour.

He had not thought himself a vengeful man. Or a bloody one. Even now, his determination to bring Joffroi down was less a matter of vengeance than one of justice. On behalf of all those his half-brother had destroyed, all those innocents whose deaths were of his making. Starting with the false attainder and unwarranted execution of Lucius de Chartreux, and culminating with the even more terrible crime of fratricide.

Ranulf had been no innocent, that Guy well knew, his brother having spent his youth reiving across Chartreux's borders, finally helping Joffroi to seize control of Chartre castle and committing only the gods knew what vile acts of brutality against de Chartreux's two daughters, before taking Juliène for his mistress and siring a son on her.

Nonetheless, Ran must have redeemed himself to some extent – in their grandsire's eyes at least – or else why would Gilles de Valenne have nominated him as his heir.

And it was that, Guy knew, which had caused Joffroi to have his brother murdered, that he might more easily take the lordship of Valenne for himself. Just as he would have murdered Ranulf's infant son too if the child had fallen into his hands.

Instead Juliène had yielded herself into Joffroi's wardship, perhaps to save Val, perhaps to save herself, Guy had never been certain which. Whatever the truth, she had found herself bound to Hervé de Lyeyne, a brute and a bully if ever there was one.

Aware that he had once again been tricked into starting to feel pity for the little witch, Guy stopped short, rubbing the back of his hand across his damp brow.

Damn it, he would not feel sorry for her!

Just because the scent of honeysuckle was in his nose, delicate and sweeter by far than the dry itch of dust or the smell of his own sweat-wet shirt.

Unable to prevent himself, he closed his eyes for a heartbeat or two, remembering how Juliène had looked at her binding feast, her face beneath the chaplet of golden honeysuckle, pale and beautiful, and as unyielding as polished marble.

He could have gone further, remembered more... except he refused to allow himself to think of the moment when her frantic green gaze had met his in desperate plea across the width of the bed she had been bound to share with Hervé de Lyeyne.

Forcing his eyes open again, Guy realised in some relief that the subtle honeysuckle fragrance was not a figment of distorted memory but was real enough, the thorny hedge beside him a blur of pale golden petals and blood-red haws.

It was at that moment, and with a bitter curse for his own folly, that Guy added Hervé de Lyeyne's name to the list of those he would see justice served upon.

Though he knew the road from Rath-na-Cael to Vézière to be considerably shorter and better maintained than the one from Malvra to the crossroads, nonetheless it seemed to Guy as if he had been walking for ever.

He had slept – if slept was the word – rolled in his mantle in a succession of sheltered spots just off the highway, the first night in a tract of coppiced woodland, the second amidst thick bracken, the dark green fronds of which were already beginning to turn yellow and brown with the waning of the season.

Now with yet another night gone by, he sat up, combing his fingers through the knots in his hair. Then, running a hand over the sparkling beads of water adorning the cobweb-woven grass about him, he scrubbed the last remnants of sleep from his face, his stubble a prickling rasp against his palm as he looked about him.

He saw a misty, hazy sort of dawn, wherein meadow and moor, field and forest appeared as gauzy shadows of palest gold and grey, green and brown, the nearby river wreathed in drifting, diaphanous veils, the grass of the meadow lying quiescent beneath the dew, barely more than a soft sheen in the first hazy lightening in the eastern sky, gradually brightening to glittering silver, as of a thousand fallen stars or ten thousand shattered shards of glass, as the sun rose above the dense oak woods to glimmer down onto the lowlands of northern Mortaine.

Such thoughts might be the stuff of songs, suitable enough for wandering harper.

Reality was the grimace for the stiffness of his bones as Guy rose to his feet, walking a few paces before untying his breeches to relieve himself.

Returning to his rough bed, he pulled the remaining half loaf of bread and the much reduced lump of cheese from his pack. Having filled his belly, or at least taken the edge off his hunger, he scattered the last few crumbs on the ground before him, sitting quietly as a small flock of finches settled fearlessly at his feet, bright of eye and quick of wing.

It was a quiet start to the day, the wood doves cooing softly in the elm beneath which he had slept. Just as it had been a quiet night, the starlit silence of the darkness broken only occasionally by the flitting flight of a bat, the haunting call of a hunting owl, or the sharp yip of a fox. Once he thought he had heard the howl of a wolf, though when he had last been in Mithlondia, it had been almost unknown for the packs to venture so far south, their hunting grounds being the vast dark forests of fir and pine that spread across the uninhabited hills beyond Vézière and Lasceynes.

He had not lit a fire the night before, having nothing to cook – and a healthy caution as regards the whereabouts of Oswin and his fellows, or any other cohorts of Joffroi's Black Hunt as might be abroad and drawn to the flicker of flame. Nor, despite the disquiet that stretched his senses, had he truly felt the need of a living flame. The wolf, if wolf it had been, was so far away as to present a negligible danger, and nothing else on four legs was likely to trouble him.

Still, it made him realise yet again how much he had forgotten, how much he had come to accept as normal after five years in Kardolandia.

Not that he missed the perpetually hot nights, the heavy hedonism of the orange-blossom scented breeze, the sweat that slicked his skin, whether he was pushing himself to give pleasure to the woman whose bed he shared, dozing with her sated body in his arms or, on the rare, blessed occasions when circumstance allowed him to sleep alone, simply lying with his skin bared to the whispers of wind that blew off the sea beyond the frets of his window as he listened to the rasping song of those Kardolandian night creatures that never slept.

Safe as that life had been, he would rather risk the distant danger of the wolf, the disquieting presence of the wraith-owl or even the closer menace of Joffroi's ruffians.

At least it made him feel alive again, responsible for his own fate once more, not liable to the vaguaries of his royal master and mistress.

And if by night he dreamt of jewel-green eyes and white hands soft against his skin, he was able to push the memory aside when he woke to the unmistakable scents of a Mithlondian autumn morning.

Added to that, the cool caress of the morning air, the dew damping his mantle, the stiffness in his aching limbs, all served to remind him that he could not wander the roads for ever.

The life of an itinerant harper, sleeping rough and always on the move, had never held much appeal for Guy, and now having seen his fortieth summer it held even less.

Particularly not with the Black Hunt on the loose and looking to hang any man who had no-one of sufficient wealth or title to vouch for him.

Neither of which things Guy was likely to find, sitting on his arse in a misty meadow, no matter how serene and peaceful it might be for his soul.

With that, he dusted the last breadcrumbs from his hands, waited until the little finches – his new namesakes, he thought with a smile – had flown off in a flurry of wings, and rose to his feet.

Packing up his camp took little time and turning his back on the sheltering elm, and the wood doves still cooing comfortingly in the branches, he made his way through the dew-wet grass to the road, and set off once more, the stiffness falling from his limbs as he settled into a long easy stride.

Guy covered the first league or so in good time, the road remaining empty of other travellers, the only movement that of rabbits, the odd vole, a hind and her faun, and at one point he glimpsed the sharp nose and bushy tail of a fox slinking back into the cover of a tangle of silver willow herb, the tall rose spikes tufting now into white fluff.

Before him, thistledown danced delicately on the golden morning air, the hedges on either side were hung about with berries and hips, sloes and haws like glowing gems, black and purple, and every shade of red – vermillion, scarlet, crimson – set against yellowing leaves and a cloudless blue sky.

The road was dry, the morning peaceful, the sky clear.

Yet for all that Guy did not relax his guard, aware even without the hint of a distant horn call from the direction of the moors that he was not walking in an idyllic world spun from the stanzas of one of his own harp songs.

If further proof were needed, the closer Guy drew to his destination, the busier the highway became. This, in itself, was only to be expected, Vézière being an important provincial town and the site of the nearest Healing House to Lamortaine, as well as the seat of the de Vézière family.

It therefore came as little surprise to see that one of the groups of riders who passed him by without a second glance appeared to be a hawking party from the castle.

With the three young men, and their attendant grooms and falconers quickly out of sight, Guy continued on his way, though he had barely settled into his stride again when the sound of fast hoof beats had him stepping back, an instinctive caution causing him to seek concealment within the spreading boughs of a squat chestnut tree.

From there he could look out between the rustling leaves of brown and gold without attracting notice on his own account. He did not think it was the Black Hunt – there did not seem enough horsemen for the size of the two patrols he had seen thus far. Nevertheless there was a definite sense of purpose about the pounding beat, and when the riders came into sight he knew he had not been wrong in his surmise.

Royal guardians, two of them, headed south to Lamortaine at a fast pace.

Despite their serviceable mail, it was immediately obvious that these were not just any common men-at-arms. Well-mounted on big, powerful beasts, both men rode with that peculiar ease of those who had sat a saddle almost before they could walk, their hair long and loose, flying on the wind of their speed, the thin braids at their temples confirming their status.

One man Guy recognised immediately, having seen him a scant three days earlier, his expression just as unwaveringly grim now, if not more so than it had been then. The other, however, gave him a moment's pause before something about the slender form and fine-boned features caused recognition to spark, together with a sharp curiosity as to what had etched such a look of harsh determination into that handsome, hawk-nosed face – especially when a more penetrating glance as the huge horses thundered past revealed a man who bore the drawn, pallid look of someone riding to his own execution, though Gabriel de Marillec was under no constraint that Guy could see.

Then they were gone and with the dust settling once more over the wheel-rutted, hoof-pocked highway, Guy turned to resume his journey, wondering with increasing unease what had sent the High Commander of Mithlondia's guardians and his Second riding in such hell-sent haste in the direction of the royal court.

Had the Atarkarnan barbarians crossed the border to lay waste to the north of the realm?

Or was it a more personal errand they were engaged upon?

Cursing the paucity of his knowledge, Guy lengthened his stride, determined to reach Vézière before darkness or the Black Hunt overtook him.

He had managed one more league before the next group of travellers passed him heading south, albeit these were riding at a somewhat more decorous pace, which was scarcely surprising when Guy realised that in the midst of the half-dozen soldiers rode two women – high-born ladies both by the quality of their attire.

One was young and would have been pretty if her face had not been so utterly drained by misery, and while her hair was for the most part hidden beneath the hood of her mantle Guy did not need the glimpse of primrose gold to recognise his cousin Adèle.

Forgetting his intent to remain anonymous in his anxiety as to what had set that look of white strain on Adèle's face, Guy had taken a step towards the women and their escort, hand raised, before he realised what he was doing.

"No closer, you! The ladies has better things ter be doin' than be bothered by filthy beggars!" one of the soldiers warned him, his spear dropping to back up his words.

Aware of but ignoring the glittering point inches from his chest, Guy looked up to meet the faded blue eyes of the Lady Isabelle de Lyeyne, the distant pity in them changing slowly to a look of uncertainty... of half-recognition... and finally, thank the gods, dismissal.

As for Adèle, she never even glanced his way, so deeply bound was she in her own unhappiness.

Then they too were gone, leaving Guy to stare after them until they disappeared around a bend in the road and he could see them no more.

He was more than ever aware that things were happening that he had no knowledge of and that he was powerless to change, so that this time he was left cursing his impotence as well as his ignorance.

It was as he was turning back to continue his journey that he caught a glimpse of something silver lying among the stones and sun-hardened mud of the highway, something that he was almost sure had not been there before.

Frowning, he bent to pick it up, then as he turned the half-noble over in his fingers, he realised that in all probability he had Lady Isabelle to thank for the fact that he now had money for a meal and a bed when he reached Vézière.

Had she recognised him, he wondered uneasily?

No, for surely Guyard de Martine was dead as far as the Mithlondian realm in general, and the court in particular, was concerned.

So then, Lady Isabelle had merely succumbed to pity for a barefoot beggar... he hoped.

But if she had indeed recognised him, would she mention it to anyone?

Adèle? Possibly, since he was her kinsman.

Her daughter-by-binding? Pray gods, no!

For he had no way of knowing whether Juliène would keep such knowledge to herself, or pass it on to her mother and thence to Joffroi.

At which point his half-brother would undoubtedly unleash every man of his bloody Black Hunt after Guy.

Damn it all to Hell!

He had not yet been a month in his homeland and already the last of his joy in his return had been burned to ash, thanks to Joffroi's bloody ambition.

And, it had to be said, his own stupidity!

It was not that he had been unaware that he would have to be circumspect if he wanted to survive within Mithlondia's borders but now Guy realised that discretion would not be enough.

Changing his name was a start, but having in the end chosen not to seek out the outlaws until he had rather more information than he did at the moment, he must now find some means of supporting himself. Preferably where he could keep abreast of what was happening at the royal court without drawing unwelcome attention to himself.

Just then, his eye was caught by a flash of movement and he turned to stare at the men working in the field of a nearby village, scythes glinting as they harvested the last of the summer's standing wheat, the rippling sea of dusty gold a close enough match, both for his shoulder-length hair and the steadily thickening stubble on his jaw and upper lip – a reminder, as if he could have forgotten, that he would always stand out in a crowd.

Yes, there were men who shared his colouring – his dead brother for one, the soldier he had seen riding alongside Joscelin de Veraux three days ago for another. Unfortunately, such men were rare and, with a few exceptions, were to be found only in Valenne, where he really had no wish to go. Though he accepted, reluctantly, that it might come to that in the end.

For the moment, however, he was resolved to continue on to Vézière and then, sooner rather than later, he would find some cause to visit the Sisters of Mercy and discover whether Sister Herluva still lived amongst them, and if she did whether she recognised him for what and who he was.

If she did not, all well and good.

If she did, perhaps he would seek her advice as to how best to change his appearance, possibly by darkening his hair – though that carried its own difficulties since his beard would always grow out lighter than his dyed hair.

One thing he did know, with a certainty he did not think to question, was that whether she helped him or not, she would not betray him. Many things might have changed, and none for the better, in Mithlondia in the past five years. Sister Herluva's definition of loyalty would not be one of them.

With the last light of afternoon falling around him and gilding the dusty air, Guy finally saw the towers and turrets of Vézière castle dark against the deepening blue of the sky, perhaps a league before him, the moors rising in hazy purple shadow to his left.

Shouldering through his weariness he picked up the pace, determined to reach the town before darkfall, and he was half way through the valley when an unwary step unexpectedly sent pain shooting up through his foot.

With an exasperated curse at his ill fortune, he limped across the marshy meadow to the nearby stream and sliding down the low bank between a grey ash and a red alder allowed the chilly water to wash the dusty grime from his feet, then sat back amongst the roots to study the deep cut on one foot.

Though clean enough now, it was still bleeding freely. Here, quite clearly, was the excuse he needed to visit the healers, though in all truth he could have done without it since he still had to get to Vézière before the gates closed for the night.

He was searching in his pack for the makings of a bandage when something – nothing as substantial as the sound of hoof beats on the highway, more the sense that he was no longer alone – made him glance up, peering past the concealing trees, all too aware that a cut foot and a twisted ankle might now be the least of his problems.

He had noticed before, though thinking little of it, that while the main highway continued north to Vézière in a reasonably straight line, somewhat less than a furlong from his position a small, rough track cut away towards the rolling heights of gorse and heather.

Looking along the road, he saw that where both highway and path had previously been empty, two horsemen had now appeared, coming towards him from Vézière... then even as Guy straightened, squinting into the sun that was now sliding over the shoulder of the moor to shine almost directly into his eyes, they turned onto the narrow track leading up to the moors.

Blinking through the dazzling dance of black and gold sun specks, he saw that whoever they were, they were neither soldiers nor noblemen, not merchants nor even members of Joffroi's Black Hunt. Clad in rough jerkins and breeches in woodland tones of green and brown, they were booted for riding and bare-headed, one showing shoulder-length hair the colour of a cormorant's wing, his companion having the more muted colouring of a red kite, and while Guy could not see their faces, something about them was undeniably familiar.

As if sensing the strained observation of the man watching from the shadows by the stream, the more slightly built rider turned to stare over his shoulder, and Guy recognised the youthful features – and they *were* youthful, extraordinarily so, Jacques not appearing to have aged a day since the last time Guy had seen him five years before. Unless it was merely distance and the wine-gold light perpetuating the illusion of youth.

Illusion? He shook his head, impatiently dismissing the thought... he had been obviously been alone for too long if he was starting to *think* in song!

The harsh truth was that it mattered not at all how many summers the boy had seen when he and his companion, undoubtedly his older brother Luc, were riding into danger if they meant to take the path over the moors.

Forgetting his cut foot, Guy took a limping step towards the outlaws and perhaps catching the movement, Jacques seemed to hesitate, the mare breaking step... until Luc turned his head to speak to his brother.

Guy could hear neither tone nor speech at that distance but Jacques' reaction told him that both had been sharp enough to prevent the youth from turning back again.

Swearing under his breath, Guy let them go, watching as they disappeared over the crest of the hill.

It was too damned late to shout a warning and he had his own situation to think of.

His only consolation as he hastily bound up his foot and set off once more for Vézière, was the thought that as outlaws with a price on their heads, Jacques and Luc were probably all too well aware of the danger of being caught out on the moors by the soulless members of Joffroi's bloody Black Hunt to take any unnecessary chances.

Verse 2

The Black Hunt

"Did you tell him?"

These words, spoken in a taut, raw tone, were almost the first that Luc had uttered in the two days since he and Rowène, the latter once more clad as an outlaw youth rather than a Sister of Mercy, had ridden away from the Healing House in Vézière.

Two days during which Rowène had watched the sun rise each morning, a shield of burnished bronze above a sea of silver mist.

Two days of watching that same sun set behind trailing veils of primrose-pale lace and rich, gossamer gold.

Two days of riding beneath clear light blue skies, her face lifted to the caress of a breeze that carried with it the scents of bracken, heather and horse, rather than the stench of fear or the stale perfumes of palace life.

Two endless days of waiting for her brother to break the brooding silence that stretched between them.

And now, at last, he had!

With more than a little reluctance, now that the moment was finally here, Rowène withdrew her watchful gaze away from the scene before her – the rolling, empty moors beginning to drop down to the vast sprawl of the greenwood, now showing the first autumnal glints of gold and scarlet and tawny brown – to look across at her brother, worry warring with exasperation.

Only to find that Luc was not looking at her at all, his dark head tilted upwards in ostensible study of the red kite wheeling high in the air to the south of them, where a shifting glint of silver hinted at the distant, and deceptively tranquil, waters of Taneth-Rath Tarn.

Undeceived by her brother's attitude of apparent indifference in respect of any answer she might make to the question he had just thrown at her, she allowed her rising temper to creep into her tone, making it more than a little terse,

"By *him*?" she enquired. "I assume you mean Gabriel de Marillec?"

A grunt from Luc that she chose to take as affirmation.

"So what is it that you are afraid I told him?" she demanded.

If it is that you are hurting as much as he is, well then I think he knows it already!

"And will you look at *me*, and not the bloody sky, Luc! It is not as if you have never seen a hunting kite before."

"No, but there is more than one now, and they are not like to be gathering without a reason..."

"*Luc!*"

"Damn it, Ro!"

There was more than a hint of a snarl in his voice as he abruptly reined in and drew the dun stallion – formerly the property of Gabriel de Marillec – around so that he was facing her, so close that their knees, clad in rough leggings of green and brown wool, were almost touching.

"Hells'death! I asked, did I not?" he said brusquely. "Then the least I can do is listen to the answer! So we will talk about Gabriel. Just this once and then I do not want to discuss the matter ever again. Do you understand me, Ro?"

"Yes."

More than you think, perhaps.

"So what is it that you fear I have told him?" she asked again.

Luc shot her a scowl and she shrugged, irritated rather than apologetic, and amended her words.

"So what is it that you *think* I might have told him?"

Her brother's black brows did not relax at her rephrasing but he did finally deign to reply, his unnatural hesitancy an indication of his sorely troubled state of mind.

"I want to know if you told Ré... Gabriel, that is, about his prediction... foretelling... whatever you want to call it. That is, if you believe it to be anything more than a mindless jumble of senseless words let loose by only the gods know what cause. Perhaps he was simply worn from too many days travelling... too many nights with little sleep... drunk on guilt or wine. How would I know?"

"You know bloody well that he was not drunk!" she retorted. "Not that I would have thought that to be one of his vices anyway?"

She regarded her brother, brows raised in ironical question, and when he simply shook his head, continued flatly,

"No, I did not think so. Nor would simple weariness alone explain his collapse. Or even guilt. You *know* what he is, Luc..."

Another glance at her brother – this one less sharp, more sympathetic – showed him to have gone rather white at her accusation, his light grey eyes bleak as winter rain as she continued,

"And so do I now, and *because* of what he is, we cannot just dismiss the words that came from his mouth as *meaningless*. Or leave him to discover himself the target of vicious gossip."

"So you did tell him what he said?"

"Yes, I did. He is obviously part of this... this thing... whatever it is... and, as I said, I did not think it right to leave him in ignorance of the message he unwittingly carried."

It will never be finished... Gabriel had said. *Not between those of us here today...*

Luc, Josce, Ranulf, Rowène, Adèle de Martine, Princess Linette and Gabriel himself.

And she who watches out of the shadows of the moon...

That, she had taken to be a reference to her sister, Juliène. Not, gods forbid, their witch of a mother!

For the one who is yet to return.

The watcher who waits... and the harper...

Regardless of the identity of the watcher, the harper could only be Guyard de Martine, she thought.

Must find him... warn him...

Even now... he is closer than you think.

"But what does it all mean", someone – she could not remember who – had asked in bewilderment and perhaps not truly expecting an answer. Gabriel had given them one nonetheless.

It means that on the day the sun sets over a field of blood, and the Moon Goddess walks on silver feet amongst the living and the slain... when harper and healer stand together within her light... when the healing is done, and the last harp song... our song... is sung... then, and only then, will this thing be truly finished...

Once again Gabriel's words ran through her mind – Luc's too, she could see from the haunted look on his hard, dark-shadowed face – with a clarity that eliminated the need for them to be repeated out loud.

It might, she thought, have been possible to dismiss them, if not entirely forget them, save for the presence that night of the huge golden moon, and the terrifyingly empty look in de Marillec's citrine gaze as he muttered those barely coherent phrases.

Less uncanny and depressingly bleak had been the stark expression in his amber eyes as he had bidden her farewell, just before he had ridden south to fulfil his prince's command to formalise his betrothal with Adèle de Martine, thus knowingly condemning both himself and Adèle to a life of misery.

As for Luc...

"Did you never think that Gabriel might be better off in the forest with us?" she blurted before she had had time to consider all the implications of what she was suggesting. "If you had asked him, I think... no, I am sure, he would have come with us, rather than riding to..."

A flash of pure fury replaced the frown in her brother's eyes.

"Damn you, Ro! Do you think I would deliberately seek to destroy the man who has been my friend – my only true friend for so many thankless years – and closer to me for most of my life than my own brothers?"

"No, but surely Gabriel would be safer with us than treading the treacherous paths of court, especially if he should again fall victim to the voices in his mind. Think what would have happened two nights ago had it been anyone other than you and Rafe, Josce or I who witnessed his words and subsequent collapse! What if it had been some stranger? Or even worse, some toad in thrall to our mother?"

Despite the determination darkening her brother's eyes to storm grey, she saw the same flicker of fear that she felt. Then he spoke, his tone flat.

"I will have to take that chance. As must he."

And when she would have protested further, he added with cold deliberation,

"Now let me ask you a question! Would you wish our kinsman to give up his life as a royal guardian, his duty and the remnants of his honour, foreswear the oath he has sworn to Joscelin... in order to come to the forest, *for your sake?*"

"Our kinsman?" she whispered. "How do you know... *what* do you know about... Rafe and me?"

"I saw you together the evening you rode into the healers' enclave," Luc said stonily. "And in one of his brief moments of lucidity Gabriel told me he had seen you go into the barn together. He made it very plain what he thought the pair of you were about in there, though the gods know it must have been a bloody quick tumble."

51

He was clearly still very angry about the episode.

"No, do not say anything! Since even if de Rogé was only thinking with his prick, I would hope *you* would not act the wanton with him unless you did in truth feel something for him. That being so, I ask you again... would you willingly bring Rafe to the forest, to an outlaw's life and an unlawful liaison that would see him bleeding out in agony on a scaffold if he were caught and tried?"

"No," she whispered, shaken beyond measure. "And nothing happened between us, Luc, I swear it."

At least not then.

Lamortaine had been another matter, and memory of those few heartbeats of intimacy between them on that narrow bed in that stuffy little chamber in the Palace of Princes prevented her from defending herself any further against her brother's charge.

"I... I would do nothing to destroy Rafe," she said instead.

"So why in the black depths of frozen hell would you think I would risk Gabriel's life on a fucking whim!" Luc demanded roughly, before continuing in only a slightly more moderate tone,

"He is Second in command of the Guardians of Mithlondia and will one day be Lord of Marillec. He has his own duty, his own path to walk. And even did Josce – who is our brother and deserves some part of my loyalty – not need Gabriel by his side in battle, not to mention his eventual support in the Counsel Chamber, still I would do nothing to put the name of traitor on his head and bring him to the same bloody death that our father suffered!"

Then, when she could do no more than stare at him in mute shock and shake her head, Luc muttered another biting curse beneath his breath and guided the stallion around so that once more horse and rider were set on the faint path that ran westwards through the heather, leaving Rowène with little choice but to touch her heels to Starshine's black flanks and follow in silence once more.

Another league of steady riding and the forest was clearly visible before them, a close-locked canopy of dark green and tawny gold, extending into the gossamer grey haze of distance, wherein a keen eye could just make out the tallest towers of Lasceynes castle. Beyond which, and shrouded in even further layers of diaphanous veiling, floated the glistening snow peaks of the Guardian Mountains, the mighty range that divided Mithlondia from the almost mythical kingdom beyond, from which their ancestors had been exiled thousands of years before.

It was mid-afternoon, and with nothing to hinder them Rowène thought they would be well within the borders of the forest by dark-fall. Gods, but she hoped so! Though a mere season had passed, it seemed far longer since she had left the comparative safety of the life she shared with her companions in outlawry – all of them Chartreux-born, with the exception of Beowulf and Melangel of Mallowleigh, and Gwynhere of Valéntien. Yet even more than these trusted friends, she missed her young daughter, Lissie, and Ranulf's son, Val, who – perhaps wrongly – she had come to think of as her own in the six years since he had been given into her care.

She had left the forest in late summer, ending up at Lamortaine for the second time that year, in company with the Eldest of the healers of Vézière who had gone at Prince Linnius' behest to attend on his sister, Princess Linette who was with child, and bearing the hopes of all Mithlondians that this might be the long-awaited heir to the royal circlet of princes.

Having somewhat fortuitously been in Vézière when the royal summons came in, Rowène had been determined to go too, though she had not understood why she had felt so compelled to accompany the Eldest until she had arrived in Lamortaine and discovered her sister Juliène to be dangerously ill of a fever and close to death from the terrible internal wounds inflicted on her by her own lord-by-binding.

Never a fair or a forgiving man, Hervé – having discovered his lady to be with child and knowing it to be none of his get – had first attacked Juliène with a savage brutality that nearly killed her, and then abandoned her to the care of her tire-maid, a willing enough girl but one wholly ignorant in the healing arts. Siflaed had tended to her mistress to the best of her abilities but without Rowène's intervention it was certain that Juliène would have died. As it was, while Rowène had been able to save her sister's life, she had had to tell her that she would bear no more children.

Whether it was that, or some other factor that had aroused Juliène's jealous spite, she had turned on her sister, firstly imprisoning her, then drugging and attempting to seduce the soldier set to guard Rowène from harm. An action in which Juliène had been partially successful, at least in so far as getting Ranulf naked and into her bed, which was where Rowène had found him.

It was at this point in the proceedings that Hervé had returned unexpectedly to the de Lyeyne chambers. With no other option open to them, Rowène had persuaded Ranulf to accompany her into the tiny room where she herself slept, in an attempt to preserve both his assumed identity and Juliène's good name. In repayment for which, Juliène had accused the guardian of fornicating with the woman everyone believed to be one of the highly respected order of healers, a serious enough offence were it true.

As it had been – to a certain extent.

Certainly they had both been naked, in bed, and for a few brief heartbeats intimately joined.

Enraged at what she perceived to be Ranulf's rejection of her own charms, Juliène had ordered the lovers to be sent to Joscelin de Veraux to be dealt with, Rowène, no longer clad in healer's grey but a gown of whore's scarlet that Juliène had forced her to don under threat of telling Hervé that the soldier he knew only as Rafe was in truth his own kinsman, Ranulf de Rogé, the legitimate Lord of Valenne.

The kinsman Hervé had always hatred and thought to be dead already – and would do all in his power to see dead in truth if he were to realise that Ranulf were alive and living right under his nose.

What Juliène had *not* known was that Joscelin de Veraux, Ranulf's commander, was Lucius de Chartreux's bastard son and therefore half-brother to herself, Luc and Rowène. Nor had she guessed that Joscelin's loyalties lay with his hunted and outlawed kin, of which tight-knit group Ranulf was now a member.

Not surprisingly, given these circumstances, Rowène had not parted from her twin on good terms, and that loss still tore at her heart, in spite of Joscelin's unfailing loyalty and Ranulf's feelings for her – he had told her he loved her, and she wanted desperately to believe that it was more than the violent lust he had first displayed towards her at Chartre all those years ago.

Now, with Luc's withdrawal into the prison of his own bleak thoughts, she felt more than ever that she was alone, fighting for a cause already lost.

Never would they gain the justice they had sworn for her father, never defeat Black Joffroi and his coldly, calculating Winter Lady.

Moreover, even if they did win that final bloody battle in Gabriel de Marillec's vision, she and Ranulf could never be together in any true sense, and the bond between them would have to remain that of blood-kin rather than of lovers.

But if they lost that last battle...

Then there would be *no* winners. Luc would never take his rightful place as Lord of Chartreux, while the children would remain in the forest, little better off than peasants and hunted like beasts for the amusement of a man who was uncle to Val and Lissie, father to Nettie and Wulf.

Her eye caught by a flicker of movement, she glanced around, abruptly reminded of the hunting kites to which Luc had drawn her attention earlier, frowning when she saw the hazy sky dark with the circling birds. Where before there had been but two, now there were more like two score, and uneasily she wondered what had made them gather there.

Whatever it was, she did not think it was likely to be good.

She thought briefly about mentioning her worries to Luc but he was some yards in front of her now, slightly slumped in the saddle, his normally straight shoulders bowed from tiredness or some emotion she did not want to put a name to.

Not because she did not feel for him – goddess knew, she did – but because Luc had always been her oldest brother, the head of her divided family, the unshakeable granite foundation on which she had built her life over the past seven years since she had come to the forest. And it was as a knife thrust to the heart to see him so close to breaking.

She was a healer, yes, but how was she to cure what ailed him now? And, even with the best of motives, should she try to intrude into his private hell?

All too well she remembered the crippling pain she had felt when she had first seen Ranulf lying in her sister's bed, before she realised how Juliène had manipulated the scene to make him seem guilty of something he had not done, and had no mind to do. How much more extreme would be that pain to see him bound to another woman, even knowing it was not by his own choice?

So yes, she could sympathise all too keenly with her brother's hurt.

She might even have told him so, had not the blast of a hunting horn brazened out across the moors.

Startled, Starshine danced sideways beneath her, and hearing

Luc's curse as he was wrenched from his reverie, she followed his gaze...

"Gods above, Luc!" Disbelief and fear jolted the words from her. "It is the Black Hunt!"

"Hell'sdeath! Ride, Ro, and do not stop for anything!"

Obeying her brother's hoarse command and her own visceral fear, she kicked her mount from an ambling walk into a fast canter, then a flat-out gallop, her knees clamped to the mare's smooth sides, her hands twined in the flowing black mane, calling encouragement to Starshine as they raced across the short-cropped turf, side by side with Luc and Golden-eye, all the while praying that neither animal would put a foot down a rabbit hole.

Ground and sky flashed past in a blur of green and brown and cloudless blue until the mare was labouring, while the stallion, despite having the greater endurance and being far fleeter of foot, kept pace beside them, Luc refusing to give Golden-eye his head.

And all the while the men hunting them were slowly gaining ground...

Not that she dared to cast even the briefest glance behind, all her attention of necessity given to the open moorland unfolding in curves and coombes before them.

Certainly there was nowhere to hide and their only hope was to outrun their pursuers if they could.

Their chances of this, she knew, were not good, the thunder roll of hoof beats discernible even over the thud of their own mounts' steps, accompanied by the harsh view-halloo of the hunting horns, the excited shouts of the hunters, eager to catch up with their prey.

And then...

Well, even had they been nothing more than innocent travellers, it would have done them little good to try and talk their way free. Rowène had heard tales enough of how the Black Hunt treated anyone they found out in the Rathen Fells, and while this western side of the moors was lawfully under Justin de Lacey's jurisdiction, she did not think such a formality would hold sway with the brutes closing in behind them.

Gods! If they were taken...

She swallowed against the sick dread roiling in her gut and concentrated on staying on Starshine's sweating back, even the force of the wind battering at her face, pulling and tangling in her hair, and the nauseatingly swift passage of the ground beneath the mare's pounding hooves failing to hold at bay the nightmare image of what would happen if they were caught.

Luc would be bound, beaten and tortured before being dragged back to Lamortaine.

And she...

Once it was discovered that she was no boy but a woman grown, she knew all too well what was likely to happen, and the mere thought was sufficient to reduce her to a state of fear worse than anything she had felt that morning at Chartre when Ranulf had come to her chamber and done... the terrible thing he had done.

An act she had known for years now, if not at the time, to be utterly out of character – the result of her sister's selfish manipulations and whatever foul substance their mother had laced his wine with. Something so powerful as to override his innate inability to hurt a woman... something so lingeringly vile that even the next morning she had been able to taste it when he kissed her. She had never been able to drink Marillec wine since without remembering... and wanting to retch. Neither, she suspected, had he.

The hounds of hell behind her though – men such as he had once commanded, and kept firmly in line – gave their allegiance now to his elder brother and far from putting any rein on their behaviour, Joffroi had made them into merciless monsters, whose actions were a thousand times more cruel and callous than anything Ranulf...

Her thoughts shattering abruptly, she gasped as Starshine stumbled, lurching forwards, then righted herself as the mare regained her footing, the notion flashing through her mind that a broken neck would be a cleaner, swifter fate than to fall into the hands of Oswin One-Eye and the likes of those who followed him.

The whistling flight of a slender shaft past her ear and a shouted order to halt made her flinch, not so much at the prospect of an iron arrowhead lodging in her back but more at the realisation of just how close the hunters had come to their fleeing prey.

Risking another glance over her shoulder, she found the half-score men just within bow shot and drawing closer with every sobbing breath she took, feeling a momentary flash of sympathy for the hunters' hard-ridden horses, spittle foaming about iron bridle bits, and blood flecking their sweating black flanks from cruel iron spurs...

She caught sight of a raised bow, another arrow already in flight and yelling a warning to Luc, jinked Starshine to the left, yelping in shock and pain as an arrow sliced into the flesh of her arm.

That was not the worst of it though.

That came next.

In the moment when Luc's eyes were on her and not on his own path.

Golden-eye stumbled... her brother's body went tumbling through the air to the sound of snapping bones, followed by the terrible sound of a horse screaming in pain, all overlaid by the triumphant shouts of the pursuing men.

Pulling Starshine to a wild-eyed halt, she slid from the trembling mare and ran back to kneel beside Luc's sprawled body, reaching out a hand to him even as he rolled over, groaning, and pushed himself to his feet, the dazed look in his eyes clearing abruptly as he took in the hunters almost upon them.

His face hardening, he glanced from his mount's broken leg to Rowène, now standing at his side, her arm transfixed by a black-feathered arrow and clamped close to her chest, loyal but helpless to prevent either their capture or the stallion's agony.

Even as she drew in a ragged breath, she saw calculation set like ice in her brother's grey eyes.

"Over you go."

He nodded at the edge of the flat piece of moorland where they were standing, the hillside falling away in an almost sheer drop to the narrow valley below.

"*Now!*"

"Not without you!"

Unlike his granite steady tone, her voice came out as a breathless trickle of sliding shale.

With no time to argue, he did not bother, instead pulling the long knife from the sheath at his belt, and dropping to his knees beside the fallen stallion.

Seeing his intention, Rowène went down beside him, setting her hand on the struggling animal's straining neck, praying to all the deities to give her the strength to help her brother and ease Golden-eye's passing.

As if her frantic pleas had been heard the stallion stopped its wild thrashing long enough to allow Luc the angle he needed, and a heartbeat later the only sound on the moors was the terrifying loud rumble of hoof beats that almost drowned the lonely lament of a skylark and her own gasping sobs.

Luc looked at her across the stallion's still form, the golden hide dyed scarlet, the same bright red blood staining his hands and clothes, his face as white as death.

"Go!" he barked.

But go where?

All around her was nothing but black legs – the thinner spindles of horses, the thicker thighs of their black-clad riders – a steadily shrinking circle of bars set to cage her. As she had so recently been caged by the stone walls of the Palace of Princes. And this time there would be no escape.

"There! Through that gap! Come on!"

With that, Luc grabbed her hand and dragging her to her feet, thrust her through the one small remaining gap in the circle of horsemen, following her so swiftly that they tumbled over the edge together, sliding the first six feet on their backs until they hit the first of the thorn trees clinging to the slope, Rowène coming close to blacking out from the sudden surge of pain shooting through her wounded arm.

Then Luc was urging her back to her feet, keeping his grip firmly about her hand as he tried to steady her on their barely controlled descent of the steep hillside. In their haste they lost their footing more than once, snatching at thorny boughs to regain their balance, all the time fearing to hear the sounds of pursuit.

Yet, in spite of the apparent madness of his decision, Luc had chosen well, for the slope was too steep to permit the horsemen to ride down and the haw-laden thorn trees protected them to some extent from the arrows that hissed after them.

Coming, scratched and sweating, dirty and bleeding, to the valley floor, they were faced with a stretch of boggy grass, which Luc crossed easily enough, leaping agilely from tussock to tussock, Rowène stumbling and splashing through the mossy pools between, lacking both the strength and the clarity of sight to navigate the marshy ground as surely as her brother was doing.

Finally staggering from the bog onto the grassy bank of the coldly sparkling stream that wound the length of the narrow coombe, she would have fallen on her face if Luc had not caught her, holding her against him when her trembling legs would not support her, and gently lowering her to the ground.

"Sit. Let me look at that arm. You cannot carry on like that."

"But the hunt..."

"Cannot follow us down here. Look for yourself if you do not believe me."

She managed to turn her uncooperative body far enough to squint up at the crest of the moor, only to find it empty. Even Starshine had disappeared, fled away to find the rest of the herd, she hoped, rather than dead like poor Golden-eye.

"Where did they go? Have they given up the chase?"

Even as she said this, she knew the answer.

As she expected, when she turned back to her brother, Luc was shaking his head, his mouth set in a humourless smile.

"No, they have just split up and gone east and west, seeking an easier descent. No doubt when they reach the valley floor in a league or so, they will follow the river until they pick up our scent again."

"So we have no time to be sitting here," Rowène exclaimed, attempting to pull herself to her feet.

"Sit down, Ro!" Luc ordered tersely. "I need to get that arrow out of your arm and the wound washed and bound. Now hold still, this will hurt."

"As if I did not know th... *ahhh!*"

With a crack, Luc snapped the arrow below the point and then drew the shaft out, his face already pale with concentration, going even whiter at Rowène's ill-suppressed cry.

"I am sorry, Ro, but there is no other way."

"No, it is I who should be apologising to you."

"For what?" he demanded blankly, cupping his hands in the river and washing out the wound.

"I hope to the gods there was not poison on that arrow," he muttered. Then, more loudly,

"Hell'sdeath! It was my folly, my inattention, that got us into this bloody damned quagmire. I should have known there was something wrong when I saw the birds gathering. I *did* know it! But I could not bring myself to care. Because I was thinking about R... something else, something I had no business brooding on, and because of that I have put my sister in a danger that could have been avoided."

"I can hardly blame you for thinking about Gabriel," she said softly, and saw him flinch at the open declaration of the name he himself had almost avoided speaking. "And the blame is mine in equal measure. I have eyes, Luc, and the wit to keep watch when I knew you were not really with me. And I am sorry about Golden-eye. I know it is my fault you had to... do what you did."

"He stepped in a rabbit hole and broke his leg," Luc said flatly as he yanked his shirt from his breeches. "How can that be your fault? You could not save him, and I could not leave him to suffer as he was. No! No more words. It is just us now. And we still have to find a way to escape those filthy curs."

Drawing out his dagger, still stained with Golden-eye's blood, he slit the stitching on the seam of his shirt and ripped a broad width from the long tail. Folding the linen, he wrapped it around the freely bleeding wound on her arm, head bent, all his concentration apparently given to his handiwork.

So she said no more, but neither would she easily forget the grey shadows of sorrow darkening her brother's eyes, nor the grim set to his mouth. Or ignore how the strain of his loss etched whiter lines in the pallor beneath his weathered skin, for she knew just how much it had cost him to draw his blade across Golden-eye's throat, at once putting the animal out of its pain and sending into darkness the one link that had remained between himself and Gabriel de Marillec.

Cursing himself to hell and back for his folly, Luc tied off the bandage around his sister's slender arm, and taking another look at her pale face and the pain reflected in the grey pools of her eyes, bent once more to the river, offering her a drink with his cupped hands, now washed clean of blood, both hers and Golden-eye's.

She smiled at him in thanks – a gratitude he felt he had done precious little to deserve, since it was he who was responsible for her being in this wretched position. Wounded, and hounded by the Black Hunt no less!

The gods knew he would have taken his fists or a blade to any of his men who had been stupid enough as to get his beloved sister into such a situation, at risk of repeated rape at the hands of Black Joffroi's vile mercenaries, even if, as Lady Ariène de Rogé's daughter, her life was not in direct danger.

Unlike his. He knew he faced the scaffold as a proclaimed traitor.

But just at the moment he did not care.

In all truth, if it were not for Ro needing him to care for her wound, to get her back to the sanctuary of their forest home, he thought he might well just walk into the bloodthirsty circle of the Black Hunt and be done with it. If he were dead, Gabriel would have no cause for conflict within his heart, and might in time come to care in some way for the woman who would wear his binding band and bear his children.

But Rowène *did* need him, Luc reminded himself grimly. At least for now. And so he could not simply give up.

"Come on, Ro, up with you. We must be away."

He looked at the deepening blue of the western sky, and felt a flicker of hope.

"If we can keep the hunters at bay until we can lose ourselves in the darkness, we have a chance."

She looked up at him then with a trust that tore at his already raw heart, and struggled to her feet, pushing her tangled curls off her face with a hand that was not quite steady, despite her obvious determination not to let him down.

Looking at her, he hoped his wince was not visible, as he took in the details he had not noticed until then. The sodden state of her boots, still gently oozing stagnant bog water, damp breeches stained with moss and bits of broken rushes, the numerous bloody scratches raking the skin of hands, neck and face from passing encounters with thorny branches...

Her eyes, however – the same grey that mirrored his own – were clear despite her pain, holding a bleak determination.

"You lead, I will follow."

It sounded like an oath, and in the grim spirit of fulfilling his part of that reciprocal promise, he set off up the valley, following the stream eastwards – the direction the hunters would least expect their prey to take and where he could see the going would be a little gentler for his sister.

"Tell me if I am pushing the pace too much for you," he said.

She did, but only once, the rest of the time slogging silently at his heels.

Fortunately, the northern side of the valley was less steep than the slope they had so recently tumbled down. On the other hand, it was more open, with no possible place to hide from prying eyes save the occasional fissure carved out of the peat by a tiny splashing streamlet. These gullies were usually narrow enough to leap over but one required them to climb down and then back up again, Luc finding that he had to lend his strength to his flagging, but still stubbornly silent sister, at ever more frequent intervals.

Her strained breathing sawed at his heart and he eyed the rough terrain and lengthening shadows with equal wariness. He had ridden over this part of the moors once or twice before, not enough to recall the finer details, but he knew where he wished to go, a place where he could throw the hunters off the scent once and for all before he turned west towards Lasceynes Forest.

Since the last thing he wanted to do was lead the Black Hunt towards the only home he had left, and the women and children who depended on him to keep them safe, together with the men who had loyally followed him into outlawry.

With Gabriel gone from his life, Rowène had first claim on him.

Even so, as he thought again of those who would now be gathering around the main fire prior to the serving of the evening meal, he realised there were other reasons, other people he had to live for as well as protect. He might never be acclaimed Lord of Chartreux, or return to Chartre castle, but he had a duty to the folk of the forest, and to his family – his half-brother, his sisters and his sisters' children to whom he stood, in some part, as father since their own fathers were absent from their lives.

Though not willingly, Luc knew. Or at least not in Ranulf's case.

As for Guy de Martine, he simply did not know that he had a daughter.

Would Ro ever tell the man, Luc wondered. That is, if she survived this day, and if chance brought her and de Martine together again...

But first they had to survive this damnable hunt.

And Luc was not so sure that his sister could stay on her feet for very much longer.

She was weaving now as she walked, even though they were once more on a piece of relatively smooth, sheep-cropped grass spreading out across the plateau where he now halted.

"Why have we stopped?" she gasped, her breathing as rough and uneven as her footsteps had been.

"So that I can get my bearings," he replied, staring around him. "And give you a chance to catch your breath. How is your arm?"

"Fine," she gritted.

Then, in answer to his raised brows,

"What in bloody hell do you expect me to say?"

"You could try the truth... that it hurts like bloody hell," he retorted grimly.

"Just because I am a... Gods! What was that?"

She broke off her defence of her womanly status to look wildly in the direction of a horn's triumphant call.

Even as Luc turned quickly to stare into the reddening sun, another horn rang out from the opposite direction, muffled by distance and the rising moor to the east, and he heard his sister say quietly,

"We are trapped. Oh gods, Luc, is there no escape?"

"Not this time, I do not think," he said bleakly, unwilling to lie to her.

"Nor," he added swiftly, reading her expression all too easily. "Will I flee and leave you to face Joffroi's hell-hounds alone."

"But it is *you* they want. You they seek to hang. Go, Luc, now while you have the chance. Take care of Lissie and Val for me, and tell Ranulf..."

"Hell'sdeath, Ro! I am *not* going to leave you," he snarled, wrapping his arm around her good side. "If they hang me, they hang me! There are folk aplenty who will care for the children. You, Gwynny, Mel, Beowulf, Edwy, Nick. Even that young rogue, Aelric, would do his part..."

A great baying of hounds caused him to break off, frowning as he continued,

"Unless those bastards have acquired some dogs from somewhere, there are others out on the moor besides ourselves and the Black Hunt."

As if in testimony to that conclusion, a magnificent stag, evidently a king among his kind, appeared on the skyline heading straight towards them.

Even as Luc put himself between his sister and the terrified animal with its wild eyes and dangerous tines, and reached for the long knife sheathed at his side, the stag veered away and disappeared northwards.

It had barely vanished from view before a brace of dogs, huge, brindle-coated deer hounds, surged past, baying loudly and Luc knew what – or rather who – must inevitably follow on their heels.

Sure enough a group of horsemen appeared, following some unseen path through the heather. A nobleman and a small tail of retainers, all clad in rough garments suitable for hunting through forest and fell. But at least these were hunters of wolf and deer and boar, not Joffroi de Rogé's mercenaries who only hunted men.

Or women...

And, wounded and run ragged as she was, Luc knew that his sister was in no state to maintain the protective enchantment that persuaded those who saw her into thinking her a mere beardless youth, rather than a grown woman in boy's clothing.

He would give his life to save his sister but in the end...

Then there was no time for further thought or preparation, nothing save cool-eyed defiance as the leading horseman drew rein a yard away from him and Luc looked up into the face of the man he had been desperate enough to rob one day as the nobleman was riding through the Rathen Fells. And saw from the startled look in the suddenly narrowed gaze that he had likewise been recognised.

"Luc de Chartreux, as I live and breathe."

For all Justin de Lacey's voice was soft, it was nevertheless edged with a steely menace.

"The gods know I have waited six damnably long years for this day."

Then raising his voice and slipping into terse common speech, he spoke over his shoulder,

"Bryce, call the dogs back."

In that same heartbeat that de Lacey looked away, Luc risked a quick glance back over his shoulder to reassure himself that Rowène was still behind him and out of the direct line of sight of the vengeful nobleman, feeling a painful tightening in his chest to see her so white-faced and weary, yet still making a determined effort to hold herself together in the face of this new peril.

"We have a different quarry now," Luc heard de Lacey say. "And as luck would have it..."

Luc looked up to see the older man grinning mirthlessly down at him.

"Our hunt would seem to be done."

Abruptly de Lacey's gaze shifted to stare beyond his shoulder, a frown flickering in the hazel eyes. Of suspicion? Or confusion? What in gods' name did he see?

If only Luc knew. Did the other man merely see two bedraggled outlaws standing at his stirrup or...

The unexpected sound of a hunting horn brazening through the dusk had de Lacey's head snapping up.

"What in hell's name is that?" he demanded of no-one in particular.

"That," Luc said, taking it upon himself to reply when no-one else did. "Is the Black Hunt."

De Lacey did not reply for a moment, his frown deepening as he glanced around the open plateau, covered in knee-high heather, bilberry and bog grass, with the odd grey boulder raising its rough-hewn head.

Then he said,

"And they are after you? And your companion?"

"Of course they are, de Lacey," Luc replied, mildly scornful. "They hunt anything that moves on these moors. Even those who have broken no law."

"Not to mention wolf's-heads, like you, who quite clearly have," de Lacey remarked coldly.

He lifted his head again, this time staring speculatively out over the eastern reaches of the moors. Whilst de Rogé's scum were not yet in sight above the curve of the hill, when they did come over the summit, it was obvious that their prey and the rival band of hunters would be clearly visible to them.

"Well, this should prove interesting, do you not think, de Chartreux?"

"Interesting, Messire?" Luc kept his tone and expression wooden.

De Lacey laughed, a sudden unexpectedly reckless note in his voice.

"I have it in mind to take on Black Joffroi's hounds. Will it amuse you, I wonder, to see us fighting like dogs over your bloody carcass?"

"Fight all you like over me," Luc snapped, his hand clenching even tighter about the hilt of the knife at his side. "But let my si..."

He bit the word off as Rowène stumbled forwards to stand at his side, and he blinked at the change that had come over her in the last few moments.

"Let your sibling go free, you would say?" de Lacey picked up his sentence, albeit not quite accurately. "I think not, de Chartreux. The boy would drown in the first bog he came to, weak and wounded as he is. No, he stays with us. Bryce!"

The man he had addressed before rode forwards, a questioning look on his craggy, bearded face.

"M'lord?"

"You promised me a rare hunt today, Bryce, and so it has proved. We may have lost the stag but see what we have brought to bay instead. And if netting this pair of rogues, one of whom I have been waiting to catch for a good number of years now, was not enough, I foresee an encounter with the Black Hunt itself. Would you care to wager which of us will get to drink the hunter's ale at the end of it all?"

"Aye, m'lord, I'll take that wager."

Nodding at his retainer, de Lacey returned his attention to Luc, his thin-lipped mouth quirked in something that would never have passed as a smile, a message in his eyes that Luc could not quite read, as he finished softly,

"And whether de Chartreux here leaves this moor over the back of a horse like a gralloched stag, with his guts left on the hillside for the kites to feed on."

Verse 3

The Healer

Thankfully Luc had not left any part of himself, save perhaps his pride, on that high moorland plateau.

And while the tension between the two hunting parties had been thick enough to cut with a gralloching knife, ultimately the confrontation between Justin de Lacey and the Black Hunt had passed without blood being drawn.

To his disgust Luc had seen nothing of the encounter, though he had heard every word from his current uncomfortable position – having realised too late that the Lord of Lasceynes had meant part of his grimly jocular question almost literally, which translated into Luc spending what felt like hell's own version of eternity rolled in his cloak and bound over the back of a horse as if he had been a corpse in truth.

From which position he could only curse himself, and hope that his sister was faring better – or as well as was possible when surrounded by not-quite-enemies and with a painful arrow wound in her arm.

As it was, in the scant span of time before the Black Hunt had come upon them, Justin de Lacey had made his dispositions, commanding Bryce to give his mantle to "the boy" to cover the rough bandage and bloodstained shirt, whilst giving Luc the choice of playing the part of corpse voluntarily or at the point of a fist.

Unwilling to abnegate what little control he had left to him, Luc had chosen cooperation.

A fact de Lacey had recognised with an ironic half smile, before issuing the order to head for home, his words almost lost in the muffled rumble of rapidly approaching hooves.

This being followed by a coarse challenge in common speech from the leader of the Black Hunt, all Luc had been able to do was lie still and listen tensely to the ensuing acerbic exchange – it could scarce be termed a civilised conversation – between Justin de Lacey and the other man, who had arrogantly given his name as Oswin of Sarillac, retainer to Lord Joffroi of Rogé.

Given the generally accepted truth that his master was the most powerful man in Mithlondia – second only to Prince Linnius, and even that was questionable – Oswin had either not recognised the nobleman or else felt it within his rights to rudely demand, rather than courteously request, information concerning a pair of fugitives from royal justice, both of whom carried a high price on their heads. Adding that one of them had been wounded badly enough that they could not have run far.

Disregarding de Lacey's terse denial of any knowledge of such men, Oswin had bluntly demanded to know the identity of the "corpse", the obvious implication being that he thought the man he had accosted to be lying if not in actual collusion with the outlaws.

It was at this point that Justin de Lacey had chosen to announce his identity. Quietly – but with a lethal edge to his cultured voice – he had informed the other man that not only was he addressing the Lord of Lasceynes and the Rathen Fells but that until they produced a warrant signed by Prince Linnius himself, they were all guilty of trespassing on de Lacey land.

Belatedly realising that his bullying tactics stood no chance of success here, Oswin and his fellows had withdrawn, and de Lacey had given the word to ride for Lasceynes. Luc, with the blood pooling in his head and bound hands, sweating, bruised and near to suffocation within the confines of the woollen mantle, had gritted his teeth and set himself to working out some way of ensuring his sister's safety.

It had been full dark before the horse had come to a jolting halt and Luc felt rough hands haul him from the saddle, the grim-faced huntsman holding him upright while he fought free of his bonds and the confining folds of cloth, waiting for his blood to settle where it should and the stars to stop their nauseous spinning in a black sky lit softly by a gibbous moon.

It might have taken even longer to get his wits back together, save that just then Luc saw one of the other de Lacey retainers move to pull the hunched form of his sister to the ground, and the words tore roughly from his tongue.

"Leave he...him alone!"

A curt command from de Lacey unexpectedly reinforced his demand and sent Bryce shambling over to offer a burly arm, thus enabling Rowène to dismount without falling, though the face she turned towards Luc was as white as that of the moon itself. It being abundantly clear to him that his sister was near the end of her strength, Luc forced himself to move, albeit in a stumbling, shambling run, making it to her side just as her knees gave way.

Even as he caught her, he heard de Lacey giving quick orders for a fire, for water to be heated, and finally, blessedly, for Luc to be left free to tend to his sibling without hindrance.

Which is how it came to be that Luc found himself, weary in body and trapped in a fog of heart-sick pain, maintaining a close watch over his restlessly sleeping sister, her right hand firmly clasped in his own in order to prevent her from pulling at the blood-stained binding about her left arm, his own readiness to snap and snarl like a wounded wolf, together with the night's subtle shadows conspiring to keep the curiosity of his current captors at bay.

Indeed the darkness of the night – lit only by the waning moon and the subdued blue flames of the peat fire – formed the only real protection Rowène had at the moment. That and the boy's clothing she wore, though this seemed a fragile enough guise to Luc's anxious eyes. It had, however, held thus far.

What would happen when dawn brought the full light of day to shine upon his sister's purely feminine face and form he did not know. He could only hope that by then she would have recovered her wits from wherever they were presently wandering, or at least sufficient to present some sort of a credible facade to de Lacey and his men.

Hell'sdeath! What was he thinking? The onus should not be on her at all, damn it! It was his own bloody fault that his sister had ended the day in such dubious company, and he was desperately afraid that it might yet turn into an even worse nightmare, since only the daemons in Hell knew what those filthy de Rogé bastards had dipped their arrows in.

If he had been paying attention to their surroundings as he should have been... but he had not, and now they were both like to pay with their lives for his carelessness.

De Lacey would hang him just as soon as they reached the edge of the forest, and it seemed probable from the fever that had overtaken her with such unnatural swiftness that Rowène would die from a poisoned wound soon after, thus in one fell sweep depriving his men both of their leader and their healer, and Val and Lissie of their closest guardians and protectors.

As for Gabriel... well, here Luc could but attempt to console himself with the knowledge that Ré would be free to find what happiness he could in his binding to Adèle de Martine without the burden of betrayal on his soul. Luc could do nothing about the other burdens the man had carried for so long in secret, and to which Rowène was now privy.

"How is your brother?"

Justin de Lacey's voice intruded into Luc's tortured thoughts, jerking him back to the fire-lit night and the overwhelming need to protect the fey being who was both sister and brother to him.

"No worse," he said tersely.

No better either, damn it all!

But that he would not say, lest Ro might somehow hear him.

Ignoring Luc's narrow-eyed glare, de Lacey dropped to his heels, the better to regard the slender form curled up in Luc's arms.

While it was not easy to read the expression on the other man's face, Luc had the sense that de Lacey was frowning, and he was reminded of the way the Lord of Lasceynes had looked at Ro earlier, just before the Black Hunt came up with them – with curiosity and the beginnings of suspicion.

And possibly the man had good reason, delirious and close to betraying herself as she was.

To Luc's deep concern, she had been muttering since they stopped, intermittently and mostly incoherently, though knowing her as he did, Luc had recognised a few names. *Papa. Guy. Lissie.*

Oddly enough, given the apparent state of intimacy between his sister and bloody Ranulf de Rogé, Rowène had not mentioned his name in any of its variants.

Until now. And the timing could not have been more disastrous!

"Ranulf... wait... I love you, heart of my heart."

While it was little more than a low moan it was perfectly clear.

Nor could there be any doubt that de Lacey had heard it.

Brows lifting, he regarded Luc with a sardonic, if surprisingly nonjudgemental, shrewdness.

"Hmm. It would seem that you and your brother have more in common than a shared paternity and a price on your head."

"Messire?"

"I think you know very well what I mean. That being so, it is doubly unfortunate that your lady-mother has the tongue and temperament of a poison-viper and no qualms at all about using her position to set her first-born son up for the gallows."

"Even if you do not hang me from the nearest tree, I am bound for the gallows anyway, de Lacey. I am a traitor to the crown, remember?" Luc said, the merest hint of black bitterness underlining his flat tone.

"Ah, but just in case there should be any nobleman in the Counsel Chamber with the wit or courage to argue that it has never been proven that you had any knowledge or complicity in your father's crimes, your mother has been taking steps to ensure that you hang anyway, tarring you with the same brush she has already applied with such damnable effect to Gabriel de Marillec's reputation. Not," he added caustically. "That the young fool has ever done anything to help himself. Unlike you, he appears not to know the meaning of the word *discretion*."

Luc could not read the expression in de Lacey's hazel eyes, could barely make out the pale blur of his face. Even so, the other man's startlement was obvious, and the equal to Luc's own, when a hoarse, halting but undeniably lucid voice said breathlessly,

"Perhaps his... forthcoming binding to... Adèle de Martine will help change... public perception regarding his supposed... *indiscretions*."

"What binding?" de Lacey demanded tersely, the shadowy darkness of his eyes flickering between Luc and Rowène. "Between Demoiselle de Martine and Gabriel de Marillec, you would say? Are you sure? I heard nothing to suggest this was imminent when I was last at court."

"None of us knew until three days ago," Rowène muttered.

She struggled to sit up a little straighter, her breath catching as she jarred her arm.

"Best get you back to the Palace of Princes, Messire, if you wish to..."

Her long lashes dropped to rest against dirt-smeared cheeks.

"To witness such a... notorious event."

"Oh, I shall be there," de Lacey said grimly. "If only to see that you speak truth and this is not merely some piece of trickery on your part, though gods know what you mean to achieve by it if it is."

"It is true enough," Luc said, a little surprised at how steady his voice sounded when his very soul was torn in two. "Neither I nor my brother are likely to lie about something like that."

"No, perhaps not, given your rumoured relationship with de Marillec," the nobleman muttered, before adding in a sharper tone,

"Gods damn it! Even if I abandon you here on the moor, send my men back to Lasceynes without me, and ride straight to Lamortaine it will be a bloody close run race."

Then on an even more explosive note,

"Hell's damned depths! Can I trust you, de Chartreux, to keep your mouth shut about today and your hands off my purse in future?"

"Certainly to the first," Luc agreed tersely. "And probably to the second. My kinfolk and my men live rent free on your land and hunt your game as it is. Taking any more from you would be..." He paused, looking for the right word.

"Would be taking the piss, and you bloody well know it," de Lacey retorted. "And just in case you are wondering... if I have ignored your presence so close to Lasceynes it is *not* because I am blind or witless! But rather because I am not of the same ilk as Black Joffroi or his ice-witch of a wife. Believe me, I could have hunted you down any time these past six years if I had wanted to, but I do not persecute women or children, and I know damned well you have both living with you. As for your half-brother here, I have to say he does not look old enough to shave, let alone anything else, so unless either of you do something overtly stupid or unlawful in the days to come I will not raise my hand against you."

With which unexpected promise Justin de Lacey rose to his feet and stalked away into the night.

Luc would have been tempted to laugh in relief had it not been for the fact that Rowène was still burning up in his arms.

Nor did it escape him that this was the second time in almost as many days that he had held someone he loved in a fiercely protective embrace whilst they wandered down torturous, dark paths he lacked the ability to tread alongside them.

Gabriel had come back from the edge of Hell, only to be lost to him through his forthcoming binding to Adèle de Martine. All Luc could hope was that Rowène too returned from the realm of fevered dreams, for he could not bear to lose her as well.

She was lost!

Lost amidst a moonlit mist, her only companion a small grey cat walking a few paces in front of her, now and again turning its head to regard her with gleaming pale blue eyes. Beyond that she was aware only of the point of pain burning in the arm she carried cradled against her breast.

But where was she? *Who* was she?

Papa, she whispered, calling instinctively on the one person she trusted to see her safe.

The mist swirled and reformed, and she had the fleeting impression of grieving grey eyes set in a grim, colourless face, grey water lapping at a stone quayside, a ship flying the banner of a silver swan riding the waves nearby.

I am sorry, sweetheart, I should never have sent you away. Should have been there to protect you when you returned. Gods forgive me, Little Rose, for I cannot forgive myself.

Papa! She called again but her father was gone.

Little Rose, he had called her, and with the memory of her father's pet name for her, echoing through the sunlit years of her childhood before he had sent her away from Mithlondia, she realised she had found some small part of herself again, a single shining piece of the confused puzzle of who she was.

Then she heard another man's voice, lighter than her father's but rasping with rage,

What have you done to her? My golden rose!

A golden rose? Was that her?

And who was this man who needed to know the answer so fiercely that all his passion spilled over into his voice?

For a fleeting moment, as the mist drifted apart, she caught a glimpse of a young noblewoman, clad in a silken gown of pale gold and seated within a bower of yellow roses, sunlight glinting on long red hair the colour of fire.

Was *that* her? It did not feel like her. Or at least not the her she had become...

Before she could answer the question the breeze blew the image away and in its place she saw yellow gorse, a green headland above a white-capped blue sea, and two riders, one a slender youth, hair hidden beneath a close-fitting hood, the other a broad-shouldered man with cropped hair the colour of sunlit wheat.

Was he the unseen man whose angry voice she had just heard?

Somehow she did not think so, though she felt herself bound to this other man in some way.

A flicker of memory like the flashing wings of a flock of finches brought her the image of a child with sun-bright braids and summer blue eyes... *her* child. And his.

And she knew him again.

Guy de Martine.

Accompanying this recognition came the faint notes of a harp weeping a poignant lament for some unnamed mortal man lost in love for a woman who must, by her allegiance to the Moon Goddess of the Faennari, be set forever beyond his touch...

Perhaps even the woman who now appeared briefly, wrapped about in fast falling mist, clad in a healer's robes, dark red hair loose about her shoulders...

Then all was grey again... grey pebbles, grey sea glimmering into green with the incipient glow of dawn... a black rock rising from the gently swelling water and sunlight shimmering on the pale limbs of the flame-haired fey staring towards the shore, whence came the sound of a man's voice – the same man she was sure who had spoken of his golden rose – this time raised in a terrible oath. To take for his own what could never be his, even if it meant his own death...

Unpredictable as ever, the mist swept back down, and through the gossamer veiling she thought she glimpsed a red-haired wanton in a scarlet gown locked in the arms of a fair-haired man in loose shirt and dark breeches...

Before they too were gone, and with them the shadowy walls that had surrounded them, leaving only a solitary oak tree standing beside a silent stream, the only sound the distant music of an unseen harper, singing of falling rain beneath the stars.

A man was lying on that smooth sward, she saw now, a blood-stained sword close by his hand, his fair head resting in the lap of a woman in healer's grey... and she realised suddenly that these were the same couple she had glimpsed earlier bound in desperate embrace... realised almost too late that she must be the woman and he...

Then he was gone... and she was alone, save for the small silvery-grey cat, and walking beneath a starlit sky the same dark blue as his eyes, the words she should have spoken before the mist came down slipped softly from her lips.

Ranulf... wait! I love you, heart of my heart.

As if the moon had risen above the mist to shine down on them both with a clear-edged clarity that defied time and clouded memories, she knew herself again, in all her parts.

And him.

Ranulf Jacques de Rogé, otherwise known as Rafe of Oakenleigh.

And with the recollection of his name, and all he had been to her, she returned at last to some fleeting sense of where she was.

Not imprisoned within the deep, dark caverns of memory.

Nor treading the twisting paths of foresight by the light of a blood-gold moon.

Nor even spinning wishful illusions within the mist-wreathed reaches of eternity

Instead of her lover's face, the falling moonlight revealed the stark lines of her brother's dark-stubbled features and hearing the tight tension in his bleak voice as he spoke with some other man whom she sensed at present to be neither enemy nor ally, she roused herself with a fierce effort, somehow managing to find the words to ward off the suspicion she saw in Justin de Lacey's shadowed gaze... before slipping back into the goddess' healing embrace.

Waking to the sound of footsteps crunching ever closer, Rowène opened her eyes to see Luc striding towards her across a carpet of fallen beechnuts, the leaves above his head just beginning to show the first bronze gilding of autumn.

Blinking aside the last smoke-swirling remnants of her dream, she frowned and tried to sit up, only to let loose a muted cry as red-hot pain blazed through her left arm.

"Be still, Ro, for gods'sake," Luc ordered tersely as he dropped down beside her, his eyes keenly studying her face.

He must have approved of what he saw for suddenly his white-drawn features warmed in a smile.

"You truly are back with me again. Thank the gods!"

She regarded the strip of cloth bound around her arm – the bleached whiteness of the linen long since stained a dirty shade that defied description – and moving the limb with rather more care than she had taken before, said somewhat absently,

"Indeed, it would seem so."

Then looking up into her brother's anxious eyes, grey as the clouds presently charging like wild horses across the colourless autumn sky, added,

"How do I come to be here? The last thing I remember is being out on the moor with Justin de Lacey's men on one side and Joffroi de Rogé's scum approaching from the other."

"You do not remember anything else? Not riding with de Lacey's men, nor telling him he had better take himself off to Lamortaine if he wanted to know what was going on there rather than wait for gossip to inform him?"

She shook her head, half amused, half appalled.

"No, did I?"

"You did. *And* he went. He sent his men back to Lasceynes but agreed to lend me one of his horses so as to bring you back here more easily. On condition, of course, that I returned the beast to his stables sooner rather than later."

"That was... decent of him," Rowène said tentatively. "So... I take it he knows we are living in his forest? Living off his game, his lands?"

A grunt from her brother that she chose to take as assent.

"Did I tell you I saw him talking to Josce whilst I was in Lamortaine, and they seemed to be on some terms of trust, if not actual friendship?"

"In truth, you have not told me much at all," Luc replied, straightening and presenting her with his back while he ostensibly directed his gaze out under the bronze-tinged eaves of the forest.

"My fault, of course. I have given you little encouragement to talk to me since your return."

Rowène stared at his braced shoulders, the taut lines of his lean body, and wondered whether to mention Gabriel de Marillec... then decided against it. Instead she asked without much hope,

"I do not suppose Messire de Lacey's generosity extended as far as sharing his provisions?"

"Actually it did," Luc said, turning back to rummage in one of the bags beside her, and which they had managed to hold onto despite yesterday's mad chase across the moors. "Only bread and cheese and an apple or two but it is all reasonably fresh. Eat up, Ro. No..."

He waved off the hunk of bread she held out to him.

"That is yours, I have had my share already."

Privately she doubted it, but knew it would do no good to say so, and when she had eaten as much as she could stomach, made sure she packed the remainder away in case Luc should admit to being hungry later.

Finding herself frustratingly weak, and – with the last shreds of her fevered dreams shrouding her mind – prone to dizziness as well, she allowed Luc first to pull her gently to her feet, then boost her onto the back of the dark bay gelding, Luc electing to lead the animal along the narrow tracks between the trees once she had assured him that she was perfectly capable of remaining in the saddle by herself.

Something that was, as always, to prove much easier in the saying than in the doing.

They arrived back at the encampment at mid-day, accompanied by the steady dripping of rain drops off oak and chestnut leaves, the damp misty chill of the autumn day negated by the warmth of the welcome they received.

Desperate to be home as she was, when Luc stopped the horse just short of the clearing, Rowène was unable to restrain the look of impatient enquiry she directed at her brother, to which he had responded in a level tone that – almost, but not quite – concealed his enduring bitterness that he could not provide for her in some more fitting fashion.

"Are you ready to be Jacques again?"

Closing her eyes, she took a deep breath of the wet woodland air, allowing the illusion of the outlaw youth to settle into her flesh, her bones, her blood, her very soul... and when she opened them again she could see from the look on her brother's face that she had succeeded.

Further proof came when she slid down from the saddle at the edge of the clearing and found herself the centre of a crowd of men, women and children, some eager to slap her sound shoulder, kiss her cheek, engage in banter of dubious taste, or simply hug her tightly, as in her turn she held Lissie and Val, the latter now growing to look so much like his father that it came close to causing the carefully moulded mask of her illusion to shatter.

Nonetheless, and in spite her sudden acute pain that Ranulf could not be here, to share this home-coming, she knew this was where she belonged, with these long-time companions and friends.

Well, mostly friends, she amended, as she met Caite's vaguely disgruntled gaze over the heads of the children, wondering yet again why – having escaped the degradation and abuse she had suffered at the Black Lily – Caite had chosen to risk her freedom and her life by remaining in the forest as part of the outlaw band she had no previous ties to. Moreover, whilst it was plain that the woman would do anything for Luc – a truth he was blind to, wilfully or otherwise – Caite held everyone else, and in particular Rowène, at a clearly-marked distance.

Why she should be kept at an even greater remove than the others she did not know, though she guessed it was somehow related to Caite's freely-expressed antipathy towards the man who had once been Ranulf de Rogé – and his well-earned reputation for lechery that went with being Black Joffroi's younger brother.

The children were still shouting, demanding her attention, and Rowène was quite happy to abandon all thought of Caite and any past connection with Ranulf, catching her breath in an audible hiss as the children in their eagerness to greet their "Uncle Jacques" jarred her wounded arm.

This in turn caused Beowulf to glower, curse, and growl under his breath, Grandmère Anne to look strained and anxious, and the ever-practical Gwynhere to take immediate charge, sending Melangel running for water, salve and clean linens.

Gratefully taking a seat on a log by the fire, Rowène allowed the older woman to remove the binding about her arm, the wound beneath revealing itself to be inflamed and foul, the raw flesh oozing pus, the virulent red line reluctantly retreating back towards the wound along the pathway it had clearly been striking towards her heart.

Plainly the arrow *had* been poisoned and but for the goddess' intervention – she vaguely remembered following a small grey cat along a twisted and thorny pathway through the confusing canyons of a starless night – she thought she would probably be dead by now.

This was the second time she had been poisoned, Guy's jealous wife, Mathilde, being the first to try it, inadvertently causing Rowène to lose the child no-one knew she had been carrying.

Ranulf's child, conceived that first terrible morning following the fall of Chartre.

And whilst Rowène had survived both Mathilde's malice and the Black Hunt's filthy tactics, she had to acknowledge that a third encounter with poison might well prove to be the last...

She was distracted from this chilling conclusion by the gentle touch of a child's delicate fingers on her arm, tracing that slowly receding line of angry red, and heard Gwynny say with unusual sharpness,

"Lissie, come away!"

The child jerked back, turning blue eyes – the same shade of summer blue as those of the man who had sired her – towards the older woman.

"But, Gwynny, I can help. I know I can."

"You already have, sweetheart," Rowène said quickly, shaking her head slightly at Gwynhere before reaching out to wipe the tear that had slipped down her daughter's dirt-smudged cheek.

"You are not just saying that to make me feel better?" Lissie asked.

"No, I am saying it because you have made *me* feel better," Rowène replied firmly. "You see that red line there... look how it is growing smaller all the time." She managed a smile. "That means it is no longer a danger."

Lissie's earnest face lit in a smile,

"I did that?"

"You did."

"What else can I do? Gwynny says the wound needs to be washed and salved, and bound up again. Can I do that? I would be very careful not to hurt your poor arm any more."

"If you wish to, and if you do exactly as Gwynny says, then yes you may help."

Over the child's head, her fine fair hair tied up in two untidy braids, Rowène met Gwynhere's anxious brown eyes, and shrugged slightly.

Only much later, after Lissie had gone chasing off after Val and Wulfric and Benet, did they exchange any further words.

"The child has your healing touch," Gwynhere said quietly.

"I know," Rowène agreed with a sigh. "I would she had inherited her father's skill with the harp, rather than the gilded but dangerous powers of the Faennari. Still it could be worse, Gwynny. She might have been burdened with some other, even more troubling, gift."

Or perhaps," she added grimly to herself, recalling Gabriel de Marillec's apparent collapse into insanity. "Curse might be a better word for it."

With the return of Luc and his sibling to the forest, life settled back into its usual pattern, albeit it was some little while before Rowène's arm was healed enough to allow her to draw a bow and go hunting with her brother and the other outlaws.

She refused, in the interim, to remain tied to the camp, and instead chose to accompany Beowulf and Aelric when they undertook to return Justin de Lacey's horse to Lasceynes castle, while Gwynny, Melangel and Lissie took the opportunity to visit the market and mingle with the townsfolk under Edwy's watchful eye.

Not knowing quite what sort of welcome they might receive at the castle, Rowène was relieved to discover that Bryce the huntsman had left word at the stables that they were expected, the head groom accepting the horse with nothing more than an incurious nod and word of thanks before turning away, making it clear that the three roughly-clad men could find their own way out of the castle precincts.

Just as they were leaving, however, Bryce's burly form fell into step beside them, keeping pace with them as they crossed the courtyard heading for the gateway.

"How's the arm, lad?" he asked after a few steps, nudging aside an indignant chicken pecking in their path and giving the nearby cockerel a warning look.

"Oh no, ye don't, ye evil-tempered bird, else it'll be the pot for ye tonight. Well, lad?"

This last being clearly aimed at "Jacques", Rowène answered in softly accented common speech, her wary attention divided between the narrow-eyed huntsman and the beady-eyed cockerel,

"'Tis healing well enough, Master Bryce."

"'Tweren't poisoned then? Damned lucky, ye were," Bryce retorted. "Ye do know that, don't ye, boy?"

"Aye, that I do."

"In more bloody ways than one," the huntsman continued.

Noting the growing scowl on Beowulf's weathered features, she kept her tone calm as she turned to address the de Lacey retainer more formally.

"Truly, my brother and I are grateful, both to his lordship and to you."

"Aye, well then, see as how ye don't abuse m'lord's trust, nor kill all his deer, else I might take it personal."

"There's plenty fer all of us, huntsman," Beowulf interjected roughly.

"The name's Bryce," the other man responded with a growl of

similar pitch. "Lord de Lacey's *chief* huntsman. An' ye are?"

"Beowulf, *headman* o' Mallowleigh village in Rogé until I fell foul o' his black lordship."

Bryce gave a grunt, and Beowulf continued drily,

"An' now I'm sworn ter keep the lad here safe."

His tone said all too clearly that if Bryce chose to take his verbal warning to Jacques into the realms of violence, the huntsman would have to deal with Beowulf first.

Another throaty growl from Bryce, then a grudging offer of something approaching a truce,

"Go on then. An' mayhap next time I'm in the forest, we'll go huntin' Lord Justin's deer together, being as I'm as fond o' roast venison as the next man."

Beowulf's hackles slowing subsiding, he said,

"Aye, mayhap we will then."

With that, they passed out through the cool shadows of the arched entry passage, past the alert guards, the grey de Lacey wolf emblazoned on their armoured breasts, and thence down into the little town.

Collecting their cheerfully chattering companions, they made their way back to the forest, Aelfric falling behind to ensure that their path was not marked, and while he did not return at all that night, he slipped into the outlaw camp early the following morning with the tidings that Bryce had apparently kept his lord's side of that extraordinary bargain struck out on the moors and had made no attempt to track the outlaws into the forest.

Even so, Luc deemed it wise to move their camp to another glade, deeper in the vast sprawling greenwood, and by the time this had been accomplished, every one of the outlaws was tired, filthy and inclined to be out of temper.

Until, that is, Melangel served up a more than usually robust meal, accompanied by the best of Gwynhere's brewing. After which, and with the children abed, the men were content to settle to their normal evening pursuits.

Only Luc remained restless, and for all he had laboured as hard as any of the men, appeared unable to relax and Rowène, emerging from the shelter they would share with Lissie, Val, and Gwynny, found her brother seated on a fallen log, hunched over the horn cup in his hand.

Even as she watched, he drained it in one swallow and reached for the flask on the ground beside him.

Pausing, Rowène eyed her brother narrowly, wondering what had made him delve into the dubious oblivion to be obtained from the contents of that flask, for whatever it was she doubted it was Gwynny's honest ale, rather something far more darkly potent.

As to what had made Luc forsake his normal cautious sobriety she had no notion, unless...

A quick glance upwards gave her the answer, the previous day's clouds having been blown away by a cool west wind, to reveal the dark arch of the sky filled with a glittering array of stars... but no moon.

"Oh gods, it is tonight!"

She had not meant to speak her thought, let alone loud enough for Luc to hear.

"It is indeed."

His tone was brittle enough to snap under a single feather's weight of additional strain.

"And by now your friend Adèle will be Madame de Marillec."

He tipped the flask, filling his cup to the rim, then lifted it in mocking toast as he continued,

"The binding oath sworn, the feasting done... only the bedding to be blessed by the gods and witnessed by all those bloody damned vultures who whisper that it will never be consummated."

His hand clenched around the cup and his voice dropped to a raw whisper,

"Hells'death! Confound them all, Ré, and just bloody do it!"

Knowing that she had never been meant to hear those words, Rowène continued across the clearing to the place where Gwynhere stood, dispensing ale to the thirsty outlaws, remaining for some few moments, horn beaker in hand, listening to her companions' conversation without really taking in anything of what they were saying, the greater part of her attention focused on keeping her brother under as casual an observation as she could contrive.

Or perhaps not so casual, as she discovered when – on seeing Caite start to walk towards her impervious brother – Rowène moved swiftly to intercept the other woman without a word to her grandmother or other friends.

"Wait!"

Gwynhere laid a gently restraining hand on her good arm.

"Something is obviously troubling him, Jacques. Maybe Caite can take his mind off it."

"Let me go, Gwynny, and trust me when I say that she is only going to make matters worse."

"Just because Luc is your brother I think you sometimes forget that he is also a man, with a..."

"Damn it, Gwynny, I *know* what he is. And whatever he seeks, he is not like to find it tonight. Not in wine. Nor with Caite, no matter how willing she is to offer him the body she thinks he needs."

"I didn't mean..."

Gwynny started to say, but Rowène did not wait to hear what she had meant.

Instead, she pulled her arm free and ignoring the anxious look in her grandmother's eyes, set off across the clearing.

Caite had a head start however, reaching Luc before Rowène was more than half way back, and so she slowed her step, watching with concern as whatever her brother said to the woman sent her stumbling away, face averted from any watching eyes.

Sighing – since whatever the lack of warmth between them Rowène had no wish to see Caite hurt – she resumed her ambling approach to the spot where her brother sat, determinedly drinking his way to self-destruction.

When she was a scant spear's length away from him, he turned his head towards her, his face in the flickers of amber and shadow thrown by the chancy light of the campfire revealing deeply-carved lines of bitter pain.

"Oh, it's you."

His voice was low, steady, carrying only the faintest edge of a slur. It was not much by way of greeting but neither was it outright rejection.

"May I sit with you a while, Luc," Rowène asked, striving not to let her worry invade her voice. "Share whatever it is you have in that flask?"

He shrugged ungraciously,

"Be my guest," and passed her the flask. "But somehow I don't think you'll like it."

Aware of the disquieting glint in his grey eyes, she took a cautious sip of what she had taken to be mead but which turned out to be wine.

Marillec wine!

Even as it rebelled in her belly, roiling amidst memories of that far-off morning at Chartre, she choked down another swallow.

"Where did you get this?"

"You don't want to know," Luc retorted. His eyes, she saw, were still dangerously narrowed and her temper flared.

"Would you rather I left you alone?" she demanded. "With your wine, to drown in whatever memories it holds for you?"

"No, you can stay," he muttered after a taut moment, adding acerbically, "Just do not try and pry into my soul. And I will stay out of yours."

"A bargain then," she murmured. "Just know that I am here, if you need me."

With that, she seated herself on the log beside him and with a hard sigh, took the flask from his hand and filled first her own cup and then his with the memories of blackberries and honey and a man's warm, firm mouth...

True to her word, she kept her grimly silent brother company through the long moonless night, waiting patiently until the fire had burned down and the embers were banked, until first one and then another of the outlaws sought their beds, and finally both the clearing and the flask were empty.

Only then did Luc speak, and while his voice was no more slurred now than when she had first taken her place beside him, clearly he was drunk enough to forget his habitual caution with her identity.

"Why do you bear with me, Ro, when you know who it is I drink to forget?"

"You cannot help who you love," she said softly. "Any more than I can. Or Josce, for that matter. As for why... there is too much violence and malice rending our lives already for me to set any love aside as worthless or wrong."

Luc gave a bark of bitter laughter and lurched to his feet with a rare clumsiness.

"A single star in the sky, Ro, that's what you are."

"No, Luc!" She spoke with quiet vehemence to his back. "I am not the only one to think like that! Josce, Rafe..."

"Tolerate what is between Gabriel and me, for the sake of our kinship. If it were not for the blood we share, they would be quick enough to condemn us both for what is..."

He broke off and turning, smiled mirthlessly down at her.

"I should say, what was once between us."

His face settling into bleak lines, he looked down at his open hand, slowly clenching his loose fingers into a fist, hiding the scar that ran across his palm, the twin, Rowène knew, to the mark that Gabriel de Marillec carried.

Feeling utterly helpless, she murmured,

"Come on, Luc, call it a day, you have kept your vigil long enough. Whatever was due to happen in the Palace of Princes tonight, it is long over and cannot be amended."

Carefully keeping her thoughts from venturing any further into what did not concern her, Rowène saw her brother – still remarkably quiet and steady on his feet in defiance of the quantity of wine he had consumed – to his bed.

He was out cold before she had even removed his boots, let alone covered him with his mantle and the bed furs.

With resigned forethought she fetched a bucket and set it beside his bed, made sure he could not roll onto his back, and wearily sought her own pallet, her tasks made the more difficult for only having one sound arm to work with.

Stripping down to her shirt, she wrapped herself in her own blankets, her good hand seeking out the small carved wooden box she usually kept beneath her bed but which was now tucked beneath the folded cloak that did duty as a pillow.

Opening the lid, she took out the silver cloak pin nestled within, her fingers running over the intricate design of a falcon within a circle of thorns, almost as if she was caressing not cold metal but the beard-stubbled cheek and firm, warm lips of the man who had once owned that brooch.

With a silent prayer to the gods to keep safe those whom she and her brothers loved, she closed her fingers about the brooch and settled her cheek on her hand. Weary though she was, she found she could not sleep after all, even the soft soughing sound of the two sleeping children failing to soothe.

Instead she lay awake, edgily awaiting the inevitable violent result of Luc's attempt to drown his regrets in Marillec wine.

It was, in many ways, a mirror of the night she had kept a healer's watch over the man Luc called foster-brother and friend.

A man that almost everyone else would have left lying in the dust where he had fallen.

Gabriel Aurélien de Marillec.

A night of holding the man while he vomited, soothing him when he shook, walking alongside him in his dreams, guarding his mind from that which he most feared – so that when he woke he knew who and, perhaps more importantly, accepted *what* he was.

A night that had left him open to her in ways he could not possibly have imagined, and was as yet uncomfortable with, linked by a bond neither of them had foreseen, though Rowène felt that she at least should have done.

A bond that could never quite be broken, even by distance.

Different to the bond she shared with Ranulf, but in its way just as strong.

So that now, rolling to her feet as the sound of Luc's retching ripped through the darkness of the moonless night, wrenching her mind free from the memory of all she had shared with Gabriel de Marillec, Rowène found herself wondering just how badly wrong his ill-fated binding had already gone?

Or whether there was a chance, however remote, that he and Adèle might find some way of living together without both of them being utterly miserable.

Certainly Gabriel had given her his word that he would try, and perhaps Adèle would be prepared to do likewise?

Unless – and far more likely, as Rowène knew from experience – the vicious under-currents of court gossip had put paid to any attempt at understanding, even before they had been bound together.

Verse 4

False Friends, True Friends

With the deliciously decadent nature of Gabriel de Marillec's prospective binding almost the only subject being discussed by the gossips of the court, and Juliène de Lyeyne the only person at court completely uninterested in either the prospect or the protagonists, it was fortunate that Princess Linette's continuing absence made it possible for her to escape the interminable conversations – as well as her mother's unrelenting determination to discover the whereabouts of Guyard de Martine – by retreating to the relative sanctuary of the de Lyeyne apartments in the south wing of the vast palace.

Whilst the princess remained at Vézière Juliène had no official duties to perform and, saving the necessity of avoiding her mother, she could please herself how she spent her days.

The nights, goddess help her, were another matter entirely!

Her recovery from the injuries Hervé himself had inflicted, combined with his obsession to sire another son to secure the de Lyeyne lordship – undiminished by his temporary banishment to Lyeyné – meant that he was visiting her bed again with increasingly fervent frequency, and while she still had the vial of poison her mother had intended her to use on Guyard de Martine's loyal retainers, that was a resort only to be used in extremis.

By contrast to the harsh reality of those brutal nightly couplings with Hervé, the thought of giving herself to the gentle and honourable Guyard de Martine seemed no more real than a dream or a line from a harper's song. Certainly it no longer induced in her anything approaching the panic and protest she had felt when her mother had first mooted her scheme.

Even so, Juliène still prayed daily that it would not happen.

Not because she did not want it, but more because she wished to be saved from making the choice between her estranged son's safety or the destruction of a man who, far from ever having done her any wrong, had done all that lay within his power to see her safe – the only man in Mithlondia of whom she could say such a thing.

Val or de Martine? Guyard or her son?

Goddess, why did it have to be one or the other! Why could she not have...

A soft knock at the door made Juliène glance up, startled and starting to shake.

It was too early for Hervé, and he would never knock in any case. But, goddess! What if it should be her mother, called here by her own tumultuous thoughts?

Instinctively her fingers tightened on the harp she held on her lap – Guyard de Martine's harp that her mother had ordered her to destroy, along with Edwy, his body-servant, and Geryth, his groom. None of which she had done, and reminded now of her dangerous act of disobedience she scrambled to conceal the instrument, praying that the gods would grant her that grace.

They did not!

Even now her tire-maid was opening the door, bobbing a curtsey, stammering a welcome to the person who stood outside.

"Oh, my lady, come in, do. Lady Juliena'll be right pleased ter see ye, as down as she's been since Sister Fayla left us so... er... sudden-like."

Even from across the chamber Juliène could see the colour rise in Siflaed's cheeks. Everyone in the palace, from Prince Linnius down to the lowliest scullery maid and spit boy, knew the gossip regarding the Sister of Mercy who had been sent away in disgrace, having been caught very much in flagrente with one of the royal bodyguards, who had likewise been removed from his post and sent north to the Atarkarnan border. Where, Juliène hoped viciously, her sister's lover – and her son's father – might die painfully on some barbarian's blade.

"Daughter?"

A softly diffident voice, utterly unlike the Winter Lady's silk and ice, brought her head up.

"Madame de Lyeyne!"

Still scrabbling for composure, she met the faded blue eyes that held more than a trace of sadness.

"I would you did not feel the need to keep me at so formal a distance, Juliène. Despite being Hervé's mother I am not your enemy, and the gods know we have more in common that you might think."

"Your pardon, Madame Isabelle," Juliène said stiffly. "I was surprised to see you, that is all. You will take a glass of wine?"

And when Siflaed had served them both and been dismissed, she continued in some puzzlement,

"Is Princess Linette returned from Vézière then?"

"No, indeed, but I am here at her request, as company for Messire de Marillec's betrothed on her journey from the Healing House. I will remain here in Lamortaine until after the binding ceremony has been completed, and then return to Vézière."

"De Marillec's betrothed was at the Healing House?" Juliène asked blankly. "In Vézière? What in the name of the gods was she doing there? Is she sickly?"

She snorted delicately.

"Scant chance then of her giving de Marillec the heir his father will be no doubt be expecting from this binding."

"You mistake the matter," Lady Isabelle said in some distress. "Far from being sickly, Adèle *chose* some years ago to live among the Sisters of Mercy as a healer. I believe it came as... quite a shock to her to learn that her father had betrothed her to Jean de Marillec's eldest son... and then almost in the same breath to see him there before her."

"No doubt!" Juliène agreed waspishly. "Personally I would not want to see him at all."

Other than to watch him hang!

"Unfortunately, Adèle seems to share your feelings," Lady Isabelle murmured.

Adding, with a troubled sigh, more to herself than Juliène,

"Which does not bode well for their binding, especially given the inauspicious circumstances of their meeting."

"Oh? There was... some trouble between them?" Juliène asked, curiosity stirring, tinged with more than a little malice.

"No, not at all! Indeed they barely exchanged a dozen words."

The older woman's voice reflected the nervous strain in her eyes.

"Messire de Marillec was... or at least he seemed..."

"What did he seem?"

"Not... himself. He... well, I suppose you might say he collapsed in the courtyard just after meeting his betrothed, and as I understand it one of the healers..."

"He *collapsed*?" Juliène interrupted again. "Passed out, do you mean? Was he that sickened by the thought of what he must do?"

"No, no, nothing like that! It is a long journey south from the Atarkarnan border, and he had ridden himself into exhaustion, or so Sister Fayla said."

"*Fayla!*"

Juliène ground out her sibling's assumed name between clenched teeth.

"And just what did *she* have to do with it all?"

"Sister Fayla was the healer who attended Messire de Marillec when he broke down in your br... when he collapsed, and, as I understand it, she sat by his bedside all night," Lady Isabelle went on hurriedly before Juliène could question what she had started to say.

Then, with a frown deepening the lines on an already care-worn brow, the older woman added,

"Was it not Sister Fayla who tended you when Herv... back in the summer, and restored you to health? Yet you sound as if you are not... kindly disposed towards her?"

"Hardly! Considering what an arrant slut she proved herself to be!" Juliène said viciously.

"Surely that is a little harsh..."

"You would not say that if it had been you who found her in bed with that guardian! As it is, I would not put it past her to try her whore's tricks on de Marillec, save that given what rumour has to say about *his* preferences, I will accept that on this occasion she did sit chastely by his bed, rather than pleasure him in it. Unless, of course, he is one of those who will take his pleasure any way he can get it!"

"Juli·ène!"

Lady Isabelle was white with shock.

"You should not speak such slander. Especially as there is no proof that Messire de Marillec is... that he would..."

She stopped, swallowing, her blue gaze clouding, as if seeing something Juliène could not. It was not difficult to guess what.

"Of course he *is*... and he *would*," she said, putting a different emphasis completely on the older woman's broken sentence. "Nor do I care what he is, providing it is not my b... providing it is no-one I know that he is doing it with!"

Then, with a sweetly derisive smile,

"So, Madame, now that we have disposed of de Marillec and his proclivities as a topic of conversation, perhaps you would tell me why you are here at all, since it is obvious do not care for my company."

With a shaky sigh, Lady Isabelle reached into the pouch at her belt, and retrieving a neatly folded and sealed missive, said simply,

"Princess Linette asked me to bring you this."

Taking it with some reluctance, for she did not see how this could possibly contain any tidings she wished to hear, Juliène ran her finger under the red wax seal, unfolded the parchment and began to read.

Finally she raised her eyes with a calm that masked the myriad of emotions in her mind – disbelief and irritation being only the most readily identifiable – to regard her mother-by-binding.

"Do you know what this says? What the princess is asking me to do?"

Lady Isabelle nodded, her faded blue eyes regarding Juliène more than a little warily.

"Linette felt that you would be best-placed to stand as Adèle's friend, should she feel the need of one in her... unhappy situation."

"But I do not even know the girl!" Juliène exclaimed.

"True, but you are of an age, and I believe Adèle shared a brief but sincere friendship with your sister Rowène, when they were both at court. This, of course, was before your sister's tragic demise... what was it, five years ago?"

"Six," Juliène said curtly.

She felt like scowling but refrained, not only because she did not wish to wrinkle the smooth skin of her face but also because she did not want Lady Isabelle to guess at the less-than-loving feelings she held for her not-so-dead sister. Instead she said,

"I still do not see why Linette is asking *me* to befriend this provincial nobody who has, according to what you said earlier, spent the last few years living among the healers at Vézière. What in the name of all the gods would we have in common?"

Lady Isabelle fidgeted with the dangling tassles on her gold-embroidered belt before looking up, her eyes soft with a sympathy that made Juliène squirm.

"Linette knows that you have known little happiness in your binding. And she fears that Adèle will likewise know only misery. All the princess asks is that you befriend her, be a sympathetic ear if she needs to unburden herself. After all," she said, suddenly astringent. "I cannot imagine that Adèle will be able to confide in her mother, Mariette de Martine having done her utmost to..."

"What?"

Juliène's wandering attention was jerked back by that single name.

"You are telling me this girl is a *de Martine*?"

Lady Isabelle blinked, looking perplexed.

"Of course she is, did you not know? Surely someone must have mentioned it, since I imagine gossip has been rife on the subject of this binding, poor child!"

"To be honest, I have found the whole affair tedious beyond words."

Or I did until now.

"I seem to have heard that her father was a minor castellan in Valenne," Juliène admitted. "But I confess I thought no more about it."

Now, however, she remembered all too clearly the harper who had come to Chartre calling himself Guy of Montfaucon. And Montfaucon was a village that lay just south of Valéntien.

Juliène hesitated, but she had to be sure before she committed herself to any course of action.

"So if your Adèle is a de Martine, presumably her father's holding is Montfaucon, and there is therefore some kinship between her and..."

No! She dared not speak his given name aloud, fearful lest the Winter Lady should somehow hear it and descend on her again with questions she did not want to answer and orders she did not want to obey.

Lady Isabelle was not so reticent.

"Between her and Lord Joffroi's natural brother, Guy de Martine? Yes, his mother, Lady Alys, was Adèle's father's sister, so they are..."

Lady Isabelle blue eyes were suddenly opaque.

"*Were* cousins, I should say."

She eyed Juliène with an uncharacteristic intensity as she continued,

"More than that, I seem to remember there being some closeness between Adèle and her kinsman before she went to live with the healers and Messire de Martine... disappeared. But why do you ask, Juliène? Does it make a difference?"

"No, why would it?" Juliène replied coolly, and knew she lied.

For if Guyard had indeed returned to Mithlondia, from whom would he seek assistance if not the only member of his family who held any feelings save disdain and dislike for the de Rogé cuckoo in the otherwise unremarkable but strictly respectable de Martine nest?

"Of course," Juliène said now, borrowing something of her mother's silken charm. "I will do what the princess has requested. Indeed, I shall seek Adèle out at the feast this very evening. Perhaps you would be so kind as to introduce us, Madame?"

Accordingly that evening, rather than leaving the hall immediately the feasting was done, Juliène waited until Lady Isabelle approached the place where she sat, accompanied by a slender, pretty, fair-haired young woman who had the same summer blue eyes as Juliène remembered – with an inconveniently sharp thorn-stab of regret – Guyard de Martine as having.

Except where Guy's had been clear and confident – until that last day when, gods help her, they had been near blind with pain – his kinswoman's gaze was clouded with suspicion and a sullen unhappiness.

Having performed the introductions, and eyed the two staring, unsmiling young women for a moment or two, Lady Isabelle sighed and suggested that they withdraw to the Hall of Fire where they would find conversation far easier in the shadowy quiet than amidst the growing uproar of revelry in the Feast Hall.

Adèle agreed, but with such an apathetic lack of interest as made Juliène's own underlying dissatisfaction at the situation burn that much brighter.

Nevertheless, she held her silence until they reached the otherwise deserted fire-lit chamber, and then she rounded on her companion with an exasperated exclamation,

"For gods'sake! Have you no pride in yourself! You are here at court to take part in a binding, not an execution!"

"Pride, you say?" Adèle demanded, with the first show of spirit Juliène had seen in her. "You expect me to be *proud*... or... or *joyful* that I am to be bound to such a man? A... a... I do not even know the words for the likes of Gabriel de Marillec!"

Juliène regarded the other woman – little younger in years but separated from Juliène by an unbridgeable sea of inexperience – with a distinct lack of sympathy.

"Gabriel de Marillec is many things, Demoiselle de Martine – and *sodomite* is the politest of the words you are looking for – but whilst I cannot think of a man I dislike more, even I cannot see him taking his fists to your face or a whip to your back, let alone a blade to your most private of parts."

Adèle stared at her in horror for a moment, evidently discerning more than Juliène would have wished. Then her gaze went distant and unfocused, as if seeing something far away from the fire-lit chamber with its soft amber glow of dancing flames.

"How strange! That is almost exactly what Row..."

She stopped, guilt putting hot colour in her previously ashen cheeks.

"What Rowène said," Juliène finished for her, trying to keep the brittle note of bitterness from her tone. "Oh, do not worry. I have known for years now that my sister is alive. I know too the disreputable guise she chooses to hide behind."

"There is nothing disreputable about the Sisters of Mercy!" Adele said sharply, abruptly roused from her misery to defend the healers amongst whom she had lived for so long.

"Forgive me," Juliène said insincerely, striving to suppress her satisfaction that Rowène had not taken Adèle, supposedly her friend, into her confidence regarding the guise she wore most often, and only just restraining herself from reminding the other woman that as a Sister of Mercy, Rowène had recently acquired a distinctly disreputable name for herself *and* the order of healers.

"They work amongst the poor and misfortunate of the realm, expecting and gods know receiving scant thanks for doing it," Adèle continued hotly.

"Indeed, they do," Juliène murmured soothingly, before continuing with a reluctant curiosity,

"So what exactly did my sister have to say about the... ah... man with whom you are to swear the binding oath?"

"She told me..." A pause. An unsteady breath. "That there are far worse men to whom I could be bound!"

A flicker of the dark gold eyelashes suggested that Adèle knew Rowène had been alluding to Hervé de Lyeyne with that acerbic remark.

"And that if Messire de Marillec was the sort of man to practise violence against a woman, her brother could never have lo..."

She stopped, utterly aghast at what she had so nearly implicated Luc de Chartreux in.

"A man your brother could never have called friend," she amended hastily.

Juliène regarded the other woman with no shred of warmth or forgiveness in her narrowed eyes.

"*Never,*" she said with icy precision. "Unless you wish to make an enemy of me, will you ever say anything of that nature again. Regardless of whatever my witless and undiscerning sister may have said, there is *nothing* between my brother and the man to whom you will be bound save a distant boyhood friendship, long since outgrown."

Evidently chastened by Juliène's freezing fury, Adèle nodded, blue eyes huge in her bone-white face, perhaps also belatedly realising that if de Marillec were to be arraigned and convicted of indulging in unlawful and unnatural acts with another man, Adèle herself would be left little better than a beggar in the gutter. Especially if she had not conceived the next heir to Marillec by then – which, gods knew, seemed the unlikeliest of eventualities.

Satisfied that she had cowed the younger woman into guarding her tongue, Juliène turned the subject to one more to her own purpose, though she was careful not to allow more than a thread of interest to embroider her tone of bland tedium,

"Given the circumstances of your upcoming binding, I do not suppose you have heard from your... ah... cousin?"

"My cousin?" Adèle looked utterly – and apparently genuinely – confused by the unexpected question.

"Do you not acknowledge him then, base-born as he..."

"Base...? You mean *Guy*? Well, of course I acknowledge him! Why would I not?"

The scorn for those who did not – her grandsire, her father, her mother, possibly Juliène herself – burned like fire in her eyes, then something resembling a sorrowful frown creased her pale brow.

"But Guy is dead. He died five years ago."

"No. He *disappeared* five years ago," Juliène corrected her.

Then, with more than a tinge of tartness creeping into her tone, added,

"Disappeared is by no means the same as dead, as my sister can testify."

She regarded Adèle's rising blush with malicious satisfaction. The girl made a very poor liar, and almost certainly knew her kinsman was alive. Whether she knew his present whereabouts was another matter.

Almost, Juliène did not pursue the subject, until a shaft of icy pain cleaving through her skull warned her that her mother was aware of the conversation, and that she must therefore follow it through.

"I was told," she said now, as steadily as she could. "That he tired of being taken for granted in his legitimate brother's service, and instead went south to seek a harper's position at the royal court of Kardolandia."

Goddess, if only he had taken such a course of his own volition, rather than being thrown into the shameful life to which her thoughtless words had condemned him!

With an effort she managed a smile, hoping it might invite the younger woman's confidences.

"I wish him well if that is so. Except... I heard a rumour just recently that he had been seen in Mithlondia again, and since he has not contacted Lord Joffroi, naturally I wondered if he had sought you out?"

"No. No, he has not," Adèle said jerkily. "If indeed rumour tells truth for once, and Guy has returned, and is not dead as I thought. But I am sure you must be mistaken."

"Perhaps," Juliène made a show of conceding the debate. "But wherever he is, I should like to know that he is safe, since he is by way of being my kin too, at least by binding."

Then, as Adèle gave her a doubting glance, she added casually,

"For my sister's sake, as well. Rowène loved your cousin, and he her."

She took a swift moment to calculate the effect of her next words, then said coolly,

"Indeed, she must have done, must she not, since she bore him a child without the benefit of a binding band."

And when Adèle merely regarded her with a fixed blue gaze, added with spurious candour,

"You *did* know my sister has a child? A daughter, I believe."

"Y... yes."

It took the other woman two blushing attempts at the affirmative.

"But I... I thought it was J... Joscelin de Veraux's babe."

Nor was it a flush of dainty embarrassment, such as might be expected given the delicate subject.

Instead Adèle's previous pallid skin was blotched a deep and hectic red.

Now *that* was interesting, Juliène thought, even as she said in a tone of polite indifference,

"No, I have seen the girl and she is unmistakably Guyard de Martine's child."

Juliène swallowed a sudden raw rise of bitter jealousy.

"She has your kinsman's dark fair hair and light blue eyes. You might like to tell him that if you ever see him again. He should know, do you not think, that he has a daughter?"

"Surely..." Adèle swallowed again. "Surely Rowène would have told him if he was the father of her child?"

"You do not believe that any more than I do," Juliène remarked, scornful now. "The truth is that my sister has not told any of us, let alone her former lover, even a quarter of the secrets she keeps."

Particularly not that she had betrayed Guyard in his absence by taking his own half-brother to her bed.

That, however, was not something she intended to tell Adèle.

Not just yet.

Maybe never.

No, Juliène intended to keep that truth to herself for the moment. Then, when she deemed the time right, she would tell Guyard to his face. And when he broke, as he surely would, she would be there to patch his heart back together.

After which, if she followed her mother's command – and she had no choice if she were to save both Val and herself – she would break him again. And when that happened, there would be no-one to heal the shattered pieces of his riven soul.

Gods save it does not come to that! But if it does... Guyard, forgive me!

The final few days until the binding ceremony passed by in a flurry of ever-more extravagant feasting, seasoned by the ongoing orgy of gossip.

Juliène took her expected part in the former whilst striving to ignore the latter, and in fulfilment of Princess Linette's request, kept Adèle de Martine company through it all, though the goddess knew, with the other girl existing in such a miasma of misery it was tedious work.

Tedious but necessary if Juliène was to convince her mother that she was pursuing the matter of the harper's seduction and betrayal. That was the real reason why she tolerated Adèle's snivelling presence, but thus far she had learned nothing more about Guyard de Martine's whereabouts, though she was almost certain the wretched girl knew more than she was telling.

The answers to the two questions that acted like twin thorns stabbing into her head and heart, day and night, came to Juliène one afternoon when, in her desperation to escape Adèle's depressing company, she accompanied her maid, her mother-by-binding and Adèle's mother out into the palace gardens seeking flowers for the bride's binding crown.

Having no interest whatsoever in the outcome, Juliène left it to the older women to fill the basket Siflaed was carrying and, pleading a headache, wandered away to seek some peaceful place where she might perhaps take refuge from the very real turmoil in her mind.

The rose arbour where she had once tried to seduce Guyard de Martine was now little more than a barren lattice of branches arching over a moss-slimed bench, home to snails and spiders, neither of which she cared to sit with.

The green sward by the lake was a squelchy, smelly haven for waterfowl of all sorts and sizes, the herbs in the walled garden dying back into drab insignificance, leaving only dry scentless stalks, the lavender edging fading to a dull grey.

Only the fishpond in the centre showed any sign of life and as Juliène seated herself on the raised edge and wrapped her mantle more tightly around her, she found herself joined by Princess Linette's pet cats.

Three pairs of green eyes regarded each other across the dark water with a sort of wary aloofness, before the two cats fell to watching the carp swimming within the confines of the pond, and after a moment Juliène found herself doing the same.

It was then that it came to her, slowly, softly, stealthily as a summer's sunrise slips over the darkness of the starlit night, that what she needed was a way to encircle some small part of her mind, somewhere it would be safe to hold her thoughts secret from her mother's probing, as the fish were kept safe from the cats' clever paws. But could she do it?

Goddess help her, she must! For now she had something to hide!

Her heart quickening as her determination grew, she looked up to find that the cats had abandoned the lazily circling fish and were watching her instead, their green gaze steady, unblinking and clear as the sunlit waters of the Southern Sea.

Seeing the intensity with which they regarded her, a sick trepidation rose in her throat, almost choking her with the fear that the cats might somehow be servants of the Winter Lady... before her common sense suddenly reasserted itself, combined with the memory of how Jade and Amber had reacted to her mother's presence that other time they had all met by the pond.

Taking a deep, steadying breath, and with Jade's soft, furry dark head butting against her fingers on one side, and Amber's gentle purring resonating on the other, Juliène slowly and with a cautious concentration began to build an invisible wall to keep her mother out. Then, when she sensed no hostile, icy invasion she carefully concealed the knowledge of Guyard de Martine's whereabouts therein.

Or at least she *thought* she knew where he was.

Or perhaps, more accurately, where he had been a scant three days ago. For if Adèle had seen him, as Juliène guessed she must have done, it could only have been on the road between Vézière and Lamortaine, and while Guyard would surely have more sense than to come anywhere near the royal palace, it was entirely possible that he might seek and find a refuge with Lord Nicholas of Vézière.

She dared not examine that thought at any great length though. Instead, she made sure to seal it away behind the secret wall she had constructed in her mind.

Then, hearing Siflaed's anxious voice calling for her beyond the walled garden, she rose to her feet and walked back to her companions, both cats leaping down from the rim of the pond and disappearing into the disorder of dying herbs, just as Juliène caught a flash of green silk from the archway in the wall behind her.

"Ah, there you are, my dear," Lady Isabelle said, as she appeared in the entrance ahead of Juliène, her gaze flitting over Juliène's shoulder as she continued,

"I trust your headache is better for some fresh air, but it is starting to rain and we should go in. Siflaed's basket is full, so unless your mother needs you for anything..."

Juliène dared not turn around, fearing the command she might see in the Winter Lady's eyes

Instead, she shook her head with a motion Lady Isabelle could not mistake.

Blue eyes widening, the older woman extended a visibly shaking hand and said quickly,

"Come then, my dear, we have a binding crown to make for the morrow."

Thus the day of the unwanted, ill-fated and much-talked-about binding of Adèle de Martine to Gabriel de Marillec finally dawned... in spitting rain and drear grey clouds, to the sound of black crows cawing in harsh mockery from the storm-stripped branches of the beech trees lining the north road.

It seemed a fitting omen. And gave the gossips further cause to mutter amongst themselves.

Caught up in her own concerns, Juliène sat heedless of whispered gossip, dark weather or avian chorus, in the cramped de Martine chambers, together with Lady Isabelle, while Lady Mariette fussed in strident form, harrying the servants who were doing their best to carry out her conflicting instructions.

Eventually, however, Adèle was arrayed in the specially sewn gown of tawny-gold brocade embroidered with acorns and vine leaves, her long primrose-pale hair brushed out and left loose, so that it cascaded well beyond her hips, longer even, Juliène observed with more than a little annoyance, than her own.

Then, with the placement of the binding crown – a band of late honeysuckle woven with autumn berries – Juliène's feelings underwent an abrupt reversal.

Momentarily forgetting her jealousy, she succumbed instead to the pain of memories she strove ever to forget.

For she herself had worn honeysuckle to her binding... but where the pale petals had glimmered like pure gold when set upon the midnight-silk of her own tresses, against Adèle's sunlit locks the flowers were simply lost, the thorn berries by contrast standing out like drops of fresh blood... reminding Juliène most unpleasantly of the crimson-flecked, straw fair hair of the man whose head had once rested so briefly in her lap.

"No!" she said sharply, almost at the same time as Lady Isabelle stepped forwards.

"You must find something else for her to wear!"

"There *is* nothing else," Lady Mariette objected pettishly. "It is far too late. We had trouble enough finding these flowers. The palace gardens are bare, save for purple mourning daisies which would scarce be fitting for such a joyous occasion."

"No, indeed," Lady Isabelle interjected before Adèle – who up until this point had been as lifeless as a child's wooden doll – could speak the thought that Juliène could see reflected in her suddenly rebellious blue eyes.

"I have a circlet that might do," Juliène offered. "Not living flowers, it is true, but with petals of amber and leaves of beryl, all set in a band of red-gold."

She had never liked it.

"Shall I fetch it?"

"That would be kind indeed," Lady Isabelle spoke quickly before Adèle's mother had a chance to object, her washed-out blue eyes regarding Juliène with surprised approval.

Juliène herself cared only to escape the bloodily vivid memory of the day Guyard de Martine had been beaten almost to the point of death by his vengeful older brother. And as he undoubtedly would be again if Joffroi ever succeeded in laying hands on him.

Shuddering, Juliène almost ran from the room.

According to palace officials, the formal joining of Jean de Marillec's heir and the castellan of Montfaucon's daughter was due to take place at the propitious moment when the pallid autumn sun should reach the height of its low arc – or where the sun would be could it even be seen, Juliène mused as she waited in the cavernous hall, hidden as it was behind cloaking clouds the same rain-grey as her brother's eyes.

And then found herself wondering whether Gabriel de Marillec was thinking the same thing as he waited, alone with his thoughts in the small chamber adjoining the Hall of Binding, perhaps looking out of the window at the sheeting rain, his long slender fingers clenched on the stone surround as he readied himself for what must come, knowing the eyes of the whole court would be upon him, watchful for any betrayal, any weakness of will, any sign that he was pining for the man rumoured to be his lover...

Back within the seldom-used hall with its carven pillars and vibrantly coloured hangings, impatiently waiting for the ceremony to begin, Juliène gladly abandoned all thought of Gabriel de Marillec, fighting instead to keep from drowning in memories of her own binding, these coming like waves, some washing over her in a nauseating blur, some shining clear as crystalline shards of sunlight...

The innate pride that had striven to hold her quivering spine straight but which, without the presence of Guyard de Martine at her side would scarcely have been strong enough to enable her to survive the day without breaking down.

The comforting warmth of his shoulder so close to hers as she stood before the prince, Hervé's sweating hand gripped painfully tight about her own ice-cold fingers.

The look Guyard had given her when she had first entered the great ceremonial chamber, his eyes as warmly translucent as the Southern Sea beneath a summer sky... a flash of heat, swallowed immediately by a plea that reached into the depths of her very soul, as if to demand of her why in the name of all the gods she was doing this?

The solid presence of the man, seated beside her at the binding feast, so close she could have touched him if she had dared.

And she had wanted to! Goddess, how she had wanted to!

To feel his strong arms fold about her in an embrace that said she was his, and his alone, and that he would protect her to the death from any who sought to cause her hurt or harm.

Instead she had made herself endure Hervé's repulsive groping, and smile through it all because her mother and all the court were watching her, and she must not reveal her nausea and the desperate conviction that she had made perhaps the greatest mistake in a life already filled with erroneous judgements.

Guyard had begged her not to bind herself to such a man, and he had been proved right almost before the blood that sealed the binding vow had dried upon her hand.

Set against that – the hideous brutality of that binding night to which Guyard had perforce had to abandon her and the endless years she had yet to endure in Hervé's bed – what did that ninny Adèle have to fear?

Glancing at her now, Juliène wanted only to shake or slap her out of her state of listless misery.

So what if the girl fancied herself in love with Joscelin de Veraux?

The man would never look twice at her, all his attention being of necessity given to the task of holding onto his title, position and lands in the face of Joffroi's determination to deprive him of them. As for de Veraux's other needs, no doubt he took care of them at the Crimson Rose.

As, Juliène reflected cynically, did most of the noblemen presently filling the ceremonial chamber, including her own lord-by-binding.

Though there was one man who Juliène did not expect to be found visiting the courtesans of the Crimson Rose.

Quite possibly, she thought with a slight smirk, Adèle would find him more acceptable if he did...

A sudden whispering stir, like the ripple of wind across a field of flowering flax, informed her that the man himself had entered the chamber, and she turned her head just enough to watch his approach.

Completely unattended by family or friend, Gabriel de Marillec walked across the crowded chamber.

Looking neither left nor right, head held high, jaw set in a surprisingly hard line, he stopped before the throne, and after making his obeisance to Prince Linnius, turned to acknowledge his betrothed with a bow and something that might have been meant as a smile but which showed more clearly than anything else the strain he was under.

Getting no response, de Marillec's face took on a blank expression as he assumed his place at Adèle's side. He made no immediate move to clasp her trembling hand in his own though, his tension obvious as he glanced over his shoulder, just as Prince Linnius leaned forward in his great carved chair to ask in an impatient undertone,

"I see your father is here." Albeit standing a good six feet away from his son. "But where is your other witness?"

"I do not know, Sire," de Marillec replied, his level tone betraying nothing of the emotions he must be feeling. "My younger brother, Bayard, agreed to stand with me but why he is not here I cannot say. He has sent no word, either that he had been taken ill, or... or that he has changed his mind."

Linnius sat back, impatience rapidly darkening into annoyance on his pale features.

He drummed his fingers on the polished arm of his black oak throne for a moment or two and then announced abruptly,

"Well, you will just have to find someone else then, and quickly. Before I start wondering whether you are deliberately seeking to make a mockery of my word given before the High Counsel that this binding will take place today?"

"I assure you, Sire, that is the last thing I would seek to do!"

Given the unmistakable threat contained in the prince's terse tone, Juliène was scarcely surprised to see that de Marillec had gone white beneath the weathering of wind and summer sun, since whatever his private wishes regarding this binding, he could not fail to see it through in public without risking what little standing he had left. And even his life, if Linnius decided he was disloyal rather than merely reluctant to do his duty to his name.

With a half shrug of tight shoulders, de Marillec returned the prince's burning stare and said flatly,

"Forgive me, Sire, there *is* no-one else I can call upon."

"No friends, Messire?" Linnius sneered, before raising his voice to address the watching courtiers,

"Is there anyone here who is willing to stand at Messire de Marillec's side and witness his binding to Demoiselle de Martine?"

Apparently not, Juliène concluded, as none of the assembled noblemen – not even Hal de Vézière, whom she vaguely recalled as claiming friendship with her brother and de Marillec many years ago – took a single step forwards from the comfortable anonimity of the crowd of courtiers massed within the chamber.

With the silence stretching out into hundreds of heartbeats some of the younger ladies began to giggle nervously as the tension continued to thicken around them, and when Juliène glanced covertly at the noblewomen most closely connected with the affair, she saw that Lady Isabelle's blue eyes were bright with sympathetic tears, Lady Mariette's face was suffused with fury and embarrassment, whilst the faintest glitter of icy amusement in the Winter Lady's green eyes revealed the enjoyment she was experiencing at Gabriel de Marillec's blatant discomfiture.

Most of the older noblemen, Juliène saw as she glanced rapidly from face to face, were maintaining a stony sort of dignity, staring straight ahead of them, only Justin de Lacey frowning grimly at the flagstone beneath his feet, but before she could wonder at it, she caught sight of Joffroi's face.

Goddess, help her! She had seen that look of triumphant malice on his face more than once before, and feeling slightly sick she turned her gaze quickly away, only to alight on Hervé and Léon, dark heads bent close together, neither of them making any attempt to hide their sniggers at de Marillec's solitary state.

Glancing away in sudden revulsion, she looked again at the slender, glittering figure standing before the throne... and any momentary softening she might have felt towards him was lost as she remembered what he was to her brother, all her old animus returning with the force of white water crashing over a high cliff, and if she had possessed the power she would have consigned him to the icy depths then and there, thus setting both Luc and Adèle free.

Only then did Juliène look back at the woman whose friend she was supposed to be, finding the girl standing as still as a carved effigy in a Kardolandian crypt, her tightly entwined fingers, and the faint, erratic movement of her silk-covered breast the sole sign that she was in any way aware of the debacle her binding had descended into.

Slowly the head beneath the glittering circlet turned to look at the man standing in almost visible isolation at her side, hope briefly showing on her pure profile. Since if no man could be found with the courage to stand alongside...

"I will do it, Sire!"

Juliène saw Adèle jerk as if struck through the heart, felt her own blood freeze at the sight of the man pushing his way forwards from the back of the hall, his clipped "stand aside" unnecessary by the time he reached the front rank, which parted of its own volition so that he stood straight and tall, and almost as solitary as the man he had come to support.

A sudden draught set the flames of a thousand candles to dancing, their chancy light flickering over the lean lines of his face, setting swan feathers of white in his dark hair, and shards of ice to glitter in his sleet-grey eyes...

Luc!

Even as her brother's name screamed through Juliène's stunned mind, she saw the shock on Gabriel de Marillec's face fade, and he was once more in control of himself, brought to his senses – just as Juliène had been – by Adèle's low moan,

"Oh gods! Joscelin, no! Anyone but you!"

And Juliène realised that both she and de Marillec had been deceived by flame-cast shadows and a flickering superficial resemblance between Joscelin de Veraux and the man they both loved in their different ways

It is but a glancing likeness, Juliène assured herself frantically. *No more substantial than starlight on still water, or the mist-shrouded moon.*

Then, as de Veraux turned slightly to look at the man at whose side he now stood, she was able to study him more closely, seeking out the very obvious differences between him and her brother. Or at least how she remembered Luc from the brief glimpse that was all she had had of him on the Vézière highway last summer.

De Veraux was clean-shaven for a start, his hair much longer and tidier than Luc's ragged shoulder-length crop, while his nose – unsurprisingly for a nobleman who was also illegitimate and had spent most of his formative years fighting – showed signs of having been broken and badly reset.

Yet these things, striking as they seemed at first sight, counted for nothing when Juliène realised that the straight locks falling over his broad shoulders were not only as dark as Luc's but also touched by the same frost, unusual for men in their twentieth decade.

And if de Veraux's nose had not been broken, it would undoubtedly have shown the same long – and very familiar – line as Luc's.

Thus, what Juliène had taken to be differences were, she realised with growing dismay, barely sufficient to conceal the identical bone structure beneath.

Yet why should they not share such lineaments, she argued desperately with herself.

Was it not only to be expected, when she knew what few others did, that Luc's father, Lucius de Chartreux and Joscelin's father, Prince Marcus, had both been sired by Prince Raymund of Mithlondia.

Except, if that was all it was, how did Joscelin de Veraux come to possess the same clear grey eyes as Juliène's father, brother and sister?

The conclusion was inescapable. Damnably so!

Gods above!

Was it not trial enough that she had been forced to accept Lucien, the man who had commanded the Chartre garrison until his death on a de Rogé blade, as her half-brother, without discovering yet another one of her father's indiscretions flourishing here, and in considerably better circumstances than the offspring of a mere washer-woman could ever have achieved.

It had been possible for her to ignore Lucien of Chartre.

Joscelin, Lord of Veraux and High Commander of Mithlondia, was another matter entirely, damn him!

Had her mother and Joffroi guessed whose son he was?

But of course they had, she answered herself. Hence their ongoing and vicious vendetta against him.

As for Luc and Rowène, they must know too, she realised as another black tide of bitter anger swept over her.

Once again her brother and sister had not trusted her.

Once again they had rejected her, chosen to hold her outside of the family bond.

Gods knew, she expected little else of Rowène, but that Luc should turn away from her too...

Or perhaps, she thought, scrabbling after a tiny hope, he did not know that Joscelin de Veraux was his half-brother... *her* half-brother, damn him to Hell!

Yet even as she cursed him, she saw that her father's last-born bastard had gone down on one knee in front of the throne, a supplicant's stance though his head was held high.

To judge from the scowl on Prince Linnius' face, he did not approve in the slightest of his High Commander's intervention.

Nor was he the only one, Juliène having caught de Marillec's hissed,

"For gods'sake! You do not have to do this, Josce."

Followed by de Veraux's curt,

"Yes, I do."

Adding so quietly that almost Juliène did not hear the words,

"I will not leave a man I call *friend* to face these bloody vultures alone."

Finally, after a few more moments of irritated finger tapping, Linnius waved his hand in dissatisfied consent, causing the tall figure in the formal dark green and silver robe to rise to his feet and take his place once more at Gabriel de Marillec's side.

And the question of what Luc knew or did not know had to be set aside for a quieter moment.

As to what Adèle might be thinking... the simple truth was that Juliène neither knew nor cared.

Verse 5

Coming to Terms

With the formal binding ceremony being completed without further delay – though for a single, shining moment Adèle had truly thought she might be granted a reprieve – the court settled to enjoy the full-scale feast that always followed the more serious business of oath-swearing.

Terrible though this was for someone as accustomed to quiet as Adèle – the occasion made almost unendurable by the fact that *she* was now the focus of all attention.... she and the tense, silent man seated by her side – there was, of course, something far worse to come.

The part of the day Adèle had been dreading even more than the oath-taking or the feasting – the moment when she would be alone with the man to whom she was now bound until death.

It was close to midnight now and almost everyone – from the noblemen and their ladies to the tire-woman who had been assigned to her – had either left, or were leaving, the richly-furnished chamber that henceforth she would share with her lord-by-binding.

Thought of which left her caught between an overwhelming urge to burst into hysterical tears or vomit up what little of the rich food she had managed to eat at the feast.

Neither of which actions she could – for the sake of her own pride and self-respect – indulge in while there were other people in the room.

Dear God of Light, why could they not all just *leave*!

And take her unwanted lord-by-binding with them!

That, of course, was not going to happen but *finally* the last of the courtiers were departing, Lady Isabelle giving her the maternal embrace her own mother would never have dreamed of offering, and which Adèle so very badly needed. By contrast, Juliène de Lyeyne – the woman who was supposed to be her friend – had regarded her with distinct lack of anything resembling either compassion or kindness in her cool green eyes.

The womenfolk having slipped quietly away, the noblemen remained a little longer before they too – with one notable exception – made their drunken departure, and while they had laughed and exchanged the crude witticisms common to any binding night, there had been a bitingly raw edge to some of their comments, so that even when Adèle had not fully comprehended their meaning, the tone alone was enough to make her cringe.

God of Mercy! Will no-one stop what is to come?

In frantic desperation, but very little hope, her restless gaze settled on the one man who lingered yet.

With his tall, leanly-powerful body clad in the formal court robes of a Lord of Mithlondia, and the long, frosted dark hair at his temples bound up in warrior braids, Joscelin de Veraux was so sternly handsome that even to look at him hurt her heart.

Unlike his peers, he was stone-cold sober – she had not seen him drink more than a single cup of watered wine all evening – and was presently standing by the door leading to the passageway, seemingly impervious to her trembling presence as she tried not to listen to his deep, crisp voice as he spoke with the man who was his Second.

Second of the Guardians! Ha! As if she could ever have mistaken such a gilded jay for a soldier!

As it was, she had been doing her best *not* to look at him but now, when he stood so close to the man about whom she had recklessly dared to dream for the past five years, she had no choice.

Gods, if only Joscelin de Veraux were not her distant kin.

If only he had showed even the slightest interest in her at all.

But he never had, and she had to accept that with her binding to the man he had publicly called *friend* he never would.

That being so, all she could do was try and pay heed to the advice – unpalatable though it was – offered by the two women to whom she had once felt closest, and make the best of a situation she could not escape save by her own death. Or that of the man to whom she was now bound!

And unhappy though she undoubtedly was, she had no desire to escape this barbed binding by such extreme measures. Not on her own account certainly.

On the other hand, could she, who had been a healer for five years, truly wish for the daemons of death to steal the soul of a man who had done her no harm?

Or at least, she amended with an uncontrollable lurch of her queasy insides, he had not done so yet.

This nightmare of a day was far from over, however, and there would be time aplenty to discover just how far adrift Rowène and the Eldest had been in their reading of his character.

On that thought, she slanted another look at her lord-by-binding where he stood, gaudy and glittering in the candlelight, his fine-boned face reflecting all the pride and arrogant beauty of a golden falcon.

He looked, she thought in sick horror, every inch what she knew him to be!

Revolted, she turned quickly away. Nothing, however, could prevent her hearing enough of his Commander's low-voiced valediction to know how this night must end.

Then Joscelin was gone, and she was alone with *him*.

The man who was heir to one of the wealthiest provinces in Mithlondia as well as Second of the Guardians.

Gabriel de Marillec.

Her lord-by-binding.

And – she had seen the irrefutable proof with her own eyes – another man's lover.

She swallowed bile and clutched after her courage, wishing desperately that she had never seen him that night with Luc de Chartreux, the pair of them mercilessly revealed by the eerie light of the rising moon. De Marillec, lying on the trampled earth of the healers' enclosure, held in the fiercely protective embrace of the dark-haired man she had not needed Linette's subdued murmur to put a name to.

Shocking though that scene had been, it had degenerated still further when the fair-haired soldier of the royal bodyguard had gone to kneel beside his commander, not even twitching when de Marillec had reached out to touch his face, raving all the while in a barely coherent whisper about fields of blood and unfinished harp songs, the great golden moon rising above his head reflected in his blazing citrine eyes.

Even now, Adèle was not sure which had been the worst to watch – de Marillec's obvious descent into madness, or the disgusting intimacy he displayed not only towards the outlaw leader but also the soldier under his command.

And this was the depraved creature to whom Joscelin had so callously abandoned her, all but ordering the man to secure the de Marillec blood-line!

So much for Rowène telling her she had nothing to worry about...

"Would you like some wine?"

De Marillec's voice – lightly urbane, and lacking any emotion whatsoever – broke into her frantic thoughts, setting them to eddy and scurry like autumn leaves in the cool wind seeping through the shuttered window behind her.

"It may warm you, Madame. If only a little."

Only now aware that she was shivering, she forced herself to accept the goblet he was holding out towards her with one long-fingered, heavily-beringed hand. Indeed such was the weight of gold and gems on his fingers that she wondered he had the strength to lift his arm at all!

"Thank you."

Regardless of the tone of her thoughts – a constant skitter between contempt, disgust, fear and a wavering determination to follow her friend's pragmatic advice – she managed to match the indifferent courtesy of her lord-by-binding's manner.

Raising the chased silver goblet to her mouth, she took a sip, feeling the warmth slide down inside her frozen body.

Alas, it left no perceptible thaw in its wake, only a heightened sense of nausea, caused as much by the thought of what must shortly take place as the underlying sweetness of the spiced wine.

Swallowing a rising retch, she hastily set the goblet down on the table.

"No more, my lord. If... if you do not mind, I am weary and would... seek my b... bed."

Her tire-maid having already removed her bridal finery, clothing her instead in the thin silken garment her mother had designated as fitting for this night, there was no further excuse to delay the dreaded moment.

And so, with the vague but terrified thought that it was better to be done with it as quickly as possible, Adèle forced herself to walk on trembling legs towards the massive bed with its oppressive purple hangings, thick sable furs and gold-embroidered coverlet of murrey and blue brocade, and shakily climbed upon it.

Scrambling hastily beneath the heavy layers of fur, silk, wool and linen, still not quite able to believe this was happening, she risked a glance across the room and found the proof before her.

Swallowing, she watched de Marillec slowly divest himself of his own clothing...

Soft leather shoes... silk hose as fine as any she herself possessed... the formal court robe made up in his family colours of mulberry and blue... finely embroidered linen shirt... and finally, with a clink of metal on wood, all the jewellery that had made him glimmer and shimmer like the gilded jay she had likened him to in the privacy of her mind.

Except, devoid of either the mail shirt he had been wearing at Vézière or the more subtle armour of jewels and rich raiment he had worn this night, with his slight – but, as she observed now, strongly-muscled – frame clad only in a pair of close-fitting linen braies, he seemed suddenly a different man completely.

And, gods help her, even more of a stranger than the effete nobleman she thought she had been bound to.

"Move over," he said quietly. "There is sufficient room in that bed that we need neither of us trouble the other at all."

"But..."

Adèle stared at him as she attempted to rearrange her thoughts.

"But surely J... Messire de Veraux said you were... you had to..."

She stopped again, her disarray complete, the flare of anger in de Marillec's agate-hard eyes unmistakable.

"Joscelin de Veraux may be my commander on the battlefield, and about my only friend off of it, as today has proven beyond all doubt. However, that means nothing in this chamber. Whatever happens, or does not happen here tonight, it concerns no-one save us two."

"You mean... you will not... t... touch me?"

She could hardly believe what he was saying. Surely the gods would not be this kind to her?

Ah, but given what rumour and her own recent observations told her of his inclinations, he was probably just as reluctant to join his body with hers! Could he even manage the act, she wondered.

And with that malicious thought in her mind the jibe slipped from her mouth before she could think better of it,

"Because you do not want me? Or because you are incapable of bedding a woman?"

"It is quite true, I do not want you," he agreed, his voice still level. "Any more, if my memory serves me correctly from that evening at Vézière, than you want me, Madame."

Then his expression changed slightly, became even less readable if such was possible.

"For what it is worth, Madame, I have bedded just as many women as men..."

She almost blurted out *how many*, before deciding that she really did not want to know the answer.

Unfortunately he must have seen something of the incredulous revulsion in her face because he said in a tone of lazy mockery that set her teeth on edge,

"Content yourself, Madame, with the knowledge that, regardless of the exact numbers involved, I *would* know what to do to make it bearable for you, were the circumstances right."

He eyed her for a moment, then picked up his shirt and shrugged back into it before continuing evenly,

"Which we have just established that they are not. May I?"

One calloused, ringless hand reinforced his request and when she managed outwardly to neither recoil nor refuse – though inwardly she was doing both – he seated himself at the foot of the bed, a good yard and a half away from her, and after a frowning moment continued with none of his former mockery,

"Aside from any lack of desire on either of our parts, Madame, I gave your kinsman my word that I would not cause you hurt or harm."

"My kinsman?" She shook her head in confusion. "Do you mean my... *father?*"

Frankly incredulous, she tried and failed to imagine Gaston de Martine caring whether her lord-by-binding hurt her or not, provided he upheld his part of the binding oath and made her Lady of Marillec in truth as well as name.

"Of course not your self-serving sire!" There was scorn and impatience in his voice now. "Rather, the only one out of all your kin who, as far as I can see, actually cares about you."

"Guy," she breathed.

Then, eagerly,

"You have seen him? Spoken to him?"

He considered her in silence for a handful of heartbeats, a flicker of citrine in his wary amber gaze, before long shadow-dark lashes swept down to hide that odd, disquieting glint.

"Not recently, no," he said softly and relapsed into silence.

Not knowing whether to be disappointed or relieved, but determined to keep her own counsel on the matter of her cousin, she watched de Marillic until he looked up again, narrow, dark brows still drawn together over his thin, aquiline nose, and though she said nothing, when he spoke it was as if he felt the need to refute some silent accusation, his tone as dry as summer dust,

"Difficult though you may find it to believe, Madame, I *can* keep my word without the necessity of being reminded in person of the terms of the oath I swore."

"And it is because of that oath that you will not... consummate our binding?"

She hesitated, then forced herself to wade into deeper, murkier waters,

"I know I am not the person with whom you would chose to... to be with... like..."

She swallowed, gestured to the bed they both occupied, albeit at opposite ends.

"Like this... but we are bound now... and... and..."

She halted momentarily at the look of loss on his face, but she needed to be sure.

"Do you not wish for a son, Messire? An heir to the lordship that will be yours in time?"

He winced at the word *heir*, his rather beautiful mouth thinning into the bleakest of smiles.

"Believe me, Madame, my father would be delighted were I to die childless, thus leaving the way clear for him to make my younger brother, Bayard, Lord of Marillec after him."

God of Light, did his father hate him that much? Because he was... as he was?

Even Adèle did not *hate* him, she just wished she did not have to be bound to him.

Unfortunately she was, and still struggling to understand this man she was gradually coming to see as a tangle of contradictions, she asked tentatively,

"And you would be content to be displaced like that? But surely..."

He did not wait to hear what else she might say, a trace of the same astringency he had employed when speaking of her father entering his voice again,

"If you must have it said bluntly, Madame, I want no part in siring a child. *Any* child!"

The flicker of pain in his eyes turned the amber to shadow as he continued hoarsely,

"Surely you need not ask why? You have seen with your own eyes *what* I am! Would you truly wish to give life to a child... a *son* who had the potential to grow up to be... just like me?"

Sick with remembered horror, she merely shook her head, watching the feral light fade from his eyes, as he finished more calmly,

"In that case, Madame, you are safe from my touch."

"And you will not change your mind?" she asked, though she did not really doubt his word, not given the vehemence of his voice, the dark shadows in eyes that should by rights have been light.

He gave her a considering look, then a hint of a wry smile touched his mouth,

"I think that about as likely as you changing yours. In the meantime, and until the gods choose to put an end to our binding with my death, we are stuck with each other. Oh, do not look so anxious, I do not intend to remain in Lamortaine any longer than I must..."

The smile widened unexpectedly into a grin, his eyes showing the first spark of humour she had seen in him.

"Believe it or not, Madame, I make a far better soldier than I do a gilded jay..."

She started, wondering how he could have snatched the derisive words right out of her head, for she was sure she had never spoken them aloud.

"Come, Madame," he continued, his tone level, reasonable even. "Whatever you think of me, surely we can manage to be civil to each other for the few days I am here? For my part, I will undertake to do nothing to make you a laughing stock or the butt of court gossip..."

He paused, grimacing, then lifted his slender shoulders in an eloquent shrug.

"Or at least no more than the misfortune of wearing the binding band of a shirt-lifting sodomite is apt to do."

Evidently perceiving her shock, he dropped his gaze for a moment, then looked up to say stonily,

"I have perforce become accustomed to being reviled in such terms, and while I will spare you anything cruder, others around the palace may not be so reticent, so you should be prepared to hear..."

"No! Please!" she interjected. "Do not say that again, let alone tell me whatever other coarse terms are used to describe you. I do not want to know."

"Very well, but if I cannot change what others say of me, I can at least apologise for the way in which my reputation must now unfairly soil you."

He took a breath.

"And though it cannot provide much by way of amelioration, you should know that whilst much of what the gossips say about me *is* true, none of my enemies are slow to blacken my name with lies either."

"And you have no lack of enemies," she commented, more to herself than him. "Men who hate you. Women who despise you. All of whom want you publicly shamed, if not dead."

"True enough," he agreed evenly, his eyes on her face, as if wondering whether she was one of them. In truth, she was not sure herself, though she said dully,

"No, not me."

She rubbed her fingertips over the intricate band of amber-studded bronze about her wrist, reminding herself that they were now bound together, and that what touched one, also touched the other.

Then she looked up to say,

"Joffroi de Rogé is one of those enemies, is he not?"

"Him! That vicious, hell-born witch who would bend us all to her rule. And..."

He must have seen the look on her face and read it accurately enough, breaking off before he had completed the listing, though she suspected she knew who would have been next.

"Ah!" He drew in a sharp breath as understanding struck. "You may dislike *me*, but you hate the de Rogé brood more! Perhaps because you suspect they had a hand in your kinsman's untimely... disappearance?"

She gave a small nod.

"Yes, that of course. But also because of what they, and in particular that beast Ranulf, did to Rowène, forcing her to submit to his filthy lust!"

Her tone was low, fierce, rippling with disgust, directed as much at her lord's apparent indifference as de Rogé's unmitigated brutality.

"Oh yes, Messire, I know what happened at Chartre, what he did there! And I would have seen him hang for it, if Hell had not claimed him first."

His amber eyes went blank and unfocused as if he were looking beyond her at something she could not hope to see, his tone emotionless, eerily even, not quite his own.

"Ranulf de Rogé may not have stood upon the public scaffold but you can be assured that he has long since paid in blood and pain for whatever crimes he committed against Rowène de Chartreux."

He blinked, seemingly returning to himself, a glinting hint of a smile in his amber-gold gaze.

"I tried to kill him myself once, you know. Not so long after Chartre had fallen into his brother's blood-stained hands. Needless to say it did not go well."

He shrugged in deprecating fashion.

"Even with a knife in my hand, it was like pitting a dragonfly against a bull."

"*You* attacked *Ranulf de Rogé?*" Adèle asked, eyeing him with a glimmer of respect.

She had never knowingly seen Ranulf de Rogé but if he was anything like his elder brother in looks, build or temperament, de Marillec would not have stood a chance.

"Because of what he did to Rowène?"

A grimace twisted that finely-shaped mouth.

"Ah... no! Though circumstance and that damned blood-gold moon have brought us together, so close that there is little, if anything, that Rowène does not know about me, or I her... the truth is that seven years ago when I rashly tried to bury my dagger in Ranulf de Rogé's beating heart I had no thought of her at all. Loath though I am to forfeit your good opinion, I did it for Luc."

"Because he was your lover," she said flatly, then wished as the silence spun out between them, that she had not thrown such a provocative accusation at him, destroying what they had started to build.

"Perhaps, Madame..."

There was steel in his voice now.

And a lethal light in his eyes.

"We can agree to simply call him my friend, or my foster-brother, since that is all he can ever be to me now."

She swallowed and nodded jerkily, not a little ashamed of herself.

For whatever reason de Marillec was trying his best to be level-headed about this whole wretched affair, while she appeared to be doing the exact opposite. But it was just so hard not to...

"For gods'sake!" he snapped. "I may be many things, Madame, but I am *not* stupid! I *know* this is hard for you."

She blinked in shock. That was the second time he had plucked the thoughts from her head.

Even as she stared at him, he drew in a harsh breath, exhaled it as a barely audible curse, and then having flattened almost all trace of emotion from his tone he continued,

"Just try and accept that it is damnably difficult for me as well. I do not expect you to understand, or even condone what is between Luc and I..."

"No, I cannot," she said in a muffled voice. "I wish I was like Rowène and could... but I cannot. I... I think I might be able to, or at least I would try... if... if I were not..."

"If you were not bound to me," de Marillec finished quietly. "I understand it is much to ask of you but it *is* in the past, and I have more than enough enemies without wanting to make one of the woman I am bound to and must share what remains of my life with. Hell knows, it would be hard enough even if we did have some commonality of purpose but without that..."

He shrugged and evidently considering the discussion closed, stood and walked back towards the table and the forgotten pitcher of wine.

She watched him for a moment. His face in profile told her nothing. His hand, however, pouring the dark red wine pressed from the grapes of his own province, betrayed him... as did the way he drained the goblet to its dregs... filling it once more...

"We do have... one thing... in common," she said uncertainly as she watched his lips close about the silver rim, saw him swallow as the dark wine flooded his mouth, again and again, his long lashes coming to rest against the shadowed hollows below his shuttered eyes.

He looked lost, unbearably alone, adrift in memory and shattered dreams.

"You said it yourself, Messire," she added in a louder, more determined tone. "Joffroi and Ariène de Rogé are my enemies as much as they are yours, as would Ranulf be were he still alive."

"Forget Ranulf," he said sharply, opening his eyes with a snap and finally turning to look at her. "He can trouble you no more. As for Joffroi and Ariène... there may be something in what you say."

He stopped, his narrow brows drawing together over that aquiline nose that saved his face from crossing the line from simply handsome into an ethereal beauty.

"What about Juliène de Lyeyne? Where does she fit into your reasoning?"

"Juliène?" Adèle repeated in blank surprise. "Why do you speak of her in particular?"

"Because she has seemed very much your friend these past few days. As much, would you say, as Rowène is?"

"In all truth," she said tartly. "I think Rowène is more your friend now than mine! Certainly she was swift enough to spring to your defence when she took me to task about my... unwillingness to accept this binding of ours."

"Perhaps," he acknowledged. Then, his gaze darkening again,

"No, you are right. Rowène *did* stand my friend, gods help her. It cannot have been easy for her."

He sent Adèle the most fleeting of glances before continuing,

"I can see you find that hard to accept, considering what I am, and what I have been to her brother."

"Yes, well..."

She was not going to think about that. Besides, they were talking about Juliène now, not her. And if it came to that...

"Just do not make the mistake of thinking that just because Rowène has accepted you, Juliène will do the same," she warned him. "Sisters though they are, they are as unlike as fire is from ice."

"Do you think I do not know that already," he said, his mouth twitching in grim amusement.

There was a moment's silence, then he continued in that same soft, somehow dangerous tone,

"You never did answer my question as to whether you are on the same terms of friendship and trust with Madame de Lyeyne as you were with Rowène? Oh, and since you seem to believe her friendship with me has ousted that which she felt for you, I should tell you that Rowène took me to task too before I left Vézière, and probably a good deal more bluntly than she did you. Because she cares about *your* happiness. Can you see Juliène doing the same?"

Adèle did not even hesitate.

"No, I cannot. Indeed, I think I have known all along that she is not the friend she took such care to appear."

One slim – surely plucked – eyebrow lifted in question, simultaneously distracting her and spurring her to examine further the lie of that false friendship as de Marillec said sardonically,

"Try asking yourself what was so important to her that she risked smirching her own reputation by keeping company with the woman who would soon be bound to..."

He shrugged.

"I will not say it, since you have asked me not to... but a man like me? A man she most certainly hates beyond any reasonable measure."

Adèle hesitated, running her fingers over the bronze and amber bracelet, considering. Then as the fog of misery that had surrounded her for the past se'ennight finally lifted, she was left feeling foolish for not having seen the truth before.

"Dear God of Mercy! I think... I think she wanted to find out what, if anything, I knew about Guy's whereabouts."

"And you told her... what exactly?" he asked, the line of his jaw hardening, and his narrow dark brows snapping back in that increasingly familiar frown that changed the whole look of his face, turning him from a gilded jay into something infinitely more disturbing.

"I knew nothing *to* tell her!" she retorted, though it was not entirely true. "Why? Do you?"

"Only that de Martine is in danger if he is ever seen in Mithlondia again," he replied evenly.

She might have let the matter drop if she had not glimpsed something in his eyes, a shift in colour, transient as a rainbow, from amber to gold and back again.

"The harper... And the one who watches from the shadow of the moon..."

Her voice an incredulous whisper, she repeated the words he had spoken that night beneath the blood-gold moon at Vézière.

Then as understanding belatedly struck her, exclaimed,

"God of Light! You think *Guy* is the harper? And Juliène... a spy for Lady Ariène?"

"What I think is that neither of us should try and make sense of whatever madness I was spewing that night," her lord-by-binding said bitterly, his troubled amber gaze dropping to study the dark liquid lapping the sides of the silver goblet he still held in his hand, adding harshly,

"Forget whatever you think I said. I was drunk! Out of my senses!"

That was the truth, she thought, though somehow she doubted it had been an excess of wine that had deprived him of his senses.

At least, not then.

But now... perhaps? She cast a dubious look at the goblet and he set it down on the table so forcefully that a few blackberry-dark drops spilled across the polished table.

"No, I am not drunk. I cannot afford to be when we have the rest of this damnable night to get through, not to mention the days that will follow. Days when we must somehow face down the busy-bodies of the court. Either separately or together, the choice is yours!"

He rubbed a hand over his lightly-stubbled jaw, his eyes showing a momentary indecision, then coming back to the bed he looked down at her, his gaze bleak, considering.

Seeming to make up his mind, he continued carefully,

"We have already agreed, have we not, that we have enemies in common, so what do you say to making some sort of common cause? In this matter at least? And deprive the gossips of their meat?"

Surprised though she was, it was not such an odd notion as it sounded. Moreover it was not an offer he had been obliged to make – he could simply have forced himself on her, for the sake of appearances, insulted her publicly or ignored her completely.

Instead he had taken the time and trouble to truly talk to her... and as she looked at him she was reminded of the moment when he had stood in the binding hall, alone in the midst of that crowd of vulpine courtiers, in those endless moments before Joscelin de Veraux had slammed into the cavernous chamber and thrust through the vultures to stand at his friend's side.

Now he stood, slight and slender, one hand loosely gripped about the bedpost, his fine-boned face impassive, seemingly impenetrably armoured against his solitary, friendless existence – and why should he not be lonely, she asked herself, when that was surely all a... man like him deserved!

Then, bright and brilliant and ephemeral as a shooting star, she heard Rowène's haunting voice inside her head.

Would you put him in the pillory simply because he has the misfortune to love where he should not?

If that were so, who amongst us would not be joining him there?

The words put an abrupt rein on her resurgent disgust, pulling her up sharply, making her think again... and she knew that, if she were honest, if she judged herself by that condition, she would certainly be in the pillory alongside this man she had, until now, regarded as being so much less worthy than herself.

It was too much to say that she either understood the friendship Rowène had unaccountably extended towards Gabriel de Marillec, or felt she could do likewise.

Nonetheless, she *could* finally acknowledge some fellow feeling with the man.

For not only did she love where she should not, she too was lonely here at court and very nearly as friendless as he, albeit for very different reasons.

Now, when it was far, far too late to recall her pointed words, she deeply regretted her petty needling regarding his relationship with Luc de Chartreux – the gods knew it was no affair of hers how he had conducted himself in the past – her malice now shown up for what it was by the fact that, despite all provocation, *he* had refrained from descending to her level in order to taunt her with her own unrequited affection for his commander, since those feral amber eyes now masked by long, unnaturally dark lashes seemed far too keen not to have seen how she felt about Joscelin de Veraux.

Given that her lord-by-binding must be labouring under a strain at least the equal to her own, Gabriel de Marillec had behaved considerably better than she had any right to expect.

The least she could do was meet him halfway.

"That is a fair offer," she said now, finally meeting his eyes. "And one I would like to accept. For my part, I will undertake not to discuss what happens behind the closed door of our bedchamber, with anyone. Nor speak out against you, my lord-by-binding."

"Then we have a truce and an understanding of sorts," he said, his smile holding something close to a companionable warmth. "That being so, and since I am weary to the bone, will you permit me to share the rare comfort of that bed with you?"

And when she could not quite repress her nervous recoil, he added with a return to his former dryness,

"Even had I not already given my word, first to your cousin and more recently to Rowène, that you will come to no harm as my wife, someone else I... care about very much bade me treat you gently. So... if I promise not to move until you give me leave, will you take your eyes from me long enough to assure yourself that it is as I have said, and there is room enough for both of us to sleep in that bed without trespassing on each other's territory?"

Taking him warily at his word, she glanced around her, and without fear muddling her mind and shrinking the dimensions of the bed, she realised just how wide it actually was, in her relief almost missing what was clearly an afterthought to himself,

"And in the morning..."

His words faded into silence, and Adèle returned her questioning gaze to her lord, only to find him frowning in unfocused fashion at the great, purple-hung bed,

"What... what about the morning?" she asked, a quiver of renewed trepidation in her voice.

The curve of his mouth was closer to grimace than grin as he said quietly,

"Trust me, Adèle."

It was the first time he had called her by her given name, and so far as they had come already that night, she found it almost reassuring – that he saw her as a person, rather than simply a shackle banded about his arm.

"It is nothing that can hurt you. Nor is it anything for you to lie awake worrying about. Best if you just leave me to deal with it in my own way."

And if that was not liable to make her lie awake worrying, nothing was!

It was perhaps not so surprising that she did not sleep well that night, the first night of her new life as Adèle de Marillec.

The feather bed was comfortable, and the thick curtains would have held the autumn draughts at bay had they been closed. Except she could not bear to be shut in such dark intimacy with the man lying beside her, almost within reach if she stretched out her hand. And her lord-by-binding, for reasons she could only guess at – perhaps he felt something of the same distaste of confinement after the relative freedom of life in the northern wilds, sleeping rough in a soldiers' encampment with the whisper of danger borne on every breeze – had neglected to draw the curtains on his side of the bed either.

While she found herself trusting in his word that he would not touch her – and even more in his obvious disinclination to take part in any sort of carnal intimacy with her – still she found it unsettling after so many years sleeping in the Grey Sisters' dormitory at Vézière to be alone in such close proximity with a man.

Not that she could accuse him of being a restless sleeper, nor did he snore in an uncouth way. To the contrary he slept neatly and quietly, effortlessly keeping to his own side of the wide bed.

Nonetheless, Adèle spent many long endless moments listening to the sound of his even breathing before finally allowing herself to relax. She had been living on the edge for so many days now, fearing this binding, and the bedding that must inevitably follow and now...

She was relieved, of course, that de Marillec did not intend to force either of them into something that would bring neither any pleasure.

Yet at the same time she wished he had just gone ahead and done the deed anyway – given that he had admitted that he could – since then it would have been over and done with.

And perhaps, just perhaps, she might have quickened with a child.

Then again, as he himself had pointed out, did she truly want to bear a child of his? Merely to consolidate her own position – a position she had never wanted – as Lady of Marillec?

Perhaps if he had been another man the answer might have been *yes*. To the chance of a child at least.

She could not, however, forget what she had seen that night at Vézière. Not so much his familiarity with the other two men – she valiantly tried to repress a shudder – but the other.

A s...

She swallowed and forced herself to form the word in her head, knowing she would not be able to avoid hearing it spoken aloud in the days to come. She only prayed she would not hear worse.

A sodomite she could – and would – manage to deal with.

A madman, gods help her, was another matter entirely!

Although – and here she rolled over, staring into the darkness, nervously nibbling at her lip – she had to admit that de Marillec had appeared perfectly sane throughout the length of this whole long, wretched day and night, his eyes perfectly lucid, showing none of the madness that had so terrified her before. He had even at times shown a rare glint of wry humour.

Nevertheless, she realised now that her most abiding impression of her lord-by-binding was the loneliness he wore beneath his gilded trappings, so close to his skin that it seemed an indelible part of himself.

Almost as much as the guardians' mark pricked into his upper arm, and which she had glimpsed briefly before he had put his shirt back on.

She thought again of his comment that Joscelin de Veraux was his only friend.

That was undoubtedly true, yet the fair-haired guardian – Rafe, she remembered his name now – had also appeared close to him in some incomprehensible way.

As for Luc de Chartreux...

No, she would not go there again! Nor put her lord in the pillory of shame with that scornful name branded upon his brow.

Henceforth she must think of him only by his given name, now that she and... *Gabriel* had come to some sort of agreement as to the way their binding would unfold.

She shivered as another cold draught found its way through the shuttered window to touch her face with chilly fingers, and tugging the heavy covers closer about her silk-clad body, curled up into a ball, trying to wrap her frozen feet in the inadequate folds of her flimsy nightshift, another – and eminently practical – resolve forming in her mind.

As soon as her lord-by-binding had left court and gone back to the barracks or the battle line, or wherever else it was that he intended to go, she would visit all the cloth merchants in Lamortaine in order to find the softest, finest woollen cloth available, out of which she would sew herself a warmer nightrail...

It was to such oddly tangled thoughts that she must have fallen asleep eventually, and in her sleep migrated to the only source of warmth in the bed, waking with a start to find her cold nose in contact with fine, warm linen that smelt of male skin, male sweat and some heady exotic scent, her frozen feet brushing against strong legs covered with soft, warm hair, her cold fingers burrowing beneath a firm, warm body...

Even as she started back in shock, a light male voice, deepened by sleep, muttered something caustic about icicles and...

Gods above! Had he really just said... what she thought he said?

Appalled, aghast, and terribly tempted to giggle – that must be the residual effects of the wine – she scrambled hurriedly away, to lie clutching the far side of the goose-feather mattress until she was as certain as she could be that he was not going to wake fully or say anything else.

The frantic beating of her heart gradually calming as his breathing returned to its former steady rhythm, she finally slipped back into an uneasy sleep.

Only to find herself wakening to see the first pale grey smudge of dawn showing between the shutters. Wondering what had woken her so early she checked first to see that she had not inadvertently rolled back into her lord-by-binding's warmth.

She had not, and indeed was still clinging tenaciously to the outer extremities of the bed.

So what then had brought her awake? It was far too early for her tire-woman to be coming to rouse and ready her for the day, and indeed there was no noise at all from the sleeping palace, except...

Except for some soft, indefinable sounds coming from just behind her... and which must have somehow penetrated her broken and nightmarish dreams.

The first sound, now repeated, seemed no more than a steely whisper, making her think of a blade stealthily sliding in or out of a scabbard... and she felt an immediate, stark fear that de Marillec meant to murder her, the woman to whom he had never wanted to be bound!

Deceived by his reasonable attitude last night, she had allowed herself to be convinced that he meant her no harm, unless...

Unless in the depths of the night his madness had descended again!

Finally, after many long moments of frozen stillness, she released the breath she had not known she was holding when she realised that whatever the man behind her was doing, it did not involve cutting her throat or sliding a knife between her ribs to pierce her frantically beating heart. But what in the name of all the gods *was* he doing?

Whatever it was he was making little noise about it, save for one odd constrained sound that was part grunt, part groan.

God of Light! Was he ill?

The healer in her told her to look, to see if there were something she might do to help him.

The maiden she still was shrank from the implied intimacy of touching her lord-by-binding in any way.

Eventually the healer won and she started to sit up, to ask if there was anything wrong...

Except he spoke before she could complete either movement or question.

"No, nothing! Go back to sleep!" His voice was taut, strained. "I did not mean... to disturb you!"

Still unsettled, she nevertheless lay down again, obedient to his command, saying only,

"If you are sure you are all right?"

She sensed that he had rolled over onto his back, perhaps flung an arm up over his eyes.

"All is well... or as well as it can be between you and me."

A heartbeat's hesitation and then he continued flatly,

"Since you are awake, I will tell you now what I intend to do, rather than leave you to discover my absence in a note."

"Are you leaving already?" she asked, suddenly glad she did not have to look at him. Or he her.

"Only for a ride before the palace starts to stir. And I will probably spend the day with Joscelin and the rest of the guardians, though I will return in time to escort you to the hall for the evening meal. Until then, you can keep to this chamber or not as you please, but wherever you go, and whoever you see, whether it is merely your tire-maid or the noblest of court ladies, you will find yourself the butt of curious looks and probing questions about my... abilities in the binding bed. And you may find it easier to face all that without the embarrassment of fabricating some fantasy in my presence."

"Yes... yes, I think I would," she agreed, feeling a flush rise in her cheeks.

"If it is any consolation I will face a similar barrage," said the voice behind her.

Except, she imagined, it might be even worse for him, judging by those comments she had overheard the previous night.

No wonder he wanted some time to prepare himself, or perhaps...

"Are you truly going for a ride?" she blurted out.

"For what it is worth, Madame, yes, I *am* going for a ride. On a horse. Alone, if you need any further proof that I meant what I said last night. Hell knows, I did not want to take the binding oath with you but now that I have, I will not break it to take another to my bed, man or woman."

"That does not seem very fair," Adèle said, her voice little more than a whisper, though only he and the gods could hear her. "I... I do not think I would mind if you..."

"If I... assuaged my desires elsewhere, providing I was discreet?" he finished for her, when even an approximation of those words failed to leave her tongue.

Embarrassed, she merely nodded her head against the soft pillows that smelt of her own lavender perfume and more subtly of his, whatever it was.

"And in return, would you wish me to extend a similar generosity to you?" he asked, his level voice revealing nothing whatsoever of his feelings. "That you may take a lover of your own choosing?"

"No," she choked out. "No, there is no need for that."

"No *need*, you say? Because you are a woman and think you should not own to such crude needs?"

It was not a question she wished to answer and after a moment he continued in that same carefully unthreatening tone,

"I may be wrong but certain observations make me think that your very understandable reluctance to take the binding oath with me was perhaps less because of what *I* am, and more because your heart is already given to... some other man?"

"Perhaps," she admitted, feeling tears struggle past the lump in her throat. "But he has no thought of me."

"And if he did?" the man behind her pressed. "Would you have me give my consent for you to break the terms of your binding oath to lie with him?"

Even as she shook her head, her heart leapt with hope.

"You might then have a child free of my tainted blood."

He spoke her own thoughts, quite softly, without judgement.

"If, that is, you wish for children, Adèle?"

"I would like to have... a child of my own," she confessed unsteadily, thinking back to the two happy, fair-haired children she had seen last summer in Vézière's market square and who had rarely left her memory since. And if she took him at his word, she too could have...

Abruptly her sense of morality reasserted itself.

"No! It would not be right, Gabriel. Not like that! How could I ask you to acknowledge another man's child as your own, or expect your father to accept that other man's get as the heir to Marillec?"

"If I care not for what my father might think," his voice came bleak as a winter's wind. "Then neither need you! But it is not something we must decide today," he added, his breath steady and warm against her shoulder. "If I live long enough that your desire for a child overcomes your loyalty to an oath you never wanted to swear, then we may have this conversation again. For now..."

There was a sudden upheaval as he sat up, flinging back the covers.

"I beg your forgiveness, but I cannot lie here any longer."

"With me, you mean? I am sorry, my lord, I should not have..."

"No, this is about me, not you. Nothing you have done or said has caused me offence. I just need to be alone for a while."

The next moment she felt his weight leave the bed, heard him pad barefoot across the floor to open the wooden chest on his side of the chamber, followed by the rustle of clothing as he hurriedly dressed himself in the near darkness.

Then she was alone, and he had gone to seek out the solitude that clearly meant so much to him.

Even as the door closed quietly behind him, Adèle gave a shaky sigh.

The first night of her binding was over, and it had in no way been as terrible as she had feared.

He had not ill-used her, either verbally or physically, and save for the odd flashes of bitterness directed at himself, had seemed perfectly sane and in command of himself throughout the night.

Far more than she if truth were told.

He had even defied his commander and convention and refrained from taking what was his by right of binding, for the sake of an heir. She was a maiden still...

And, as she knew well enough, a very poor liar.

130

How then was she supposed to convince the servants who would shortly be coming to attend her, let alone the inquisitive noblewomen of the court who would doubtless make excuse to corner her during the course of the day, that Gabriel de Marillec had successfully played the stallion's part last night?

Lack of experience was no excuse she told herself firmly. They had a bargain of sorts, she and her lord-by-binding, and she must keep her side of it, as oddly enough she had no doubt that he would keep his. How he would do it, she had no idea, and even less how she might...

Sighing again, she rolled towards the middle of the bed and then sat up with a small shriek of shock.

Tossing back the blankets and furs, she stared in bemusement at the small patch of opaque wetness surrounding a few spots of scarlet in the centre of the bed.

Frowning in uncomprehending distaste, she tentatively touched her fingertips to the damp linen... and belatedly understood.

This was how her lord-by-binding intended to keep his side of their bargain, having spilt not only his blood but his seed on that sheet.

So all she had to do in return was behave as if she had been an equal participant, willing or otherwise, in that supposed act of consummation.

Adèle survived that first day as Gabriel de Marillec's lady, and the ones that followed, by keeping her mouth firmly closed on their private dealings, and letting the stained bed-linens serve as irrefutable proof that all was as it should be between a man and his woman.

In accordance with the bargain she had struck, she told no-one what really happened in that bed – not the quietly sympathetic Lady Isabelle, and certainly not the sharp-eyed, sharper-tongued Juliène – and was careful to speak no word that could be construed as criticism against her lord-by-binding.

For his part, Gabriel de Marillec maintained an air of distant courtesy towards her in public, and shared the binding bed with her every night, keeping strictly to his own side of the goosedown mattress and doing what he must – either to maintain the illusion that all was well between them or to ease his own needs, she was never quite sure which – when she was safely asleep.

Following that first occasion of something approaching intimacy between them, he found little enough to say to her in private and never of anything personal to either of them. Whether he was regretting the bargain he had made, or his tacit permission for her to cuckold him, she could not say.

She knew only that his sleep became increasingly restless with each succeeding night, so that sometimes he seemed not to sleep at all, at other times he muttered incoherently, a victim of his troubled dreams, and she could not help but fear that the madness that had taken him at Vézière was returning to torment him.

Regardless of how well or ill he slept, he rose every morning well before the first servant was stirring in the palace and rode out with the dawn, later going to the guardians' quarters to join in with weapons practice with the men.
Or at least she assumed that was how he spent his time when he was not with her.

After that first morning he did not say, and she did not ask, feeling it no part of their bargain for her to question his activities. He had told her that he would not dishonour their public binding vow – or their private bargain – by taking another to his bed, and for some reason she trusted him to keep his word.

As it was, once he had left their chamber, she knew she should not expect to see him again until the short autumn day had faded into darkness, and while she did not miss his absence during the day she found herself looking for his almost soundless return in the evenings.

It seemed that one moment she would be alone with only the candlelight, her stitchery and Princess Linette's two cats, who seemed to have taken a liking to her, for company.

The next, she would look up and there he would be, standing just inside the door, his fine-boned face set in strained lines, his slender body clad in sweat-stained shirt, padded leather jerkin, torn breeches and muddy boots, his long hair tied back off his face in an untidy tail.

Knowing her duty as his lady, she would summon the Marillec servants and order the wooden tub to be filled with hot water, though only when the servants had all been dismissed would her lord begin to strip off his clothes, and she, sensing if not understanding this unusual need for privacy in which to make his ablutions, would retreat to the far side of the chamber and take up her stitchery.

Nonetheless, even with her head bent over her embroidery frame, she could not help but be aware of the moment when he shed his clothes, and stepped naked into the tub.

Curiosity made her peep more than once, catching a hint of sun-warmed skin, smooth muscles, scarred limbs...

God of Light, she had not realised until now how dangerous must be the life he led, how close to death he had already come!

More than that, she had with reluctance to admit that he was a well-made man.

Such glimpses, however, were few and far between, since for the most part he was careful to keep his back towards her, presumably out of consideration for her modesty. Or perhaps he merely guarded his own privacy?

Whatever his motive, it served to temper what had started as the merest curiosity on Adèle's part into a rare determination.

Thus she began to watch him more closely, whereas he – once settled in the water, sometimes with a hiss for the heat, sometimes a sigh for the soothing warmth – seemed to disregard her presence entirely. Taking up the small square of rough cloth, he would wash himself thoroughly, using the soap purchased especially from a merchant in Lamortaine who dealt in exotic, foreign goods, and scented, so he told her when she dared one evening to make enquiry, with bergamot – an oil she did not know, it being an expensive import from the southern kingdom of Kardolandia.

When she had somewhat anxiously questioned the cost, he simply laughed with that increasingly familiar note of bitterness in his light voice, and informed her that the Marillec revenues were more than adequate to cover it.

It was a pleasant perfume, she had to admit, and suited her lord-by-binding as if it had been made for him.

Or rather, she amended cautiously to herself, it suited the man who rose from the linen-lined bath every night to array himself in pale blue silk and mulberry velvet, a twisted gold torc about his throat, every slender finger encircled by a ring, many of them flashing with polished stones of lapis and turquoise, citrine and agate, these last two a disturbing reflection of the unusual colour his eyes could occasionally appear.

By the side of such magnificence, she felt herself drab indeed, even though she was no longer clad in healer's grey. Indeed, the gold-embroidered amber silk was the most expensive gown she had ever owned, and while she could not help but take a certain guilty pleasure in it, she would willingly have exchanged both it and the binding band about her arm for the plain robe and linen headrail of a Sister of Mercy.

Such would never be her lot again though, and she told herself she had to accept it. And perhaps she would... when she had found some other worthwhile life to replace it, though gods knew she would not find it here at court as Gabriel de Marillec's barren, unwanted wife.

This particular evening, a se'ennight since the binding ceremony that had made her the Lady of Marillec, she sat waiting for her lord to finish readying himself for the long evening of formality and feasting that lay ahead of them and which, she had gradually come to realise, brought him just as little pleasure as it did her.

For once she had not taken up her stitchery and Amber, the more friendly of Princess Linette's cats, was stretched out upon her silken lap, purring placidly, her sister Jade seated some little distance away, green eyes wide and watchful, fixed with a sort of aloof concentration upon the man who was now sliding rings, one by one, onto his long fingers.

Having completed this task, he picked up a small stick of charcoal and with the aid of Adèle's silver-backed hand mirror, began carefully darkening his brows and lashes, as a final outrageous touch outlining his eyes with kohl before adding a less than subtle line of malachite paste to his eyelids.

Following the direction of Jade's unblinking gaze, Adèle found herself frowning at a thought she had never consciously been aware of before.

Why in gods' name did her lord-by-binding, who surely did not employ cosmetics like a whore whilst living a soldier's life amidst the dirt and danger on the northern border, feel the necessity to do so when at court? Moreover, he had been growing steadily more heavy-handed in their application, having worn none at all on their binding day and now to look at him...

Still frowning, she watched him comb the day's tangles from his long hair and then, rather than tying it carelessly at the nape of his neck as he did in the mornings, pulled it back from his temples and held out a narrow strip of leather.

"Can you bind it for me?"

It was not the first evening he had asked her to do this.

It was, however, the first time it had struck her as being in any way odd.

Setting aside the cat, with a murmur of apology in response to Amber's look of reproach, she crossed the chamber to take the tie from his hand.

Waiting until he had seated himself on the stool in front of her dressing table she took the lank dark brown wings in her shrinking hands and, disliking the feel of his unwashed hair against her clean skin, made swift work of her task.

It was only as he came to his feet with a courteous thank-you and turned towards the door, giving her the opportunity to surreptitiously wipe her fingers on the linen cloth beside the ewer, that the inconsistency of Gabriel de Marillec's actions became suddenly, glaringly obvious.

He was so careful about the perfumed, painted and gilded appearance he presented to the court, being quite fastidious about his own cleanliness after a long, hard day obviously spent handling weapons and horses, yet not once had she known him to wash his long hair.

She realised then that she had never seen its natural colour, and could only guess that it would be similar to the light brown of his undarkened brows and lashes, or the morning stubble she had caught glinting bronze on his jaw before he shaved, the short soft hair that spread lightly over his chest, or grew more thickly on his arms and legs, all hidden now beneath layers of linen and silk. As was the coarser hair she had very occasionally glimpsed curling about his manly parts when he stepped into or out of the wooden bathing tub, and which she now realised only she – and whoever he had shared his bed with before their binding – had been permitted to see, since the servants were always gone from the chamber before he stripped...

Before she could blurt out the half-formed question in her mind, he dropped his hand from the door latch, and turning on his heel to face her, gently placed his hands on her shoulders, startling her considerably and making her forget what she had intended to ask.

"My lord?" Her voice came out as little more than a squeak.

"I think it only right that I tell you what I mean to do tonight," he said quietly. "Since it will affect you too."

Her heart gave a sickening lurch at the serious look in his eyes and she asked somewhat breathlessly,

"What? What are you going to do?"

"Do not look so worried, Adèle. It is to your benefit after all. But I need Prince Linnius to release me from attendance at court so that I may return to the northern borderlands."

And in answer to her unspoken protest,

"Yes, I am aware that there is a signed truce between Atarkarna and Mithlondia. None better, since I had some small part in bringing it about. Even so, I do not know Attan, the new chieftain, well enough to put any more trust in his word than I did in his predecessor's."

It was the first time he had spoken to her of anything concerning his other life, and she could not help but be pleased. For a few heartbeats at least.

"The gods know I would trust Rafe to guard my back or hold the line but still..."

"Rafe?" she interrupted, all her pleasure abruptly frozen at mention of that name.

Once again she heard in her memory Joscelin's crisp voice as he shouted for one of his soldiers, the same man who, before he had gone to kneel at Gabriel's side, had appeared with the woman she had known as Sister Fayla.

"You are talking about the fair-haired guardian I saw you wi... I saw that night at Vézière?"

The long, charcoal-darkened lashes dropped briefly, then lifted with a disconcerting flash of green to reveal a glittering golden gaze.

"Yes, Rafe was there. *With me.* That *was* what you were going to say, is it not? Do not lie to me, damn it."

Adèle took a step back and nervously cleared the constriction from her throat.

"Yes. Yes, it was."

The flash of feral anger that had momentarily lit his eyes from amber to agate faded, but his jaw remained hard.

"You are wrong in what you are thinking, Adèle! But whether you believe me or not, Rafe is up on the border with a mere handful of men, and that, damn it, is where I need to be too!"

She stared at him for the length of several stomach-lurching, heart-juddering moments, into the depths of his oddly changeable eyes, and it was as if something dawned in her, an understanding she had gradually been approaching, and would have reached much sooner had she not been so concerned with her own misfortunes or the unsavoury reputation Gabriel de Marillec wore like a cloak to conceal the man beneath.

"You hate it here at court, do you not?" she demanded softly, lifting her hand to finger the stiffly embroidered silk of his sleeve.

"Hate acting the gilded jay!"

Adding, with a small wisp of an uncertain smile,

"Though the gods know you do it as if born to it."

"Yes, I hate it," he agreed emotionlessly.

"Then *why* do you do it?"

His fine, firm mouth twisted in something akin to an answering smile, though it was far more darkly mirthless than hers had been.

"Necessity? Circumstance? Something else entirely? Whatever you decide, I will not be around to hear the answer. Or at least not if Linnius grants my request."

It was only then that it occurred to her to ask somewhat blankly,

"If you are going back to the border, what am I supposed to do?"

"That is why I told you now, so that you would have time to think about it. My father is leaving Lamortaine to winter at Marillé. You could go with him. You are, after all, the Lady of Marillec now."

"In name only," she reminded him drily. Then, lest he think she was complaining about that state of affairs, said swiftly,

"My choice as much as yours, of course. Even so, if I went with your father to Marillé I should feel I was living a lie, with the added burden of your people's expectation in the matter of an heir.

"And in the unlikely event that at any time in the years to come I should find myself with child, watching them wonder whether it is even yours, my lord," she finished pointedly and watched his face harden even more.

"I would never deny any child you bore," he said flatly. "You know that! I have given my word that you will not be made more unhappy in this wretched, misguided bitch of a binding than you must, and if a child is what it takes, then so be it. Go ahead and cuckold me. I shall not care."

She flinched at his tone and he continued, less savagely,

"If you do not wish to go with my father to Marillé, and I can scarce blame you for that, you will have to stay here at court."

"Ha!" As his own temper cooled, so hers abruptly flared.

"Why would I want to stay here and live the meaningless life you yourself are so intent on fleeing? You are a soldier, I am a healer. We each have our own callings. And if Linnius gives you the freedom to pursue yours, will you in turn set me free to follow mine?"

"You want to go back to Vézière?" For once his tone was unguarded. "Rejoin the Grey Sisters?"

"Do you find that so surprising? But yes, my lord, I do! At least until you return and I must fulfil my public role as Lady of Marillec once more. Besides, the princess is there and having trained as a healer and served as one of her companions, I may be of some use to her during her confinement."

Adding on a barbed afterthought, thinking the scars that marred his fine-framed body,

"And perhaps I may also be of use to you, my lord, when the next barbarian blade makes its mark upon your flesh. Or your enemies weary of trying to bring you down by means of vicious rumour and simply slip hemlock into your wine instead."

He looked a little startled as if the simplicity of such a method of ending his existence had not previously occurred to him, then gave her that slight, almost amused smile she was coming to know.

"Very well, then. Let us strike another bargain. When I ride north, you will accompany me as far as Vézière. The least I can do is see you safe to the healers' enclave, whereupon you will have the freedom to follow your calling or cuckold me as you see fit. And then... well, you have but to wait for my death – either by blade or poison – to set you free completely."

"I... I do not wish for your death, my lord," she stammered, appalled that he could think she might. But perhaps he...

"Nor do I wish for yours," he said quietly, despatching her horrified conjecture even before it was fully formed. "And while neither of us sought this binding, I think there is an understanding of sorts between us. Is there not, Adèle?"

And when she managed a nod, continued drily,

"Best if we leave it at that for now. And when... *if* we meet again this side of the sunset path, then we can look again at the terms of our bargain. Agreed, my lady?"

"Agreed, my lord."

And to her surprise, Adèle found their hands joined.

Not reluctantly as on their binding day but with something that, if not quite friendship, was at least an acceptance of the union neither of them had wanted and which they now found themselves in the difficult position of having to make the best of.

With the prince's permission formally obtained – Gabriel making his request whilst Linnius was feeling pleasantly mellow after the evening meal – all was set in train for their departure from Lamortaine the following morning.

In consequence, neither Adèle nor her restless lord slept at all that night, instead lying awake, silently watching for the dawn, both of them as ready as the other to abandon their comfortable chamber, the unobtrusive but watchful servants and the lonely tedium of the gossip-ridden court, not to mention the more subtle danger contained in any close association with Juliène de Lyeyne.

Eager as she was to return to Vézière and her former life, Adèle rose well before her tire-maid arrived and, dressed only in shift and shawl, did what she could to ready herself whilst Gabriel – clearly equally keen to be on his way – washed and shaved in cold water.

Storing her beautiful amber gown in the same wooden chest as Gabriel's court clothes, layered with lavender and dried rose petals to keep them fresh, she packed only the barest necessities and when the maid finally arrived with hot water, washed and gladly donned the nondescript travelling garb she had arrived in a se'ennight before.

Lady Isabelle having returned to Vézière some days previously, and neither Adèle nor Gabriel finding it necessary to be encumbered by a servant, they had thought to slip away unnoticed... until they came down to the stable courtyard and found Joscelin de Veraux and Juliène de Lyeyne waiting to see them off.

It was a most unlooked-for gesture of friendship and, frankly, one Adèle could well have done without.

Feeling all the awkwardness of the situation, she glanced over at her lord-by-binding in an attempt to gauge his reaction... and learned precisely nothing.

Clad once more in guardians' mail, Gabriel was in the process of mounting a tough-looking, rough-coated stallion the likes of which Adèle had seen often enough being offered for sale in Vézière's main square on market days. So dark a brown as to be nearly black, the horse had a splatter of white spots on its rump and a star between its dark eyes.

Ostensibly a belated gift from Joscelin to his friend to mark the occasion of his binding, Adèle could not help but think that it had a more practical – and possibly dangerous – purpose since such a mount might serve a man heading north to the borderlands far better than a fancier steed more in keeping with a nobleman's status.

The farewell between the two men had likewise been muted and sober. A simple arm clasp, a few quick words exchanged in low voices, then Gabriel swung easily up into the saddle, leaving Joscelin free to turn to Adèle.

Cupping his hands, he helped her mount, then stood beside her mare, looking up at her, a smile warming his normally cool grey eyes, so that her heart fluttered in her breast like a trapped butterfly and bright colour suffused her face as he lifted her gloved hand to his lips in a formal kiss.

God of Light! She thought she might have died then from the poisonous mix of emotions flooding her blood – joy, bitterness, pleasure, shame – and could only be thankful when Gabriel drew everyone's attention to himself by saying, somewhat drily, that they must not delay further.

Nor had he alluded in any way to that moment since, though he could scarcely have failed to notice what had been happening beneath his thin, aquiline nose.

Caught up as she had been in her own embarrassment, Adèle had still noticed the puzzling but very pointed manner in which Juliène had ignored both the High Commander and his Second. And whilst Adèle had every sympathy with Juliène's ongoing antipathy towards the man who had once been her brother's lover, try as she might, she could think of nothing that Joscelin had done to deserve such a blatant show of contempt.

Even more disorientating had been the moment when Juliène had held her close in an uncharacteristic embrace, using the opportunity to whisper in her ear a reminder to keep an eye out for Messire Guyard, adding the scarcely audible but apparently sincere reminder that she wished Adèle's kinsman nothing but good.

It was a claim that Adèle, still shaken from her encounter with Joscelin, had almost believed, so credible had Juliène sounded, her green eyes aglimmer with what looked like heartfelt tears.

Yet with Lamortaine out of sight behind her, the highway to Vézière snaking away before her, a treacherous quagmire of mud and fallen leaves, the emotion in Juliène's plea seemed scarcely more real than Adèle's illusory relationship with Gabriel de Marillec.

A comparison that led Adèle to conclude that Juliène's words were no more than a snare designed to determine Guy's whereabouts.

A piece of information Adèle had no intention of sharing with Juliène, even if she should manage to discover it herself.

In the meantime, she found herself truly alone with her lord-by-binding for the first time.

No silent servants.

No blank-faced guards.

No avid-eyed, sharp-tongued courtiers.

Just herself and Gabriel.

Though in truth she rarely addressed him so informally.

Or he her, for that matter.

As it was, there was little enough talk between them, and for long stretches of the journey the only sound was that of horses' hooves sucking in and out of the mud of the highway, the bright jingle of harness, and the increasingly cheerful song of the birds as the sun warmed the chilly autumn air, drying the glittering droplets left by the previous night's rain from leaf and blade, twig and branch.

At the edge of sight hawks soared untamed over the dark moors and in the fields closer to hand, men laboured with oxen and plough, sweating and swearing, hard eyes watching the high-born couple who rode past on their horses, apparently free of all care.

Appearances, as ever, were deceptive.

Gabriel's brows, now their natural light brown, were drawn together in an almost perpetual frown, his slender shoulders braced against some burden Adèle could only guess at.

As for herself, she found herself worrying more and more about her kinsman, wondering whether the man Lady Isabelle had seen begging by the wayside could really have been Guy.

When Lady Isabelle had first told her, with some hesitation, about the fair-haired beggar carrying what looked like a harp at his back, Adèle had given it no further thought, being too caught up – as she now admitted to herself, with a feeling of shame – in her own misery to consider anyone else, even her own kinsman. The man she had held in such deep affection and whose loss she had never quite got over.

Yet even when she *had* found herself able to reflect on Lady Isabelle's nervous suggestion, she had *still* dismissed the notion as ridiculous.

Now, however, the combination of Juliène's questioning, coupled with certain things Gabriel had said, meant that she had to accept the possibility that Lady Isabelle had been right in her identification and that Guy was not dead after all.

Please gods, let it be true!

Adèle had never known exactly what had happened to her kinsman when Guy's regular letters to her at the Healing House in Vézière had ceased. Gossip from Lamortaine and the provinces came seldom to the Sisters, and when it did it was generally late and rarely accurate.

As it was, the generally-accepted conclusion had been that Guy de Martine had died in some unpleasant manner – as his legitimate half-brother had done – and the whole affair hushed up at Lord Joffroi's behest.

The validity of that assumption now called into doubt, Adèle had initially regretted that she had not questioned Lady Isabelle more thoroughly when she had had the opportunity to do so, but as she considered it further, she was glad that she had not, since to deliberately drag the older woman into a conspiracy against someone as ruthless as Joffroi de Rogé would be a poor return for her kindness.

Gabriel, however, was a man – and if the scars on his body were any indication, more than able to look after himself. And yet...

Ah! There was always a 'but', Adèle thought, as she slid another sideways glance at her companion's fine-cut profile, and slender mailed form, chewing her lip as she considered whether she should seek to involve him in her quest.

As she well knew, Gabriel de Marillec had enough dangerous secrets of his own, without being asked to shoulder any more.

Set against that, he did seem to have some respect for her kinsman, and was undoubtedly still angry about the manner of his disappearance.

Besides, she reasoned, all she needed from Gabriel was information, and once he was up on the northern border he would be well out of whatever happened in Lamortaine or Vézière... or wherever Guy proved to be.

Verse 6

Return to Vézière

As keen as Adèle knew Gabriel to be to reach Vézière – and slough off all responsibility for his unwanted wife – he was yet considerate enough to hold the pace to that which a lady unused to riding long distances could manage.

Though even had he been alone, she reflected, he would still have had to break the journey when darkness fell, since not even the most capable horseman, with a change of mounts every few leagues, could ride from Lamortaine to Vézière in a day.

That said, when they did stop for the night it was not, as Adèle had expected, at Rath-na-Cael.

Arriving in the drear light of late afternoon, she made by instinct for the inn with the sign of the Three Hares swinging gently outside, only to come to a puzzled halt when Gabriel leaned over to place a commanding hand on her bridle.

A jerk of his head invited her to look around, and in doing so she quickly realised that the village appeared to be playing unwilling host to a patrol of grim-faced, black-armoured men, the sight of whom had brought a harder than usual look to her lord-by-binding's stonily handsome countenance.

In answer to her whispered question, he replied in curt tones,

"It is Joffroi de Rogé's Black Hunt, the gods help whatever poor wretch they have taken this time. Come on, we cannot stop here. I may not be much use to you in our binding but I *can* protect you from such vile company."

Adèle merely nodded meekly, one look having told her that for once she agreed unreservedly with her lord's judgement. Only when they were out of sight of the grimly silent town, its sullen inhabitants and the sly glances of the black-clad soldiers, did she dare to ask,

"You think they are after your..." She baulked at using the word 'friend' and said instead, "After Messire de Chartreux, and his men?"

"I bloody well know they are!" Gabriel snapped back, his state of mind betrayed by his language.

Adèle said nothing more, instinctively turning her gaze away so that she need not see what his eyes betrayed.

With the relative comfort of the inn at Rath-na-Cael behind them, they spent the night instead in a tiny but surprisingly homely tavern a little further along the road, eating their fill of mutton stew and herb dumplings before withdrawing to the single bedchamber the inn could supply.

Leaving Adèle to settle in – and to question whether her lord intended to return at all, being, as he had said, no use to her in the binding bed – Gabriel had taken himself off to the stables to check on their mounts.

Convinced she would not see him again that night, she was sitting on the bed, pleasantly surprised by the depth of the straw-stuffed mattress, the thickness of the woollen blankets and the freshness of the rough linen sheets...

When something made her look up, to see Gabriel standing just inside the door, in that silently casual stance she had become accustomed to when they had lived within the palace walls, but which now seemed startlingly intimate.

"My lord!"

Disconcerted, she came to her feet, suddenly more unsure of herself or him than she had been at any time since their binding night.

Without moving, he said quietly,

"I came to tell you that I will bed down with the horses tonight if you wish to be rid of my unwelcome company."

His unsmiling gaze went beyond her shoulder.

"That bed is by no means as wide as the one we have been sharing."

This was undoubtedly true but just as Adèle opened her mouth to accept his offer, she felt a shiver of icy cold wind swirl around her ankles and heard a handful of hail hit the shuttered window, and with an inner sigh she realised that she could not send him out in that.

"There is no need for you to sleep in the stables," she said. "Or the floor," she added as she saw his gaze drop to survey the rough boards beneath his booted feet.

He shrugged slightly.

"It is no hardship. Compared to some of the places I sleep whilst keeping the border-watch, the stables or indeed the floor would be luxury indeed."

"I have no doubt about that," Adèle said.

And found herself unable to repress a shudder as her mind suddenly presented her with the image of her lord lying wrapped in his cloak on the rocky floor of a shallow cave, shivering as a white-flaked wind whistled around the crags outside... or blasted the bare branches of some rotted-out oak tree, in the hollow trunk of which Gabriel lay curled up on a bed of damp leaves, not daring to light a fire lest barbarian scouts discover his presence and slit his throat in the night...

"It is not normally *quite* that desperate, Adèle."

His light voice, holding a hint of his rare humour, pierced her horrified imaginings, seemingly able to track her thoughts in that uncanny way he sometimes demonstrated.

"That said, I am more accustomed to such rough conditions than a feather bed. Besides which," he added on a dryer note, "There is warmth in the company I keep..."

And when she could not prevent her gaze flying to his in startled question, he added with a lift of his light brown brows,

"We never go out on patrol alone. It would be folly to do so. Why, what did you think I meant?"

Then as Adèle flushed, part in mortification, part in anger that he had seen fit to deliberately mislead her, he added quietly,

"My apologies, it has become habit with me to treat everyone the same, hold them at a distance, give them what they expect to hear..."

"Oh, surely there must be exceptions!" she snapped. "Somehow I cannot see your commander appreciating your flippant desire to shock?"

"He has no choice but to tolerate it in public," he agreed. "In private, it is a different matter. Then I can be myself... as I can with so few others... Luc, Rafe, Rowène..."

A small flicker of a wistful smile shifted amongst the shadows in his eyes, and he cast a glance around the tiny, candlelit chamber, empty save for themselves and the night's shadows, almost as if he were looking for those he had just named.

"And what about me?" Adèle demanded, feeling a sharp prick of unaccountable annoyance. "Can you not be yourself with me?"

145

"I doubt, Madame, that you would want to know the full extent of the darkness within me, or see the daemons that ride me."

She swallowed at his harsh tone.

No, she was not ready for that. She doubted she would ever be.

"That said," he went on. "We are bound until death and perhaps deserve what truth I can give you."

"So tell me a smaller truth then, my lord. I know you are restless tonight. More restless than usual. Is that because you left... a lover behind in Lamortaine? Or is there someone waiting up on the border to warm your bed?"

"No," he said. "Neither lover nor mistress. I gave you my word, Adèle. And just as I have kept it whilst I have been at court, so I will continue to keep it when I am not."

She nodded, trying not to think of how he must deal with his body's inevitable need for release, and said instead,

"Sleep in the stables, or on the floor, wherever you will. Just know that if you wish to, you are welcome to share the bed with me. I think..." she finished with an attempt at a smile. "You will find it warmer, and certainly more comfortable than the floor, even if you must take my company with it."

He nodded, his hands – once more bare of all jewellery – lifting to unpin his thick, royal blue mantle, then dropping to release the buckle on the heavy belt that held both dagger and longsword, before seating himself on the bottom of the bed to remove his mud-splashed boots.

She did not wait to see what came next, instead pulling off her thick over-gown and diving beneath the covers still clad in her shift, shivering at the touch of the cold sheets, freezing despite the hot stone the tavern keeper's good-wife had placed in the bed in an attempt to ward off some of the autumn damp.

A draught of chilly air and the rustle of straw told her that Gabriel had chosen to join her after all.

It was, she realised then, a *very* small bed, even smaller than she had originally thought. Barely big enough for two of them, his body lay considerably closer than she had become accustomed to. So close in fact that she did not even have to stretch out her fingers in order to feel the warm linen that covered his limbs.

After that first night in Lamortaine, he had always slept naked and it had not troubled her in the least.

Here, however, he retained both shirt and braies, possibly against the cold, possibly for some other reason.

Whichever it was, Adèle found it disturbing in ways that were wholly unconnected with Gabriel de Marillec.

It made her wonder things she should not wonder... such as how she would feel if it were Joscelin lying there beside her?

To imagine his mouth on hers, his long lean body pressed against her... rising above her... moving within her...

Struggling against the rising surge of heat born of her desire for another man, she rolled over onto her side, as far away from Gabriel as possible, and it occurred to her that possibly he too was thinking of someone he would rather be with, and that the garments he wore formed some sort of armour against his own heated thoughts, and the need to wrap his clenched fingers about his aching flesh.

It was not, however, a question she intended to ask him. Ever.

Determinedly banishing both the longed-for lover and her unwanted lord-by-binding from her mind, she closed her eyes in the hope of falling asleep, only to open them again as she remembered the candle still burning on the low stool beside the bed.

She half reached out towards it, hesitated and glanced over her shoulder at the man lying on his back beside her, one arm flung over his eyes, then left it alone, watching as the small golden flame flickered and steadied as the wind rose and fell outside, while behind her Gabriel's body slowly relaxed, his breathing deepening into sleep. And finally, she slept too.

She was wrenched from dreaming into wakefulness by a most terrible sound. Not the wail of the wind howling around the tavern – though that too was making its voice heard – but a cry that sounded like a soul being riven asunder.

Her heart thundering in her ears, she sat up, instinctively turning towards the man she had last seen sleeping peacefully at her side, a state she had hoped might last through until dawn – although it would be the first night his sleep had been remained unbroken since their binding.

Her first thought was a useless wish that she had not left the candle burning!

For then she need not have seen him as he was, sweating and shaking, his narrow brows, long lashes, the stubble on his jaw and every hair on his body not hidden beneath the fine linen of his shirt, sparking bronze in the gilding light.

And his eyes... dear God of Light, his eyes!

Normally a clear – if impenetrable – amber, they now blazed bright citrine within a ring of pure gold.

"No!"

The hoarse shout burst from his heaving chest and before Adèle could reach out to him or utter any of the soothing nothings she had murmured in the darkness of every other night, he had flung himself from the bed and stumbled to the window, throwing open the shutters and letting in a drenching downpour of icy rain.

Soaked within a half-dozen heartbeats, he stood there, thin linen clinging to his wet body, gripping the sill with bone-white fingers, staring out into the night as if he could see... what, Adèle did not know.

Hastily grabbing his thick mantle from the nail behind the door, she threw it around his shoulders, and tried to draw him away from the window, wilfully deaf to his barely coherent words, thankful that he was whispering now, rather than shouting loud enough to reach whatever wraiths or daemons were abroad in the darkness.

"Luce! Gods no! Luce!"

"My lord, come away."

He, in his turn, ignored her pleas and with the sudden memory of Rafe kneeling at his commander's side, calling him by his given name, she said more forcefully,

"*Gabriel!* Look at me!"

Much to her surprise, he turned those bright, feral gold eyes towards her. He did not know her, that much was plain, though that might yet stand to her advantage.

"Gabriel, come away from the window. Luc... *Luce* is safe, and Rafe is waiting for you."

He stared at her without comprehension, and she added in desperation,

"They *need* you, Gabriel. Come away now. Please!"

Long bronze lashes dipped, and when he opened his eyes again, she saw to her relief that something of the fervid brightness had dimmed with the retreat of his madness.

By dint of patience and persuasion, she managed to get him to the bed, pushing him down so that he was sitting on the edge.

Then, confirming that he was far enough away from the stool that he could not knock the candle over if he moved suddenly, she darted back to wrestle the shutters closed again. If she had not been wet before, she certainly was by the time she finished.

Her satisfaction that she had shut out the night was short-lived, however, ripped apart by the realisation that the man she had left silently staring into the candle flame was now sobbing quietly into his hands.

"Blood... so much blood! Rivers of blood... fields of blood... washing the silver feet of the goddess of night... while the harper sings the last lament... and the healer... oh gods! Please! Let the healer come in time..."

And Adèle recognised, as if a frost had crept over her heart, words similar to those he had spoken that night at Vézière and knew the madness she dreaded had come upon him again.

"The healer will be there," she heard herself saying, as she pulled away his soaking mantle and replaced it with her own dry one. "The harper and the healer both. Just as you said. And all will be well."

"I cannot see her! Gods, why is she not there? I saw her before..."

He looked up suddenly, and Adèle let go the breath she had not realised she was holding when she saw that the terrible glittering brightness was fading.

Finally, when his eyes were very nearly their natural shade of light amber and almost completely lucid, she heard him mutter,

"Rowène... hear me. Be there! You are the only one who can save... something, *anything* from the bloody shambles in my dreams..."

Something or *someone*, Adèle wondered, but did not ask, the healer in her unwilling to do anything to destroy the frail hold Gabriel was establishing over himself.

Even if he was talking to a woman who was not there.

A woman with whom he could – and evidently did – share a bond of trust the like of which he had made no attempt to extend to Adèle, who merely wore his binding band.

Repressing her sense of ill usage, Adèle repeated firmly,

"It was just a dream, my lord. Just a dream."

If only she could believe it.

Dream... madness... whatever it was, she could only pray it would not take hold of his mind when he was alone on the road north, for who then would keep him from destroying himself.

And once he reached the border, she believed – she *had* to believe – that she could trust the soldier, Rafe, to keep his commanding officer safe and – by any reasonable means possible – sane.

Two days later, in a clear dawn of blue-ice skies and silver-frosted branches, Adèle rose, dressed in the plain blue-grey woollen gown she deemed appropriate for her new surroundings, and having bidden her lord-by-binding a subdued farewell, now stood in the gateway of the healers' enclave. Shivering beneath her mantle, the hand she had half raised to wave if he should look back at her fell to her side.

Still she stood and watched the slender, solitary figure until the man whose binding band she now wore disappeared into the poplar copse that spread its yellowing leaves over the green path that would take him into the desolation of the distant borderlands.

She could not help but wonder if she would ever see him again.

That, however, seemed too much like ill-wishing him, which she certainly did not. So instead she muttered a hasty prayer to the God of Light to guard his journey. A journey Gabriel would have embarked upon yesterday if he had had his way.

He had indeed protested most vehemently on their arrival about spending any time, let alone the night, at the Healing House.

The Eldest, however, had taken one look at his face, at the careful blankness of his amber eyes and the dark bruising beneath that told of strain and sleepless nights, and to Adèle's unspoken relief had overridden not only Gabriel's objections but also the tight-lipped disapproval of Sister Winfreda.

Having given his reluctant agreement to accept the healers' hospitality, Gabriel had allowed his horse to be taken away to the barn by Sister Aldith and meekly followed the Eldest towards the infirmary.

At the same time Adèle had excused herself to wash away the inevitable taint of travel and present herself to the princess and Linette, after a moment's startlement at her unexpected presence, had welcomed her graciously and suggested she might wish to withdraw to unpack her clothes.

Adèle, who had not brought more garments than could be fitted into one small saddle bag, had blinked, then returned Lady Isabelle's anxiously questioning look with a smile she hoped conveyed reassurance, and made haste to retreat.

Restless and ill-at-ease with no useful occupation, she had found herself heading for the infirmary, where in the small chamber at the far end normally only used for patients needing to be kept apart from the others, she found her lord-by-binding.

He was sitting, fully-clothed, on the side of a low bed, a red earthenware bowl of bean pottage balanced on his knees, a hunk of bread and cheese on a wooden platter resting on the grey blanket beside him.

Hearing her footsteps, he looked up, a slight smile lighting his wary gaze.

"I thought you might be that sour-faced besom I upset the last time I was here," he grinned.

"Sister Winfreda?"

Adèle bit back a sympathetic laugh, though the circumstances had been anything but amusing at the time, and she still winced inwardly when she thought about that night.

"I doubt it was personal. She hates having any man within the enclave's walls. She is just as fiercely outspoken against Jos... Messire de Veraux."

Feeling herself flush, she continued with much haste and little thought,

"But you must admit that Rafe did not help the situation by his pursuit of Sister Fayla, and then you and..."

"Me and Luc!" he finished her truncated statement with a stony lack of emotion. "Being out of my wits at the time, I can only guess how depraved that must have appeared to bigoted eyes."

He lifted the spoon to his mouth, grimaced and dropped it back into the bowl, pottage untasted.

"Indeed, there are not many who could have witnessed that scene with any forbearance. I do not blame you for what you must have thought."

Not knowing what else to do, Adèle said helplessly,

"You should try and eat something, my lord. You have a long ride ahead of you. If, that is, you still intend to leave in the morning?"

"I do! Hell knows, there is nothing wrong with me! Nothing beyond the obvious, of course," he finished with a hint of the biting self-mockery that underlay so many of their conversations.

"Nevertheless, a good night's rest will not come amiss," she suggested.

"You have not been sleeping well since our binding. Or before it either, I dare say," she finished with some difficulty, trying and failing to banish the recurring image of Gabriel in Luc de Chartreux's fiercely protective embrace.

"No," he admitted. "But then I do not expect sleep came any easier to you once you had received your father's letter informing you of our betrothal."

Wordlessly she shook her head, and his finely-formed mouth hardened. He said nothing more for a few moments, merely regarding her in silence, eyes narrowed as if trying to make up his mind about something. Finally, he said,

"Come, my lady, sit and share my meal with me. If, that is, you do not mind using the same spoon and cup."

And at her look of surprise,

"Only the gods know how long I will be gone, or even if I will return. That being so, there are things that must be said between us, and I fancy the Eldest does not mean to allow us to be alone together under this roof, though what she thinks will happen I cannot imagine! I doubt she is blind to the truth about either of us."

And when she could not meet his perceptive gaze, he added with the unlooked-for gentleness that always took her by surprise,

"I know it is Josce you are in love with."

"As long as... gods, as long as *he* does not know it too!" she muttered, the coarse red surface of the clay floor tiles blurring through the mortified tears she would not shed.

"I have seen no sign that he does," he assured her. "Nor – while I am not in the habit of keeping secrets from the man who is my commanding officer as well as my friend – will he hear of it from me."

"Thank you, my lord," she managed. Then, pulling herself together, "What did you want to talk to me about?"

Now, watching him ride away without once looking back, Adèle pushed that last conversation into the back of her mind, not wanting to think about it any more. Then he was gone, leaving nothing of himself save a few terse, stilted words to set her free and the impersonal touch of his warm mouth against the back of her hand.

In truth though the only freedom either of them had within the bounds of their binding was the liberty to pursue their opposing callings, as they had for the past several years.

Hers to heal. His to kill.

That being so, she guessed that he had probably put her from his mind already.

Unfortunately, she did not think she would find it so simple to forget him.

She looked down at the band about her wrist and sighed as she rubbed the warm bronze, studying the amber insets that so closely resembled the colour of his eyes, and knew that whether she thought of him not at all or imagined him in battle, sunlight flashing off the sword in his hand, his fine features and slender form splattered with barbarian blood from lank brown hair to booted feet, or lying awake in the darkness beneath the cold loneliness of the northern sky, perhaps seeking his own pleasure, she would still be here in Vézière, still be bound to him in ways he, being a man, could never comprehend!

"He will be all right."

The Eldest's voice broke into her thoughts, and Adèle turned a confused look on the woman who had appeared at her side.

"Your lord-by-binding," Sister Herluva said softly. "He will find peace for his tortured thoughts and scarred soul once he reaches the borderlands and the men under his command."

"Peace in the midst of slaughter and death?" Adèle asked with a huff of humourless laughter.

"Well, perhaps he will. Certainly, I cannot ever imagine him happy walking among the vineyards around Marillé, a small son riding on his shoulders, his lady back at the castle directing domestic matters for his comfort."

"No," Sister Herluva sighed, her blue eyes misted with sadness. "I cannot see that either. The gods know I wish I could. Wish you might both be happy."

Then her tone changed, her words brisk,

"What we cannot change, we must learn to live with as best we may. With your lord's departure, your duty lies once again with Princess Linette. And mine with making sure this house runs smoothly. Please excuse me, my lady."

So saying, the Eldest seemed to retreat into herself. Being the recipient of a distantly courteous smile, Adèle knew she would henceforth be treated an honoured guest, rather than a fellow healer and with another inward sigh watched as Sister Herluva tucked her hands into her wide sleeves and walked back towards the long, low wing housing the infirmary.

She cast one more look north, then turned back into the enclave, feeling oddly bereft.

An unwarranted feeling since, as the gods and everyone else knew, Gabriel de Marillec had never been hers to start with.

Céline de Veraux, otherwise known as the Eldest of Vézière's Grey Sisters, continued on her way, the careful serenity of her expression marred by the slightest of anxious frowns. Beneath her habitual calm she was deeply worried.

About many things, but at this particular moment mostly about Adèle.

And, yes, her lord-by-binding also.

So much so that Céline felt she barely had any room left to worry about the things she should be concerned with, such as the welfare of those who sought aid from the Sisters, and for the smooth daily running of the Healing House.

Coming to the kitchen, she stepped inside to see plump Sister Gilda already stirring the morning porridge, while Aedgyth, the lame, mute girl who assisted her, was carefully carrying wooden bowls and spoons through to the refectory.

"'Twill all be ready in two flicks of a lambkin's tail, Eldest," Sister Gilda assured her with a cheery smile. "An' I did feed that young man afore he left, just like ye telt me last night. Lad looks as though he could do wi' a deal more feeding up, so slight as he be."

Céline found some of her anxiety lifting at this sign that not all of the healers regarded Gabriel de Marillec's presence within their walls as they might a malignant growth of black mould.

Alas, this tolerance was not repeated when she joined the rest of the household for the morning meal.

Sister Winfreda naturally enough had the harshest words to say on the subject, and whilst even she had not dared to openly question the Eldest's decision to allow the weary nobleman to remain overnight, she had made it very plain that she thought his departure a good riddance... until catching the look of icy rebuke in Céline's eye, decided at last that it might be wiser to hold her tongue and apply herself instead to her porridge.

Finally able to spare a quick glance at the three noblewomen seated nearby, Céline felt more than a flicker of pity to see Adèle de Marillec sitting rigid, very white of face, her eyes fixed on her porridge. Beside her, it was clear that Princess Linette, while remaining tactfully silent, nevertheless agreed with Sister Winfreda and the majority of the other healers. Only Isabelle showed no sign of taking sides, but then given the life her sister had suffered as Henri de Lyeyne's lady, Céline could well understand her nervous inability to venture an opinion.

With the morning meal over, the Sisters rose to go about their allotted tasks, Adèle hesitating visibly, before overcoming five years of habit and following Linette and Isabelle from the refectory.

Watching the slender figure in the blue-grey gown, Céline sighed under her breath, wondering whether Adèle would truly be content to serve as lady-companion to the princess in the same environs where previously she had lived the busy and hard-working life of a healer.

She was still pondering the matter when, having completed her morning tour of the enclave, delivering praise, advice and command where due, Céline came at last to her own airy, austerely furnished chamber, the place where she slept by night and by day conducted the administration of the house.

Disregarding the pull of the infirmary, where the sick and injured were tended most competently by her fellow healers, Céline seated herself at the table and drawing parchment, ink and quill towards her began her daily reckoning of supplies and provisions – some of their own cultivation and making, others donated by the generosity of Lord Nicholas de Vézière – all of which needed to be accounted for and used wisely.

As Céline's quill continued to scratch its inky reckoning, the crisp clarity of the dawn yielded to grey clouds and by mid-morning the sort of chill rain that penetrates every crevice of clothing to soak a body through to the skin was beginning to fall.

Reduced to working by chancy candlelight, with her window shuttered against the increasingly unpleasant weather, Céline was far from unhappy for the excuse to pause, looking up as a knock sounded at her door.

Setting aside her quill, she absently rubbed her aching fingers – the joints were swelling again, she noted with a frown, a reaction to the cold, the damp and, quite possibly, her own underlying and constant concern for those she loved.

Her mood was scarcely improved by the sight of her senior healer. Repressing her sigh, she instead enquired in a calm voice,

"Yes, Sister Winfreda, what is it?"

"'Tis a man," the other woman stated, her voice high and tight with disapproval. "At the gate, askin' fer ye. That soldier, I reckon, though he's no' wearin' mail. Him as was here afore. He's back!"

"What soldier, Sister?" Céline asked as patiently as she could. "The Guardians' Second? He who left this morning?"

"*Him?* No." The words were practically spat out. "T'other debauched lout. The one that slut Fayla's been liftin' her skirts for."

Holding onto her temper with difficulty, Céline spoke with a distant coolness her son would have recognised as being very much his own manner.

"*Sister* Fayla is not within these walls at present, and I will not discuss her in her absence. As for the guardian, please do not keep him standing about in the rain, and in future bring him to me at any time he asks to speak with me."

As the senior healer's footsteps disappeared down the passageway and into deluge of rain beating against the shutter, Céline came to her feet and pouring a generous amount of mead into a beaker, picked up the poker and thrust it into the brazier to heat.

Whatever had caused Ranulf to ride south, it could not be good, and given the weather outside he was bound to be wet and cold.

By the time a second knock was heard, the mead was warmed and waiting, and Céline's anxiety such as made it hard for her to answer with the serene dignity expected of her.

The door opened and instead of the skinny, grey-clad form of Sister Winfreda, there stood a big, broad-shouldered man, rain dripping from a mantle so dark with rain its original colour was impossible to judge.

But when he threw back the hood shadowing his face, the flickering candlelight danced off the wheat-fair hair she had been expecting.

"Rafe!" she exclaimed. "What in the name of the gods has brought you back here so soon? Did you not see..."

She stopped abruptly, watching as the visitor's eyes narrowed in a manner very like that of the man Céline had just named.

156

And yet, she could see now that those eyes under thick blond brows were a lighter shade of blue than the dark ice of the man who was presently known as Rafe of Oakenleigh, and a heartbeat later the stranger confirmed it.

"I am not Rafe, whoever he may be."

"No, forgive me, I see now that you are not."

Indeed, she saw very well who he really was, but needing a few moments to realign her thoughts and speaking more for the benefit of the woman she could hear shuffling her feet in the passageway, continued,

"Will you not tell me your name, and why you wish to speak to me. And please, take a cup of spiced mead to warm yourself."

"Thank you, Eldest."

Extending a calloused hand from beneath the dripping cloak, he accepted the cup she held out to him.

He took a small wary sip, then another more appreciative mouthful, his blue eyes meeting hers over the rim with a considering look, before saying,

"My name is Finch, and I am a harper, until recently at the royal court in Kardolandia, now in the service of Lord Nicholas."

"Welcome to Vézière, Master Finch," Céline said after a moment, ruthlessly capturing all her random thoughts about harpers and healers, death and danger, battening them down firmly beneath common sense and courtesy.

"And your visit today? Are you in need of healing? I noticed you were limping."

And to her subordinate,

"That will be all. If I need assistance, I will call."

With that she firmly shut the door in Sister Winfreda's face, and turned to face Guyard de Martine.

"Speak softly, Messire, and in Mithlondian. And tell me what has brought you here thus unexpectedly?"

"Ah!"

Despite his obvious surprise at being thus addressed, his voice did not rise much above a low murmur.

"I came to see you, Madame. To see if you would recognise me."

He grimaced slightly.

"Which, quite clearly, you do. And also to ask whether you have any tidings of Adèle?"

"Your kinswoman is here," she confirmed quietly. "Would you like to speak to her? She can tend to your... Leg? Foot?" She raised questioning eyebrows at him. "At the same time."

"I cut my foot on a stone the day I arrived in Vézière. It is healing well enough but it will serve if you need a reason for my visit..."

She looked down at his feet, only now noticing that they were not shod in boots, nor even sturdy leather shoes but a pair of sandals which to judge from their intricate design were unlikely to be of Mithlondian workmanship.

Raising her eyes to study his face more closely, she saw that his skin beneath the scattered glimmer of raindrops bore the darker kiss of a hot southern sun rather than the lighter weathering of northern winds, and wondered how she could possibly not have realised at first sight which of Jacques de Rogé's younger sons was standing in her doorway.

As she probably would not have done if Sister Winfreda had not described him as *that soldier... him as was here afore'* so definitely that the return of a man Céline had thought to be a thousand leagues away was the last thing on her mind.

"Adèle will be so pleased to see you returned safely," she said, surprised at her own calm. "And I am sure you have much to tell each other. Wait here, and I will bring her to you."

She was very nearly out of the door when she heard his voice behind her,

"Eldest! Who is this Rafe you mistook me for?"

After a moment's hesitation she turned to look at the man who believed his brother to be dead.

Nor was it her place to tell him the truth.

"He is, or was, one of the royal bodyguard. Now he is simply a soldier serving under Gabriel de Marillec's command on the northern border."

"He is still with de Marillec then?" Guy asked, his voice taking on an edge Céline had heard all too often lately in reference to the Second of Mithlondia's Guardians, and which she really did not care to listen to again.

"Yes," she curtly and walked away, determined not to be drawn into any further discussion regarding either of the two men who kept at least as many secrets as she did.

Entering the Eldest's private chamber a little later, Adèle glanced at the man standing warming his hands at the brazier, taking in all at once the shoulder-length fair hair... eyes the same light summer blue she saw reflected in her mirror... the familiar, longed-for face.

"Guy!" she whispered on a breath that was half laugh, half cry. "Oh, Guy, it *is* you. Thank the gods you are alive."

She was across the room and in his arms before another beat of her heart, her hands sweeping up his chest to touch the soft, blond beard he had not worn the last time they had met – indeed, as a nobleman should, he had always been clean-shaven before.

Barely able to see the warm affection of his smile for the tears in her eyes, she said again,

"Oh, Guy."

"Well, at least someone is pleased to see me," he murmured, his strong arms closing tight about her, his light voice huskier than she remembered it, as if he was as affected by emotion as she.

The words, however, returned her to some sense of reality, and she drew back sharply, her gaze darting from the shuttered window – outside which she could still hear the comforting defence of the autumn rain – to where the Eldest stood quietly, her back to the closed door, before returning her attention to her kinsman.

"What are you doing here, Guy?" she hissed.

"Visiting the healers and seeking tidings of you."

"No, not *here* in the Healing House. I mean, *here* as in Vézière. In Mithlondia at all! Gods above, Guy, you must know you are in danger if word gets to Lord Joffroi that you have been seen."

"Yes, I know that." Her kinsman shrugged broad shoulders. "And I promise you I have been, and will continue to be, careful."

"Not nearly careful enough!" Adèle snapped, fear overtaking her joy.

"You mean Lady Isabelle?" he asked ruefully. "I thought she might have recognised me when you passed me that day on the highway."

"She will say nothing," the Eldest assured him, at the same time as Adèle said unhappily,

"It is someone much closer to your brother you need to be wary of."

"Juliène!"

It was not a question this time, simply a flat statement.

"Yes, she suspects, I know she does. And she will tell her mother and..."

"Perhaps," Guy interrupted her rising tones, blue eyes looking beyond her at something only he could see. "Then again, perhaps not. I know only that I have been five years away from my homeland, and can remain an exile no longer, whatever happens to me now and whoever was responsible for sending me to Kardolandia in the first place."

"Please, Guy, promise me you will stay away from Lamortaine. And Juliène," she begged.

"I cannot do that," he said gently, taking her hands in his warm clasp. "All I can promise is that I will not deliberately put myself in her path. But whether you like it or not, there *is* unfinished business between Madame de Lyeyne and me."

"Unfinished business! Oh, gods!" She gave a laugh that bordered on hysteria. "Not you too. I do not think I can bear to hear those words ever again."

With that, she tore her hands from her kinsman's grasp, putting them instead over her ears and closing her eyes to Guy's astonished stare, in a futile attempt to escape the memory of her lord-by-binding lying in his lover's arms, eyes as hard and unfathomable and brilliant as citrine, his normally pleasant light voice hoarse with strain as he spoke of the nightmare only he could see.

It will never be finished. Not between those of us here today, and she who watches out of the shadows of the moon for the one who is yet to return.

And later, just before he had slumped into unconsciousness,

On the day the sun sets over a field of blood, and the Moon Goddess walks on silver feet amongst the living and the slain... when harper and healer stand together within her light... when the healing is done, and the last harp song is sung, only then will this thing be truly finished.

Opening her eyes, wondering how much of Gabriel's ravings she had repeated, Adèle's frantic gaze fell first on the Eldest's face, her normal serenity gentling into compassion, and then on her kinsman's openly bewildered countenance.

"Oh, gods," she moaned, bringing her hands up to cover her face. "Forgive me, Guy, I must have become infected by my lord's madness."

"Your *lord?*" he queried, his eyes widening in a flash of blue, then narrowing as he belatedly took stock of her raiment, evidently realising the significance of her fine woollen gown, the way her hair was braided about her hair in a pale gold circlet beneath the light veil she wore in place of the concealing linen headrail.

"Lady Adèle is no longer here as one of our healers," the Eldest confirmed his unspoken conclusion, broadening her explanation at his frowning look. "Both you and she knew that her time here was finite. And with the blessing of the gods, she had five years of peace before her father remembered her existence."

"So why is she here now?" Guy asked blankly.

Slowly he turned to survey Adèle more closely, his speculative gaze fixed on her midriff rather than her face.

"Are you with child then?"

"No!" Adèle felt the blood seep from her cheeks at his blunt question, and struggled for composure. "But Princess Linette *is*, and I am here to bear her company during the months of her confinement."

"And where is your lord that he does not desire your company at his own side?"

Guy's voice, though still gentle had taken on the slightest hint of his half-brother Ranulf's rough-edged steel.

"On the northern border," Adèle replied with what calm she could muster, and watched comprehension flare in her kinsman's eyes.

"The northern border, where the guardians keep their watch. So... given that my ambitious Uncle Gaston would not have seen you bound to a common soldier, that means either Joscelin de Veraux or Gabriel de Marillec. Please tell me it is de Veraux."

Gods, if only she *could* tell her cousin that she was bound to Joscelin, that she was carrying his child! How happy she would be if that were so.

"Unfortunately, Lady Adèle and Lord Joscelin are blood-kin," the Eldest answered when Adèle could not.

"Distant it is true, yet still within the limits of prohibition as set out by the High Counsel."

"Then it is de Marillec."

Anger flashed within the depths of Guy's eyes as he read the answer in the stillness of her stance, the pallor of her face.

"Damn the miserable cur, he gave me his word he would not bring harm to you."

"Nor has he," Adèle snapped, surprising herself, let alone Guy, by the speed with which she sprang to her lord's defence.

"Indeed I think he has treated me better than I deserved, given the... the attitude which I brought to our binding. And before you say anything else in his disparagement, Guy, let me tell you that he has not forgotten that oath he swore to you, and if Prince Linnius had not made the matter of our binding a royal command, Gabriel would *never* have broken his word or taken me in any way."

"And has he? Taken you? And yes, I *do* mean that in the most obvious sense of the word."

Adèle felt herself flush as red the glowing heart-wood in the nearby brazier.

"That is none of your business, Guy. He has not hurt me. And he... he respects me, or at least my calling as a healer. That is as much as you need to know."

Guy stared at her for a long moment, his blue eyes searching, then as if becoming aware of the Eldest's silent support for the younger woman, shook his head.

"Very well, it is done and there is nothing I can do to undo it. But if ever you change your mind – or de Marillec's dangerous proclivities take him to the scaffold – at least you know where you can find me if you need my help."

She blinked stupidly at him.

"And where is that?"

"Here in Vézière, of course. Did the Eldest not tell you? I have a permanent position up at the castle, as Lord Nicholas' household harper."

"So you mean to stay here? Oh Guy, is that wise?"

No matter how hard she tried, she simply could not put aside as meaningless Gabriel's warning that if and when the harper returned, he would be in danger. Nor could she forget what else Gabriel had said – about the watcher waiting within the golden shadow of the beautiful and sinister blood-moon, a watcher she very much feared must be Juliène de Lyeyne.

Guy, however, had not been there that night, and so could have no notion of the terror that had taken her then, and still did every time she thought too much about that tangled tapestry woven of moonlight and madness.

"What then would you have me do, Adèle?" he was saying. "If those words you spoke earlier prove true, I am part of whatever fate the gods are spinning for us, and I will see it through to the end. And here is as good a place as any to do it from. Lord Nicholas is an honourable man by all accounts and, as I have found in the se'ennight since I entered his service, he is more than generous to the musicians he retains. Furthermore, here in Vézière, I am close enough to Lamortaine to hear all the gossip from the court without arousing unwelcome attention in turn."

He must have seen that she remained unconvinced, and put forward one final rueful point.

"Do not worry, Adèle, no-one is going to take any notice of a base-born harper in the entourage of a near-blind nobleman."

Remembering Juliène's sly questioning in the days leading up to her binding, Adèle wished she could be so sure.

At the same time she well knew the futility of trying to change a man's mind, and while Guy and Gabriel had absolutely nothing else in common, they both had in full measure the same stupid, senseless stubbornness that all men seemed to be born with.

That being so, she merely nodded unhappy acquiescence to her kinsman's plan.

"Now then, before I go, is there anything else I should know?" Guy asked.

It crossed her mind that she should tell him that Rowène lived and was occasionally to be found here in the Healing House when there was need of Sister Fayla's particular skills.

She also considered doing as Juliène had suggested and telling him that he had a daughter living with her outlawed kinsmen in the great Forest of Lasceynes, just across the moor from Vézière.

Two things stopped her.

The first being that the only woman Guy had mentioned since his return had been Juliène de Lyeyne.

The second that she did not trust Juliène one jot.

Moreover, she found herself belatedly wondering why it mattered so much to the other woman that Guy should be told a truth Rowène had quite clearly chosen to withhold from him.

If it were a case of deciding which of the sisters had Guy's well-being closest to her heart...

Rowène had her faults, Adèle knew, but she was before all else a healer.

Juliène on the other hand had chosen allegiance to a cold-blooded witch and a black-hearted murderer, and on her own account took a malicious delight in the humiliation of those whom she believed had offended her in some way − as witness her treatment of both Gabriel and Joscelin.

With such a choice before her, Adèle took a decision she prayed would not rebound on either her or Guy in the months and years to come, and said nothing to him.

Either of his former love.

Or his daughter.

Neither, she noted, did the Eldest, who almost certainly knew the truth about both.

Much to Adèle's relief, life continued quietly in the days and weeks following her reunion with her kinsman, nothing untoward occurring to cause her to second-guess her decision.

Which was not to say that she did not continue to pray to the God of Mercy that neither Rowène nor Lissie would have reason to come to Vézière at any time when Guy's duties to Lord Nicholas should take him beyond the castle walls and down into the town.

Then again, when Adèle considered the viciousness and tenacity with which Joffroi de Rogé's brutish men-at-arms pursued their prey, it seemed to her unlikely in the extreme that any of the outlaws would be venturing out of the forest, least of all in the very direction in which the Black Hunt were known to prowl most frequently.

She should, she was to think later, have known better!

Verse 7

Mulled Ale on Market Day

Well wrapped up against the brisk wind blowing down off the moors, and idly wondering whether she might see her cousin today, Adèle was content to amble around Vézière's market square in Linette's wake as, with her thick fur-lined mantle hiding the growing bulge of her belly, the princess made her slow, slightly waddling progress around the stalls, Lady Isabelle at her side, and the burly bodyguard, Rhys, grim as a grizzled wolfhound, ever watchful, at her heels.

Linette's attention being caught by a display of carved wooden toys, amongst them a gaily painted rattle, Adèle took the opportunity to glance around the square, hoping to see Guy, who was quite often to be seen about the town in pursuit of some errand for Lord Nicholas.

Instead, her gaze clashed against that of a tall, roughly-clad man standing outside the building Adèle knew housed the town's brothel, the rope bridles of a pair of ponies, similar in markings to the one Gabriel now rode, looped over his arm.

The man's raggedly cut dark hair blew unheeded around his lean, stubbled face while his eyes – the cool grey of moorland rain – settled on her face with a sort of wary curiosity that yet carried a hint of hidden pain.

Then much as Guy had done at their first meeting, the man allowed his gaze to drop to study her belly, outlined as a gust of wind flattened her cloak against her.

The inference was obvious and Adèle hardly knew whether she should be angry at the intimacy of de Chartreux's perusal or pity him for his need to know whether or not she was carrying his l... carrying her lord's child.

Much as she loathed the idea of Gabriel with this man, she was dismayed to realise that she did understand something of the pain de Chartreux must be suffering now – if only because she knew how she would feel if she were to find herself facing a woman she suspected of carrying the child of the man she still loved.

Alongside this unexpected flicker of fellow-feeling with Luc de Chartreux came the mad impulse to tell him that while Gabriel had indeed lain by her side for some dozen nights, he had never lain *with* her...

And then, before she had a chance to talk herself out of it, she had murmured some excuse to Linette, and ignoring Rhys' stare of startled disapproval, was heading straight towards the outlaw.

Despite the bodyguard's obvious consternation, she felt no trepidation in venturing beyond his protection.

After all, she knew these people, for the most part recalled the names of the stallholders, the good-wives, even some of the itinerant traders who had been bringing their wares to the weekly markets for as long as she could remember... including the scarred man lounging against the wall of the bawdy house, recognising him as one of de Chartreux's men, though the young lad who kept the outlaw leader company most frequently was nowhere in sight.

Coming to a halt in front of Luc, she found she had to tip her head back so as to look up into the leanly-handsome face she had only seen at a distance before, and for some reason found she had no breath to speak the words she had intended.

"Good day, m'lady. Happen you're wishful of buying a pony?"

Luc's voice, lightly accented and very slightly mocking, broke the taut silence.

"How about this one?" he went on. "A fine little beast of sturdy moorland stock on the dam's side, though I'll not make claim to know which noble stallion had the siring. Well, m'lady?"

"No," she blurted, flushing both at the unsubtle insinuation and the underlying bitterness to his patter. "I... I just wanted to tell you..."

His narrow dark brows rose in an ironical look that made her think of Joscelin de Veraux, and for the second time her words dried in her mouth.

Knotting her fingers together, she took a deep breath and said abruptly,

"I just wanted you to know that I am not. And I never will be."

She saw from the flicker of silver fire in the storm-grey depths of his eyes that he understood what she was saying. And that it was not the pony she was talking about. But then, she was sure, neither had he been.

"That is all I wanted to say."

166

She was turning away when she heard him say, quick and rough and low,

"R... Gabriel? He is well?"

"I have no idea," she replied, struggling to contain her sudden rising nausea and wishing she had never started this.

"All I can tell you is that a se'ennight after our binding he returned to the Atarkarnan border and since word has not yet been brought to me that he is dead, I must assume that he is alive and still in control of his... daemons."

With that she swept away, scarcely heeding Luc's muttered oath, and so completely blind as to where she was walking that she did not see the youth approaching until she heard his startled warning and felt something warm and wet splash over her cheek, before dousing her gown from shoulder to stomach.

She recoiled with a gasp of shock, felt a hard hand steady her from behind, and found herself staring into a pair of clear grey eyes that, unlike Luc's, were on a level with her own, and heard an irritated curse that made no concessions either to her gender or noble birth.

"Bloody damned hell! Look where you're going, can't you. That's three marks' worth of Willow's best mulled ale you're now wearing. Three marks I can't bloody afford to waste."

"Here now, Master Jacq," the burly brute behind him growled. "Let the lady be! Here, ye can ha' mine."

"Don't be daft, Beowulf," the youth retorted, visibly regaining a grip on his temper. "'Twas just as much my fault as hers."

And to Adèle, with a slight bow and a milder tone,

"Beg pardon, m'lady. I should have been looking where I was going."

"No, you were right the first time," she replied. "It *was* my fault. Please allow me to pay for some more ale. It must be chilly work standing around the market, waiting for buyers for your ponies. It... it cannot be an easy way to make a living."

She studied the lad standing in front of her, noting the way his face was moulded in the same lean lines as Luc's, yet at the same time lacking the older man's harder edges so that he resembled most closely the woman who must be his sister, the only difference being that his hair was a shining chestnut brown rather than a dark fiery red.

"You must be Rowène's other brother," she said softly. "Jacq, is it not?"

There was a perceptible moment of hesitation as if the youth might be ashamed to admit to his illegitimate connection to the outlawed de Chartreux family – although his irregular birth mattered not a whit to Adèle – but then he bent in a more formal bow.

Straightening, he answered her question with a tight smile,

"Aye, m'lady, I am Jacques."

Though he still used the language spoken by the common folk of the realm, he spoke his given name with the softer pronounciation of the high tongue.

"And is your sister here with you?" Adèle continued. "Or the children I saw you with last summer?"

The young outlaw shook his head.

"Too dangerous, m'lady, what with the Black Hunt riding the moors and highways, right up to Vézière's gates."

"Yes, of course."

Relieved though she was to hear that those two happy, carefree children – one of whom must be Guy's daughter, and therefore her own kin – were safe, and much as she would have liked to know more, she found herself distracted by the way the autumn sunlight danced over the outlaw's shoulder-length curls, striking bronze sparks amidst the brown, and for no good reason at all it occurred to her that Gabriel's hair might be of a similar shade if she were ever to see it clean.

Alongside such frankly foolish speculation, a far more practical thought made its way into her head, since if there was one thing Gabriel *had* given her, it was an abundance of money.

"Jacques, you *must* let me pay you for the ale I spilt," she reiterated more firmly. "Three marks, I think you said? With perhaps a little extra that you might take some honey cakes back for..."

"No need," interposed another voice, clipped, cool, commanding, and sufficiently familiar to make Adèle's heart begin to churn like a mill race.

"By your leave, Madame de Marillec, I will take care of this matter. Moreover, to save you from any further distress or discourtesy, I would suggest that you stay away from itinerant horse traders and the like. Now, if you will give me a moment to deal with the lad here, I will escort you back to your companions."

Much as Adèle would have liked to argue with Joscelin, there was something in his unyielding countenance that made her hold her tongue and turn away... although not so quickly that she missed the way Jacques inclined his curly, chestnut head and upper body in an abbreviated bow, the smile lurking in the depths of his grey eyes undeniably impudent as he acknowledged the nobleman.

"Lord Joscelin. I reckon that'll be ten marks ye owe me, if you're going to pay the lady's debt."

"Ten marks! You thieving scoundrel, do you think I do not know the price of ale hereabouts?"

"Oh, but I was going to give him something extra for..."

Adèle abruptly curtailed her hasty interjection, withered by the wintry look Joscelin slanted in her direction.

"I said, let me deal with this, Madame."

By contrast, the outlaw appeared utterly *un*withered by the Lord of Veraux's blighting tone. Tossing the empty beakers to Beowulf, the lad wiped his wet fingers on his ragged, holly-green breeches and then held his hand out expectantly.

In response, Adèle saw Joscelin smile grimly, his long fingers dipping into the purse at his belt, drawing out a handful of copper coins which he dropped into the grinning outlaw's hand.

"Thank 'ee, m'lord." The boy's accent was suddenly thicker, his grey eyes openly laughing. "Us'll drink a toast ter yer continued good health. Won't we, Beowulf?"

His gaze flicked, light and quick as a stone skimming across still water, from Joscelin to Adèle to the more distant princess and back again as he added less mockingly,

"An' that o' her highness an' her ladies, o' course."

He was about to turn on his booted heel when Joscelin stopped him with a soft,

"A moment, Jacques."

After a rapid glance around the market square that missed Adèle's sudden surge of swiftly concealed curiosity by a heartbeat, Joscelin brought out a small leather bag that chinked distinctly as he tossed it to the youth, who took a moment to gauge its weight before thrusting it hastily beneath his leather jerkin.

"From Rafe and myself," Joscelin said quietly, evidently in answer to the outlaw's silent question. "In case neither of us makes the Midwinter quarter day."

Then catching the look Adèle was not quick enough to hide this time, added with crisp clarity,

"For the filly and the colt. You understand, boy?"

"Aye, m'lord."

With no further explanation, Joscelin waved the outlaw lad away and held out his arm towards Adèle with a coldly formal,

"Madame de Marillec?"

Putting aside her dislike of all that name implied, Adèle took the arm he offered and began to walk the short distance back towards Princess Linette and Lady Isabelle, both of whom were smiling a warm welcome at Joscelin, and both of whom she wished anywhere but here. Since that was impossible she told herself to make the most of this brief moment of pleasure in Joscelin's company.

A little disappointingly, she could detect no individual aroma to set him aside from any other of a dozen men. He smelt of horse, sweat, leather and metal – not unpleasantly she assured herself – and with the sleeves of his mail shirt ending level with his elbow, only a thin layer of linen prevented Adèle's fingers from touching the warm skin of his arm. It did nothing to hide the steely strength beneath, a match for the sword-steel grey of his disconcertingly hard eyes.

Fearing she might simply babble gibberish if she spoke, she dared not open her mouth, and her guilty enjoyment at being so close to this man she had loved since she had first seen him six years ago pushed aside her lingering disquiet.

For the moment at least.

It was only much later, after they had all returned to the Healing House, Linette having retired to rest and Joscelin ridden on up to the castle, that Adèle had the leisure to wonder exactly why Mithlondia's High Commander should be engaged in *any* sort of trade with the outlaws he was responsible for bringing to justice – since in addition to the colt and filly Joscelin had paid for today, he must also have bought the distinctively marked stallion he had given to Gabriel.

Not, of course, that she could bring herself to believe that Joscelin would actually hunt down and *hang* the brothers of the woman to whom he had once been betrothed. That said, there was a deal of difference between hauling Luc and Jacques to the scaffold with his own hands and... whatever it was Joscelin de Veraux *was* doing in partnership with two known outlaws.

Adèle was still trying to puzzle this out when her fragile presence of mind was disturbed once more by the discovery that Joscelin would be dining at the Healing House, as a guest of Princess Linette.

There was nothing particularly remarkable about that, Adèle assured herself as she took her seat, whatever a scowling, tight-lipped Sister Winfreda might think about it. The princess was Joscelin's half-sister, Lady Isabelle was his mother's sister, and it was simply a matter of courtesy to invite the Eldest as well.

Her own presence at that table, Adèle thought a trifle dispiritedly, was due to the simple fact that she could hardly be excluded without Linette appearing guilty of gross discourtesy. Yet in spite of this, she was determined to enjoy the evening.

As it seemed were her companions.

Lady Isabelle, so often sad and withdrawn, glowed under the influence of Joscelin's grave kindness, chattering and laughing, a brown wren transformed into a songthrush, while beside her the Eldest said little, though her cornflower-blue eyes rested frequently on the man facing her.

Seated at the head of the small table, with her half-brother at her right hand, Linette was clearly beyond happy to have him there, her eyes sparkling like the brightest stars in the frost-clear sky.

As for Adèle, she was content to sit quietly, watching Joscelin beneath her lashes, observing the golden glow of candlelight as it gilded the lean, clean lines of his face, and rippled over the uneven ridge of his nose. Saw too how it danced like mist shadows across water, now revealing, now concealing those eyes she had never been able to read, and could not now.

It did not matter.

She had her own thoughts to guard.

And an oath of fidelity to her lord-by-binding to keep, a small cold voice reminded her.

An oath that meant that even had Joscelin shown her anything beyond the formal courtesy he gave her, she would not have been able to take it any further.

Whatever his feelings, she was tied by the bonds of blood-kinship and her binding oath, and so she simply watched, with slightly heated cheeks, listening to the low, level voice that could only ever whisper in her dreams, and his infrequent laugh when Linette said something that amused him.

How she wished that *she* could make him laugh with such a rare carefree note. Or at the least knew something that might capture and hold his attention. Alas, nothing came to mind.

Not then. Not later, when the Eldest was called away to deal with an admission to the infirmary and Linette excused herself for a moment to visit the privy, Lady Isabelle electing to accompany her, and Adèle found herself unexpectedly alone with the man she loved.

For several heartbeats there was nothing but a daunting silence between them. Then Joscelin set down his wine cup, and levelled a more than usually cool look on her.

"I have heard from Gabriel," he said abruptly.

"Oh! Have you? Is he... is everything well with him?" she stammered.

With a glint in his sleet-grey eyes that said she should have asked such a question long before now, he replied,

"As well as can be, considering his situation. According to Jarec – the lad he sent with the message – an Atarkarnan warband surrounded and burned out the temporary camp he and the rest of the scouts had been using. Only the gods know how any of them survived the assault by such superior numbers. As it was none of his men escaped without injury. In addition he lost three men, two dead outright and one taken prisoner, no doubt to be tortured until his tongue loosens, unless Gabriel can get to him first."

He paused a moment, his eyes chilling to winter's ice.

"It might just as easily have been Gabriel. And you would not give a damn were he lying now in some rocky grave among the fells or burned alive on some barbarian's impromptu pyre? Would you, *Madame de Marillec!*".

She gasped, at the sharp condemnation of his tone as much as his harsh words, her eyes dropping to the binding band about her wrist.

What she could not do was look Joscelin de Veraux in the eye and say she did care.

Not, at least, in the way Joscelin meant. In truth, she could think of only one person who did.

"Luc de Chartreux would care," she said instead, finally looking up. "Why did you not tell *him* these dire tidings when you saw him earlier today. Since I am perfectly well aware that you must have recognised him!"

Dark lashes narrowed over eyes that glittered like sun-shot icicles. "Because," he started to say. "I do not consort with outlaws, and..."

"And what do you call what you did today if not *consorting*? Whatever it was, my lord High Commander, it is surely enough to merit a charge of treason!" Adèle hissed.

"And because Gabriel is *not* dead," Joscelin continued coolly, apparently impervious to her own fear-fuelled attempt at a rebuke. "Else I should have contrived to let his foster-brother know somehow, no matter what the risk to myself."

She started to sneer at his choice of words, wanting desperately to fling in his perfectly controlled face the terrible truth about Gabriel de Marillec and Luc de Chartreux.

That her lord-by-binding – Joscelin's friend and Second-in-command – and the hunted outlaw with a price of five hundred gold crowns on his head were, or at least had been, lovers.

Except that would result in Gabriel being charged with high treason – with Joscelin the one who would have to arrest him!

Thankfully, at that moment she heard the door open behind her and as Princess Linette came back into the room Adèle took the opportunity to flee, the evening in which she had previously found such pleasure now reduced to something more nearly resembling the burned-out ash of an Atarkarnan torture pit.

With her heart pounding so hard she thought she might be sick, and her cheeks as hot the brazier warming the princess' chamber, she hesitated, then turned towards the quiet sanctuary that stood at the heart of the healers' enclave.

Fixing her gaze on the twin flames kept burning there, day and night, she gave belated thanks to the Gods of Light and Mercy that Gabriel still lived, adding a prayer for swift passage beyond the sunset for those of his men who had not been so fortunate.

Eventually, feeling a little more composed, she made her way back slowly towards the two rooms set aside for Linette's use.

The meal having been all but over even before she had fled the room, she expected to find the table cleared, the princess and Lady Isabelle preparing for bed, and Joscelin returned to the castle.

The last thing she thought to see was Linette standing in the middle of the room, leaning against her half-brother, her head resting against his shoulder, his hand splayed over her rounded belly.

Even as Adèle came to an abrupt halt on the threshold, stuttering shocked and largely incoherent apologies, Linette's eyes flew open and something that looked very much like fear flickered through the blue depths. While the look of soft-eyed wonder Adèle had fleetingly glimpsed on Joscelin's face was gone so swiftly she could not be sure it had ever been there in the first place.

Confused, and sensing she had stumbled onto something she was not meant to have seen, Adèle took a step backwards, straight into the woman who had come up behind her without her noticing.

"Excuse me, Lady Adèle," the Eldest said politely, as she moved past Adèle.

Then seemingly untroubled by the tension that tied everyone else in the chamber to silence, continued with barely a pause,

"Well, Lord Joscelin, did you feel the little one move? It is a most amazing thing is it not, your highness, and so kind of you to allow *your kinsman...*"

Was there the faintest emphasis on the term, Adèle wondered.

"To share such a wonderful feeling with you."

"Yes, wonderful indeed, Eldest," Linette agreed, a little unsteadily. "It was fortuitous that... my..." The word 'brother' seemed to stick in her throat and she said instead. "That Lord Joscelin was still here."

"And I thank her highness for granting me the privilege," Joscelin said equally formally, his hard, handsome face betraying no more emotion than the blankly moulded full-face helms worn by the royal bodyguard.

He stepped away from the princess, and bowed low. First to Linette, then to Lady Isabelle who had just emerged from the inner bedchamber and was looking in nervous bewilderment from face to face, and finally to the Eldest, who was regarding him with her usual unruffled calm.

"I thank you for your hospitality and forbearance," he said quietly. "With your permission, I will wait by the gates until Rhys has returned, and then relieve you of my presence."

"You are welcome to visit the princess here at any time, Lord Joscelin," the Eldest replied placidly. "As, of course, is Prince Linnius. Please tell him that."

It was noticeable that the Eldest did not mention Prince Kaslander, even though when all was said and done he was the child's father.

After a moment Joscelin inclined his head in acknowledgement of the Eldest's words, and after bowing to her, hand on heart in the familiar gesture of respect, turned to look at Adèle.

"Madame de Marillec."

That was all he said, curt and cold, the words accompanied by the merest inclination of his head, the movement far more indicative of contempt than courtesy... and then he was gone, and Adèle realised that she was not alone in staring after him, though surely she was the one who felt his loss most keenly.

It had, she decided as she made ready for bed, been an utterly miserable day.

She had angered Joscelin... been subtly mocked by her lord's former lover... had ale tossed over her clothes, probably ruining them beyond redemption... angered Joscelin a second time by a lack of proper concern for Gabriel's welfare... needlessly frightened the woman who was also her friend when she was in a delicate condition... and in so doing had angered Joscelin a third time.

Thank the gods today was over.

As for whatever the next market day would bring... surely all she had to do was keep away from the bitter-eyed outlaw leader and his reckless younger brother. What could be simpler?

Only when sleep finally took her did she allow the tears caused by Joscelin's unspoken rejection to seep from under her closed lids to trickle silently across her cheek.

Verse 8

Thorny Walls

With winter coming early to Vézière, Adèle found it very easy to keep the resolve she had made following her confrontation with her lord-by-binding's foster-brother and, by keeping strictly within the walls of the Healing House, avoid any chance of contact with the outlaws.

Until the morning when Linette looked up from desultorily spooning honey and cream onto her boiled oats, to say with something of a sigh,

"Since Joscelin has requested that I do not leave the enclave until after the child is born, would you go up into the town for me this morning, Adèle? The Eldest tells me that it is the first market of winter and thus bound to be busier than normal."

She sounded more than a little wistful.

"That is, if you are sure you do not mind?"

"Of course not, your highness, it would be my pleasure."

Since they were in the refectory, seated amongst the quietly eating Sisters, Adèle maintained the formality Linette would not allow in private.

"Was there anything in particular you wished me to look at or purchase for you?"

"Some more white and green thread, if you would, and if the man is there with his wooden toys..."

"You would like the painted rattle that caught your fancy last time," Adèle finished for her, smiling into the royal blue eyes that laughed ruefully back at her.

"And I may look for some furs on my own account," she continued thoughtfully. "I know from experience how cold it can get here in Vézière during the winter, when the wind whips down from the moors."

"When winter gets here, you would say?" Linette enquired with a mock shiver. "I thought it had already arrived!" Adding more pensively, "I had not expected quite such a difference between Vézière and Lamortaine. It is not *that* much farther north."

What she meant, of course, was that it was far colder in the Healing House – and much less comfortable, though the Sisters had done their best to make it so – than the Palace of Princes. Being by nature both courteous and gentle, and grateful beyond words to the Eldest for giving her sanctuary from Lady Ariène's venomous malice, she said nothing of this though.

What she did do was offer to send Rhys with Adèle for protection.

Adèle, having a very clear notion of what Joscelin de Veraux's reaction would be should she deprive the princess of her bodyguard, for however short a time, and with absolutely no desire to arouse his ire again, simply shook her head and declined, adding at Linette's doubtful look, that she was unlikely to come to any harm in a place so familiar to her, and where everybody knew her as one of the princess' lady-companions.

Stepping out of the enclave a little later, accompanied by the sweet chiming of the bronze bells hanging amidst the deep pink fruits of the spindleberry bush by the gate, Adèle took a deep breath of the bracing air and felt her heart lift, realising only when she was outside how much like a prison the walls had become.

It was a strange thought for she had not suffered such morbid fancies when she had been living there as a healer, yet with so little to occupy her hands and mind, the very air seemed to have become scarce and stale, and she was glad to escape.

If only for the morning...

Catching Sister Winfreda's sour look as the senior healer stood in the gateway, watching her go, Adèle could not quite repress the lilting smile she knew would annoy the older woman still further.

"Ye're as bad as that Fayla!" Sister Winfreda had muttered when Adèle had informed her in passing that she was going up to the market place on an errand for the princess. "An' ye'll come ter the same bad end, jus' mark my words."

"You *also* said she would be back when she fell with child," Adèle had felt impelled to point out. "And since she has not, you should admit that you were wrong to judge her so harshly, and therefore owe her an apology."

Undaunted, Sister Winfreda had merely sneered back,

"I know her sort. Run off wi' that soldier what was sniffin' about her skirts, she has, an' once he's done wi' her, she'll be..."

"She is with her *brother!*" Adèle had snapped, all patience gone. "Not a lover! And I will not discuss her further. Good morning, Sister Winfreda!"

With that she had stalked out of the gates, her dampened spirits rising immediately at the caress of the clean, cold moorland air... hence that smile over her shoulder at the sour-faced healer.

As she walked up the winding cobbled street, however, the other woman's spiteful words came back to her and something of Adèle's certainty as to her friend's whereabouts leached away.

She was troubled far more than she cared to admit by Rowène's familiarity with the big, fair-haired guardian that terrible evening when the shadow-light of the blood-gold moon had let loose her lord's hidden madness, unwanted memories of which still plagued her dreams more than a season later.

As for what that night may have meant to Rowène, Adèle could not believe – or rather, she did not *want* to believe – that the woman who had once been her closest friend would have betrayed her outlawed brothers or abandoned her young daughter in order to run off with one of Mithlondia's guardians. To become, in effect, a camp follower, and no better in general parlance than a common whore.

In her days as a healer, Adèle had treated all three of the brothel's women for some cause or other – whether customer-inflicted injury or customer-inflicted ailment – and she refused to give credence to the nagging fear that Sister Winfreda might be right and that Rowène de Chartreux would come to a similar 'bad end'.

And all for the sake of a certain hard-eyed, coarse-tongued soldier who was far too close to her own lord-by-binding for Adèle's comfort.

Tripping over a cobblestone, she once more took herself to task for not enquiring of Rowène's brother and half-brother, when she had had the opportunity to do so, as to whether their sister was presently living with them, just to reassure herself that Rowène was indeed safe, and not to be found sleeping at some soldier's side, amidst the burned, barren and bloodily fought-over wilderland between Atarkarna and Mithlondia.

Which thought prompted yet another anxiety to rear its ugly head.

For Adèle had discovered – to her surprise, and very much too late – that as a result of Joscelin's brutally honest description of the risks run by any guardian in the disputed borderlands, she had actually started to worry over her lord-by-binding's safety. Recollecting that he had claimed to make a better soldier than a gilded jay, Adèle could only hope that it had been no vainglorious boast and that he was indeed capable of defending himself.

That being so, he would have killed, maimed and perhaps even bloodied his hands by torturing any enemy prisoners he and his men had taken. Just the thought of it was sufficient to make Adèle feel sick.

Though, gods knew, not as much as the possibility that Gabriel himself might end up on the receiving end of fiery brand and hot iron, if he should have the misfortune to fall into barbarian hands.

She had not thought she would care what happened to him once she was free of his company, and yet...

Yet it would seem that she did.

She also wondered, with a flash of uncharacteristically ironic humour, whether Joscelin or Gabriel would be the more incredulous if they knew.

Having by this time reached the market place, she hesitated for a moment and then continued on up the steeply winding cobbled street until she had gone as far as she could go before towering walls and watchful guards prevented folk without legitimate business in the castle from venturing any further.

This proximity to the castle walls and its careless soldiery meant that it was not, perhaps, the most salubrious of places but at the same time it had the advantage of being the highest point in the town itself, with a view that more than repaid the smell.

Holding a fold of her mantle over her nose, she picked her way carefully through the rubble, rubbish, rotting vegetables and other fouler stuff she declined to put a name to, until she came to the open space between the curtain wall and the nearest dwelling and then wary of the almost sheer drop to the next level of the town below her, she pulled her cloak closer against the tug of the wintry wind and gazed out over at the lands spread before her like a crumpled tapestry.

It being a beautifully crisp day on the cusp of winter, and the sky a brilliant blue undimmed by even the lightest skim of cloud haze, she could see for leagues, only the view to the east being blocked by the castle walls looming behind her.

The Healing House and the adjacent orchard partially covering the southern slope of the hill were also out of sight, though the road leading to the western entrance of the town was plainly visible, empty save for a woman and a boy herding a gaggle of wayward geese along it.

Lifting her gaze beyond the frost-frilled mud of the highway, she allowed her gaze to roam over the rolling moors, now dull with winter-brown grass, the occasional smudge of smoke rising above the curve of the land revealing the existence of isolated farmsteads, the hillsides dotted with brown and white sheep, their maaing muted by distance.

It all looked very peaceful and placid, but observing a small group of wild ponies grazing the nearer slopes, she found herself wondering with a shiver of unease whether the outlaws or, gods forbid, the Black Hunt were abroad today.

While she did not like Luc de Chartreux – for what she considered an eminently reasonable cause – neither would she see him in the hands of Joffroi de Rogé's brutish hunters.

As for his younger brother, Jacques had done nothing – a few oaths and an ale-splashed gown scarcely counted – to merit such a vicious fate.

To her considerable relief she saw no sign either of the outlaws or the scum who hunted them, only the vast empty stretches of the moors, beyond which the somnolent colours of the leafless forest seemed to merge without pause into the dark feet of the Guardian Mountains, the ragged peaks glimmering snow-white in the winter sunlight. Soon the moors themselves would be sleeping beneath the same white mantle, and by Adèle's reckoning this could well be the last market before travel across the moors became too difficult.

The highway south to Lamortaine would probably remain open, but as for what had once been a broad, well-maintained road running north beyond Vézière, none but Mithlondia's guardians ever travelled in that direction now and it had become a mere grassy track that led the eye into a forbidding haze that defied sight by mere mortal eyes.

Somewhere up there, in the bitter cold of the north, amidst dark fells and darker holly woods, rocky hills and snow-tipped ridges, the Tarkan River splashed and crashed between craggy cliffs, forming a border *both* sides seemed to ignore when it suited their purpose – since not for one heartbeat did Adèle suppose that Gabriel and the guardians under his command would be content to simply sit on their hands when they had fallen comrades to avenge.

God of Light, do not let him fall, either to sword or flame! And bring him back safely!

Shaking her head at the realisation that she was actually asking the gods for grace on behalf of a man for whom she held such ambivalent feelings, she stepped away from the edge, and with a quick glance at the castle gateway on the off-chance of seeing Guy, set off back down the hill towards the main square.

Pausing where the narrow shadows of Castle Street opened out into the bustling market place, Adèle looked instinctively towards the far end where she had seen the outlaws before.

No half-broken ponies tossed their heads in the shadow of the brothel, so she thought at first that the men who usually brought them were not there either... until she caught sight of the distinctively tall figure of Luc de Chartreux, alongside the shorter, slighter form of his young half-brother.

Neither looked adequately dressed against the chill wind, but while Luc appeared impervious to the snow-scented cold, Jacques was blowing on his cupped hands and shuffling from one booted foot to another in an obvious attempt to keep from freezing.

In instinctive response, Adèle wriggled her own fingers in their fur-lined leather gloves, and pulled her hood tighter, feeling a flicker of shame that she was warm and would be well fed through the winter when all four of the outlaws – she vaguely recognised the other two men lurking nearby – looked pinched with hunger and evidently lacked the wherewithal to buy so much as a mug of mulled ale between them. And if the men were in such a bad case, how much worse off were the children?

Sudden determination outweighing her antipathy towards Luc de Chartreux, she set off towards the outlaws to offer... she knew not what, since she had a feeling he would reject her charity with the same contempt he treated her person.

Before she had taken more than a few steps, however, the approach of a group of richly-clad riders forced her to retreat into the shelter of the covered walkway running along the north side of the market, wondering as she did so exactly what Juliène de Lyeyne was doing in Vézière.

She was, Adèle reflected, almost the last person she wanted to see at the moment. Or be seen by.

Thankful that her hood was up and her mantle not such as to attract attention, Adèle shrank a little more into the shadows, while the noble lordling, his guests and attendant servants continued to mill around on the edge of the market, causing consternation just by their presence, not least in Adèle's breast.

Even if they were here for the most innocent of causes, there were a number of men in Vézière whose freedom – and lives – were at risk should they be recognised. Though she, of course, was only concerned with one...

Guy!

Gods! She must warn him that Juliène was here...

Except she had no reason for entering the castle, curse it! Then again, she consoled herself, Guy was hardly witless. He would hear of the new arrivals and surely find some excuse to stay out of their way.

Almost convinced, she started back towards the Healing House...

And found she could not do that either.

Turning her back on Hal de Vézière and his guests, she hastened along the covered side of the square and then struck out across it, slipping between gossiping matrons, ignoring the importunities of the various stallholders... to have her feet measured for a new pair of winter shoes, to sample a dish of braised sweetbreads, to buy a fat goose for the Midwinter feast... a set of amber beads to adorn her neck and ears... the finest rabbit and squirrel skins to...

"Yes," she said breathlessly. "How much for that bundle?"

"Twelve silver nobles to you, Mistress."

It was an outrageous price for the small bundle of brown and russet-red pelts and in other circumstances...

"Done! But I only have half that amount on me. Here... take it!"

She fumbled in her purse and evidently taken off guard by the arrival of a customer with more coin than good sense, Luc de Chartreux accepted the handful of silver in silence, and it was left to his younger brother to peer into the shadows beneath Adèle's hood and say dubiously,

"Lady Adèle, is that you?"

"Yes," she hissed. "But do not speak my name again..."

"Mistress?" The boy sounded even warier now. "Is something the matter?"

"Yes! Gods know I would not be here else! Now, please just listen to me."

She risked a harried glance over her shoulder, and turned back to look into Luc de Chartreux's narrowed grey eyes just as he thrust his hand back towards her, saying with a biting ferocity,

"Keep your bloody charity, and pi..."

"Luc! Look!" Jacques' urgent exclamation cut through his brother's coarsely-worded dismissal. "There! Surely that is Ju!"

"With Hal de Vézière, amongst others," Adèle added. "But they are the important ones and if you have any sense at all, you will not let them see you."

"Juliène is our sister. She would not betray us," Luc said curtly, his grey eyes as ice-laden as the wind presently nipping at her exposed cheeks.

"She might me," Jacques observed, somewhat dubiously.

Adèle looked from one brother to the other, trying to decide which of them was right, and what Jacques could possibly have done – apart from being born – to upset his half-sister to such an extent that he thought she might yield him up to his enemies.

Not, of course, that it really mattered.

What *did* matter...

"Would you truly trust Hal de Vézière to hold his tongue, considering how high is the price on *your* head, Messire?" she demanded, making very sure she was looking straight at Luc as she said it.

"Fifty gold crowns is a lot of money, especially to a man like him, with expensive tastes and little to support them save his expectations as his father's heir. He may have been your friend in years gone by but would you risk your life and your brother's on his willingness to stand by that friendship now, when you are a proclaimed traitor to the realm."

She saw that he was not convinced and added in a voice so brittle she thought it might crack,

"You and he and my lord were friends in your youth, yes? Yet when your lov... your *foster-brother* needed a friend to stand at his side on our binding day, de Vézière denied that friendship. Only Joscelin de Veraux had the courage to call Gabriel *friend* that day."

She saw Luc go white beneath his wind-chapped colour, but all he said was,

"I cannot for the life of me see why you would want to help me, Madame, bearing in mind what you think I have been to your lord, but..."

"*Why?* Because Gabriel would never forgive me if he knew I had stood by and done nothing to prevent... whatever is going to happen if you do not make yourselves scarce! And quickly! Before the Black Hunt are alerted to your presence here."

"They'm lookin' this way, m'lord," the whip-scarred outlaw interpolated gruffly. "Best make yer mind up and go, quick like the lady says. Ye an' Master Jacq both. In there..."

He brandished a cold-reddened hand towards the nearby brothel.

"Me an' Beowulf'll stay here, let ye know when 'tis safe ter come back, an' then we'll get the hell outta here."

"And if Ju should recognise *you* as Luc's man?" Jacques enquired through gritted teeth. "Damn it, Nick, she saw you often enough around Chartre castle that she would know you again."

"Na! Won't happen, lad," the other man, Beowulf, grunted. "Don't ye know by now, high-born noblewomen like her don't trouble theirselves over peasants like us."

Then he grinned, showing an array of uneven teeth.

"Savin' Lady Rowena, o'course."

And evidently catching sight of Adèle's indignant expression added,

"Well, mebbe ye as well, Lady Adela."

Then turning back to the younger of the de Chartreux brothers,

"Now, away wi' ye, lad. Nick an' me'll be safe enough. We might even sell some o' these here furs fer a goodly profit if there's any more customers as generous as Lady Adela about!"

While Jacques' eyes reflected a glimmer of the other man's grin, he still did not move. Instead he threw another glance at his sister, who was staring with bored disinterest out over the little market.

"But what is she doing here?" Jacques muttered.

"No doubt her excuse will be that she is here to visit the princess," Adèle replied, more than a little cynically. "Though clearly she does not mean to remain at the Healing House. Not when she can manipulate Hal de Vézière into offering his father's hospitality."

She drew in a sharp breath,

"Which reminds me, I need to warn Guy that your sister is..."

"*What* did you say?"

The wry grin that had started to lift Jacques' fine mouth – no doubt at the ludicrous notion of the luxury-loving Juliène reduced to the humble comforts of the Healing House – flattened now into a hard line as he continued in that same sharp tone,

"Guy? As in Guy de Martine? And he is here in Vézière? *Damn it, Luc!* I thought it was him I saw at the edge of the moor that day but you would not let me go back! And he is still here, you say?" he demanded of Adèle.

"Yes, up at the castle," she confirmed. "He found employment as harper to Lord Nicholas." Then on an irritated huff,

"He *said* he would be safe enough. But if Juliène should see him there... oh gods, I fear what she will do!"

"You and me both!"

"But of course Guy will stay out of her way..."

Adèle found herself looking hopefully at Jacques, disconcerted when he muttered grimly,

"You would think so, but... bloody hell!"

Then before he could offer anything more constructive, a blast of icy wind ripped her hood back, tugging off her gossamer-fine veil, sending it flying over the market, and as Adèle snatched impotently after it, she heard a soft, silken, subtly sinister voice behind her say in Mithlondian,

"Goodness me! It that you, Adèle? Does your lord know what low company you keep in his absence, I wonder?"

"I expect he would rather keep it himself," Adèle muttered bitterly as she held Luc de Chartreux's hard grey eyes for a heartbeat before he turned away, dragging his hood up over his hair, leaving Adèle to take a deep breath of the freezing air and spin on her heel to face Juliène de Lyeyne.

Apparently noticing nothing amiss, Juliène continued,

"Whatever are you doing here dressed like that, Adèle? I would have taken you for some humble good-wife, rather than the Lady of Marillec, if I had not caught sight of your hair."

All too aware of her plain attire, and the way her loosened hair was blowing in wild tangles around her wind-reddened face – Juliène by contrast contriving to look as delicately perfect as a winter frost lily – Adèle gritted her teeth and hoping that de Chartreux and his brother had managed to meld into anonimity, tried to infuse surprise and pleasure rather than guilt and dislike into her voice.

"Juliène, how lovely to see you again. But how do you come to be here? Surely it is late to be travelling. I heard one of the locals say it will snow soon."

Switching back into common speech, she waved her gloved hand at the man Jacques had called Beowulf, and said with as much hauteur as her naturally diffident manner could maintain,

"You, there! That bundle of furs, have it delivered to the Healing House immediately. I will be returning there shortly and will arrange for payment to be made to you then."

"Aye, Mistress," the outlaw said, his stoic demeanour and weathered countenance giving nothing away. "Reckon I kin do that fer ye."

"If you are going to the Healing House, I will accompany you," Juliène said with a smile that chilled Adèle to the bone and reinforced her resolve to be far more wary of Rowène's green-eyed sister than she had ever been before her binding to Gabriel de Marillec had belatedly taught her caution.

"It is so long since we have had the opportunity for a good gossip," Juliène continued. "And of course I should pay my respects to the princess sooner rather than later."

She turned to the man who had followed her across the square, carelessly abandoning the others in his party.

"Hal, do you come with us?"

"No, I must let my father know that we have guests, and make sure all is made ready."

There was a less than subtle look of banked lust in his dark eyes and it was clear he intended to make some very special arrangements for the Lady of Lyeyne.

"I will come down to the Healing House and escort you up as soon as I have done that. If that is acceptable to you?"

Juliène, with no indication that she thought his certainty misplaced, gave gracious approval to this plan and then, linking arms in friendly fashion with Adèle, set off across the market.

Telling herself that all the time Juliène was in her company she could not be making mischief for Guy, Adèle allowed herself to be drawn in the direction of the Healing House, one last glance over her shoulder giving her a glimpse of two hooded men – one short, one tall – as they negotiated entry with the woman standing in the brothel's doorway, a bright red shawl draped about her naked shoulders.

As if sensing her gaze the younger outlaw glanced back, his grey eyes briefly meeting hers, then he was gone, following his older brother into the brothel, and Adèle could only put her faith in Jacques' last few, silently mouthed words,

"Go. I will warn Guy."

Except... Jacques had no idea of the name by which Guy was now known. And no way of getting into the castle even if he did!

Leaving her brother to deal with Mistress Cherry's abundant charms in whatever manner he saw fit – after all, Luc was no naïve novice in carnal transactions of any sort – Rowène shot through the brothel's main downstairs room, along a narrow, dark passageway and into what was clearly the kitchen, startling the young servant girl chopping carrots at a stained wooden table into nearly chopping her finger as well.

Her shriek of shock, and the shout that succeeded it, followed Rowène as she burst out of the back door and skidded onto the turned earth of a surprisingly neat vegetable plot.

"Hey, what's yer hurry, boy! If ye'm wantin' the privy there's a fellow out there already."

"I can wait," Rowène called back over her shoulder as she paused to survey the scene.

Like most of the gardens on this south-west side of town, it was long and narrow, sloping steeply down and ending, as Rowène had hoped, where it met the stone wall encircling the healers' enclave.

A small cat, brindled grey and black, was crouched on top of the wall, quite still, only its tufted ears twitching in the wind as it stared down at some hapless creature it was intent upon catching.

Hearing a stranger's approach, it turned its head, fixing an unblinking golden gaze on Rowène as she slipped and slithered between the orderly rows of cabbages and leeks, her booted feet finding little purchase on the frost-slick mud of the rough path leading to the privy.

She went down twice.

Once landing jarringly hard on her backside.

The second time sliding through a pile of rotting cabbage leaves before rolling to her feet again, pausing momentarily to brush away the worst of the accumulated slime and assorted slugs clinging to her clothes.

A heartbeat later she was running again, determined not to lose her balance a third time.

Then she was scrambling up the pile of fire wood between the wall to the neighbouring plot and the privy. Just as the badly-stacked logs rolled away beneath her feet, she landed safely on the roof of the privy, causing the man within to let out a yell of outraged alarm.

Ignoring both the vitriolic curses and the nose-curling stench emanating from the creaking shed, she mentally measured the distance from the roof of the privy to the top of the wall, and then leapt... in the same breath as the whole rickety edifice fell away beneath her feet.

It was far from the best of landings, and for a moment she thought she was going to tumble headlong off the other side. The crash and clatter of the collapsing privy and the roar of rage as the man stumbled out from the broken timbers, clutching his bleeding head in one hand, his breeches in the other, made her think such a precipitate descent might have been no bad solution. Instead, she maintained her precarious perch as she looked where she wished to go, grimacing again at the depth of the drop. Too far to jump without risking a broken limb...

A shout from behind her, warning of a wrung neck and sore arse, informed her it would not be wise to linger where she was either.

Feeling something brush against her arm, she nearly jumped out of her skin, if not off the wall, then let out a choked laugh when she realised that it was only the brindle cat.

"So what would you suggest?" she asked it, more than half seriously.

While this was not Mist, the mystical creature who had appeared to her before, she did recognise the animal. When she had last been in the Healing House, it had been a tiny, starvling, wild-cat kit, all bedraggled dark fur, black-tufted ears and great golden eyes that had put her in mind of Gabriel de Marillec in one of his more feral moods.

Despite this resemblance she had considered taking the little cat back to the forest for Lissie, who would have loved it dearly, but in the end Rowène had left it with Sister Aldith, who cared more for animals than she did people.

Whether there was after all some feyness about the creature or whether it had simply had enough of clumsy people who landed in its territory, frightening away its prey, Lyra suddenly let out an odd little "purr-ow" and stretched, unsheathing a set of sword-sharp claws from its tufted paws.

Then before Rowène could blink, it was away down the wall, graceful and sure-footed, leaping from branch to branch of the thornberry tree trained against the layered stones.

Once on the ground, it promptly sat down in the grass, tail curled over its paws and looked up expectantly.

Rowène glanced incredulously from the cat to the flimsy branches, the hanging clusters of blood-red berries, the hooked black thorns, as wickedly sharp as Lyra's claws...

Set against which there was an incandescently irate man alternating between shouted abuse and threats of violence, a prostitute her brother could not possibly afford to pay, and most important of all, her friend was depending on her to do what Adèle herself could not.

So, with a muttered "needs must", Rowène swung herself down, feeling for the first foothold.

After that, her descent was swift, though it otherwise bore no similarity whatsoever to Lyra's delicate feat of agility, and the next thing Rowène knew, she was standing somewhat shakily in the long grass of the orchard, her much-mended clothing torn beyond even Gwynny's skilful repair, her hands, arms and legs bleeding from several deep and painful scratches.

Thanking the gods that the thorns had missed her eyes – although not by so very much – she ran her hands impatiently through her hair, dislodging broken bits of twig and squashed berries.

Judging from the silence on the other side of the wall, she assumed the unfortunate fellow in the privy had hitched up his breeches and retreated to lodge a complaint with whosoever would listen, while in the now tranquil orchard a flock of tiny jewel-bright finches flew down from the bare branches of a nearby apple tree to feast on the gleaming winter fruits her descent had damaged or dislodged.

Leaving Lyra to watch the birds and wait for one foolish enough to fly within reach, Rowène set off at a limping run through the orchard, heading for the distant range of buildings that made up the Healing House, evading the pecking beaks of the belligerent geese more by luck than any turn of speed on her own part.

She was breathing in noisy gasps by the time she staggered between the kitchen and the barn and into the centre of the enclave.

Pressing a bleeding hand against the pain stitching her side, she made directly for the Eldest's private chamber.

She was nearly at the entrance to the main wing of the Healing House when a figure in pale grey robe and white headrail emerged into the sunlit courtyard.

Briefly Rowène knew the hope that it might be Joscelin's mother... only to grit her teeth as the rigidly disapproving face of Sister Winfreda turned towards her.

"Here! What d'ye think ye're about, boy?"

Damn it all, I do not have time for this!

Barely pausing, Rowène brushed past Sister Winfreda, muttering in thick common speech,

"Message fer th' Eldest."

"Now jus' ye wait up," Sister Winfreda retorted, grabbing at Rowène's tattered shirt sleeve.

On the brink of losing her temper Rowène wrenched free, leaving Sister Winfreda staring owlishly at the scrap of dirty linen in her bony hand.

"Ye young hellion! How dare ye show such disrespect..."

"What in gods' name is happening here, Sister? You, boy! Hold, right there!"

The clear, cultured voice cut through Sister Winfreda's grumbling and at the same time brought Rowène to a reluctant halt, a quick glance at the woman in the rich, royal blue velvet gown, and silver embroidered veil causing her to execute a brief, clumsy bow.

Straightening, she saw Linette's eyes go wide with shocked recognition.

"I will deal with this, Sister Winfreda," the princess said firmly, her bemused gaze still tracing the blood-streaked, mud-smeared lines of the face that, as far as she knew, belonged to an outlaw lad called Jacques de Chartreux.

Sister Winfreda opened her mouth as if to protest and then closed it again, so tightly it formed a thin white line.

"Please, Sister, carry on with whatever you were doing," Linette commanded, at her most regal.

"Very well, yer highness, if ye're sure, but that boy looks a right ruffian to me. Most likely he's a thief, if not worse."

"Thank you for your concern, but I know this boy, and I assure you he is neither ruffian nor thief."

Then waiting only until she was certain the disapproving healer had gone on her way, Linette said urgently,

"Jacques! What are you doing here, and in such a state? Are you in trouble?" Her hand went to her swollen belly. "Gods forbid, not the children!"

"No, your highness, the children are safe and well and far from here."

"It is your brother then?"

As a natural extension of that thought, she looked beyond Rowène, almost as if she expected to see armed horsemen thundering past the peaceful enclave.

"Has he been taken by the Black Hunt?"

"No, my lady."

Rowène had managed to catch her breath by now, though her voice still sounded laboured and hoarse.

"None of those, but begging your forgiveness, I cannot explain... and by your leave I need to speak to the Eldest without further delay."

A candle-notch later a wary-eyed Sister of Mercy emerged from the barn with a placid donkey in tow, and – having made certain that Adèle and Juliène were heading for Linette's quarters and were not looking her way – mounted up, and riding sedately when her sense of urgency urged her to prod Muriel into a faster pace, followed the narrow, twisting street up to the market square, and then up again, finally drawing to a halt outside the castle gateway, giving a deceptively tranquil reply to the guard's bored challenge.

"I am Sister Fayla, and I bear a message from the Eldest of the healers of Vézière to Lord Nicholas' harper, Master Finch."

"Looks like ye could do wi' a bit o' healin' yerself, Sister," the guard said, disinterest giving way to a grin. "That's a right nasty scratch ye got there."

"Yes, it is," Rowène agreed primly.

She also made sure to keep her bandaged hands hidden beneath her wide sleeves as far as possible, at the same time hoping that word had not spread this far about the raggedly-clad lad who had gone over the wall from the brothel into the grounds of the Healing House, tearing down the best part of a carefully nurtured thornberry tree in the process. Not to mention destroying a privy and making a mess of the Mistress Birch's winter vegetables on the way.

As to that, and despite the Eldest's necessarily hasty ministrations, Rowène could still detect a faint whiff of rotted cabbage about her person, though the mud and blood had been washed away and the worst of the scratches salved and bandaged by no less a personage than Princess Linette herself.

Only when this task had been accomplished to the princess' satisfaction had the Eldest managed to persuade Linette to leave her alone with Jacques, pointing out that the less Mithlondia's princess knew about anything a known outlaw might have to say, the better for all concerned.

With her impatience by then bordering on desperation, Rowène had left Joscelin's mother in no doubt of the need to get Adèle's message to their kinsman in the castle, whereupon the older woman had immediately offered to take it herself, but even had Rowène considered yielding to her suggestion, one of the other healers had come knocking on the door with word that a patient recently admitted to the infirmary had set her feet on the sunset path and was asking for the Eldest.

Relieved that the woman she loved so dearly would not be able to involve herself any deeper in the murky affairs of Gilles de Valenne's hunted descendants, Rowène had practically pushed her from her own chamber, with a loving smile that combined rueful apology with silent farewell, only to have the Eldest turn back at the door with a similar expression on her softly-wrinkled face.

Pointing at the small wooden chest at the bottom of her neatly-made bed, she had said serenely,

"Your robes are in there, waiting for you, as always. When you are ready, go to Sister Gunhilda in the still room and tell her I said to take a flask of the thyme and honey mixture for Lord Nicholas' cough. Then see Sister Aldith in the stables and tell her you have my permission to ride Muriel up to the castle."

And at Rowène's indignant look, added gently,

"It will be quicker, and you will attract much less attention to yourself than if you go running through the streets of the town. Now go, with my blessing and that of the gods who watch over us all. Oh, and my regards to Messire de Martine."

Guy was in the process of mending a broken wire on his harp when he first heard what might have been a scratch at the door of the topmost tower chamber he shared with the four other musicians Lord Nicholas had gradually gathered into his service in the seasons since he had first realised he was losing his sight.

They had originally come from every corner of Mithlondia, itinerants all until they arrived in Vézière and found their wandering days were done, if they so wished. Aelfraed, the young flute player, still admitted to itchy feet, but the remainder, Beorn with his drum and cymbals, Halfiren and his gittern, and Maury the rebec player all seemed content enough to remain where they were guaranteed a stone roof quite literally above their heads, a flea-free bed to sleep in, a new set of clothes once a year and regular meals to fill their bellies. And perhaps most important of all, a lord who truly appreciated the music the gods had put in their hands.

Initially wary in the wake of Guy's unexpected arrival, it had taken no more than a couple of evenings to change their minds and welcome him into their group, even while there remained a small, barely perceptible distance between them. Possibly because he had travelled foreign roads they themselves had not trod, and seen exotic sights they could barely envisage, none of them having ever ventured beyond Mithlondia's borders. Possibly too because they suspected he was something more than the unwanted, unacknowledged bastard of a minor Valennais nobleman he had presented himself as.

It had perhaps been reckless to admit as much, Guy knew. On the other hand, he had decided that it would be even more stupid to deny the blood-lines his fair hair hinted at, and so he had simply told a version of the truth. Like it or not, he *was* a bastard by birth, and certainly the minor Valennais nobleman who was his maternal grandsire had never openly acknowledged his existence, although his father, Lord Jacques de Rogé, had had the inherent decency to do so.

As for Lord Nicholas... being uncertain how much the older man could see of his newly-employed harper's appearance, but mindful that the older man's lack of vision had probably taught him to sharpen his other senses, Guy was careful to keep any trace of a more cultured accent from his common speech without lapsing into the opposite extreme of the rough Rogé dialect he had grown up with.

Under normal conditions, it was not strong enough that anyone from the northern reaches of Mithlondia would recognise it for what it was. Aelfraed, however, came from Chartreux and Maury from Rouvraine, both these fiefs bordering on Guy's home province.

Still, to all intents and purposes, he had been accepted and for the most part Guy was content to be in Vézière, especially as it meant he could keep an eye on Adèle in her lord's absence. He still did not approve of her binding to Gabriel de Marillec, though the gods knew he had no choice but to accept it.

Even so, it still felt good to be close to the only one of his family yet living for whom he cared, and who cared about him.

Set against that, Vézière was within two days' ride of the royal court, the highway between regularly patrolled by a band of ruthless men who answered only to the most powerful man in the realm after the prince.

A man who would see his bastard half-brother dead in a heartbeat.

As for the more subtle sense of danger emanating from Juliène de Lyeyne, the distance between Lamortaine and Vézière *should* have been sufficient to keep his mind clear.

Dreams, however, yield neither to long leagues nor high walls and it was rare indeed for Guy to sleep the night through without some image of Juliène de Lyeyne walking wraith-like through his mind... whether his first sight of her in her mother's bower at Chartre, or his last sight of her in the Palace of Princes... or any of the occasions in between, none of which he had ever forgotten.

Nor could he prevent himself from wondering what she would do if she ever saw him again.

Would she betray him to her mother and his brother?

Or let him live the life he had made for himself in peace?

He had no way of knowing the answer, and common sense told him he should have little inclination to put it to the test...

Another, louder scratch at the door brought him from his rueful musings, and even as he laid his harp carefully on the bed and rose to his feet, the door opened and a child – he recognised the grinning, freckled face as belonging to the son of one of the garrison soldiers – stuck his head around the wooden edge.

"Yes, what is it, Brec?"

"Da says can ye come down ter the gate, Master Finch, there's a healer askin' fer a word wi' ye. Says her's got a message fer ye from th' Eldest."

Abandoning his task, Guy grabbed his cloak from the peg on the wall, and followed the boy out into the chilly courtyard, keeping his disquiet to himself.

While he frequently went down to the Healing House to see the Eldest or his cousin, this was the first time any of the women from the enclave had come up to the castle asking for him.

"This healer... did she give a name?" he asked the boy.

"Aye, Sister Feather or Faillan, or sommut like that."

Guy having heard of neither, this information proved of questionable assistance. All it told him was that it was definitely not Adèle, which had been his first worried thought.

"There she be, Master Finch!"

Pointing one grubby finger at the grey-robed figure standing in the lee of the gateway, hands tucked into her wide sleeves, Brec darted away, and as Guy drew closer he heard Brec's father say,

"Here he be now, Sister," and saw the healer's head lift slightly as she sent a fleeting glance his way.

The wind within the tunnel of the gate arch was strong, tugging fiercely at the grey robe and white linen head-rail and Guy's first words to the woman were not so much a greeting as gentle command,

"Come with me, Sister. Let's get you out of this wind."

He had the odd notion that she would have much preferred to remain in the freezing courtyard, but then she nodded and still with modestly lowered head, followed meekly at his heels.

Nevertheless, the idea that this silent, grey mouse of a healer might be reluctant to accompany him grew ever stronger as he took her further into the castle precincts until he reached the great hall, empty at this time of the day save for his fellow musicians practising up in the gallery.

Frowning slightly, and keeping a suitably respectful distance between them, he gestured her closer to the fire burning in the huge hearth halfway along the length of the hall and directly opposite the gallery, an almost infinitesimal break in the music enough to inform him that their arrival had been observed, leaving him in no doubt that he would be the subject of a certain amount of good-natured ribaldry later.

"Now, Sister," he kept his voice low and unhurried. "Perhaps you will tell me your name, and what I may do for you. Brec said you had a message for me from the Eldest."

In response, the healer extracted a small flask from the pouch at her belt, and held it out to him with a hand wrapped about in a pale linen bandage.

"For Lord Nicholas," she said quietly, her gaze fixed on the flask rather than his face. "The Eldest sent it in the hopes it might ease both his cough and the tightness in his chest."

Except, thought Guy, as he reached out a hand to take it, with carefully incurious courtesy, Lord Nicholas did not have a cough at present, nor to Guy's knowledge had he ever complained of any sort of trouble with his chest.

As his fingers touched the linen binding about the healer's small hand, he felt a quiver go through her, and the flask nearly slipped away from them both.

"What is it? Did I hurt you?" he asked in concern, as soon as he had the flask safe. "I see your hand is..."

"No!"

A single snapped word repudiated his concern, and the white-wrapped hand disappeared swiftly back into the grey sleeve.

"But surely...?" he tried again.

"It is no matter, Master Finch. Please, just let me speak my message before it is too late."

"Of course, Sister..?"

"Fayla," she muttered. "My name, if it matters at all, is Fayla."

And then before he could say anything else, she added in a low, terse tone,

"Lady Adèle would have you know that Lord Nicholas' son has returned to Vézière, bringing as his guest the Lady Juliène of Lyeyne."

Forgetting what he had been about to say, Guy barely succeeded in strangling his startled exclamation.

He could do nothing, however, to control the painful clenching in his gut, or the sudden cramping tightness in his chest at the thought that the woman in his dreams would soon be before him in the flesh.

Ignoring the urge to ask whether the medicine intended for Lord Nicholas might ease his own malady, he said instead, quite steadily,

"Thank the Lady Adèle for these tidings, Sister Fayla. I will..."

"Stay out of her way if you have any sense," the healer hissed, finally raising her head and impaling him with a glittering gaze the same grey as the sea-washed pebbles of Black Rock Cove.

And when all Guy could do was stare at her in bemused disbelief, she added only a little less vehemently,

"Lady Adèle said you would know why."

"Yes, I... know why," he agreed.

Except he had no idea *what* he was saying, the words simply a way of riding out the wave of shocked comprehension that crashed over his mind.

She murmured something else to which he paid no heed, and sensing that she would be gone from his presence if he so much as blinked, he held her gaze as he would that of a wild creature, lifting his hand slowly, fingers stopping just short of tracing the prominent line of the blood-encrusted scratch running from the outer edge of one dark copper eyebrow to rip open the sun-browned, wind-weathered skin of what had once been a smooth, rose-petal-soft cheek.

"What happened?" he asked obliquely, and even he did not know whether he meant to her life in general, or her face in particular.

Her cloud-grey eyes showed a similar confusion, and for the most fleeting of moments he thought she might permit the gentle touch that was all he meant to offer...

A silent echo of the single demand his mouth had uttered.

A tacit acknowledgement of the truth that must remain unspoken in this public place... and perhaps might never be spoken, given what they were.

She, a Sister of Mercy.

He, a man who bore the scars of slavery on his heart and mind as much as on his body.

Then, just as Guy felt the warmth of her skin beneath his fingertips, she drew back.

Not, he thought, in fear. Or distrust. Or anger.

More as if an invisible wall of thorns had sprung up between them.

Allowing his hand to fall back to his side, Guy closed his eyes – for a heartbeat or untold more, it mattered not – and when he opened them again, the woman who had presented herself to him as Sister Fayla was gone.

And he knew he had given up what would likely be his only chance to settle the questions that disturbed his dreams and troubled his waking thoughts as persistently as did his doubts – one might almost say obsession – regarding Juliène de Lyeyne and her dangerously shadowy loyalties.

The opportunity was lost, he knew that.

Yet when he was back in the sanctuary of the small chamber high in the north tower, a prey to loneliness, betrayal and regret, he could not prevent the words still circling in his mind from slipping from his tongue, accompanied by a faintly bitter laugh.

"Fayla! The fey one! How damned, bloody apt!"

Then a cry from the heart, that emerged as little more than a hoarse whisper to the still emptiness surrounding him,

"Gods damn it, why could you not trust me with the truth I have stumbled over today? And how many other wretched truths are you hiding from me, I wonder?"

Except, he realised, he already knew the answer to that. In part, at least.

Some truths did not need to be put into words, not when he had already read them in the guarded depths of Sister Fayla's bleak grey gaze.

He could not, however, guard himself from the harsh hurt of his own thoughts.

Damn it, Rowène, whatever else you have done with your life since you left me... left me thinking you were dead, for gods'sake... if after all this, I find that your daughter is also my daughter... I swear I will never forgive you!

For not telling me at the time, when I was sure you loved me.

And for not telling me today, when I am no longer sure of any bloody thing...

Verse 9

From First Snow to Midwinter's Morn

Only when he was sure he had his hurt under control did Guy finish restringing his harp and make his way back to the hall. Once there, he climbed the narrow wooden stairs to join his fellow musicians in the gallery, and seating himself beside Aelfraed became to all intents and purposes absorbed in his music.

He would not allow himself to think of Rowène, yet at the same time he could not entirely dismiss her warning from his mind – or rather Adèle's warning, Rowène having admitted to being but the messenger.

So... what *had* brought Juliène de Lyeyne so suddenly to Vézière?

Was it merely duty to the princess?

Or did she have some more sinister motive for her visit?

It was not beyond the bounds of possibility that some rumour had come to Joffroi's ears concerning Lord Nicholas' new harper, and Juliène sent to confirm his identity.

Or, he thought wryly, he could simply be making too much of this, and her presence in Vézière nothing at all to do with him.

And if that were so, was she visiting the healers on her own account? Because Hervé had hurt her in some way!

Gods, no!

She did not deserve that! Whatever she had done to Guy himself.

A convulsive clench of his fingers calling forth a slightly off-key note, Guy became aware that both Maury and Aelfraed were sending him sidelong glances, and forced himself to concentrate his attention on the music they were to perform that evening for the entertainment of Lord Nicholas – rather than the motive of his unexpected guest.

As it turned out, Guy need not have troubled himself.

Just as the muffled notes of the horn calling everyone in the castle to the evening meal drifted up to the small chamber beneath the intricate stone-tiled roof, where the five men were in various stages of readiness, one of Lord Nicholas' pages appeared at the door.

Guy eyed him with some misgiving, remembering what had followed young Brec's appearance earlier. His voice, however, expressed only the mildest of polite interest.

"Aye, lad?"

"Message from Lord Nicholas."

"Well then, get on wi' it, boy," Halfiren growled, his head emerging from the neck of a hastily-donned clean tunic. "We're runnin' late as 'tis."

"Lord Nicholas says as how Master Finch and Master Aelfraed are to go down to the Healing House to play for Princess Linette tonight."

Guy felt a flicker of a frown drawing his brows together but he left it to the suddenly wide-eyed Aelfraed to give an awestruck assent on behalf of them both.

It was only when he arrived at the Healing House and saw the quickly concealed look of relief on Adèle's face as he followed Aelfraed into the princess' chamber that his suspicions as to the underlying cause behind this sudden summons was confirmed.

He did have a moment's qualm lest the princess recognise him and, without thinking, call him by his given name, though this turned out to be a needless worry, the princess seeming tired beyond thought – no doubt wearied by the burden of her advancing pregnancy – and apart from a brief, abstracted welcome for the musicians so kindly sent by Lord Nicholas, took little further notice of them.

Even so, Guy kept to the edges of the shadows and bided his time – there were things he wanted to say to his cousin before the evening was out and he did not intend leaving until he had done so.

The opportunity came later that evening when meeting his kinswoman in the moonlit darkness, seemingly by accident as he sought out the privy from which she was returning, he stopped her by the simple expedient of speaking her name.

"Adèle! A word, if you please."

"Guy?"

She sounded surprised – possibly at the grim note in his uncharacteristically curt voice – but nervous as well. Whether because of fear for him or her own guilty conscience...

"Is something wrong, Guy? Is..."

She hesitated.

"Is it Juliène? Did you not get my message in time? I hoped..."

"Yes, I got your message," he interrupted, his tone as terse as his thoughts. "Thank you. But what I want from you now is the knowledge of Sister Fayla's whereabouts?"

"Sister Fayla?" she echoed, and while her astonishment appeared unfeigned, there was definitely a worm of guilt beneath. "W... why would you want to know that?"

"I should have thought *that* was obvious!" he snapped.

"N..o..."

The halting answer told him all he needed to know about his cousin's involvement and his temper, rare to rouse though it was, roared into life, fully as unforgiving as that of his father and brothers.

"You can tell me where Sister Fayla is, Adèle. Or you can tell me why you deliberately withheld from me the knowledge that Rowène de Chartreux is alive and well and apparently living right under my bloody nose? Well? Your choice!"

And when she merely stared at him, hurt and hesitation and confusion, in her eyes, he added cuttingly,

"Tell me the first, and I may – possibly – forgive you the second."

"I do not know how you found out... about Fay... Rowène, but please believe that I never meant to... deceive you or... or cause you pain..."

She seemed so distressed, his anger against her faded somewhat and he managed a rueful, almost reassuring smile.

"No, I do not suppose *you* did. But you must see that now that I know Rowène... Fayla... whatever name she goes by... now I know she is alive, I need to speak with her about... Never mind what about, that is between her and me. So, please Adèle, tell me where I can find her. Before I have to start asking the Sisters themselves."

"No!"

There was definitely panic in her voice, and he frowned, wondering what she did not want him to learn.

"Then you tell me."

"Very well... but truly, Guy, it is little enough."

He watched as she took a deep, difficult breath, and the last residue of his anger died.

"I... I do not know where exactly she lives when she is not here... at the Healing House," Adèle said unhappily. "I only know that she is not here at the moment. Indeed I have not seen her since... since the night before I left for Lamortaine and my... binding. By the time

Gabriel and I returned a se'ennight later, she was gone, and I have not seen her since."

"Well, I can assure you she was here in Vézière today," Guy said flatly. "Standing no further away from me than you are now."

"I do not understand it," Adèle replied helplessly. "Unless... unless she came to Vézière with her brothers, though she was not with them when I saw them earlier... in the market square."

"Then if she was not with her brothers, nor here among the Grey Sisters, who else might she be with?" Guy asked grimly... and watched his cousin flush.

He had known since this morning that there was some other man, and was surprised only that it did not hurt as much as he thought it would to have it confirmed.

"Who is he?"

Adèle shook her head, clearly torn between loyalty to Rowène and her affection for him. He waited patiently and eventually she swallowed and in little above a whisper said,

"It is only a rumour... court gossip, Guy. I do not know whether there is any truth in it or not."

"But you think there must be a spark before there is fire?"

"I... maybe... I do not know..."

"Just tell me, Adèle."

He kept his voice level, then added with something of an edge,

"I am a grown man, and after the past five years in Kardolandia there is nothing you can tell me that would surprise or shock me, but I *do* need to know."

"Yes, I can... understand that."

He saw a flicker of... *something* in her eyes that told him just how deeply she did sympathise with his need to know the truth, however unpleasant it might be to hear.

"Very well then, but bear in mind it *is* only gossip."

Another breath, then she said unsteadily,

"There is a soldier... one of the royal bodyguard. Or at least he was until..."

"Until he entangled himself with Rowène." It was not a question.

"Perhaps. There was... a rumour of some scandal involving him and... her. They were both sent away from court."

"So where is he now, this soldier?"

"Up on the Atarkarnan border. He is one of Gabriel's men now."

"And they were... or are... lovers," Guy concluded with a frown.

"*No!* He is under Gabriel's command. That is all! Oh!"

The rose blush darkened to crimson in her cheeks.

"Oh, you meant he is *Rowène's* lover?" She shook her head, frowning slightly. "I cannot say for sure what they are to each other. All I know is that there was... something, a familiarity between them that night that made me think they were... close."

"And this guardian's name?"

"Rafe," she said after a long, hard heart-beat of hesitation.

Of course it bloody was.

The same damned Valennais bastard Guy had first encountered on the highway between Chartre and Marillé, his back rendered into bloody stripes at Gabriel de Marillec's command in punishment for his dubious dealings with Jacques de Chartreux.

The same man the Eldest had mistaken Guy for a mere two seasons ago, so close must be the resemblance between them.

Was that why Rowène had taken up with the man?

Because, as she had seen it, Guy had not been there for her when she needed him? Not only by reason of his enforced absence but also by the binding band about his arm?

Or did some other, even darker reason lie behind her betrayal?

Only the gods knew how a woman's mind worked. Certainly Guy did not.

And with one final silent curse, he accepted the futility of pursuing any further the fading rainbow fire that marked Rowène's fleeting presence in his life.

The truth about her daughter – *their* daughter? – was another matter entirely. Lissie, he would not give up so lightly.

Having returned to the castle, accompanied by the first pale drifting flakes of snow, Guy and Aelfraed were making for the kitchen to see what they might be able to coax out of the cook by way of food when they were intercepted by Alfgar, the household steward, with orders that Master Finch attend upon Lord Nicholas in his private chamber immediately.

As puzzled as Aelfraed, but considerably warier as to the cause of this unexpected summons, Guy muttered something about the medicine brought up earlier in the day by – what he somewhat bitterly thought of as – the false Sister of Mercy.

Given what Adèle had told him, Guy was more than ever aware that he had no idea where – or what – Rowène de Chartreux was now, and whatever he felt – or did not feel – for her, he certainly did not care for the possibility that if the mother of his child had been reduced – or chosen – to live the dubious life of a soldier's leman in the dangerous environs of the Atarkarnan border, she could well have taken the child with her.

So what, he wondered, had brought Rowène to Vézière today? Apparently alone, and wearing the robes of the Grey Sisters as if she had some – surely spurious – right to be recognised as a healer...

It was then that he recalled the very disturbing tale Ranulf had once told him of how Rowène de Chartreux had healed the scratches she herself had gouged across his cheek the morning after the fall of Chartre. The morning his brother had edged far too dangerously close to rape for Guy's peace of mind.

Setting aside his brother's disgraceful, unprecedented – and as far as Guy knew – unrepeated descent into mindless brutality, the healing skills Rowène had, by Ranulf's admission, displayed that day seemed to skirt far too disquietingly close for Guy's peace of mind to the dangerous enchantments practised by the Faennari.

Furthermore, Guy could not escape the insidious conviction that the grey robes and white headrail she had worn today had been no more than a guise, hastily assumed and imperfectly aligned, to conceal the fey creature composed of witch-fire and moonlight she truly was.

On a spurt of angry laughter he wished the soldier Rafe well in his dealings with her!

Gods pity the man! Did he have any *notion what sort of creature he had chosen to entangle himself with, merely for the sake of a warm body in his cold bed?*

As far as Guy was concerned, Rowène de Chartreux – or whatever she called herself now – had revealed herself today to be no less devious or duplicitous than her far more beautiful sister.

And Juliène Eléanor de Lyeyne, Guy reminded himself firmly, was the last woman, either in the five mortal realms or the fey lands beyond the moon, that any man, himself included – *especially* himself, when he was still attempting to salve the bleeding pieces of his heart following his bitter experience with her sister – should be stupid enough to entangle himself with...

Except – and in direct contradiction to all common sense – the mere thought of that dark-haired, green-eyed enchantress was enough to set his blood burning in familiar, shameful fashion. It also made him glance uneasily about him, first over his shoulder and then down the length of the long passageway ahead of him.

To his relief, there was no sign of her and he guessed she had already retired to the guest chamber that would have been prepared for her – either alone or accompanied by Hal de Vézière, who must surely be the latest in the long line of her reputed lovers.

Not that Guy, with his own five years of infidelity to Mathilde, was in any situation to put her in the pillory for betraying her lord-by-binding. Nor, if he were honest with himself, could he blame her for her present choice. The heir to Vézière was young, healthy and handsome, and – more importantly to Guy's way of thinking – lacked anything approaching Hervé's reputation for vicious brutality.

Indeed, Guy reasoned as he surreptitiously eyed the blandly closed doors as he passed, wondering which one Juliène might be behind, almost anyone would make a better bedmate for the fragile – if fey – woman he remembered from that last bloody day in Lamortaine.

Even him.

Not, of course, that it would ever come to that!

Coming to the end of the passage without sight or sound of Juliène or her lover, he took the stairs up to the floor above where Nicholas de Vézière had his chambers, raising his hand to knock on the door just as his lordship's manservant, Eadric, came out.

"There ye are, Finch. Ye took yer own bloody time." He gave a sniff of disapproval. "His lordship's been waitin' these past four candle-notches fer ye. Go on in, an' see ye don't keep him from his bed any longer than's needful. Bad enough he has to be plagued by these noble guests Master Hal's put on him, wi'out ye addin' to his troubles."

Guy merely raised his brows and said mildly,

"'Twas his lordship himself as sent for me, Eadric, so doubtless he had good reason. Even so, I'll do my best not to burden him further."

Then with a light rap of knuckles against oak and a quick,

"It's Finch, my lord," he went in, pausing just inside the doorway to allow the occupants to accustom themselves to his presence.

The elderly nobleman half buried in furs and blankets, seated in the chair in front of a well-stoked fire, looked up at the sound of Guy's voice. As did the huge brindled hound lying at his feet, his wolf-bright eyes taking in the visitor before his grey-muzzled jaws opened to show two rows of sharp, yellow teeth... his initial alertness turning after a moment into a yawn of bored acceptance.

At least, Guy reflected, it wasn't the snarl the dog had been known to turn on some members of the household.

Meanwhile the younger of Lord Nicholas' constant companions shook himself to his feet and trotted over to take Guy's held-out hand in a massive mouth, teeth closing on his flesh, as the beast worried it back and forth in what was both test and greeting. Unperturbed, Guy rubbed the great tawny head and greeted both dogs by name.

"Hé, Cavall. Hé, Cub." And then when Cub had returned to flop down on the stone floor before the hearth. "You sent for me, my lord?"

The older man raised his head, cloudy dark eyes seeking out the shadowy form of his harper.

How much could the man see, Guy wondered. Perhaps no more than a bulky blur of brown, topped by another blur of fairish hair, limned to dark gold by the candlelight? Perhaps not even that much?

"Yes, Finch."

And then irritably throwing off the blankets and furs.

"Gods above! Does that fool Eadric want to cook me? I am not as young as I once was, and half-blind to boot, but I am not teetering on my death-bed quite yet."

Obviously hearing the snort Guy could not quite repress, the old nobleman added in much the same tone,

"Come closer, man, for gods'sake. Find a stool and sit on it. No point standing on ceremony here."

Glancing around, Guy found a stool and when he was seated, he said again,

"My lord?"

"Tell me about your visit to the Healing House, Finch. Is the princess well?"

"Tired, I think. As you know the child will be born some time around the Midwinter feast, and she is very... er..."

He hesitated and Lord Nicholas smiled, his grey brows rising wryly.

"Very round?"

"Meaning no disrespect, but yes," Guy agreed.

"No disrespect at all," Lord Nicholas grinned. "It is just what happens with women, from royal princesses down to the humblest peasant, and all ranks in between. I remember how it was with Hal's mother, the Lady Hélène..."

But Guy was no longer listening.

He had memories of his own.

Of how Rowène had looked when he had seen her that day in the palace gardens just before she had given birth. When he – blind, trusting fool that he had been then – had carried her undeniably rounded form to the refuge of Joscelin de Veraux's chamber.

Gods damn it!

If only he had known at the time that it was *his* child she had been about to give birth to. But it had not occurred to him then.

Indeed, he was not even sure now that Lissie was his daughter.

His!

Not Joscelin de Veraux's.

Not – a sudden, horrified thought struck him – not, gods forbid, Ranulf's child born of something Guy would never have thought possible of his brother... but no – reason overtook icy panic – the timing was wrong. Nor could Ranulf have betrayed him like that.

No, Lissie must be his. But, gods above, how could he not have recognised that truth when it had been right before his eyes?

Pain shattering through his heart, Guy lived again those few precious moments after her birth when he had held his daughter in his arms... before Luc de Chartreux had taken her away from him!

And while Guy could not truly fault Luc for wanting to see his sister and her child out of the hell their life would have been at court, still he begrudged the loss of his daughter...

"Finch? Finch! Damn it, answer me, man!"

Lord Nicholas' querulous voice drew him from the reckoning – bitter as rue – of that which could not be changed to the perilously uncertain nature of his present situation.

It was, he reflected as he made automatic answer, a little like stepping off a solid stone path to find himself stumbling through the treacherous shadows of a moorland mist.

"Your pardon, my lord. I was thinking."

"Of your own woman and children perchance."

It was less a question than a statement from the half-blind nobleman who, Guy was beginning to think, might *see* far too much.

"Child, my lord," he said abruptly, jerkily, the words torn from him. "A little girl. Lissie."

His tone gentled as he spoke her name, soft as the snowflakes falling past the shuttered window, concealing the secrets of castle and moor alike in shimmering silence.

"She is... seven summers old."

Gods! Seven summers old already. And I have not seen her since the day she was born!

"And her mother?"

"Gone to live as a soldier's whore!"

Only as the harsh words left his tongue did he realise the true depth of the hurt and anger he still felt at Rowène's betrayal.

Lord Nicholas looked momentarily shocked, then said,

"Surely that cannot be good for the child, living with her mother in such circumstances?" His voice a mixture of curiosity and something far warmer than the normal condescension of a nobleman to his retainer, he continued, "If you wish, Finch, to have little Mistress Lissie here with you, she will be a most welcome addition to my household. I can arrange..."

"No need, my lord."

Guy interrupted whatever else the man had been about to offer in his generosity, and fought to keep his voice even.

"I think... believe..." He *had* to believe, else he was like to do something stupid next time he saw either Rowène or her bloody brothers. "That Lissie is living with her mother's kin."

Gods knew it was dangerous enough for the child to be under the care of her outlawed uncles! Better that though, than that Lissie should be living with her wild and wayward mother and the rough soldier Rowène was presently sleeping with, in defiance of everything she owed her name – and her brothers.

As to that... Guy mentally considered the two men, grimly assessing their ability to protect his daughter and – he suddenly remembered – Ranulf's son, Val.

Luc de Chartreux, for all his tarnished reputation, Guy had no doubts about. The man was clever, wily and strong. He had to be, to have survived, both his brief experience as a galley slave and, for the past seven years, as a hunted outlaw.

There was something definitely odd about Jacques though – Guy had thought it when he had first met the boy in Chartre castle, and then again when the youth had appeared in Kaerellios and somehow saved his mangled hand – and whilst Guy was well aware that he owed the young outlaw his life twice over, he still did not quite trust him.

"Good, good. But if you change your mind at any time," Lord Nicholas was saying. "Remember, there is a place for Mistress Lissie here, all the time you are in my service. And, given that her father is one of the finest itinerant minstrels I have ever heard, the child may have some talent of her own?"

"I would not know, my lord," Guy said stonily. "Communication between myself and her uncles is... sporadic to say the least. And, as far as I can see, not like to improve."

There was a moment of awkward silence before Lord Nicholas cleared his throat and said,

"Whilst on the subject of music, you would not know, having been absent this evening, that one of the noblewomen my son invited here, Lady Juliène de Lyeyne, has the most lovely singing voice you have ever heard."

It is indeed, Guy thought, recalling that afternoon in the honeysuckle-scented intimacy of the small, walled garden of Chartre castle. *The voice of a daughter of the moon sent to lure mortal men to their doom.*

"Hmm, yes. Most interested in my musicians the lady was. In the subtlest of manners, of course. I should not expect a daughter of Lady Ariène to be anything else."

This last comment, a mere mutter to himself, was clearly not intended by Lord Nicholas to be a compliment.

"She wondered that I did not have a harper amongst my household," the old nobleman continued. "Skilled as the trio entertaining us undoubtedly were."

"Oh?"

The word was tight, constrained, only uttered because Guy knew he had to say something.

"So naturally I told her I *did* have a harper."

The other man's voice took on a faintly disparaging note.

"A good enough musician in his way but nothing to mark him out from the ordinary. Certainly not when compared to the likes of Guyard de Martine."

Guy's gut lurched.

"Have you not heard of him in your wanderings?" the old man mused. "Certainly Lady Juliène knew who he was."

Guy took a breath to steady himself and then, with the very slightest suggestion of an edge to his voice, said,

"Aye, well, she would have done, would she not? She being the former Lord of Chartreux's daughter and he the old Lord of Rogé's bastard son."

"Ah! So you do know who he is." Lord Nicholas' words fell light as feathers, heavy as lead. "I heard him play at court once, many years ago. I have never forgotten."

There was a long silence, broken only by the throaty breathing of the dogs, the muted roar of the fire, until finally Lord Nicholas said,

"Lady Juliène seemed most disappointed to hear that you were not of the same skill as de Martine."

For which Guy breathed a sincere thanks to the gods – and Lord Nicholas.

Until the old nobleman added,

"For which injustice I must apologise, Finch."

A heartbeat of stillness at these astonishing – and worrying – words, before Guy forced himself to ask the obvious question.

"And *why*, if I may be permitted to ask, did you do me what you call an injustice, my lord?"

"Chiefly, because you are *my* harper," Lord Nicholas replied flatly.

His sightless gaze lifted to stare straight at Guy as if he could truly see him, even as he fingered the heavy gold signet ring on his left hand.

"And because, Master Finch, as I am very sure you are aware... oaths of fielty work both ways."

The old man hesitated before adding heavily,

"Also, there was something in Lady Juliène's voice that I... misliked."

He stopped again, and for a moment Guy thought the other man had said as much as he meant to, then Lord Nicholas continued musingly, a grim edge to his seemingly random reminiscence,

"I doubt the lady herself is aware of it but I first met her when she was no more than a little lass herself, of six or so summers. It can be no secret that in those days her father and I were..."

Guy thought the word *friends* lay on the other man's tongue. In the end, Lord Nicholas went for a more prudent description.

"We were allies then, in the days before Black Joffroi and his marauding brothers destroyed Lucius de Chartreux's reputation beyond redemption, making his name a byword for treachery."

Guy winced but could scarcely take issue with Lord Nicholas' words. Mostly because he spoke no more than the truth. Though not the whole truth. De Vézière himself had played a part in his friend's downfall, as had every member of the High Counsel of the time, with the sole exception of Gilles de Valenne.

"I visited Chartre often enough," Lord Nicholas was saying. "Back then. When the castle was still home to his children. Before his son had gone to Marillé and his daughters to Kardolandia. And what I remember most clearly about the young Juliène was her singing. Her voice was as sweet and pure as that of the lark high in the summer sky. She was a pretty child too, as I recall, with hair darker than midnight and the most unusual green eyes I have ever seen."

As Lord Nicholas continued his reflections, his unseeing gaze moved as if to study the flames dancing in the hearth.

The logs were from an apple tree and the flames burned green at their heart, as mysterious and unlikely a green as Juliène de Chartreux's eyes.

"My son tells me she has grown into a beautiful woman."

The very lack of expression in the older man's tone told Guy that Lord Nicholas suspected his son to be unwisely enamoured of their guest.

"Have you seen her yourself, Finch?"

Not here. Not yet.

But unless she had changed a great deal...

"I have, my lord, and your son does not lie. She is..." Or at least she had been. "Very beautiful indeed."

As exquisite in her perfection as a figurine limned by the clear light of the blush-dawn sun rising over the Star Isles.

As untouchable in her beauty as a white lily on a mountain lake.

And as dangerous, and treacherous, as only a woman – or man, he conceded, though he knew of none – who owed their allegiance to the Moon Goddess of the Faennari.

"Beauty is not everything though," Lord Nicholas sighed, evidently still concerned over his son's infatuation with a woman who wore the binding band of another man. And that man a murderous bully like Hervé de Lyeyne.

"I should not be saying this to you, Finch... and would not, save I sense you hold secrets of your own and can therefore be trusted to hold mine also."

"You can, my lord."

It was the only answer Guy could give.

Whether he *wished* to hear Nicholas de Vézière's most private thoughts was another matter.

"As I was saying, when I first saw Juliène de Chartreux, young though she was she seemed bound already to her mother's side. But whenever she could escape, it would be to follow her brother about, eager as a puppy. And to do the boy justice, he suffered it without complaint and looked after her as well as a lad of that age is wont to do. In return she adored him."

The blind eyes sought out the flickering light of the fire again.

"It must have been a sad day for her when Luc was declared traitor and outlaw in the wake of his father's attainder and execution."

Guy made some sort of indistinct noise in his throat and Lord Nicholas sighed again.

"Yet, for all her childish innocence and the love she lavished on her brother, I sensed something... cold in her even then. There was a stable boy at the castle, a good-looking lad and, as all with eyes could plainly see, de Chartreux's bastard get. Young as she was, Juliène knew it too, and she hated that boy with an icy malice that knew no mercy. Unfortunately, it is a trait I sense in her still, grown greater through the passage of the years, forged stronger by her brother's misfortunes, and her own unhappy binding."

"It cannot be easy being bound to scum like Hervé de Lyeyne," Guy said grimly, and with scant regard for discretion.

"Even so..."

I would not have her destroy my son.

The words were unspoken, save perhaps in the hiss of dampness in the burning logs, but plain enough in the silence.

"De Chartreux had another daughter," Lord Nicholas said after a moment or two of brooding.

His head turned away from the hearth, unerringly towards Guy.

"As different from her sister as two girls born to the same parents on the same day can be. A scrawny, freckled lass, all arms and legs and torn clothing, Rowène was her name."

Guy had no need to ask how *she* had treated her illegitimate half-brother. Regardless of his own bitter anger towards her now, he could not entirely discard his memories of the unaffected acceptance, the warmth she had extended to Lucien of Chartre, the stable boy who had grown up to become the castle's garrison commander, ultimately dying on a de Rogé sword.

It was the same manner she had displayed towards the itinerant harper Guy had presented himself as, even when she realised he too was of bastard birth, and worse than that, that his father was Jacques de Rogé, Chartreux's old enemy.

As if Lord Nicholas had picked up his thought, he continued with a trace of a wistful smile.

"I wonder what sort of a woman she would have grown into had she lived? I saw her at court once, while I yet had my sight. She was Joscelin de Veraux's mistress then, and big-bellied with child."

Guy was glad the old nobleman could not see him flinch.

"Not that I saw much of her," Lord Nicholas was still meandering in melancholic manner through his memories.

"She kept out of public view as much as she could. With good cause – her father's head barely picked clean by the crows, her brother hunted as an outlaw... and her own precarious situation, betrothed to the very man who put the noose around her father's neck, and who for whatever reason refused to put the binding band about her wrist that would at least have given her child a name. And then after all that, to die in childbirth."

Lord Nicholas stared mournfully in the direction of the fire, one hand dropping to stroke the head Cavall had laid in his lap, the other reaching down to gently pull at Cub's silky ears.

"I prefer to remember her as the child she was when I saw her at Chartre, half feral, half fey, more boy than girl, with her red hair in wild tangles and her eyes as bright as starlight..."

Something flickered through Guy's mind... like lightning across a midnight sky or a single shaft of moonlight glimmering on an endless onyx sea... and, then as Lord Nicholas' manservant walked back into the room, his face dark with displeasure, his footsteps heavy with eloquence, once again the thought was gone.

"Ah! That sounds like Eadric," Lord Nicholas said, raising his blind gaze to track his manservant's approach. "Come with a posset to help me sleep."

And as Guy rose to his feet to take his leave,

"I hear you had a visitor today, Finch. One of the healers? No doubt she brought some more of the Eldest's vile-tasting medicine for me?"

Lord Nicholas sounded ruefully resigned, and Guy remembered with something of a shock the small bottle he had been carrying around all day – and completely forgotten until now – the contents of which he had no intention of permitting the other man to drink until he himself had tested it.

He could see no reason why Rowène would wish harm to a man who had once been her father's friend... unless it were some belated and elaborate way of taking revenge for Nicholas de Vézière's betrayal of her father.

"Forgive me, my lord, I do not have it with me," he lied. "I will bring it to you in the morning..." *If it proves harmless.* "Unless you need it now?"

If he said yes, Guy would have to think of some other excuse...

"No, no, the morning will be soon enough. Thank you, Finch. Good night."

It was dismissal, and Guy was glad enough to take it. In addition to his doubts regarding the contents of the flask in his pouch, Nicholas de Vézière's conversation had provided a very uncomfortable end to what had already proved to be an extremely unsettling day.

Nor was it quite over yet, as Guy discovered after he had closed the door to Lord Nicholas' chamber and started to descend the broad spiral to the floor below where he guessed Juliène's room was situated.

He had been walking slowly, thinking over certain of those things the elderly nobleman had said, and his soft leather shoes made little or no noise on the stone steps. So he had no difficulty in hearing a woman's sweetly, sensual voice saying,

"Hal, no! We must not..."

And a man – evidently de Vézière's heir – murmur something in reply, his words inaudible, his tone low, persuasive, clearly determined on the seduction of his guest.

"Hal, we cannot. Not under your father's roof."

"Then where, my love?"

Though still low, the young man's voice was rising in frustration.

"We cannot be together at court because of that oaf you are bound to. I thought once we were away from there, somewhere you might feel safe, you would be free of him..."

"I can never be free of Hervé," came Juliène's reply, the strain evident in her voice, to Guy at least, beneath the softly yearning note that was all her lover was interested in listening to.

"These past few days with you have been a blessing, Hal, but still only a reprieve. I cannot linger long before I must return to Lamortaine – and my lord-by-binding."

"Then let me make this night a delight for you, my love."

De Vézière was persistent, Guy would give him that, even if he did not appreciate being put in the position of eavesdropping on another man's amatory aspirations. Particularly not when the woman in question was Juliène de Lyeyne!

"Let me in, love."

"Hal, no, please..."

Guy caught the unmistakable note of panic in her voice and pushed off the wall against which he had been leaning. He could recognise, even if the other man could not, that this was not mere coquetry designed to further inflame an already ardent lover.

"Let me share your bed tonight, my dearest love, and I promise you..."

Guy did not wait to hear what carnal delights de Vézière might be about to describe. Drawing out the small earthernware bottle Juliène's sister had given him earlier, he scraped it against the dressed stone blocks of the stair wall...

Heard a quick drawn breath from Juliène.

"What was that? Hal, you must go!"

"It was nothing, love. A mouse in the wall. My father's manservant moving about upstairs."

"I loathe mice. And your father's servant is not nothing, Hal. He will tell your father and all the other servants, and I will be disgraced. If you cared for me, you would not seek to dishonour me like this!"

"If you let me in, no-one will see us together. No-one will ever know. Not my father. Not the servants."

Bollocks! Of course they would, servants know everything. Besides, she said 'no', *you prick!*

With difficulty, Guy kept his snarl between his teeth and scratched the bottle down the wall again, adding a couple of shuffling footsteps for good measure.

"Someone is coming," Juliène hissed. "Good night, Hal."

There came the sound of a door firmly closing – in Hal de Vézière's face to judge by the muted curses coming from the passageway below.

Guy thought for a moment the disappointed lover might come seeking the cause for his dismissal, then heard him stamping away, evidently in search of some other, more willing woman, on whom to slake his frustrated lust.

Grimacing, Guy sat down on the steps, not wanting to walk past Juliène's door until he was sure she was asleep and would not be opening it again until morning brought her maidservant.

The last thing he wanted to do, since Lord Nicholas had chosen to put her off the harper's scent, was carelessly reveal his whereabouts to her.

It was long gone midnight when Guy finally slid beneath the blankets of his own bed, by which time the snow that had been but a scatter of feather-soft flakes when he and Aelfraed had walked back from the Healing House had begun to drift into every roof hollow and sheltered corner of the courtyard.

He woke to find town and highway covered with the first white of winter, only learning after a day of avoiding any place where he thought Juliène might be that she had seized upon the excuse offered by the weather and returned to Lamortaine before she become trapped in Vézière, thus – she had been heard to say – putting her host to the inconvenience of housing her over the winter.

It occurred to Guy that the true reason might lie somewhere between her failure to find her quarry – him – and a desire to escape her would-be lover's importunities before they became too forceful.

Whatever the cause, Juliène's departure served at least to give him a breathing space, time to decide what he would do if – or rather when – he finally did come face to face with her.

Nor could he quite prevent himself from wondering whether Rowène had returned to the Atarkarnan border and her low-born lover, before shrugging the thought aside.

All he truly cared about now was that Lissie should be kept safe from winter's freezing grasp.

Lissie was indeed safe, though for a while it had been in the hands of the gods whether her mother and uncle would get back to her before the weather made the moors too dangerous to cross.

It was a race the outlaws had won by the smallest of margins, no more than the skein of lace spun between one snowflake and the next.

Waking to a white morning, watching Lissie laughing as she ran about the clearing with the other children, trying to catch snowflakes on her tongue, Rowène was more than willing in the wake of her recent experiences to fall in with Luc's very firmly phrased suggestion that she remain there for the foreseeable future.

She therefore spent the early winter months hunting game in the forest with the other outlaws – and occasionally with Bryce, Justin de Lacey's chief huntsman – and until midwinter the farthest she had ventured was into Lasceynes with Beowulf, trading furs for grain.

Then just short of the Midwinter feast, on a night when moonlight drenched the forest, setting the snow-covered branches to silver-shot crystal, Rowène woke from a dream and knew she would have to leave again, if she were not to break her promise to one of the men she held closest to her heart.

As cold as it was, she had lain down fully dressed beneath the wolf pelt and blankets of her bed, and now in obedience to some silent summons, she rose and went to look outside, grimacing at the sight of the trampled snow of the clearing, frozen once more to a crisp hardness.

In the darkness behind her, Luc was still asleep, and knowing she could do nothing until he woke, she returned to bed, there to lie awake and plan her journey... and wonder whether Ranulf might have requested leave from his commander to come south for the Midwinter quarter day.

Though even if he had asked, and Gabriel been in a mood or position to release him... even if weather and road conditions permitted travel... even if Ranulf managed to make it to their usual meeting place... common sense told her that he would have returned to the Atarkarnan border long before she herself reached Vézière.

That being so, she did not need to hear it from her brother as well, least of all for it to be the first thing he said when he woke at dawn and she told him what she meant to do.

"Hell'sdeath, Ro! What madness is this?" he demanded tersely, his eyes going from sleet to storm in a heartbeat, and his voice dropping to a low growl, "If this has anything to do with bloody Rafe..."

"It has not!" she snapped back. "I am not such a fool!"

"Who then? Guy de Martine? I thought you had decided to stay out of his way."

"I have."

He frowned and very, very hesitantly spoke the name of the man who must always be foremost in his thoughts,

"Is it... though I cannot think why it would be... is it.. Ré?"

Unable to speak for the swell of pity in her throat, she simply shook her head.

While she comprehended well enough the nature of Luc's preoccupation, there was nothing she could tell him. Her dreams were unpredictable in every way and this last one had not given her so much as a glimpse of Ranulf, let alone Gabriel de Marillec.

What she had seen was a tall man restlessly pacing the palace walls, starlight glimmering off the swansdown feathering in his hair.

A man who so nearly resembled the one she was facing.

"This is for Josce," she said now, somewhat sharply. "Our brother, need I remind you, who puts his life at risk every day for our sake."

The grey eyes so like her own narrowed, the lean face hardening in a manner she knew well, as Luc said grimly,

"Very well. But you do not go alone."

"Beowulf will..."

"No, not this time. Since this concerns *our* brother, it is me and not Beowulf who will be travelling to Vézière with you."

It took Rowène and Luc five days to reach Vézière.

Five days of slogging through melting snow, slush and sludge, sleeping rough in sheep byres and what other dubious shelter they could find.

Fortunately Luc knew the moors as another man might know his mistress' moods and guided Rowène unerringly by the easiest – if such a term could be applied – pathways.

Even so, it was an exhausting task she had set for herself, and if not for her brother's presence, she would undoubtedly have pushed herself beyond what was wise. Perhaps he had known that when he had made the decision to accompany her, for where she might possibly have managed to persuade Beowulf to bend to her will, Luc was adamant that she take time to rest, to eat, to sleep.

"How else," he had pointed out bluntly. "Will you be of any use to the princess? Though gods know what you mean to do when we finally reach the Healing House."

To which Rowène had no answer at all.

There was nothing she *could* say to Luc that would not cause him to regard their brother without suspicion deepening in his eyes or hardening his heart to something approaching the old coolness Luc had felt when he had first realised that Joscelin de Veraux was their father's son too.

Pausing in the shelter of some gorse bushes just before they dropped down off the moors, Luc put on the robe that had once belonged to Justinian de Valenne and which, Rowène hoped, would shield his identity from such curious glances as might be cast his way, at the same time giving him entrée into the Healing House without raising too many unwanted questions.

She herself meant to slip into the Eldest's chamber and change into Sister Fayla's robes on their arrival, and then present herself to the princess – if it should prove that Linette was indeed in need of her peculiar skills.

It was late in the afternoon when they finally arrived at the Healing House, the last fires of the setting sun streaking an otherwise sullen, snow-bound sky, and disturbingly there was no sign of Sister Aldith who usually kept watch over the gate when she was not caring for the enclave's animals.

Accompanied by Luc, the deep hood pulled up to hide his frost-flecked dark hair, Rowène went straight to the Eldest's chamber. Her disquiet mounting when she found the chamber empty and cold, the wood in the brazier long since reduced to grey ash, she changed clothes with a rapidity bordering on urgency whilst Luc kept watch beside the door.

Tightening her rope belt to an almost savage tension, she gestured to her brother to follow – as if she could have stopped him, the grim look in his eyes told her – and made her way to the rooms set apart for the princess.

As they entered the inner bedchamber the reason for the strange air gripping the enclave became obvious.

Not only was Linette in labour, but clearly all was not as it should be.

Lady Isabelle sat in the shadows to one side of the bed, her hands held tightly within her lap, her features grey with weariness, and while Adèle was still on her feet, engaged in decanting something from a pitcher on the table, the face she was careful to keep turned away from the princess was white and rigid with fright.

The Eldest herself was bending over Linette, murmuring gentle instructions as she conducted an examination of the princess' sweat-soaked body, which now twisted and tightened in a renewal of agony, Linette's gasping scream making Luc step back involuntarily, and slicing Rowène's already shaken composure to the quick.

Bowls and pitchers of water, hot and cold, had been placed on the table, together with neat stacks of cloth. A little gown warmed near the brazier, folded over the side of a beautifully carved and polished beechwood cradle, while one of the younger Grey Sisters stood ready to assist the Eldest or receive the babe.

All that was missing, gods help them, was the child itself.

With an effort Rowène cleared the choking bile from her throat and said,

"Is there anything I can do to help?"

The Eldest straightened sharply and turned, the sternly-held expression of serenity shattering in a heartbeat before settling into place again, the merest remnant of it remaining to belie her barely steady tone.

"Sister Fayla! I have been hoping – no, I have been *praying* – that you would come."

Her blue gaze – normally so clear but now hazed by the same exhaustion shadowing every other face in the stifling chamber – slid warily towards the tall, grey-robed man standing silently at Rowène's shoulder.

"Who... who is this?"

"This is Brother Justinian, Eldest. He accompanied me from Lasceynes."

The blue gaze sharpened from something close to despair to determination even as she traced the lean lines of his darkly-stubbled face.

"Good Brother, I realise you have been travelling for many days in treacherous conditions to get here but..."

A faint glimmer of relief showed in the otherwise well-armoured grey gaze.

"You have some task for me, Eldest?" he enquired.

"Yes, and if... if you will step outside for a moment, I will tell you what I... need you to do. If, that is, you are willing to risk your life in the snow once more."

His eyes flickered from the pleading face of the woman who had once been his father's mistress to the figure in the bed, the princess alternately panting and moaning, tears trickling from under the closed lids of her eyes.

Finally he met Rowène's stark gaze, and she saw from the grim line of his mouth that he knew already what the Eldest was about to ask him to do.

With a slight inclination of his head to their brother's mother, and the faintest of grim smiles for Rowène, Luc turned and left the room, followed almost immediately by the Eldest, even as she despatched the other healer on some errand to the still-room.

With Luc out of the way, Rowène wasted no more time but went straight to the bed and ignoring Adèle's astonished gaze – though she felt the weight of it well enough – took Linette's lax hand between both of hers.

"Your highness?" she said softly. "Linette?"

For several heavy heartbeats there was no reaction, then with aching slowness the reddened lids lifted to reveal eyes from which all but the barest spark of life had been worn away.

For a moment this spark glimmered with blue fire and the cracked lips parted enough for the princess to croak,

"Who..? I feel I should... know you?"

Then as the flicker of life burned low again,

"Why are you here?"

"Not knowing which of her incarnations Linette had recognised, Rowène said steadily,

"I am Sister Fayla. I came to the palace last summer with the Eldest." *And left in disgrace, under suspicion of seducing your bodyguard, but before that...*

"I promised Lord Joscelin then that I would see you safely through this ordeal, and I will."

"Josce...lin..."

The whisper was little more than the lightest of winds through winter-dead willows.

"Tell him..."

"You may tell him yourself when he arrives," Rowène spoke with an assurance she was far from feeling. "My br..."

She grimaced inwardly at her mistake, then glanced fleetingly at Adèle and Lady Isabelle who were both staring at her as if they could not quite believe their eyes, before concluding firmly,

"Brother Justinian has gone to fetch him."

"We will... be gone long... before Joscelin gets here..." Linette breathed as her weighted lids slid closed again. "Me and... the babe... both."

Rowène met Adèle's terrified gaze, then Lady Isabelle's despairing one, and shook her head stubbornly.

"No, your highness. Too much depends on this for you to give up now."

Goddess help me, I did not come this far through snow and ice and bitter fear, risking Luc's life, which is worth more than my own, just to see Josce's living heart ripped out and torn into a thousand bloody pieces. Nor did I come to watch you or your child die.

Looking across the bed as another contraction twisted Linette's straining body, causing the sweat-soaked linen shift to tighten across her swollen belly, Rowène asked quietly,

"How long has she been in labour?"

"A day and a night already," the Eldest answered as she glided soundlessly back into the chamber.

Her voice was low and steady, and no-one would have guessed at her anxiety if they had not, like Rowène, been able to perceive the emotion hidden behind the mask of serene confidence.

"And the babe?" she asked now.

"Was lying the wrong way but I contrived to turn it. There is no reason why all should not be well. It is just a matter of time."

And of praying that Linette's endurance is equal to the task.

She did not speak the words, but then she did not need to. They must all have reached that bleak conclusion for themselves.

What only Rowène knew – and possibly the Eldest had guessed – was that there was another reason why things might turn out very ill indeed.

The contraction over, Rowène took a seat beside the bed, leaving Joscelin's mother, Lady Isabelle and Adèle to care for the princess in their separate ways.

Retaining Linette's hand in her own, Rowène closed her eyes and reached deep into herself, seeking the strength and skills the Moon Goddess had set in her soul, and which she had gradually taught herself to harness and use, though it was still a haphazard business at the best of times, with no guarantee of success.

This time, however, she was determined not to fail.

Dawn was trembling below the sun-gilded horizon when a black-maned, moon-grey stallion bearing an incongruous pair of riders came to a halt outside the gates of the healers' enclave.

The man riding pillion slid wearily to the ground, staggering slightly as he caught his balance, his outflung arm brushing against a branch of the nearby spindleberry bush and inadvertently setting the bronze bells to chiming.

His companion remained in the saddle a heartbeat longer, staring at the closed gates, the last shattered rays of moonlight glittering off the spurs at his heels and the silver brooch wrought in the shape of a stag that fastened the dark mantle hanging from his broad shoulders to the tops of his boots.

Then, with a scathing glance at his companion, he too dropped to the ground, setting his spurs to chinkle in tune with the tinkling bells, his voice a low, barely audible growl,

"If you have not already alerted everyone to our presence, *Brother*, do you think there is a single, solitary chance in Hell that we might do this with a modicum of discretion?"

"As discreet as you bloody please," Luc shot back. "Considering you have damned little excuse to be here, being neither Linette's brother-by-blood nor her lord-by-binding."

"No, but I am the only one who *can* be here," Joscelin snapped. "Linnius is bound by protocol to his bloody throne, and Kaslander simply does not give a shit whether Linette lives or dies."

"And you do."

"Yes, I fucking do."

And that, as Luc well knew, was a testament to Joscelin's inner turmoil, his customary constraint over his language having been long abandoned – somewhere amongst the moonlit shadows of the highway between the place some leagues south of Vézière where they had so unexpectedly met and the spot where they now stood, arguing, outside the healers' enclave.

As it was, Joscelin had said nothing to explain his presence that far north of Lamortaine and Luc had not asked, choosing somewhat grimly to ascribe it to their sister's far-reaching and undoubtedly fey influence.

Now, he made the effort to shrug off the uncomfortable feeling compounded of anger, envy, fear and bitterness that any reminder of the Faennari inevitably provoked in him, and turned from the locked gates to survey the encircling stone wall.

It was only a couple of feet over his own, and Joscelin's, height.

"If you give me a leg up," he offered. "I will climb over and open the gate."

Without a word Joscelin bent over, and hitching up the folds of his robe with a muttered oath, Luc put his foot in the stirrup of his brother's linked hands.

He was already reaching for a grip on the wall, accidentally setting the bells to jangling again, when one side of the double gates creaked open.

"Lord Joscelin? Brother Justinian?"

"Yes."

They spoke as one, swift and low, their voices – one granite, the other steel – barely distinguishable one from the other.

"Who is there?"

"I am Sister Aldith," came the hushed tones from the widening crack in the gate. "The Eldest bade me keep watch for you. Come you in, and... oh!"

Her courteous tones melted into a crooning murmur as her gaze went beyond the brothers to the big stallion, her appreciation rendering the men all but redundant.

"And bring that fine fellow with you."

Exchanging a glance that, for the first time that night, held something other than antagonism, Luc and Joscelin handed the tired horse into Sister Aldith's care, and then turned to make their way to the chamber where Luc had left the Princess of Mithlondia in the torturous throes of childbirth, the small amount of relief that moment of shared humour had brought him dissipating as quickly as it had come.

From what little he had seen before he had left Linette's chamber, Luc did not hold much hope that he was bringing his brother to a scene of gladness and joy.

With the memory of his own feelings when he had found Rowène in a similar situation flooding into his mind, he braced himself to deal with Joscelin's grief in the moment when they would open the door to find the woman their brother obviously cared deeply about lying dead, and the babe with her.

Hearing the door open behind her, Rowène glanced around and felt her strained features stretch into a smile as her exhausted mind put names to the two tall, grey-eyed, dark-haired men standing shoulder to shoulder just inside the room's shadowy limits.

Then, looking more closely, she saw that for all the superficial similarity between her brothers, neither the shade nor the expression in their eyes was the same, for while Luc's were set into the stone-grey of guarded suspicion, Joscelin's gaze held the dark storm-grey shadows of wordless dread, his lean features pale with a fear that was not for himself.

For several long moments the silence in the chamber was oppressive, nobody moving, nobody daring to utter a sound, until the white-faced woman lying against the pillows slowly opened her eyes, and seeing the man she had been waiting for, whispered,

"Joscelin..."

In the same moment the tiny babe in Rowène's arms responded to her ministrations and let out a single, mewling wail.

Then another, louder one.

And finally a full-blown cry that held all the music of life.

Taking a moment to thank the deity who had aided her that night, Rowène placed the blanket-wrapped bundle into Linette's trembling, eager arms, watching as the princess instinctively guided the little mouth to her breast, tears of unfettered emotion coming to the eyes of every woman in the room.

Only then daring to look at Joscelin, Rowène saw him fighting to keep his own feelings from showing on his face as he took first one, and then another unsteady step towards the bed.

He cleared his throat but plainly could think of nothing to say that would not immediately give himself away, his eyes remaining fixed in wide, unwavering wonder on the pale, unkempt woman in the stained linen shift, and the babe, still covered in blood and birthing fluids beneath its blanket, that she held to her breast.

By the look on Joscelin's normally unreadable face, it was the most beautiful, glorious and heart-binding sight that he had ever seen.

Then, even as Rowène's overwhelmed mind was wondering how best to contrive to divert Adèle's suddenly frowning gaze from Joscelin's face, Luc stepped between them, breaking her line of sight and deliberately drawing her attention to himself.

"Messire de..."

"You mistake me for someone else," he cut across her coolly in common speech. "I make no such claim to noble name or blood."

At the sound of his mocking voice Linette glanced up briefly, her gaze touching only on his dark grey robes without rising to his face.

"Thank you for bringing Joscelin to me," she murmured, her fatigue stronger than the flicker of confusion raised by his tone.

"I did very little, your highness," Luc said quietly as he watched her drop a kiss on the slick dark hair of the babe nursing at her breast. "If truth be told, he was already on his way."

He glanced across at Rowène, their eyes meeting in perfect understanding, as he added more grimly,

"As must we be."

"Oh, but surely you and Sister Fayla mean to rest and eat before you return to... Lasceynes, was it?"

"No, your highness, it is better that we go now. We have a long way to travel and it is less treacherous to walk the moors by daylight."

"Besides," he grinned humourlessly into Adèle's stormy blue eyes. "I think Madame de Marillec's stomach will be the more settled for my absence."

Clearly seeing the dawning comprehension and hint of uncertainty on Linette's face as the princess looked up again, he added with unerring and emotionless accuracy,

"As no doubt will you be too, your highness."

Then catching Rowène's eye,

"I will wait for you outside. Take as long as you must."

With that he bowed, turned, and was gone.

"I must go," she said distractedly to the room in general.

And giving Linette no time to protest – always supposing the bewildered princess had meant to make any – Rowène slipped past Joscelin's instinctively outstretched hand, following hard on Luc's heels, determined not to put him in any further danger by lingering over her farewells.

Almost, she stopped when she glimpsed the distress on the Eldest's face as she was forced to watch her lover's son and daughter walk away, ignored and outcast once more.

Then a moment later – catching the murmured request Linette addressed to her lady-companion and unable to resist the temptation to watch – Rowène *did* stop.

Only for a heartbeat, but it was enough.

So that the last thing she saw before the door closed behind her was the unguarded look of love and adoration on her brother's face as Adèle, her light blue eyes openly yearning, leaned forwards to gently place Mithlondia's youngest royal princess into the tenderly protective embrace of her 'Uncle' Joscelin.

PART II

SUMMER

1203

Verse 1

Summer Celebrations

Even as the frozen white of winter finally thawed into a green and vibrant spring, so the uneasy peace that had slumbered across the moors and fells melted away with it.

Once more the Black Hunt rode the rocky passes and rushy valleys, scattering flocks of spotted sheep across the grassy hillsides, ruthlessly searching every outlying hut and farmstead, leaving bloodied men, bruised women and terrified children in their wake.

Led by Oswin One-Eye – whose name had swiftly become as well-known and loathed in the northern provinces as his master's was in the south – the mercenaries who owed allegiance only to Black Joffroi and paid mere lip service to the notion that they answered to Prince Linnius and the Lords of the High Counsel, continued to sweep the hills and highways up to the very gates of Vézière and Lasceynes.

They stopped short of entering either of these towns, however, prevented by the forceful representations made in the Counsel Chamber itself by Nicholas de Vézière and Justin de Lacey against what they saw as unnecessary and unwarranted incursions into their demesnes.

As for Lasceynes Forest itself, though no writ prevented their entry, the men of the Black Hunt gave it a wide berth, finding it easier to bully peasants than summon up the steely courage required to tread the silent avenues of beech and chestnut guarding the edges of the greenwood, let alone invade the impenetrable and uncharted depths of dark holly and hoary oak. Not when the rash few who had dared it had never come out again.

In the midst of all this mayhem, Joscelin de Veraux did what he could to maintain the rule of law, though it was proving an unequal struggle, being on the one hand hamstrung by the lack of men – the campaigning season was underway and the greater part of the army was engaged in the fight along the Atarkarnan border – and on the other by the stranglehold Joffroi de Rogé and his lady maintained over Linnius' mind.

In spite of this, the Prince *had* shown some signs of independent thought, and renewed interest in the ruling of his realm, following the birth of his sister's child.

He had ordered days of feasting and celebration when Linette finally returned to Lamortaine under Joscelin's escort, accompanied by her two faithful lady-companions and the little princess Elanor Lysette de Mortaine – or as she was less formally known by those who loved her, Lilia.

The court, and indeed the whole realm, took their lead from Linnius and there was much joy in Mithlondia that spring, though the babe was not the heir everyone had hoped for.

And surely, the courtiers and gossips murmured one to another, Linette's next child would be a boy.

If, they added, as the season turned towards summer, Kaslander ever went to her bed again.

For it was a truth that gradually became known beyond the trusted circle of her lady-companions, that Kaslander – having been given the tacit freedom to lie where he wished during Linette's confinement – showed no sign now of playing the faithful lord to his lady, nor of being a loving father to his child. Indeed he appeared to regard both Linette and his daughter with the utmost indifference, and rarely went near either of them if he could avoid it.

Living deep within the protective embrace of the vast greenwood though she did, Rowène was not unaware of events happening further afield, and even while she could not help but worry about those she loved, she had her own life to lead and concerns much closer to home.

Not least her brother Luc, who seemed to become more remote with every day that passed, even as he strove to ensure the safety of the men, women and children who had followed him into outlawry and whose presence made the rough encampment a home.

Here everyone played their part, men and women alike, from Lady Anne, increasingly frail though she had become with the passage of the seasons, to Melangel and Gwynhere, and Rowène herself.

Only Caitlyn seemed to have no place, no purpose. Unfortunately, neither Luc nor Rowène trusted her enough to encourage her to make a life for herself elsewhere and so Caite remained.

In addition to her anxiety over Caitlyn's loyalties, Rowène had also to contend with her constant, underlying fear for Joscelin – walking as he did that narrow, thorny path between loyalty to his prince and loyalty to his outlawed kin, with the knowledge that at any moment he might be denounced as a traitor's bastard.

Then there was the more obvious danger to Ranulf, who faced death at the point of a barbarian blade every day.

And in spite of the manner in which they had parted Rowène could not help but be concerned about Guy – he was Lissie's father, after all – and what dubious fate Juliène might have in mind for him once her sister realised who Lord Nicholas' harper really was, as sooner or later she was bound to do.

She even worried about Gabriel de Marillec, the goddess alone knew why! No, that was a lie, she knew very well why. And she would not see Luc broken because Gabriel could not control his daemons.

Not that she did not have daemons of her own.

They lay in wait, cloaked in dark webs of terror, lurking in the hidden corners of her mind, striving ever to deprive her of the pure light that now and then illuminated her dreams, seeking to slay the hope she held in her heart that one day all would be well.

Barely a day went by when she did not think of Gabriel's words that night at Vézière when the Moon Goddess had thrown the protection of her golden veils around him.

Had that been a message of hope or doom that he had brought, the words deep carved in her mind through constant consideration.

That on the day the sun sets over a field of blood, and the Moon Goddess walks on silver feet amongst the living and the slain... when harper and healer stand together within her light... when the healing is done, and the last harp song... our song... is sung... then, and only then, will this thing be truly finished...

How that was to come about, Rowène had no way of telling.

For good or ill though, it served to strengthen her resolve – the resolve that had kept her going through all these years of outlawry that one day she would see her father vindicated, her brother restored to his rightful place – and the hope that she and Ranulf might yet be together...

Or if not that, since Mithlondian law would always hold them apart, that they might be able to watch Lissie and Val grow to live lives of their own in a realm where peace and justice were more than words, and where they would not be hunted as the misbegotten dregs of a traitor's spawn.

Sounds of childish laughter and shrieking echoed suddenly amongst the trees, firming her resolve, reflecting her hope and buttressing the cautious belief she held in her heart that all might yet be well.

Narrowing her eyes, she could just make out the pale blur of Val's hair through the summer green leaves as he hung head downwards over the branch of a chestnut tree... saw Lissie run to help Beowulf's daughter, Merry, to her feet when the toddler tripped over a root, rubbing a healing hand over the angry graze on the younger child's chin.

"All better now," she heard Lissie say comfortingly.

And it would be, Rowène knew. For Merula at least.

But Goddess! What was she to do about her daughter's gift, as dangerous as it was?

If that was not worrying enough, she heard Val yell something both bloodthirsty and crude at Wulf and Benet, his companions in the rougher boys' games they played, and felt her breath catch.

God of Light! What was she do about Ranulf's son?

The boy was running wilder with every season that passed without a father's presence in his life, and if not for Luc's firm hand on the boy's leash, she feared Val would be almost unmanageable.

Even so, Luc, however loving an uncle, was not the same as a father. Or at least not in Val's eyes.

He and Lissie would have seen seven summers this year and aware of just how fast the seasons had skimmed by, Rowène could not help but feel the next seven years might likewise be gone with the effortless ease of a swallow swooping after a fly.

If, of course, they had not all come to grief before then.

Best they make good use of what time they were granted, she decided grimly, before any part of Gabriel de Marillec's moon-mazed prediction became bloody truth.

Rowène was still attempting to salve the ragged dark edges of Gabriel's distant mind as she dropped down onto a stump at the edge of the clearing and abruptly found the gossamer connection between them broken.

Wondering slightly at the cause, she glanced up at the clear blue afternoon sky and with a sigh stretched the strained muscles in her neck.

There were, gods knew, any number of useful tasks she should be undertaking, but for the moment she did not particularly wish to do any of them.

Not on this first truly warm afternoon of the year, with the sun turning the new green of the leaves to jewel-bright gems and the sound of distant cuckoos calling-in the summer falling sweet upon her ears.

Breathing deeply, she allowed her abstracted gaze to settle on Beowulf, diligently engaged in fletching a new set of arrows outside his sod-roofed hut, and apparently paying no attention at all to her.

It was an illusion, Rowène knew. If the man caught so much as a whiff of a suspicion of a threat to her, the bow would be in his hands, arrow ready to fly.

Just as Edwy, presently engaged in a reasonably friendly wrestling match with young Aelric, yet managed to keep one eye on Val and Lissie, while Nick... she glanced around in time to see Luc and his bodyguard come striding into the clearing from the direction of the Daemon's Chain, a pair of coneys and brace of wood pigeons between them.

The scarred man gave her a nod and then veered off to take the game to Melangel and Caite at the central fire pit, leaving Luc free to drop down onto the grass beside her, stretching his long, booted legs out in front of him with a soft grunt as he lifted his face to the sunlight.

Before he could say anything, however, Lissie and Val came running up, almost as if they had been watching for his return.

"Uncle Luc, Uncle Jacques," they chirped together. "We want to ask you something."

Their *something* turned out to be an artfully innocent demand to know whether their kinsmen had decided how they were to celebrate their seventh-year days.

In all truth, Rowène had given very little consideration to the matter, and knew without even looking at her brother that Luc had thought nothing at all about it. Grandmère Anne and Gwynny would certainly have done so, however, having always managed to contrive something by way of celebration for each of the children of the forest, from Linnet, the eldest, on down to little Merula, the youngest.

"You took me to Vézière last year," Lissie reminded them a little plaintively.

"And we want to go again this year," Val said more bluntly.

He shot a look at Luc's face, evidently noted the sardonic rise of the narrow dark brows, and added hastily,

"If you please, Uncle."

"I had a new dress," Lissie continued.

She looked down at the kingfisher-blue rag of a gown she was wearing, her lip quivering a little.

"It's not new anymore."

Then she brightened.

"*And* we saw the princess. She was pretty and smelled like flowers. I showed her Popette and she... she asked about my mama."

The soft mouth was definitely trembling now but before Rowène could say anything, or do more than reach out a calloused hand to cup her daughter's cheek, Val put in rather more loudly than necessary,

"And *I* talked to the princess' bodyguard, *and* I held his horse, *and* he would have let me hold his sword if the princess hadn't called him away."

"Yes, well, even if we could go to Vézière, you are not like to see either Princess Linette or... or the guardian again," Rowène said placatingly. "The princess will be at the palace in Lamortaine with her babe, and all of Uncle Joscelin's soldiers are fighting up on the northern border according to the tidings Aelric brought the other day, and that includes..."

"Don't call him *the guardian* or *the soldier* like you don't know him," Val interrupted, his sun-browned face flushing with the temper he had so clearly inherited from his father, his voice rising angry and accusing. "When I know damned well you do!"

"Val!"

One word from Luc, his tone low but edged with steel, was enough to stop the boy.

Ignoring the oath, Luc waited until he had captured Val's sullen, stubborn gaze before continuing,

"Yes, we do know the guardian you were talking to. His name is Rafe, and he is one of your Uncle Joscelin's most loyal companions and therefore our friend, and because of that he is in great danger from those who wish us and your uncle ill."

He waited a moment, watching the boy's eyes widen.

"And now I have trusted *you* with his name."

"And me!" Lissie piped up.

"Yes, and you too," Luc confirmed, with the smile he could never quite repress around his niece.

"So can we go to Vézière?" Lissie asked again. "Even if we don't see the princess or Uncle Joscelin or..." She shot a smug look at her cousin. "Or Rafe, we still want to go, don't we, Val?"

"Aye, that we do."

He was looking at Rowène when he said this, the Rogé accent he had picked up from Beowulf and Edwy suddenly very plain to hear. Then he switched the focus of his attack.

"Pleeease, Uncle Luc."

Young though he was, he clearly understood that it was Luc who would make the final decision, Luc who was the head of their close-knit little family, as well as the outlaws' chief, and so he kept his gaze fixed firmly on his uncle, his eyes as innocent as the sunlit leaves whispering in the soft summer wind, as limpidly clear as the waters of a forest pool where only the fey ones ever swam...

It was that thought that jolted Rowène out of her state of drowning enchantment.

Damn the boy! He knew very well what he was doing. She could see it in the faintest shadow of calculation in the very back of his ingenuous green eyes!

It was rare indeed that she thought of Val as being anything but her own son, but just now she saw very plainly his true mother in him.

"Val, stop it!" she said sharply, and watched the illusion crumble.

No longer did her sister look mockingly at her out of those luminescent eyes, only the boy Rowène loved – bewildered and not a little frightened by the power he had obviously felt within him, and which at the moment quite clearly controlled him rather than the other way around.

She thought he might succumb to the brief mercy of tears and would have drawn him into her arms if he would have tolerated it. Instead he set his wobbling jaw and straightened his thin shoulders, looking so like Rowène's illusory visions of his father when Ranulf had been a boy playing in his mother's garden at Rogérinac that she could have cried herself.

"What about Lasceynes, Lissie?"

Luc's voice came to her from the distance beyond her dreams and she forced herself back to the forest clearing, reaching for the sunlight of the present time, anchoring herself to the birdsong and blue sky and wood smoke, and her brother's solid presence at her side.

"Would that not do just as well as Vézière?" he continued persuasively.

"Lasceynes is boring," Val dismissed the suggestion flatly.

"And we always go to Lasceynes," Lissie pointed out.

Then with a little more ingenuity,

"I really want to go to Vézière, Uncle Luc. The honey cakes are better there, and we haven't seen Grandmère 'Louise for a-ges."

Lissie had elongated the last word into a plea, her summer blue eyes taking on a doleful expression which, even though her mother suspected it to be exaggerated, nevertheless won the day.

At least with Luc, though none but Rowène would have known it from the stern note in his voice as he said,

"We will consider the matter and let you know our answer after the evening meal is done."

With the children clearly knowing better than to argue further, they ran off to rejoin their companions, leaving Luc to say reasonably,

"She does not ask for much, poor child, and it is true that she has outgrown her gown again."

"Yes, but Vézière," Rowène protested, not because she did not want to give the children the treat they so plainly hoped for, but because of the danger involved.

"Yes, I know," Luc replied, his voice hard. "And if it all goes awry, I will take responsibility for it onto my head."

"That will not be much comfort to me if anything should happen to Lissie or Val. Or to you."

Then with something of a wry smile,

"You *do* know that Lissie is trying to manipulate you?"

Her brother let out a short laugh that for all its harshness still contained a hint of humour.

"Yes, of course I do. Just as Val will always try to play on *your* heart-strings."

The glint of amusement faded from his eyes, leaving them cool and unreadable beneath dark quirked brows.

"Like father, like son, hmm?"

"One day, Luc, you are going to make one clever remark too many!" Rowène snapped as she came to her feet.

"And what is more, *you* are in a very poor position from which to throw stones!"

She started to walk away, then turned back to say,

"I am going to talk to Aelric. Since he only returned to the forest yesterday, he is the one who will know best what is happening out on the moors. And in Vézière too, like as not!"

The decision having been taken, it was on a soft day in early summer that Rowène set out once more for Vézière, her emotions in something of a tangle, anticipation rubbing shoulders with the inevitable lingering doubts.

Lissie and Val, whose state of high excitement admitted no qualms, rode along happily between her and Luc.

They were accompanied by Gwynhere, her placid manner and kindly face giving their party the unthreatening appearance of a normal family group, if one did not also observe Beowulf, Nick and Edwy riding in a flanking and rearguard position, whilst Aelric – whose tracking and spying skills, honed on the Atarkarnan border, were second to none – scouted ahead on foot.

Whatever reservations Luc might be experiencing on his own account, he hid them well, Rowène thought, his lean face with its heavier than usual stubble betraying nothing more than a keen, if guarded, observation of the countryside through which they passed, his expression becoming steadily more impenetrable as they rode through the town gates and into the market place... only to find the revelries, ribbon dancing and music that marked the summer festival well under way.

Rowène muttered an oath under her breath and would have retreated if she could.

Too late! Luc's look said, as his flat grey gaze met hers, leaving her to hope that amongst the assorted musicians, jugglers, tumblers, dancers, food sellers, liveried servants from the castle, and townsfolk dressed in their summer finery, the outlaws – clad in what passed for best with them – would pass unnoticed.

Particularly, she thought grimly, by the big, fair-haired harper presently taking a seat between a paunchy rebec player and a skinny lad with a flute who were playing for the girls dancing about the tall, beribboned pole set in the centre of the square.

Damn it all to Hell, she had known this could happen!

That Guy could be here!

Nevertheless, she had persuaded herself that the likelihood of him being in the town at the same time as they were was negligible.

Her assumption had been reasonable enough.

Her folly had been in forgetting about the festival when she and Luc had made their reckoning of the risks.

Now all she could do was pray that Guy did not set eyes on his daughter.

Or that Lissie would not come face to face with her father.

Setting his harp on his knee, and glancing at the laughing young women as they wove gaily-coloured strips of ribbon around the flower-bedecked pole, Guy could not help thinking that this was his favourite out of the Mithlondian calendar of celebrations.

The Kardolandians having their own gods and their own high days, he had missed all such festivities for the past five years, so that now he was resolved to make the most of this one, in whatever manner the folk of Vézière kept it.

It was not so different, he soon realised, to the summer celebrations of his childhood when Lord Jacques and Lady Rosalynde would invite the folk of the surrounding land – fishermen, hill farmers, even the healers from Silverleigh – to Rogérinac to partake of roasted meats and richly spiced cake.

As he remembered it, Joffroi had been overly inclined to grumble and sneer at the untrammelled enjoyment exhibited by folk who generally had very little to be cheerful about, before taking himself off elsewhere. The absence of his scowling countenance had certainly not been considered a loss by anyone.

Guy and Ranulf, however, had thought it wondrous fun to see the somewhat bleak castle on the cliffs come alive with laughter, to find themselves free of lessons for the day, to be allowed to eat standing around the huge fire burning in the courtyard, instead of being expected to sit quietly at the linen-covered table on the dais in the great hall and display the manners commensurate with their high birth.

They were young gentlemen, Lady Rosalynde had been wont to say to them in gentle rebuke for dirty nails, torn clothes and runny noses, before kissing them and sending them off again with a smile to enjoy themselves.

Young gentlemen or not, neither Guy nor Ran had thought much of the dancing – that was for giggling girls, and the grown-ups who would sneak off later to lie together in the soft grass of the headland – but after the contests to find the swiftest runner, the most cunning wrestler, the most skilled at tossing the ring or hitting a mark, Guy would wait for the moment when the setting sun rivalled the flames of the summer fire and Lady Rosalynde would take her small harp upon her lap and sing for those who might appreciate the more melodic music after the raucous, whirling gaiety of the day.

He and Ran would sprawl out on the ground at her feet, with full bellies and the odd bruise or two acquired from wrestling with the local lads, listening as the soft sea-scented dusk settled around them, until first Ran, then he, would fall asleep, untroubled as puppies, fine fair hair falling over brow and shoulder to mingle with the dust and discarded flower petals, not even waking when their father and Guthlaf came to carry them to bed.

They never had managed to stay awake to hear the end of Lady Rosalynde's singing, though each year he and Ran made a solemn vow to do so.

Then, when they were eight and Ran had already begun to think more of weapons than his mother's harp music, Lady Rosalynde had died.

Their father had continued to hold the festival every year. The heart was gone from it, however.

By the time Joffroi became Lord of Rogé there had been no money in the coffers, nor any inclination on his part towards merrymaking with the common folk of his demesne. Summer would come whether they celebrated or not, Joffroi had told his brothers the year their father died.

Except, it seemed, summer had never come again and when Guy had once half-humorously said this to Joffroi, all he had earned was a fist in the face and a dozen lashes from Oswin One-Eye's whip.

Ranulf, having more sense, had merely shrugged when Joffroi turned a black glare in his direction, and then spent the early part of the evening washing the blood from his brother's back and spreading some foul-smelling salve on it under Guthlaf's direction, before putting Lady Rosalynde's harp in Guy's hands while he himself had taken one of the servant girls out onto the headland in a bid to ease his own barely acknowledged feelings of frustration and sorrow.

Now, years later, Guy had a harp in his hands once more and he hoped that wherever Ran was, his brother would spare a thought for those long-gone days of carefree childhood. Before either of them had heard of the Faennari or foreseen the day when – somewhere in Mithlondia – a son or daughter of their own blood would even now be celebrating the coming of summer.

Guy was still idly thinking about the old days, as he packed his harp into its bag and slipped it over his shoulder. Lord Nicholas, who had come down to the square, accompanied by Cavall and Cub and his surly, over-protective manservant, had decreed a pause in the dancing to allow his musicians the chance to wander about and enjoy the festivities for a while.

Maury, who was a genial, gossip-loving fellow had disappeared immediately into the crowd, like a hound on a scent, dragging Aelfraed with him, while Beorn went off in search of beer, Halfiren choosing to remain close to Lord Nicholas, his fingers idly plucking a soft tune from the strings of his gittern.

Guy would probably have remained too, save that his belly was telling him it had been a long time since the dawn meal and the scents of chicken and herbs rising from the huge iron pan nearby had him heading in that direction.

Yet even such pragmatic concerns could not quite obscure the returning memories of his distant childhood...

Of the incoming tide washing over the seaweed-covered rocks beneath Rogérinac castle on a summer's evening, in and out, placid and rhythmic, a music in itself... shoals of little fishes darting in sun-warmed pools, mussels and whelks gleaming on the sides... and a little way off, two other barefoot boys, one as fair of hair as himself, but both scrambling sure-footedly over the sharp ridges of rock, startling the oyster catchers into flight, as they searched the pools for sea-stars and sea-gems and other impractical treasures, all the time keeping a very practical watch out for the red sails belonging to the pirate ships of the Eastern Isles.

They had been, Guy thought, perhaps ten years old then, and with no mother to see either of them decently clothed, he and Ran might have been mistaken as being of peasant stock as Edwy was rather than the Lord of Rogé's youngest sons, save no commoner would have had such long, light hair.

Hair Guy now kept clipped short, and for the most part concealed beneath a linen coif such as might be worn by any man in the more northerly provinces of Mithlondia.

That said, it was hot now in the middle of the day, and he would have taken the cap off if he had deemed it wise, to let what breeze there was riffle through his damp hair. Yet even here, surrounded by the friendly folk of Vézière, lulled by the mingled scents of summer flowers, cooking meat and honest sweat, he did not dare drop his guard.

It was not, he knew, beyond the bounds of possibility that Joffroi had set a spy in the heart of Lord Nicholas' fief, and Guy was of no mind to give such a one any cause to report to his master.

Not when he wanted to stay in Vézière.

He liked it here for one thing and Lord Nicholas was, even apart from his appreciation of music, a good man, fair in his dealings, and generous to those who served him well. Take today. He had made sure that all his retainers had received their quarterly wages, plus a bit extra, and then given all save a skeleton guard left up at the castle the day off to enjoy the festival.

Guy, with his board and bed provided for him and little reason to spend his coin – having no taste for gambling and even less for whoring – had accumulated a satisfyingly heavy purse during the three seasons he had served as Lord Nicholas' household harper.

He had brought some bronze marks and a silver half-noble or two with him today, leaving the bulk of it untouched beneath his pillow.

For Lissie.

Though only the gods knew when, or if, he would ever be granted the opportunity to give the money to his daughter or her guardians...

Becoming aware of the darker direction his thoughts had taken, he made haste to banish them, refusing to permit such grim speculation to spoil his pleasure in the day, his eyes seeking out instead the bright crown of flowers topping the dancing pole, the ribbons beneath lifting and fluttering in the slight breeze, unclaimed until the dancing should begin again.

Finishing the bread and herb-flavoured chicken, Guy licked the last smears of sauce from his fingers before wiping them dry on his tunic hem with a rueful apology to Lady Rosalynde's wraith.

A mug of good ale would wash it all down rather nicely, he decided, as he headed across the square to the trestle set up in front of the

Wheatsheaf. And then, he told himself, he really should return to his duties. He was no longer a carefree child, nor yet a high-born nobleman with nothing to do than look on and enjoy the pleasures of the day. No, he reminded himself, he was in service to the Lord of Vézière and should be earning the coin he had already received.

Yet when he did stroll back to the place where Lord Nicholas was sitting, face lifted towards the sunlight, he did not have the chance to do more than take out his harp before a brusque gesture from Eadric told Guy that his presence was required.

No sooner had he approached the cushioned chair that the guildsmen of the town had set up for their lord's comfort, Nicholas de Vézière dismissed his hovering manservant, bidding Master Finch to fetch his stool over and be his eyes for a while, Eadric having all the lyrical imagination of a bad-tempered turnip.

This last was said softly though, for Lord Nicholas was keenly aware of the devotion displayed towards him by his irascible servant.

Despite Guy's surprise at the request – though on reflection he did not know why he should have been when had already observed the interest Lord Nicholas continued to take in his people's affairs, his lack of sight notwithstanding – and with his own thoughts still floating pleasantly, lulled by heather beer and the distant music of that long-ago tide lapping the shores of his boyhood memory, he let his fingers stray to the strings of his harp, the small, rippling notes providing a lyrical background to his more prosaic words.

Finally Guy drew to a close, and in the ensuing silence the sound of a hand cracking across a cheek, followed by loud laughter and ribald commentary was probably more noticeable than it might ordinarily have been.

"What is that?" Lord Nicholas asked immediately, his head cocked as if to compensate for his lack of sight.

Guy glanced in the direction of the curfuffle, grimacing slightly when he realised what was happening.

"There appears to be some sort of altercation taking place outside the C..."

He cleared his throat.

"Outside the brothel, my lord. Between one of the women of the house and, I would assume, some man known to her through her profession."

"Indeed," Lord Nicholas murmured. He exhaled heavily before continuing,

"Between you and me, Finch, I should be loath to close it down and deprive the women of their livelihood, but this is not the first time they have made the place notorious. I am sure your fellows have acquainted you with the gossip?"

"Yes, my lord," Guy agreed. "Apparently one of the... patrons fell over the balcony rail during a fight with another man, or so Maury said."

"Smashed his head against the cobbles, just like an egg... or so I was told," Lord Nicholas replied pensively. "Which was unfortunate for him. Worse, he landed right at the feet of Lord Joscelin of Veraux, and as the man responsible was one of his own guardians and the dead man, so I later learned, some weasel in the pay of Lord Joffroi of Rogé, it caused quite a stir in the High Counsel."

"I should imagine it did," was all Guy could find to say, though the mention of his older half-brother had made his gut tighten uneasily.

"Indeed," Lord Nicholas continued. "I learned later that the guardian, who according to my son was rumoured to be of some bastard Valenne blood, had barely escaped hanging for murder. Instead, the Counsel sentenced him to five score lashes at the hand of the man who now so infamously leads the Black Hunt."

Guy, with nausea and premonition mingling with memory to form a bitter bile in his already cramping belly, said with as much indifference as he could muster,

"I do not suppose you know this guardian's name?"

"I believe Hal did mention it but it has slipped my mind for now." Lord Nicholas frowned. "Is it important, Finch? Do you know the man?"

"Perhaps. If it is the man I am thinking of."

Unwillingly he recalled a summer's day five years before, sunlight flickering through poplar leaves above the Marillec highway, blood dappling blond hair, broad shoulders braced to the cut of the lash.

Remembered also the gusto with which Oswin One-Eye had wielded his whip of old, when the man had been merely one of the Rogérinac garrison soldiers, long before his greed for blood had led him to became Joffroi de Rogé's head henchman.

Oh yes, I know Oswin One-Eye.

As for the soldier de Marillec had flogged...

"Rafe! That was it, I knew it would come to me."

Lord Nicholas sounded triumphant.

Guy just felt sick.

"Rafe of Oakenleigh," the old nobleman continued. "That was the guardian's name. Does this have some significance for you, Finch?"

"No, my lord."

Except that I look sufficiently like this Rafe of Oakenleigh for the Eldest to mistake me for him!

As if sensing what Guy had left unsaid, de Vézière turned to regard him with a bland, blind gaze.

"They tell me you have something of the Valennais colouring yourself, Finch?"

"If I have, 'tis not something in which I had any say, m'lord. All I can tell you is that my mother was regarded as a whore by the kinsmen who turned their backs on her, and that she died soon after giving birth to me."

And not one word of that a lie, he reflected.

He did not think Lord Nicholas would make any comment on his history, which was by no means out of the ordinary in Mithlondia, but even if the nobleman had meant to enquire further, a clear piping voice made itself heard first.

"Gwynny, why is that lady kissing Uncle Luc? If she's sorry she hit him, she shouldn't have done it in the first place and made everyone stare. I don't like her, Gwynny, do you?"

Lord Nicholas turned as if to see the speaker, then tilted his head back towards Guy.

"Can I assume from the child's observation that peace is at least partially restored?"

Guy glanced briefly in the direction of the brothel and the couple clasped in close embrace – Mistress Cherry, he assumed, from the resplendently bright colour of her gown, and a man he could see only to be above the average in height and dark of hair.

"It would seem so, my lord."

"And thank the gods for that," the old man sighed. "I would not have such a merry day spoiled by discord or complaint. Particularly when those particular women are involved."

He smiled slightly.

"Do you remember that incident last winter? The day of the first snow-fall, it would have been?"

Guy remembered the day of the first snow-fall all right! That had been the day he had seen Rowène de Chartreux for the first time in six years and let her walk away from him, taking the truth with her.

"I had the head guildsman up at the castle," Lord Nicholas was saying. "Complaining because some lout was running amok in the town. What he expected me to do about it when the lad was long gone and the healers had made no complaint of theft or disturbance within their walls, I do not know."

"Oh, the collapsed privy. Yes, I remember Maury telling me about it."

Maury had laughed so much when regaling his fellow musicians with the tale they had all thought he was going to choke, and even Guy had managed a smile, though the gods knew he had not felt much like smiling that day or for many days afterwards.

Even now he had not forgotten the bleakness in the grey eyes of the woman he had loved, her beautiful dark flame hair completely concealed beneath the white linen headrail, the fresh scarlet of the blood-beaded scratch on her sun-freckled face, the bandaged hands she had hidden in her wide sleeves...

Something nagged at him. The same annoying something that had been nagging at the back of his skull ever since he had returned to Mithlondia. If only he could see what it was...

"Finch!"

Guy shook off his irritation as a horse might a fly, careful to keep his frustration from colouring his tone.

"Yes, my lord."

"I would know more about the child I heard just now. A girl-child, I think, but not I would judge by her accent one of my folk. Is she still close by?"

Even though he knew Lord Nicholas could not see him, Guy kept his surprise from his face, scanning the crowd with an inward sigh. The square was filled with children, at least half of them girls, and he had not seen this particular one after all, only heard her voice.

Then, suddenly, he heard it again.

"Please, Gwynny, it is *my* day after all, and Uncle Luc said I might choose something for myself."

"Well, it is my day too," put in another voice, this one belonging to a young lad, Guy thought. "And what you want is just silly. Almost as silly as..."

"Ah!" Lord Nicholas said with a smile, as the boy broke off with a subdued grunt. "Siblings then by their squabbling. Can you see them, Finch?"

Casting around him, Guy saw them almost at once.

A little girl of perhaps six or seven, dressed in a faded kirtle of what might once have been kingfisher-blue and which now was too short in sleeves and length. She was holding the hand of a woman whose gentle loving face and soft brown eyes made the shabbiness of her attire unimportant.

A boy of about the same age as the girl was standing close by. Clad in much-mended brown breeches and a shirt of holly green, he stood with legs apart, arms folded defiantly across his thin chest.

Both children wore the linen headgear of the northern provinces and each was glaring at the other. Definitely brother and sister, Guy thought, deducing from their garments and general appearance that they were of poor, if respectable stock – possibly moorland folk – come to Vézière with their kin for the day.

Except Lord Nicholas, whose ear was almost as finely tuned as Guy's own, had said they were not from around here.

Moreover, the children were quarreling in earnest now, not minding their words, and it was very plain indeed from their speech that they were from somewhere other than Vézière.

Then the boy spat a word that made Guy start.

Very, very far from Vézière, he amended with a frown, as he heard what was definitely a man's voice, chiding the boy, his accent much more pronounced and all too recognisable to one who had grown up hearing it spoken all around him every day.

"Go, Finch, see what they are about," Lord Nicholas instructed, his mouth twitching in amusement.

Approaching the small group gathered in front of a bird-seller's collection of cages, Guy had a moment to observe them all before they were alerted to his presence.

As well as the two children and the woman, there was a man – the one Guy had already heard, and now saw with no surprise at all to be broad-shouldered and brown-haired, clothed in the same rough fashion as the boy before whom he was kneeling.

Indeed, the only surprise as far as Guy was concerned was the unexpected presence of the Eldest of the Sisters of Mercy.

"Ah, Master Finch!" she said now, and while her voice was soft and welcoming, it had the same effect on her companions as a falcon's scream.

The respectable-looking woman – who he now belatedly recognised as Gwynhere of Valéntien – turned the wide brown eyes of a startled hind in his direction, her clasp tightening on the little girl's hand.

The man tensed and slowly straightened to his feet.

Then even more slowly turned to face Guy, one hand coming to rest on the boy's shoulder. Tension hardened his mouth and bearded jawline but he said nothing.

He did not need to.

Guy had already heard him speak, had known him by his tone and accent long before he saw the other man's face.

"I thought I recognised your voice," Guy said now with deceptive calm. "How are you, Edwy?"

"Well, Master G... Sir."

His boyhood friend and former bodyguard choked off any further incriminating statements, whilst the relief Guy had first felt on realising that Edwy had escaped Joffroi's violent eradication of anything connected to his bastard half-brother yielded to the overwhelming weight of suspicion now pressing down on his skull.

A suspicion that had him staring beyond Edwy, sorting through the shifting mass of faces in the crowded square, almost immediately catching sight of the man he had seen with Mistress Cherry earlier. Then Guy had only seen the back of his head.

Now, as he grimly identified Lucius de Chartreux's outlawed son, a flicker as of sunlight glancing off chestnut hair made him look for Luc's younger brother, and in so doing Guy saw yet another face he knew, that of Beowulf of Mallowleigh.

It was entirely conceivable that Beowulf should be here at the same time as the outlawed de Chartreux brothers.

But as to what Edwy was doing in Vézière was a mystery to Guy. Let alone in company with a child who used the gutter vernacular of Rogé no less. That the man had settled down to an honest trade, with a family of his own seemed... unlikely.

"Your children, Edwy?" he remarked now, keeping his tone as pleasant as the summer breeze.

"Only if ye're bat-blind or sodden drunk!" came the reply, blunt as a bludgeon, before the man clamped his mouth shut tight as a trap.

Aware that he would get no more from Edwy, Guy looked at the Eldest, willing her to tell him what he wanted to know. This time, damn it, he meant to have the truth.

"Not here!" she said suddenly, discarding her serene silence as if she could read his mind. "Not now!"

"Then where?" Guy demanded. "And when?"

"Come to the Healing House tomorrow."

"By which time the birds will have long since flown," he said softly, his narrowed gaze telling the Eldest that he knew well what she was about. "Will they not?"

"See, it's not silly. *He* said it too. So I don't see why I can't do it!"

The little girl's impatient statement took him – and apparently everyone else as well – by complete surprise, and as all eyes were directed at her, the boy said scornfully,

"He wasn't talking about that, Silly! And it's still a silly idea."

"What is?" Jacques de Chartreux asked, coming to stand between the two children, giving Guy no more a hunched shoulder and a single, unreadable glance.

"*She* wanted to let all the birds out of their cages," the boy said. "And if that's not..."

"It's *not* a silly idea!" came the tearful interruption. "Is it Uncle Jacques?"

"It is when we don't have any money," the boy pointed out before that young man could reply.

"We have got money, so! Otherwise Uncle Luc wouldn't have said I could have a new dress. Well, I don't want a new dress. I want to set the birds free."

"That's..."

"Don't you *dare* call me silly again, Val! You know Rafe said you weren't to. Or be unkind to me. Or... or..."

"That is quite enough! From both of you!"

Luc de Chartreux's voice effortlessly quashed the developing quarrel, and effectively cut through the complete and utter sense of disbelief currently clouding every corner of Guy's mind.

"Nobody here wishes to listen to your squabbling. Nor do I see the need to discuss how much or how little silver we can muster between us."

"But I only wanted to..."

"*No, Lissie!*"

And there it was!

Of course, Guy had suspected who the child must be, almost from the start of this increasingly surreal encounter.

But this... this was stark, uncompromising confirmation.

From Luc de Chartreux's own mouth.

And the boy, Val, must surely be Ranulf's son...

Yes – Guy spared a brief glance at the boy – now he was looking for it, he could see his brother in every line of that youthful face... catch an unmistakable glimpse of the black de Rogé temperament in the scowling expression.

But it was the girl who held the better part of Guy's attention.

Clearly upset by her kinsman's stern voice, she had turned to bury her face in Gwynny's skirts.

Look at me, little one, he begged silently.

As if she felt the gentle tug of his thought, she turned around and looked up at him.

And he knew.

Oh, gods! It is true then!

She had her mother's face, the skin faintly golden from the sun or her Faennari blood, the pure lines of the high cheek-bones and the long nose softened by youth but still the same lineaments he could see in her uncles' far harder features.

The eyes below the dark gold brows were not the distinctive de Chartreux grey, however.

They were the light blue of the summer sky at dawn, shimmering with a sheen of tears like sunlit rain.

Guy had not looked in a mirror for years. Nor did he need one now to know that his eyes, even without the tears, were the same shade of blue.

Or perhaps he did have tears in his eyes, he did not know.

The one thing he did know was that his daughter was returning his stare with an intensity that rivalled his own.

"I know you," she said suddenly. "You were playing with the other minstrels."

Then, the confidence abruptly leaving her voice, she almost whispered,

"You... you had a harp. Is... is it your own, sir?"

"Yes, it is," he replied, not understanding her unexpected descent into diffident formality, only that his answer was important to her.

"Why do you ask, lass? And please... please do not call me *sir*. I am... just a harper."

She simply shook her head, looking almost as overwhelmed as he felt, and slid a sidelong glance at her cousin who was staring at him with a fierce concentration, his thin mouth set hard, his thick fair brows drawn together in a manner Guy recognised with a painful twisting in his gut.

It was, he found, more than a little disconcerting to see Juliène's green eyes staring at him so unwaveringly from that youthful face instead of his brother's dark blue gaze, when everything else about the boy proclaimed from earth to sky that he was Ranulf's son.

"You look like..." Lissie's soft, shy voice drew his attention partially away from her cousin.

"Like someone else we know," Val intervened abruptly.

"And who might that be?" Guy asked evenly, thinking he already knew the answer.

He wished to the gods that one of her kinsmen would close down the conversation.

Yet at the same time he found himself hoping desperately, selfishly, that they would not... wishing that there might be some way to hold on to this moment without enacting it under the gaze of every man, woman, child or cat who should chance to wander this way.

"Just a soldier we know," Val answered, just as the great, golden form of Cub padded past Guy to sniff at the boy's hand, the hound's presence warning enough to Guy that Lord Nicholas himself must be close by.

"And this soldier's name?" Guy asked gently.

"Rafe," Val answered grittily, after a fleeting glance at his uncles. "But *why* do you look like him... sir?" Val continued, his fingers absently playing with Cub's ears, neither the presence of the Lord of Vézière nor the manners obviously bred into him by his uncles strong enough to prevent the question, nor his determination to have an answer.

Guy hesitated, sent a quick, searching look at the two de Chartreux brothers – the elder grim, the younger pale – then at the two Rogé men, reading the truth in four pairs of eyes that held the same grim expression.

It was a truth he should have known from the start... *had* known from the start, even if he had not admitted it.

252

Now it seemed the time had come for him to do so openly, with Lord Nicholas as witness like as not, damn it all!

He took a breath.

"Because, Val, improbable as it sounds, your fa..."

A sharp shake of a head, just glimpsed from the corner of his eye gave him pause and he quickly amended what he had been about to say,

"Because *your* Rafe, Val, is most likely *my* brother."

What might have followed – whether wary reconciliation for the sake of two innocent children, or the breaking of a violent verbal storm between Guy and those he believed had wilfully deceived him – was lost in what actually did happen.

Completely without warning, a manic shriek made itself heard over the merriment in the square,

"Told ye, I did! There he be! Luc de bloody Chartreux! An' his men wi' him! Cursed traitors all!"

Between one breath and the next, the joyous celebrations in the square descended into a chaos of screaming women, scattered children, overturned stalls, trampled flowers, torn ribbons, and outraged bellows as, with sparks flying from iron-shod hooves and steel blades flashing in the sun, more than a dozen men of the Black Hunt bore down on the corner of the square where the outlaws stood.

With very little chance of escape, Luc snapped a command at his companions to disperse as best they might, thrust Lissie and Val in the direction of Gwynny and Sister Herluva and then set off at a run, first towards the Black Hunt and then, when he was sure he had their undivided attention, in the opposite direction, deliberately drawing Joffroi's hunters after himself and away from the women and his sisters' children, a burly, whip-scarred man Guy had not noticed before pushing through the crowd to follow at his heels.

Seeing that Edwy, Jacques and Beowulf still hesitated, Guy instinctively snapped a command at his former retainer,

"Edwy, go! The children will be far safer without the complication of a Rogé turncoat's presence."

He would have repeated a variant of the same advice to Jacques save that he could see from the stubborn look on the youth's beardless face that it would not be taken, and instead turned his attention towards Beowulf.

"Get your master out of here. Now! Unless you want to watch him hang as a bastard offshoot of a traitorous family tree!"

Good, sound advice, seconded by the Eldest as she laid a trembling hand on the young outlaw's arm.

"Go, Jacques. Gwynny and I will take care of the children. The Black Hunt will not look at them or us if you are not here."

And indeed such reasoning might well have produced the desired result – if the roiling tide of the panicked crowd had not surged into their midst, separating the children from their protectors and each other.

There were horsemen all around them now, weapons catching and splitting the sunlight, their horses rearing with rolling eyes, lethal hooves cutting the air before dropping down to pound the ground, and anything so unlucky as to be in their path into minced meat.

Ignoring his unarmed state and cursing Joffroi's ambition and his bloody minions with equal viciousness, Guy fought his way through the fretting, sidling, sweat-streaked, spur-goaded horses, determined to find and protect his daughter and Ranulf's son...

Saw, from the corner of his eye, a black rider bear down on Val and the Eldest.

Even as Guy caught his breath to shout a warning that would probably never be heard in this mad medley of ear-battering noise, was forced to watch, powerless to prevent the violence or the indignity as the Eldest of the Sisters of Mercy of Vézière – a healer whose grey robes should have afforded her some protection, even with these shit-scum maggots – was knocked carelessly aside when she dared to stand in their way, while Val was simply swallowed up by the hungry maw of the mob.

Mistress Gwynhere was down, as well, Guy saw, his fury surging anew, though she had some protection in the form of a lean, feral youth who appeared from nowhere to stand over her, knife in hand, slashing and snarling at anyone who came within reach of his blade or vitriolic tongue.

Casting frantically about in the ever-changing tide of movement, Guy saw a scrap of kingfisher-blue, lost it again, ducked under a sweeping cudgel blow, taking it on his shoulder instead of his skull... and was granted another momentary glimpse of Lissie, her small hand held safely within her kinsman's tight grasp.

Rashly, Guy allowed himself a sigh of relief.

This turning within a heartbeat to bowel-loosening terror as he saw Jacques and Lissie torn apart... heard the outlaw's frantic desperation vibrate in his own bones as they searched from opposing sides of the melee for any sign of the lost child.

They were both calling her now, and even in these extreme circumstances there was some note in the outlaw's high, strained voice that was odd enough to catch Guy's attention.

"Lissie! Lissie, where are you?"

With Jacques' frantic words echoing above the roar, Guy spared a single, shocked glance through the black wall of bodies at the white-faced outlaw... then put all his strength, all his attention where it was most needed, his own voice hoarse with a heart-stopping fear as he added his own harsh calls to the tumult,

"Lissie!"

There! He could see her now!

She was on the ground, perhaps a dozen yards away, her small body having been sent flying by the force of the surging bodies.

And, gods! She was not moving!

All around her horses were circling, stamping, rearing, spurred into madness by their riders who shouted and cursed and laid about them with blade or staff. She could be trampled at any moment in that hell-wrought whirl of steel and iron-shod hooves.

With no time to think and certainly no time to look again at the slender outlaw fighting like a crazed animal to get to its cub, Guy dragged the nearest rider from the saddle, grabbed the trailing reins, hauling the maddened horse out of the way by brute force, and shouldered through into the heart of the seething, heaving mass, seeing the daemons of death staring at him out of every rolling dark brown eye, catching their reek in every pungent breath, hearing it in every whistle of a descending weapon, every grunted curse, every crack of iron on stone...

Saw the huge hoof about to stamp down.

And flung himself over his daughter's crumpled body.

Pain shot through him at shoulder, knee, buttock and temple.

The last thing he heard was a woman's voice screaming his name.

His true name.

"Guy! Oh, gods! Guy!"

Verse 2

Master Finch & Mistress Lissie

Guy woke to find his eyes stabbed by a thousand shafts of spear-bright light... and immediately shut them again in self defence, holding them closed for a dozen heartbeats, then with an effort forced them open enough to be able to squint through his lashes.

He tried to move, discovered his body to be one throbbing, stiffening sore, vaguely felt the cool rim of a cup being held to his lips, heard a soft voice he thought he should recognise urging him to drink, and having managed to swallow some of the liquid carefully dribbled into his mouth, lay back on the bed, dropping down once more into a featureless void.

The next time he woke he discovered he could open his eyes without inviting an immediate surge of nauseating agony, and further, that the blinding golden light – which previously had been a seamless extension of the pulsating pain that had assailed his aching head – had now dwindled to the draught-driven flicker from the single night candle, its soft light subtly illuminating the grey-clad healer seated by his bed, chin resting on her breast as she dozed upright, her back against the wall, the white wings of her wimple falling forwards to conceal her face, her small, capable hands folded in her lap.

Even so, he knew her.

Or rather, he knew who she was not!

As it was, he could only hope that it had been no more than another part of his painful phantasmagoria that he had imagined Sister Fayla kneeling by his bedside all night... or day... or however long he had been lying here.

He did not want to feel under an obligation to her for *anything*, let alone his life.

Not when he considered what she – or rather the *she* who wore the guise of the healer's grey robes – had deprived him of.

Just now he did not want to think about that at all, since it hurt too bloody much.

What he did want – *need* – was a drink – well, he needed a piss too, but he thought that could wait – and with an effort he moistened his dry throat enough to say,

"Eldest?"

Immediately she was awake, turning towards him, the anxiety in her blue eyes softening into a smile.

"You are awake. How do you feel?"

"Thirsty," he croaked. "But better."

He drank gratefully from the beaker she held to his lips, tasting honeyed water rather than the bitterness of pain-deadening herbs.

"And at least I can see again, even if my body feels as if it has been trampled by a herd of maddened horses."

"That would be because you were," the Eldest reminded him drily. "In truth, I think the gods themselves must have held their hand over you, that you escaped with your life."

"Oh, gods!" he groaned, as he suddenly remembered it all. "Lissie?"

"Frightened, bruised. But alive too, thanks to you."

"And Val, and the others?"

"Safe for the moment. I must say, you missed an epic brawl when your wits were knocked out of your head."

"Between de Chartreux and his men, and my brother's scum?"

"At first. But seeing Val attacked and Lissie nearly trampled proved too much for the townsfolk to stomach. They began to join in with whatever weapons they could find – stones, staves, the dancing pole even, once Beowulf and Nick had uprooted it."

She smiled a little at the memory, before saying more soberly,

"By the grace of the gods no-one was killed, though there were bruises a-plenty to go around before the castle guard came down to restore order, and when Lord Nicholas could finally make himself understood, he turned the Black Hunt out of Vézière in no uncertain terms. They were battered enough by then to slink away without argument, their tails temporarily between their legs, but I am very much afraid that they have not gone far. And that they will be back with the full force of the High Counsel's writ behind them."

"But you said they were safe. The children. De Chartreux. His... brother. The rest of the outlaws? That being so, surely they are well away from Vézière by now?"

"No, not yet. Lissie, Val and Gwynny are here in the Healing House. The men are... elsewhere," she said, regarding Guy with a rueful smile. "I am sure you will forgive me if I do not tell you where."

"And Jacques?" he asked flatly, forcing himself to speak the outlaw's name. "Where is he?"

The serene blue gaze did not waver but he did see the healer swallow.

"He is here. With Lissie."

"Can I see her? Lissie, that is?"

"Yes, of course. They are waiting only for word that you have woken with all your wits still in your head. If you are ready, I will bring her to you now."

"I would rather you let me clothe myself decently first," he muttered as he struggled to sit up straighter in the bed, bare as the day he had been born. "And... er..."

The Eldest regarded him with something between exasperation and understanding before saying blandly,

"There is a chamber pot beneath the bed."

She rose to her feet.

"Now might also be a good moment to mention that Edwy is here also, since he is by way of being the children's bodyguard, a duty he feels he failed at most miserably yesterday. But since, as I understand it, he was once in your service in a similar capacity, perhaps you will have no objection to him serving you again."

"Even if I did, my lady, I doubt you would listen," Guy muttered as the door closed behind her.

Leaning back against the straw-stuffed pillow, he closed his eyes, which still had a disconcerting tendency to see double, opening them only when he heard the door, and looked up to see Edwy standing on the threshold regarding him warily.

"Come in and shut the door, for gods'sake!" Guy said, with as much of a snap as his fragile state permitted. "All you need do is help me out of this damned bed and into my clothes. Oh, and find that bloody pot for me."

"Aye, Master..."

"*Finch!* The name is Finch now, Edwy. And I am not your master. Not any more."

"No, sir," his former retainer replied. "Don't mean I can't keep an eye on yer little lass an' Master Ranulf's lad."

"You know then?"

"Not blind, am I?" Edwy retorted, with a flicker of scorn. "Growed up alongside ye an' Master Ranulf, I did. Course it didn't tek me long ter figure out which one of ye had fathered which one o' them. And there 'twas. Ye were gone, Master Ranulf were gone, one way nor t'other. Lord Luke offered me a place in the forest an' a task ter do. So I took it. An' I ask yer pardon, sir, fer failin' in that task yesterday. If 'twere not fer ye, the lassie 'ud be dead now, trampled inter the ground by yer bastard brother's pox-ridden scum."

"Setting aside Joffroi's legitimacy, you did *not* fail, Edwy. Or do you think I did not see you get Val out from under Oswin's whip before he could use it on the boy."

"Aye, an' if I e'er get wi'in bow shot or knife throw o' that one-eyed midden rat ag'in, I'll make him rue the day he dared ter think 'bout tekin' a lash ter the lad."

Since Guy felt much the same way, and knowing also that he had no real cause to quarrel with Edwy, he allowed the man to help him don his clothes and empty his bladder without further words, then sat back on the bed, breathing through the blinding pain that was once again hammering his skull and shooting fire through every limb, while Edwy went to tell the Eldest that he was ready for his visitors.

Whether he was ready in mind or heart was another matter entirely.

Looking up as he heard the door open, Guy found it impossible to do more than stare in dumbstruck silence, and while aware that Lissie was not alone, could not take his blurred gaze from his daughter long enough to see who those other someones might be.

He had thought he had control of his wits.

Had thought he was prepared for this moment.

The breathtaking reality of it, however, had him lurching with a subdued groan to his feet, putting a hand out to the wall to keep himself upright, and possibly to prevent his pounding head from rolling off his shoulders.

"Sit down, do, Master Finch," came the Eldest's gently scolding tones as she hastened across the room to his side.

"Afore ye fall down!" Edwy's low growl sounded in his other ear as he eased him back down onto the bed. "Aye, that's the way, sir."

Guy closed his eyes for a moment, then cautiously opened them again.

There was a blur of pale grey to his left – the Eldest, he thought – a blur of green and brown to his right – Edwy, without a doubt – and directly in front of him a blur of kingfisher-blue and gold.

Not a simple monotone gold either, but a shining, shimmering fiery gold, like a misty sunrise, or a waterfall shot through with the last rays of the setting sun.

"Master Finch?" It was a soft, sweet voice, overflowing with childish sympathy. "Are you still poorly? Grandmère 'Louise said you was feeling better, else she wouldn't have let us come to see you."

Ignoring the parts of that speech that remained incomprehensible, Guy put all his efforts into saying as reassuringly as he could,

"Indeed, I am much better now."

"You don't look it," Lissie said dubiously.

"Bloody right, he don't," Edwy muttered darkly, though hopefully the child did not hear that forthright assessment.

Guy felt the flutter of butterfly soft fingers touch his bruised temple and incredibly the sickening drumbeat of spiking pain faded to a more manageable level, a mere thrumming ache, while the distorted melange of blurred colours resolved itself into actual figures and faces, and at last he could see who was in the room with him.

The child, the healer, his former retainer and... that bloody lying outlaw!

Holding back his fury with an effort that brought sweat beading on his brow and nearly made him retch up the honeyed water burning like acid in his gut, Guy stared straight into the drowning depths of Jacques de Chartreux's grey eyes, and said bitterly,

"What are *you* doing here?"

"I came with Lissie, of course."

"Of course," Guy muttered.

"But before that Uncle Jacques was with *you*, Master Finch. Weren't you, Uncle? He stayed with you all yesterday and last night, when Grandmère 'Louise was called away, 'cos we all thought you wasn't going to wake up. But you did!" Lissie finished with a bright smile.

"Why did you stay?" Guy asked, still looking at the youth and wondering how he could not have seen the truth before.

His blindness was even more incomprehensible considering as he had already seen through another, different, mask.

"I thought I could help," came the emotionless answer.

"And you did not think you had already done enough?"

Despite his best efforts, Guy could not keep all the violent anger he felt out of what was otherwise a reasonably bland question. Then becoming aware of Lissie looking between him and her kinsman with puzzlement and dismay, added quickly,

"Perhaps you will allow me a few words in private before you leave. To discuss the debt I obviously owe you."

And saw from the flicker in the otherwise well-guarded grey gaze that the other understood well enough the nature of the reckoning to be made between them.

Gods give me the strength to see it through.

"Come along, Lissie, we must not weary Master Finch."

His eyes closed, it seemed to him that he heard the outlaw's voice from some great distance. As if many long leagues lay between them. As far away as Valéntien. Or Chartre. Or even the great palace of kings in Kaerellios with its marble pools and peacocks calling *pee-or, pee-or* under a blue, blue sky...

"Now would be the time to say what you came to say, Lissie." Jacques' voice came more firmly, recalling him to an even more bitter present. "And then we must rejoin the others and leave Vézière. We can go home, now we are assured that Master Finch will recover."

"Master Finch?" That was Lissie's voice, causing him to open his eyes again.

"Yes, Poppet?" The endearment slipped out before he could recall it.

Fortunately Lissie did not seem to mind or think it odd, though she did giggle and say,

"That's what I call my doll."

Then her little face turned serious, her dawn-blue eyes solemn.

"Thank you for saving me from the horses and those horrid men."

Unable to speak for a moment for the lump blocking his throat, Guy reached out and took her delicate little fingers into his own calloused hands, cradling them delicately as if they were tiny birds, then lowered his aching head to kiss them gently.

"I would give my life to keep you safe," he told her.

The child's eyes widened until all he could see was the blue of a summer sky. A Mithlondian one this time. Almost he could hear lark song, smell the heather of the high moors...

Until she broke the spell by saying,

"But I don't want you to die, Master Finch."

"Well," he smiled. "I do not particularly want to die either. Not when I have the notes of a new song in my head."

"What is it about," she asked, eager enough to be distracted. "Is it... is it about what happened yesterday?"

"It is about a little girl..."

"Me?"

"In a kingfisher-blue gown."

"It *is* me!"

"With eyes as blue as... as..."

"As yours!"

Again it was an effort to speak at all, let alone naturally.

"If you like. And hair like sunshine on a field of ripe wheat."

"Just like yours. Except mine is much longer."

"It is indeed."

It had been brushed out of the tight plaits she must have worn it in under yesterday's head-rail and it fell now in soft shimmering ripples to below the waist of her shabby gown.

"Val's hair is almost the same as ours," Lissie continued thoughtfully. "Though not quite. More like Rafe's, Val says. But then he would!"

She did not dwell long on the apparent iniquity of her cousin's obvious partiality before continuing,

"Most everyone else we know has brown hair. Not Uncle Luc, of course. That is black like... like the rocks of the Daemon's Chain, and sometimes Uncle Jacques' is as red as fire. Until he makes it brown again with walnut dye," she confided.

Grimly Guy refrained from looking beyond her at her kinsman, as Lissie – evidently catching the gently admonishing look directed at her by the Eldest – continued hastily,

"Anyhow, it's because our hair is so light that Uncle Jacques made me and Val wear those horrid caps yesterday. We only ever wear them when we leave the..."

She started guiltily as Edwy cleared his throat.

"Sorry, Master Finch, I'm not supposed to tell anyone where we live."

Guy thought there were probably any number of other things she had told him that her kinsmen would much rather she hadn't.

No matter. He would keep her trust. Nor would he press her to reveal anything she had categorically been told she should not.

"I forgot last year and told the princess," she whispered. "But I was only six then. I'm seven now. That's why we came to Vézière. It was supposed to be a treat. For Val and me."

Her mouth quivered and tears came into her ears.

"We didn't think it would be like this. You got hurt, and Rafe wasn't here, though I know Uncle Jacques meets him here sometimes."

"Oh, gods!"

The muttered oath came from the far side of the chamber.

Guy ignored it, never taking his eyes from his daughter's face as she continued tremulously,

"And then there were those horrid men. The Black Hunt. We thought they were far away, down in the Fells, else Uncle Luc wouldn't have let us come. But then they were *here*! And the horses were so big, and the men were shouting and slashing with their swords, and I was so frightened!"

Tears were running freely down her face now and Guy pulled her thin, unresisting body into his arms, letting her sob out her terror against his bruised shoulder.

"I lost Val, and Gwynny and Grandmère 'Louise, and then I lost Uncle Jacques, and all I could see were the horses and those horrid men, and I thought we were all going to die. And it would be my fault. Mine and Val's, 'cos we both wanted to come here. Uncle Luc wanted to take us to Lasceynes but... but..."

"Hush, now, Lissie. You are safe, and Val is safe."

He glanced over her shaking shoulder, eyeing her guardians with grim disfavour.

"Your uncles are safe, and Edwy is safe."

"As are the rest of your friends," the Eldest – Grandmère Louise, as Lissie had called her – added firmly as she put a scrap of linen in the child's hand.

"Now blow your nose, Lissie, rather than wiping it all over Master Finch's clean shirt. What will Lord Nicholas think of his household harper if he goes back to the castle with green streaks all over his shoulder?"

"It will match the green and purple bruises on my ar... er... backside," Guy whispered in his daughter's ear.

Lissie gave a choked sort of giggle and said,

"It's all right, Master Finch, Edwy says much worse things than that, and then Gwynny gets cross with him because she says Val and me shouldn't be hearing words like that. Except mostly I don't understand them anyway, though I think Val might."

Guy shot a glance at his former retainer's reddening ears and grinned, glad only that Lissie's tears had dried, even if the tension still sparking between him and her thrice-damned uncle remained.

Yet even as he stared bitterly into those wary grey eyes, Guy accepted that he could keep his daughter here no longer.

"Lissie, poppet, you have to go now. Back to your home, wherever that is. No," he held up a hand as she opened her mouth. "I am not asking you to tell me, I do not need to know. I only need to know that you are safe."

"And you are better now? Truly?"

"Truly," he confirmed, though his head was still a tight knot of contrary thoughts.

That maleficent tangle, however, was not something Lissie could cure.

"So this must be farewell, Mistress Lissie. One day perhaps we will meet again, and I will play your song for you. For now, may the gods go with you and give you joy in your seventh year, and beyond."

"Farewell, Master Finch, take care of yourself," she replied with grave courtesy, and turned to take the Eldest's waiting hand.

"Come along, Lissie, let us go and see if Val has eaten all the honey cakes or whether Gwynny has prevailed upon him to leave some for the rest of us."

A single look had Edwy following the Eldest and the child from the chamber, leaving Guy alone with the outlaw youth.

Or as Guy now knew her to be, Rowène de Chartreux.

The mother of his child.

The woman he now knew had betrayed him twice over.

For the count of sixty heartbeats there was silence in the candlelit room, neither of them seeming in any great haste to speak first, though the gods knew there was much to be said, and precious little time in which to say it.

Guy continued to sit on the bed, staring bleakly at the slender form clad in coarse linen shirt and sleeveless jerkin, the long legs concealed by soft boots and sturdy breeches, chestnut hair falling in tangled curls to her shoulders, her cheeks warmed to golden-brown by the sun and faintly freckled.

Despite his close study of the face and form he felt he should have recognised long since, he had to admit that there was absolutely nothing about her to betray her true identity. Furthermore, if it had not been for that moment in the square when terror for her daughter had shredded the protective enchantments that kept her safe from discovery, he doubted if he would ever have known.

She was waiting for him to speak, he realised, and below the apparently casual stance of the outlaw youth was the stillness of a hunted vixen hiding in the bracken waiting for the hounds to discover her scent.

Did she know she had betrayed herself back there in the square?

He thought she probably did. Rather than fling it in her face, however, he asked possibly the last question she might be expecting, yet one that was important to him just the same,

"What is Lissie's real name?"

"Alysiène Annette de Chartreux," she replied, without either hesitation or surprise.

"Ah! Some form of my mother's name and... your own, Rowène?"

He spoke her given name quite deliberately and this time he did surprise a flicker of something – consternation, perhaps? – in her suddenly narrowed gaze.

If she was disconcerted by this unexpected revelation of his knowledge, however, it was not apparent in her reply, a single curt word in affirmation of his guess.

"Yes."

What would it take to shake her control, he wondered.

Not him, obviously.

As witnessed by the fact that six years ago she – or rather the smooth-faced outlaw youth she had seemed – had ridden right past him in Valéntien, the infant Val in her arms, and given him not the smallest sign of recognition. A year after that she had faced him across a yard of steel in the governor's quarters in Chartre castle, and later yet, when their relative positions of power had been severely reversed, they had met again in the palace at Kaerellios. And it had been she who had healed his hand, bargained to get him out of the pools and into the queen's personal service.

She had done all those things, and all without giving him the slightest cause to suspect that Jacques de Chartreux was anything other than the outlaw lad he seemed to be.

Even when she had appeared to him a mere two seasons ago in a healer's grey robes, it had only been instinct on his part rather than betrayal on hers that had allowed him to see 'Sister Fayla' for what she really was.

Galling as it was, Guy doubted that he would ever have guessed that she had this second mask to hide behind. One she was so accustomed to wearing that it fit her like a selkie's skin. One moreover that no-one, least of all himself, would have suspected her of wearing.

Or... had he?

He remembered now that nagging sense that there was something about Jacques de Chartreux that he should recognise. Something... not quite right.

Yet it had just been too incredible to contemplate that the outlaw lad might not be a lad at all.

Even though he had seen her once, years before, riding astride, clad in boy's gear, for gods'sake! She had spent a month – a month, damn it! – with him on the harvest circuit, travelling the high moors and coastal lands of Rogé, and during that time he had watched her revel in the freedom granted by the simple exchange of her skirts for breeches.

Hell take it! With the force of that evidence in front of him, how could he *not* have realised the truth!

That said, it was not just him she was lying to, was it? If it had been, he thought he would not have cared so much, but she was lying to Lissie too. And that he did care about, very much.

It was that which finally set the embers of his anger blazing into life, turning his former mild tone to one of searing accusation.

"So exactly when, Rowène, are you going to start telling the truth?"

"Of what?" she asked as she straightened away from the wall, her grey eyes now distinctly wary.

"That Lissie is my daughter," he replied. "And when in hell's name are you going to tell *her?*"

For the first time her eyes would not meet his.

"I cannot tell you... either of you... that."

"Why? Because it is not true?"

"No, because I swore an oath that I would not."

"An oath to whom?"

"To your brother Ranulf, for one."

"You told *Ran*! But not me? For pity's sake, woman, did you not think I had *the right* to know I had fathered a child in a moment of unthinking madness?"

She went white, almost as white as she had been in the square, but did not bother to argue.

"Yes, you had the right. I admit it! Even so, I could not argue with R... with your brother that it was better for your peace of mind that you be kept in..."

"In ignorance! Of my own daughter's existence! Hell take the pair of you, you and my bloody interfering brother both! Gods above, did you think me so damnably weak that I would shatter like glass from the knowledge? If you remember, I grew up reiving alongside my father and brothers along Chartreux's border, and have seen and done many worse things than merely breaking an oath of fidelity to the woman who has never hesitated to cuckold me. More than that, what do you think I have spent the past five years in Kardolandia doing, if not whoring myself!"

"You had no choice in Kaerellios," she retorted, before a raw honesty forced her to add, "And little enough the night of the Mallowleigh harvest fire."

"So you forced me into breaking my binding oath, is that what you are saying? The gods know, I had broken it often enough in my mind so I dare say it took scant exercise of your enchantments to make my body yield to your will that night. And since we are being honest – or at least I am! – even had I known what I was doing, the truth is I should probably have done it anyway."

He smiled, entirely without humour.

"Set against *five years* of adultery, do you expect me to feel guilty over a single night I cannot even remember!"

"It was not just that," she protested. "If it had been that, I would have told you. But there is something else, a truth I only discovered when it was far too late. That you and Ranulf, Ju and I are all blood-kin within the prohibited degree for... for any physical union. Which makes Lissie and Val not only illegitimate but something far worse. And doubly dangerous when combined with their Faennari heritage.

So the fewer people who know, the easier it is to keep their secret. To keep *them* safe."

His anger cooling somewhat at this pointed reminder that it was not he but his daughter who would suffer from any public acknowledgement, he contented himself with saying grimly,

"Even so, you should still have told me. *Me!* Not my damned brother who has run away from his own responsibilities for too long to have any say in how I deal with mine."

Breathing hard, he turned away, grappling for control over his temper.

"Please, Guy! I know you are angry with me..."

Against his better judgement he shifted his stance so that she was once more within his line of sight, regarding her with a hard-won dispassion that barely shielded the tearing pain beneath.

"Yes, I am angry with you," he agreed.

Gods! Was that his voice? Dull as weathered rock, lacking even a hint of the emotion that threatened to rend him apart.

For a moment he looked at her, from tousled chestnut hair to booted feet, only the soft dove-grey eyes remaining of the girl he had fallen in love with at Chartre when he was merely an itinerant harper, and a treacherous one to boot. He thought she had fallen in love with him. Yet it had all been so long ago and if she had become a fey creature he did not know, assuredly he had changed too.

"We had two seasons together," he said stonily. "During which we became..." He corrected himself. "I *thought* we had become friends, and then lovers, if only for that one damnable night. In the seven years since, we have met what... three or four times? I can understand that your feelings have changed, that you no longer love..."

"But I..."

"Do not say it! The time for lies is done!"

Something of his vast anger and hurt sharpened his voice, and only by some great effort did he manage to return to the level, emotionless tone he had affected before.

"As I said, I can understand that you no longer love me. As for the man whom rumour has it is your current lover... be very careful, Rowène, for you are playing with fire. In more ways than one."

He watched her flush, but she said nothing in defence, either of herself or the common soldier gossip said she was sleeping with.

The fact that Rafe of Oakenleigh was so much more than that merely made it worse!

Gods! She had left him for his own damned brother!

The one man he would never have believed could have betrayed him in such a manner. How *in hell's name* could he bear it?

And yet, he must. For he would not give either her – or his brother, for that matter – any hint of the depth of pain they had inflicted upon him.

So it was only when he was sure that he had his anger and hurt under control that Guy said coldly,

"Not, of course, that I care who you bed down with, provided Lissie is safe. You can sleep with the whole damned Mithlondian army if you want!"

He felt his temper starting to slip out of control again.

"What is important... what I really want to know... is why you felt you could not *trust* me? We are still kin, damn it. I would *never* have betrayed you!"

"I... know." She shrugged helplessly. "And I should have told you. Forgive me, Guy?"

Then, because he could no longer keep it within him any longer, he told her the bleak, hell-spawned truth.

"Maybe. One day. At the moment forgiveness is beyond me. What I feel... it goes beyond anger... deep, deep into an endless hell of hurt that nothing and no-one, least of all you, can heal. So... just go, get out, leave me alone to lick my wounds in peace. By the grace of the gods we will never have to meet again!"

So she had left.

She had no choice really. She could see how deeply she had hurt him, and while she had been able to ameliorate the terrible effects of the trampling he had sustained in protecting Lissie – Rowène could only hope he never realised just how close he had come to not regaining his wits at all – only time and distance would serve to heal the justifiable bitterness he felt towards her.

Leaving Guy was simply a matter of walking away from the Healing House. Leaving Vézière proved another matter entirely.

As the Eldest had feared the Black Hunt had not gone far away, and while excluded from the town itself by Lord Nicholas' edict, the hunters continued to prowl the lands all about, waiting for the inevitable moment when the outlaws would be forced to leave the protection of the town's walls.

Trapped but determined not to involve the blind lord of Vézière or the innocent townsfolk any further in his dangerous affairs, Luc had sent Aelric out to assess the likelihood of them being able to escape unseen.

Knowing her brother as she did, and the burden of responsibility that lay so heavy on his shoulders, Rowène shared his gratitude that no-one had actually died in the imbroglio, though there had been more than enough broken bones, bruised limbs and bleeding flesh to keep all the healers – including Rowène – busy for the rest of that disastrous day and beyond.

As it was, Rowène was unsure whether Guy would ever walk without a limp.

She had done her best for his shattered knee, but like the hand his older brother had so viciously maimed, there was only so much a healer – even a fey one – could do, especially when her main concern had been the kick he had sustained to his head.

Thank the goddess it had only been a glancing blow.

Even so, she had asked the Eldest to keep as much of an eye on him as circumstance permitted.

Though even if Guy did have further need of her skills there was very little likelihood that Rowène would be able to return to Vézière to tend the hurts of a man who clearly wanted never to see her again.

Always supposing she and her companions managed to get away at all – Aelric having returned from his scouting expedition with the expected tidings that the Black Hunt was watching every gate out of the town and that they had as much chance of escape as a rabbit trapped in a warren with a dozen ferrets at each exit.

It was not an analogy Rowène much cared for though she had to admit, looking at the grim faces of her brother and the other men, that Aelric was probably understating the case if anything.

This being so, she was still at the Healing House with Gwynny, Val and Lissie, even though Guy had gone.

He had left perhaps a candle-notch after their confrontation, limping heavily and with a frown carved deep between his brows, but insisting on returning to the castle nonetheless, whether to avoid any chance of meeting her again or because of some other reason Rowène could not say.

All she knew was that he had refused the Eldest's offer of Muriel the donkey, and so she had sent Edwy to follow his former master as inconspicuously as possible to make sure Guy did not collapse in the street.

He had not, Edwy later reported, but only because whatever was eating at him – here Edwy had given her a straight look, though otherwise refrained from speculation – had also fuelled his determination to stay on his feet.

Passing through the market square, however, he had altered his course, heading away from the castle and over towards the western end of the square.

"He did not see Luc or the others?" Rowène asked anxiously.

"Don't think he was lookin' fer them, ter tell truth," Edwy replied. "Arter all, he's got no quarrel wi' any o' them, has he?"

"Maybe, maybe not," Rowène said dubiously. "So what did he do?"

"Only told that fancy-arsed bird seller he wanted to buy all his stock, emptied his purse into the dirt at the little weasel's feet, an' ordered him ter open the doors ter all the cages.

"Bird seller, he protested, o' course. Told Master Guy he were drunk or mazed in his wits ter be throwin' down good coin, only to see it fly away. Master Guy, he jus' stands there, proud as only a son o' Jacques de Rogé can be! Like he'd forgotten as he weren't still governor of three provinces, wi' me an' a whole troop o' men-at-arms ter back his word. Or even when 'twere just him an' me an' Master Ranulf 'gainst the rest o' them shiftless buggers as made up the Rogérinac garrison."

Edwy sighed a little in recollection of those days, then after a moment or two, continued caustically,

"Bird seller, he twitches a bit, then does as he's told. An' as all them finches an' larks an' what-have-ye takes off in a whirr o' wings, I hear Master Guy say plain as ye please, *this is fer ye, Lissie*."

Edwy let the words settle into silence, before taking up his tale again, a faint, reminiscent smile lighting his hazel eyes.

"Well, after that, Master Guy he turns an' heads off ag'in. He's limpin' pretty bad by this time, an' as he goes past he says ter me as how p'raps he should ha' rid the donkey arter all. He's all done in by then, don't even try ter send me away when I gi'es him me shoulder ter lean on. So we gets up ter the castle, and damn me if Lord Nicholas ain't waitin' fer ter see him. An' e'en though Master Guy don't say nothin' 'bout who I be, jus' thanks me fer seein' him back safe, his lordship seems ter know wi'out bein' told. An' him as blind as a mole, so they say. Anyhow, his lordship gives me a message fer ye and Master Luke, that he wants ter see... well, mebbe not see exactly..."

"Edwy, just tell me what he said!"

"I were getting' there, Master Jacq," Edwy said reproachfully. "But I thought ye'd like ter know 'bout Master Guy settin' them birds free..."

"Yes, I did. And I thank you," she grinned. "When this is all over and we are safely back in the forest you may tell Lissie about it too." Her smile faded. "For now though, what did Lord Nicholas say?"

"Just that he wants all o' us, the little master and mistress included, ter come up ter the castle ternight. Says mebbe there's somethin' he can do ter keep his folk safe *an'* help us out at the same time."

Accordingly, just before the sun set and the curfew horn was blown, Luc de Chartreux and his various kin and companions were shown into the great hall of the castle, to find Nicholas de Vézière ensconced in his comfortably cushioned chair, alone save for the two great hounds sprawled at his feet and his household harper seated on a stool a little to one side.

As the doors closed behind them, Rowène saw Guy look up, his gaze immediately seeking out his daughter where she stood, clutching Gwynny's hand.

Laying his harp aside carefully, he rose to his feet, the faintest of grimaces crossing his bruised face and said quietly,

"My lord, they are here. *All* of them."

"Come forwards," Lord Nicholas said firmly, and when the soft shuffle and scrape of shoes and boots had ceased, he added, "I have given you safe conduct here tonight for one reason, and one reason only."

"And what might that be?" Luc asked flatly.

"To get you out of my town! In order that my people are no longer endangered by your rash and reckless presence," the old nobleman said sternly. "I could always hang you, of course. I would be within my rights, and would no doubt gain the approbation of the High Counsel for my actions."

Then his harsh expression momentarily softened,

"However, I would not wish harm to come to the children you have with you, and so I must choose another way, one that fortunately for you will give you another chance at life."

"Thank you, my lord."

Lord Nicholas cocked his head, his expression sardonic.

"For all your words of gratitude, I sense a coolness in you, young man."

The blind eyes seemed to move from face to face.

"Will you in courtesy tell me your name, and let those with you introduce themselves to me."

Luc regarded the old nobleman for a moment, shrugged assent, and then apparently remembering Lord Nicholas could not see him, said in Mithlondian with a slight bow,

"Very well, Messire, I am as I am sure you must already have guessed, Luc de Chartreux."

He nodded at Rowène who, after one fleeting glance at Guy's expressionless face, said in a tone that defied contradiction,

"And I am Jacques de Chartreux, Luc's younger brother."

And so it went first right and then left down the line, with the diverse tones and accents of Mithlondian common speech.

"Nick of Chartre."

"Beowulf of Mallowleigh."

"Gwynhere of Valéntien, my lord."

"Aelric of Anjélais."

"Edwy of Rogérinac."

And then finally the children, one so shy as to be barely audible, the other perhaps a little too loud.

"I am Lissie, my lord."

"And I am Val... sir"

At that, the grim expression on Nicholas de Vézière's face shifted subtly, and he smiled.

"Ah! The little lass who wanted to let the birds fly free. And the lad who thought the notion silly, eh?"

"Well, it was," Val muttered, though he was sufficiently intimidated as to make sure his words did not reach his host's ears.

"Quite a collection you have gathered around yourself, de Chartreux," Lord Nicholas said now. "Who would have thought to find men – and women..."

His gaze turned unerringly in Gwynny's direction. "From Chartreux, Rogé and Valenne bound together in... friendship."

"Why do you not simply say bound in reckless folly to a *traitor*," Luc interjected harshly. "Since that is what I am, courtesy of the High Counsel declaration that you yourself signed, Messire! Just as you signed the order that sent my father to the scaffold!"

"And it is because of that debt of dishonour," de Vézière said quietly. "That I am willing to help you now. I was wrong to agree to your father's arrest on nothing more substantial than Joffroi de Rogé's word, and while nothing I do tonight will bring your father back to life, nor restore your title or lands..."

"It may perhaps assuage your guilty conscience somewhat if you let Lucius de Chartreux's sons and grandchildren go free?"

While Rowène understood her brother's bitterness, she could wish he might soften the arrogance of his stance in the current circumstances, given that Lord Nicholas held them all in the palm of his hand.

Gods help them all if Luc angered the old nobleman beyond his present unexpected forbearance...

"No, young man, it will not ease my guilt. It is, however, the best I can offer you."

"Then for the sake of all my companions, but most particularly my sisters' children, I accept whatever help you can give us."

As Rowène breathed a sigh of relief, he added,

"And if we can but get away unseen from Vézière, you have my assurance that I will not put you or your people at risk again by returning."

"Uncle Jacques, does that mean we can't come back," Lissie whispered, pulling at Rowène's hand to get her attention. "That we won't see Master Finch ever again?"

Before Rowène could think what to reply, Lord Nicholas put in gently,

"Never is a long time, Mistress Lissie."

His hearing must be as acute as a hunting owl's, Rowène thought, wondering with some misgivings what else he might have heard.

"Then again, child, I notice that your... uncle did not make any promises on your behalf, only his own. So one day, perhaps, it will be safe for you to return to Vézière. If that day ever comes, both Master Finch and I will welcome you back gladly. Will we not, Finch?"

"Yes, my lord, most gladly," Guy said softly, and the look on his face was enough to make Rowène weep for the hurt she had caused him.

"Good."

So saying, de Vézière straightened in his chair, his voice taking on the authority of his position.

"Now to the matter at hand. Finch, will you summon Eadric..."

And when Guy had left on his errand, Lord Nicholas leaned forwards in his chair and said with a grimly conspiratorial smile,

"Every castle has its secret passages and portals – I am sure Chartre was no exception, eh, de Chartreux? – and Vézière's is more elaborate than most."

"Ah! The caves," Luc murmured.

"You know about them then?"

"Only that they exist. Your son told G... told me about them years ago, said he had tried to find the entrance but never could."

"And he still does not know where it is located," Lord Nicholas said. "And before I show you, I will have your word, de Chartreux, that you will not attempt to use this secret way again. Or pass on your knowledge to anyone else. Even..."

The blind gaze seemed to stare straight through him with a disconcerting clarity.

"Even someone as close to you as young de Marillec is reputed to be."

"My word, de Vézière," Luc said curtly.

"Can you speak for all those with you?"

"They can speak for themselves," Luc retorted.

A chorus of confirmations endorsed his sharp statement.

"Lissie and Val, however, are perhaps too young for such a heavy responsibility," Luc added blandly. "But Jacques and I will stand surety for them."

"So be it. Now, unfortunately, I cannot show you the secret ways myself. It is too long since I travelled them and in my state I would only slow you down too much. However, my body-servant Eadric knows what must be done, and you can trust him not to lead you astray. I have not told him who you are, of course. He may guess, but he will not know for sure. And now, if there is nothing else I can do... you have water, provisions?"

"We do."

"Very well, I hear footsteps. That will be Finch returning with Eadric. So now, I will bid you all farewell, and hope that if we do ever meet again it will be in happier circumstances."

They travelled the dripping caves and twisting tunnels by torchlight, Eadric at the front, Guy limping along at the rear, with the outlaws strung out between them, Lissie alternating between Edwy's arms and Aelric's back, Val disdaining to be carried at all.

By the time they reached the entrance and saw a light that was not the smoky red-gold flame from the burning torches but rather the murky grey of a misty dawn, it was not only Guy who was limping. Rowène was stumbling despite herself, and Gwynny was leaning heavily on Beowulf's sturdy arm. Lissie was asleep against Edwy's shoulder and even Val had succumbed to slumber, carried in Nick's strong, scarred arms as he walked close behind Luc.

Aelric of course had already disappeared, slipping past the shuffling line at the first sign of light, sliding from the cave's mouth with the sinuous silence of a marsh snake, to scout out the land before any of the others should venture outside.

"Right then, I'll be headin' back," Eadric announced abruptly when they were within a dozen yards of the cave mouth.

They were the first words he had spoken since leaving his master's side, and these begrudgingly uttered.

"I thank you for your guidance," Luc said, curt with weariness but courteous as a nobleman should be to one who has rendered him a service, however unwillingly.

Eadric gave a grunt that could have meant anything or nothing, and turned to head back into the twisting labyrinth of dark, dripping tunnels.

"Wait!" Guy said, putting out an urgent hand to stop the man as he went past. "Give me a moment, please."

Another grunt. Then,

"I'll wait o'er there. Don't be long, else ye'll be findin' yer own way back, Master Harper."

"Obligin' soul, ain't he?" Edwy muttered as he knelt on the wet, rocky floor to set Lissie on her feet, albeit he kept a solid, supporting arm around her.

"Wake up, little one," he murmured with a gentle insistence that baffled Rowène, weary as she was.

"Edwy? Are we there yet?"

The child yawned and blinked around in confusion.

"Aye, 'tis me, lassie. An' see here... yer da's waitin' ter bid ye farewell an' gods'speed."

"Edwy! For gods'sake!"

It came as a shocked snap from Rowène, followed by a disgusted growl from Guy,

"Damn it all, man! When did you get to be such a loose-tongued meddler?"

"Since I seen *ye* hurtin', an' a little lass of Lord Jacques' blood wonderin' why her da don't want her..."

"You know I do, curse you!"

"Then tell her so."

"It's not that simple, Edwy, and if you've been around *him*..." He flicked a lash-like look at Rowène. "As long as I think you have, you must know it too! You're not witless."

"No, I'm not!" The rough accent was suddenly far crisper. "Nor am I goin' to stand by an' watch while my... my *brother* damn it, is brought to his knees, his heart broken an' bleedin' out."

Silence.

The stunned silence of bemused surprise.

Then, as Rowène looked from one man to the other – Guy quite clearly as speechless as she was, Edwy looking defiant and sheepish in equal measure – the silence finally splintered into boundless possibilities as she spoke directly to Guy for the first time since he had dismissed her from his life.

"You did not..."

Well, of course he hadn't known! He was still looking like a beached fish as it was.

"Suspect?"

A shake of that fair head as he continued to stare at the man he had known all his life... and yet not known that they shared the same blood. She turned then to look at Edwy, her daughter still drowsy and soft as a sleeping kitten in his arms, and raised her brows in silent command.

Finish this. Now!

"Aye, well."

He cleared his throat, lapsing back into the rough accent she was accustomed to hearing from him.

"Ye knowed what Lord Jacques were like," he muttered, looking into his half-brother's eyes. "Did ye think ye was the only by-blow he got in more'n a score o' years o' wenchin'?"

"No, I... I just never thought that you were one of them."

"Aye well, tha's the diff'rence atween us. Lord Jacques acknowledged ye, ye ma being a high-born lady."

"And *your* mother?"

"A fisherman's daughter from Rogérinac village. Lord Jacques..."

"Don't bloody call him that!" Guy snapped. "He was your father just as much as he was mine. And don't you dare call me *Master* Guy again after what you've just told me. Damn it, Edwy, all these years... Why didn't you tell me before? You and Ran and I grew up together, for gods'sake."

"Didn't seem ter matter then. I reckon Ma were happy enough wi' the coin Lor... our father give her ter bring me up, an' after her died he had me brought up ter the castle an' given over ter Guthlaf ter train wi' the rest o' the garrison. It suited me better'n a fisherman's life would ha' done, that's fer sure, an' if he never told no-one as he were the one what sired me, I can't say as it bothered me.

"But it do bother Lissie," he said pointedly, bringing the subject ruthlessly back to the original starting point. "She knows her da is a harper, Master Jacq told her that much, an' havin' seen ye, how could she not wonder if ye was he? An' there ye are, denyin' it, an' bleedin' inside the whole time. 'Tain't right, M..."

A scorching look from Guy stopped him.

"*Guy*, damn it! You said it yourself – I am your *brother*! As is Ranulf, damn his lying soul. So bloody well get used to saying it all the time, Edwy! As for Lissie, the gods know how much I want her to know the truth, to tell her openly that I am her father but..."

"Truly?" A sleepy little voice said, as Lissie stirred and stretched in the cradle of Edwy's arms, staring somewhat owlishly in the uncertain light at broad-shouldered, fair-haired man she knew only as Finch the harper. "You are my papa?"

"Yes, Lissie, I am your father," he admitted.

"Good! I hoped you were."

She still sounded half asleep, but as he bent over to kiss her brow, a contented smile curved the soft lips she in turn pressed to his beard-stubbled cheek.

"G'night, Papa."

And with that Lissie snuggled back against the shoulder of the man who had been her bodyguard for the past five years, the man who was also – astonishingly – her kinsman by blood. Another uncle, no less. For Val as well as Lissie.

As for Rowène, she was still trying to assimilate that unexpected bit of information – although why the truth of Edwy's birth should come as a surprise she did not know, considering Jacques de Rogé's reputation for lechery.

Then she realised something she did not think had occurred to either man yet – if Edwy were Guy and Ranulf's half-brother through the de Valenne line, that made him *her* kinsman too.

"Welcome to the family, cousin," she murmured to Edwy, who gave her a somewhat wild-eyed look. "So no more *Master* Jacques, eh?"

She was tempted to add, *No more Lady Rowena either,* but thought that might be pushing Edwy just one step too far at present.

Then she looked at Guy, and realised the moment had come.

"Give me a moment with your brother," she said to Edwy. "And then I will be with you."

She tipped her head towards the mouth of the cave where Gwynny, Luc and Nick, with Val still asleep bundled in a cloak in his arms, were waiting, alongside Beowulf who was casting more than the occasional concerned glance towards her beneath his grizzled brows.

Taking the hint, Edwy gave a brief, awkward nod of his head towards his half-brother, his words emerging thickly accented and hoarsely hesitant,

"The gods go wi' ye... Guy."

"And with you, brother," came the half-smiling, half-raw reply, as he gripped Edwy's shoulder in lieu of the arm clasp that was impossible under the circumstances. "Take care of Lissie for me."

Rowène thought Edwy was going to say something else, probably the same something that was lying heavy on her own tongue, but in the end he simply turned and walked to join the others at the cave's mouth.

Leaving Rowène alone with Guy.

Once her lover.

Still the father of her beloved child.

And, whatever else happened between them, her kinsman by blood as well as affection. Which left her with a choice, to speak or remain silent. And if she asked, and he accepted...

Everything will be different. Difficult and awkward, in a dozen damnable ways.

On the other hand, could she deliberately stand between Guy and the daughter he had just discovered?

No, damn it, I cannot.

That being so, she had to make the offer, and cope with the emotional – and practical – ramifications of the situation later.

"You know you are... welcome to... to come with us," she blurted, holding his gaze, wanting him to see that she meant what she said, that it was no token offer, no mere sop to her conscience.

"Perhaps... but I cannot."

Sheer relief deluged her. Then guilt.

"You do not want to be with Lissie? Or is it me?"

He gave her a tight, humourless smile.

"Of course I want to be with my daughter. To watch her grow as a flower towards womanhood. And to do my part in keeping her safe from Joffroi's bloody hunters, as well as your mother's icy clutches. But *you* do not want me there... wherever *there* is. Do you, Rowène?"

And while she sought for a reply that would not wound him further, he shook his head.

"I may have been blind where Edwy is concerned, but not with you. It would be too uncomfortable for us both, even leaving the truth about your treacherous lover out of the bargain. And while, for Lissie's sake, I would try to come to terms with that and..."

He waved a hand that took in the entirety of her appearance.

"With Jacques de Chartreux, but still she would sense something awry between us, and I would not see her unhappy or hurt any more. At least now she knows that she has a father. One who loves her."

"And what reason am I supposed to give her when she asks why the father who loves her does not wish to live with her?"

"I am sure you will find a suitable reason if you try hard enough," he said, something of the anger he must still be feeling at her betrayal hardening his tone. "You have had seven years to practise, after all."

"Guy, I would not have had things turn out this way by choice, and you are still my kinsman by blood..."

"No! No more. If you want the plain truth, I will not go with you because I cannot look at you without feeling my gut burn with bile. And as for the thought of seeing your lover there..!"

He shook his head.

"But that is not the only reason. I have a place here, and a position whereby I can still hold my head up. More than that, there is... something... binding me here..."

"Something or *someone*?" Rowène enquired, the uneasy suspicion stirring in the moonlit shadows of her mind giving her tone an unmistakable edge.

"Listen to me, Guy. I know you think I have betrayed you with R... with your brother. And I... I suppose I have. But please, I beg you, do not seek solace in my sister's arms. If it is Juliène who keeps you here in Vézière be very, very careful, Guy. I would not see you bound in her twisted schemes. Granted, she saved your life once, and Edwy's too, but she cannot be trusted not to betray you if you cross her path again. For your own sake, Guy, stay out of her bed."

"What is sauce for the goose..." he said, bitterly mocking.

Then, before she could reply,

"You may be right, but it is *my* risk to take," he pointed out, his voice even, his eyes unnaturally dark in the moonlight.

"Always supposing," he finished, somewhat ironically. "I ever find myself in the position of being invited to share a bed with her."

He was in an odd mood, Rowène thought, with a pang for the loss of the gentle harper she had loved, but then the events of the day, and indeed the past five years, had to have changed him.

Between them, she and Ju had brought him to this.

"Very well, Guy, if you will not come with us, will you at least promise me that you will be careful?"

"Yes, that I can do," he replied, his demeanour softening slightly. "And there is something you can do for me in return."

"Look after Lissie? You know I will."

"No, not that." He brushed it aside, obviously taking it as read. "Will you take this..."

He pulled the harp bag from his back, together with a small pouch that chinked of coins as he untied it from his belt.

"Take the money for her keep, and give the harp to Lissie when you think the time is right."

He shrugged broad shoulders, bitter once more.

"For now, this is all I can give her. Other than the clothes on my back, and aside from being too big, I think one fey changeling in the family is quite enough."

There was perhaps the faintest flicker of humour discernible in the look he gave her, though Rowène had no doubt that he was hurting still, and would for a very long time to come.

Despite her misgivings, she took the bag he held out and slipped it over her own shoulder, tucking the purse into the breast of her shirt.

"But what will you do now, without a harp? Surely, Guy, your position depends on it?"

"I will commission a new harp, I have silver enough still for that. And in the meantime there is a lute lying around gathering dust. I can use that."

He glanced beyond her, his attention caught by something behind her.

"Ah, I see that slippery young fellow – Aelric, is it? – has returned and your brother is looking this way. Time you were away, and I must go too, before Eadric loses what little patience he has with me."

He held out his arm.

Instead of gripping it, Rowène stepped in close enough to brush a kiss across the warm, weathered skin of his cheek, the bristle of his beard soft beneath her lips.

"The gods go with you, Guy," she whispered.

And walked away before he could return the gesture or make any reply... always supposing he felt any need to reciprocate her goodwill.

When she paused at the cave mouth and turned to look, he was already gone, swept up into the shadows, with no more than a diminishing flicker of torch flame to show where he went.

She was, she found, fighting hard to hold back her tears, though whether it was Guy or Lissie or even herself she wept for, she could not say.

What she did know was that could not stand there snivelling all day. So, after wiping her wet eyes and runny nose on the sleeve of her shirt, she set off after her companions.

Stepping out of the cave she found herself within a dense knot of thorny trees, a close tangle of shadows and frothy pale flowers, beyond which the silvery grey glimmer of the dying moonlight yielded to the advance of a misty dawn.

Ducking beneath the last clawed branch, she find herself facing north-east into the wilderness, Vézière's walls and towers lost in the darkness behind her.

There was, thank the gods, no sign of the Black Hunt, and surely this would be the last direction they would look for their prey.

Nevertheless Rowène still felt the warning touch of a searching gaze and glanced around, knowing as she did so that the watcher was not one that she would see.

Unless it be in the silver reflection of a mirror, or through the moonlit waters of a scrying bowl...

Yet even as she sought frantically to hide her thoughts, her very presence in this place, she heard her sister's voice whispering with sly spite in her mind.

Now I know where he is.

And from this night onwards, Guyard de Martine is mine!

Your part is done, Ro. Oh, I know you tried to warn him, and perhaps if you had not lied to him these past eight years, he might have paid more heed to your words now. As it is, it is your betrayal that has left him raw and vulnerable, ready for me.

And I am going to break him!

There, that is a thought to take with you, Sister, wherever you go!

"No, Ju," she started to say, frantic, pleading. "He has been hurt enough! Yes, by me! Though the goddess knows I never meant for it to be so. But what has Guy ever done to you, that you would seek to destroy him? But if you do... then may you be damned to the outermost reaches of the starless depths of hell."

She heard a laugh – cold as ice, and almost as brittle – and then nothing, and thought her sister gone.

Then, very faintly and almost beyond the stretch of her senses, as if it were no more than the distant passage of a falling star, she heard her sister say,

I have no choice, Ro. Would to the gods that I did...

Verse 3

A Confusion of Cats

Now I know where he is...

Her own maliciously vindictive words sliced with vicious emphasis through her sleeping mind, causing her to toss and turn in her soft bed, and to throw off the heavy covers of brocaded silk lest she suffocate under their stifling weight.

Yet nothing Juliène did could free her emotions from the prison she had made for herself when she had chosen to aim that ill-timed taunt at her sister.

Now I know where he is!

Why, oh why, had she been so foolish as to utter those poisoned, doubly dangerous words?

Yes, she had wanted to hurt Rowène.

Unfortunately she had realised, far too late, that if Ro had heard her, it was almost inevitable that their mother would also.

That being so, even in the depths of her uncomfortable dreams, Juliène accepted that there would be no going back from this night. Even though by some unlooked-for gift of the gods – and a terrifying reliance on luck – she had managed to delay the moment of revelation for three nerve-racking seasons.

But no longer!

The game – though the goddess knew it was no game for her – was over.

With dawn's first light, the Winter Lady would be at her door. Moreover she would come expecting Juliène's plans for Guyard de Martine's seduction and ultimate betrayal to be formulated and ready to be put into effect.

Goddess! What have I done?

Worse, what must I now do?

And how can I ever bring him to my bed, with all that lies between us?

Yet even as she sat up, arms held tight about her knees, despair and distress creeping cold along her limbs, she found she could see an image forming against the blackness of her closed lids... the image of a pair of lovers...

Naked and so closely entwined it was impossible to see where one began and the other ended, the woman's long dark tresses spread out upon a living pillow of green moss starred with tiny white flowers, the man's shorter hair glimmering gold in the light of the late afternoon sun slipping through the leafy canopy above, their sighs and moans barely audible over the sweet music of birdsong and brook.

Blatantly erotic as the image was, causing a forgotten heat to suffuse long-numbed parts of her body, there was nevertheless an innocent joy about the lovers that brought tears to her eyes, even as she allowed herself to be drawn back into the power of that moment beneath the lavender sky, losing all sense of time...

Until eventually, as if a soft kiss had brushed across her cheek, Juliène awoke with a sigh, to find that daylight had overtaken her moonlit dreams.

A heartbeat later she realised that it had not been her dream lover's lips drifting across her skin at all!

Or at least not unless Guyard de Martine's dark blond beard had grown longer, sparser and paler, less like a man's bristles and more like a... *cat's whiskers?*

On that startled, incredulous and appalled thought, she opened her eyes to find that both of Princess Linette's pets had managed to inveigle their way into her chamber, the one they called Amber presently engaged in nuzzling her cheek, while Jade sat observing her sister's antics with aloof disdain from the foot of the curtained bed.

With a shriek that pitched somewhere between shock and distaste – as much for the alarmingly close proximity of the cat on her chest as the belatedly appalling notion that she, a noblewoman of Mithlondia, had been reduced, even in a dream, to being tumbled on the ground like some peasant wench – Juliène once more sat up in bed, abruptly enough to send the feline intruder to the floor in an undignified whirl of white paws and amber-tipped tail.

Picking itself off the polished boards, the cat stalked to the window seat, leapt upon the cushioned surface and sat down, presenting its back in silent indignation.

Juliène, who had never shared her sister's affinity, or affection, for creatures whose only place in any household should be as a deterrent to small, squeaking things or their larger, more rapacious relatives, rubbed her face on the sleeve of her night rail, subdued a sneeze and then glared from one uninvited visitor to the other.

Unwelcome though their presence was, Juliène was also aware that it would be impolitic to eject the animals from her chamber if she wished to retain what small amount of Linette's favour she possessed.

Perhaps more disturbingly, she found herself unable to shake the compelling image of the entwined lovers from her mind.

Disquieted by the undeniably earthy nature of the dream, and irritated beyond measure by her rude awakening, she called sharply for her maid.

It must have been Siflaed, she thought crossly, who had let the creatures in, and she was determined that her wretched servant would not make the same mistake again.

Then, in the moment when her tire-maid appeared at her side, Juliène recalled that she herself had made a far greater error, and as a result of her folly would shortly be receiving another, even more unwelcome visitation than that of the princess' pets.

Shivering violently, in spite of the golden, summer-scented sunshine now chasing the shadows from her chamber, Juliène shied away from the memory of the scene she had glimpsed amidst the deceptive moon-shimmering reflections moving below the waters of her silver scrying bowl.

Swallowed too the dread that rose in her throat at the realisation that she knew beyond doubt where Guyard de Martine had found refuge.

She had, in all truth, used every excuse possible to delay the moment... until last night when something her mother had said had warned her that she had prevaricated long enough and that promise must now be transformed into purpose.

Not that her excuses had been without a base in truth.

Despite her mother's most diligent instruction, Juliène was still lamentably lacking in skill with a scrying bowl, anything she did glimpse in the water being fragmented and far from clear. Moreover, she could only work when the Moon Goddess was at her most powerful, any wisp of cloud veiling the Lady's silver light proving an impossible impediment to Juliène's imperfect efforts.

Beyond all that, Hervé – pig though he undoubtedly was – had at long last proved himself of use since, as Juliène had told her mother, she could scarcely be expected to sneak from her lord's bed for the purposes of exercising the dubious skills that would brand her a witch beyond all doubt.

Therefore, her scrying must be conducted in the strictest solitude, for who in their right mind would trust Hervé not to spill such dangerous secrets when he was awash with wine, as he all too frequently was.

It was an argument her mother had no defence against.

For while it was one thing for courtiers and common folk alike to call the Winter Lady and her daughters *witch* in the same casual manner as they used the terms *slut* and *whore*, it was quite another for such slander to be publicly proclaimed as the truth.

It had been over three hundred years since anyone – man or woman – had been brought to trial before the High Counsel on a charge of witchcraft, and Juliène had no intention of being the first since that grim time to walk into the flames.

Certainly not by way of drunken testimony from her despised lord-by-binding.

All these more or less cogent arguments she had used in turn since Guyard de Martine had returned to Mithlondia nearly a year ago, until she had recognised during the course of yesterday evening's meal that the Winter Lady's patience had reached its frozen limits.

Therefore, she had made a determined attempt last night to read the waters, and her decision, guided by a bitter jealousy of her sister to focus on Rowène rather than Guyard himself, had brought unexpectedly accurate results.

With this impetus providing the key to last night's revelations, she had driven herself to delve deeper than ever before into the shadows behind the shimmering waters, until finally she reached the disclosure she sought.

Ironically, it had been Rowène's voice, speaking her sister's name, which had crystallised the, as yet indistinct images, rendering them as clear and sharp-edged as moonlit steel.

And it had been in those moments of clarity during which Juliène had spied on her sister's parting from her former lover, that she had heard Rowène speak of Vézière, and of Guyard's position there – though it seemed he was, for the moment, a harper without a harp.

Even as Juliène pondered what use she might make of this knowledge, she found herself wracked by rage and humiliation as she remembered how, when she had questioned Lord Nicholas about his new harper, the old nobleman had contrived to put her off with a quiet yet – in hindsight – determined deliberation.

And Juliène had been so desperate to find an excuse to escape Vézière and its heir's importunities to share his bed that she had accepted Lord Nicholas' casual dismissal of his harper's skills at face value.

Now, however, she was close to grinding her teeth at the thought that she had been outwitted by a near-blind, apparently witless, old man.

But, she promised herself, when she returned to Vézière – as now seemed inevitable – she would be far more wary.

Both of Lord Nicholas and his lecherous son, to whom she had developed a decided aversion.

Not least because at the height of the de Chartreux family's power Hal de Vézière had claimed friendship with her beloved brother... and then chosen to publicly deny that friendship when Luc had been proclaimed traitor and outlaw.

Unlike Gabriel de Marillec.

And whatever other grudge Juliène might justifiably hold against the man, she could not fault his loyalty to her brother, a loyalty that sooner or later would take him to the scaffold.

Given that same choice, Hal de Vézière had shown himself to have too much regard for his own skin and his inheritance to risk either for the sake of a mere boyhood friendship.

Nor had he displayed the slightest qualm before attempting to seduce his former friend's sister into becoming his mistress.

Juliène had managed to evade the ultimate intimacy so far, but if that was what it took to regain entry into Vézière castle, and thence into Guyard de Martine's arms...

With a heavy sigh, she dragged herself from the huge bed, thankful that Hervé had been too drunk the previous night to demand his binding rights and had chosen to sleep elsewhere – in some whore's bed or the gutter, she cared not which – and wrapping a light shawl about her shoulders, went to sit at her dressing table and there, in the silver reflection of her mirror, studied her flawless face.

Or rather, the face that had been flawless once.

Now the translucent pearl-toned skin that had first captured Guyard de Martine's gaze showed ash-grey smudges beneath weary eyes.

Worse, lines had appeared between her slender arched brows, set there by the blinding headaches that invariable followed her attempts at scrying, with yet more lines deepening about her mouth, carved by bitterness and discontent, the whole underlain by the sickly pallor of fear.

The same fear that coiled within the slender body with which she must soon entice a man – a man who had more integrity in his little finger than Hal de Vézière could ever hope to possess – and then betray him to his destruction.

Even so, she had to admit that where fear *for* her son, and fear *of* her mother made her shake with nauseous shivers, there was something that was *not* fear – a nervous apprehension, perhaps – at the thought of indulging in carnal intimacies with Guyard de Martine, since whatever else she had to do, it was unavoidable that if she were to contrive his destruction, she must first incite his desire.

She had been able to do it once.

But that, Goddess help her, had been six long years ago.

Before her binding to Hervé de Lyeyne had blighted her ability to feel.

Before Guyard's exile to Kardolandia, and what must have been five years of hell to the honourable man who had refused her own casual advances amidst the golden roses of the palace garden.

And now?

Now, when Guy had returned and she must seduce him in earnest?

Suffice to say, she was painfully uncertain whether she was capable even of arousing his lust, let alone gaining his trust sufficiently that he would spill the secrets of his heart at the same time as he spilled his seed into her beautiful, barren body.

A brisk knock, sharp as cracking ice, caused Juliène to start violently, dropping the pot of scented unguent she had been about to apply to her face, then drawing in a harsh unsteady breath, ordered Siflaed – who was hovering behind her, eyes downcast and almost as pale as Juliène herself – to see who it might be.

At the same time, the cats who had been curled up peaceably together on the window seat, shot out of sight, one disappearing under the big bed, the other clawing its way up the curtains to take refuge in the concealing shadows of the canopy.

"Oh, m'lady, ye don't think as 'tis his lordship?" Siflaed stammered in a strained whisper as she bent to pick up the lavishly brocaded gown that had slipped from her shaking hands.

"Of course not, you silly girl," Juliène snapped as she watched her tire-maid walk with dragging steps across the room.

"Lord Hervé would hardly knock at his own door. I expect you will find it is my mother."

Scarcely reassured, Siflaed cast her another frightened glance and went to lift the latch, cringing back into an unsteady curtsey as the Lady Ariène de Rogé swept past her into the chamber on a rippling wave of gossamer green silk and elusive perfume, jewels glinting on her graceful wrists and about her white neck, her fiery red hair bound up in two gold net cauls.

Immaculately attired, impossibly beautiful, showing no perceptible signs of age, she made Juliène – who was, under normal circumstances, perfectly confident of her own allure – feel like an unpolished pebble set next to a glittering gem.

"Mother!"

Juliène rose to her feet, all too aware of the ravages wrought upon her features by the passage of the night, not to mention the fact that she was still in her under-gown, her hair falling in knotted snarls about her shoulders.

With a desperate attempt at composure, she said,

"Wha... what brings you to my chamber so early, Madame?"

Her mother regarded her with dispassionate disfavour for a frozen heartbeat or two, then spoke in the same soft, silken voice, with its dangerous undercurrent of ice, that she used most often to Juliène,

"It is scarcely early, Daughter, and besides there are tidings from Vézière that I thought you would prefer to hear from me first."

"Vézière?"

Her heart thumped once with a leaden fear she fought not to show, then in one final, frantic, and probably futile, attempt to feign indifference, she forced herself to continue with no more than polite curiosity in her own tone.

"What about Vézière, Mother? Can it be that Messire Nicholas has finally admitted that his infirmities have overtaken his usefulness, and ceded his seat in the Counsel Chamber to his son?"

"No. Unfortunately for your ambitions in that direction, your callow lover must wait a while yet before he steps into his father's place."

There was a delicate edge of scorn to her mother's voice.

"Though the Goddess knows that interfering old fool cannot live for ever, blind as he is and on the brink of losing what few wits he ever had. That said, it would do no harm if you were to draw his son closer into your web. He may yet prove himself of use to us when he does eventually come into the lordship. And if not..."

An indifferent shrug accompanied the succeeding words.

"He shall follow his father into oblivion most speedily."

Indifferent to Hal de Vézière's fate but almost ill from the strain of concealing her anxiety over the man about whom she feared to ask, Juliène barely managed to say,

"If not a change in the lordship, then what are these tidings you have heard?"

"If you would but listen, Child, I am trying to tell you," her mother said somewhat sharply.

"Indeed, I am listening, Mother," she said meekly.

"Very well. Now, according to Oswin's latest report..."

"Oswin?" Juliène interrupted with an uncomprehending frown.

"The captain of the Lord Joffroi's huntsmen! Really Juliène, where is your mind wandering this morning?"

"Nowhere, Mother, I am just tired. So this Oswin..?"

"Brought tidings to my lord late last night regarding that feckless traitor you persist in calling your brother..."

"Because he *is* my brother," Juliène protested numbly, even as she was thinking,

So this was not about Guyard, after all.

She could feel no relief, however.

Goddess, I beg you, let nothing terrible have happened to Luc.

"Brother!"

Her mother almost spat out the word, her contemptuous tone inciting a spark of rebellion in Juliène's terrified soul.

"Yes, brother. Luc and I... we are one blood, Mother. Why can you not understand what that means to me?"

"Perhaps because your sister is of your blood also yet her fate does not seem to trouble you half as much as that of your degenerate *brother*. Or your wretched bastard brat's, come to that."

Her mother's green eyes glittered with cruel amusement, like winter sunlight on ice, as Juliène winced at this brutal description of her beloved brother and son, then continued with chilling distaste,

"I have warned you before about the unfortunate sentimentality with which you persist in regarding them both. As you know very well, Lucius Valéri de Chartreux is a man doubly damned. Once by the tainted blood he inherited from your traitorous father, and again by his own perverse predilections."

Lady Ariène's level voice was frosted with the crisp disdain she reserved exclusively for her former lord-by-binding and his sons, legitimate or otherwise.

Then, incredibly, her voice changed, revealing a rare vulnerability.

"If it is a brother you need, you have one, Juliène. One who truly needs you. Raoul is but a child, I grant, but he longs for a sibling's affection. Moreover, he is lonely here at court for the boys of his own age and rank who should be his companions shun him. Fools! They will pay thrice over for their short-sighted folly when he is grown to full manhood!"

What her mother had omitted to say, though Juliène knew it well enough, was that when Raoul was at home in Rogérinac or Chartre, he was prevented from associating with the boys of his own age who lived alongside him, and thus had no companions there either, and as a further consequence had no chance of forming the friendships that would bring him the sort of loyalty that both his grandsires and his three uncles had earned.

"If I could give him a brother, I would," Lady Ariène continued, her trembling voice revealing a bitter yearning Juliène had not heard before. "One to guard his back. One whose loyalty would never, *ever* fail."

It was plain who her mother alluded to so bitterly. The loyalty of Raoul's own father's brother and half-brother having long since crumbled into dust under the unbearable strain Joffroi had put on it.

"Alas," her mother continued. "The Goddess has seen fit to bring my child-bearing days to an end... but I know that Raoul would be glad of an older sister's kindness."

There was the merest hint of a plea in the normally unyielding depths of the Winter Lady's green eyes, this unexpected love for her last-born child the only sign of weakness Juliène had ever detected in the otherwise cold and untouchable woman who had given her life.

Anger burning dark within her heart, Juliène lowered her gaze in a submission she could not bear to put into words, before drawing a deep breath and asking the question that was rubbing her raw,

"So what exactly did Oswin say about Luc? Did he... see him?"

There were, she knew, frequent rumours of sightings along the highways or out on the moors, though thank the Goddess they had always come to naught on further investigation, her brother being too canny to be caught so easily. At least until now...

"Oh, this is no will-o'-the-wisp glimpsed once and then lost in a moorland mist," Lady Ariène murmured, seemingly reading her thoughts with ease.

"This time your brother was flaunting himself in full view in Vézière's market square. With a scarlet-clad slut on his arm, no less! As if a deviant wolf's-head such as he has the same rights as any other man to peruse and purchase a whore's services."

"And why should he not?" Juliène snapped before she could stop herself. "He *is* a man, Mother. And it was scarcely his own fault that he was outlawed. As for the other... well, if it is acceptable in King Karlen's realm, I do not see why it should not be so here."

Then, quickly, before her mother could pour further vitriol on her eldest son's Kardolandian tendencies, Juliène added hastily,

"Besides, how does Oswin know anything about what Luc was doing in Vézière? I thought the Black Hunt had been banned from entering the town. Did Oswin then gain permission from Messire Nicholas as was agreed by the Counsel."

It seemed unlikely, with what she knew of Oswin One-Eye, who took orders only from his master.

Nor would she easily forget the frightening sight of Joffroi de Rogé almost frothing at the mouth with rage following the High Counsel session when Nicholas de Vézière and Justin de Lacey had banded together and, reinforced by the moderate voices of Robert de Vitré and Jean de Marillec, had persuaded the prince that it was in no-one's best interest to allow the Black Hunt the unfettered freedom to rampage through town and countryside alike.

"Well... no," her mother conceded. "If you must know the truth, Oswin did not waste time applying for permission, the information he had received being such that he needed to follow it up most urgently."

"Information from *whom?*" Juliène enquired with a breathless sort of bitterness.

In her experience the folk of Vézière, Mortaine and Lasceynes had proved themselves stubbornly unforthcoming in the past, particularly towards the Black Hunt, and she had silently rejoiced that no-one had seen fit to betray her brother to those who sought to take and hang him.

If that wall of silence had now been breached...

"Information from a woman who claimed to have been close to that worthless cur you persist in calling brother."

"Luc had a mistress?" Juliène strove to keep any trace of surprise, or animosity, out of her voice.

Her mother's perfect mouth curved in contempt and a flicker of chilly amusement showed in her ice-green eyes.

"Only in her mind! From what Oswin had to say, it would seem that your brother took the wench from a brothel here in Lamortaine, for what perverted reason I cannot guess. She, on the other hand, seems to have fallen victim to his handsome face and spent the intervening years hoping that he would turn from his own unnatural desires for her sake, which just goes to show how stupid she must be!

"Having finally realised that this would never happen, it was inevitable do you not think that she should have decided to take her revenge upon him for all those years of indifference?

"And having reached this decision, she must have thought the gods were with her when she crossed paths with my lord's men outside Vézière, and told them that your brother was in the town, along with a few of the worthless curs who follow him. And that should have been an end to it. However, in Oswin's haste to catch the man she was so eager to betray, and being regrettably over-confident in his own ability to lay them all by the heels, he neglected to discover from the woman the exact location of your brother's lair, only that it is somewhere in the depths of Lasceynes Forest.

"Nevertheless he *will* find and destroy it, if he has to burn the whole wretched wood to the ground."

"No! You cannot permit him to do that! Not when my son is living there too!"

A flicker of irritation showed in the cool green eyes at Juliène's rash outburst.

"Of course, if your brother had simply yielded himself up, such drastic action would not be necessary. Or if Oswin had shown more concern for his duty and refrained from taking out his frustrations at losing his quarry by indulging himself and his men with the woman before getting the necessary information out of her. And then what must the fool do but compound his error by leaving her unwatched!"

"She ran away," Juliène said, less in question than statement, since if the woman had had any sense left to her after a half dozen men of the Black Hunt had taken their protracted pleasure, she should have fled as far and fast as possible.

"I do not believe she was in any condition to run," Lady Ariène murmured with cool cynicism. "Crawl, maybe. But no, she did worse, contriving instead to open her wrists. Lost to remorse – or so one supposes – at the betrayal of the man she must have belatedly realised she still loved," the Winter Lady concluded without a trace of any such emotion softening her own dispassionate tones."

"And Luc?" Juliène asked, her hands clasped tightly together to still their trembling, needing to hear the truth of his fate in plain words.

"Escaped, curse him!"

Such a heady feeling of relief washed through her at her mother's hissed reply that Juliène nearly fainted, even as the Winter Lady continued icily,

"Together with every last one of his misbegotten companions! Of whom, I have no doubt, your wretched sister was one. It was not an entirely wasted mission however," Lady Ariène continued smoothly, her voice a dash of cold water against Juliène's reeling senses.

"Oswin also reported seeing a pair of brats in your brother's company. A young girl and a boy, of about seven summers."

She raised artfully darkened brows, and Juliène felt her heart drop.

Val! No, no, no!

Oh, gods, Luc! What possessed you to drag my son into danger...

"A boy with fair hair and green eyes!" the wintry voice penetrated her frantic fears, wrenching her from her silent recriminations.

"Oh yes, Daughter, if matters had turned out otherwise, you might even now be reunited with your precious bastard – slightly damaged no doubt, since Oswin will never be anything less than a vicious lout with a taste for inflicting pain, and a child is as fair game to him as a woman!"

"What happened?" Juliène's voice was a thread of sound, her fingers knotted tightly together in her lap. "Where is Val now?"

"As to that, I do not know," her mother replied, her eyes dark with a dangerous anger Juliène could only be glad was not directed at herself.

"Unfortunately Oswin was thwarted in his attempt to grab the boy by a man he swears was for many years one of the Rogé men-at-arms, before he broke his oath of fielty and instead gave his service to your thrice-damned brother."

Something in the Winter Lady's ice-green stare suddenly made Juliène think that her mother's anger was directed at her after all.

Especially when Lady Ariène continued glacially,

"Does the name Edwy of Rogérinac not mean anything to you, Daughter?"

"No." She shook her head in uncontrived puzzlement. "Is there any reason why it should?"

"What if I were to tell you that when this man was last heard of, he was serving as personal retainer and bodyguard to Guyard de Martine!"

Juliène suppressed, with some difficulty, her nervous start.

Thankfully her mother did not seem to notice, instead continuing in chilly tones,

"Since it seems I must remind you, this Edwy was also one of the two men that *you* were supposed to have dealt with six years ago as a small token of your loyalty to me and to Joffroi! A loyalty that, to my sorrow, you have so often given me cause to doubt."

"No!"

Juliène shook her head again, this time in an effort to remember what she had tried so hard to imprison in the darkest corner of her mind.

"*Six years* ago, Mother? How should I remember one man among so many you have had me *deal with?*"

Abruptly some shard of recollection shifted in her mind, and she saw herself in her mother's still-room mixing poisons, carefully pouring the deadly draughts into two vials, one tied off with a blue thread, one with red...

"I did as you told me to, Mother, I swear it."

Or did I?

What had Rowène told her last summer...

Do you not remember helping Edwy to escape from the palace...

"Hmm." Her mother was regarding her closely. "While I would like to be able to accept your word for that, in the light of Oswin's report it seems I cannot.

"So... if you would see your son safe you would be wise to bring me some proof that this rash fool who risked himself by stepping between the Black Hunt and their lawful prey is no more than some chance stranger who bears a tenuous resemblance to Guyard de Martine's child-hood companion and most loyal retainer, and that Edwy of Rogérinac is dead these six years past by your hand!"

Juliène started to ask how she was supposed to accomplish such a feat so long after the event when a tearing pain in her scalp caused her to round on her tire-maid, snapping,

"If you cannot dress my hair without pulling it out by the roots, you stupid girl, I shall send you back to Lyeyné, and have your sister brought here in your stead. It is *just* possible that she would prove less clumsy than you."

"No, please, m'lady. Millie'd never manage here at court, she do be better off lookin' after the childer..."

"And you think I care a snap of my fingers for any of that?" Juliène demanded coldly, her tone more than a match for the Winter Lady at her iciest.

"No, m'lady, o' course not, an' I'll try not to be so clumsy, I'll..."

"Oh, stop snivelling, girl, and give me the comb, I will do it myself. Why I ever thought you would make a suitable tire-maid is beyond me. The only thing you have ever been good for is keeping Lord Hervé out of my bed! And just lately you have even failed in that! "So if you want to keep your place here, you would do well to take more care with your duties. Now get you to the kitchens and fetch back a plate of almond pastries and some elderflower cordial to break my fast. Well, go on, girl, do not just stand there with your mouth open!"

"Aye, m'lady."

With a sniff and a bob of a curtsey, the girl was gone, leaving Juliène alone with the woman who had given her life, who had taught her to use the fey power that tingled in her blood, and with whom she was presently engaged in a very dangerous game of deception.

"I cannot understand why you bother with that witless wench," the Winter Lady commented in common speech, her cool contemptuous words directed at the shrinking servant girl as she fled from the room.

"Then again, I suppose it is your own concern if you chose to have Hervé's leman waiting on you, and have his by-blows brought up in your own household."

"And *you* did not have my father's by-blow brought up in *your* household?" Juliène could not resist asking.

"Admittedly the stench of the stables did not reach your bower, Madame, but you must have known Lucien was within the castle bounds, all the same."

"I had no choice," her mother snapped, an unusually raw edge to her smooth tones. "Your father would not have his bastard banished beyond the walls. But as you know very well, I made sure they paid for their arrogance in the end! *Both* of them!"

Lucius de Chartreux on the public scaffold.

Lucien of Chartre at the point of a de Rogé sword.

"And their blood has washed away the insult that between them they put upon me," Lady Ariène continued with a satisfied smile.

Goddess!

While Juliène had not loved her father beyond the duty of a daughter, and had certainly felt no affection for her half-brother, the venom in her mother's voice made her feel more than slightly sick.

Nor had the Winter Lady finished yet.

"All that remains to make my vengeance complete is to ensure that your father's last remaining and best-loved bastard – the one he tried so hard to hide from me – will meet the same bloody fate."

Juliène swallowed, hesitated, and then said,

"You know then?"

"What? That our base-born High Commander who masquerades as a prince's by-blow has not one single drop of royal blood? Of course I know. I have always known. There is nothing that can be hidden from *my* sight. Remember that, Daughter!"

"I do, Mother," she mumbled, trying not to let her guilt – or her knowledge that Joscelin de Veraux was indeed of royal blood – colour her tone.

Fortunately her mother seemed to hear nothing amiss, being too taken up with her own malice.

"That slack-thighed bitch Céline may have lain with both Marcus and your father, sharing her favours indiscriminately between them, at the same time and in the same bed like as not, but for all that her precious son is no prince's get. And you know how I know that?"

"Because de Veraux has my father's eyes," Juliène replied dully, as a child repeating a well-worn lesson.

Inside, however, her resentment seethed like a bitter, bubbling stew.

Luc, Rowène, Lucien of Chartre, Joscelin de Veraux – all her siblings, save Raoul who did not count in this case and who she scarcely thought of as her brother anyway – had Lucius de Chartreux's clear light grey eyes.

It gave them an indefinable bond that she – with her fey green gaze – must always lack."

"What will you do about de Veraux?" she enquired of her mother.

"Nothing as yet. He knows we know the truth, Joffroi and I, but the bastard's hands are tied by his mother's lie, and all he can do is wait for the rope to tighten about his neck. As it will, when I deem the moment right.

"As it is, I perceive the signs of strain biting ever deeper into his mind, visible with each separate strand of silver that twines through his hair. Look for yourself, if you do not believe me, next time the cur pretends to bow over your hand or presumes to dance by your side in a courtly roundel."

Juliène nodded dutifully. Then, having scant sympathy for Joscelin de Veraux but a very great desire to rid herself of her mother's presence before her guilty thoughts betrayed her, said quickly,

"My maid will be returning soon, and though she does not speak the high tongue, if there is anything else of a private nature we should speak of, it should be now."

"Yes, there was something else... something concerning Vézière..."

Her mother looked momentarily confused, an expression so fleeting and inconceivable that Juliène was almost convinced she had misread it, until Lady Ariène glanced swiftly around the room, a tiny shadow of a frown marring her smooth white brow.

"Have you a cat in here, Daughter?" she demanded suspiciously.

"A *what?*"

Juliène was so astonished, she nearly laughed. Until she recalled that she had not one but *two* cats in her chamber!

On the brink of confessing, she bit back the words and instead told a different truth,

"You know I cannot be in the same room with such creatures, Mother, they make me sneeze. How Princess Linette can abide that mewling pair following her about, shedding their hair on her skirts and shaking their filthy fleas onto her skin, I do not know. I would drown them in the fish pond if I had my way."

"Hmm, that can perhaps be arranged," the Winter Lady said with soft venom, making Juliène regret having spoken so heedlessly.

A tentative knock at the door heralded the return of her servant and seeing the girl's laden tray, Juliène could do no less than extend a reluctant invitation to her unwanted visitor.

"Will you not join me, Mother?"

"No, I must go. I need to speak to Joffroi before the Counsel session begins."

She glided towards the door, the watered green silk of her skirts whispering against the polished floorboards, only to turn back as if suddenly remembering what else she had meant to say.

"I wonder..."

"Wonder what, Mother?"

Here it comes!

She has just been playing with me until now, Luc and Val no more than a means to set my nerves on edge.

Now she will tell me she knows about...

No! No, I must not even think his name!

"I wonder," Lady Ariène said, darkly musing. "Whether there might not be more to the matter of this man, Edwy, than I first thought. If it *is* the man Oswin swore it was, would it not be logical to suppose that he might be in Vézière for some reason of his own, rather than because he has some connection with your wolf's-head brother? For I cannot believe that a sworn Rogé man would serve a de Chartreux in *any* manner, the ill-will between them being too ingrained to be overcome by any... dubious inducements your brother might offer."

"Yet he saved Val," Juliène pointed out quietly.

And the gods bless him for doing so, whoever he is.

"And Val is himself a de Chartreux. So perhaps that proves that this man is not Edwy of Rogérinac, but merely some stranger acting out of unthinking kindness towards a child threatened with violence. Such men *do* exist, Mother."

Guyard de Martine, for one.

"Perhaps..."

The Winter Lady pursed her lips in thought.

300

"On the other hand, if it *is* the man who was de Martine's child-hood companion..."

"That is the second time you have said that, Mother. How can you possibly know such a thing?"

"Oswin, of course. Besides, it makes sense that Jacques de Rogé's bastard would make friends with the local whore's son. Like calling to like, hmm? That being so, I suppose it is just conceivable that this Edwy would act on that old friendship once he realised the kinship between de Martine and young Valéri, as he surely must have done, since according to Oswin your son looks just like his own father did at that age.

"But of course," she added blandly. "You would not know that, not having seen the brat since you abandoned him to your sister's care when he was little more than a puling infant."

Juliène shook her head, unable to say anything.

Contrary to her mother's supposition, she *had* seen her son, albeit only briefly, a year ago, and knew just how closely Val resembled the brutish de Rogé boar who had sired him.

"And for your son's sake," her mother said with a shiver-inducing smile. "I suggest that you seek out any truths that Oswin himself may have missed when he was forced to leave Vézière. Too much is happening in that insular little provincial town for any of it to be coincidence..."

Abruptly, her tone changed from contemplative to brisk.

"Now, as you know, I shall be leaving court soon, taking Raoul back to Rogérinac for the summer."

For such was the Winter Lady's devotion to her precious last-born son she would not risk his health amidst the foetid humours of Lamortaine during the fever months, unhesitatingly accepting her isolation from the centre of power for his sake.

"So, Daughter, you have until I return from Rogérinac, not only to discover the truth about this man who saved your son but also to ensnare your harper and bring him to his knees. In both of which endeavours, I suggest you start with Vézière."

And with that pointed valediction she was gone, leaving Juliène alone with her tire-maid, both of them shaking as badly as the other.

Releasing her breath on a shaky sigh, Juliène took one look at her tire-maid and said sharply,

"For goodness sake, Siflaed! Put that tray down before you drop it!"

And, ignoring the girl's startled surprise at the rare use of her given name, continued irritably,

"Help yourself if you are hungry, I have quite lost my appetite."

And when the girl simply shook her head in bemused refusal,

"Well then, if you are not going to eat and your hands have stopped shaking, you can finish doing my hair."

The fear and confusion did not leave the brown depths of her tire-maid's eyes. Nevertheless, she took the comb and began with carefully gentle strokes to untangle the snarls until Juliène's hair hung like a shining fall of midnight black water straight down her back to within a foot of the floor.

"There, m'lady, 'tis done."

Juliène remained seated, reaching out to pick up the silvered mirror from the dressing table, then tilting the polished surface so that she could see her servant's eyes, she said softly,

"Now tell me why the name Edwy of Rogérinac means something to you?"

Siflaed trembled at the question, the delicately carved bone comb slipping from her fingers to clatter on the wooden boards at her feet, but before she could stammer anything by way of answer, Juliène felt herself engulfed by a rising and inexorable wave that emerged from her nose as a far from dainty sneeze.

Even as she groped for a piece of linen on her dressing table, she spun around on her stool to glare at the two cats, one crawling out from under the floor-length bed cover, the other shimmying down the hangings.

Both felines, Juliène could not help noticing, looked every whit as wild-eyed as she herself felt in the crackling aftermath of her mother's nerve-racking visit.

At the same time, the first drifting mists of suspicion began to form that it had been the hidden presence of the cats that had somehow thrown up a wall of fog to keep the Winter Lady from piercing the depths of Juliène's mind in order to pick through the bones of her dreams, thus discovering that Guyard de Martine had indeed taken refuge in Vézière.

And while it did not make the slightest sense to Juliène, nevertheless she was prepared to accept it and even to make some sort of wary truce with Princess Linette's pets. In the spirit of which she found herself staring into their unblinking golden-green eyes and murmuring a surprisingly sincere apology regarding her earlier rejection of their presence, following this with a silent plea to the Goddess to keep them safe from any violence of her mother's instigation.

A momentary quiet filled the sunlit room and then, as if the cats had understood and deigned to accept her apology, they both flopped down to wash their ruffled fur, allowing Juliène to return her attention to her pale and trembling tire-maid.

Fixing her with a glinting gaze, Juliène said softly, yet with the undertone of steel she had heard her despised half-brother use on occasion,

"I repeat, Siflaed, what is it about this man Edwy that affects you so much?"

"'Tis naught, m'lady. How can there be when he be *dead*."

The tire-maid's voice shook suddenly and the fear in her eyes overflowed into tears as her words dissolved into almost unintelligible dialect,

"I... I was allus afeared as ye or yer ma had sommut ter do wi'..."

She swallowed nervously.

"Wi' his death."

Juliène had a sudden memory, long since suppressed, of a man's light autumn-brown eyes glowering down at her, as arms folded across his broad chest he refused to take the draught – half poison, half incredible chance of life – she offered him.

"But when he were alive," Siflaed continued, tears still thickening her tone. "He were bodyguard an' servant ter Sir Guy... ye know, Lord Joffroi's half-brother as was. Sir Guy an' Edwy, they was good ter Millie an' me when they came ter Lyeyné that one time afore your betrothal."

She smiled tremulously at Juliène.

"Sir Guy, he were like somethin' outta one o' his own songs, courtly an' kind an' fair. But Edwy were good ter me too, in his own way, an' that I weren't expectin'. Not from a soldier, an' a Rogé one at that. An' fer all I doubt he e'er thought of me again once he left Lyeyné, I ain't ne'er forgot *him*," she finished with a defiant sniff.

Juliène debated within herself for a moment before saying with a certain amount of caution,

"You obviously heard my mother mention Edwy's name without understanding the rest of what she was saying... but there is a chance that the man may be alive after all."

"Alive? Oh, m'lady."

Siflaed's brown eyes brightened and a faint flush rose in her pale cheeks, making her almost pretty.

Then with a flash of intuition Juliène would not have expected of her somewhat woolly-witted tire-maid, Siflaed added,

"Does this mean Sir Guy bain't dead neither?"

As if in extension of that thought her gaze slid slyly towards the carved wooden chest at the foot of the bed.

"An' if that's so, m'lady, mebbe he'll be wantin' his harp back?"

"What do you know of that?" Juliène asked sharply, causing the girl to blanch and tremble anew.

"Naught, m'lady. 'Tis just I seen the harp an' I wondered if 'twas Sir Guy's... I thought as how he'd mebbe gived it ter ye... I mean, I could see as how he cared about ye when he came ter Lyeyné that one time. Nigh on came ter blows wi' Lord Hervé o'er ye, he did."

Juliène felt her brows rise and her heart fill most inconveniently with something that might be mistaken in another woman for a tender hope. Ruthlessly quashing this treacherous emotion, she kept her voice composed as she said,

"Is that so?"

The girl swallowed again before adding in a whisper,

"Aye, m'lady. An' once, when Lord Hervé were in his cups, he let slip as how Sir Guy had threatened ter kill him if he hurt ye in any way."

At these words, this promise from the past, Juliène felt something sharp and painful like a shard of broken glass pierce her heart.

Guyard had tried so hard to protect her, to help her, and in return she had tried to poison his bodyguard – his friend – and had sent the man himself into a degrading exile...

Her head swam and she had a wavering memory of herself kneeling on the hard flag-stoned floor, Guyard's head resting in her lap, her tears mingling with the blood streaking his bruised and battered face, as she begged his brother not to kill him...

"M'lady?"

Her tire-maid's tentative tones dispelled the image, sending it back into the black oblivion where it belonged.

304

"What is it, Siflaed?"

"Edwy... ye said as how ye thought he might still be... alive. Oh, m'lady, I know ye've no reason ter do anythin' fer such as I but it'd mean a lot ter me ter know, one way or t'other."

"As to that," Juliène answered slowly, as she rapidly considered the ramifications of her new-found knowledge. "I *may* be able to help you."

And, more importantly, myself.

"However, before I can discover the truth as to whether your Edwy lives, I must prove to my mother beyond all doubt that the Edwy who was Sir Guy's bodyguard, is dead."

Understandably Siflaed looked confused.

"But... but they be the same man, m'lady."

"Yes, *I* know that," Juliène sighed, and for some reason beyond her immediate understanding deigned to explain her thinking to her servant.

"It is complicated, Siflaed, but put simply, if I can convince my mother that Edwy of Rogérinac is dead and buried these six years past, then she will not set her hounds to look for him – or his master – now."

She transferred her pensive gaze to the cats, who having finished washing themselves were now both sitting upright and alert, watching her.

"All well and good for you two to look smug but how in the name of all the gods am I to prove a man, who is most probably still alive, to have been satisfactorily dead for the last six years?"

Jade's dark ears twitched, while Amber simply maintained her unblinking regard.

Well, what had she expected, Juliène thought irritably, an answer?

Then to her eternal surprise, she *did* get an answer.

Not from the cats, of course, but from a source almost as unexpected.

"Well, m'lady, I reckon as I knows how ye can do that," Siflaed said nervously, hope rinsing the last residue of confusion from her soft brown eyes.

"Really?" Juliène raised her brows. "Well, go on then! Tell me how you think it can be done."

"Well, m'lady, as I remember it, they... Edwy an' Sir Guy that is, was here in the palace when... when whatever it was happened."

"Yes. And so?"

"So all deaths in the palace an' Lamortaine has ter be reported ter the High Commander, an' the... the body taken away by the guardians so as it can be dealt with proper-like."

"And you know this how?" Juliène asked, curiosity overcoming her irritation.

The servant girl flushed with every appearance of discomfort.

"I dare say ye'll not know this m'lady, but happens I spent some time wi' one o' Lord Joscelin's men, back along when ye was taken ill."

"Indeed! Well, I hope he treated you better in bed than Lord Hervé does?" Juliène asked caustically.

"'Tweren't like that wi' Beric 'n' me," Siflaed confessed. "If'n ye wants the truth, I'm afeared ter go ter any man's bed after that night when... when *they* all had me."

The night Siflaed had been abused, even beyond Juliène's capacity for indifference, by a drunken Hervé, his dissolute brother and his precocious, petulant son.

Juliène, with her own experience at the hands of the de Lyeyne brothers all too clear in her mind, merely nodded, a sliver of sympathy with her maid contriving to maintain the rickety bridge circumstance had thrown up over the usual distance she kept between herself and Siflaed.

"So if you did not share this Beric's bed, what were you to him?"

"I reckon, m'lady, as ye might say we was friends. I told him 'bout Lord Hervé an' he talked ter me 'bout what 'tis like being one of the royal guardians. Anyhow tha's how I knows what happens when a body's found in the palace. So if 'tis proof o' Edwy's death..."

Her voice shook.

"Ye're wantin', ye'll need ter talk ter Lord Joscelin hisself, bein' as 'tis the High Commander's task ter keep the records o' the dead."

Waiting only until Siflaed had returned from the royal apartments with Princess Linette's permission for Juliène to attend to her own affairs that morning, she set her feet towards the distant chambers occupied by Mithlondia's High Commander.

Juliène had only once before ventured into the guardians' wing of the palace, and on that occasion it had been Gabriel de Marillec whom she had encountered, looking very much the soldier and secure in his role of Second of the Guardians – a very different image from the effete courtier that was all most people would ever see him as. Though Luc, Juliène reflected, must see yet another reflection of the man.

How much of any of it was truth and how much illusion, Juliène could not be sure. All she knew for certain was that she did not care for Gabriel de Marillec in any of his forms, and she was glad she would not have to deal with her beloved brother's enigmatic, golden-eyed lover today.

Whether she would find it any easier dealing with the coldly-controlled, impervious man she knew to be her bastard half-brother was another matter.

"Yes," she insisted haughtily to the guard standing outside his commander's door. "I *do* want to see Lord Joscelin. And what is more, I want to see him without any further delay."

The guard scratched his bearded jaw, looked from Juliène – almost as richly-attired and bejewelled as Gabriel de Marillec on a court day – to her plainly-clad, and plainly nervous servant, muttered something under his breath, and finally banged a fist against the door behind him.

"Lady Juliena an' her maid ter see Lord Joscelin," he said gruffly to the dark-haired lad who answered his rough summons.

On observing Juliène, the boy's eyes opened wide and his narrow dark brows rose in surprise.

Nonetheless, his manners did not fail him and as he straightened from his very correct bow, he said,

"Come in, my lady, and I will tell Lord Joscelin that you are here."

With that the lad retreated into the inner chamber and Juliène heard a murmur of male voices, followed by a heartbeat's silence, then a crisp order,

"Show her in, Dominic. Beric, we will finish this later."

Juliène felt Siflaed start and sent her a warning glance as a young man with curly brown hair, clad in guardians' mail emerged from the inner chamber. He made a slight bow, hand on heart, divided equally between Juliène and her maid, and said in barely accented common speech,

"Lord Joscelin will see you now, m'lady."

Then he was gone and with a

"Wait here, Siflaed,"

Juliène swept past the boy politely holding the door to the inner room.

To her surprise – for some unknown reason she had been expecting de Veraux's lair to be as dark and shadowy and secretive as the man himself – the chamber she now entered was filled with a shimmering gilded light reflected through the window from the sunlit lake beyond, to fall full on the face and form of the tall, dark-haired man who rose to his feet as she came to a halt before his parchment-littered desk, hands clenching involuntarily in the folds of her silk skirts.

"Messire de Veraux."

"Madame de Lyeyne."

The curt courtesies over, he regarded her for several long moments from grey eyes so like to Luc's it made her heart clench in pain, before he finally broke the dragging silence, his tone clipped and cool.

"Clearly you would not be here did you not want something from me, Madame. It would perhaps bring matters to a conclusion more swiftly, and thus allow me to return to my work, were you to tell me what that is."

Not a little disconcerted, Juliène stared at her father's bastard for a heartbeat longer, holding his gaze and rapidly readjusting her thinking.

This man was quite unlike the competent yet diffident Lucien.

This man was wrought of ice and steel, the only hint of his vulnerability betrayed by the strands of silver weaving down through the narrow braids from his temples. Proof – or so her mother would have her believe – that Joscelin de Veraux was all too aware that he was under a silent sentence of death.

Possibly that was true, Juliène reflected. Yet in spite of his knowledge, she sensed that this was not a man who would allow such a threat to stand in the way of what he felt was right to do.

He must, however, have a weakness. All men did.

While she herself had been trained by the Winter Lady to seek out such subtle cracks in a man's armour.

She simply had to pry deeper than usual to find Joscelin de Veraux's.

With that inner core of certainty... of belief... of honour... whatever name one cared to put upon it, he was, she thought bitterly, more like to his father and his legitimate brother than he perhaps knew.

As far as she was concerned, however, this man with his long, straight raven-dark hair and clear, cool, rain-grey eyes was not, and never would be her brother.

He was merely Céline de Veraux's by-blow, the visible symbol of her father's faithlessness.

And the only reason she was here with him now was to discover if there might not be some way of confusing the scent that presently led directly to Vézière and Guyard de Martine – if only for long enough to give Juliène time to formulate and put into action her own plan where the harper was concerned.

"You, Madame, may have time to waste! I, however, do not."

De Veraux's steel-edged voice made her start and served as a pointed reminder that he was still waiting.

Stung, she said baldly,

"I want to know if you have a record of the death of one Edwy of Rogérinac. My maid..."

She gestured towards the girl just visible behind the door, left discreetly ajar when servant and soldier had left the room.

"Lost touch with her lover six years ago. It has now come to her ears that he may have died rather than simply abandoning her as she believed he had done. And I thought it would be of some comfort to her to know the truth."

The look in Joscelin de Veraux's eyes, glittering through narrowed black lashes, bright and hard as the sheathed blade he wore at his hip, told her that he did not believe a word she said.

"I do have Princess Linette's permission to make enquiries of you in this matter," she continued sweetly, holding his cool, light gaze, watching the grey darken to the colour of storm clouds over Chartreux Bay as she delivered this less than subtle barb.

"Knowing how great a regard she has for you, both as the High Commander of Mithlondia's Guardians and her *half-brother*, I should be loath indeed to report any deficiency on your part, either in courtesy or assistance, back to her."

She watched de Veraux's white teeth bite back a word that might have been 'witch' – but was more likely 'bitch', certainly it was no compliment that had formed on his anger-thinned lips – before he said brusquely,

"Sit down, Madame! This may take some time."

He himself remained standing, only waiting until she had seated herself on a rough campaign stool, arraying the folds of embroidered wine-dark silk about her with every appearance of composure, before striding over to the shelves arrayed on the wall behind her, his long fingers running along the line of leather-bound books until he reached the one he sought.

Pulling the heavy book from the shelf he carried it back to his table, cleared a space with the back of one strong, sun-browned hand, the single signet ring he wore glinting with the movement, then dropped the book down, untied the thong that was holding it closed and allowed it to fall open in a swirl of dust that made her nose itch.

"It would help if you could be a little more precise in your direction than merely six years ago?" he said coldly.

"If it is precision you need, Messire," she said stiffly, trying neither to sneeze nor yield to the almost overpowering urge to scratch her nose. "The man I am enquiring after disappeared exactly one day after Midsummer's Day 1197."

De Veraux's head jerked up, his sword-steel eyes glittering harder even than before.

"The day after your binding to that boor, Hervé?"

She regarded him with a startled frown.

"Yes, but... why would you remember that?"

Because you are my half-sister.

The unspoken words hung stark in the silence, but all he said in a flat, emotionless tone was,

"Certain events have a habit of searing themselves into one's mind, Madame."

He lowered his gaze to the book, a single glance at the date inscribed in fading ink at the top of the page causing him to flip the stiff leaves backwards until he came to the one he sought.

"It was also," he commented, without looking up, his calloused finger running down the lines of neat script. "The same day that Joffroi de Rogé's half-brother *disappeared*. In circumstances that, to put it bluntly, stank worse than the palace privies in the midsummer heat. But I suppose you will disclaim any and all knowledge of those circumstances, even now?"

When she declined to acknowledge either his words or the swift, searing look he sent her through his lashes, he continued his search until a soft grunt under his breath informed her that he had found something.

Turning the book around so that Juliène could see where he pointed, he asked,

"Is this the man you seek?"

Coming to her feet, Juliène rested her hand lightly against the table and bending over the book, read the few lines of flowing script.

Received in the morning following Midsummer's Day the corpse of a man identified as Edwy of Rogérinac, bodyguard and retainer to Guyard de Martine, in whose chamber the body was found. Cause of death thought to be poison, administered either by his own or by an unknown hand. None coming forward to claim him, the body has this night been despatched for burial in the city's common ground.

The signature of the over-seeing officer was in the same neat, educated hand.

Gabriel de Marillec,
Second of the Guardians

"Well," de Veraux demanded. "Is that the proof you sought?"

"It is, yes," Juliène replied.

Proof of more than one thing, did de Veraux but know how to read between the lines his Second had written.

"And to me must now fall the sad task of telling my maid that her lover is indeed dead. I give you my thanks, Messire, for your... co-operation."

She gave him a sly smile.

"And will now take my leave of you."

He gave her the faintest inclination of the head, a mere mockery of the courtesy she was due, the lean lines of his handsome face set in a cool, inscrutable mask, so that his resemblance to Luc – or at least the adored brother of her childhood – was far less obvious.

Nevertheless she found she could not ignore the chains of their kinship entirely.

Feeling his keen eyes following her as she glided towards the door, and being unable to resist the intensity of his gaze, she turned to look back at the man she despised for being her father's bastard, and brows lifted in enquiry, waited for him to tell her why he watched her thus.

He hesitated, unusually she thought, then said with a grim tilt to his mouth,

"What really brought you down here today, Juliène?"

It was the first time he had ever called her by her given name, and for a heartbeat she merely blinked stupidly at him.

In that moment, his expression more quizzical than guarded, he looked so much like the brother who had always stood by her, from her mild childhood scrapes to taking her illegitimate son into his care, that she nearly told him everything. The past years, however, had taught her to trust no-one save herself. So instead, she said calmly,

"No more and no less than I have told you. If you seek any further truths, I suggest you ask your Second, but only if you truly wish to hear the answers. Good day, Messire de Veraux."

Turning her back, she thought their small exchange was done, until he surprised her by appearing suddenly – and soundlessly – at her shoulder, and belatedly she realised he was wearing neither mail shirt, nor spurs on his boots, his wolf-lean body clad simply in dark green breeches and shirt, his thick fall of black hair startlingly stark against the bleached linen, save for those intriguing tendrils of silver that hinted at a more sensitive side to this man she scarcely knew.

He did not speak to her though, merely stooping so that he could look into her tire-maid's widening eyes to say with grave courtesy,

"I am sorry for the loss of your man, but at least now you know he did not leave you through his own choice."

And as Siflaed glanced in confusion at Juliène, tears beginning to well in her brown eyes, she snapped with unfeigned anger,

"I asked you to leave the telling of these tidings to me, Messire. All you have achieved is to upset the girl further!"

And to her tire-maid,

"Come, Siflaed, we will go into the gardens. You need to have a moment in peace and I need to breathe a fresher air than can be found in here."

"Oh, gods, he's dead! He's truly dead!"

The girl was beginning to weep hysterically and as Joscelin de Veraux straightened to his full height, with another murmured word of intended consolation, Juliène sent him a poisonous look, then with an arm around her maid, ushered the sobbing Siflaed out of the High Commander's chambers. How much either of them was playing a part at that point she could not have said.

They had not gone far down the passageway when the dark-haired lad who evidently served as de Veraux's page came running after them.

"Beg pardon, my lady," he said. "If you would follow me, Lord Joscelin sent me to guide you by the quickest way from the guardians' quarters to the palace gardens. No need, he said, for Mistress Siflaed to be exposed to more prying eyes than necessary."

Juliène nodded a stiff acquiescence and did as the boy suggested, following him along a different passageway from that which she had used before, across the guardians' courtyard, then through an archway on the southern side and thus into the palace gardens.

Reluctantly she turned to thank the boy, managing only the barest courtesy before the words shrivelled on her tongue as she looked full into clear grey eyes set beneath level dark brows.

Clearing the sudden raw roughness from her throat with an effort she said,

"Please give your... please tell Lord Joscelin he has my gratitude. And thank you too... Dominic, is it?"

"Yes, my lady."

"Just Dominic?" she queried with a brittle curiosity. "No birthplace? No Fitz to your name? You *do* have a father, do you not? Perhaps one of noble blood?"

A faint flush showed along his high cheekbones, though the granite grey gaze he must have inherited from his father neither wavered nor cracked.

"Does not everyone have a father, my lady?" he answered with an unexpected bravado from a lad in his position.

"Even if we do not wish to own them. Yours was a traitor who bled out his lifeblood on the scaffold. Mine was a soldier who died in some drunken brawl before I was ever born. That being so, why would I wish to claim his name."

Ignoring the flagrant discourtesy, Juliène continued to prick at his defences,

"How then did you come to be one of Lord Joscelin's personal retainers?"

"My grandsire Rhys, who is captain of Princess Linette's guard, asked Lord Joscelin to take me on as his servant when Prince Marcus made him Second of the Guardians."

He shifted slightly.

"If that is all, my lady, may I go now?"

So, she thought, Joscelin de Veraux had not cared enough for his chance-got son to acknowledge the truth of his siring, even when the boy had been placed in his direct care.

Perhaps the man truly did have the heart of ice that rumour credited him with.

Seeing the boy was still watching her with those grey de Chartreux eyes, she dismissed him sharply,

"Yes, go."

Dominic regarded her for a moment longer, then nodded and disappeared back through the archway, leaving Juliène with the still sobbing Siflaed.

Repressing the urge to slap her servant into silence, Juliène merely snapped,

"Oh, do be quiet, girl. There is none here to be impressed by your tears."

"But Lord Joscelin said 'twere true, an' that Edwy be dead."

Juliène cast a quick look around but to all intents they were alone and unobserved.

"For pity's sake, girl, have I not told you already? That is what we *want* everyone to believe! But if I am right, he is not actually dead at all but is... or rather he was in Vézière a few days ago, possibly in company with my outlawed brother..."

Siflaed gasped and then gaped as Juliène continued,

"Or possibly with the same man to whose service he was sworn six years ago."

"Sir Guy, ye mean?"

"Sshh, girl, not so loud! Because if my mother and Lord Joffroi, not to mention Lord Hervé, should learn of this, both Edwy and his master will hang together. And this time there will be no mistake as to their deaths. So you must say nothing, Siflaed, do you understand? Nothing at all about Sir Guy, or his one-time bodyguard. To *anyone*. And then, if you promise to guard your tongue, next time I go to Vézière I will give you the chance to discover whatever you can about Edwy of Rogérinac."

Leaving me free to pursue my own quest to seek out and seduce a certain high-born harper.

Needless to say, this latter thought she had no intention of sharing with her maid.

Juliène had originally thought that she would again have to make use of Hal de Vézière's infatuation with her in order to find an excuse to travel to his home town.

Siflaed's remark about Guy wanting his harp back, combined with a half-remembered comment from her dream, gave her a different idea however.

Accordingly that afternoon, when she attended on the princess, Juliène begged the indulgence of yet another morning's leave from her duties – a boon which Linette appeared perfectly happy to grant – and taking Siflaed to attend her, together with Beric as escort – a favour de Veraux had been distinctly *un*happy about and had conceded only because Juliène had been clever enough to make her request in Princess Linette's hearing – had gone down into Lamortaine, to the small workshop owned by the master craftsman, known throughout Mithlondia, for the quality of his instruments.

This, or so Juliène reasoned, would be the first place Guyard de Martine would go if he were in need of a new harp.

Afraid that she might already have missed her chance, Juliène put her plan into action without further delay, even though she was well aware that her mother had not yet left the palace and might come to hear of her daughter's odd behaviour.

Ignoring that dread possibility as best she could, Juliène wrapped Guy's harp in an old cloak and donning the soberest gown and the plainest veil she possessed, she and Siflaed went down to the guardians' courtyard to meet the clearly-puzzled Beric, who was clad as she had requested in a plain leather jerkin without insignia.

Then, taking three nondescript horses from the guardians' stables, they went to pay a visit to Master Gilraen.

The tale she spun the elderly craftsman was simple enough – that she was a widowed lady of few funds and fewer resources, but possessing an instrument she could not play and wished to sell to someone who might, thus benefiting all parties, since Master Gilraen would of course take a generous commission out of the price paid to him on her behalf.

The instrument-maker, dazzled by her beauty and beguiled by all the fey charm Juliène did not hesitate to employ against him, agreed without demur to the bargain she offered, including the one condition she had thought he might think peculiar – namely that she wished to be advised regarding whosoever enquired after a harp, any sale to be made only after she had personally viewed the prospective purchaser.

Her man, she said, would call in at the workshop every other day and report to her.

With that she swept from the dusty premises, thankfully before Master Gilraen could observe the look of stunned displeasure which Beric made no attempt to hide.

Helping Juliène to the saddle outside the shop, he told her quite bluntly that Lord Joscelin would not like it.

"Lord Joscelin does not have to like it," Juliène replied. "And neither do you. You just have to do as I say until this matter is settled to my satisfaction."

Beric opened his mouth to protest a second time, then catching Siflaed's distraught look shut it again, though it was plain that he wondered what hold the Lady Juliène de Lyeyne could possibly have over his commander that Lord Joscelin would thus bend to her will.

She could have told him it was because she was Joscelin de Veraux's half-sister and that he felt a duty of kinship towards her, but that would not have been true.

The real reason was far darker, a secret Juliène had stumbled on purely by chance the preceding afternoon and meant to make full use of before it became common knowledge – as it surely would in time.

For now though, all her thoughts and hopes were focused on a certain shop smelling of wood shavings, copper wire and beeswax polish, and the harper who would – gods willing – go there soon.

But not too soon, she hastily amended.

Goddess, let him not come while her mother was still at court, lest next time she ventured into Lamortaine town she failed to evade the Winter Lady's merciless green gaze.

As it was, by good fortune or the blessing of the goddess, it was on the evening of the very day her mother departed for the south that Beric brought word to her that a man calling himself Finch of Vézière had come to Master Gilraen's workshop enquiring after a harp, and had promised to return on the morrow to view the instrument.

Torn between relief and impatience, Juliène told herself it was only her imagination that, with the delivery of these tidings, Princess Linette's two cats had seemed to turn their backs on her in regal rejection, an expression gleaming in their golden-green eyes that Juliène found she did not wish to put a name to at all.

At the same time, she felt a flicker of anger piercing her shame. For by what right did such simple creatures judge her own damnably complicated life, where the danger to her beloved brother and estranged son must constantly be set against the downfall of a man she could never allow herself to care for.

If the man who had come to the instrument-maker's shop was even the harper she sought.

It is.

It has to be.

The anticipation alone was sufficient to set her heart to fluttering, so that when she lay down to sleep that night, Hervé's gross, sweat-soaked, revolting body close beside her, it was hardly surprising that she should once more dream of a bed of green, velvety moss and the two lovers who shared such sweet pleasure upon it.

Now all she had to do – goddess help her – was make it happen in truth.

Verse 4

A Single Grain of Midnight-Black Sand

Guy was fully aware that he was risking much in venturing so close to the Court, his life not least. His livelihood, however, made the visit an inescapable necessity.

Having begged leave of Lord Nicholas to travel to Lamortaine in order to replace his missing harp – he had with considerable reluctance told the old nobleman something of the truth of how the instrument had come to be lost – Guy did not immediately leave Vézière, instead taking a little time to allow the dust kicked up by the Black Hunt's near capture of Luc de Chartreux to settle again.

Admittedly, that had been by Lord Nicholas' suggestion, the old nobleman having proven generous indeed in Guy's estimation, demonstrated not only by his readiness to keep in his service a harper whom he now knew to have links to a proclaimed traitor, but also by allowing Guy to take a horse from his stables, rather than having to walk to Lamortaine and back.

Why Lord Nicholas should have such faith that he would return to Vézière, rather than simply absconding with the animal, Guy did not know. Then again, perhaps the old nobleman was secretly hoping that he *would* disappear.

A feat that would be all too easy to accomplish since, with a sound horse between his knees and silver in his purse, Guy could have gone anywhere... even in search of his daughter and her outlawed kin if he chose, more especially as he now had a fairly good idea of where to look for them.

As it was, he could admit to himself that he was tempted to do just that – although if he went, it would be on his own two feet and not on a horse stolen from a man who trusted him against all the evidence against him.

Yet in spite of his almost painful yearning to be where his daughter was, Guy had every intention of returning to Vézière, not only for the reasons he had already given Rowène but also because he could not think that his joining the outlaws would be looked upon as anything more than another mouth to feed. Better, he reasoned, if he should stay in Lord Nicholas' service, earning the silver he continued to hoard for the day when Lissie would have most need of it.

It had grieved him more than he could say to see his daughter and Ranulf's son clad in a manner so ill-befitting their noble birth. At the same time he could not deny that they had seemed content with their lot. Certainly he could no longer doubt that they were loved and well protected.

As for Edwy, it still gave Guy a small jolt somewhere between his gut and his heart every time he thought of the man who had been his and Ranulf's companion through their childhood years, before they had grown up to go their separate ways, Edwy taking his place first as one of the Rogé garrison, then as Guy's personal servant and loyal bodyguard... and all that time they had been brothers, damn it!

Such thoughts, not unnaturally, served to remind him even more painfully of Ranulf.

The brother to whom he had once been so close.

The brother who had callously betrayed him in his absence with the woman Guy had loved and then – as a direct result of that betrayal, perhaps – had chosen to disappear from his life for good.

And finally there was Joffroi, no more nor less of a brother than Ranulf or Edwy by blood, yet a thousand leagues away in every other respect. The same thousand leagues perchance that lay between Lamortaine and Kaerellios, every step of that heart-shattering distance a betrayal of the father whose blood should have bound them all.

His thoughts turning over with such unaccustomed bleakness, Guy found himself standing in the shadows of the stable, watching as one of the grooms – a young man who wore a face a hundred years older than his true age, out of which looked the bitterest brown eyes Guy had ever seen – turned from his tasks to saddle the sturdy moorland mare Lord Nicholas had bidden Guy take to Lamortaine.

"Here ye are," the groom grunted, holding out the reins ungraciously. "See as ye brings her back safe 'n' sound."

He muttered something further, and likely derogatory, under his breath which Guy ignored, merely saying pleasantly,

"Thank you, Gryff. Rest assured, I will do my best."

Then, taking the reins he swung up into the saddle, fighting the impulse to address the other man by another name.

If Geryth wished to hide his past here in Lord Nicholas' stables, so be it.

It was, after all, no more or less than Guy himself was doing, and while he had recognised Geryth not long after he had come to Vézière the previous autumn, the younger man had said or done nothing to make Guy think the reverse was true, and so he had kept his knowledge to himself.

He was simply glad to know that both his former retainers had survived Joffroi's violent desire to erase all trace of his bastard half-brother's existence, though he did find it curious that Vézière was the connection that had drawn them all back together.

For now, however, it was a fine summer's day, he had a good horse beneath him for the first time in far too long, and he was minded to enjoy the journey, more especially as he saw no sign of the Black Hunt as he rode south.

Then, on the second day, he came within sight of the fluttering banners and tall towers of the prince's palace rising high against a cloudy sky further stained by the smokey smudge from Lamortaine's chimneys, and his tension returned ten-fold.

Regardless of the growing tightness across his shoulders, not to mention the trickle of sweat pooling in the small of his back, he was on an honest errand.

Or so he told himself as he momentarily drew rein on the cusp of a small rise, reminding himself at the same time that the likelihood of seeing, let alone meeting Juliène de Lyeyne, was as chancy as finding a single grain of midnight-black sand on the dawn-pink shores of the Astran Archipelago.

Mere common sense, however, could not prevent his heart beating just that little bit more quickly at the sense of danger, tangible as the scent of wood smoke and sweat borne on the damp breeze.

Nor could pragmatism stop his body from stirring unquietly with long-repressed memories of a desire that was as shameful to him now as it had ever been.

It was late afternoon when Guy rode past the guards at the town's northern gate and headed towards the Artisans' Quarter, taking advantage of the excuse offered by the soft, drifting mizzle of summer rain to keep his mantle wrapped closely about him, his features concealed within the deep hood.

Having some knowledge of the town from years past, he rode straight to the White Hart inn where he intended to put up for the night, and thence made his way to the workshop he sought just off Argent Street, the busy road that led through the bustling streets to the shimmering silver expanse of water that separated town from palace, with its sprawling gardens where he had once offered his aid to the woman who was now Juliène de Lyeyne.

Curbing a nagging need to walk down to the lake's edge, on the off-chance of catching a glimpse of that same young noblewoman, Guy turned his steps instead towards Master Gilraen's workshop.

He had gone there occasionally in the past, and at least some of his underlying tension was relieved when the old man showed no recollection of having met him before, either because Master Gilraen's eyesight had grown worse in the intervening years or because his memories of Guyard de Martine could have little in common with the carefully nondescript harper who stood before him now, brows, beard and hair darkened by some beneficent artifice of the Eldest's, and his speech tinged with the hint of a Vézière, rather than his native Rogé, accent.

Having greeted 'Master Finch' and professed himself perfectly agreeable to crafting a new harp, the old instrument-maker tentatively broached a quite different proposition, the gist of which was that a lady had recently visited his shop and requested that he arrange the sale of a perfectly good instrument she had in her possession and which she herself had no use for.

Despite his suspicion that this was not simply the fortunate coincidence it seemed to be, Guy agreed to return the following day at noon and try out the instrument before making a final decision, and then in a mood of brooding disquiet retreated to the White Hart, there to eat a supper of fish stew and bread pudding, and after a mug or two of ale, seek his bed in the men's communal sleeping loft.

Lying awake on his pallet, ignoring the snores and snufflings of those around him, he listened to the town bells toll away the hours of night and watched the silver specks of moonlight dance across the ceiling beams, and all the while his thoughts drifted back and forth between the two sisters with whose lives he and his brothers had become so inextricably entangled over the course of the past ten years.

Despite his simmering anger with Rowène regarding her double deception – and his blazing fury over her betrayal of him with his own bloody brother – he realised in a cooler dash of hindsight that he could to some extent accept that she might have some justifiable cause for her reluctance to reveal the truth to him.

He might choose to look upon his actions as no more than a strict adherence to the dictates of honour but he had to concede that there might have been something of the straight-laced prig about him when he and Rowène had first met at Chartre and later roamed the wilds of Rogé together.

Nor could he deny that the knowledge of their blood kinship had come as a shock to him, and that being so, only the gods knew how *she* must have felt when she had first realised the full ramifications of her irresponsible actions the night of the Mallowleigh harvest fire.

None of which excused her taking Ranulf as her lover in his stead!

That matter aside, he found he could understand, and even to some extent forgive her keeping Lissie's birth and paternity a secret from him – if not his damned brother – as well as her own dangerous masquerade as an outlaw youth, and along with that acceptance came the realisation that Rowène had made it very easy for him to look on her with the dispassionate affection of a kinsman, even while his not-completely-deadened sense of honour informed him that he still had a duty towards her as the mother of his only child.

Whether he could extend that same undemanding acceptance to *Juliène* was another matter.

Particularly if – as he had to admit was not beyond the bounds of possibility – she too was about to betray him.

She had, after all, done so once already.

Six years before, it had been her word that had seen him sentenced to servitude in the warm, translucent waters of Kaerellios' infamous bathing pools, where courtesans of either gender came two to a Kardolandian penny but skilled harpers – fortunately for him – were somewhat rarer.

And now, having escaped that life at some cost to himself, was he about to find himself betrayed a second time – if, that is, Master Gilraen's mystery woman proved to be, as Guy suspected, none other than Juliène de Lyeyne.

Then again, it was always possible that he was seeing deceit and danger in every shimmering, shifting shaft of moonlight, when the stark light of day would reveal that none existed save in his own tormented mind.

Still, better that he be prepared for another betrayal than ignore the possibility altogether, and so he considered once more the few facts Master Gilraen had been persuaded to part with concerning the woman he was acting for.

It *could* be Juliène, Guy thought.

And if it were to prove so, was he so stupid as to take pleasure in her presence in his life once more?

Certainly if the stutter of his heart and the flash of heat in his groin was any indication, he did.

Which, of course, only proved him thrice a fool!

Unable to deny the charge, he moved restlessly on the bed, resolutely turning his back on the moonlight reaching through the crack in the shutters to touch his hair and naked shoulder with all the softness of a lover's caress, and dragged the blanket more closely around him despite the stifling warmth of the summer night.

Yet if he set aside his instinctive reaction – difficult when his mind was fogged by need and his body hardened to the point of pain by a desire he would not yield to – there was nothing beyond the mystery woman's dark hair to suggest a link between the beautiful, wealthy, high-born Lady of Lyeyne and this other outwardly respectable woman who, according to Master Gilraen, was selling a valuable instrument simply because she was in need of money to pay her debts.

As for Guy's own need for coin, he had not so much that he could ignore this chance-come bargain – if chance it was, rather than cunningly contrived trap.

If the harp proved suitable to his purposes, he would be able to return to Vézière with half the silver he had brought still in his purse.

Which could only be to the good, for who knew when Lissie might have need of the coin, and regardless of whatever objections Rowène had it in mind to make, Lissie *was* his daughter and it was both his right and his duty as her father to help feed and clothe her – and Val too if his bloody, treacherous brother was lacking the means or, worse, the will to support his son.

There was, Guy thought balefully, a certain inevitability about it all, and unless he was prepared to turn his back on Lissie and Val –

which he was not – he was resolved to return to Master Gilraen's workshop at the appointed time.

All being well and no trap springing closed about him, he would take the bargain offered to him and be on his way back to Vézière before the sun had set, and think no more of Juliène de Lyeyne.

His decision made and feeling somewhat more at ease because of it, Guy rolled back so that his shoulders were flat on the thin mattress, and with the glittering, seductive moonlight once more softly playing on his skin, he closed his eyes and did what he had to do to bring a similar ease to his tense and aching body.

Having wandered the streets of Lamortaine for the better part of the morning – during the course of which he had succumbed to what he could not help but feel to be a fool's impulse to purchase a length of kingfisher-blue ribbon, in the hope that one day it might be used to tie up his daughter's sun-bright braids – Guy found himself at last standing on the well-trodden strip of ground at the town edge of the lake, directly opposite the palace gardens, and attempting to keep his nerves at bay and his person out of the way of the women who had come there with their baskets of laundry and were now gathered like a gaggle of noisy geese, linen headrails flapping as they scrubbed and gossiped together.

Despite his determination to keep his appointment with Master Gilraen, Guy was still in two minds regarding the likely consequences, and was considerably relieved to learn from half-heard snatches of the women's conversations that Lady Ariène de Rogé had departed with her young son the day before, which meant that any trap set for him would likely not be of her making.

Joffroi, of course, was still at court, his position as Prince Linnius' chief counsellor not sufficiently secure that he would carelessly allow it to slip from his grasp as a result of any extended absence – even for the purposes of seeing his lady-wife and heir safely to their destination.

That said, Joffroi's presence in the nearby palace did not cause Guy half as much anxiety as Lady Ariène's would have done, since by contrast to his witch of a wife, Joffroi having about as much subtlety as a blacksmith's hammer, and experience gained during those blood-drenched years of following Joffroi when the three – no four, for Edwy had ridden with them too – de Rogé brothers had gone reiving across the Larkenlye into Chartreux had given Guy a very good notion of how Joffroi would act in any given situation, including the possibility that his despised half-brother was currently in Lamortaine.

That being so, Guy had decided that if he picked up even the slightest hint that Joffroi had set a guard on Master Gilraen's workshop, he would settle his account at the White Hart and be back on the road to Vézière – empty-handed but with his neck intact – before the next hour bell had been rung.

Whilst his livelihood might dictate that he replace without further delay the harp he had given away, he considered his life and the information he held about the whereabouts of his daughter and his brother's son – and which it was not inconceivable that Joffroi would try to torture out of him – too high a price to pay for a mere object wrought of wood and copper wire.

Lord Nicholas, he reasoned, would surely understand if Guy returned with his errand unaccomplished, and there were other places, other ways, in which he might obtain a new harp.

After all, he had only come to Lamortaine because it was quicker and easier, being relatively close to Vézière and knowing Master Gilraen's reputation as a fine craftsman...

Not because Juliène is here?

The question came unbidden and unwelcome, the familiar voice of Rowène de Chartreux no more than the softest of sardonic murmurs in his mind.

Shaking his head roughly to dispel the spectacularly stupid thought that he might have put his own freedom at risk and – which meant more to him – endangered his daughter's very existence into the bargain, merely that he might catch a glimpse of a woman who, however warmly enticing in his moonlit dreams, surely had ice instead of blood coursing through her heart.

If so, you are a fool, the voice answered his silent conjecture.

Nor could he do other than concur.

For who but a mad fool would risk putting his trust in the very woman who had sent him into slavery?

As for recklessly yielding to this damnable craving to see her... he must be out of his mind!

The voice in his head waspishly agreed with him.

And yet, he reminded himself – and the voice – it had been Rowène herself who had told him that Juliène had tried to save both him and Edwy from setting their feet on the sunset path before their natural span was done.

How then to settle the argument as to what had really happened?

He had been unconscious, and Rowène had not been there.

The only person who knew the truth, and might possibly be induced to tell him, was Juliène.

If he saw her again, and in a situation where they could speak plainly and in private.

Not something he could foresee happening soon, if ever.

Not when she was the Lady of Lyeyne and he little more than a rootless, nameless harper.

Shaking his head again, though less violently this time, he turned away from the water's edge and made his way back to Master Gilraen's workshop just as the noon bell rang out across the red-tiled roofs of the town.

Striding down the narrow street, avoiding pedestrians on one hand and the malodorous gutter on the other, Guy arrived to find two saddled horses standing patiently outside Master Gilraen's premises.

He surveyed both animals – a pair of well-cared for, if nondescript, bays – then turned his attention to the groom who stood at their heads talking to a woman dressed in sober servant's clothing, and even though Guy recognised neither, another rapid glance was enough to confirm his first suspicion that the groom bore himself less like a stable hand and more like a soldier.

Not a Rogé soldier, Guy concluded, still wary, as the younger man courteously dipped his curly head at him as he approached the doorway. The serving woman shied back out of his way like a nervous filly, yet still he had the uncomfortable notion that he could feel her eyes fixed on his back as he ducked under the low lintel and took the step down into Master Gilraen's workshop, the elderly instrument-maker immediately setting aside the lute he was working on to shuffle forwards, his lined face lit by an unshadowed smile.

"Master Finch, welcome, welcome."

"Good day, Master Gilraen, you have the harp?"

"Of course, of course," the old man wheezed.

Turning, he picked up a covered object from a nearby work bench, and drawing off the wrapping – a fine length of sea-green silk – he placed the instrument into Guy's hands with another beaming smile.

"There you are, Master Finch, a fine harp indeed. Yes, very fine."

Ignoring the old man's reiterations Guy stared at the instrument in his hands, his fingers absently smoothing the wooden frame as the harp found a home against his shoulder.

A ripple of notes, sweet as lark song, flowed from his fingertips into the expectant silence, eliciting Master Gilraen's enthusiastic approval. Guy barely heard him, struggling as he was against successive waves of shock, recognition and stunned realisation.

His head snapped up.

"Where is she?" he demanded, quick and low.

"She? She?" Master Gilraen repeated, consternation now plain to read on his face. "You mean Mistress Nell? Come now, come now, Master Finch, you know it was no part of this bargain that you..."

"Never mind."

Putting the old man aside with a careful restraint, Guy stalked towards the curtain separating workshop from living quarters.

Before he could lift his hand to wrench the concealing cloth aside, dainty white fingers performed the task for him, and with considerably more grace and less violence that he would have used.

Still in shock, but with no surprise whatsoever, he found himself facing Juliène de Lyeyne.

Though if it had not been for the disturbing eyes that lifted to his – green as a bed of verdant moss in the sun-dappled shade of some ancient wood – he might yet have been deceived into thinking her the soberly-clad and unknown woman she had presented to Master Gilraen rather than the Faennari witch he himself had been expecting to see from that first heart-jolting moment when he had felt the harp come alive beneath his hands.

Not some stranger's dusty instrument but his own harp that his father had given him so many long years ago.

The harp Guy had left in his chamber the day he had gone to confront Joffroi about their brother's supposed murder.

The same day he had been beaten senseless and sent south to Kardolandia in chains, with a hole torn in his heart, all the bones in his right hand crushed, and little hope of ever reclaiming, let alone playing, his harp again...

A whisper of perfume, a brush of air brought him back to himself, and he realised that Juliène was gliding past him, slender and graceful, long feathery black lashes lowered to pale cheeks as if to shelter her secrets... and before he could decide whether it was wisdom or folly that prompted him, he put out a hand, stopping just short of touching her, his murmured plea for her ears alone,

"Juliène, wait..."

She glanced up at him, the smile on her strawberry-soft mouth as suddenly bleakly empty as the expression in her jade green eyes.

"I think not," she said, her tone as distant as the High Moors of his home. "Give you joy of your new harp, Master Finch."

Then she was gone, leaving Guy frowning after her.

He would, he thought later, have accepted her rebuff, would have let her go without further attempt at speech... if she had not then paused in the doorway, a hesitation so slight he was not even convinced it had happened at all.

He met her gaze for the briefest of heartbeats, and in that moment glimpsed the shadows swirling darkly beneath the seeming clarity of the clear green pools that were her eyes... and even as the door closed and the latch dropped with a soft metallic snick behind her, Guy was moving, his thigh colliding bruisingly with the workbench, made clumsy by the urgency of his haste.

"Look after the harp for me, Master Gilraen. I will be back for it shortly. Here..."

He fumbled in the purse at his belt and almost flung a handful of silver nobles beside the harp, the chime of coins loud in the troubled silence, one rolling off the table to spin on the workshop floor.

The old craftsman stooped to pick it up, straightening to regard Guy with a pensive expression.

"The harp'll be waitin' fer yer return, Master Finch, don't ye worry none 'bout that," he said with none of his usual repetition.

Before adding with a worried sigh,

"An' I'll beg ye ter be careful what ye're about, if ye mean ter go after that woman. There's a feyness about her I should ha' seen before, an' a dangerous music bides in her soul."

"No blame to you," Guy threw over his shoulder as he strode towards the door, pausing with his hand on the latch to add,

"Master Gilraen, if I do not return, get word to Lord Nicholas of Vézière, if you can, of my fate. Oh, and sell the harp. Mayhap it will bring better luck to its next owner than it has to me."

"A moment, my lady, if you will?"

He caught up to Juliène just as she was settling in the saddle of one of the waiting mounts, and risked laying his hand on the dainty booted foot showing beneath the hem of her gown.

She stilled, making no protest at his familiarity, merely staring down into his eyes for the longest moment possible, her green gaze unreadable, before giving the smallest nod of acquiescence, at the same time waving off the groom who had started towards Guy, his hand moving in a manner Guy recognised all too well as one searching for a sword hilt that was not there.

"Do not trouble yourself, Beric," Juliène said, with a calm Guy was nowhere near sharing.

"It seems my business is not yet concluded. Master Finch and I will take a walk down towards the lake. You and Siflaed will accompany us, of course, at a discreet distance."

Beric gave her a dark look that expressed perfectly well the objections he did not allow his tongue to utter and returned to the horse's head, plainly leaving the way clear for Guy to help her dismount.

Very well aware that he was under sharp scrutiny, both from the guardian – of course he was, he could not be anything else! – and the tire-maid – very belatedly, Guy recognised the lass he and Edwy had tried to help at Lyeyné – he set his face into blankly polite lines – a necessary mask he had perfected at the Kardolandian court – and held up his hands, accepting without visible emotion the warm, slender weight of Juliène de Lyeyne into his arms.

It was the first time he had held a woman so close in nearly a year.

It was the first time he had ever held *this woman* so close.

His body's response was as he might have predicted – he was a man, after all.

Even so, he had not expected anything approaching the intensity of his reaction. Though, gods knew, he should have done – having experienced something similar that day in Joffroi's chambers.

When she had pressed her breasts against his chest, and sent her hot tongue into his mouth... and then a heartbeat later had killed his arousal stone-dead by informing him coolly that they were blood kin. A relationship that should have excluded the sort of intimate kiss – no matter how brief it had been, there had been no mistaking the blatant carnality of it – that *she* had chosen to initiate.

Now, as then, the same roil of conflicting emotions surging through him were so violently out of control he thought he might actually be shaking.

Gods help him, if this was what she did to him, perhaps he should have followed Rowène's unwelcome advice and stayed as far away from her sister as possible.

With this worthy, if tardy, intention in mind Guy waited only long enough to ascertain that Juliène's feet were firmly on the ground before removing his hands from her waist and clenching them behind his back. They were indeed trembling and he would tread Hell's darkest depths before he let Juliène see the effect she had upon him.

He did not offer his arm, and after a curious look slanted at him from those mysterious, dark-lashed eyes, Juliène fell into step beside him, Siflaed and Beric following some little way behind.

Gritting his teeth, Guy held his silence as they walked, fighting to ignore the flagrant and outright folly of his actions as much as the escalating argument inside his head.

She betrayed you once – you are a fool if you think she will not do so again!

Is it betrayal that she saved my life the only way she could?

Gods help him, he thought he might just be sick if he could not manage to calm the painful pounding behind his breastbone, or put a stop to the voices rebounding off the inner walls of his skull.

Keeping his hands locked behind his back and his mouth firmly shut, he walked down the street towards the lake, his booted feet kicking up small spurts of dust and other less readily identifiable debris while Juliène kept pace beside him, as lyrically graceful as moonlight on water, apparently as content as he to wait until they came to a more private place before she spoke.

In this manner they came eventually to the water's edge and then, still in silent accord, turned to walk along the reedy shore, past the gossiping laundresses, through the flapping linens of the drying grounds and into the shade of the adjoining wood, grey-green leaves bent by the breeze to flicker like silver in the sun, the footpath dwindling into shadow as it meandered beneath down-swept gilded boughs.

Here they came to a halt, barely a dozen paces along the path yet deep enough within the trees that they were free of observation – Beric and Siflaed having remained just outside the arching willows.

Alone at last with the woman he had every cause to be wary of, Guy found himself sighing softly under his breath as he wondered which of the many questions bouncing around inside his head he should ask first.

Then, prompted by the shadow of a bruise, a faded mauve against the water-lily whiteness of her skin, and the utter vulnerability of her glass-green eyes, he lifted a hand to touch the tips of his fingers to her throat, an intimacy she surprised him by permitting, and asked quietly,

"How goes it with you, Juliène, in your binding?"

He felt her swallow... saw tears shimmering in her eyes as they had the last time they had been this close, that morning in Joffroi's chambers.

She shook her head with its incongruously respectable headrail that covered every single strand of her beautiful midnight-dark hair.

"Do not ask me that, Guyard. Not when you must know the answer. After all, you warned me what Hervé was like, and I would not... *could not* allow myself to listen."

"Is this..."

He brushed his fingers once more over the fading bruise, taking great care despite his surging anger to be as gentle as possible, then seeing her flinch, dropped his hand.

"*This!* This is Hervé's handiwork!"

It was no longer a question.

"Not the work of his hands," Juliène whispered unsteadily, reaching out to catch his falling hand, returning it to the place it had rested a heartbeat before.

"He did it with his mouth. And that is not the worst. See!"

With that, she slipped the neck of her gown down over her shoulder to reveal a series of fresher purple-red blemishes branding her skin from fragile collar-bone to the delicately rising swell of her breast, exposed almost to the tight bud of the nipple outlined by the straining decency of her gown.

And in each livid blotch Guy could see the marks left by the individual points of a man's teeth.

"*The bastard!*"

Guy ground his own teeth until his jaw ached, and with infinite gentleness straightened her gown, being very careful not to brush against her breast.

"I always knew de Lyeyne to be a vicious brute, with a bestial taste for inflicting pain and drawing blood, but to treat you so basely is beyond vile."

"Oh, Guyard!"

She choked on something more than the words, and Guy would not have been surprised if she had vomited.

Not when he could taste the searing bile of disgust in his own throat.

"He... Hervé has always been... rough and... and violent in... in his couplings, but lately he has grown worse. I am frightened that one night he will go too far and tear out my throat."

"I will crush the breath out of *his* throat first," Guy muttered, his vision still tinged with red rage. "And rip off his balls for good measure."

"No! No, you must not go near him."

She laid one soft hand over his flexing fingers, catching his clenched fist with her spare hand, so that she held him captive.

"I cannot go through another day like that other one... the day Joffroi nearly killed you."

She must have read something in his expression because she released him immediately, bringing both hands up to rest on his chest, her green eyes wide, pleading and awash with tears, her words tumbling one after another, lacking all coherence.

"I have not had a chance to say this before. Not to your face. Please forgive me, Guyard. When I said what I did... I was trying to save your other hand from being broken too. I thought.. remembered that my brother Luc had been a slave in Kardolandia, and that he had escaped. But if you had lost the use of both your hands you would never have lasted long enough to escape... And then, gods forgive me, my mother seized upon my foolish words, twisting them into something I had *never* intended. Guyard, you must believe me."

Did she mean what she said?

As her green eyes proclaimed, and he knew all too well, she was of the Faennari and it was impossible for a mortal man to tell whether it was truth or lie she spoke.

Tears glittered and sparkled as a stray shaft of sunlight danced across her face.

Caught in the net of her long dark lashes, he found himself remembering...

Juliène... weeping as he lay barely conscious on the granite floor of Joffroi's chamber. Kneeling at his side, she had lifted his bleeding head onto the silken pillow of her lap, her tears falling onto his raw face, warm and salty...

As warm and salty as were the droplets on his lips today as, unable to stop himself, he bent to touch his mouth to the closed lids of her eyes.

"Gods help me, but I do believe you," he said as he drew back.

"Don't," she sighed

And then, when he frowned down at her in surprise, she opened her eyes again to fix him with a look so speaking he nearly threw all his good intentions into the ice-cold depths of Hell in order to take her into his arms again.

"Oh Guyard, I did not mean *do not touch me*. I meant, do not draw away. Do not leave me cold and alone, not when I have risked everything to arrange this meeting."

"Then you *knew* I would come to Lamortaine?"

That gave him an uneasy queasiness in his gut, to have his suspicions thus confirmed.

"So you are not acting at Lady Ariène's behest? Or Joffroi's?"

"No, no! This has nothing to do with my mother or your brother. Joffroi does not know you are here, and my mother has left Lamortaine until the autumn. This... today... this is for *me*, Guyard. Because I wanted – *needed* – to see you again. To see for myself that you have survived the hell I unwittingly sent you to."

"And is that the only reason you wanted to see me? Well then..."

He smiled, trying to bring some ease to the almost unbearable tension between them.

"As you can see, I am returned from Kardolandia sounder in body than I arrived there, and will happily disappear back into obscurity once I have collected my harp from Master Gilraen."

He gave her a considering look.

"And just how did *you* come by it, if I may ask?"

"I have always had it," Juliène replied. "I took it from your chamber when my mother bade me take and destroy everything of yours, and I have kept it safely hidden since. It was the only thing I had to remind me of you."

And, reaching up, she ran her fingers through his hair, her thumbs smoothing the weathered skin of his cheek, the lines etched at the corners of his eyes, by wind and sun and the passing years.

"To remind me that not everything in my life is ugly and cruel. To give me hope that one day you would return to me..."

Gently, very gently, he put a few more inches of distance between them, trying to ignore the devastation in her eyes.

"Juliène..."

He stopped, drew a deep, hard breath, and continued,

"If you are saying we might be..."

"Lovers? And why should we not be?" she demanded with breathless passion, snatching off the confining headrail to let her dark hair tumble about her shoulders, sending it streaming down over his hands as far as his groin, and releasing a scent that made him think of honeysuckle, sweet and heady beneath a midnight moon.

Except the sun was still high in the sky and he was yet sane enough to know what was right.

"We cannot be lovers," he said, holding her eyes. "Apart from the fact that you wear another's binding band..."

"As do you," she reminded him, reaching up to touch the place where it should be above his left elbow, frowning when her fingers met nothing but sun-warmed linen and warmer skin beneath.

"You took it off? Because you no longer consider yourself bound to Mathilde after..."

She hesitated, before whispering,

"After all that has happened?"

"No, I did not take it off. And am still bound to Mathilde, whether I like it or not."

He saw her confusion and added even more stonily,

"The Master of the Baths in Kaerellios ordered me stripped of the rags they gave me to wear when I left the slave market, but since the binding band was metal and could not be removed in any other way, he had the ring heated until it was soft enough to be cut from my arm."

He saw her wince.

"No, it was not pleasant," he agreed. "But then neither was having a slave collar fitted around my neck and hammered shut."

He ignored the questing touch of fingers against his upper arm and throat, circling with heart-breaking care beneath the coarse linen of his shirt as if her caress might erase the visible scars left by binding band and slave ring.

In much the same manner as her words had finally erased the scars left by what he had once believed to be her betrayal.

Finally, he said as evenly as he could,

"There is another reason... another *law* I will not knowingly break, even though circumstance has consigned the shreds of my binding oath to hell. Moreover it is a law you cannot claim ignorance of since it was you who first told me that we are blood-kin."

He wondered for a moment, as he watched the shadowy thoughts flicker behind her eyes, if she would argue, or worse, let her fingers drift even further down his body to where his rampant prick gave the lie to his words of rejection, and desperate to give her some other rock that she might hold onto in her despair, gave her the only thing he had any right to offer.

"Perhaps though, if there were trust enough between us, we could..."

He halted, the words sounding feeble even in his own mind, let alone spoken aloud, fair game for Juliène's mockery.

"What?"

She mustered a smile as shaky as his, evidently trying to hide the hurt his refusal had so clearly inflicted, and murmured,

"We could be as close as lovers are to each other yet not share a bed? Is that what you would say?"

"No, I did not mean even that. Friendship, kinship, I daresay it does not sound like much to a woman as beautiful and fey as you... but that is all in honour I can offer you, Juliène."

Expecting her to reject his sincerity with scorn, he was surprised when after a moment or two of studying the ground, she looked up to say,

"Oh Guyard, you can have no idea how sweetly seductive such an offer sounds to me."

And with that she leaned into him, resting her cheek against his chest.

"I have had more lovers than I can count," she sighed, a bitter note threading her barely audible voice. "Or perhaps I should say men in my bed, since I loved none of them, nor they me."

"Not even..."

His throat hurt as if he had swallowed shards of sharp iron but he had to ask.

"Not even my brother?"

"No, Ranulf was never more than a means to an end."

She looked up.

"Does that shock you? That I have traded my body and my *beauty...*" She practically spat the word. "For what I thought he could give me? As for the others, they did not even serve my ends, but rather my mother's."

She gave him a small, twisted smile.

"So what does that say about me?"

Sensing that astringency rather than sympathy was needed now, he allowed his mouth to form the same faintly derisive curve as hers.

"You think I am in any position to judge you? You grew up at the Kardolandian Court at Kaerellios and must have spent enough time in those warm, flower-bedecked pools that you can have no illusion as to what I did there or with whom."

Her head moved slightly in negation.

"I am only glad you survived... whatever hurts and humiliations you had to go through to win your freedom."

"Galling though it is, I have your..."

He hesitated and changed his mind about what he had been going to say, instinct advising that it was probably best to avoid bringing her sister – in any of her forms – into this conversation.

"Galling though it was, it was not unendurable. Some might even call it an education."

He had been trying to lighten the conversation but the sudden tension emanating from the slender body in his arms told him that Juliène had recognised his effort for the partial lie it was, and without thinking he added,

"At least by the end I was more harper than whore."

"Do not say that!"

Juliène's head came up so sharply he felt the snap in his own neck. Her green eyes were glittering with fierce golden sparks.

"Do not call yourself that. If anyone is the whore here, it is me. Even my own mother says so. *The harper, the healer, the guardian and the whore.* That is what she calls us four – you, Rowène, Ranulf and... me."

"Curse her for a bloody-minded, foul-mouthed bitch!" Guy growled, his simmering anger at Ariène, Hervé and every other person who had hurt her, taken from her, broken and destroyed her, boiling over into rage.

"You are *not* a whore, damn it! And *she* is nothing more than a manipulative witch with an ice-encrusted rock for a heart."

"Do you think I do not know that?" she asked, her smile still edged with a brittle bitterness.

"Or at least tell myself that. And surely you can see that with the Winter Lady for mother, a murdering madman for foster-father, a drunken bully in my bed and my only child irrevocably lost to me, that is why I value your offer of friendship. And why I will do nothing to put you or that friendship at risk."

He nodded.

"Yes, I do see. And you must know I will do anything – short of lying with you," he added hastily, and far too tautly. "To help you. Know too that if ever you need me, I will come."

"That is good of you, Guyard. And it is true that Vézière is but thirty leagues distant," she said, shocking him anew with her knowledge.

"Princess Linette visits the Grey Sisters there often, and I can contrive to be among the ladies who accompany her. I will be able to see you, and we can talk more easily there. Perhaps you will bring your harp and play for me as you did in Chartre. Except this time my mother will not be there to put a blight on our... friendship."

"So long as such friendship does not leave you at risk of Hervé's wrath."

"If it means I can see you, I will find a way to handle Hervé," she promised. "I have..."

A sharp whistle from Beric made her start and glance over her shoulder.

"I must go before I am missed. But before we part..."

She looked up at him with the first hint of light-heartedness he had seen in her.

"A kiss to seal our friendship?"

A kiss?

The last time – the *only* time – she had kissed him before, it had not been a kiss between friends. And the remembered sensual heat of it not only made his cock twitch but also made him regard her narrowly.

Evidently noting, if misinterpreting his look, the slight, bewitching smile retreated once more behind that fragile facade of distance that made him ache in a different way.

"I know what you are thinking, Guyard! And how could you not? That the last time I kissed you, you lost your freedom and almost your life. Even now you wonder if I mean to betray you. You are wary lest my kiss be the signal for Joffroi's men to leap from their hiding places and take you prisoner ag..."

"No, that is not what I was thinking," Guy interrupted. "Not now, when you have told me the truth of what happened that day in Joffroi's chambers."

He gave a soft grunt.

"It is not fear of betrayal that makes me wary of your... of the intimacy of your mouth on mine."

He grinned mirthlessly at his own arrogance.

"But there! I take too much for granted, and I dare say you meant nothing more than the sort of light kiss exchanged between kin. Did you not?"

Her fingers brushed across his cheek above the close-trimmed beard, then across his mouth, leaving fire in her wake.

"There will be no kiss at all," she said. "Intimate or otherwise, unless you tell me what makes you so wary of my touch."

"I will tell you that if you first tell me why you kissed me that day in Joffroi's chamber. The truth please, Juliène, if we are to be friends."

She hesitated, clearly reluctant to dredge up her memories of that occasion, then squaring her slender shoulders, said with a sigh,

"Guyard, do you remember what had happened the day before?"

"I am not like to forget such a hellish occasion."

"Or that I had spent my first night in Hervé's bed?"

Once more a shudder shook the slender body, even as his brows snapped together at the needless reminder.

"I thought I knew what to expect after Kaslander and R... your brother. But even then, after all you had told me and the gossip going around the palace, it turned out to be far worse than anything I could have imagined, foul beyond words!

"And I was still in a state of shock when I saw you that morning. I felt that if I could only touch you in some way, I could be assured that there was something good and gentle in a life that must now feel only the blight of Hervé's vile possession. And so I kissed you, and while it was wrong of me to use you like that, I could not stop myself. Forgive me, Guyard?"

He gave her a somewhat terse smile.

"Believe me, I have been used far worse, for less cause..."

He saw her swallow and added quickly,

"But we are not going over that again. It is over and done."

"Do not *tell* me... *show* me you forgive me," she pleaded softly as she slid her hands up to his shoulders, and rising on her toes, placed her softly alluring mouth against his lips.

Lips that were – gods forgive him – already partly open in anticipation of the touch of her warm tongue.

"And I shall show you there is no need for you to be wary of me, for whatever cause."

And then she kissed him.

Sweetly and far too chastely.

Nevertheless, that sweet, chaste kiss did exactly as he had feared it would... setting the simmering heat in his already tense body ablaze with all the searing swiftness of Kardolandian night-fire, sending him to another place where moonlight shimmered on the southern sea, and he was surrounded by the heady scent of midnight-blooming flowers, and the sensual sounds of lovers moving together beneath the stars.

Oh, gods...

He kept his groan locked in his throat, opening his eyes to see Juliène looking up at him, the faintest blush of pearlescent sunrise pink colouring her lily-pale cheeks, a tremulous smile on the mouth he ached to kiss again. And again.

Not as a friend but with all the tender passion of a lover.

Damning himself to the icy caverns of Hell he fought for control, for a sense of himself as her kinsman, for the strength to uphold her flawed perception of him as the honourable man to whom she had offered the precious gift of her trust and friendship.

"Thank you, Guyard."

Her voice brushed soft and delicate as starshine across his heightened senses.

"For what?" he asked, his own voice emerging a little more rough-edged than usual.

She shook her head, bundling her hair into the plain linen coif with hands that were as unsteady as his voice.

"Just for being you. The man who gentles my dreams when my life is a waking nightmare."

Her hand lifted to touch his face once more, her fingertips smoothing his short beard, his thick brows, finally combing through the cropped mud-brown hair, a hint of curiosity combining with censure in eyes that were no longer closed and secretive but now seemed as clear and open to him as sunlight welling through the clearest spring-water in some deep green dell.

"I understand the reason," she murmured, adding with the hint of a smile,

"Though I confess I do not care for the colour. I hope this dye, whatever it is, washes out soon, so that you will once more be my golden-haired harper when I see you next."

He shrugged and smiled, trying to maintain some semblance of indifference to her touch, to ignore the possessive quality of her words.

"If it does not wash out, it is but to wait until it grows enough to cut off the brindled bits. In the meantime there is none in Vézière to care how I look."

"No casual mistress?" she asked archly. "To give you relief?"

"No mistress, casual or otherwise. Now go, Juliène, before yon guardian decides he ought to haul me before his commander for making so free with a noblewoman of Mithlondia."

Obedient at last, she turned to walk towards the horses and her two attendants – Siflaed anxious, Beric frowning with impatience – then paused to glance over her shoulder.

"I will see you soon, Guyard. At the Healing House in Vézière. Before the moon is full again. Until then, give me your word that you will take care, and keep out of the way of Joffroi's Black Hunt."

"I will," he promised, adding under his breath as she walked away,

"May the gods guard you, and keep *you* safe from Hervé and anyone else who would cause you hurt or harm."

He moved until he stood at the very edge of the dappled willow shadows, watching as she mounted from Beric's cupped hands, and with Siflaed riding pillion behind the guardian, rode back the way she had come.

He did not expect her to look back.

Nor did she.

But still he kept watch until she was out of sight, knowing that his plain garments and dye-darkened hair made him nearly invisible to anyone looking towards the trees from the drying grounds.

"Gods above, I must have taken leave of my senses," he muttered when she had finally gone beyond his straining sight, taking with her all sense of magic and mystery, the strident horn call from the nearby palace walls serving to reinforce his abrupt return to reality.

"And if I do not end up in a dungeon or on the scaffold," he continued grimly. "It will be by the grace of the gods who watch over lack-witted fools, rather than because of any soundness of judgement on my part."

Still half expecting to find himself surrounded by royal guardians or his half-brother's black-liveried soldiers, he returned to Master Gilraen's workshop to collect his harp and thence to the White Hart.

Guy had intended to leave that same day.

Yet in the end there was one other bit of business that kept him in Lamortaine another night.

This accomplished to his satisfaction, he was back on the road to Vézière as soon as the gates opened at dawn the following morning.

Two days later, Guy came within sight of the walls of the town that had become his home, still with no sign that Juliène had betrayed him, or that he was being hunted for any other reason.

Despite his somewhat extended absence he did not immediately head up to the castle, instead making a small detour to the Healing House where he begged word with the Eldest, and when this was granted answered her unspoken question with a rueful request for salve and linen.

Although he was not normally a violent man, he could not pretend to be sorry for what he had done, and the healer, whilst clearly startled at his actions and concerned for the consequences, had said nothing by way of rebuke as she pursued her calling.

It was therefore late afternoon by the time he eventually dismounted in the castle courtyard and handed the mare over to the grooms.

He then presented himself to Lord Nicholas and being dismissed until it was time for the evening meal, hesitated a moment or two before making his way up to the castle battlements.

Once there, he rested his forearms on the warm stone of a merlon, watching as the sun set the westerly sky ablaze with gold and amber, silver and amethyst, the last glimmering light lingering on the green orchard and grey walls of the Healing House far below him.

Absently flexing his bandaged fingers, he ignored the resultant twinge of pain from his sore and swollen knuckles in favour of remembering Juliène's last few words to him, while behind him a sliver of a sickle moon rose, a token of her promise, the untarnished silver bright against the deepening blue of the evening sky.

Soon, she had said. *Before the moon is full again.*

Until then... well, he had his old harp back – though it would be a few days before he would be able to play it properly – and in the meantime he could hear the words of a new song burgeoning in his mind, growing apace with the waxing moon. By the grace of the gods, and the Eldest's care, he would have it fit to play for Juliène by the time she came to Vézière.

Following Guy's return the summer days continued to flow by, placid and uneventful, his hands healing swiftly, much to his relief.

Try as he might not to keep a count of the steadily passing days, he found himself doing just that... until the morning Lord Nicholas summoned him to the castle garden perhaps a se'ennight before the full of the moon, and time seemed to seize the reins and ride a swift course all its own.

Walking from the cool dimness of the castle into the bright sunlight of the garden, Guy drew in deep breaths of the morning air, still fresh from its journey across the moors and carrying the scent of the nearby lilac trees and the fragrant purple flowers of the vine climbing over the garden's outer wall and which, Lord Nicholas had told him on another occasion, he had planted to please Lady Hélène who had seen one similar in the palace gardens, and now in his blindness it brought him much pleasure too, both in the sweet scent and in the sweeter memories it gave him of the woman he had loved and lost so many years before.

Knowing where the old nobleman would be found, Guy walked towards the far end of the garden, greeting the great golden hound who came bounding up to him with a word and his hand to sniff, Cub giving it a lick of acceptance before turning to trot back to his master.

The old dog lying at the seated man's feet raised his grey muzzle, then dropped his head back onto his crossed paws, in the same moment as Lord Nicholas raised his blind gaze.

"Ah, Finch, there you are."

"My lord?"

"Oh, don't sound so surprised, man. Even if I had not sent for you, do you think I do not know your step by now? Or perhaps you think me lacking in wits as well as sight?"

The old nobleman was obviously in one of his more irritable moods, Guy thought, and wondered what had brought it on so early in the day. Normally it was only in the evening when he was tired...

"Well, man?"

"No, my lord..."

"Stop humouring me as if you were some mindless lackey with your head stuffed full of wheat-straw, rather than it merely being the colour of the stuff that grows on your head. Speaking of which, I have been hearing some odd stories from Eadric following your return from Lamortaine."

"My lord," Guy replied patiently, somewhat self-consciously running his fingers through his hair, now after several washes a mishmash of pale brown threaded with fair.

"I would be a fool indeed if I deemed you witless or diminished simply because you no longer have the vision of a hunting hawk."

He ignored the older man's deep-throated grunt.

"And since you did send for me...?"

He left the question open, an invitation Lord Nicholas answered with something between a growl and a sigh.

"My son arrived late last night."

"Alone?" Guy queried before he could stop himself, memory of the guest Hal de Vézière had brought with him last time he visited his father still all too raw in his mind.

"Aye, thank the gods," came the barked retort.

"Mark my words, Finch, there can be no happiness for any mortal man who tangles with a Faennari witch, and my son is a fool if he thinks to slake his lust with this particular one! She would suck the life out of him and shrivel his balls into the bargain. And so I told him last time he came home, but since nothing in this castle stays a secret for long, I expect you know that already."

"I did hear something of the sort," Guy confessed, adding in a harder tone. "I also happen to know that the lady in question did not... invite your son's... attentions."

"Then why in gods' name did she come here with him, if not to act the wanton in his bed?"

"I do not know, my lord."

I wish I did.

"Aye, well, she is not come with him now, which is all that concerns me."

De Vézière let loose an exasperated sigh.

"That said, we must prepare ourselves for visitors nonetheless."

"Aye, who, my lord?" Guy asked, a tightness growing behind his breastbone.

"Prince Linnius and half the feckless fools of court, that's who," Lord Nicholas growled.

"They arrive in three days' time, and will expect the finest of foods and the best of entertainments. Fortunately – or perhaps not, as far as you are concerned, Finch – I have the best harper in Mithlondia in my service.

"So get your fellow minstrels together, sort out what you have that is fitting for royal ears, and then practise until you can play every last ballad and roundel in your sleep. Come to that, have I not heard you picking out the notes of a new tune in your spare time?"

"Aye, my lord," he agreed cautiously.

"Good. You have three days to make sure it is fit for public performance."

"I will do my best."

He hesitated.

"My lord..."

"Yes, Finch, what is it?"

"Do you know exactly who will be accompanying the prince?"

If Lord Nicholas thought this request from the man who was merely his household harper strange, he did not show it, merely saying,

"Linnius' closest friends and counsellors, naturally, together with Prince Kaslander, all of whom will be accommodated here at the castle. The ladies, however – that is, Princess Linette and her companions – will be staying down with the Grey Sisters at the Healing House, though they will of course spend much of their time here in the castle. And before you ask, I have no idea for how long we will have to endure this royal visitation. Until Linnius becomes bored, I suppose.

"Now get to it, Finch. I have already sent Hal and the huntsmen out over the moors, and no doubt by now Alfgar and his good wife will have set the dust to flying in their efforts to make ready the guest

344

chambers. *I* am going to be damned uncomfortable until after this precious royal party has been and gone, and see no reason why you should escape the upheaval either."

"No, my lord, I had not thought to do so," Guy assured him, not entirely truthfully. "By your leave?"

And with a wistful look around the quiet garden, the sunlit serenity disturbed only by a blackbird's song, the plop of a fish in the nearby pond and the cooing of doves in the dovecote beyond the wall, he made his way back into the castle shadows, turning over Lord Nicholas' words.

Would Joffroi and Hervé be among the courtiers accompanying the prince?

And if they were, what were the chances that either or both of them would see Lord Nicholas' household harper for the man he really was?

He shrugged broad shoulders.

He would face that problem when, and if, it arose.

Far more dangerous – and alluring – was the possibility – probability, even – that Juliène would be one of Princess Linette's chosen companions.

And if she was?

He could only pray to the gods that with half the court around, she would have the sense not to acknowledge him, and that neither would she be so reckless as to seek him out if he did not find some way of approaching her discreetly.

Then again, perhaps in the intervening days she would have thought better of pursuing their *friendship.*

Not that Guy considered that the most fitting word to describe what lay between them – he merely hoped to convince himself that friendship was all it was.

All it could ever be, he reminded himself grimly, as he went to fetch his harp from his room before seeking out his fellows.

Three days later, and with the castle still in a state of ordered chaos, Lord Nicholas despatched Guy to the Healing House with a request for as much mead as the Eldest could provide.

Although the royal party was expected before the end of the day, there was no sign of their arrival when Guy took a quick look from the castle walls just before making his way down into the town.

The weather had been dry for the past three days – a gods'sent gift to the harassed servants trying to air musty hangings, dry bed linens and wash flag-stoned floors before laying clean rushes – and with such a large cavalcade coming up the highway from Lamortaine the dust haze marking their passage would be clearly visible against the hot blue of the summer sky.

The horizon remained unblemished, however, and after another glance south Guy descended the stone steps beside the gatehouse somewhat less hurriedly than he had ascended and made his way to the stables.

With the place in much the same turmoil as the keep, he was fortunate enough to find the head groom close by the door, caustically directing his minions in their labours.

"Aye, Master Finch?" the man said, spitting out the piece of straw on which he had been chewing. "Come wi' more orders from his lordship, is it?"

Guy gave the other man a conciliating smile.

"I'm afraid so. Can you lend me one of your lads and a pack pony for the rest of the morning."

"Aye, ye can tek that lazy bugger, Gryff. I'll tell him ter get Molly tacked up an' send them along if ye'd care ter wait in the yard, Master Finch."

"And get out from under your feet, I suppose?" Guy said drily, and the normally dour stableman gave him a quick grin.

"Aye, well, I reckon 'tis just as mad in the castle too?"

"You could say that," Guy agreed, and retreated to the yard.

Leaning against the mounting block, he enjoyed a rare moment of doing nothing, watching the swallows diving over the courtyard as they went about their business of catching flies for the young still in their nests below the high eaves, whilst the servants – both man and maid – scurried with equal diligence about the task of making the castle fit for royal habitation, more than one of them directing a questioning glance at the idling harper.

His reverie broken by the sound of hooves against the courtyard cobbles, Guy straightened away from the sun-warmed stone of the mounting block and set off towards the gateway, Molly the pony and Geryth – or rather Gryff, for this morose young man bore no resemblance to the cheerful lad Guy had known at Rogérinac – following after.

Far from displeased to be released from the ordered mayhem within the castle precincts, Guy did not make any particular haste down to the Healing House, and despite Geryth's subdued grumbling allowed his attention to wander over the varied stalls and pitches crowding the market square.

Even more crowded than usual for a market day, he amended, and catching snippets of the excited chatter, realised that the imminent arrival of the prince and half his court was scarcely a secret. Not only in the town, but also for several leagues around.

All of which made him wonder just why in gods' name the horse-traders he could see in their accustomed position at the western end of the square had chosen this particular day to come to Vézière with their stock!

After a moment of exasperated reflection, however, wherein he reminded himself that it was no business of his what they did, providing they were not endangering his daughter or Ranulf's son – and there was no sign of either child in the square – Guy carried on his way to the Healing House, intending to check that neither child was there. Only then would he make any approach to the two outlaws he had seen – and recognised amidst a roiling tumble of emotion.

Arriving at the Healing House, Guy found the Grey Sisters going about their tasks with an enviable tranquility and lack of excitement over the impending arrival of the royal visitors.

But then as the Eldest placidly pointed out Princess Linette and her favoured ladies were scarcely unknown strangers within their walls, while little Princess Lilia had been born there.

Nevertheless, all was in readiness for their arrival, the Eldest confirmed, her impressive calm relaxing momentarily into a sympathetic smile as she watched Sister Gunhilda load the pony's panniers with the earthernware bottles of mead destined to augment the castle's wine supply.

This accomplished, with minimal assistance from a scowling Geryth, Guy turned to thank the Eldest on behalf of Lord Nicholas. Only to find his words drying in his mouth as he saw Molly start to sidle, throwing up her dappled head in response to the arrival of a troop of strange horses.

"It is the princess and her entourage," the Eldest informed him quietly.

An entirely unnecessary piece of information as he had already recognised a number of faces amongst the riders, not least Joscelin de Veraux's lean unreadable visage and Princess Linette's openly smiling countenance, made more noticeable by contrast with his cousin Adèle's shuttered expression.

Then, a moment later he discarded all thought of Adèle as his searching eyes met the secretive green gaze of Juliène de Lyeyne.

Gods! She came! She is really here!

Did his heart truly halt its beat within his chest for a single painful moment?

Or was that merely his imagination?

Either way, he had no place here and no desire to be recognised, either by de Veraux or the princess. As it was Adèle was staring fixedly at him, her blue eyes wide and wary.

"I should be going," Guy murmured to his companion. "And give you the chance to greet your noble visitors without the hindrance of a scruffy harper by your side. My lord's thanks for the mead, Eldest."

"It is the least I can do," she murmured back. "I shall see you soon, Master Finch, with all the latest tidings from court, should you be interested."

He shot her a quick, sideways glance, only to find that she was no longer looking at him, her blue eyes resting thoughtfully on his cousin Adèle and – as he forced himself to remember – his only slightly more distant kinswoman, Juliène.

She, it seemed, had not taken her eyes from him, and now de Veraux had noticed the unwavering nature of her attention and had turned his habitually cool grey gaze on him too.

"Go," the Eldest said, more firmly this time.

And with a curt word to Geryth, he went... though only after bowing low as Linette swept past, her hand on Joscelin de Veraux's arm, her ladies following after in casual order – Adèle unnaturally pale and quiet, others Guy did not know chattering gaily amongst themselves and giving him no more than the briefest of curious glances. After these came the nursemaid carrying the little princess, and finally, languidly bringing up the rear, Juliène de Lyeyne.

Guy straightened from his obeisance just as a pair of sea-green silk slippers passed within his line of sight, and the merest breath of a promise reached his ears.

"When darkness falls, I will find you."

Verse 5

Meet Me At Midnight

The promise implicit in Juliène's few whispered words had been enough to send Guy from the Healing House with his mind in a state of distraction sufficient to shield him from Geryth's continued complaints but which very nearly resulted in him being ridden down by a troop of horsemen who came clattering up the cobbled street behind them.

Becoming aware of them only at the last moment, Guy flattened himself against the rough wall of the nearest dwelling, waiting alongside a cursing Geryth and restless Molly until de Veraux and the half-dozen guardians of the princess' escort had clattered past, heading for the castle.

Once they were gone, Guy continued on up the hill at a brisk pace until he came to the market square. There, he came to a halt and turned to his sullen companion.

"I have business here. You go on up to the castle. Oh, and make sure you deliver the mead to Alfgar with the Eldest's compliments."

Then he waited. From what little he had seen of the man Geryth had become, he did not expect him to take the orders of a mere harper without argument. Nor did he.

Guy allowed his former groom's grumbling defiance to ramble on for a while, then interrupted him to say,

"Just do it, Geryth," and while his words were mild enough, the harsh Rogé accent underpinning his tone was not. And had an immediate effect.

"Aye, Master G..." Geryth started.

Then suddenly realising what he had been about to say, stopped and stared across Molly's laden back, his brown eyes wide in a face now so pale as to show every freckle and fleck of dirt.

"Master *Guy*," he whispered. "Oh, gods, sir, 'tis truly ye?"

"Aye, it is. For if I were not, how would I know that Gryff is in truth Geryth?"

"Aye... but... but I thought ye was dead, sir."

"No more than you, it would seem. Now, please, will you just do as I ask and return to the castle without further argument. There is someone here that I must speak to."

"Oh, aye, sir?"

The younger man glanced about the crowded market place, a spark of the old quickness of wit in eyes that had shown only a dour disregard for life since his sister had died, then indifference returning, he shrugged and said,

"Aye, whatever ye say, Master..."

"Finch," Guy cut in before he could complete his sentence. "No 'sir', Gryff. Just Finch. Or Master Finch, if you must."

"Aye, Master Finch, I'll not fergit again. I'd not see ye dead alongside yer murderin', midden-maggot brother. C'mon, Molly-lass, let's go."

And with that Geryth continued on up the hill, the faintest of thin, tuneless whistles drifting back to his former master. Whilst it was not a particularly joyous sound, it was nonetheless considerably more welcome than his previous undertone of relentless grumbling.

Left to his own affairs at last, Guy made his way through the market, exchanging greetings with those tradesmen and merchants he knew, pausing to reply to excited questions from groups of townswomen who, recognising him as one of Lord Nicholas' household, wanted to know exactly when the royal visitors were expected to arrive and which of Mithlondia's great noblemen would be accompanying the prince.

Between the promptings of discretion and the plain truth that Guy knew little more than the women, he was not able to satisfy their curiosity to any great extent, though his habitual gentle courtesy softened their disappointment in his uninformative replies.

In this halting manner he came eventually to the far end of the square where the horse traders were making ready to depart, having sold all the ponies they had brought with them. There were, in fact, three men all told, rather than the two he had originally thought.

One was Beowulf of Mallowleigh.

The second was the sharp-featured young man he remembered from that previous, never-to-be-forgotten occasion... Alaric?.. no, Aelric, that was it.

And the third was his half-brother, Edwy of Rogérinac.

All three stopped what they were doing as Guy came up to them, Aelric's pale gaze flicking from Guy's face to the space behind him as if checking he was alone, Beowulf nodding his head in circumspect greeting, only Edwy coming forwards with his arm tentatively outstretched.

Guy took it without hesitation, saying quietly,

"Edwy, I did not look to see you here but I am glad nonetheless."

At which the other man's wary look warmed into the grin Guy remembered from those distant childhood days.

"Guy."

The single word emerged somewhat stiffly, but Guy did not care. Edwy had called him by his given name as a brother should, and that was all that mattered. No doubt the man would find it easier in time to slough off the ingrained habits of more recent years.

"So, how goes it with you, Edwy? And Li... the others? All are safe, I trust? And very far from here?"

"Aye, to all of it," Edwy continued. "An' I'll tell ye 'bout yer little lass, if ye'd like. Jus' not here in the street fer any busybody ter see. It don't matter a damn ter me but I misdoubt Lord Nicholas would care fer his harper havin' any truck wi' the likes o' us, 'specially after what happened a couple o' months back."

"What you really mean is that you don't care for the thought of facing Lord Nicholas again so soon after that last time?" Guy offered, with a wry smile to take any sting out of the comment.

"Aye, though it could ha' been a bloody sight worse. His lordship's a good man, right enough. Then again, I reckon he'll be like a cat on hot bricks right now."

"You've heard the gossip about the forthcoming royal visit then?"

"Who hasn't? Seems like the whole bloody province is talkin' 'bout it."

"That being so, and tempers being a mite strained up at the castle at present, you're probably right about us being seen together. That said, I would like to buy you all a drink and hear... whatever you can tell me about Lissie, and Val too."

He glanced around.

"The Cock should be quiet enough at this time of day and I have it on good authority that Mistress Birch has a skilled hand..."

He ignored the snicker young Aelric made no attempt to suppress, and Beowulf's sudden, frowning stare to finish his sentence evenly,

"When it comes to brewing ale."

Edwy merely grinned, and with an *I could have told you that* look tossed at his companions, said,

"I reckon we could manage a mug or two afore we need ter be gone."

Interestingly, Guy thought, Mistress Birch had taken one look at him and his companions and poured four beakers of ale without making any attempt to interest them in the principle service offered by the establishment.

Furthermore, even as Guy was counting out the requisite amount of copper marks onto the trestle between them he was very aware that her dark eyes were fixed not upon the coins in his hand but rather upon his face.

"Ye'm not goin' ter cause no trouble, are ye?" she asked abruptly as she reached out to sweep the coins into her hand.

"*Me?*"

Guy looked up at her, startled.

"Aye, I don't want no fightin' this time, nor no corpses neither. Not when Lord Nicolas said next time it happened, he'd ha' no choice but ter close us down."

"I think you are confusing me with someone else," Guy said drily. "This is the first time I have ever set foot beneath your roof."

"Aye, the hair's diff'rent, I'll grant ye that," she conceded, peering at him with shrewd brown eyes. "But yer face though... I reckon ye an' that other one could be one an' the same."

"I think you will find that the *other one*, as you call him, is a soldier in royal service, whereas I am merely a harper, currently in Lord Nicholas' household, and therefore unlikely to cause you trouble in any way. I am here simply to share a peaceable ale with my friends..."

"Aye, that's what *he* said, that he were just here ter sit an' think an' drink, an' see what come o' that! A wrecked room an' a payin' customer – fer all he were a rat-arsed little weasel – tossed out o' *my* window, ter spill his brains in the street outside *my* house. Not but what I wouldn't ha' said good riddance, save it brought his bleedin' bastard lordship down here. Him wi' his eyes like grey ice an' a voice fit ter freeze fire! Unsettled ev'ryone, he did. An' I tell ye straight, that sort o' thing, 'tis bad fer business."

"From the gossip doing the rounds up at the castle, I had rather supposed it had been good for business," Guy murmured. "But if you prefer that we left, we will."

"Nay then, ye can stay, since I reckon ye're tellin' the truth 'bout who ye are. Or rather who ye aren't."

She eyed him reflectively.

"Now I comes ter think on it, I seen ye at the Summer Festival jus' gone. Seen what ye did fer that little maid an' all. An' 'cos o' that, I'll tell ye somethin' fer nothin', which is a thing I don't normally do. If *them's...*"

She jerked her pointed chin at the outlaws, waiting nearby.

"The sort of friends ye keep, ye'm headin' fer trouble, Master Harper. I knows who they be, see?"

"Thank you, Mistress Birch, I know who they are too," Guy replied pleasantly, and picking up the mugs walked over to the table where the three outlaws had found seats.

Beowulf, he saw, was looking vaguely uncomfortable to find himself in such sordid surroundings, while Aelric had his lively gaze trained on what little he could see of the sunlit square through the open door, and Edwy...

Guy met his half-brother's wryly questioning look with an equally rueful smile.

"As long as we behave, she will not throw us out."

"Don't think I'll gi'e her the chance," Beowulf muttered. "I'll take my ale outside, if 'tis all the same ter ye, Master Guy. Leave ye an' Edwy ter talk like."

"I'll come wi' ye," Aelric said. "Someone did oughta keep an eye out fer trouble."

With that the two men rose and, with a chary look at Mistress Birch who was still watching them, arms folded beneath her bounteous breasts in a manner that had absolutely nothing of enticement and everything of warning about it, they walked out, beakers in hand. They did not go far, however, remaining within sight, sipping their ale, talking quietly between themselves, and Aelric at least keeping a keen watch for anything untoward.

Guy regarded them for a moment, with something of a smile, then turned back to Edwy to say,

"I still find it odd to see a Rogé man and a Chartreux one in amity."

"Aye, we're an odd lot all told," Edwy agreed. "Those of us who keep company, for whatever reason, wi' the attainted Lord of Chartreux's sons."

Ignoring the plural, Guy swallowed the mouthful of ale he had just taken and put down his mug.

"Ahhh! That's good. Beorn was right about the brew here! Now, Edwy, tell me what happened after you left Vézière that morning."

So Edwy told how, having returned to the forest, Luc had immediately ordered them to move camp again, reasoning that if Caitlin had betrayed them to the Black Hunt she would also have told Oswin One-Eye everything else he wanted to know.

Joffroi's huntsmen had indeed made several forays into the forest, burning as they went, until Justin de Lacey had managed to persuade Prince Linnius to call a halt to the destruction.

Since then, the outlaws had been left to lick their wounds – three had died in the forest raids, and all had suffered wounds or burns of varying degrees – though Edwy hastened to assure Guy that Lissie and Val were unharmed and safe.

Or as safe as they could ever be.

Edwy then went on to explain how – urgently needing the coin they earned from their semi-legitimate horse trading but being banned from Vézière – he, Beowulf and Aelric had gone south and west, taking the half-broken animals to sell in the more distant towns and villages of Valenne and Vitré.

It had been a long, hard journey with precious little profit to show for the venture, and in desperation they had decided to return to Vézière with the remaining horses. These sold, and Lord Nicholas hopefully none the wiser as to their presence, they would be heading back to the forest forthwith – there to face Luc's wrath for breaking their collective oath not to return to the town.

"Worth it though," Edwy said, patting his purse, which released a soft chinking sound. "An' his anger won't outlast the sight o' the little 'uns tuckin' into good wheat bread an' the Sisters' heather honey fer a change."

He grinned.

"Soft as butter, Master Luc is where his sisters' bairns is concerned."

"And you are not with your brothers' children?" Guy said knowingly. "I have seen you with them, remember?"

Before Edwy could reply, even had he intended to defend himself against the charge, Beowulf had come briskly back into the brothel and setting his empty beaker down on the table, said gruffly,

"Yer pardon, Master Guy, but I reckon we ought ter be on our way. An' Aelric says there's somethin' as ye might both want ter come an' see."

Exchanging a look, Guy and Edwy drained their own almost untouched ale and with a nod at the watchful woman behind the trestle, walked towards the doorway, Guy – whether by chance or Edwy's design – a step or two behind his half-brother.

Looking over Edwy's shoulder Guy saw the most ill-matched, discreditable troop of hard-faced horsemen he had ever seen – not excluding the Black Hunt – riding through the square, the townsfolk falling over themselves to get out of their way.

It was not a large troop, the horses covered with the dust of the summer roads, what armour the men possessed dubious in comparison with the glittering ring-mail the guardians accompanying Joscelin de Veraux had worn.

Indeed Guy was not even sure whether these men were soldiers or merely a band of armed ruffians, so lacking in uniformity and cohesion was their appearance. They looked as if they had been living rough in the wilds of Mithlondia for uncounted years... and with that thought, some distant bell of reason rang in his mind.

His gaze snapped to the two men heading up the cavalcade, and a curse hissed between his teeth as belatedly he recognised them both, though neither bore much resemblance to the men he had once known.

Of the two, Gabriel de Marillec was perhaps the most changed, his long, light brown hair bound up in a myriad of tight braids threaded with beads of raw amber, and where he had previously been clean-shaven as a nobleman should be, the almost effeminately beautiful lines of his face were now obscured by a barbarian's beard, braided and beaded in similar fashion to his hair.

Moreover, in contrast to his former indolent public manner, alert amber eyes glittered between bronze-tipped lashes, his once delicately drawn dark brows, now their natural colour, almost meeting over the thin, hooked nose that appeared to be the only aspect of the man unchanged from the last time Guy had spoken with him.

Which, if Guy remembered right, had been the day when Gabriel had offered his friendship and sworn to keep Adèle safe from harm as some recompense for having refused to share any save the most basic details regarding the guardian Rafe of Oakenleigh.

The very same man who, unless Guy missed his guess completely, was presently riding in easy companionship at the Second's side.

Yet if it was the same man whom Guy had watched being flogged beside the Marillec highway – as a result of his questionable actions towards the outlaw known as Jacques de Chartreux – he too had changed out of all recognition over the course of the past six years. The cropped flax-fair hair was now almost as long as his commander's and braided in the same fashion, save only that the pale plaits were bound together at the nape of his neck, while his light blond beard was neat and devoid of any ornamentation.

What Rafe of Oakenleigh – if it was him – lacked in decoration he made up for in weaponry, having a battleaxe on his saddle, a sword at his back, a long knife sheathed at his hip and another in his boot. Dressed in the same worn leather and dirt-greyed linen as every other man in the group, he looked no less dangerous than any royal guardian and far more disreputable.

What he did not look like was a high-born nobleman's son.

Not that the Second did either, but Guy was not concerned with de Marillec just now.

What Rafe of Oakenleigh was, did he but realise it, was confirmation of all the doubts and questions that had tormented Guy for the past six years.

Just then the roving dark blue gaze reached out over the heads of the milling townsfolk, narrowing suddenly as something caught his eye as he glanced in the direction of the brothel.

He could not possibly have seen Guy, standing as he was within the shadows of the doorway. Nevertheless, draw rein he did and with a word first to his companion and then to the lad riding just behind them, dropped down from the saddle to stride across the square, men, women, children and chickens scattering at his forceful approach.

With the younger man following closely at Rafe of Oakenleigh's heels, Gabriel de Marillec remained where he was, watching their progress, the reins of all three horses held loosely against his thigh, a flicker of something that might have been acerbic amusement in his otherwise expressionless gaze.

Then, with a shrug of his slender shoulders, he turned to lead the rest of his troop on up the hill towards the castle, plainly leaving Rafe to settle his own affairs in whatever manner suited him best.

For his own part, Guy was only vaguely aware of Aelric crushing the brown-haired youth into a roughly fraternal embrace as the big, fair-haired, almost-stranger came to a halt in front of Edwy, demanding curtly,

"Is he here?"

"Who?" Edwy asked, though Guy had the feeling he knew the answer already.

"Jacques, damn you."

"Nay, 'tis jus' Aelric, Beowulf an' me."

At the mention of the former Mallowleigh headman's name, the dark blue eyes flicked a baleful glance in his direction, for all its swiftness every bit as cutting as a lash stroke.

"Then something's amiss. I've never known Beowulf desert his master before."

He glared at Edwy.

"What in hell's happened? And why wasn't I sent word? I swear if any ill has befallen Jacques..."

"Jacques's fine. An' yer son too," Edwy replied, a faintly reproving note in his rough voice – and something else that evidently served to put the other man on his guard.

"What is it, curse you! Why do you look at me so?"

It was at this moment that Guy chose to step out of the shadows of the brothel's doorway.

"Ran." He spoke quietly, the word both a greeting and all the other things he dared not allow his tongue to express more fully, the edge of a rarely-roused temper underlying his level tone a warning that he was liable to either pull his brother into his arms or smash his fist into the face that, despite the passage of the years, was still so very similar to his own.

He saw the dark blue eyes widen, read the reflection of his own contradictory thoughts and emotions in the flicker of light and shadow across the features that were even more weather-beaten than the last time he had seen him, and finally the hard mouth relaxed in the merest hint of the deep-rooted affection that had always bound them one to the other, twins in all but name.

Ranulf spoke but a single, heartfelt word.

"Guy!"

Then the fleeting emotion was gone and it was an excoriating, narrow-eyed glare he turned on Edwy.

"Why in bloody hell did no-one see fit to send me word that my brother was here?"

"Which brother?" Guy asked with a deceptive mildness before Edwy could reply.

And ignoring Edwy's choked off protest, added tersely,

"We are all brothers here, Ran."

Once more the dark blue eyes flared wide, before Ranulf's startled expression warmed into a grin as he reached out to snag Edwy's arm.

"Why in bloody damnation did you not say so before, man?"

"Ye doesn't doubt me then?" Edwy asked, dropping back into the rough Rogé speech of their childhood.

"Would *you* doubt anything Guy told you as being the truth? Hell knows, I would as soon doubt that he is my brother as that you are."

"I wish I might have the same confidence in *you*, Ran," Guy put in, his cold anger gaining the upper hand in the roil of emotions fighting for supremacy.

"Or I suppose I should call you *Rafe* now. Though I could think of other things a damned sight more fitting. Hell take you, you let me think you were *dead*! You seduced secrets out of the woman I loved, *slept with her* for gods'sake, and kept the truth about my only child from me! How brotherly was any of that?"

And as Ranulf opened his mouth, he continued sharply,

"No, do not bloody tell me you did not mean to, or that any of it was for my own good! I have already heard all that well-meaning sort of *shit* from Rowène herself."

"You have seen her?"

His brother was pale now and sweating.

So much so that Guy would not have been surprised if Ranulf had suddenly doubled over and spewed his guts up, there in the public street.

Then he seemed to snatch back some control over himself, and ground out,

"I never seduced anything out of her, damn you. Or... slept with her. Whatever she gave me, it was..."

He grimaced and broke off.

"It was of her own free will, was it?" Guy finished for him, a furious disbelief lifting his brows and harshening his level voice. "Even back in Chartre in '94!"

"No, not then," Ranulf muttered, a flush rising beneath his weather-worn skin. Then, more forcefully,

"I am talking about *now*. Or at least how it was with us the last time we were together. That was at the end of last summer, nearly a year ago, damn it, and I haven't seen her since."

He shook his head impatiently.

"It was just before you returned to Mithlondia. We knew you were coming, of course, but..."

"And just how did you know I was coming back at all?" Guy demanded. "I sent no..."

"Gabriel."

"*Gabriel?* You mean de Marillec told you! And just how did *he* know such a thing? Unless... no, I would swear he had not seen me."

"No, he... he had some sort of... fit." Ranulf 's voice, already quiet, was now almost inaudible. "He said you were near... and a lot of other things that none of us could make sense of, even Luc who knows him best. Something about a harper and a healer, standing together in the moonlight amidst a field of blood..."

Guy could not quite repress the shiver than ran through the muscles of his shoulders at this imperfect echo of the words Juliène had spoken, but Ranulf was still talking, his voice low, strained, rough as gravel.

"Whatever is going to happen, however this... business... is to be finished, it would seem that we are bound together until the end of it, the four of us... Ro, Juliène, you and I."

"So it would seem. If, that is, de Marillec's words have any more substance than can be found at the bottom of one of his own wine barrels."

"He was not drunk that night. He very rarely is. Damn it, Guy, I saw what the speaking of those words did to him! And I believe him."

Guy himself did not know what to think, though to a certain extent his belief or otherwise was irrelevant to the matter at hand.

Holding his brother's eyes, he said firmly,

"Whatever the meaning behind de Marillec's words, you need not trouble yourself further on Rowène's account. She and Lissie are *my* concern now. As Val should be yours!"

He easily read the flare of hot temper in the dark blue eyes, and curious to see how far Ranulf would trust him, said with deceptive mildness,

"So where does Jacques fit into this mess? And what is he to you that you must needs speak of him to Edwy before anything else? Or have you been so long on the border with de Marillec that you have taken his dubious preferences for your own?"

Ignoring Edwy's sudden frown and sharply questioning glance, Guy watched as the dark blue eyes narrowed at what, for most Mithlondians, would be a deliberate insult.

Ranulf, however, merely said in grating tones,

"Gabriel is my sword-brother and Jacques is my kinsman. Neither of them is my lover. But even if one or both of them did share my bed, it is none of your fucking business! And while I thank the gods that you survived your exile, brother, I would have thought living amongst the Kardolandians, however unwillingly, would have taught you some degree of tolerance. Unfortunately, I see you are still the same self-righteous prick you always were in such matters..."

"If by that you mean I still do not condone rape..."

"Nor do I, curse you! I never bloody have! That was not my meaning, and you fucking well know it."

Ranulf drew in a harsh breath and visibly strangled his temper back into submission.

"Whatever our differences, I hope now that you are back in Mithlondia you will have the sense to stay out of Joffroi's way. He had a long arm before, Guy. He has a longer one now, and this time he *will* kill you."

His black look lightened into a brief grin as he gave his other, new-found, brother a slap on the shoulder.

"As for you, Edwy, look after yourself. Give my greetings to Jacques when you see him, and this to Luc for Val's keep." He dropped a purse in Edwy's hand. "And tell Val..."

"And tell Val what?" Guy enquired when Ranulf stopped. "Have you no word of greeting to send to your son? Nothing warmer than cold coin?"

"It is all I can give him," Ranulf said stonily. "Do you do even as much as that for your daughter? As for Val, he knows me only as Rafe of Oakenleigh, a man with the guardians' mark on his arm and nothing more. It is better that way."

"For whom?" Guy queried. "For you, obviously, if not for Val. At least my daughter knows the truth, knows me."

Ranulf gave him a look of dark brooding rancour that gave warning to one who knew him as well as Guy did that his violent temper was barely held in check.

"Is that so? Well, you are more fortunate than I then, Guy. And now, given the differences the past six years have wrought between us, I think it is probably better if we part now before we come to blows, you and I."

He flicked a quick glance at the lad standing with Aelric and Beowulf, all three of them clearly pretending to be unaware of the quarrel that had broken out so swiftly between the brothers.

"Come when you are ready, Jarec, but I have kept Gabriel waiting long enough."

With that Ranulf turned and stalked back towards the road leading to the castle, leaving Jarec to follow or stay as he pleased.

Guy simply watched him go, his thoughts and expression bleak.

It was interesting, he thought, that Ranulf had not contradicted him when he had implied that Jacques and Rowène were two separate people.

Did that mean that his brother did not know the truth?

Or that he believed Guy did not know, and meant to conceal that knowledge from him, for whatever reason.

And if that were so, were there any other secrets his brother would deliberately keep hidden?

Though of course such doubts ran both ways, as Guy realised when he caught Edwy's unhappy look at the unresolved tension that had sprung up like rampant hedge of thorns between his two half-brothers.

And Guy had every sympathy with his distress.

Far from proving a joyous occasion, it seemed that all his long-anticipated reunion with Ranulf had shown was that he did not trust Ran any more than Ranulf trusted him.

Damn it all to Hell, what had happened to them?

A witless question if ever he had heard one! He knew what had happened to them.

The same thing that had come between them the last time they had met in Chartre in '95.

With much the same depth of pain, disappointment and anger as he had felt then, made worse by Ranulf's more recent betrayal, Guy cursed the Faennari for coming into his life, and for driving the wedge of violence and doubt between himself and Ran, brothers who – in spite of their differences – had always trusted each other to the death.

"Hell take it! Ran... and bloody, sodding Geryth!"

"What?"

Edwy picked up on Guy's muttered curse and, on the point of departing himself, turned to look back over his shoulder.

"What's that ye say?"

"Do you remember a girl called Gerde, back in Rogérinac?" Guy asked rapidly, still staring up the hill after his brother, all sign of his pale braids now lost amongst the crowd.

"Aye, o' course, I do. Quiet little lass, sister to the Geryth what used to be..."

Edwy stopped abruptly, his gaze slanting upwards to the castle walls, looming against the blue summer sky.

"Bugger it! He's not, is he?"

He stopped again.

"Yes, that Geryth," Guy confirmed. "And yes, he is up at the castle. He's a groom in service to Lord Nicholas now, has been for the past six years."

Guy was talking as he walked, threading his way through the market crowds, Edwy keeping pace beside him for some unfathomable reason.

"And that's a problem for..." Edwy stumbled over his half-brother's name then got it out. "For Ranulf?"

"Aye. Do you not remember how Gerde died?"

"In child-bed, weren't it?"

Then, as it apparently all began to make a disturbing sort of sense.

"Ah! Our whoremongering brother?"

"Yes, it was Ranulf! Curse it, I will never be able to think of him as Rafe! Anyway, it was his babe Gerde was brought to bed of, and rightly or wrongly, Geryth blames him for their deaths."

"An' ye think even after all this time..."

Edwy did not bother to finish his question, instead quickening his pace, as he added more or less under his breath,

"I've no doubt Rafe can take the little sod with one hand behind his back but he deserves to be warned. An' the gods only know what'll happen if he's held responsible fer causin' a ruck right under Lord Joscelin's nose. Not ter mention Prince Linnius an' his retinue're due ter arrive anytime now."

Guy and Edwy reached the edge of the crowded market together, and as they stepped into the cobbled street leading up towards the castle, both men broke into a run.

It was a hot day and they were soon breathing heavily, sweat matting their hair and soaking their linen.

In addition, Guy was limping badly, the leg that had been damaged by a kick from one of the Black Hunt's nags never having quite recovered its former strength.

Even so, he struggled on at Edwy's side, knowing the gate guards would never let a stranger in, today of all days, without his say-so.

Possibly not even then. And indeed the soldiers on duty were just dropping their spears across the entrance as Guy limped up to them.

"Hey, Master Finch, what's yer hurry? Is it hell's own daemons or the prince hisself at yer heels?"

"Neither, Brett. Just let us pass, will you? This man..."

He waved a hand at Edwy, who looked rough enough to fit the role Guy was hurriedly assigning to him.

"This man is one of the northern scouts, come with a message for Sir Gabriel. Have you seen him?"

"Aye, he just come through, wi' a dozen or so horsemen an' then two more soldiers on foot what said they belonged to his company," Brett confirmed.

"Ha' ye seen them, Master Finch? Call themselves guardians? Huh! A wilder-looking pack o' wolves I ain't ne'er seen," he concluded as he spat to one side, raising his spear at the same time.

Relieved at this sign, Guy said quickly,

"I'll take him along then. Someone will know where his commander can be found."

"Try the stable yard," Brett suggested, bringing his spear upright and nodding to his companion to do likewise.

"That's where they was all headed, an' if Sir Gabriel's not there no more, I don't doubt Alfgar will know where he's gone."

The stable yard?

Hell and damnation!

Guy heard Edwy curse rather more explicitly under his breath and much as he felt like echoing it, merely said tersely,

"Come on!"

Guy heard the serving maid's scream long before his limping step carried him into the stable yard, the sound having served to propel Edwy ahead of him through the arch.

Following as fast as he could, he stumbled into the yard just in time to see Edwy push his way through the press of bodies and barrel into the two figures struggling beside the water trough, short brown hair and unravelling pale braids flying as they fought.

The serving maid stood by the kitchen door, still screaming, and those horses that had been in the process of being untacked were stamping and rearing, ears flicking in agitation, tugging on their ropes and generally keeping everyone – grooms and guardians alike – busy just preventing them from running amok.

Seeing that Edwy's best efforts had still not managed to loosen Geryth's death grip on the leather rein he had wrapped about the neck of the man he was evidently taken unawares, and that Ranulf was rapidly losing all strength as his body was starved of breath, Guy made haste to grab hold of Geryth's other arm, and between them, he and Edwy managed to wrestle the vengeful madman away from their brother.

Finding himself free and able to breathe again, Ranulf clawed the leather noose from about his neck and collapsed heavily onto hands and knees, uncaring of horse dung or puddles of piss, harsh breaths hissing painfully in and out of his damaged throat.

Surmising from the strangled sounds that Ranulf was recovering, Guy set aside his instinct – intact despite his underlying anger – to go to his brother's assistance, retaining his tight grip on Geryth's arm.

"*What* in the frozen depths of *Hell* is going on here?"

The cultured, frost-cold voice cut through the clamour with ease, carrying all the icy menace of death itself.

Recognising it, Guy ignored the leaden lump in his gut and straightened with a grunt, dragging Geryth – still struggling and shouting nearly incoherent abuse – with him, cursing under his breath as he looked up to discover that not only Joscelin de Veraux but also Gabriel de Marillec had arrived on the scene.

Gods knew, one of them would have been bad enough!

That *both* senior officers were here to witness his brother's past indiscretions coming home to roost in such fashion was a complication he could have done without!

"I said," the cold voice continued. "What..."

"That whoreson shit-scum killed me sister!"

Geryth spat the words at the plainly-dressed nobleman, either not recognising or not caring exactly who he was dealing with.

"An' murdered his own hell-spawned brat what he put in her belly. An' if no-one else'll give me justice, I'll make the filthy bloody bastard pay meself."

His last screamed words were all but lost, however, as the blaring of horns and thunderous clatter of hooves from the outer bailey announced the arrival of the royal visitors, causing Edwy to mutter,

"Bugger it! We're in the shit now if we wasn't before."

Evidently hearing this unfortunate comment, Joscelin de Veraux shot him a glance and said in a voice like the snap of cracking ice,

"The voice of experience, no doubt!"

Then, as he looked more more closely at Edwy, a faint frown developed between his dark brows as if thinking he should know the man, before he transferred his attention briefly to Guy.

It was no more than a fleeting glance but one that swiftly – and probably accurately – assessed the lines of his face and the colour of his hair, still a mottled mix of brown and fair, with the same hint of silver that less noticeably threaded the paler strands of his brother's loosened braids.

Finally, that frost-edged grey gaze dropped to Ranulf, still on hands and knees, his breath coming in heaving rasps, and though de Veraux did not address him directly it was abundantly clear that he was not pleased with the situation.

Then, switching from common speech to the high tongue, his tone warming not one whit in the transition, Joscelin de Veraux turned to address his Second.

"You certainly pick your time to return to civilisation, de Marillec. But now you are here, you can damned well get this mess sorted out, since it is your man who seems to have caused it with his indiscriminate actions. Beyond that, I want this yard cleared, *now*, and I do not care how you do it."

"And the Prince?"

"Leave Linnius and his cronies to me."

With that de Veraux turned on his heel and strode towards the archway, spurs ringing in metallic counterpoint to his firm booted footsteps.

Left to his own devices, Gabriel de Marillec paused beside Ranulf only long enough to put out a slender, sun-browned hand and, with a soft grunt of effort, hauled the bigger man to his feet, pausing at his sword-brother's side only long enough to say with a fair amount of irritable restraint,

"Get yourself out of sight, for gods'sake, Rafe! At least until these damnably ill-timed new arrivals are out of the way! Then take yourself down to the Healing House. I will deal with what is left of you after the good Sisters have finished with you."

"Sir," came the croaked acknowledgement.

De Marillec raised his voice,

"As for the rest of you, get on with whatever the hell it is you are supposed to be doing."

As the gaping grooms and guardians began again to attend to their tasks, Guy spared one anxious look at the livid bruising around Ranulf's throat before turning to say something – anything – to Gabriel de Marillec in instinctive support of his brother.

The guardians' Second, however, was clearly not of a mind to listen, either to extenuating circumstances or Geryth's continued accusations.

He took three swift steps until he was directly in front of the three remaining men, took a moment to judge his aim and then, with neither word nor warning, let fly with a fist that impacted right on the point of Geryth's jaw.

Abruptly silenced, Geryth's head snapped back, his whole body jerking against the two men holding him, before collapsing to hang limply in their grasp.

Guy blinked at Edwy, seeing his own shock mirrored in his half-brother's autumn-brown eyes, before glancing back at Gabriel de Marillec who was absently shaking out his bruised fist, his fine-boned face blank and unreadable.

Catching a flicker of movement, Guy glanced beyond the lean, leather-clad figure to see his cousin Adèle peering curiously through the arch.

If Guy had been surprised by the Second's swift if brutally effective action, it was nothing to the horrified disgust on the face of the woman who wore Gabriel de Marillec's binding band. A disgust she appeared to extend to the two men still holding up the sagging body of the unconscious man.

A heartbeat later she was gone, and the last glimpse Guy had of her, she was walking towards the main entrance to the castle, one trembling hand clutched about Joscelin de Veraux's arm, the other held to her white lips.

The rest of the day passed without further incident, much to the relief of everyone in the household concerned with the smooth running of the royal visit.

Once dismissed, the guardians of the prince's escort joined the men of the northern patrol and Princess Linette's guard in the stable yard and having tended their mounts, were settling – more or less amicably – into the cramped quarters they were sharing with the garrison's soldiers.

Geryth, having been half-dragged, half-carried to the castle lock-up – where he had been dumped unceremoniously on a pile of straw and left to regain his wits – and with the outer bailey finally emptied, the way was clear for Ranulf to walk out of the castle, accompanied by a grimly silent Edwy.

Wasting neither time nor words, Edwy delivered his half-brother into the Grey Sisters' care, then, having located Aelric and Beowulf who had been skulking nearby, made all haste to leave Vézière before he fell foul of Prince Linnius' chief counsellor. Even if Guy and Ran had chosen to accept him as their brother, Edwy knew – they all knew – that Joffroi never would.

Just as they all knew that considerations of shared blood would in no way prevent Joffroi from having any of them tortured and killed as traitors and oath-breakers if they were so unfortunate as to fall into his hands.

Meanwhile, Guy – having seen Ranulf and Edwy out through the gatehouse, and watched their descent into the maze of narrow, winding streets – retreated to the chamber where his fellow musicians had gathered and thereafter spent the remainder of the day ostensibly practising those tunes they had prepared for that night's entertainment.

Behind his placid facade, however, he was prey to a number of nagging worries, and while most of them concerned his cousin Adèle, Juliène de Lyeyne was certainly not absent from his thoughts.

It was early evening before Guy saw any of the royal party again, and then it was from the relative obscurity of the minstrels' gallery, from which he could look out and see them... whereas they – the assorted guardians and gentlefolk now crowding all four corners of the normally quiet hall – did not as a rule raise their collective gaze from their platters or wherever else in the lower reaches of the candlelit chamber they perceived their interest or their duty to lie.

There were, Guy decided after several moments of surreptitious observation, three very different elements within the royal party.

Firstly there was Linnius and his principal cronies – mostly the younger Mithlondian noblemen, the majority of whom Guy could not even put a name to, though he recognised Hal de Vézière well enough, as well as Prince Kaslander.

Then there was Princess Linette and her lady-companions, two of whom Guy did not know, three of whom he did, these being the Lady Isabelle de Lyeyne, her daughter-by-binding – Juliène looking as coolly beautiful as a white water lily floating on the secret waters of some far green pool – and his cousin Adèle.

And finally there was Joffroi, observing everything out of familiar dark eyes, an ill-fitting expression of affability on his florid face.

Yet when Guy came to look at the man more closely, it seemed to him that Linnius' Chief Counsellor was beginning to look his age, shadows lingering in the sagging creases of his ruddy skin, his long hair white brindled with the occasional streak of black, rather than the mere sprinkling of silver it had held for so many years.

As for Joffroi's position within the royal court, it was noticeable that even seated amongst the other nobles at the high table, he appeared very much apart, separated as much by the indefinable aura of menacing power that clung to his black-garbed bulk as by any superficial difference in age.

It was abundantly clear that the man Guy had once called brother had no friends among the younger courtiers. As for the rest – and this latter consideration had nothing whatsoever to do with Joffroi – Guy could not quite suppress the satisfied smile with which he noted Hervé de Lyeyne's unusual absence from his kinsman's side.

Much less amusing, however, was the necessity of watching Hal de Vézière taking full advantage of this lack in order to engage in very public flirtation with the glitteringly beautiful Lady of Lyeyne, who far from repelling his advances – as Guy might have supposed from their recent conversation that she would have done – seemed entirely taken with de Vézière's virile figure and handsome face, combined with the impetuous charm of a man little older than herself in years, all three of these qualities representing a marked contrast to her ageing, flabby, dissolute lord-by-binding.

And – as Guy would have been the first to admit – himself as well, though he was, gods knew, neither fat nor debauched.

Then again, *he* had no intention of competing with any man for a place in Juliène's bed and if she was content to share it with Hal de Vézière then it was no affair of his.

Rather, he reminded himself, he should concern himself about his cousin's welfare.

Adèle, he saw, as he turned his gaze towards the slender figure clad in a plain, if loose-fitting gown of soft tawny-gold, was as pale as she had been when he had first caught sight of her earlier that day, her pallor accentuated by smudges the colour of cold ash beneath the blue eyes she kept fixed on the platter before her, and from which Guy was certain she had eaten nothing whatsoever during the course of the long, elaborate feast.

If it had been any other woman he might have wondered if she was with child. Except, as far as he was aware, Gabriel de Marillec had been serving on the northern border ever since his binding to Adèle nearly a year before. And for all her reluctance to take de Marillec as her lord-by-binding, Guy could not really see her making a cuckold of the man. Whether de Marillec had kept faith with her was another matter...

Suddenly he saw the blood rise abruptly in her face, a hectic flush of colour almost as painful to witness as her previous pallor had been... and glancing in the direction of the doorway, whence her gaze was directed, he saw two men walk into the hall, both immediately recognisable even from his partially obscured viewpoint, the one by his unusual height, the other by his barbaric appearance.

But which one, Guy wondered, had caused that betraying blush to cover Adèle's white rose-petal countenance?

Her lord-by-binding? Or, gods forbid, his commanding officer?

As if realising she might have betrayed herself, Adèle glanced quickly away from the men now making their obeisance before royalty, clearly seeking something else upon which to concentrate her attention, and in the heartbeat before her lord-by-binding slipped into the empty chair beside her, her gaze lifted to the minstrels' gallery, fixing on Guy, her blue eyes awash with emotion, amongst which embarrassment and distress were easily uppermost.

Even at that distance Guy could see her pale lips move.

Unfortunately he had no notion what words they formed, whether exclamation, plea or prayer.

It was only after the feasting and dancing were finally done for the evening, the assembled courtiers ambling from the hall, and Guy and his fellow musicians were making their way down the narrow, wooden staircase to the hall, that he found out exactly what Adèle had been trying to say to him.

He had just set foot to the hall floor when he felt her stumble against him as if she had lost her footing in the press of people.

"Meet me in the garden at midnight."

He barely had time to murmur an acknowledgement of her whispered plea before she was swept away by the surprisingly strong arm of her lord-by-binding, his amber eyes glittering gold in the candlelight as for a moment they flicked over Guy where he stood half concealed in the shadows beneath the gallery, and then they were both gone, and all Guy could do was watch her disappear into the crowd, a single fallen autumn leaf aswirl on a river of brightly coloured silks and glittering gems.

With the hall finally empty of all but the weary servants come to clear away the wine and sauce-stained linens and whatever edible remnants of the feast Cavall and Cub had overlooked, Guy and his fellow musicians were at last free to seek their own beds. Aelfraed was yawning, Maury humming a few strains of Guy's latest composition, and Beorn and Halfiren arguing good-naturedly between themselves when they stumbled through the door into the small chamber they shared.

Guy was in the lead and when he spotted the folded square of parchment, pale against the brown and blue weave of his blanket he came to an abrupt halt, only to start forwards as the others collided with him.

Bending down, he seized the note before Maury – that inveterate seeker and retailer of gossip – could snatch it up.

Even so, he had to endure more than a few moments of ribald enquiry and speculation over the assignation they assumed he was about to embark upon, while they themselves made such preparations for sleep as suited each of them.

Ignoring them all, Guy dropped down to sit on the edge of his bed, slowly stripping off the formal tunic in the de Vézière colours... before turning his attention to the note, studying the delicately curving script that formed his name – his assumed name, that is – then the blob of green that held the folds of parchment closed and private, the wax showing no seal, for which minor discretion he was grateful.

The contents of the note, when he finally broke the seal, proved to be equally discreet, with no salutation, no signature and very few words.

Meet me in the garden at midnight.

It was, Guy thought with a flash of very wry humour, almost as unlikely a coincidence as those plot devices used by the Kardolandians in the plays they were as enamoured of performing as they were in indulging every other aspect of their hedonistic lives. Needless to say the theatre, like their bathing pools and the subtle contrasts of sweet and spicy food, was not something that had ever found favour at the Mithlondian court.

Only Juliène, he thought, would appreciate the farcical nature of the dilemma he now found himself in.

Not that she would be amused if he failed to meet her at the appointed time because he had chosen to answer another woman's plea first.

It had been a damned long day, and heart-sore and weary as he was, he was tempted simply to ignore both of his importunate kinswomen, save that he had promised Adèle that he would be there.

Just as he had promised Juliène at their last meeting beneath the willows...

Know too that if ever you need me, I will come.

With those sincerely meant, if rashly spoken, words echoing in his mind, he accepted that he really had very little choice in the matter.

Somehow he would have to find a way to honour his word, both to Adèle and Juliène.

A quarter candle-notch before the appointed time, Guy slipped from his chamber and made his way cautiously through quiet passageways, lit only by low-burning candles and torches, and thence into the whispering warmth of the walled garden just as the midnight bell rang out from the tower in the town, the deep sound of the heavy bronze bell making the moonlight dance and shimmer about him in time to the waves of sound.

Even after the last echo had faded, and the warm summer night had settled into stillness once more, he remained in the shadow of the keep wall, letting his eyes accustom themselves to the looming patches of deeper darkness marking trees and bushes, the lighter grey of flowers and walkways lit only by a scatter of starlight and the dull glow of the golden moon.

While he could *see* no-one, away to his right where the interlocking branches of the fruit trees of Lord Nicholas' small orchard held the moonlight at bay, he could hear a low murmur of conversation – to which he listened only long enough to assure himself that neither voice belonged to Adèle or Juliène.

Easy enough since it was obvious that both speakers were male, one voice as cool as deep water, the other somewhat lighter in pitch, carrying a biting edge of anger. Then Guy realised there must be three men all told, every muscle locking taut as he recognised the last voice with its hint of a harshly familiar accent.

Fists clenched, he stepped out into the moonlight, making no effort to conceal his presence, the scuff of his footsteps sufficient to immediately kill the other men's conversation.

Deliberately turning away from the taut silence, Guy forced himself to walk in seeming aimless fashion through the flowered borders, their mingled scents heady in the warmth of the night. He had no idea if either of the women were here or if the presence of the men would have driven them away before he arrived but reckoned they would find him if they wished to speak to him that much.

If not... well it was a soft summer night and he was not so tired that he could not enjoy the tranquil beauty of starlight and shadow...

On that thought one of the shadows moved, and suddenly Adèle was standing before him, moonlight turning her loose primrose-fair hair to silver, her gown to the same colour as the moon itself.

"You came!"

"Surely you knew I would," Guy murmured back.

He saw her cast a baleful glance at the sky, another hunted look around the treacherous shadows of the garden, before slipping back into the denser darkness, clearly expecting Guy to follow her.

Which, with a silent sigh, he did.

It still had all the elements of a Kardolandian *farcire*.

Any idea he might have had of sharing the rueful nature of his thoughts with his cousin died the moment he joined her in the shadow of a rose arch, and she threw herself, overwrought and trembling, against his chest.

Abandoning humour as a lost cause, Guy simply wrapped her in his arms.

Gods knew, he could do no less than to offer comfort in her distress, whatever had caused it. And he had a very good idea what that was.

He rested his chin against the top of her head, murmured soothingly as he stroked her soft hair, and waited for the shivering to stop. At least, he thought with relief, she was not weeping.

Eventually, when he felt her regain control and pull away, he said gently,

"What is it, Adèle? Why did you ask me to meet you here?"

"I hate that moon!"

It was almost the last thing he had expected her to say. Perhaps some comment about her lord-by-binding's changed appearance or his unexpected return. In any case, violent antipathy towards the distant entity who ruled the night skies – and which might or might not be the face of the mythical Goddess of the Faennari – seemed misplaced.

"Surely you did not risk your reputation and my position to bring me out here to tell me that?" he asked, mildly incredulous.

"No."

She shivered again, and he drew her back into his arms.

"But then I saw the moon, and I remembered how it was that night."

"What night?" he asked, keeping his voice steady even as he looked into the darkness beyond her, wondering uncomfortably whether Gabriel de Marillec had remained with his companions, or was somewhere within earshot. The man could walk as silently as a cat when he wanted to.

"Tell me, Adèle. Even if I cannot make it right, just telling me about it may help in some way."

"Thank you, Guy. Truly, I do not know what I would do without you."

She snuggled a little closer against his chest, a child seeking comfort.

Save that she was no child. She was a woman grown, with a man's binding band about her arm.

A man who was quite possible not as far away as she thought – if she had thought at all about Gabriel de Marillec's whereabouts, which Guy rather doubted.

"Tell me," he said again.

And this time she did.

"That moon... you know some people call it a blood moon when it is that colour?"

"Some superstitious country folk perhaps," Guy allowed.

"Not just superstitious country folk," Adèle retorted briskly, then hesitated before saying in a voice barely above a whisper.

"Just the sight of it was enough to make my lord start talking of blood. And other things I defy anyone to understand. He spoke of you too. Or at least he spoke of a harper."

"Ah! And a healer perhaps? And possibly fields of blood?" Guy asked.

"Yes, but how did you know?"

"Others have spoken of it too. Indeed, you told me a little about it when we first met, but as you have not mentioned it since I thought you must have forgotten."

"No, I have not forgotten, though the gods know I have tried! I hoped for a while that perhaps I had. Until I saw the moon tonight," she said, her soft voice bitter in the darkness. "And it brought it all back."

Guy heard her swallow.

"Not only my lord's words but how he looked..."

Her voice dropped to a near soundless breath of an agonised whisper.

"Lying in Luc de Chartreux's arms."

Guy frowned down at the silvery blur of her head, and grimaced. After all, this was not Kardolandia where such things were common-place. That being so, and whatever Gabriel and Luc were to each other, he truly doubted they would betray themselves in public as Adèle's words implied they had done.

"Where were you when all this happened?" he asked curiously.

"At the Healing House here in Vézière."

Which made it even less credible, this image she had woven of two lovers lying together, bound by treacherous moonlight and distorted memory.

Moreover he guessed from what Ranulf had said earlier that his brother had been present as well, and possibly there had been other witnesses too.

"I am not doubting you, Adèle, but was there anyone else there who saw this thing?"

"Everyone that matters," Adèle sighed. "The princess, the Eldest, Messire de Veraux. Oh, and the guardian they call Rafe of Oakenleigh. He is here now as well. At least I am almost sure it was him I saw on his knees amidst the filth of the courtyard earlier. But can you not see, Guy, that is what makes it all so much worse for me. We are *all* back in Vézière, under the same terrible moon, and I am meeting my lord-by-binding for the first time in nearly a year... and... and nothing seems to have changed!"

"Some things may not have changed but the situation is far from the same," Guy pointed out quietly. "We are not at the Healing House for one thing. Nor is Luc de Chartreux anywhere near here."

"But my lord still... feels for him as he did then! I know he does!"

"Adèle, you cannot know that."

He hesitated but she had not spoken of love, perhaps she *could not* in such a context, and so neither did he.

"No matter what the songs say, Adèle, feelings between two people *can* change over the course of the seasons, passionate love becoming a deep if... less possessive sort of affection, or..."

"Perhaps that is so, for some people. All I know is that *my* feelings have not changed. The gods know, I wish they had, it hurts so much to love where it is not returned."

"You love him?" he asked tentatively. "Your lord-by-binding?"

"I am not such a fool!" she replied. "But... but there was something between us for those few days we were together after our binding, before he went north. A... a shared loneliness perhaps. A sort of honesty. We... we had a bargain, Guy, though I doubt you will think it an honourable one. My lord promised not to bring public shame to our binding by any affair of his, and gave me leave to... have a child if such was my wish."

"Not *his* child, I assume?" Guy said drily.

"No. Nor, in case you are wondering, have I availed myself of his generosity... indifference... call it what you will. Even though..."

She sighed again.

"I would dearly love a child of my own. It is doubly... oh gods, Guy, it is *impossibly* difficult now that Linette has Lilia."

"I am not advocating adultery or cuckolding the man, but perhaps if you talked to him..." he started to suggest.

"Talk! To the man who, rather than talking, would choose to use his fists on another who was held helpless by two other men. One of whom," she added, pushing away from him. "Was you! Oh, how could you, Guy? I thought you too gentle a man to have any part in my lord's violence."

Even through the darkness, he could sense her shutting herself away from him.

From any man who demonstrated the sort of forceful brutality – carefully measured though it had been – that Gabriel de Marillec had meted out earlier to Geryth in the stable yard.

"I thought we might come back to that," Guy said now. "What you saw... it was not quite what you think, Adèle."

"Was it not?"

Adèle's voice shook with the same disgust that had been on her face earlier that day.

"No, it was not," he said firmly.

"The truth is that if Edwy and I had not been holding Geryth back he would have choked the life out of the man you call Rafe. And if de Marillec had not silenced the lad as swiftly as he did, we would have had Prince Linnius, Joffroi, and half the court as witness to it all. Including my presence there."

"Oh! You are saying that your brother would have recognised you? Yes, of course, the bright light of day is somewhat different to the shadows of Lord Nicholas' hall. I am sorry, Guy, I did not think."

"Nor was it just me," Guy offered gently, deprecatingly. "Both Edwy and Geryth were once Rogé men, and Joffroi knows their faces as well as he knows my own. Six years ago they were in *my* service, and because of their loyalty to me Joffroi ordered them killed. Believe me, he would do no less if he saw them today."

He did not mention Rafe again, thinking it possible that Adèle would not have recognised him as the man formerly known as Ranulf de Rogé, and for all that he and Ran had quarrelled bitterly still he would do nothing to put his brother's life in any more danger than it was already.

Instead he said,

"De Marillec did the only thing he could in that situation."

"Yes, I suppose so." Adèle's admission came on a soft sigh from the shadows. "But there is something else, something I have not yet told you, the thing I brought you here for."

"And that is?"

"Few people know this but when this visit to Vézière is done, Linette and Kaslander will be travelling south to Kaerellios, with Lilia, at the invitation of King Karlen and Queen Xandra."

"That does not sound so very troubling, Adèle."

"You think not? What if I told you that I am one of the two lady-companions who will be accompanying Linette to that dissolute place. Away from... those I love. From you. And away from all that I know."

"Flattered though I am, and licentious and depraved though Kaerellios undoubtedly is by Mithlondian standards, it is still a king's court with all the luxury thereof," Guy pointed out calmly. "And while both you and the princess are like to find it uncomfortably hot after these cooler climes, you will grow accustomed as I did. Or is it that you are worrying yourself about the ability of the men who will accompany you to resist whatever favours are offered them by the courtesans of the bathing pools..."

"Linette would not upset herself over something as trivial as Kaslander's infidelities," Adèle interrupted. "As for Gabriel, I trust him to be discreet. I... I can ask no more of him."

"What then?"

"It is not the behaviour but the *composition* of Linette's bodyguard that worries me," she hissed, plainly expecting him to understand.

Guy gave a soft grunt of surprise and, it had to be admitted, incomprehension. He knew women thought differently to men, considered different things of importance but still...

"Does she not have a competent guard any more? What happened to that gruff old bear who used to watch over her?"

"Rhys? He is remaining in Mithlondia with Prince Linnius, the original plan being that Joscelin would head up the royal guard in his place and accompany the princess to Kardolandia, and my lord retain his command of the northern patrols."

"And now?" Guy queried, beginning to see where this was headed.

"Now, Gabriel has been put in charge of Linette's guard and Linnius has decreed, at Lord Joffroi's prompting, that Joscelin must take his place in the north, where..."

Her voice shook.

"Where the fighting is! I cannot prove it, Guy, but I know your brother wants Joscelin dead. That is the only reason I can think of that he would have convinced Linnius to change all the arrangements like this."

"From what I hear, the border is quiet at the moment," Guy said calmly. "Besides, I doubt very much that Joffroi would be content to see de Veraux perish in obscurity. When he decides to take the man down, he will make sure it is done as publicly as possible."

"Are you sure?" Adèle asked, an odd mix of hope and horror in her voice that told Guy much of what he had not already guessed.

"Very sure," Guy retorted. "Joffroi may mean murder now but we grew up as brothers and I know the dark ways in which his mind works. Take my word for it, de Veraux will be as safe on the northern border as he is in his quarters in the Palace of Princes. As for the rest of it... I can only suggest you actually talk to de Marillec. You have done it before, surely you have courage enough to be honest with him again?"

"Indeed, Madame, your kinsman has the right of it."

The light, cultured voice, as silvery sharp as moonlight glancing off the honed edge of a knife blade, accompanied the man who stepped silently out of the shadows, causing Adèle to flinch back in alarm and Guy to say coolly,

"You know what they say about eavesdroppers, de Marillec? How long have you been listening?"

"Long enough to hear my lady-wife's opinion of me as a brute and the sort of man who will be comfortably at home in Kardolandia's depraved court. All of which is quite possibly true. Now, if you will forgive me, de Martine, there are certain things she and I must discuss. In private."

Guy hesitated, sensing Adèle's fear and dismay, and Gabriel's voice hardened.

"I gave you my word and my friendship six years ago. I have not broken it yet. Nor will I."

"In that case..."

378

Guy reached out in the moon-speckled darkness for Adèle's hand, bringing it to his lips in formal farewell.

"Talk to him," he said again, quietly, firmly. "And trust him, as I do."

"But then," she said tartly, snatching her fingers away. "You are a man. Even as he is. And I have never yet met a man who could understand a woman's heart."

"Damned if I do, damned if I don't," Guy muttered to himself in the rough Rogé dialect, eliciting a subdued snort of laughter from the man standing nearby, the amber beads in his braided bronze hair glinting softly in the shadowy golden light as he moved.

Somewhat reassured, Guy released his grasp on Adèle's hand, gave de Marillec a curt nod and left them to whatever degree of honest conversation they chose to exchange.

He had another lady to find.

Keeping to the shadows, Guy walked quietly to the far end of the garden until he reached the bench set amongst its fragrant curtains of pendulous purple flowers and finding it unoccupied, seated himself, his gaze fixed reflectively upon the golden glow of the amber moon as it swam on the still, dark surface of the pond.

A blood moon, Adèle had called it, making him think about de Marillec's words concerning fields of blood, the harper and the healer.

Did it mean anything, he wondered. Or nothing?

The deep tolling of the hour bell across the empty garden intruded into his wandering thoughts, reminding him how far past the time it was that Juliène had set for their meeting.

She would be long gone from the garden by now, and he might just as well seek his bed.

"Guyard."

His name came as barely more than a murmur on the night breeze, almost unheard, yet when he looked up sharply it was to find her there before him, radiantly beautiful in the moonlight, stars caught in her long dark hair, her white gown shimmering as it clung to her slender body, bare toes peeping beneath the silver-shot silk.

He came to his feet, slowly, as if caught in the enchanted strands of a shadowy dream wherein she stood, revealed and revelling, in the full glory of the Moon Goddess' light.

"Juliène."

Without thinking, he reached out his hand, more than a little surprised that she took it, but when she resisted his attempt to draw her into the safety of the shadows, he went to her, fully aware that while she would have no cause to fear the White Lady of the Night that same grace would not extend to him.

Releasing her hand, he said quietly,

"I thought you would have gone long since. I am sorry to be so late. To make you wait for me."

Seeing the hard glitter in her eyes he more than half expected her to slice his apology into shreds but then her expression softened.

"It is no matter. You were with Adèle and of course her claim on your kinship is greater than mine. I knew you would come to me when you were done. Or at least... I hoped you would."

There was a hint of vulnerability about her trembling mouth that made him want to take her in his arms as he had held Adèle. This, however, was Juliène and kinswoman though she was, he could not trust himself to treat her with the same undemanding affection he felt for Adèle.

That being so, he kept his hands to himself, hoping she would not realise the power she held over him, frowning when a distant sound from the castle walls gave his thoughts a different turn.

"If the princess has returned to the Healing House, as she surely must have done by now, how do you come to still be in the castle? I can understand Adèle's presence, since her lord-by-binding is here..."

He just caught the expression that flickered across Juliène's face at this reference to Gabriel de Marillec but chose to ignore it, instead saying,

"But you have no such excuse to remain since de Lyeyne did not even accompany you here."

He hesitated, then added,

"How... *where* is he?"

As he had hoped this question distracted Juliène from her obvious antipathy towards de Marillec – the gods knew what the man had done to deserve it – and she gave Guy a smile that mingled warmth and mischief.

"Hervé is still at court, recovering from his injuries and swearing vengeance on the band of ruffians responsible for robbing, beating and... er... unmanning him as he went about his lawful business in Lamortaine one night."

"There is precious little lawful business going on in the Marish at any time of day," Guy commented drily. "Let alone at night."

"No, nor was it a pack of thieves who attacked him, was it?" Juliène asked, though there was no uncertainty in her tone. "It was just one man."

Guy held her eyes for a moment, then feeling the brush of petal-soft fingers, glanced down to see her hand, white in the moonlight, laid against the bare skin of his forearm. Her whisper was equally soft.

"Thank you, Guyard."

And rising she kissed him on the mouth, her lips parted and slightly trembling.

"I know you did it for me."

Resisting the temptation to prolong the embrace, to deepen the kiss, to draw her closer against him, into the unbroken circle of his arms, he simply waited until she settled back onto her heels, whereupon he managed to say quite calmly,

"You are my kinswoman, Juliène. I could do no less than to fight for you. Luc would have done the same, had he been there..." A thread of remembered rage edged his reasonable tone. "And did he but know what that bastard did to you."

"But Luc was not there. You were. And you risked everything for me. What if Hervé had recognised you?"

"He did not."

"What if you had damaged your hand?"

She slid her fingers down his arm, a caress in itself, and catching his right hand in both of hers, lifted it to her lips.

Gods help him, he felt her tiny kisses running like fire up his arm, setting off sparks in the blood that surged so hotly through his loins.

His voice remained steady, though the effort to keep it so brought sweat to his temples and upper lip.

"My hand is fine."

"It is now," she murmured. "Though I confess I was worried, until I heard you play in the hall tonight and I knew whatever hurt you had sustained, you must be healed."

A small silence fell between them. Then,

"Guyard, that song the gittern-player sang tonight... you wrote it, did you not? For me?"

There seemed little point denying it.

"It was after I heard it that I slipped away to leave the note on your bed."

"And you knew it was my bed, how?" Guy asked before he had thought better of it.

"I just knew it was yours."

Still teasing his fingers with her lips and tongue, she glanced up at him, green eyes dark and mysterious as the starlit night.

"If you truly want to know how I knew..."

He had a feeling he was not going to like what was coming.

"Your pillow, your blankets... they smell of you."

He groaned, wordlessly. The last time he had taken a bath had been in the river, a se'ennight at least ago...

"It was not unpleasant," Juliène assured him.

"Sweat and wood smoke and wet dog?" he countered in deprecating disbelief.

"Better than to stink of spilt wine, stale perfume and vomit as Hervé does," Juliène retorted with no trace of humour at all.

"Whereas you smell far sweeter than either of us," Guy said, his tongue once more outrunning his common sense. "Like flowers and starlight and..."

He coughed and closed his mouth before he could complete his downfall.

"And?"

"Nothing," he said hurriedly. "I know little of women's perfumes."

"Even after five years at the Kardolandian court?"

Gentle as the mockery was, it stung, and obviously sensing his recoil, Juliène added quickly,

"But mine is a simple Mithlondian scent. Do you not recognise it? I wore it for you before."

What he did know was that he should not be having this conversation at all. Should not be doing anything as intimate as breathing in the scent of the soft skin at her throat, the sweet allure of the silken shadows between her white breasts, the subtle fragrance caught in the flowing darkness of her hair...

Oh, gods!

Straightening slowly, his hands moved down her shoulders to grip her trembling fingers, before letting her go, even as he struggled to recall the question, to regain some thread of control....

"It is honeysuckle." The unnecessary reminder came as a soft sigh.

"I know."

Admitting the truth did nothing to douse the fire of unlawful desire licking his already burning groin, fanned by a thousand memories. Of the times he thought he had caught her scent... in the air, in his dreams. The times he had caught it in truth... in the garden at Chartre, the hedgerows of Valenne and Vézière.

"I have not worn the scent for many years," she said wistfully. "Not since the day you went away, but I thought tonight..."

I would wear it for you, her smile seemed to say.

"And you will find it all around you when you lie down to sleep tonight. On your pillow. On your sheets."

"As it was at Valéntien," he muttered to himself.

"You slept in my bed at Valéntien?" she asked, suddenly wide eyed.

"What *had been* your bed," he corrected.

"Just as I lay in your bed tonight," she murmured, everything about her – voice, words, eyes, hands – the living embodiment of feminine provocation.

"You took a risk," he managed, trying to sound stern. "One you should not have done. What if anyone had seen you?"

"No-one saw me. Everyone was in the hall or busy about their own affairs. And in truth when I went to your room, it *was* just to leave the note. But once I was there... once I had discovered your scent on the pillow, I wanted if only for a moment to lie in your bed, to feel you with me when I... But you did not come and without you what followed was empty, meaningless..."

And just like that Guy snapped out of his state of lust-induced enchantment as he realised just how Juliène had managed to remain in the castle when all the other women, save Adèle who was with her lord-by-binding, had returned to the Healing House.

"So who else's bed did you lie in tonight?" he demanded. "And for far longer than the few moments you spent in the empty bed of one who can never be your lover?"

She flinched back, and in the moonlight he could easily read the expressions flitting across her face. Ignoring the state of his still rampantly out-of-control body, he said steadily,

"No, Juliène, I am not jealous, I merely express a kinsman's concern for your reputation... your safety."

He frowned slightly as the answer – the only possible answer – came to him.

"It was Hal de Vézière, was it not? It was from *his* bed you came to meet me here?"

"Yes, but he did not... I did not let him..."

"What? Couple with you? Make love to you?"

Anger prompted him to say something much coarser – a far more accurate a description of the act that must have taken place in de Vézière's bed.

He restrained himself, reminding himself that *he* was not his brother and that Juliène was a gently-bred lady.

"It was none of those things you said," she answered him quietly. And still holding his gaze, "Nor the one you did not say."

"What then?" he demanded. "After five years at the Kardolandian Court I am not like to find anything you did with him a surprise. Or a shock."

Distasteful perhaps, but he was not going to tell her that.

As it was she had lowered her eyes, and half turned away from him as if ashamed.

Gods! Perhaps she *had* done something she found more terrible to admit to than a simple fuck with de Vézière, something worse than anything she had done with the multiplicity of lovers she had already told him about during their conversation beneath the willows at Lamortaine.

The sight of her distress caused his innate gentleness to rise over his more unruly emotions.

"What is it, Juli? What did you do?"

"You remember I told you that I would find a way to handle Hervé if it would ensure our... friendship would remain our secret."

"Yes, but what has that to do with whatever you did or did not do in Hal de Vézière's bed tonight?"

"I have a... potion. A poison of sorts though it is not lethal in small quantities. I use it sometimes... or rather, I used to use it to keep Hervé from... molesting me. Mixed with wine it brings sleepiness and... and a temporary impotency."

"And you gave this potion to de Vézière? Will he not suspect something when he wakes?"

"No."

Juliène smiled. With no pleasantry and very little humour, her eyes hard and diamond-bright in the moonlight.

"A useful little potion," she continued with unruffled calm.

"It also induces sensual dreams in the mind of the sleeper, with the inevitable physical manifestation following, so that even if he wakes alone..."

She raised her brows, inviting Guy's sardonic, somewhat crude conclusions, and he was shaken enough by her self-confessed familiarity with poisonous potions to give them.

"So having spilled his seed in his sleep, he wakes to wet sheets, and thinks himself the greatest lover in all the five realms."

"Precisely. I said it was a useful little potion, did I not?"

Guy merely shuddered, feeling the sweat chill on his skin, and his body return at last to his own control.

"Remind me never to take wine from your hands," he said, not entirely in jest.

"I would never do anything like that to you," Juliène protested, her fey calm surging suddenly into a fierce sincerity Guy could not find the will to doubt.

"Certainly not to force you into my bed, since you have told me often enough we cannot be lovers. Nor, if you did for any reason change your mind, would I use it to make you believe that something had happened between us that did not."

Her gaze blazed with emerald fire.

"If ever you come to me, Guyard, I want you awake and aware of everything we share. Every kiss, every caress, every movement of your body within m..."

"Enough, Juliène! It is not going to happen. For gods'sake, we are blood kin! Not only that, you have a son by my brother, I have a daughter by your sister..."

"So we are damned already."

"Unwittingly. I will not knowingly break that law again, and in so doing risk giving another child life, thus condemning him or her..."

"I cannot bear a child!"

Her distraught cry broke over his denial.

"What?"

Without thinking he reached out for her. She was shaking. Tears splintering silver on her pale cheeks.

"What do you mean? You have Val..."

"I cannot bear *another* child," she whispered. "Not to you. Not to anyone. Thanks to Hervé I am barren, my womb dead and lifeless."

"What did he do to you?"

His voice was level, carrying no trace of the violent need for vengeance presently stabbing his gut, tightening his fingers into ominous fists while he waited for her to tell him exactly what Hervé had done.

And when she did, with an ice-cold precision he could never match, he could not help himself. Bending over, he vomited into the shadows beneath the low-hanging wisteria flowers.

Straightening at last, he wiped his mouth on the shoulder of his short sleeve, thinking distantly that Juliène would scarcely find him any more fragrant than Hervé now, while with the greater part of his mind he tried to keep his renewed rage under control.

"I should have killed him when I had the chance," he grated, and spat out another mouthful of vile-tasting bile, followed by a hoarse apology for his ill manners.

Despite the undeniable reek of vomit that now clung about him, Juliène did not move away, instead reaching up to push his damp hair away from his face with cool fingers.

"If you had killed him, my mother would merely have found someone else to bind me to, quite probably his brother Léon who is no less a beast than Hervé."

The deep sound of the night bell rolled over the moonlit garden... once... twice... causing Guy to swear under his breath.

"Two bells past the midnight mark! I must take you back to the Healing House. Unless you want to return to de Vézière's bed?"

"No! Or at least, not if you can get me out of the castle without getting into trouble yourself."

"That is easy enough, if you can play the wanton for me as you must have done earlier for de Vézière?"

"I only did that so that I might talk to you," she reminded him. "But perhaps it would be better if we talked after you get me out of the castle."

She glanced around with the first sign of unease he had seen in her.

"Too many people already this evening have chosen to make their rendezvous in this garden and the longer we remain, the greater the probability of discovery."

He thought it unlikely himself, for while the moon's amber glow was noticeably paling, the first grey glimmers of dawn would not lighten the shadows of the garden until the great bell had rung out twice more. Everyone, save the guards on watch duty, would be snug in their beds by now – either alone or with their chosen companion of the night.

Nevertheless, if Juliène was eager to be away, he would not gainsay her decision.

"Where did you leave your clothes?" he asked, frowning at the sudden realisation that she had been wearing a different gown when he had seen her earlier in the great hall and would have arrived at the castle wearing a mantle and veil as well.

"In a bundle beneath a lavender bush just by the door into the garden," she replied, turning to walk in that direction. "I did not want to return to Hal's chamber unless I had to."

She glanced over her shoulder with a swift coquettish smile.

"But surely you do not want my appearance to be *too* respectable?"

"No, I just want you to keep your face concealed from the guards and any other curious eyes as may be watching us when we leave."

"I thank you for the thought but it is far too late to protect my reputation," she told him, bitterness underlying indifference. "My mother has already seen to it that it was destroyed long since, and that no *honourable* man would ever want me."

It was plain she meant him by that description but Guy had had enough of being manipulated for one night.

"To take a nobleman such as Hal de Vézière as your lover is acceptable enough," he reminded her flatly. "To take a tumble in the grass with a low-born harper is asking for trouble. Not only on your own account but mine as well."

"Oh! I did not think."

"No, you and Adèle are very much alike in that regard," Guy said, exasperation, frustration and the late hour beginning to tell on him.

"The gods know, I would do all in my power to help either one of you. But I can hardly stand your friend if I am tossed into one of Joffroi's hell-pits or chained in a cage by the highway and left there until my bones have been picked clean by the crows."

Even in the fading moonlight he could see her blanch.

"I saw a cage like that on the way here," she whispered.

"At Rath-na-Cael, yes, I know. That was my first intimation on my return that Joffroi's power – and likewise your mother's – had grown rather than weakened during the years I had been away."

Having reached the door into the castle, he stooped and after a moment hauled out a bundle of cloth.

Shaking out the velvet mantle, he flung it around her shoulders, pulling the hood up to hide her face.

Then picking up the remaining garments – a shift, a diaphanous headrail, an embroidered over-gown, a pair of stockings and two dainty leather shoes – he rolled them all together and thrust them at her.

"Here, you will have to carry these."

"Why cannot you..." she started to say as he carefully opened the door and peered inside.

"Because," he said briskly, turning back to her. "I am going to carry you."

So saying, he swept her up into his arms and set off down the dimly-lit passage towards the main entrance.

She gave a small squeak of surprise, quickly muffled against his linen-covered shoulder, and relaxed into his embrace. Sylph-slender, fine-boned and fey, she was the lightest of burdens, weighing even less than he had expected. He felt like a cart horse carrying a child.

Except Juliène was no child. Nor even the essentially innocent girl he had first seen at Chartre.

This was a woman he held... and with his momentary flare of temper gone, it was damned difficult to forget that truth, to ignore the temptation to push aside the concealing hood and bury his nose in her fragrant hair, her honeysuckle scent mingled now with the lavender clinging to her mantle.

Not least because it was a far sweeter smell than that which lingered about his own person.

Gods above! He wondered how Juliène could bear it without covering her nose with her hands.

Those same hands that were now clasped about his neck, fingers idly tangling in his hair.

"I am not so dainty as all that," she murmured, seemingly picking his thoughts out of his head as she seemed alarmingly capable of doing on occasion.

"I do not care about any of that, Guyard, I am just content to be here with you, in your arms. And no, you cannot drop me just because you do not want to hear such things. Not when it is merely a part I play," she added meaningly, her eyes on the gateway ahead of them.

She followed this with a giggle, and said in clearly audible if slightly slurred common speech,

"I do give satisfaction, do I not, Master Finch?"

"You do indeed, my sweet," he managed to say as she nuzzled his neck, her mouth marking him with a trail of warm, moist kisses.

He dared not remonstrate with her, lest the guards overhear, instead firming his grip and gathering her closer as a mail-clad form stepped towards him.

"Here, now, Master Finch, what mischief're ye about at this time o' the night?"

"Nay mischief, Dickon. I'm just taking Mistress... er..."

"Nell," she supplied with another giggle.

"Mistress Nell back home."

"'Tis past the middle watch, man! An' we'm not supposed ter open the gates fer no-one 'til dawn."

"Aye, but ye knows me," Guy pointed out in a thick, vaguely drunken accent. "An' ye wouldn't want fer Mistress Nell not ter be in her bed when dawn comes ter light the sky an' long noses start quivering over garden walls?"

"Well, 'tis true as I've not known ye behave so recklessly foolish afore," the guard admitted. "Beorn, aye, many a time, but not ye. As 'tis I reckon ye'll ha' all the daemons outta hell poundin' inside yer head in the mornin' if ye've drunk half as much as ye must ha' done ter git tangled up wi' some respectable woman from the town."

"'S'worth it though," Guy slurred. "So're ye goin' to let us through, Dickon, or do we have to bed down in the stables? I don't mind it for meself but..."

"Oh, very well, I'll let ye through," the guard sighed. "But if ye'll tek my advice, nex' time stick ter the whores down at the Cock."

"I don't do whores."

Guy drew himself up and announced with false dignity,

"Takes yer coin, gives ye the pox. I'd rather do meself."

He felt Juliène quiver in his arms and wondered if he had gone too far down the road of tasteless, drunken vulgarity, but then she said with a meaningful laugh,

"Not while I'm around to do you, love."

"Oh, get on wi' ye," the guard said, inadvertently rescuing Guy from Juliène's searching hands and another onslaught of wet, hot kisses.

"Go find yerselves a bed, ye can't do that here."

"I can do it anywhere," Juliène argued, with a lazy, slumberous laugh. "Can't I, my lover?"

Guy did not bother answering.

Not only because they were almost out of earshot of the guards, but also because he had a notion that it was no more than the truth.

The third bell after midnight was sounding, deep and mellow, when Guy finally stopped outside the gates of the Healing House.

They had walked without talking through the silent streets of the town, winding ever downwards, Guy holding fast to Juliène's hand to prevent her slipping on the night-slick cobbles.

Until, that is, she had stumbled once too often for his liking, and then he had caught her up in his arms again and carried her, ignoring the grinding pain in his bad leg.

She had fallen asleep against his shoulder.

Now standing before the closed gates, with the night breeze riffling through the bronze bells in the nearby spindleberry tree, he had no choice but to wake her, setting her gently on her feet.

And because he was as tired as she, it was the accent of his own province that came most readily to his tongue.

"Juli-lass, we're here."

She stirred and clutched at him as if fearing he might disappear between one heartbeat and the next.

"Guyard? Is it time already?"

"Aye, lass, slip inside now and seek out your bed. You're asleep on your feet as it is."

"Not before I tell you..."

"Tell me tomorrow, Juli," he said with a yawn. "Or rather, later today, if you accompany the princess up to the castle."

He managed a wry smile.

"I am sure you will find some way of..."

"You do not understand," she interrupted, the sharpness in her tone cutting through his weariness. "I will not *be* coming up to the castle tomorrow. I will not even be in Vézière. Linette is travelling south to Kardolandia tomorrow and..."

"And you are the other one of the two ladies who will be accompanying her," Guy finished for her, now very much awake.

"Yes."

"When will you return?"

"To Mithlondia? Or to Vézière?"

"Either. Both."

"I do not know. It might be two seasons... a year... three... five... who knows? Certainly I do not."

Her voice broke.

"Oh Guyard, just this once, kiss me as if you mean it. For it is in the hands of the gods and the goddess whether we will ever meet again."

Instinct, common sense, those damned voices screaming in his head, all told him to be wary.

To refuse her request.

Warning that if he yielded to her now he would be paying the price for all eternity.

That to kiss her as they both wanted would be to put his soul into her hands – a gift she would undoubtedly use to destroy him, and then laugh as she walked away.

Leaving him broken, and regretting his rash moment of trust forever more.

With such thoughts in his mind he put his hands on her slender shoulders to put her away from him.

Then, knowing full well what he did, drew her close and kissed her as if he meant it.

Because, gods help him, he did.

PART III

WINTER

1207

Verse 1

Bitter Tidings

"Well? What *do* you think?"

Despite the slight edge to her companion's soft voice – an impatience that informed her that it was probably not the first time she had been addressed – Rowène neither replied nor moved from her position in the window embrasure where she had been standing for some considerable time, alternately watching the activity in the muddy courtyard far below and staring out over the bare brown branches of the forest towards the grey haze of the distant moors, the view obscured here and there by the first fragile flakes of winter's snow.

Then, her mind still on the steadily thickening whirl of white, she finally made answer,

"What I think is that with this hell-sent snow coming this early, it is going to be a damnably long time until spring..."

Then, belatedly becoming aware from the slightly shocked quality of the silence behind her that she had said something wrong, she turned around, making rapid assessment of the situation, including her own appearance and that of the only other person in the room, cursing with silent vehemence in the privacy of her mind.

Whilst she did not usually forget herself this was not the first time she had been caught with words or actions more suited to a guise other than the one she happened to be wearing.

Not surprising perhaps when circumstance had caused her to assume a variety of identities, ranging from Jacques, the free-spirited outlaw youth – her first venture into the realms of enchanted illusion, and still her favourite – to the dutiful and mild-mannered healer, Sister Fayla, or the quiet yet firmly independent Brother Justinian.

The one person she never allowed herself to be was... herself.

And circumstances would have to be exceptional indeed to permit the Demoiselle Rowène de Chartreux to return from the wraith-lands, and thus far such a situation had only arisen within the secret shadows of her dreams.

She was wide awake now, however, with a mask to be mended, and so she made a deliberate effort to banish the carnal thoughts an innocent like Sister Fayla would never have harboured and fixed a spuriously limpid stare on the young woman seated in comfort before a merrily crackling fire of fragrant pine boughs.

"Forgive me, Lady Nerice, it is just that I am anxious, as I am sure you must be, about the coming season. I fear it will be a bleak and bitter winter."

"And my lord not yet returned home," the Lady of Lasceynes replied with a soft sigh as her pale blue gaze dropped to the tear-spotted embroidery in her lap.

"I was hoping he would leave court before this. I do so wish to show him his son."

"I am certain Lord Justin will be home soon," Rowène said soothingly. "Given the state of the roads, the messenger you sent to Lamortaine may well have been delayed."

The highway would indeed be a mire, it having been a particularly wet autumn and now...

Rowène cast another look out of the window at the floating feathers of white and hid her foreboding behind Sister Fayla's mask of calm, which – whilst not nearly as convincing as the Eldest's habitual serenity – appeared sufficient to reassure the youthful Lady of Lasceynes.

Had she ever been as naïve and trusting as the former Nerice de Vitré? Rowène wondered. Surely not.

Yet even as she dismissed the thought, recollection came of her younger self, just seventeen years of age, returning home to Chartre from Kaerellios, filled with an innocent joy and – in spite of her underlying fear of her mother – far, far too trusting...

The first subtle cracks in that trusting innocence had appeared as a result of her unexpected meeting with Ranulf de Rogé on the Chartreux highway, and then shattered completely by what had taken place between them in her chamber the following morning.

Now, thirteen years later – *thirteen!* Gods where had those years gone? – she seized what happiness she could amidst the dangers that surrounded her, and gave her unequivocal trust to none save her brothers, her bodyguard and the man she had come to love with all her heart.

In truth, she would have given *him* anything he asked for...

Except that he had never once over the course of the past five years asked her for anything save the companionship of a kinsman, and the only times he had allowed her to touch him, had been in the exercise of her odd healing power.

She had never been quite sure whether the desire he had undoubtedly felt for her at Chartre had simply died through lack of fulfilment or whether he had become more skilled at hiding it, tacitly joining the conspiracy her over-protective brothers had entered into to keep them apart.

A task that had proven easy enough over the last three years, since Ranulf had not even been in Mithlondia, having been sent south to Kardolandia to rejoin Princess Linette's bodyguard...

"Besides," Lady Nerice said suddenly, interrupting her dismal reflections. "The little one should have a name, should he not, lest anything should... happen to him. He is so small and..."

"You must not worry so," Rowène said firmly, abandoning her own wistful thoughts. "The babe is just as he should be – and believe me, you would not have wished to birth a giant," she smiled, trying the effect of gentle humour, her reward a small but genuine chuckle from the younger woman.

"He is a healthy little fellow and will await his father's return quite happily. Besides," she added, a little wryly. "I thought all the de Lacey firstborn males were named Justin."

"This is true," Nerice agreed. "And so it is settled, all save the formalities. It will be very confusing, I expect, to have both my lord and his son answering to the same name, but I should not like to set my own wishes against the long-standing traditions of my lord's family. It would be bad luck."

"Surely not," Rowène protested, ignoring what she knew about the only time that tradition had been broken.

Then in an effort to lighten the conversation again, as much for her own sake as the other woman's, added with a hint of almost genuine mischief,

"Besides, it may be that Lord Justin has his own ideas as to his son's name."

"Well, if that is so, then I shall of course abide by my lord's decision," the other woman said with a contented docility that caused Rowène to sigh silently under her breath.

She liked Nerice de Lacey and truly appreciated her many kindnesses, including the generosity of spirit that had allowed her to extend a welcome to the dangerous guests her lord had placed in her household. Even so, she could not help wishing the girl would show herself a little less reliant upon Justin de Lacey to order every aspect of her existence.

What, for instance, would Nerice do if the worst happened and Joffroi de Rogé and the ruffians of his Black Hunt descended on Lasceynes castle with fire and steel, as in another life he and Ranulf had brought death and destruction to Chartre?

In all truth, it did not bear thinking about, and with a slight shiver that had little to do with the thickening swirl of white beyond the snow-spattered cobwebs adorning the window, Rowène allowed herself to be distracted by a soft knock at the solar door.

Gwynny was the first to enter, carrying the three-day old heir to the de Lacey lands – the babe who was the reason why Rowène had broken the rhythm of the past five years to spend the summer and autumn here in Lasceynes as Sister Fayla.

Behind them came Lissie, who at twelve years of age divided her time between absorbing the skills of a healer in company with the woman she still did not know was her mother and learning to comport herself as a noblewoman should.

Not that Rowène could foresee the day when it would ever be safe either for her daughter to be known by her rightful name or to acknowledge the man who had sired her, let alone take her place amongst the highest in the land.

"Lady Nerice, Sister Fayla."

Gwynhere dropped a small curtsy as she spoke, Lissie following suit as she gave her own greeting to the Lady of Lasceynes, her summer blue eyes – her father's eyes, Rowène thought with a slight pang – bright with happiness and an underlying excitement.

"Good afternoon, Lissie, and what have you been about today?" Lady Nerice asked kindly, watching the child's light steps with an indulgent smile. And to the older woman,

"Yes, Gwynhere, I will have the little one now."

"Well," Lissie replied. "I started out by reading to Grandmère Anne, then I worked on my letters with Val until he spilled ink all over..."

A cough from Gwynhere made her discard any further information on that subject.

"After that, Gwynny let me help with the babe until he started fussing and she said it was time for him to feed, so we brought him down to you. Oh, and I practised my harp for a bit, and Gwynny says that one day I may be able to play as well as my..."

Her golden skin acquired a slight rose flush and she glanced guiltily at Gwynhere who was bending to lay the shawl-swaddled babe in Lady Nerice's arms.

"As well as your cousin," Gwynhere finished for her, her placid tones at odds with the loving warning in her warm brown eyes. "It is but to practise a little more diligently, is it not, Lissie?"

Lissie pulled a face that said well enough what she thought of the concept of any sort of practise, diligent or otherwise, then in her usual mercurial fashion dismissed the subject, dancing over towards Rowène, and it was all she could do not to reach out to draw her beautiful, golden-haired daughter close.

Lissie, however, had no such qualms and when she flung her arms around her mother's waist, Rowène knelt to return the embrace.

"What have *you* been doing this morning, Sister Fayla?" Lissie asked with determined courtesy, before adding in an anxious whisper, the words muffled by the thick folds of pale grey wool,

"I did not mean to mention Papa."

"Nothing half as exciting as you, Lissie," Rowène said out loud. "I was working in the garden until it became too cold, then I came up here to keep Lady Nerice company."

And in a merest breath against her daughter's ear,

"Do not worry, Lady Nerice heard nothing amiss."

Thanks to Gwynny. Goddess, where would we all be without her? Or Edwy for that matter?

"I would not have mentioned Papa, except I had just seen Edwy from the nursery window," Lissie continued in an aching whisper, seeming to sense the reflection of her father's brother in Rowène's mind.

"I thought Edwy might have been to Vézière and seen Papa?"

"We will ask him later," Rowène murmured.

Rising to her feet, she glanced over at Nerice de Lacey, letting out a small breath of relief when she saw that Gwynny was keeping that young woman's attention firmly fixed on the babe nuzzling hungrily at her breast and well away from the low-voiced conversation concerning Lissie's absent father.

Just then Lady Nerice lifted her head from her absorption with the babe at her breast to say,

"Mayhap, Lissie, you could show us the results of your practising after the evening meal and before you retire to bed."

For a moment the young noblewoman's eyes rested thoughtfully on the child's face, and the fair hair spilling from the braids only partially concealed beneath a linen coif, before she continued,

"Though it has to be said that no matter how diligently you practise I doubt you will ever rival Guyard de Martine when it comes to harp song."

"Oh, who is that?" Lissie asked, with an absent-minded curiosity, just as Gwynhere straightened, the unaccustomed frown marring the natural sweetness of her face glimpsed in the moment before Rowène closed her eyes for a painful heartbeat.

"Guyard de Martine," Lady Nerice repeated. "He was the b..."

She cleared her throat delicately, and amended her explanation.

"He was, as you may have guessed from his name, of high birth and Lord Joffroi of Rogé's right-hand man at one time."

She paused, looking vaguely troubled by that connection, since even living the sheltered life she did in Lasceynes she could hardly remain in ignorance of the foul deeds attributed to Joffroi de Rogé and, by default, those who rendered him loyal service for whatever reason.

"Yes, well," Lady Nerice hastened on. "In spite of... um... the position he held in Lord Joffroi's household, Guyard de Martine was the gentlest of men and the most wonderful harper I have ever heard. He stopped the night at Vitré once, oh, many years ago, when I was little more than a child myself, but I tell you now it is not the sort of thing I would forget."

Her reminiscent smile slipped into sadness.

"I believe he died not long after that. Not that he was old by any means. It was the summer sickness that took him, I suppose. But then as you already know, child, having lost your own mama and papa, life is indeed a fragile thing and the daemons of death lurk ever close at hand."

With that, her distant regret for the death of a once-seen harper turned into a more personal fear, her arms tightening visibly around her son's tiny body, a haunted look entering the gaze she settled on the babe nuzzling her breast.

Lissie looked from Rowène to Gwynhere, a faintly questioning look in her wide eyes, then made a politely indeterminate noise that Lady Nerice could interpret how she pleased.

Whether she heard it or not, the young noblewoman seemed to make an effort at composure, and looked up to say,

"You have worked hard today, child. Would you like to go down to the kitchen now, and see if Mistress Melangel can find you some bread and honey to stay your belly until the evening meal? I expect you will find Linnet there."

"Yes, my lady," Lissie answered carefully, with another look at Rowène and Gwynhere. "I would like that."

In truth, Rowène thought that if her daughter were to seek out any of her kin, it would be her male cousins rather than Nettie, who though she was officially Lady Nerice's handmaid, still spent much of her time in the kitchen with Melangel, her mother.

Val and Wulf, however, would be about their own business somewhere in the stables or courtyard, and if Lissie did indeed go looking for them, Rowène had no doubt she would also take the opportunity to quiz Edwy about his recent absence from the castle.

With Lissie gone, Lady Nerice waited a moment or two before asking of no-one in particular,

"Far be it from me to question my lord's judgement, or trespass against his prohibition to probe into what does not concern me, but is it at all possible, do you think, that Lissie is Guyard de Martine's natural daughter?"

"It is possible, of course, my lady," Gwynhere agreed with a calm Rowène did not think she was capable of matching at that particular moment.

"Then again, any fair-haired man might have had the siring of her. Lord Gilles was notorious for passing on his own colouring to his offspring, and there are many who can lay claim to his blood in Valenne, let alone elsewhere. I doubt it means anything..."

"And the boy, Val?" Lady Nerice interrupted, with a rare and exceedingly unwelcome display of tenacity.

"He is so very like to Lissie they could be brother and sister. Do you not find it strange indeed that my lord should extend hospitality, protection *and* education to two orphaned, *fair-haired* beggar children, given the enmity that existed between Lasceynes and Valenne when old Lord Gilles was alive."

"Lord Justin is a kind and generous man," Rowène murmured into the subsequent, slightly uncomfortable, silence when Gwynhere did not – could not – reply, the Valennaise woman's tongue tied by memory, her brown eyes clouded with a never-forgotten pain.

"Indeed, are we not all in Lord Justin's debt?"

"He is, and we are," Lady Nerice agreed with a disconsolate sigh, and then rather like a squirrel returning to nibble on a half-eaten nut.

"I do wish he would come home, Sister. I cannot help but worry about him when he is away at court."

And rightly so, Rowène thought grimly, though she did not say the words out loud.

She might have no great belief that it had been kindness or generosity that had prompted Justin de Lacey to take any of the forest folk into his household, but she did, nonetheless, share his lady's wish that the Lord of Lasceynes would hasten his return, if only because he would bring with him all the latest tidings from Lamortaine and the royal court.

For while Edwy could well have brought word from Guy in Vézière, it was of their other brother whom Rowène yearned – quite desperately – to hear.

As it was, Justin de Lacey kept them waiting for a further two days.

Then, when Rowène was beginning to fear that the unseasonably early snowfall would prove too heavy to allow him to safely travel either the shorter, rougher road that led over the moors or the longer but less hazardous highway that skirted the Rathen Fells and what remained of Lasceynes Forest, he confounded all expectations by riding into the castle courtyard just before dark-fall.

Pausing only to toss his wet mantle into the outstretched hands of his steward, and pull off his muddy boots and wet hose, leaving them to dry by the hall fire, he ran barefoot up the spiral stairs that led to the solar, notwithstanding the chill of the stone, eagerness to see his lady and his son imbuing an uncharacteristic lightness to his step and overcoming the weariness that long days of travel must have added to the weight of his years.

Not that Rowène concerned herself with Justin de Lacey's private life, or his reasons for leaving it so late to take the binding oath and beget a lawful heir for Lasceynes.

She was only too grateful that when he had, he had chosen a sweet-natured young woman who was more than happy to live far from the royal court and, for the most part, exhibited little interest in delving into her lord's secrets.

In truth, Nerice de Vitré had visited Lamortaine just once in her twenty-one years, and that on the occasion of her binding to Justin de Lacey. A match made by her father but one with which she appeared content, despite the considerable difference in age between herself and her lord.

Sheltered as she had been, she had not even taken her turn, as Rowène had, as one of Linette's lady-companions, the princess having already departed for Kardolandia by the time Nerice had gone to court.

Five years later Linette had still not returned to Mithlondia, and Rowène frequently found herself wondering whether the princess – and by default her entourage – would ever come back to the Palace of Princes.

And when – if – she did, cocooned as she was by the trappings of court life, would Linette ever know – or care – what had happened in her absence to those who had taken refuge in Lasceynes' great greenwood?

There was, after all, no particular reason why a royal princess should trouble herself over the fate of those proclaimed outlaw and traitor. Even so, Rowène knew beyond all doubt that Linette would wish to assure herself that the two children she had so visibly been enchanted by during their brief meeting were safe.

Which was where – five years before – Justin de Lacey had entered the scene.

With Linette's departure for Kardolandia, and Joscelin's subsequent posting to the Atarkarnan border, it was as if their absence had removed the last fragile restraint over Joffroi de Rogé's actions, giving him leave to direct every vicious effort at his command into capturing the sons of his old enemy, together with any man, woman or child who had dared to give their support, assistance or allegiance to Lucius de Chartreux's outlawed offspring.

Bearing the High Counsel's writ, the Black Hunt had ridden every furlong of the moors and fells, killing and torturing as they went. Finding no sign of those they sought, the hunters had returned to torch the forest and this time, deprived of Joscelin's backing in the Counsel Chamber, Justin de Lacey had been unable to persuade Prince Linnius to call a halt to the burning until more than half of the greenwood had gone up in flames.

At which point, and knowing that he had won only a temporary reprieve, de Lacey had taken the extreme step of entering what was left of the forest, the beech and oak and chestnut all gone, leaving only dark-shadowed avenues of pine and silent glades that opened amongst the tangle of holly, hazel and silver birch where the last herds of fallow deer had taken refuge, alongside the outlaws who hunted them for their meat and hides.

Accompanied only by Bryce, his chief huntsman, de Lacey had laid his naked sword upon a fallen log and waited for the outlaws to find him, and hen, when Luc and Jacques had finally stepped silently from the trees, he had put his proposition to them.

An offer of assistance, which de Lacey had presented as the only meaningful way in which he could show his support for the two men who were his distant kin through Aneta de Lacey's long-ago and tragically short-lived union with her lover, Gilles de Valenne.

It was, at best, a tenuous connection and Rowène has as little belief that it provided Justin de Lacey's motivation as she had in his kindness.

To her mind, it seemed far more likely that he was using her and her brother to thumb his nose at Joffroi de Rogé, and she knew Luc shared her somewhat cynical assessment.

The lives of the children, however, meant more to them than anything else, and by then matters were desperate enough that they had little choice other than to put their trust in Justin de Lacey's word of honour – this proving less hard than one might have thought.

Neither Luc nor Rowène had forgotten that the Lord of Lasceynes had held them in the palm of his hand once before and had refrained from handing them over to the Black Hunt, and so they had put their faith in the belief that he would not do so this time.

In truth it was either that or wander the roads of the realm until they all perished of hunger, or were taken and hanged – either as anonymous thieves or known traitors.

Luc might have risked it for himself and the men who had sworn loyalty to him, but that was not the life he wanted for the children in his charge. Nor for his sister, or any of the other womenfolk for whom he had assumed responsibility.

He had therefore accepted de Lacey's offer on their behalf, and had seen Gwynhere, Melangel and the children – Lissie, Val, Linnet, Wulf, Benet and little Merula – safely settled in Lasceynes, leaving Justin de Lacey to swear the binding oath with Nerice de Vitré.

An event that provided reason enough, or so de Lacey said, to expand his household without arousing unwelcome speculation.

Luc had wanted Rowène to stay in Lasceynes too, though he must have known he would have a fight on his hands. Not only did she not wish to leave the brother she had lived and fought alongside for so many years, she had known it would be impossible for her to fit into the de Lacey household in any capacity. Having roamed the forest and the fells as an outlaw youth for the best part of eight years, she could not simply step tamely back into her skirts. Moreover, the things she had seen and done over those years made her unsuitable in every way to be a companion to Lady Nerice.

As to any other role in the castle household, she was too independent to bow her head and act the servant's part, even if she had possessed any skills in that direction. Unlike Melangel, who having been found a place in the castle kitchens had fitted in so well that she was now the undoubted ruler of that domain.

Nor, much as Rowène loved her daughter and Ranulf's son, could she bring herself to stay with them in safety, if it meant leaving Luc to struggle alone. So she had entrusted the children to Gwynny, who was more than content to continue caring for them in much the same manner as she had always done.

With the women and children settling into their new roles within Lasceynes' sheltering walls, and his men waiting for him just within the green mantle of the forest, their scant possessions slung at their backs alongside their bows, Luc had found himself with only his recalcitrant sibling left to deal with.

In the end they had compromised, as Rowène had always known she would have to, and in all truth the bargain she agreed to was far from the gilded prison she had feared Luc meant to sentence her to, making her realise that he understood her much better than she had supposed.

In return for spending the harsh winter months in the relative comfort and security either of Vézière's Healing House or Lasceynes castle, Luc agreed that she might live the better part of the year with him – on the condition that she accompany him as 'Brother Justinian', the guise Luc believed offered her the best protection from those who would henceforth be her companions.

At that point she had still not guessed where he meant to go and Luc had answered her frowning question with the last direction she – or indeed anyone else, including Joffroi de Rogé – would have expected him to take.

So, north they had gone and when she, Luc and his remaining men reached the craggy hills and stony vales of that disputed land, they had managed, with sword and bow and healing herb, to make a place for themselves alongside the company of guardians who ranged along the border with Atarkarna, now under the command of Joscelin de Veraux.

And while it had filled Rowène's heart with warmth to be with both her brothers, at the same time, she had been deluged with something close to pain at seeing Ranulf again.

A pain that had only deepened when he kept the same respectful distance as the other men from 'Brother Justinian', and for which she considered he had scant reason since he knew only too well the truth hidden beneath the dark grey robes she wore.

Regardless of her lingering hurt she had healed the wounds he brought to her, and concealed her love for him as best she might, striving always to treat him with the undemanding friendship she extended to all the men of the camp, guardians and outlaws alike.

Thus she had lived through the turning seasons of the past five years, wearing the clothes and character that best suited her surroundings, spending the winters with Lissie and Val in Lasceynes, or at the Healing House in Vézière as Sister Fayla, then the spring, summer and early autumn on the Atarkarnan border with her brothers, her healing skills in demand wherever she went.

When they had first joined the ranger company, she had been very much afraid of the likely consequences should any of the guardians – all of whom had sworn an oath of fielty to the Prince Linnius – guess at Luc's identity as Lucius de Chartreux's only legitimate son – and a proclaimed traitor and outlaw in his own right.

And perhaps some did.

Yet once accepted into that group, a man's birth name and past was put aside. What mattered were his deeds *after* he joined the northern company of rangers, within which close-knit band there was much trust but little formality.

So that while their commander merited a respectful "sir" everyone else was known simply by his given name. Or if there were two men of the same name, by some additional descriptive.

Rafe, when he had been part of the company, had been Rafe the Fair, a reference to his barley-pale hair rather than any good looks he might once have possessed, before years of war had weathered them away into wind-scoured granite.

There being no others sharing her brother's name, he was known simply as Luke of Lasceynes.

As for 'Brother Justinian' it was inevitable that those men who had not known her before would find something odd about her ability to heal wounds and broken bones so swiftly.

Yet, to her knowledge, the matter had never been mentioned aloud. As it had not been between her brother's men.

And after that first summer of fighting alongside each other, guardians, outlaws and healer had become one, bound by blood shed, and lives spared by the grace of the goddess, though even then Rowène could not save them all.

As for the other, tamer part of her life, Rowène rather thought that Justin de Lacey had his own suspicions regarding the identity of the healer he courteously addressed as Sister Fayla, though she could not say for certain that he knew that she was Luc's sister, since it had been through the Eldest that de Lacey had requested the attendance of a healer named Sister Fayla these past two seasons at Lasceynes castle in order to see Lady Nerice through the last stages of her confinement.

With all they owed Justin de Lacey, Rowène could scarcely refuse.

And so in the autumn of 1207 she had relegated her ever-present fear for her kinsmen – and the increasingly lurid rumours emanating out of Kaerellios – to the darkness of her dreams, and had gone to Lasceynes to do a healer's duty, at the same time seizing the opportunity to spend as much time with Lissie and Val as she could.

It was, she knew, a precious gift from the gods she could not expect to be granted again.

Nonetheless, as summer leached into autumn and autumn teetered on the edge of winter, Rowène could not help feeling trapped, uncomfortable within the stone walls of castle and town after so many years in the wild.

Even her guise as Brother Justinian, dangerous and bloody though it frequently was, allowed her a freedom of thought, word and action greater than she could ever find in Lasceynes castle.

Moreover, until Ranulf had been sent south to Kardolandia, life in the rangers' border camp had offered the lure of something more... sweet as rising sap, fierce as a wind-blown flame, and heady as mulled Marillec wine...

And now, if Justin de Lacey was to be believed, the man she loved with all that sweet, fierce, heady passion, had finally returned to Mithlondia.

Not that Lord Justin had spoken of Ranulf by name. What he had said was that Prince Kaslander, Princess Linette and their daughter, together with the rest of their entourage – which Rowène, listening silently in the shadows, took to mean Juliène, Adèle and the men of the royal bodyguard, including Gabriel and Ranulf – had arrived in Lamortaine just as he himself had been about to depart, and de Lacey had therefore remained a few more days in the Palace of Princes to attend to various Counsel matters that had arisen following their return.

He had said no more to Nerice but there had been a darkness in his hazel eyes and a grim set to his mouth that Rowène had recognised.

It was the look of a man who knew far more than he was telling. And that knowledge, whatever it was, weighed heavy on his soul.

Her opportunity to question Justin de Lacey came later that night, when long after everyone else had retired, she found herself in the nursery.

She had been returning from the privy and was hastening back to her warm bed, her linen night rail ill protection against the wintry chill pervading the passageways, the cold bitter enough to penetrate the thick, rabbit-fur lining of her mantle.

Shivering, rubbing her arms vigorously in an effort to generate some heat, she paused as she heard a noise beyond the door to the chamber where de Lacey's infant heir slept, something between a half-hearted hiccough and a cry, and without thinking she opened the door and walked in.

Then stopped abruptly as she perceived the man standing at the edge of the shimmering stream of moonlight, the child held against his shoulder.

"Come in, Sister, and shut the door," came the quiet instruction in common speech.

Then as Rowène approached silently, de Lacey added,

"I knew you would seek me out. And now seems as good a time and place as any for this conversation."

"What is it?"

By some effort she remained calm, although her heart had quickened its beat.

"What has happened that you could not speak of in your lady's hearing?"

She looked up at his face, lit by moonlight, shadowed by emotions she could not define, then glanced out of the window at the light filigree covering of snow, fear overcoming her normal caution, making her reckless.

"Oh gods! Tell me this does not concern Josce or Luc or... or Rafe?"

"The first two, of course, being your brothers."

De Lacey spoke now in Mithlondian, keeping his voice soft for the child's sake, and as cool as the slowly settling snow.

And when she said nothing in reply,

"Wise of you not to deny what has been obvious to me for many years now. Who is Rafe though? And what is he to you?"

"He is a member of Princess Linette's guard," Rowène said flatly, determined to give nothing further away.

"Ah! Big fellow? Fair hair? And with the same dark blue eyes as the last true Lord of Valenne?"

"Yes," she grated.

"This would be the same Rafe as was brought before the High Counsel once for killing one of de Rogé's retainers in some sordid squabble in a brothel. In... Vézière, I believe it was. As I remember it, he had de Rogé frothing at the mouth with rage, and accusing him of being his dead brother of all mad things."

The hazel eyes were intent on her face.

"He was sent down for a flogging and then to all intents and purposes disappeared from the Counsel's sight."

De Lacey tilted his head, eyeing her from rumpled curls to bare toes.

"So what is he to you? Your lover?"

It should have been insulting, given her present guise as a Sister of Mercy, yet de Lacey clearly did not mean it as such.

"No."

He waited a moment but she had nothing further to say.

To claim 'Rafe' as her kinsman would be to yield up his identity to this keen-eyed, level-spoken nobleman, and only the gods knew what use he might make of such information, bearing in the mind the old enmity between Valenne and the de Lacey family.

"Well, whatever he is to you, he is once more confined to the cells beneath the palace, along with…"

"What in gods' name has he been charged with?" Rowène interrupted. "According to you, he and the rest of Princess Linette's party only returned to Lamortaine a few days ago. Not even Ran… Rafe can get into so much trouble so soon."

"Let me finish, my dear. As I said, he is confined but not, you will be relieved to hear, charged with any offence. The High Counsel merely wishes to assure itself that he will be there to stand witness when the time comes to put Gabriel de Marillec on trial."

"On trial… but why? When?"

Oh gods, Rafe! And when Luc hears about Gabriel…

"De Marillec was arrested the day he returned to court."

"On what charge?"

At that question de Lacey's countenance turned bleak, leaving him grey in the silvery light.

"Bearing in mind where the man has been for the past five years, and the reputation he took with him, I am sure you can guess well enough the crime of which he stands accused."

"No! He would not do that, would not betray…"

She choked the words off. Far too late.

"Betray your brother? Or commit the unnatural act with which he has been charged?"

De Lacey turned to stare out of the window, his hand absently smoothing up and down the soft curve of his son's small back as he continued with a bitter edge to his otherwise emotionless tone.

"Perhaps it is true. Perhaps not. Either way it is poor recompense for the loyal service de Marillec has given to the princess these past five years. Moreover, I suspect it to be no more than a lie concocted by Joffroi de Rogé, since it was he who persuaded Prince Linnius to issue the warrant for de Marillec's arrest."

"What about Josce? Do not tell me he carried out the arrest?"

"No, he refused point blank in front of the whole Counsel, and in consequence of that ill-considered act of..."

"Loyalty!" she interrupted, her tone low but fierce.

"Of folly, I was about to say, but you may have the right of it. Whichever it is, your half-brother is now under guard in his own quarters. Not free, but not yet under arrest either. He is still Lord of Veraux and that position carries some privilege and protection. For the moment at least.

"As for your other brother, you had better pray that he has more sense than to recklessly put his neck in the noose he has managed to evade so successfully for the past dozen years."

"And what about you, Messire?" Rowène dared to ask. "What will you do, if I may be permitted the impertinence of enquiring?"

"Will I act the hypocrite or take a similar stance to de Veraux's, you mean?"

"Yes."

Justin de Lacey looked down at his new-born son, moonlight weaving silver tendrils through his thinning brown hair, laying impenetrable shadows across his taut countenance.

"Before I answer that question, I have one for you," he said grimly.

"Are *you* prepared to stand or fall by my judgement? For if I have to think first of the welfare of my lady and child, you yourself must take thought for the children you carry responsibility for.

"So consider well before you answer, because if I choose the wrong side in this farce of a trial, and end up forfeiting my life and lands, they will all be cast out into what is shaping to be the worst winter in living memory."

"I have lived rough before, as have Lissie and Val..."

Her voice trailed off at the thought of the children – *her* children – returning to such an existence.

Of Grandmère Anne, forced back into danger and discomfort...

Of Gwynny hunted again by the men who had murdered her lover and brother...

Of the gently-bred Nerice and her new-born babe cast adrift into snow and freezing wind...

"And this time," de Lacey's voice took up her thought. "You will not have the forest to shelter you. De Rogé will burn what little of it as is left to the ground if I dare to cross him and a verdict of guilty is still returned on Gabriel de Marillec."

"When will you return to Lamortaine?" Rowène asked, her tone dull and defeated.

"Linnius has given me leave of absence for a se'ennight to see to the naming of my son, after which he will expect to see me back at court. It took me three days to ride here, and I must allow for the same to return. That leaves me with less than a day in Lasceynes to settle my affairs. Hence why you find me here now with little Justin."

His thin mouth formed a faint, decidedly mirthless smile.

"After all, given the likely outcome of de Marillec's trial, this may well be the only time I see my son, or hold him against my heart."

Rowène had left Justin de Lacey soon after that, returning to the chamber she shared with Lissie and Grandmère Anne and, until recently Gwynny, who now slept in a little chamber adjoining the nursery and had either been unaware of Lord Justin's visit earlier or maintaining a discreet distance. Rowène suspected the latter.

She also suspected that Gwynny would be unsurprised by the decision she had reached over the course of that long, cold, moon-drenched night.

Not that it had taken Rowène more than a single heartbeat to make up her mind, the subsequent hours of anxious planning however had been far less straightforward. Still, she had slept a little towards dawn.

Once awake, while Grandmère Anne was still dozing in her warm nest of blankets, she went to sit on the foot of Lissie's bed, and when her daughter regarded her questioningly, said without preamble,

"Lissie, sweetheart, I have to leave."

Clear blue eyes regarded her for a moment.

"Why?"

"Because I have to find your Uncle Luc."

She had been prepared for questions or even argument but Lissie offered neither. What she did say was far worse.

"I saw him in a dream last night. There was another man with him, a man with light brown hair and strange eyes like Lyra's."

That was the cat who lived at Vézière's Healing House.

"I do not know who he was but I think... I think they were going to hang him, this other man."

Lissie's blue eyes glittered with fearful tears as she scrambled out of her blankets to bury her head in Rowène's breast, the sobbed words barely audible.

"Then he... the other man... was gone but Uncle Luc was still there... and he was hurting. There was blood everywhere... so much blood! That's why you're going, Sister Fayla, isn't it? So that you can save Uncle Luc from getting hurt?"

"I will try, Lissie. If I can stop him from going to Lamortaine, that might be enough. But to do that I must leave now, this morning. Be a good girl for Gwynny and Grandmère Anne whilst I am gone."

"I always am."

The next words were still muffled but the tone was fiercer.

"Come back soon, Sister Fayla. Promise you will come back!"

"I swear it, Lissie."

She hesitated.

"But if you have need... if something should happen here in Lasceynes before I return, you must go to Grandmère 'Louise in Vézière and she will take you to your father."

"What about Val and Wulf and Nettie?"

Her daughter's tear-stained face lifted to look at her, and Rowène thought it interesting that of all the children of the forest, Lissie had named the three who shared her de Rogé blood.

"What about them? May they come too?"

"Yes, them too. Edwy will take you all."

Because you and Val, Wulf and Nettie, are his blood-kin, and if I know Edwy he would give his life to see you safe. As for me, goddess help me, I must somehow keep Luc from recklessly putting his head in a noose, all the while trusting that Josce and Rafe know what they are doing and do not end up joining Gabriel on the scaffold. Gods! It would kill Luc to lose Gabriel like that.

She steadfastly refused to consider what it would mean to her if she lost Ranulf to a similar shameful end.

Having selected the garments she would need from the bottom of the clothing chest she shared with Gwynny, Rowène dressed carefully before donning Sister Fayla's loose pale grey robes, finally hiding her flame-touched curls beneath the linen headrail.

This done, she took a brief but heartfelt farewell of Grandmère Anne and Gwynny, a more formal one of Lady Nerice that allowed no leeway for questions, kissed a tearful Lissie, withstood an accusing look from Val's green eyes and a frowning one from Wulfric's dark gaze, before heading towards the stable to ask Beowulf to saddle Starshine and meet her at the edge of the forest.

Last of all, she snatched a few moments to seek out Edwy and tell him what she had learned from Justin de Lacey, and perhaps more importantly, what she intended to do about it.

He regarded her with grim disapproval but obviously realising he could not stop her, let her go with no more than a bleak warning to beware of wolves – both the four legged and two legged variety.

Edwy thought, of course, that Beowulf would be going with her. If he had realised she meant to travel alone, she knew he would never have let her go.

Ignoring the fear sitting like a cold stone in her belly, she trudged across the muddy snow of the courtyard, glancing up one last time at the walls of the tall, square keep.

Lissie was leaning out of the small unshuttered window of their room, fair hair tumbling down unbrushed and unbound against the grey stone, a fall of tangled glinting gold lit by the same early morning sunlight that glittered off the tears still showing against the child's soft, wild-rose skin.

For a heartbeat Rowène hesitated, torn between Lissie and Luc.

Then she caught sight of Justin de Lacey, standing at the larger window of the solar, his tiny son once more held in his arms, a bleak and bitter expression carved across the countenance only Rowène was able to see.

Whether he had made up his mind or not, Rowène did not know. De Lacey must act as his conscience bade him, all she could do was follow the promptings of her own heart.

The children would be well protected and cared for in her absence, she assured herself, as she turned to walk steadily through the trampled slush towards the gateway.

Frost was chill in the still air and she shivered. Not so much at the knife-sharp cold but more at the memory of Lissie's terrified words.

Uncle Luc was hurting... and there was blood everywhere... so much blood.

Pray gods she would be in time to stop him riding into danger.

Or failing that, that she could indeed save him from the daemons of death lurking in Black Joffroi's foul shadow.

Rowène found a place to wait beneath the snowy branches of a gnarled oak at the edge of the sad remnant of what had once been a great greenwood stretching from the Rathen Fells in Mortaine to a point in the wilderness many leagues north of Lasceynes town.

Seeing that she was completely alone and unobserved, Rowène removed her headrail, shaking her hair loose over her shoulders, before stripping off the enveloping folds of her robe.

At least, she amended, she had been alone, the frost-encrusted meadow grass untouched save for the narrow trail of her own footprints leading from the small, coldly splashing brook, spanned by a simple bridge... the wooden planks of which were now humming to the clipped sound of hoof beats.

Beowulf, of course. And Starshine.

Then struggled to free her hands from her sleeves as she realised there was more than one horse.

Tossing the robe hastily aside, her hand was at the hilt of the long knife sheathed at her hip before she saw that it was indeed Beowulf.

Except where he should simply have been leading or riding the mare, he was riding his own mount, with Starshine on a lead rein following docilely behind.

Her heart slowly resuming its normal pace, she uncurled her fingers from the dagger and folded her arms across her chest, lifting her chin as she waited for Beowulf to approach.

"What in bloody hell do you think you are doing?" she demanded as the man drew level with her and held out the mare's reins.

"What do it bloody well look like?" Beowulf grunted.

"You are *not* coming with me," Rowène snapped.

"Aye, that I am," her long-time bodyguard growled back.

He looked her up and down, from booted feet to loose curls, taking in the patched breeches, the jerkin belted over a shirt of rough linen, the fur-lined mantle of forest green pinned on her shoulder with a round silver brooch the size of a man's fist.

"I don't care who ye be right now nor where ye'm goin', 'cos where'er 'tis ye're goin' ter need me along."

"You've been talking to Edwy," Rowène accused him.

Beowulf made a sound of disgust in his throat.

"I got eyes an' ears an' all me wits yet. I don't need the likes o' Edwy o' Rogérinac ter tell me when aught's amiss. Ye wanted the mare an' provisions. Well, I brung what I could lay me hands on, an' yer bow as well. So mount up afore we're all frozen stiff as bloody corpses, an' then get on wi' whatever madness you've got in mind this bloody time."

"Beowulf, you can't come."

Much of the rough hostility left her voice then, a pleading note replacing the flat, cold tone.

"What about Mel? She has made a place for herself here in Lasceynes, for you, for the children..."

"Aye, that she has. An' in doin' so, she's forgot what we owe ye an' Master Luke."

"That was twelve years ago, for pity's sake, and you have more than repaid any debt. Not that I hold there to have been one to begin with."

"Twelve years or a score an' two," Beowulf replied stubbornly. "I don't fergit. An' I'll not stand by an' let ye go off alone, whether ye look like a boy or a healer or the noblewoman ye really are. I've looked out fer ye since the night o' that harvest fire at Mallowleigh, an' I ain't about ter bloody stop now."

It was the first time Beowulf had ever made reference to her true birthright or the many masks she had worn over the past thirteen years since he had first made the acquaintance of the Lady Rowène de Chartreux.

And while she would be only too glad of the stalwart companionship of the man who had become both bodyguard and friend over the course of those years, Rowène made one last attempt to persuade him to change his mind.

"Even so, Beowulf, you cannot abandon Melangel and the children in Lasceynes just to nursemaid me. You know what she said last time you did it. She'll not forgive you again."

"Aye, 'twill be a colder welcome than I'll get in Hell, I reckon," Beowulf agreed with a grim, gap-toothed smile. "But I'll not let ye hare off on yer own, an' Mel'll either have ter live wi' that, or not. 'Tis her choice. So now that's settled, Master Jacq, ye'd best tell me where we'm bound. East, is it?"

He paused, brown eyes glinting like pebbles in a sunlit river.

"Or north?"

They went north.

A journey that even in the best of summer weather would take a se'ennight to complete over some of the wildest, uninhabited, pathless hill country in the realm.

A journey now dragged out into twice that by the bitter travelling conditions that currently held sway between Lasceynes and the rocky slopes overlooking the roaring brown rage of the Tarkan River.

As they rode, the wind blew without pause, bringing flurries of snow to freeze their faces within their hoods... their hands within their gloves... their feet within their boots... their very bones within their bodies.

Whilst they were still within the de Lacey lands, they managed to beg or buy food and shelter for themselves and their mounts, but the farther north they travelled, the fewer dwellings they found, until in the end there was only themselves, the silent forests and the empty white fells.

They paused only to forage and hunt when they must, the tough moorland ponies pawing the snow aside to crop on the rough winter grass.

And all the time as they moved slowly north and east, as a counterpoint to the instinctive sense of urgency driving Rowène to seek out her brother and prevent him from riding into danger, the howl of the hungry wolf packs rose and fell upon the wind, distant at first, then closer, and closer yet, until the feral song was all around them and only the flickering golden flames of the camp fire kept them at bay...

Until even this was not enough, and when the emptiness of their sunken bellies finally overcame their fear of fire, the pack closed in, eyes agleam in the red-gold light, teeth bared in slavering snarls.

Having made what preparations they could, Rowène and Beowulf found themselves one frozen night facing the attack they had known must come.

Back to back they defended each other, first with bows, then with stout staves and flaming brands, and at the desperate end with fire-gilded, blood-wet steel, until at last the wolf pack turned on their own wounded, tearing the life from their brothers amidst growls and snarls, before dragging their bleeding bodies beyond the reach of the firelight, there to slake their ravening hunger.

Rowène watched them go, fingers clenched about the slippery hilt of her dripping blade, then catching the scent of fresh blood above the mingled reek of sweat and fear and wolf, turned aside to vomit into the trampled, reddened snow.

A curse from her companion made her straighten, wiping her mouth on her sleeve, then keeping a wary eye out for another attack turned her attention to tending the ragged gash in Beowulf's arm.

She herself was unhurt only because Beowulf had stepped between her and the wolf leaping for her throat, but at least she had repaid him by driving her dagger into the wolf's skull, though not before those sharp yellow teeth had done their wretched work.

Beowulf's wound having been washed clean with snow water, anointed with an unguent of lavender and chamomile – part of the small stock of herbs and linen she always carried in her pack – and bound up, they had settled down in a state of uneasy watchfulness to wait out the night.

Waking to a wraith-watch stillness broken only by the snap and thump as a pine bough broke and shed its load of snow just as the rose light of dawn spread to soften the darkness from the sky.

Indeed, so quiet was it that even the chilly trickle of the nearby steam seemed to have been silenced, and the sun slipping over the wooded heights shone with a pink glow over the pristine shroud of white crystal-sewn silk laid down by the gods some time during the latter part of the night to cover the bloody shambles of their fight with the wolf pack.

Without speaking, or pausing to perform more than the necessary tasks to start the day, Rowène and the man who had once more proved his courage and unstinting loyalty in her service, mounted up and with the faint warmth of the sun caressing their right cheeks, continued on what had always been a journey of desperation but which now seemed to Rowène to be without either hope or end.

They rode into the guardians' camp five days later, so cold and stiff they were barely able to stay in the saddle.

After the blessed grace of that clear rose-gold dawn, the weather had worsened again, bringing hail and freezing sleet when it was not simply snowing, all borne on a wind that cut like a whip through every layer of clothing they were wearing, reducing even the stoical moorland-bred ponies to misery.

There had been no trace of recent occupation at the first camp they had come to – of course it would not be that easy, if anything about this hell-cursed journey could be called easy! – nor at the second, and it was not until they rode through the narrow pass into Ferndale's hidden valley that they saw the signs they had been seeking.

On the sheltered slopes, close to the small grey-waved lake, tiny tendrils of smoke were rising from the roof holes of stone hovels that, left to fall into ruin long years before by the folk who had once lived in the dale, had now been repaired by the northern company of rangers to serve as their winter quarters.

Men Rowène recognised, outlaws and guardians alike, were visible about the dale, tending the horses, fetching firewood, bringing in the spoils of their day's hunting – here a deer, there a brace of red-legged partridge – while from the ridge above the pass a horn rang out, sharing the wind-swept heights of the winter sky with the wailing cry of a snow eagle calling for its mate.

While the horn did not sound the harsh, urgent blast warning of danger but rather the more melodic notes denoting 'friend', heads came up regardless of the reassurance, hands going to dagger hilt and arrow shaft until every man of the company had ascertained for himself who approached.

They kept their distance, however, watching as a curly-haired young man wearing a wolf pelt and worn leather emerged from one of the huts and stood waiting, shielding sharp brown eyes from the low noon-tide sun with a hand almost the same colour and texture as his jerkin.

Dropping his hand when the newcomers drew rein a yard or so away, he sent a grimly assessing gaze over them both, noting the weary state of the bedraggled ponies and the bloodstained binding around Beowulf's arm, before bringing his eyes back to Rowène's face, which despite dirt and wind burn was as white as the snow lying thick on the shoulders of the hills.

"Brother Justinian?! What in hell's name are you doing here?"

The same doubt and disbelief underlying those few words flickered across the young man's face and was gone, leaving it as bleak and hard as the icy peaks above them.

"What?"

Rowène made a brief attempt to reorientate herself – for she thought of herself as Jacques rather than Justinian in this garb –

before deciding that which name she went by was the height of irrelevance at this particular moment.

"Does it matter?" she said tersely in reply to Beric's question.

What was important was finding her brother, yet her frantically searching gaze could not pick him out amongst the men moving about the camp.

"Beric," she said urgently. "Where is Luc? I must speak with him."

So absorbed was she in her continuing search of the valley that she barely registered the guardian's reply, his tone roughening with impatience,

"For gods'sake, Justinian! You must be out o' your mind, coming here, now, what wi' winter closin' in..."

"I told you, Beric! I'm looking for Luc. Now for pity's sake, let me go and find him."

"Well, you won't. Not here at any rate."

Finally she brought her attention back to the man who was clearly in command of the camp in Joscelin's absence, fear rising in her throat.

"What..."

She swallowed hard.

"What are you saying, Beric? Is he out on patrol somewhere?"

"No, I mean, you're too late. He's gone."

"Gone? Gone where?"

A curt shrug of the ranger captain's shoulders.

"How should I bloody know? He asked me for leave of absence, a needless courtesy, seein' as I've no official command over the man, but I gave it anyway."

"Damn it, Beric!"

The gritted protest was out before she could bite it back. She had come all this way, put Beowulf into danger... for nothing!

She wanted to hit something. Preferably her bloody, reckless, hell-born brother!

What she knew she must not do was relieve the violence of her feelings by suddenly turning before Beric's eyes from the healer he respected into a highly-strung, hysterical noblewoman whose one desperate aim was to save her brother and his lover from the gallows.

"How long has he been gone?" she asked, trying to sound calm, despair seeping through her blood like snow melt.

"Three weeks ago now, I reckon."

And then, when she could not keep back her moan, added,

"For what 'tis worth, I'm sorry, lad. Whatever errand brought you here in this..."

Beric's gesture took in the snow clouds once more hanging grey and heavy on the northern heights, and closer at hand, the man hunched in his cloak at her side, shivering slightly, brown eyes worryingly bright with fever.

"Clearly it means a lot to you."

Saying that, Beric brought his narrowed gaze back to bear on her again, taking in her rough garments in forest shades of green and brown, so different from the dark grey hooded robe of the healer she had worn in his sight for the past four years, then shifting his scrutiny to touch fleetingly on the hair curling just past her shoulders, chestnut shot through with fire.

His brows drew together in a frown as if some memory – of another time, another place, another woman, another face – pulled at the edges of his mind.

Then he shook his head, evidently dismissing the stray thought.

"I can't tell you where Luke has gone, Justinian. Or why. I wish I could."

He hesitated. Grimaced.

"'Tis no secret though that his sleep was much troubled by dark dreams the night afore he left."

"Ah!"

"That means something to you, Justinian. Don't it?"

"Aye, Beric, it does. I wish to hell it did not."

She slid stiffly down from the saddle, holding tight to the moulded leather as her legs trembled beneath her, her cheek resting against the warm, faintly damp satin of Starshine's neck, while the mare turned to nuzzle her hair, blowing hot, horsey breaths beneath the collar of her cloak.

Despite the implied comfort, she was very close to tears.

"Oh, gods, what am I to do now?"

Verse 2

"So Now You Know!"

Even as the blood-red sun sank below the skeletal trees at the western end of the lake and rooks settled noisily to roost in the branches of the beech trees lining the highway, a swift darkness swept down from the hills of Mortaine to the accompaniment of a strident horn call from the high walls surrounding the Palace of Princes.

Almost before the last note had fallen silent those guards on duty, whether aloft on wall walks or down by the gates, half-frozen in the bitter wind and consequently eager to go off duty and seek the welcome warmth of the refectory, were tramping down stairs or making fast the portals that stood open during the daylight hours, the soldiers at the great north gate putting their shoulders with a will to the two halves of the massive iron-bound door, causing it to grind slowly but inexorably shut.

Accustomed as he had been since early childhood to the guardians' routines and the daily patterns of life within the palace and barracks, Dominic paid little heed to the soldiers as he made his way across the courtyard, absently acknowledging the onset of night and the arrival of the late watch.

It was only when he heard a more than usually profane curse from one of the guards on duty, instead of the shuddering thud as the gates locked together, that he had the first intimation that something was amiss.

Glancing over his shoulder, he found one of the huge doors still standing open, two mail-clad guardians blocking the gap, faces turned towards the snow-laden darkness beyond, while the pair just coming to relieve them were lurking by the red heat of the brazier, from which sparks were being sent whirling up into the sky by the same icy whistling wind that whipped the soldiers' cloaks from their determined grip, tugging their tunics awry and setting eyes to water.

In spite of the freezing weather, it seemed that some hapless latecomer stood outside the gates, and whoever it was Dominic did not wager much on their chances of gaining entry, this conjecture being confirmed a heartbeat later when he heard one of the guards growl,

"Curfew's blown, ye'll ha' ter wait 'til mornin'."

"But I cannot wait until then," came a muffled voice, its flat tones of weariness underpinned by a faint hint of desperation that unexpectedly caught at Dominic's well-armoured heart.

"I need to speak to..." A pause. "To your commander. To Lord Joscelin, that is. Or... or his Second."

"Well, ye can't talk ter neither of 'em, so ye'll just ha' ter bugger off back ter whatever hole ye crawled out of," came the brusque reply as the guard once more leant his weight against the iron-studded timbers of the gate, ready to push it closed.

"Now wait up, Siward," his companion protested, even as he blew on his chilled fingers and stamped frozen feet. "I wants ter get out o' this perishin' bloody cold same as ye but..."

"Ye don't half piss me off, Ulric! Jus' bleedin' well stay out of it this, will ye, an' we'll all be inside the sooner," Siward snarled back.

At the same moment as the stranger raised his voice to address the only one of the four guards who seemed to have even the slightest sympathy with his plight.

"Is Lord Joscelin not here then? Or Sir... or, no, he's Lord Gabriel now, is he not?"

"Oh, they'm here all right," Siward replied with a sniggering laugh before his companion could speak. "Both of 'em. But 'twon't do ye no good nohow, since neither of 'em'll be tellin' anyone what ter do fer a good long while, I shouldn't think. We takes our orders from Lord Joffroy o' Rogé now."

There followed a deeply stricken silence that impelled Dominic to ignore the caution ingrained into him over the past twenty-one years and edge closer towards the gate, just as Siward lowered his spear with the clear intention of making his point more brutally.

Before he could complete the vicious movement, however, Ulric grabbed his arm and, addressing the man beyond the gateway, said brusquely,

"Look, stranger, 'tis getting' late, an' we're all freezin' our balls off here. Why not find yerself a bed fer the night in the town an' come back in the mornin'. Or better yet, gi'e it a couple o' days. Lord Joscelin's been relieved of duty fer... well, I don't know fer how long.

'Til after the trial, I suppose. *Then* he'll be back, just ye wait an' see!"

This last he accompanied with a scowling sideways glance at Siward who was now venting his impatience with a stream of heated curses divided equally between the stranger and his fellow guardian.

"Who... whose trial?" The stranger asked shakily, ignoring Ulric's good advice. "Lord Gabriel's? Or..."

"Na, the Counsel's done wi' *him*," Siward interrupted, spitting into the snowy night. "Not but what he's still hangin' around, like a sewer stench what won't blow away!"

"'Tis the old Lord o' Chartreux's son they've got their teeth into this time," Ulric added with considerably less venom, while Siward gave another raucous laugh.

"Reckon we'll be havin' another traitor's head up aloft soon enough."

He gestured rudely upwards to where the fast falling darkness had thrown a merciful cloak over what was left of Lucius de Chartreux's crumbling skull, then spat once more into the trampled snow.

"Lord Joscelin'll be next, ye mark my words, stranger. An' t'other unnatural bugger too, wi' a bit o' luck. An' be damned ter all such maggot-shit, I say."

Then, in a sharper, decidedly more dangerous tone,

"What's the matter, stranger? Ye're lookin' sick. P'raps ye're thinkin' there shouldn't be no punishment fer wolf's-heads, degenerates, traitors an' the like? Mayhap ye're one yerself?"

"No, no, I just need to see Lord Joscelin. Or failing him, Lord Gabriel if... if as ye say he is still here. My business here has naught to do with traitors or outlaws... nor anything unnatural, I swear."

"Oh aye, like we'm goin' ter believe the likes o' ye," Siward sneered. "An' it wouldn't do ye no good e'en if we did. Now..."

He took a menacing step towards the stranger.

"Bugger off, afore I stop bein' nice an' decide ter haul yer sorry arse in front o' Lord Joffroy!"

Ulric, however, perhaps from sheer perversity, chose to take a different stance.

"Back off, Siward. We ain't got no cause ter do nowt like that."

And to the man outside the gate.

"Now, look'ee, stranger, ye put back yer hood, an' tell us yer name an' yer business. An' then we'll see."

He stamped his frozen feet.

"An' hurry up about it, man, afore me bollocks go past freezin' an' just drop off."

Still the stranger hesitated.

Then, apparently realising that he had no choice, he freed a slender, cold-reddened hand from the ragged folds of the mantle he had huddled about him and dragged back his hood, revealing a face that abruptly revived a deep-buried memory in Dominic's mind, though for the life of him he could not immediately think where and to whom such a memory belonged.

Annoyed with himself for any number of reasons, he shook his head impatiently.

It was bone-aching cold, his belly was empty and the face he sought belonged to the past, where it could damned well stay.

Whoever this youth was, Dominic was certain that he had never seen him before, despite that elusive sense of familiarity. Likely enough it was no more than an illusion wrought by the winter's night... just another thin face white with weariness and hunger.

So what if it was also framed by a tangle of curling hair the shade of chestnut brown that hinted at red under the ruddy light of the brazier and the torches burning to either side of the gateway...

Feeling anew the bitter bite of the encroaching night, Dominic abruptly dismissed the fanciful flicker of recollection that showed him a woman with witch-fire hair, gentle grey eyes and healing in her hands, and he was already turning towards the warmth of his lord's quarters when a certain ugly note in Siward's voice had him whipping around so fast he nearly slipped on the icy cobbles.

"Aye well, 'tis a pretty enough face ye have there, whelp. Reckon our shirt-liftin' Second 'ud find a good use fer ye if'n we was ter let ye in! An' after *he's* done wi' yer pretty arse, you'll be only too glad ter stop off an' see us on yer way out. Eh, lads?"

It was hard to judge by the torchlight but Dominic thought the youth went even whiter at this.

Small wonder perhaps, given the turn of recent very public events and the barely concealed leer in Siward's own voice.

"Shut up, Siward," Ulric snarled. "An' ye, boy, speak up now an' tell us what yer business is wi' Lord Joscelin."

The stranger's stance seemed to shift slightly and Dominic felt another unwilling stab of sympathy with this nameless youth – he looked unutterably weary and beyond recalling even his own name.

After a moment, however, he drew himself up and his gaze lifted beyond the guards to connect for the first time with Dominic's watchful gaze, causing him to suffer another, troubling flash of half-recognition, made worse – much, much worse – by the stranger's words.

"Very well," the youth said stonily. "My name is Jacques of Oakenleigh. And I am guardian to Lord Joscelin's daughter."

What?!

Even as Dominic gasped in shock at this utterly unexpected claim, Ulric was pursuing a different point.

"Oakenleigh, eh? Ye're claimin' ye're kin ter Captain Rafe then?" He cocked his head consideringly. "I ha' ter say, ye don't look much like him."

And *that* was an understatement.

Even given the obvious difference in age between the strange lad and the royal bodyguard, the two men looked *nothing* alike.

Not that Dominic paid any heed at all to the stranger's subsequent attempt to trace the intricacies of his relationship with the bull-like soldier who shared his place of birth.

Rather, he reeling at the thought that Joscelin de Veraux – his liege lord and the man who was all the father he had ever known – apparently had a daughter of his own blood living somewhere in Mithlondia.

Nor did it help his inner turmoil when Ulric said dubiously,

"I ain't ne'er heard naught 'bout Lord Joscelin bein' da ter some little lass, but I s'pose it could be so."

"Take it from me, he is," Jacques of Oakenleigh said flatly, just as Dominic found himself stepping into the circle of flaring reddish-gold light, and to his own amazement heard himself say crisply,

"I'll deal with this, Ulric. Let him pass."

"Ye'm goin' ter take him ter Lord Joscelin, lad?"

So saying, the soldier who had watched Dominic grow from child to young man shot a look at the openly sneering Siward and then lowered his voice as he added,

"D'ye reckon that's wise, young master, what wi' all else as is goin' on?"

"I see no reason not to," Dominic replied as mildly as he might.

"If it's true that this does concern Lord Joscelin's... daughter..."

Gods knew, the term tasted sour in his mouth.

"Then 'tis hardly a matter for the Lord of Rogé, is it? As for *him*..."

He gestured at the waiting youth, who on closer appraisal seemed barely old enough to shave and so slender it was a wonder he could stand against the icy winter wind that whipped about the gateway.

"He doesn't look much of a menace to me."

"Happen not," Ulric agreed cautiously, peering in his turn at the shivering stranger who was now regarding them watchfully through the smoky shadows.

"E'en so, not one step do he go beyond this gate wi'out bein' searched fer weapons."

"I'll do that," Siward offered with a sly eagerness that made Dominic's skin crawl. Nor was he surprised to see the stranger take an instinctive step back.

"Oh no, you won't," Dominic snapped. "Ulric or I will do it. Or..."

He glanced at the two soldiers waiting by the brazier but they were clearly not going to interfere in something that had started before their watch.

"Nay then, better I do it, young master," Ulric said, a task he performed with a brisk benevolence.

"Not e'en an eatin' knife," he reported. "Nowt of any value in his purse neither, just a couple o' copper marks. Enough ter buy a mug o' beer or mayhap a loaf of bread. Least ways it would ha' done this time las' year. 'Twon't buy naught as things stand now," Ulric continued dourly, adding with a glare at Siward,

"Don't reckon he's no threat ter no-one, let alone his black lordship."

He turned back to Dominic with a gruff,

"Go on then, young master, take him along o' ye, an' see what Lord Joscelin has ter say 'bout it."

Dominic nodded his thanks, keenly aware of what he owed the older man. Siward was a nasty-minded sod at the best of times, and would undoubtedly have proved far more awkward to deal with without Ulric's hulking presence and stubborn loyalty to Lord Joscelin, and by default Dominic himself.

Shaking free of the thought, he addressed himself to the stranger.

"Come on then, you!"

Scarcely waiting to make sure that the lad who called himself Jacques of Oakenleigh was following, Dominic set off across the outer courtyard, the ice-slick cobbles wickedly treacherous beneath his booted feet.

Only when he was half way across the inner courtyard did Dominic realise that the capricious wind had tossed the snow clouds aside, leaving the moon free to rise beyond the stark black turrets and crenellations of the palace – a pale, shimmering wraith, or a glimmering goddess gowned in cloth of silver.

Odd as the whimsical thought was for a Mithlondian male, not for nothing had he crept into the great hall on feast nights in years gone by to listen as Guyard de Martine drew forth an almost fey magic from his harp, the harper's soft-spoken words giving life and breath to what were surely no more than silver-spun myths or dark-woven dreams.

Yet even with reason and good sense on his side, Dominic still could not quite suppress the shiver that caressed his skin, and almost without any awareness of what he was doing, he muttered a warding curse against all those who bore the witch-blood of the Faennari.

"You need not fear, the Moon Goddess will not harm you."

The hoarse voice came from close at hand, and with a start Dominic came back to an awareness of himself and his companion.

Glancing sideways, he started to say something, then realised that the youth had already retreated into the concealing folds of his hood, his mantle drawn close about his sapling-thin body, and finding himself once more fighting the almost tangible sense of familiarity and danger that hung in the bitter, wintry air alongside their warm breaths, Dominic said bluntly,

"Whoever you are, I *know* you are not Jacques of Oakenleigh. So who in the daemon's name are you?"

"Certainly my name is Jacques," the other replied with a level note that carried its own conviction. "And like it or not, I *am* kin to Rafe of Oakenleigh. Best if you leave it there."

He walked on for a few more steps, and Dominic became aware with some shame that the other was limping quite badly, and that he had not noticed until now.

Before he could ask him about it, however, Jacques voiced his own hesitant question.

"Is Rafe still in... still being held at the Counsel's pleasure?"

Dominic hesitated in turn, but it was common knowledge about the palace.

"He is no longer in custody at least. Princess Linette demanded his release after Lord Gabriel's trial was done. That said, I would not suggest you try and see him."

And before Jacques could ask anything else,

"Now it is *my* turn. You are not really guardian to Lord Joscelin's daughter, are you? For one thing you are too young, and for another he does not have a daughter... does he?"

He cursed the sudden quiver of uncertainty in his voice and hoped the other did not hear it.

As if to confound him, Jacques favoured him with sidelong glance in which Dominic thought he read a certain amount of sympathy. Or pity. Neither of which he wanted, damn it. Before he could snap at the other, however, Jacques had replied to his heated question.

"Does it matter so much to you that your lord may have more than one child of his blood living in the wide lands of Mithlondia?"

"No, damn you!" Dominic spat, pride forcing the denial from him, even as he knew he lied.

He suspected Jacques knew it was a lie too. Thankfully the boy did not call it, merely saying,

"Well then, in answer to your question, yes, despite my apparent youth, I *am* guardian to the child for whom your lord has claimed responsibility."

Little though Dominic wanted to believe this to be the truth, he found he could not doubt it, and the resulting knife-twist of jealousy in his gut was so strong that it took him several moments to bring his bitterness sufficiently under control to be able to ask,

"What is her name? And where does she live?"

"Hmm?"

From the absent tone, it was plain that Jacques' thoughts had wandered far away from the subject that so ensnared Dominic.

"Lord Joscelin's daughter," he said curtly. "Your ward. What is her name?"

For a long time he thought he would get no answer. Instead they continued to trudge across the courtyard towards the candlelit palace in silence, the only sound a whinny from the nearby stables, a curse as a groom slipped on the treacherous cobbles, and the splash of their own booted feet through the puddles of icy slush.

Finally, in a thread of a voice that was barely audible, Jacques said,

"Lissie. Her name is Lissie."

Belatedly realising that the answer had come from somewhere behind him, Dominic paused and looking back, saw that his companion had stopped walking completely.

Then even as he watched, the cloaked form seemed to sway like the sapling he had earlier compared him to, borne down by the weight of too much snow.

Forgetting his impatience and his pain, Dominic started back, reaching out a swift hand to help the other.

"No! I can manage..." Jacques protested, struggling to push him away.

"Aye, I can see that," Dominic retorted. "So well that in another moment you would have fallen flat on your face in the mud."

Not waiting for any further arguments he slipped an arm around the younger man, hauling an unresisting limb over his own shoulders, before struggling on towards the palace, listening in growing dismay as his companion's breathing grew increasingly ragged with every step, more and more of his shivering weight coming to rest on Dominic's somewhat equivocal support.

By the time they reached Lord Joscelin's quarters Dominic was breathing heavily, a nagging pain needling his side with every step.

Ignoring the black-clad door-guard's suspicious stare, he walked straight past the man, dragging his increasingly substantial burden along with him.

Staggering himself now, Dominic crossed the antechamber where his narrow bed was neatly made up, heading towards the inner door that gave onto the two rooms where the High Commander of Mithlondia lived and worked – and where, gods help them all, Lord Joscelin had been under house arrest since the beginning of winter.

Long habit made Dominic sound a cursory knock, but without waiting for an answer he pushed against the unlatched door, almost falling through as it opened under their combined weight.

Regaining his balance, he looked up in time to catch the look of shock on the faces of the two men within as they rose hastily to their feet, the grating sound of Lord Joscelin's chair barely covering his uncharacteristic curse.

Startled to find that his lord had company – and this particular man at that – Dominic allowed his burden to slip completely from his sweat-slick grasp, Jacques slumping soundlessly to the floor where he lay in a heap of wet leather, sodden wool and limp limbs.

Struggling against shame that his unguarded reaction to the presence of his lord's visitor had caused him to misuse the stranger he had been trying – however reluctantly – to help, Dominic made to kneel by the fallen body, only to find that his lord had beaten him to it.

How Lord Joscelin had managed to cross so swiftly from the far side of the room Dominic did not know but the glimpse he caught of his lord's strained, ash-grey face through the concealing fall of white-woven black hair made his heart contract in a twist of love and hate, as disillusionment and bitterness and a dozen other emotions he could not name tied in a nauseating knot, leaving him panting under the force of the attack.

Grasping for control, he glanced down at the long, calloused fingers resting against the life pulsing in the youth's exposed neck and would not have believed, if he had not seen with his own eyes, that his lord's hand was shaking.

That, if nothing else, destroyed the tattered, fine-spun thread of Dominic's last remaining hope that Jacques had been lying. Obviously this chance-met midwinter stranger was no stranger at all to Lord Joscelin.

Moreover, as Dominic stared down at that pale profile, he felt yet again that elusive pull of familiarity, the sense that beyond some imperceptible veil was a face he knew, and that if he could only tear aside the shrouds wrapping his memory he would find a name to go with that face. A name that most definitely was not Jacques of Oakenleigh.

Except his lord was calling the youth by that name, and swearing under his breath as he did so.

"Jacques? Jacques! Damn it, damn it, damn it!"

And then, looking across the chamber at the other man – who, having righted the stool he had sent crashing over in those first moments, now remained at a careful distance, his face unreadable in the light of the branch of candles burning on the table behind him – Lord Joscelin continued with a violence Dominic rarely heard from him,

"Bloody damned hell! This is all my fault, Gabriel. Mine and bloody Justin de Lacey's! Hell'sdeath! I should have expected this, and done something... *any* fucking thing to prevent it."

Stunned at this display of temper from his normally cool and emotionless master, Dominic found himself staring at the older man as if he had never seen him before, flinching as Lord Joscelin's eyes – blazing now with a fire that was very far from cold – met his.

"How does he come to be here with you, Nic?" his lord asked, his voice quieter now but far from his own.

Dominic held that dangerous grey gaze as steadfastly as he could and then, in spite of his worries about how much he should say in Gabriel de Marillec's presence, told his lord everything that had happened since he had first heard the oddly compelling voice of the stranger at the gate.

Still listening, Lord Joscelin gently turned Jacques of Oakenleigh onto his back, smoothing the dirty, chestnut curls away from the thin, haggard features, and then set back the dark folds of the concealing mantle to reveal what had not been apparent to Dominic until now, although on reflection it should have been obvious.

One leg of the boy's green breeches, the left shoulder of his deerskin jerkin and the shirt beneath it were stiff and stained with blood, dried and dark and ugly against the pale linen.

Dominic saw his lord reach for the neck of the shirt as if to tear it in order to investigate further.

Then inexplicably he hesitated, moved instead to touch the backs of his fingers to one dirt-streaked cheek, then the pain-furrowed forehead.

"Hell take it! He is on fire, and hurt besides! I need to get him to a healer, and quickly."

So saying, Lord Joscelin glanced up, meeting his companion's gaze across the limp body.

"One whose discretion I can rely on – if there is such a one in this bloody treacherous outreach of hell!"

"There is Adèle."

Gabriel de Marillec spoke for the first time, his light, cool voice almost the complete opposite to the deeper, unusually abrasive tone of Dominic's lord.

"Take the boy to Adèle, Josce. Or send for her to come here. Either way, she will give you the help you need. *And* keep your dangerous secrets. The gods know, she would probably drink hemlock if you asked her to."

If there was the slightest of raw edges to these last words, his commander ignored it, saying impatiently,

"You know the terms of my parole, Gabriel. I cannot leave these chambers unless accompanied by a de Rogé watchdog. And believe me, Black Joffroi is the last person in the palace to whom word of the lad's presence should find itself. Nor would I willingly ask any gently-bred lady to risk her reputation by visiting my personal quarters."

"So be it," Lord Gabriel said, his voice still light and cool, his slight shoulders lifting in something not quite a shrug.

"I will have to take him then."

He crossed the chamber in four swift strides, and as Dominic scrambled out of his way, knelt to lift the unconscious boy into his arms.

He came to his feet with a faint grunt, and then as he settled his burden more securely against him, seemed to get his first good look at the younger man's face.

Dominic heard a curse whistle through his teeth, saw those disturbingly coloured eyes flicker like a candle flame in the wind, amber to gold to citrine as his gaze darted from Jacques of Oakenleigh to Lord Joscelin and then back again, settling into a wild wolf yellow as he said slowly,

"Yet you were not always so careful of a lady's reputation, were you, Josce? Correct me if I am wrong but did you not share your quarters once with a woman who meant something to you, a woman you would have lied and died for? A woman who, if I am not mistaken, was... indeed still is..."

De Marillec hesitated, glanced at Dominic, then back at his friend.

"A mirror image of the boy here?"

"I cannot fault your memory, Gabriel. And, as always, you see far more clearly than most folk give you credit for. So, knowing what you do now, are you still willing to involve yourself and your lady in this damnable mess?"

And for all the lack of emotion in their level voices, Dominic could not quite rid himself of the notion that the two men were talking about something very meaningful indeed.

For his own part he could not repress the shiver that ran through

433

him as he finally pinned down that elusive familiarity he had seen in Jacques of Oakenleigh's face.

So the youth was kin to the Lady Rowène then. Which in turn meant he was kin also to the man presently confined in the deepest dungeon below the palace, dying slowly, a heartbeat at a time, inch by bloody agonising inch, and breath by bloody painful breath.

Worse, it was killing Lord Joscelin too, to know what was happening, and know himself powerless to prevent it.

As for Gabriel de Marillec...

Dominic cast a sickened glance in the direction of the man who was reputed to have once been Luc de Chartreux's lover, and found him pale below the caked blood, smudged dirt and what looked unpleasantly like the product of someone's privy that now streaked a face that only this morning had – when Dominic had seen him leave the palace – been far too prettily handsome for any man.

Though the former Second could hardly fail to be aware of Dominic's curious regard, he ignored it in favour of dealing with his Commander's difficulties, which now appeared to have become inextricably interwoven with his own affairs.

"One thing is certain, Josce, Jacques cannot stay here. And if all I can do for Luc is keep his brother from falling into Joffroi de Rogé's bloody grasp, thus preventing that bastard from gaining yet another means of torturing him, it is at least something. Besides..."

He shrugged, the ripple of muscle in his shoulders far more obvious this time.

"If I am seen with the lad, it will simply be assumed that he is my latest lover. And after all, one more such charge can scarcely drag the de Marillec name any further into the gutter. Is that not right, lad?"

This last satirical comment clearly being addressed to him, Dominic felt himself flush.

His lord merely ignored it, saying with obvious sincerity,

"My thanks, Gabriel."

And then more sharply,

"Get the door, Dominic."

When his lord used his full name in that tone of voice it was as well to obey without argument, yet even as Dominic put his hand to the door it swung open of its own accord to reveal the darkly brooding countenance of the last man any of them wanted to see at that particular moment.

For a heartbeat Dominic thought he must be frozen to the floorboards, guilt writ plain across his face, his mouth dry with fear. Fortunately the newcomer did not look at him, merely shoving him aside with an impatient exclamation.

Scowling, Dominic picked himself up and glared at the bulky black-clad body of Prince Linnius' Chief Counsellor just as Lord Joscelin's ice-crisp voice made itself heard.

"These are still my personal quarters, de Rogé, and even a mannerless boor like you should know to knock before intruding your unwelcome presence into them."

"If you have nothing to hide, de Veraux," the man who was in effect his gaolor retorted. "You have nothing to fear."

Then abruptly the dark mockery shifted direction as Joffroi de Rogé cocked his head to look at the last man in the room, his deep voice taking on an even more viciously vindictive note,

"Though it has to be said, de Veraux, that you do not help your cause when, having refused to obey the legitimate orders of the High Counsel that appointed you, you persist in keeping company with this spineless piece of sewer-filth, especially when he has one foot on the gallows already, with the executioner making ready his knives."

Dominic shuddered at the implication of treason but his lord only said coldly,

"As you know perfectly well, Messire, my appointment was made by Prince Marcus rather than the High Counsel. And therefore only Prince Linnius has the power to dismiss me. Now say what you came to say, and then get out."

"Very well, I came as a courtesy to tell you that de Chartreux is close to breaking, and that you might want to be there when he does. To witness his words as it were, seeing as you are – at least until Linnius learns the truth of your bastard blood – High Commander of Mithlondia's guardians."

Dominic saw his lord's hands clench into fists at his side but while his grey eyes were frozen with an icy rage, his voice gave nothing away.

"How long before de Chartreux breaks?"

"A day at most."

"I will be there."

There was a moment's silence as if de Rogé was waiting for something.

Then, when it was not forthcoming, cast about him for another target for his malice.

"Before I go, de Veraux, I suggest you tell me the meaning of *that!*"

By this time Dominic had sidled far enough around the chamber's wall that he could clearly see the stabbing finger and de Rogé's fury-contorted face, his thick brows nearly meeting over his narrowed eyes, dark and dangerous as the wild boar of his family's insignia.

"As you know damned well, de Veraux, the terms of your parole require any visitors to be authorised by me first. So unless you want to find yourself standing in the Star Chamber alongside de Chartreux on a charge of high treason you will tell me who that boy is, and what business he has here with you."

Swallowing helplessly, Dominic dared to look in the direction of Jacques of Oakenleigh, only to discover with no little disbelief that the youth was no longer unconscious and lolling like a discarded rag doll in Gabriel de Marillec's arms but was, astonishingly, standing on his own two feet, albeit he was leaning heavily against the other man's deceptively slender frame.

"Well, de Veraux?"

"This is nothing to do with Joscelin," Gabriel de Marillec intervened sharply before Dominic's lord could reply to de Rogé's barked accusation.

"His reason for being here is a convenience to me. As to who he is, that is no business of yours, de Rogé. Unless you mean to enquire into all my acquaintances, though I doubt you would find it worthwhile since you made it perfectly plain last time I stood in front of the Counsel that I am less than nothing in your eyes. In which case, what I do with my... friend here is none of your concern."

"Filthy, buggering whoreson scum like you do not have friends, de Marillec!" de Rogé ground out, his dark eyes filled with a menacing mockery. "Fah! I cannot be bothered to grind you any further into the gutter. You are broken. A worm beneath my notice. Go on, take your catamite and get out."

"I will. Not for your say-so, but because I never intended to pursue my sordid affairs under Joscelin's roof..."

"Dominic!"

The ice-crack of his lord's voice broke Dominic's horrified trance and cut through whatever other outrageous comment Gabriel de Marillec had been about to make.

"Yes, my lord?"

"The door, if you will. My guests..."

Lord Joscelin's tone was bitingly ironic.

"Are leaving. *All* of them."

Dominic swallowed and having opened the door, stood back a little, refusing to lower his eyes as the man who was arguably the most powerful in the realm walked past him, his face dark with displeasure at his dismissal by one he so obviously despised.

Although clearly not as much as de Rogé despised the man strolling easily after him towards the door, Jacques still leaning heavily on de Marillec's supporting arm, the youth somehow contriving to make it appear amorous in origin rather than grim necessity.

Unable to tear his eyes away, in spite of his mingled disgust and doubt, Dominic watched in growing disbelief as Jacques lifted his face to his companion.

Grey eyes locked with amber, and as if in response to a message that had passed between them de Marillec bent until he was close enough to lay a heated kiss on Jacques' parted lips.

At that point the only thing that prevented Dominic from spewing on the spot was the belated realisation that Jacques' face was a shade far beyond pallid, and that he was perhaps a single heartbeat away from swooning.

Which would be much more difficult to explain away than any amount of distasteful kisses, and acting on instinct rather than thought, Dominic said with quiet desperation,

"Lord Gabriel..."

Evidently hearing that which had definitely not been meant for his ears, de Rogé broke from his own state of incredulous disgust to turn on Dominic in a roaring rage.

"*Not* Lord Gabriel, you misbegotten whelp!"

De Rogé's deep voice grated harsh as an iron file across a manacle.

"That degenerate apology for a man was stripped of all entitlement to that status by his own father's dying breath on the day his catamite of a son stood trial, and unless the lovely Lady Adèle is brought to bed of a male heir within the next three seasons – an unlikely event as anyone must know, and even if she did, it is not like to be *his* get anyway – his half-brother will be the next Lord of Marillec. And if anything should happen to Master Bayard..."

An unpleasant smile thinned those full lips.

"Well then, Marillec will be in Prince Linnius' gift."

And they all knew who would be destined to receive the gift of such a wealthy province.

Gabriel de Marillec muttered something that sounded like *over my dead body,* which only made de Rogé's mouth widen in malicious anticipation.

Dominic, however, had scant sympathy to spare for the man at the root of all these troubles, a man he did not trust, and one moreover whose unnatural predilections, as made public at his recent trial, made Dominic sick to his stomach whenever he thought about it.

Then thankfully they were all gone – Joffroi de Rogé, Gabriel de Marillec and Jacques of Oakenleigh – leaving Dominic alone with his lord, whom he had scarcely seen since this whole wretched, damnable entanglement in the affairs of Luc de Chartreux and his lover had begun.

And yet, now that he had the moment he had sought, Dominic was unsure what he wanted from Lord Joscelin... perhaps only to hear the truth, however difficult he personally might find it to listen to.

Except he was not granted the opportunity to ask anything.

Instead, he was forced to hide his disgruntlement when Lord Joscelin ordered him in a low, controlled voice that did not invite argument to follow Gabriel de Marillec and offer him any assistance he required, and further to remain with him until Dominic could bring word back from Lady Adèle as to Jacques of Oakenleigh's condition, and his chances of recovery.

With de Rogé's departure from her wavering vision and the knowledge that Joscelin was free of suspicion for the moment, Rowène managed to stay on her feet for perhaps a dozen more, increasingly unsteady steps, before the torch-lit walls of the passageway closed in on her.

A breath away from swooning, the last thing she felt as she lost all sense of her surroundings was the tightening of the steely arm around her waist as Gabriel de Marillec took her full weight, a heartbeat before he swung her up into his arms once more.

In the dark depths of her mind she knew it was Gabriel who held her thus, Gabriel who had brushed his mouth against hers mere moments before.

Yet it was the memory of another man who had kissed her and carried her against his heart that made her murmur his name out loud,

"Rafe?"

She felt Gabriel break step in momentary surprise, heard another horrified gasp from Dominic – poor lad, she would have to explain things to him, and soon – but before her woolly mind could retrieve her error, she heard Gabriel say roughly,

"It's not what you think, boy!"

But could not tell whether he spoke to her or to Dominic.

And then most definitely to her,

"No, not Rafe. It's Gabriel."

She started to struggle in his arms... to tell him that she knew already who he was, but that she needed to know what had happened to Rafe, to hear from his sword-brother rather than guardroom gossip that he had not fallen foul of Black Joffroi...

Then she felt the reassuring caress of warm lips, this time across her furrowed brow rather than her mouth, and heard Gabriel's voice soft in her ear.

"Easy, Ro, nothing has happened to Rafe that he cannot come through."

If only the same could be true for Luc. Oh, gods, Luc!

But she could not tell whether it was her own anguished thought or Gabriel's that beat its wild wings against the inside of her skull.

What she did know was that she could not fight the pain and encroaching darkness any longer, and turning her head into the warmth and comfort of Gabriel's shoulder, slipped quietly into the black shadows.

At the sound of the soft rap of knuckles against seasoned oak, Adèle de Marillec froze, then lifted her wary gaze from the woollen stocking she had been attempting to darn by the light of the one meagre candle she allowed herself of an evening.

She had no idea who might be paying a visit this late in the day to the tiny set of rooms she had occupied since her return to the palace – and that only through Princess Linette's kindness and stubborn loyalty to the woman she persisted in calling friend, despite the very public disgrace of Adèle's lord-by-binding.

Unsurprisingly in the circumstances, Adèle had had few visitors, none of whom had been welcome, and she saw no reason for that sitaution to change now.

Nevertheless when the sound was repeated, this time with rather more force, she put down her sewing and, lacking such luxuries as a servant, went to open the door herself, only to draw back in shock when she recognised the dark green livery and silver stag worn by Joscelin de Veraux's personal retainers.

For a single blank moment she could do no more than stare uncomprehendingly at the tall, dark-haired lad wearing those colours before her gaze was caught by the flicker of movement behind him which, even as her heart sped up, resolved itself into the shape of a man. Surely it could not be...

And then, as he moved into the light of the nearest flame, she saw it was not the man she had half-hoped, half-dreaded to see.

Lacking Joscelin de Veraux's height and breadth of shoulder, this was a very different man indeed and, after Joscelin, the very last person she would have expected to find at the door to her private chambers. But what – or rather who – was he carrying...

"Gabriel?"

While her voice expressed her raw incredulity only too clearly, Gabriel chose to ignore both question and implication, and instead brushed past her into the chamber that officially, she supposed, he had as much right to enter as she did. And even though he had earned her ire by his absence, to her annoyance she now permitted his intrusion without protest.

That did not, of course, prevent her displeasure from curdling from mere annoyance into the heat of anger... or stop her heart from stuttering within her breast, as the wavering candlelight illuminated his face and form more clearly.

Unable to entirely conceal her dismay, she glanced from his loose, tangled hair to the ragged cut on his dirt-smeared cheek, taking in his filthy, stinking linen, before finally settling on the limp body of the cloaked and booted man he carried in his arms.

Then, unable to keep silent any longer, but uncomfortably aware of the presence of Joscelin de Veraux's retainer, she chose to hide her incredulous anger in formality.

"My lord, what dangerous folly are you about now?"

And then, unable to suppress her concern any longer,

"And what in gods' name happened to your face?"

"What this?"

He shook his head, dislodging the matted tendrils of hair still clinging to his unshaven face, revealing more fully the lividly swollen and discoloured skin beneath the filth and glinting stubble, the sight sufficient to make Adèle wince despite herself.

"Yes, that!" she said unsteadily.

"I will give you line and verse if you really want to know. Later. *This*," he continued, indicating the silent form in his arms. "Is far more important."

"Who..." She swallowed and tried again. "Who is he?"

For a moment she thought Gabriel hesitated, and then he said with a softness that stung more than curtness would have done,

"A friend..."

Fear, anger and hurt abruptly combined, and caused her to cut short his attempted explanation. Uttering a harsh laugh that betrayed her feelings far too clearly, she said bitterly,

"As has been proved most publicly since our return, my lord, you do not have any friends. Only..."

"Do not say it!" he rasped.

His amber eyes were sparking with the feral anger she seemed always to provoke in him during their rare meetings since their return to Mithlondia. Then, even as she took an instinctive step back from the flames, he turned away from her, directing his words to the young man who waited in palpable discomfort just inside the room.

"Come or go as you please, Dominic, but either way shut the bloody door."

Having seen this blunt order obeyed, Gabriel hefted his burden higher in his arms, and casting his gaze around made a quick but thorough inspection of the tiny chamber he had never entered before.

Then returning his attention to Adèle, lowered his voice to a terse tone quite unlike the lightly satirical voice he normally adopted.

"Had you allowed me to finish, Madame, I was going to do you the courtesy of telling you the truth, rather than the lie the rest of the court must be allowed to believe."

"Why start telling me the truth now when you have not done so for the past five years!" Adèle snapped.

And at the renewed flare of anger in those narrowed, bright-burning eyes, added somewhat pettishly,

"Oh very well, what is this precious truth?"

"I swear, Adèle, one day you will push me too far! If we did not have need for you now I would..."

He broke off, breathing hard, then resumed more calmly.

"The truth is that the lad is... an acquaintance of Joscelin's and, as you might have guessed if you were to use the compassion I know you possess instead of the wasting time wielding your sharp tongue against me, the boy is in dire need of succour. And you are the only healer here in the palace that Joscelin feels he can trust."

"Oh!"

Even now, the thought of Joscelin needing her – or at least, her healing skills – filled her with an overwhelming rush of emotion.

"Of course I will help," she said with a warm smile.

And then stung by the openly sardonic expression in Gabriel's eyes, added more briskly,

"What is amiss with the lad?

"Apart from anything else, he is running a fever and..."

Pausing, Gabriel glanced suspiciously around the cramped chamber once more, as if searching for spy holes, before finishing,

"He has come a long and bloody way."

Taking the hint, Adèle asked no more, instead saying,

"Take him through to the bedchamber."

Then watched as Gabriel walked past her into the small inner chamber almost filled by the bed he had not slept in since their return, even following his release from the palace dungeons.

"Get him undressed for me, if you will," she requested.

"Not unless I must," Gabriel muttered, then threw the next words at her as he might toss down a gauntlet in challenge to another man,

"Indeed, I wonder you would ask it of me, Madame, bearing in mind my extremely unsavoury reputation in this regard."

"You were cleared of all charges!" Adèle snapped to his back.

"But not," he retorted, turning to face her, his voice suddenly savage. "Before being stripped of my position as the Guardians' Second, disinherited from the lordship that was mine by right, by my own father no less, and dragged through the shit of the streets to stand on a scaffold with a noose about my neck.

"Not to be hanged for my own crimes! Oh no, that I could have accepted! Instead I was to be used as bait to capture an innocent man!

"All so that Joffroi de Rogé can have the pleasure of torturing Luc de Chartreux until he breaks. You want to know what happened to my face, Madame?!"

Battered by this storm of unexpected emotion, Adèle could only blink at the apparent change in conversation, and Gabriel continued with no more than a heartbeat's pause to gather his ragged breath.

"I was out with the corpse collectors this morning – that being all the High Counsel deems me fit for – and I was stoned by the good citizens of Lamortaine. As a traitor and a coward! Because it was through me that the man whom gutter gossip has now publicly branded my lover – a man long regarded as a hero by the common folk for standing against Black Joffroi and his Winter Witch – was brought down!"

And with that, her anger was inexplicably gone, as easily as a candle flame blown out by the wind, her own hurt lost in his far greater pain, a running sore that helplessly she tried to heal.

"Oh, Gabriel! You must not blame yourself. What happened that day cannot be laid on your head. You *tried* to warn him away... You nearly *died*, Gabriel!"

"Would that I had, if it meant Luc remained free!"

Though his voice was muffled as he turned away from her and bent to lay his burden on the bed, there was no mistaking the passion in his voice for anything other than love.

For a moment Adèle closed her eyes and let the fresh waves of pain lap over her head. Nothing she could say or do would bring healing to Gabriel's heart... but perhaps, she thought, she could heal the youth he had brought to her at Joscelin's behest.

Dear God of Mercy! Joscelin!

Glancing behind her, her distracted gaze fell upon the young man in de Veraux livery, standing quietly in the doorway between the main room and the cramped bedchamber, and as if he had simply been waiting for her to remember his existence, he said,

"Is there anything I can do, my lady? I am sure Lord Joscelin would wish me to assist you in any way I can."

"That is kind of you... I am sorry, I have forgotten your name with everything else that has happened since you and my lord walked through my door."

The young man smiled, something she thought, from the shadows in his eyes, that he had found little cause to do of late.

"That's all right, my lady. It's been a lot to take in."

He blinked, as if he was still coming to terms with it all himself, before adding,

"If you want to know my name, my lady, it is Dominic." Adding somewhat shyly, "Though you can call me Nic if you like, as my lord does."

"Thank you. Nic."

She wondered what she had done to merit the honour of using the same familiar diminutive as did his lord... his *father*, she corrected herself with a pang, looking again at his leanly handsome, grey-eyed countenance.

"In that case, Nic, I beg you will run to the kitchens and fetch me a pitcher of hot water. And another of cold water."

"Is that all, my lady?"

He shot an uncomfortable look between her, her feral lord-by-binding and the unconscious youth on the bed.

"For the moment," Adèle said, wondering who she was trying to reassure – herself or him.

"Linens I have in plenty, and healing herbs also. And if I need help with... my patient, I am sure my lord will do what is required."

A flicker of distaste showed briefly in those clear grey eyes, then with a respectful bow, Dominic was gone, plainly eager to be away from whatever confrontation was looming between her and her lord-by-binding.

Sighing at the thought of all that still lay unresolved between them, Adèle turned back to find that Gabriel had at least removed the stranger's muddy boots, snow-wet cloak and bloody jerkin.

"Best if I leave you to do the rest," he said retreating the one step the cramped confines of the room allowed. "And while you are doing that, I will go and find some wine. We will both have need of it, I am thinking."

"I can tend to your wound," Adèle said, offering a tentative truce between them. "But I must look to... Messire Joscelin's friend first."

"You need not feel obliged to tend to my scratch," Gabriel said with a curt laugh. "Not when I can deal with it easily enough. And outcast though I am, I still have sufficient consideration not to put my lady-wife to the distress of touching scum such as myself."

Then the disagreeably sardonic tone left his voice as he gestured towards the tumbled figure on the bed,

"*He* is your only concern, and judging by the blood on his clothing, I would look to his left arm and right leg first."

Ignoring the gibe, Adèle accepted the advice.

Already bending to address the source of the blood that had soaked her patient's rough garments, she only half-heard Gabriel's final quiet words.

"Jacques needs you far more than I could ever do."

Even as she sought for the right words to respond, Gabriel was retreating, clearly intent on leaving her alone with...

Gods above!

She caught her breath as she took her first clear look at the wounded man's face.

"Gabriel, did you say... Jacques?"

She looked around but he was gone.

Surely, she thought, Gabriel had not meant *that* Jacques?

Yet even as she grappled to accept this appalling prospect, Adèle recognised the long nose, the finely- shaped mouth, the once-fair skin drawn tight over high cheekbones and deathly pale from loss of blood. Skin that, while weathered by wind and sun and smudged with the marks of fatigue and pain, was surprisingly free of any shadow of stubble.

Yes, it *was* Jacques as she remembered the outlaw youth from their meeting in the market square at Vézière.

And yet...

That had been five years ago...

Even worn and wounded, the boy did not seem to have aged a day, the obvious de Chartreux lineaments softened from the leanly masculine cast of countenance displayed by his older brother, and with the hint of witch-fire red streaking his sweat-darkened chestnut curls, the resemblance to his sister Rowène was far closer.

Indeed quite remarkably close...

The thought of Rowène de Chartreux, however, served as a nasty reminder to Adèle that if the boy was indeed as badly wounded as he appeared, his sister was the healer he really needed in this situation.

But Rowène was not here.

She, Adèle, was all this boy had and whatever her own doubts and fears, Jacques was her patient and he needed her care not her questions.

Questions he was in no state to answer anyway.

Taking a deep breath and reaching for the calm the Eldest had taught her, Adèle began her own inspection, touching fingers to brow, cheek and neck, flinching at the fierce heat of fever on his skin.

His wounds must be tended immediately, and for that he would need to be undressed fully.

She contemplated the supine body, light-boned and slender yet still difficult enough to deal with, and wished Gabriel had not chosen this particular moment to consider his reputation.

With a muttered imprecation at her lord's pusillanimity, she reached for the laces closing the grubby, blood-stained shirt and began to untie them, pausing momentarily when she found both arm and chest swathed in bandages.

The former were wet and red, the unbleached linen of the latter showing no sign of a wound beneath. Although there was something there...

A flicker of thought touched her mind from somewhere outside herself. A suggestion so wildly improbable she wondered momentarily if the recent strain and worry about Gabriel and Joscelin had caused her to lose all grip on her wits.

She hesitated a heartbeat more, then set her jaw and having finally managed with fumbling fingers to untie the knotted linen, began to pull loose the long strip of cloth bound tight around her patient's upper body.

Yet even after the truth lay exposed for all to see, her incredible guess verified, she still could not quite bring herself to believe it. Or was it that she simply did not *want* to believe it?

Hearing a soft footstep she straightened hastily and positioned herself so that her own slender body stood between her vulnerable, half-naked patient and whoever had just entered the cramped chamber.

It was Gabriel.

He stood just inside the bedroom door, a flask of wine in one hand, a clean shirt in the other, and an utterly unreadable expression in his eyes, their colour closer to gold than amber in the dim candlelight.

For a half-dozen heartbeats he said nothing at all, just looked at her.

Then in a quiet, faintly satiric tone, he murmured,

"So now you know."

The last thing Rowène had seen before tumbling into darkness had been a pair of feral yellow eyes, half-concealed behind light brown lashes burnished to bronze by the torchlight.

By contrast, the first thing she saw when she emerged from that darkness were two gentle blue eyes, the colour of a summer dawn.

"Thank the gods, you are back with us," said a low voice she knew but struggled to place. "How do you feel?"

How *did* she feel?

Stiff and sore in all her limbs, a more specific sort of fire in her left arm and right leg, a dull ache in her head and a worse one in her heart.

"Fine," she muttered, since that was clearly the expected response.

"Good!"

And though it was the same voice that went with the blue eyes, much of the softness was now gone, replaced by a certain coolness.

"Do you know where you are? Who you are? Who *I* am?"

Did she?

Warily she allowed her gaze to wander, touching in fleeting enquiry on the shabby bed hangings, the bare walls of the windowless little room, the dull brown wool of her companion's practical woollen skirts.

No, she had no idea where she was.

She remembered coming to the palace gates, seeing Joscelin's son... Gods, how the boy had grown!

Then nothing more for certain unless... yes, she could vaguely recall hearing Josce swearing at something or somebody... himself perhaps? Or even her?

Thought too that she had seen Joffroi de Rogé's brutal face sneering at her through the encroaching shadows.

Unless that had merely been part of the swirling black and bitter dreams in which she feared she would have drowned had it not been for the one steadying spark of golden light that shone through the darkness and guided her to safe ground and sanity...

The comfort of a man's strong, steadying arms, and the reassurance contained in a man's light, level voice.

A man who could hide nothing from her, and from whom she in turn could hide nothing of herself. Such transparency as she could not share with either of her brothers, much as she loved them both, nor even with her lover, if indeed Ranulf merited such a description.

Which left but one man it could possibly have been. The only man she knew with citrine yellow eyes.

Yes, Gabriel had been the guardian who had walked with her through the darkness, and she could only suppose that, as once she had been there for him, so he had now repaid the favour.

More importantly, she also remembered that he had told her that all was well with Rafe.

If only he had been able to give her the same assurance about Luc!

Damn it all, what had happened to her brother while she had been lying here... wherever here was?

At least she did not appear to be a prisoner as one, and possibly both of her brothers were...

Oh gods!

If only she had some notion of what had taken place whilst she had been wandering the outer reaches of darkness.

All she knew for certain was that she was lying in a bed, in a miserable little room, attended by a woman she had once called friend but of instinct hesitated to do so under present circumstances.

Feverishly shackling her frantic fear deep inside her, she brought her gaze back to the blue eyes that now watched her with an expression compounded of curiosity, concern and something considerably less benign, and with some distant recollection of the questions she had been asked, swallowed against the dryness in her throat and said,

"Yes, I know who I am."

It was not entirely a lie.

She did know who she was. Though she was not at all sure who Adèle thought she was – Jacques, Fayla, Justinian or even the woman once known as Rowène de Chartreux.

Holding her doubts in abeyance for the moment, she concentrated on the one thing she was certain of.

"And I know who *you* are. And I *think* I must be in the Palace of Princes."

The pale gold head nodded.

"What I do not know," Rowène continued. "Is what I have done to anger you... aside from simply being here."

"Do you not?" Adèle de Marillec demanded fiercely. "You arrived here in *my* lord-by-binding's arms. *He* knew who you were before I did myself. Until that moment of realisation, I had thought we were friends, you and I. That you would trust me with the truth. Which quite obviously you did not. Therefore I find myself wondering what exactly you are to Gabriel, that you would trust him over me? Are you his lover even as your brother is? Is that it, Ro?"

It was that single word, the diminutive of her real name, rather than the ridiculous accusations, that brought Rowène fully back to herself. That, and the belated realisation that apart from the bindings around her arm and thigh, all she wore was a man's shirt, the linen smelling stridently of herbal liniment and, far more subtly, of bergamot. Of Gabriel.

Of the man who had seen into her soul. And she into his.

That was not something that Adèle would understand however.

So Rowène kept her tone flat, her words as starkly clear as she could make them.

"No, we are not lovers. Whatever the bond between your lord-by-binding and myself, it is not a carnal one. As for not trusting you, Adèle..."

"So you admit there *is* something between you?" Adèle interrupted.

"Of course there is! Do you tell me you have lived with Gabriel this long and *still* do not know what he is!"

Pain filled the blue eyes before Adèle looked away, her voice a mere murmur of sound,

"Yes, I know what he is."

"Well, that is something. And so, you must understand him, at least to some degree."

Forcing herself to ignore her injuries, and feeling at somewhat of a disadvantage wearing Gabriel's shirt and lying in the bed he presumably... probably... possibly... shared with Adèle, Rowène struggled to sit up, feeling absurdly guilty when despite her obvious anger, Adèle pushed the two hard pillows behind her back for support.

Taking a quick, shallow breath, Rowène continued,

"That being so, to say that Gabriel thinks of me as anything more than a healer, or the sister of the man he once loved..."

She ignored Adèle's gasp of outrage, and forged ahead, since it seemed the time for unvarnished truth had arrived.

"Is beyond ridiculous. Especially since Gabriel has seen neither Luc nor myself for five very long years."

She regarded Adèle's flushed face and compressed, white lips and said with sharp emphasis,

"So, given that you believe I have betrayed your trust, both by lying *to* you and lying *with* your lord, are *you* now going to betray me to my mother and sister? After all, you have spent those same five years in Kardolandia with Juliène, and perhaps that friendship has replaced the one we once shared?"

"Hardly!" Adèle's retort was scorching. "Your sister used me before my binding, tolerated me while we were in Kaerellios, and since our return to Lamortaine she has, thank the gods, disdained my existence entirely."

"Why?" Rowène asked, then answered her own question. "Ah! Because of Gabriel, I suppose?"

Adèle started to say something, then brushed it aside.

"It does not matter now. Suffice to say I have no intention of revealing your presence here, either to Juliène or your mother, if I can help it. I have not, as the gods know, spent the past two days and nights tending your wounds only to give you up now. For one thing, neither Gabriel nor Joscelin would ever forgive me..."

And which man's good opinion did Adèle care for most, Rowène wondered, though she did not ask.

What she did say was,

"And the other reason?"

Adèle did not answer immediately, her fingers knotted in the lap of her drab gown as she searched for words. Eventually, and with some difficulty, she said,

"You must be aware that I do not... have any affection for your brother?"

"Yes, and I understand why, though he has done his best not to come between you and whatever... relationship you might have formed with Gabriel since your binding."

"I know that."

Adèle's fingers tightened still further.

"And I understand that it cannot have been easy for him. But it makes no difference to my feelings towards him. I want you to understand that."

Since it seemed expected of her, Rowène nodded, and apparently satisfied with her response, Adèle continued,

"Yet even given my... dislike of him, I still would not have seen your brother fall into Messire de Rogé's hands or suffer the... fate he has. One that Gabriel so nearly shared."

"Gods, are you trying to tell me Luc is *dead*? And that you are *sorry!*"

Rowène shook her aching head and clenched the hand of her uninjured arm over her heart.

"No, I will not... *cannot* believe that. He was alive when I arrived at the palace gates and I know he is alive still. Hurting, yes."

She glanced at Adèle.

"A living hell of agony, if you want the blunt truth."

She watched the other woman pale.

"But he is *not* dead. And all the time Luc is alive, I can hope."

She paused to take a calming breath.

"The question is, will you help me, Adèle? And if so, how far will you go?"

"How far would I go? To save the man Gabriel would have given his life for? The man Joscelin risks his position for?"

Adèle snorted softly, her gaze on her tight-wound fingers.

"I do not have any choice, not really. So, yes, I will help you, Ro. As to how far..."

She finally raised her gaze, her blue eyes blank and unreadable.

"Before we think that far ahead, you need first to eat something and rebuild your strength. I will send Dominic to wheedle some bread and some broth out of the palace kitchens, and in the meantime I have a draught of strengthening herbs I made up ready for when you woke."

"Dominic?" Rowène queried in some surprise, glancing at that narrow portion of the adjoining room she could see with a certain amount of wariness.

"As in Joscelin's so... servant?"

"Yes, that Dominic. It is hardly a common name," Adèle said tartly. "Joscelin gave me the loan of the lad's services for as long as I had need of him."

Her sharpness abruptly stuttered into embarrassment.

"We... that is, Gabriel and I... have no servants of our own now. Not since... our return from Kardolandia."

"Will you not tell me how that came about?" Rowène asked gently. "I have heard very little of what has happened here over the past few months, save what can be extracted from gutter gossip, and that is normally far wide of the truth."

Adèle swallowed and sighed.

"Yes, I think I must. Only first let me despatch Dominic on his errand..."

She rose to her feet without waiting for Rowène's response and walked swiftly into the other room.

A murmur of low voices, followed by other sounds... the door closing... the clink of metal on metal... then Adèle returned carrying a battered pewter vessel from which arose warmth and the scent of herbs.

She placed the goblet in Rowène's good hand, waited until she had slowly drunk it to its soothing, soporific dregs, and then said,

"While we are waiting for Dominic to return, will *you* not tell me how you came to be here in the palace at all? And then while you eat, Ro, I will tell you *my* sorry tale."

With the physical pain in her arm and leg temporarily held at bay, and bitterly aware that there was nothing she could do for Luc all the time she was confined to this bed, Rowène gave Adèle a brief summary of the past five years, and then a slightly more detailed account of her journey from Lasceynes to the rangers' winter camp, and thence south to Vézière...

"Not alone surely," Adèle protested in shock. "What were Lord Justin and this Beric thinking of to permit it?"

"Beowulf accompanied me from Lasceynes and he was still with me when I came south," Rowène answered. "As for Justin de Lacey, he had other things on his mind, and Beric probably considered that a healer like Brother Justinian had no need of a bodyguard."

Though there, she reflected, she might have been doing the guardian an injustice. He had been very reluctant to let her and Beowulf head into the snowy wilds by themselves. Perhaps he had been right.

"It was at Vézière that I lost Beowulf," she continued wryly.

"Not the Black Hunt?" Adèle gasped. "Or another wolf pack?"

"Nothing so dramatic," Rowène said with a smile.

"Poor Beowulf had been struggling against the winter-hag almost since we left Lasceynes but he refused to remain in the rangers' camp to await my return, pig-stubborn as he is. Of course, by the time we reached the Healing House at Vézière even he had to admit that he could go on no longer, so I left him in the Eldest's care. She would no more permit me to travel on to Lamortaine alone than Beowulf himself and so she asked Guy to accompany me."

"*Guy?* My *cousin* Guy? *Your...*"

"Kinsman, former lover and father of my child, yes!" Rowène finished with a hint of temper edging her voice.

"He asked permission of Lord Nicholas to absent himself... do not ask me what excuse he gave, I neither know nor care. All I can tell you is that Guy escorted me south to Lamortaine, and a bloody miserable journey it was for any number of reasons I do not intend to go into. Suffice to say when we reached Rath-na-Cael, the bitch in the kitchens betrayed us to the Black Hunt. Fortunately Nessa, her good-man's sister was more kindly disposed towards us – or Guy at least – and she came to warn us as we slept. Else we would not have escaped so lightly."

She caught sight of Adèle's paling face.

"Yes," she confirmed grimly. "Not all of the blood on my clothes was mine."

"Was Guy hurt?" Adèle demanded

"A fairly deep slash across the ribs. Oh, do not worry, it was well on the way to healing by the time we arrived at the palace gates," Rowène assured her.

"Guy stayed to see me inside as was our bargain and then he was to head back to Vézière with my mare and the horse he borrowed from Lord Nicholas' stables. I hope to the gods he did just that and has not stayed in Lamortaine on the off-chance of seeing my sister."

Rowène caught the look of astonishment in Adèle's eyes, and said sardonically,

"Unfortunately it would appear that our kinsman has somehow managed to become enmeshed in Juliène's web and I see no way of setting him free, until or unless she herself releases him from this enchantment she has laid upon him. Gods know how she managed it, since I would have thought Guy would have had more sense than to fall for her tricks, but then even the most sensible of men are prone to be led by their co..."

She broke off and coughed.

"Quite," Adèle said, still tart.

And then, with a certain amount of foreboding,

"So... do you think he has... they are..?"

"Are what? Oh..."

Rowène frowned as she realised what the other woman meant.

"No, I do not think they have actually lain together. After all, Juliène has been gone from Mithlondia these past five years. And I think she could not have refrained from gloating if she had managed to seduce him into her bed before she left. But now that she is back..."

"It is more than possible that they may become lovers," Adèle concluded with as dark a look as her fair face could form. "I would not normally think of preventing Guy from finding pleasure with a woman but your sister is no ordinary woman, and I fear what evil she means to wreak in his life. Can we do nothing to stop it?"

"I doubt such a thing is within our control," Rowène answered. "The best we can do is hope that Guy remains in Vézière and Juliène here at court. Beyond that... well, if you want the brutal truth, Adèle, Luc's life – and how I can save it – is the only thing I can think of at the moment."

"I suppose it would be," Adèle replied somewhat bitterly.

Then, as a sound from the other room diverted her thoughts,

"Ah! That will be Dominic."

She rose with a weary sight and went to the door, returning with a wooden tray bearing a pewter bowl of something, the smell of which actually made Rowène feel hungry.

Shaking off the drowsiness that had begun to overcome her, she began to clumsily spoon chicken broth into her mouth, directing a sharpish sideways glance at Adèle as a reminder that she was still waiting to hear what the other woman had called her *sorry tale.*

Thus prompted, and with no further excuse available, Adèle finally complied, skipping rapidly over the five long years she had spent at the royal court in Kaerellios, though it appeared that since King Karlen and Queen Xandra had made them all welcome they had not been entirely unhappy years.

Though there had been... difficulties, Adèle confided with a troubled frown.

Minor misunderstandings for the most part, arising from the differences in language and morality.

Others, though, had been of more import.

Problems that had seemed to plague Linette and her little daughter intermittently over the first two years and which, guessing at what Adèle left unsaid, Rowène felt were more than likely to be laid at Kaslander's door.

Mere mischief or deliberate malice?

The unexplained invasion of a variety of venomous creatures into Linette's apartments, could – possibly – be attributed to the former. This, however, had been followed by a series of innocent-seeming accidents for which someone – usually a slave – had been summarily punished, and then finally the far from innocent deaths of the two bodyguards who had originally accompanied the royal party.

Fearing for her little daughter's life, Linette had in desperation sought Gabriel's advice and with his assistance had smuggled a missive out of the palace and into the hands of an enterprising Mithlondian merchant, who having taken advantage of the princess' presence to open trade negotiations with the Kardolandians was about to sail from Kaerellios.

Linette's letter had eventually made its way north to Joscelin, and resulted – as Rowène had already been aware – in Ranulf being withdrawn from the Atarkarnan border and sent south to Kardolandia on the swiftest ship he could find.

And from the day Ranulf had arrived in the royal palace in Kaerellios, he and Gabriel had let no-one else have the guarding of the princesses, dividing the duty between them, and Linette and Lilia had suffered no further accidents or incidents, much to everyone's relief.

What Adèle did not say outright, though the implication was plain enough, was that it had been through this shared loyalty to the princess that she and Gabriel had finally managed to find some measure of peace in their binding.

Unfortunately, this understanding had not extended to Gabriel overcoming his aversion to siring an heir to the Marillec lordship – though it was plain that Adèle's yearning for a child had grown tenfold over the five years she had spent in Kaerellios, watching Lilia grow from a rather solemn infant into a lively, laughing little girl.

"Were you never tempted to... find another man who might... give you a child?" Rowène asked as delicately as she could when Adèle had fallen silent. "From what I know of him, I do not think Gabriel would have repudiated either you or the babe."

"No, he would not have done. He told me as much on our binding night."

Adèle considered what she had just said for a moment longer and then gave a helpless shrug.

"I would like to think that I did not take advantage of Gabriel's offer because I could not in honour break the oath I swore to him on our binding day, but the sad truth is that the only man I would have lain with outside the binding bed felt no desire for me. Thus I remain virtuous and childless."

Then, when Rowène said nothing, merely regarding her friend with a troubled frown, Adèle sighed and answered her unspoken question – or at least one of them anyway.

"And now you are wondering whether Gabriel remained faithful to that oath?"

She shrugged minutely.

"In all truth he would have had scant opportunity to break it. When he was not guarding Linette and Lilia, he was asleep. Alone, as far as I know. And so I told the High Counsel."

"They allowed you to speak in the Counsel Chamber? At his trial. That is almost unheard of."

Adèle nodded.

"I know, but Linette insisted we be heard, both of us. And Linnius permitted it, though it was clear that the majority of their noble lordships disapproved of women in the Counsel Chamber at all, let alone being permitted to speak therein."

"So tell me how it came about? This travesty of a trial," Rowène demanded. "From the swiftness with which Joffroi de Rogé levelled his accusations following your return, I can only think he has been planning this for years."

"It certainly seemed that way. We had not even been back in Lamortaine a day when some nasty little weasel arrived at Linette's apartments with a writ for Gabriel's arrest on a charge of... of..."

"I know what he was charged with," Rowène intervened. "But... well, in some ways it can hardly have come as a surprise, Adèle, considering the reputation he bore even before he left Mithlondia. And for sure, those five years at the Kardolandian court can have done him no favours."

"No, I suppose not," Adèle agreed dully. "And Gabriel *did* go to the pools... we all did! To bathe! Not to... to..."

"Fornicate in whatever unnatural or indecent manner the most noble lords of the High Counsel imagine in their furtive and frankly envious little minds," Rowène finished for her.

"So what happened after that, Adèle? I have heard various

rumours and know not which is truth and which simply wild gossip."

"When it first happened, I was more shocked than worried," Adèle replied, a frown between her pale brows. "I thought it merely one of Joffroi de Rogé's perennial attempts to discredit Gabriel, although somewhat more serious than the casual gossip-nag he had ridden before, but then the days and weeks just seemed to slip by, and all the while Gabriel was chained up in some terrible hole deep below the palace, and Rafe – the bodyguard, you know..."

Rowène did know.

"They came for him as well, though he did not make it easy for them. It took five of them to overpower him but in the end they dragged him away too and threw him in some prison cell. I do not think he was accused of anything, just needed as a witness at the trial and Messire de Rogé obviously feared what he would do if he was left free, him being by way of Gabriel's sword-brother, I suppose you would say.

"As for Gabriel, I was not allowed to see him between the time he was arrested and the day he stood in front of the High Counsel, with all the stench and filth of his cell still on him, to answer for *his vile and disgusting depravities.* Joffroi de Rogé's words, not mine."

"What about Joscelin?" Rowène asked, ignoring this trembling description of Gabriel's crimes. "Where was he in all this? I cannot believe he allowed Black Joffroi to arraign his Second and imprison one of his most trusted guardians without protest."

"Oh, he protested all right," Adèle replied. "And narrowly missed being arraigned alongside Gabriel. Thank the good gods Linnius baulked at putting his own half-brother on trial for treason, so Messire de Rogé had to be content with having Joscelin confined to own quarters. Nor could he persuade Linnius to revoke Joscelin's right to sit on the Counsel in his capacity as Lord of Veraux."

"So I suppose the time between the arrest and the trial was to allow those lords who were not then in the palace to be summoned to Lamortaine? An act as serious as that – trying the heir to the de Marillec lordship for whatever crime – would require the full Counsel to be present," Rowène said grimly. "Or a majority at least."

"He had it," Adèle confirmed. "The only man absent was Nicholas de Vézière, who sent word that he was confined to his bed with the winter-hag. He sent his son to act in his stead. Or at least Hal de Vézière was in the Counsel Chamber that day, whether by his father's wish or Messire de Rogé's contrivance I could not say. Certainly he seemed to have no qualms in speaking as de Rogé wanted him to, the duplicitous little snake. But then I should not have been surprised. He had already shown his true colours when he failed to honour the old friendship between himself and Gabriel at our binding ceremony. If it had not been for Joscelin, Gabriel would have been utterly humiliated that day."

"Speaking of Joscelin, did anyone aside from him have the guts to go against Black Joffroi and declare their belief in Gabriel's innocence?" Rowène asked, never doubting for a moment that her brother had stood by Gabriel, his sword-brother and his friend, in the same way he had done at the binding ceremony.

"No, no-one. Unless you count Messire de Lacey, who declined to vote one way or the other."

So he played it safe in the end, Rowène thought somewhat snidely, but then remembering Lady Nerice and little baby Justin, she found she could not blame him too much.

"As did Robert de Vitré," Adèle continued. "The rest followed de Rogé's lead like a bunch of witless sheep. Indeed, I do not think they even bothered to listen when Princes Linette and I spoke, damn them to the icy torments of Hell!"

Adèle spoke with surprising ferocity, her white teeth snapping together as if she were a she-wolf about to rend the flesh of those noblemen she had just castigated as witless sheep. A flush of anger lit her pale cheeks as she continued,

"But that was not the worst, Ro! Linette and I, we never did hold much hope that we would make any difference to the outcome. But I still believe that those pig-headed, high-born men might have paid some heed to Linette's defence if Gabriel's father had not already denounced him."

"He really did it then?" Rowène asked. "I hoped that was just ill-founded gossip.

"No, it is true," Adèle said bitterly. "Just as they brought Gabriel in, Messire Jean stood up and demanded that on his own death the lordship of Marillec pass to his younger son, Bayard, on the grounds that whichever way the trial went, Gabriel was *not fit* to hold the title!

"Oh, how could he do such an infamous thing, Ro? At such a moment, when his son needed him most? I know Gabriel never tried to heal the breach between them... he said his father could either trust him or disinherit him... but I do not think he ever expected him to do it."

"And having made his will public before a score of noble witnesses, Marillec's lord falls down dead in the Counsel Chamber? How very convenient," Rowène murmured.

"An apoplexy, the royal physician said, although I am not sure... it looked more like poison to me. But there was Messire Jean, choking for breath and with only me to tend him. But do you know, Ro, in all that time, he refused to speak to Gabriel, or even acknowledge his presence nearby, even though he must have known he was dying. So I was the only one of his family there with him, and I am only his daughter-by-binding, not his kin by blood. And of course Messire de Rogé was there too, hovering like a malignant vulture almost as if he meant to prevent Messire Jean from speaking. That said, he did speak once before the end, and enough Counsellors heard him that Messire de Rogé could not pretend afterwards that he had not."

Adèle paused as if to consider her memories of that day.

"What he said then... I think... I am not sure... but perhaps Messire Jean had in mind that he was doing me a kindness, because I had tried to help him. Or mayhap it was one last attempt to goad Gabriel into doing his duty, or at least as his father saw it. Whichever it was, I am sure Messire de Rogé saw it merely as one more way to twist the knife."

Rowène regarded her friend, brows rising.

"Ah! Would this be the proviso that if you give birth to a son within three seasons of Messire Jean's passing, that boy will become the next Lord of Marillec? Which we assume would assuage his uneasy conscience at condemning you to the shame and poverty you would unfairly suffer for what he regarded as his son's crimes? And Black Joffroi agreed to it in the belief that such a thing would never happen."

"Or that if I did indeed bear a child, it would not be Gabriel's," Adèle said stonily. "Thus giving Messire de Rogé the excuse to call *me* whore, Gabriel a cuckold, and tarnish the de Marillec honour almost as thoroughly as he once blackened the de Chartreux name."

With a fleeting scowl for the comparison, Rowène enquired with some hesitation,

"I suppose Gabriel has not... would not..."

"No. Nor would I ask it of him," Adèle said swiftly. "Not for so cold-blooded a reason as maintaining my own status as Lady of Marillec. Not for any reason at all," she finished with rather more passion. "Unless he himself wished it. Which he never would."

It was nothing as definite as a noise, or even so much as the flicker of a shadow that made Rowène glance towards the open door... to see Gabriel de Marillec standing there, stubble, lashes, and brows a vivid, glittering bronze against his bruised and blood-drained face, his eyes a blaze of gold.

Obviously he had heard.

The slightest shake of his head made it equally clear that he wished Adèle to remain oblivious of his presence.

Then he was gone, so swiftly and soundlessly that Rowène wondered if he had ever been there at all.

She blinked, shifted painfully against the lumpy pillows and then frowned as Adèle continued with some defiance,

"I can return to Vézière and become a healer again. It may be a hard life but at least it is a worthy one."

"And Gabriel?"

For a moment, Adèle looked lost.

"I do not know," she admitted. "I was glad when he did not die on the scaffold, but I know he wishes it were otherwise. And even though he survived, he is only half living anyway. And when your brother... *if* your brother dies..."

Rowène swallowed against a sudden upsurge of bile.

"No! I cannot let that happen. Cannot believe it will. Just let me get some of my strength back and I will think of something. Until then... you were telling me about Gabriel's trial. Please, carry on. I need to know everything."

Adèle gave her an anxious look, in which Rowène could see more than a trace of pity, then shook her fair head and continued as evenly as the distressing nature of her recital allowed.

"With Messire Jean... removed from the Counsel Chamber, the trial commenced in earnest. Linette spoke in Gabriel's defence, as did the guardian, Rafe, not that it did any good, and with them dismissed, Messire de Rogé turned his attention to me. And no matter how much I protested Gabriel's innocence, he managed to twist my words so as to make me appear both foolish and gullible for giving my trust to a man who lied to me with every breath he took. But I know... at least I am almost sure that Gabriel would not lie to me. Or hide what he was... what he did... from me. He never has, though the gods know I have sometimes wished he would!"

Rowène gave her a curious look but Adèle did not elaborate. Instead, her fingers once more writhing in her lap, she continued unsteadily,

"Then Messire de Rogé had another witness summoned, one neither the princess nor I had known about, though as it turned out we knew the man himself well enough. He was one of the Kardolandian slaves assigned to our apartments in the palace." She swallowed again, convulsively. "Oh, gods, Ro, I do not know how to tell you this part."

"You need not trouble yourself, Adèle, I can guess. This slave... was he young, beautiful, with a body as finely sculpted as any of the statues adorning the bathing pools?"

"Yes."

"And I suppose he told the Counsel that he and Gabriel had been lovers?"

"Yes."

Adèle said nothing more for a moment, before adding in a strained whisper,

"And when Messire de Rogé asked me, I could not deny that I had seen them together."

Rowène threw her a sharp glance.

"Together as in *together*? Or together as in simply being in the same room of the palace? The same bathing pool? The same bloody country for gods'sake!"

Adèle shook her head miserably.

"He... Sukash... the slave, that is... accompanied us often enough to the bathing pools. And once I saw him beyond the normal bounds of the palace. I had woken early and gone to find Gabriel. I thought he might have gone down to walk in the shallows of the sea and watch the dawn, as he often did when he had been awake all night."

"And he had? And this Sukash was there too? Did you ask Gabriel about it?"

"Yes. He said Sukash had merely wanted to tell him something he had not wanted the other slaves to overhear. Something concerning Linette's safety, or so Gabriel led me to believe."

"And now you are not so sure that he told you the truth?" Rowène murmured. "Thanks to Joffroi de Rogé's poisonous bloody insinuations, no doubt."

"No, I think Gabriel *did* tell me the truth." Adèle's soft mouth trembled in an unhappy smile. "Just not all of it. I... I fear I was not completely honest with you earlier, Ro, and I fear too that Gabriel may not have been entirely honest with me. I did not want to tell the Counsel about Sukash, but there was something about Messire de Rogé that compelled me to. Almost... almost as if he had some fey power over me."

"Black Joffroi?" Rowène snorted derisively. "He has about as much enchantment in him as a wild boar. However, if the Winter Lady was in the Counsel Chamber that day that may explain the feeling of compulsion."

"Your mother? No, she was not there. But," Adèle added slowly, as if only just now realising the significance of what she was saying. "Your sister was there, in attendance on the princess. And she has always hated Gabriel."

"And so it was Juliène who forced you to speak about that which you would rather have remained silent?" Rowène concluded. "I suppose whatever this other part of the truth was, it was enough to condemn Gabriel?"

"Oh gods! More than enough, when added to Sukash's testimony. That meeting may have been innocent enough, but according to Sukash there were many more that I did not witness. It may even have been true. I do not know. I did not walk that way again for a long time. I did not want to see... whatever may have happened between him and... Gabriel, although the gods know it would have been nothing out of the ordinary for that place."

She tried and failed miserably to smile.

"Tame indeed by Kardolandian standards."

"So you do not know for certain that they were lovers?" Rowène persisted, with a frown. "And surely Gabriel denied the accusation?"

For some reason, the notion that Gabriel could have betrayed, in one unthinking act of carelessness, both the love he bore for her brother, and the honesty he had promised Adèle, did not sit well with her.

Adèle however, appeared to have no such belief in Gabriel's sense of loyalty, either to herself or to Luc.

"Of course Gabriel denied it, but Ro... what I did see... it was enough! Oh, do not expect me to be more explicit. Not when it is *my* lord-by-binding's decadent desires we are talking about!"

Rowène regarded her companion pensively for a moment or two and then, because she was hot, hurting and uncomfortable, worried about both her brothers *and* Gabriel, she remarked somewhat acerbically,

"Make up your mind, Adèle! In one breath you tell me you do not love Gabriel, and I know for certain you never wanted to be bound to him, or share his bed. So why then would you care what he does with another? Lover, mistress, or his own hand, he must find relief for his body's needs some..."

"Oh!" Adèle gasped, her blue eyes wide with shock, even as her cheeks reddened. "How can you be so..."

"Blunt?"

"Coarse, crude. And I do not care. I just want him to..."

"Be happy? Now you *are* sounding like a fool. Happy is for winsome maidens, handsome princes and courtly harp songs."

"I want Gabriel to find some peace within himself!" Adèle snapped back, voice breaking. "To want to *live*, instead of always trying to get himself killed. First on the northern border. Then in Kardolandia. And now on a scaffold in Lamortaine's main square!"

Her words rang in the confined space of the small chamber and Rowène only hoped that Gabriel had already left the apartment as quietly as he had come.

"So tell me what happened after the trial," she sighed.

"Very little," Adèle replied, slumping in her seat. "The High Counsel brought in a verdict of guilty, of course. Gabriel was sent back to his dungeon, Rafe was permitted to return to his guard duties, and Joscelin was forced to carry out the punishment as agreed by the Counsel, even though Gabriel was the closest thing he has to a friend at court."

"Go on. I heard the Counsel sentenced Gabriel to hang, though obviously he did not since he is still walking around, while my brother is in chains."

"I know, it could have been worse," Adèle agreed sombrely. "And if Gabriel had... died like that, it would have been a more merciful death than they gave your father, or that your brother is like to suffer. But then they did not try Gabriel as a traitor. In all truth, Ro, I think he was right when he said he was no more than bait to draw your brother to Lamortaine."

Rowène did not doubt it, and indeed had known it from the moment Justin de Lacey had told her of Gabriel's arrest.

Hence her presence here, now, in the Palace of Princes, a nest of vipers and venomous Faennari into which she had promised herself she would never venture again.

Adèle was still talking, explaining how Gabriel had been reprieved once Luc had been taken prisoner in Lamortaine's Place of Execution...

Rowène heard very little of it, however, weariness and the strength of the herbal draught finally overcoming the pain of her wounds and the despair in her heart, and she fell at last into an uneasy sleep, the unremitting darkness pervading her mind lightened by the merest glimmering shimmer of a mad idea.

Whether it had any chance at all of working was another matter, and depended almost entirely on the goodwill of the gods — always a fickle foundation on which to build any plan, least of all one that also involved their silver sister of the night.

Fortunately, Rowène had far more faith in her own brothers.

First, that Luc was still alive.

And second, that Joscelin would not fail her.

Verse 3

Threads of Silver and Grey

Fists clenched, his own gut heaving in sympathy, Dominic stared in impotent misery at the closed door of his lord's bedchamber. The door was solid oak, seasoned and sturdy, an effective barrier to sight but not, gods have pity, sufficient to prevent all sound escaping.

Lord Joscelin had left his quarters midway through the afternoon, suddenly and with no explanation – though given that he had left under the escort of two men wearing the black boar livery of Rogé, Dominic could guess his destination well enough – and had returned, blank-eyed and bone-white, just as the early evening watch was sounding.

Ignoring Dominic's anxious exclamation, and indeed his very existence, Lord Joscelin had walked straight past and shut himself in his chamber.

A heartbeat later the terrible retching had begun, and he was retching still, with a painful, gut-churning, throat-burning heaving that told Dominic that whatever his lord had once had in his belly he had vomited it up long since.

Finally, and just when Dominic thought he could stand it no longer, the strained sounds settled into a silence that at first filled him with relief, and then a renewed anxiety when the door to his lord's chamber remained firmly shut.

He waited, counting his heartbeats, trying to reassure himself that all was well.

When that did not work, he hesitantly approached the door, almost convinced it would open and his lord emerge, a frown drawing his narrow brows together at finding Dominic lurking without.

But the door did not open.

And the silence continued.

Unbroken even when Dominic steeled himself to tap his knuckles softly – yet at a perfectly audible pitch to his lord's normally sharp hearing – against the unyielding wood.

That was when Dominic knew he could wait no longer without

465

fetching help – and he knew exactly who he must seek out, and where to find her. Or at least he hoped he did.

As for Lord Joscelin... well, there was every likelihood his master would despise him for revealing his weakness to someone he would surely regard as a stranger. Even so, Dominic could not do other for the man who had been all the father he had ever known, regardless of what the dubious truth of his siring eventually turned out to be.

Pushing aside all thought of his paternity, Dominic came to a stumbling halt outside the great feast hall, the two guards on duty turning what he fancied to be disapproving glances in his direction, and taking a moment to draw breath from his scrambling dash through the palace passageways, ran one faintly trembling hand through his untidy hair and tugged his tunic straight with the other.

And then, desperation lending him a confidence he was far from feeling, he walked straight at the double doors, trying to hide his surprise when neither of the guardians made a move to stop him. Of course they knew him as their commander's body-servant but even so...

He heard the door close behind him and paused to scan the assembled company for the one face he sought amongst so many.

The light from a score of torches and two hundred score candles glanced off gold thread in gowns and gem-studded jewellery, silver circlets and serving dishes, fine glass goblets, illuminating the rich colours deep-dyed into velvet and silk, brocade and wool, so that mulberry and green, black and tawny, blue and rose all ran together in a mad medley fit only to confuse the eye and mind, while the noise struck like a hammer blow against his ears.

Fighting panic and nausea, Dominic forced himself to ward off the onslaught and concentrate on his search until... there!

There she was, seated quietly at the very end of the farthest table, her grey robe and white headrail making her all but invisible amongst the bright butterfly colours.

It took Dominic a mere handful of heartbeats to work his way around the outside of the hall until he stood by her side, the blank blue gaze lifting from the untouched meat on her trencher to look up at him in silent enquiry.

Then, as she recognised him, she laid down her eating knife and came swiftly to her feet.

"What is it, Dominic?" she asked, her voice soft and low and not quite calm. "Is it...?"

"It is Lord Joscelin," Dominic spoke impatiently into her odd moment of hesitation. "You must come now. If you please, Sister," he added, courtesy a lagging rider to desperation.

"Of course I will come," she assured him, seeming to have regained her customary composure after that momentary lapse into confusion.

Dominic, however, felt his own agitation increase apace as he looked over her head -- he had not realised how small she really was, or how much taller he had grown since the occasion of their last meeting – and straight into the mocking dark eyes of Joffroi de Rogé.

The man was seated at the high table, next to Prince Linnius, and the whole length of the great hall lay between them, and thus he could not possibly be looking at Dominic and the Eldest. And yet for that single frozen heartbeat it seemed as if he was.

Chicken leg held in one hand, brimming goblet of wine in the other, de Rogé had been laughing uproariously at something Prince Linnius had said to him, until suddenly that roving, incongruously jovial dark gaze seemed to sharpen and settle...

"Hell!"

Breath catching in his throat, Dominic muttered,

"Can you pretend it is I who came to you for help, Sister? Not Lord Joscelin."

Not for anything would he wittingly give Black Joffroi cause to further despise his master.

"Certainly you look pale enough to require my assistance," the healer murmured, without asking what had caused him to lose colour so rapidly. "Bend a little closer then, else I shall be obliged to stand on the bench to reach you."

So saying, she lifted one hand to gently touch the coldly-sweating brow he presented to her.

"Yes, definitely a touch of the winter-hag. I will come with you now and brew a healing draught. The gods know I cannot stomach the thought of food just now, let alone put it in my belly."

"Me either," Dominic muttered as he straightened, his gaze drawn back inexorably towards the high table, only to find that Black Joffroi had apparently lost any interest in him and returned his attention to his meal, which he was gorging himself upon with every sign of appetite. Whilst Lord Joscelin...

"I think I am going to be sick!"

"No, you are not. Or at least not here," the Eldest said firmly, guiding him towards the doorway.

Once they were outside the great hall, however, and out of earshot of the guards she stopped and turned to look up at him, speaking such words in a grim undertone as he would never have expected from the gentle healer.

"Listen to me, Dominic. I am no fey seer but I do truly believe that one day Joffroi de Rogé will wake up to find his life lying sundered into bloody pieces all around him, and on that day I promise you that the food he eats now with such relish will be as bile in his belly and rise to choke him even as he breathes in the bitter stench of betrayal and defeat."

"And then *we* will feast in celebration of *his* downfall!" Dominic remarked savagely.

He did not really expect her to agree, healer as she was.

Nor did she, her only reply a sad little smile and a wistful sigh as she shook her head. The next moment she said briskly,

"Forget Lord Joffroi. He is unimportant compared to your own lord's welfare. Come, let us go."

Arriving back in Lord Joscelin's private quarters, Dominic found them as frighteningly still as when he had left, unchanged in every respect save that the candle he had left alight on the table had burned a little further down.

Even the unflappable Eldest appeared taken aback by the shadowy silence.

"Where is he?" she started to ask, just as the closed door to the bedchamber was flung open and Lord Joscelin himself appeared in the opening.

His black hair was wet and flat as if he had just splashed water over his face, the taut, stubbled skin lacking any trace of colour save a faint greenish sheen that put the anxious Dominic disturbingly in mind of a wraith.

His eyes though were as cold and bright as the ice laid across the lake outside the window, and very nearly as impenetrable.

Then the illusion shattered, as if an icicle had dropped onto a granite floor, and his eyes widened in shock on perceiving the grey-robed figure.

"Mother!"

Dominic felt his jaw drop.

Surely this small, serene healer could not be...

"Joscelin! Oh, my dear one, what..."

"What in bloody hell are you doing here?" the nobleman snarled, his demand over-riding the healer's distressed cry.

And then, turning his fearsome frozen stare towards Dominic,

"I suppose *he* brought you."

"*He* having a name. And yes, Dominic did," the Eldest replied with a belated attempt at calm entirely belied by the expression in her eyes. "He was worried about you, Joscelin. He feared that you had been taken ill."

And that was an understatement.

What Dominic had actually found himself telling the healer as they hastened through the palace passages – and with a lack of care for his words that made him squirm when he thought about it now – was that he had been worried witless – actually he had not put it anywhere near that politely – afraid lest Lord Joscelin had retched his guts inside out to the point where he must be bringing up blood, and had then passed out in the splatter of his own vomit.

Embarrassing as that was, Dominic's recollection of his indiscreet words was far outweighed by his present confused conjectures.

Mother, Lord Joscelin had called the Eldest of the Grey Sisters of Vézière.

And in return she had called him by his given name, followed by that heartfelt endearment *my dear one.*

"I *was* ill," Dominic heard his lord say, his voice quietening from that harsh rasp of rarely unleashed temper. "But I am well enough now that you need trouble yourself no longer, and return whence you came before you are missed."

"You do not look well," the Eldest – Lady Céline, Dominic corrected himself – replied, equally quietly. "Nor will you rid yourself of me so easily."

"No."

Lord Joscelin rubbed an alarmingly unsteady hand across red-rimmed grey eyes.

"I do not suppose I will. As to whether I am well or not, I *must* be. Must have all my wits about me if I am to accomplish what must be done."

"For Luc," Lady Céline said, voice and eyes bleak as the rocky heights of the Guardian Mountains.

Then her gaze wavered.

"Oh, no. Dear gods, no! Not... not Jacques as well?"

"No, or at least not yet. But Luc..."

Lord Joscelin visibly swallowed, before continuing in a parody of his normal even tones,

"De Rogé finally let me into the dungeons to see him. Or rather he summonsed me, as he put it, to witness the moment Luc broke under torture and betrayed his men, his kin and yielded up all his secrets."

His voice cracked suddenly, like granite under duress.

"Dear God of Mercy!"

He sank down onto the chair, and put his head in his hands.

Dominic wondered if his master was going to be sick again. Wondered if he himself might be sick just imagining what Lord Joscelin had been forced to witness.

Lady Céline went to lay one hand on her son's shoulder, the other lightly smoothing the silvering strands of damp dark hair on his bowed head.

"You do not ask, Mother, but you as much as any of us who are involved must wish to know how much of the truth Luc spilled in his agony?"

Lord Joscelin's voice was muffled by his hands, yet Dominic heard every word in his head, grating like falling scree sliding down his spine, grinding in his already roiling gut.

"However much that is, I would not blame him for it," Lady Céline said quietly. "Or you."

"Me?"

Lord Joscelin looked up briefly.

"Do you know already then how sorely I was tempted to speak in the hope of saving him from having to endure any further pain. Oh gods! How much more do you think I can take!"

It was, Dominic thought wincing, a demand flung at the distant deities rather than a coherent question asked of anyone here in this room.

"As if it were not enough..."

His lord's normally level voice was harsh, brittle, breaking under the strain of years of suppressed emotion.

"That I had to escort my father to the scaffold and watch him die a traitor's hideous death, I now have to watch my brother die a slow, even more protracted and agonising death under torture. Gods, he was barely conscious, bleeding from uncounted cuts, his skin blistered and blackened from hot iron and flame, but still he knew I was there. And all *I* could do was stand there and... bloody *do nothing*! Just as I did nothing to save my father! The man *you* loved, Mother! Daemons of Hell, how then can you love me, who has brought you nothing but misery and shame since the day I was born?"

"Joscelin, my dear, *nothing* can make me stop loving you. There was nothing you could have done for Lucius, even had you felt for him as a son should feel for his father – and how could you when you had only just learned the truth of your siring, and in such a manner? As for Luc, how in gods' name do you think you could have prevented anything that has happened to him. You have been under guard yourself – still are if that man in black boar livery at the door is any indication – and single-handedly attacking Joffroi de Rogé and his tame torturers would only have put you on the rack alongside your brother and taken away Luc's only chance of escape, of survival even."

"I know that in my head. Yet still, in my heart, I am cursed as the coward who held his tongue and left his brother to die."

"And if you had spoken," Lady Céline continued with gentle implacability. "Revealed the secrets Luc would not, you would have sold your soul for nothing."

"Perhaps..." he conceded, lifting his head to reveal a storm-ravaged countenance that was as far from his usual icy mask as to shake Dominic's perceptions of his master anew.

Whoever said Joscelin de Veraux was lacking in feeling should see him now!

Not that Dominic wanted anyone else to see the state to which the man had been reduced.

What he did want was some of that fierce loyalty and affection his master showed towards Luc de Chartreux for himself.

Gods knew he had earned it!

Then he forgot the hollow within his heart as he heard Lord Joscelin say harshly,

"Gods help us all if de Rogé does find some excuse to have me strapped me to the rack in Luc's place. For I know secrets Luc does not and therefore cannot be induced to tell, Rowène's present whereabouts for one. As for the children in her charge, the gods know I would hope to be as strong as Luc has proved in keeping Val and Lissie from falling into their vile kinsman's blood-stained hands but...."

Dominic must have made an involuntary sound at this unexpected mention of Lissie's name, causing his lord to look up sharply, only then seeming to become aware of the presence of his *servant* – since, much as he wished otherwise, Dominic knew he could not legitimately claim any closer relationship with the man who was Lord of Veraux and High Commander of Mithlondia.

His master could admit in his hearing to being the illegitimate son of a traitor and half-brother to an outlaw, but he would never ever claim Dominic as his own chance-got get. Unless...

A terrible thought struck Dominic for the first time.

Perhaps he was not, as he had come to believe, Lord Joscelin's son.

Perhaps there was no connection between them at all beyond that of nobleman and retainer...

But no, Dominic could not believe that.

He looked too much like Lord Joscelin for there to be a complete lack of blood-kinship between them.

That said, it was possible, he supposed dubiously, that his father could have been either Lucius or Luc de Chartreux...

"Nic!" Lord Joscelin's voice rasped into his distracted thoughts, bringing him back to the candlelit chamber.

"My lord?"

The strained grey gaze met his briefly before settling on the pitcher of watered wine on the table.

"Pour some of that wine for..." He hesitated, then gave a wry smile. "For my mother."

Almost grateful for the excuse to occupy his hands and distract his thoughts, Dominic turned towards the shelf of assorted drinking vessels and, having selected a goblet of polished pewter, presented it to the grey-clad healer with a respectful bow.

"My lady."

"I have not been addressed as 'my lady' for many years now, Dominic, but I thank you for the courtesy. And perhaps..."

She glanced thoughtfully at Lord Joscelin, who had risen from his chair and was now standing staring out of the window across the icy lake into the starlit darkness.

"My son could do with some wine too."

"No," Lord Joscelin said without turning. "It is the daemon's own brew I need tonight."

With some trepidation Dominic filled a small horn cup with the throat-stripping, mind-searing, barley spirit, and handed it to his master who proceeded to toss it back in a gesture that made Dominic, who had secretly tried it once, cringe in anticipation of its effect.

To his relief, Lord Joscelin neither shuddered, spat nor spewed, and when he did turn around again his countenance was tight and bleak, controlled once more, his eyes veiled in grey shadow.

"I am going to see Linnius," he announced flatly.

"Now?" Lady Céline queried, her voice betraying her surprise and disquiet.

"Yes, now." His mouth moved in a mirthless smile. "And being as there is every chance the prince will not like what I am going to say to him..."

He met his mother's anxious gaze.

"I think a word alone with Nic before I go would be in order."

Lady Céline gave a faint sigh.

"Yes, of course you must. It were better done now than later."

"Quite. You may go elsewhere, or if you wish to wait it out you may find it more comfortable in my private chamber," Lord Joscelin was saying. "I will not be... or at least I do not anticipate my... conversation with Nic will take very long."

"Why not, my lord?" Dominic dared to ask once the bedroom door had closed on the Eldest's anxious blue gaze.

"Because I imagine that once you have heard what I have to say, you will walk out of that door..."

Lord Joscelin nodded in the direction of the door that led ultimately into the dark night outside.

"Quite probably never to return. Nor would I blame you in the slightest if that is how it is to be."

"Why?"

"Because that, or something very like it, is what I did when Lucius de Chartreux, on the eve of his execution, told me that I was his bastard son."

For a moment's drubbing heartbeat Dominic could not speak, then finally he choked out the obvious question,

"And that concerns me... how?"

"Because you are *my* son and your full name, not that I suggest you use it, is Dominic Lucius Fitzjoscelin."

Gods! He had known it. Deep in the darkest depths of his heart he had *known...* and yet to hear his lord... his *father* speak the words...

Now. After so bloody long.

And damn the man to hell, Dominic knew why he had chosen this particular moment to speak those bitter-laded words.

Because Joscelin de Veraux was afraid that, like his own father, he would be dead before the sun had set on another day!

Through the roiling haze of his own ragged emotions, Dominic could see that the man who had given him life was standing still, waiting for his answer, grey eyes carefully blank, tension in every line of his tall, wolf-lean body.

Yet in spite of struggling with himself for a full dozen heartbeats all Dominic could manage by way of acknowledgement was a half furious, wholly unsteady,

"Damn you to hell, Father!" before he spun on his heel, turning his back – just as Lord Joscelin, just as his *father*, damn it, had predicted that he would.

"Nic!"

Despite his need to get away, he stopped, unwillingly snagged by the heart-wrenching note in his father's voice.

He did not look back, however, addressing his stony question to the door of black oak.

"What?"

"Since you obviously cannot stomach me for your sire, and I do not blame you for that either, go to your grandsire. And whatever happens after this, Nic, stay out of Black Joffroi's sight. I did not withhold the truth of your siring all these years – in a perhaps misguided attempt to keep my son safe from the same man who brought about my father's ruin and death – simply for you to fall foul of him now."

Dominic stared blindly at the solid unyielding wood, trying to control his voice long enough to give some sort of answer to his father, but it still hurt too much, all the words strangling themselves in his aching throat, and in the end all he could do was shake his head as he set his hand to the heavy iron latch and let himself out of the rooms that formed all the home he had ever known.

He had not paused to snatch up his cloak and with little idea where he was actually going, Dominic now found himself shivering in his shirtsleeves on the battlements above the main gate. Above him stars glittered in the black void and a pitiless moon shone full on the bleached, weather-battered bones of a broken man's skull.

Gods!

When his father had recommended him to seek out his grandsire, Dominic had no doubt Lord Joscelin had meant Rhys, that gruff bear of a man who had given his grandson the rough warmth and love he would not otherwise have known, Joscelin de Veraux never having been given to open demonstrations of affection.

Nevertheless, even with those words echoing in his head, he had not gone to Rhys, had he?

Instead he was here, alone, save for a distant, pacing sentry, the empty-eyed skull seeming to stare down on him as he stood on the frost-rimed battlements, freezing in his folly.

Or was he alone?

Could it be that the bone-chilling wind wrapping about him, whispering through the fine hairs on the nape of his neck, lifting the longer, midnight-black strands away from his shoulders, was not the wind at all but rather the wraith touch of a man who had long since yielded up his life on the scaffold, the nobleman whose blood still beat in the living heart of Dominic's father as well as his own.

No, he decided, he was not alone.

And he shivered again at that knowledge.

In spite of the stark truth that Lucius de Chartreux was now no more than a set of displaced bones and a crumbling skull – a wraith wrought of moonlight and the night breeze, who walked beneath the mid-winter stars, clothed in hazy memories drawn from the mind of a young man who had once been a solitary, fatherless, seven-year old boy – something of the man himself still lingered on in his sons and daughters.

Men and women who were his own *blood-kin. Gods, his kin!*

Up until this moment Dominic had forced himself to accept that his only family was his mother's father, Rhys.

Yet now came the realisation that he had a grandmother as well.

With that the image of Lady Céline's serene blue eyes and gentle smile rose to form a shield against the cold and loneliness that sliced at his soul, wrapping him instead in warmth and love as he recalled how she had always been kind to him on the rare occasions of their meeting over the years. Though, of course, she must already have known who he was.

As had the Lady Rowène, he remembered suddenly, something of the pleasant sensation of belonging seeping away into disquiet.

For Rowène de Chartreux had been his father's leman, had slept in his father's bed and carried his child... except Dominic's new-found knowledge made her Joscelin de Veraux's half-sister!

No! He shook his head violently. That must be wrong. He could not believe such a terrible thing could be the truth... But that his father would perjure himself to protect the half-sister he loved and her unborn child... yes, Dominic could see that happening all too easily.

What was it Jacques had said, when speaking of Lissie and Lord Joscelin? Ah yes!

I am guardian to the child for whom your lord has claimed responsibility.

Not that Joscelin de Veraux had *acknowledged* responsibility but that he had *claimed* that duty.

And that was all the proof Dominic needed.

Whoever had in truth sired Lissie – his cousin... gods, he had a cousin! – he was utterly sure it had not been his own father.

Thought of Lissie inevitably brought to mind the night the child had been born, a memory he had long since pushed aside but which now returned, borne on the biting winter's wind.

It had been a warm summer's night, he remembered, full of blood and chaos, the bitter conflict and confusion it had brought to his father's chambers ending only when both mother and child had left in company with the outlaw band who had invaded the palace.

Not long after that Dominic had heard that Lady Rowène was dead and he had wept until his pillow was sodden, unable to forget her kindness to him.

Even now he had not forgotten her, his father's sister, and absently he rubbed at his left arm, the arm Herluin de Lyeyne had broken all those years ago

Indeed, he had wanted so desperately for Lady Rowène not to be dead that when he had seen the grey-eyed Sister Fayla – the same night she had been brought to his father's quarters accused of fornication with the guardian, Rafe, whom Dominic knew to be one of the few men his father accounted friend – he had dared to ask the healer if she was really the Lady Rowène, and to his sorrow she had denied it.

No, he corrected himself again, she had not made an unequivocal denial. What she had said, word for word, had been *I wish I could tell you what you want to hear.*

She had *wanted* to tell him the truth, he thought, and loyalty to his father – her half-brother – had tied her tongue.

But whether she called herself Sister Fayla or the Lady Rowène de Chartreux, the heart that beat quick and hard within his breast told Dominic that she was still his own kin.

As were her outlawed brothers.

Luc, whom it seemed his father had in mind to save at risk of his own life if what he had said just before Dominic had stormed out meant what he thought it did.

And Jacques, the lad who presently lay weak from wounds and fever under Lady Adèle's care but who would, despite his youth, die on the scaffold as his father had already done, and as his elder brother was like to do, were his presence in the palace discovered by Prince Linnius' vengeful chief counsellor.

And as Lord Joscelin would die, if whatever he was planning tonight failed.

Gods, no!

Unable to help himself, Dominic looked up again at the empty-eyed skull, and shivered as a cold sweat of sick fear broke out on his skin.

Surely his father had not told him the truth of his siring merely so that Dominic could watch him *die*? Just as Lord Joscelin, who had learned the truth of his own paternity on the eve of Lucius de Chartreux's execution, had been forced to watch *his* father die?

With the asking of that hammer-blow question, Dominic drew in a short, hard breath of the ice-cold winter night, realising that he had been granted a choice his father had not been given.

As a man bearing the guardians' mark on his arm, his father could not have disobeyed the order of his commanding office to escort a traitor condemned by the High Counsel to the scaffold.

Moreover, if his father had been half as furious with Lucius de Chartreux as Dominic was with him, he would scarcely have risked life and livelihood to save the man who had quite deliberately withheld from him the truth of his paternity until it was too late.

Dominic, however, bore no such mark on his arm.

He could walk away from this mess. Turn his back on his new-found, outlawed kin.

He could go to his grandsire Rhys. Make a new life.

His father had in effect set him free to make his own decision.

Since you obviously cannot stomach me for your sire, and I do not blame you for that either, go to your grandsire. And whatever happens after this, Nic, stay out of Black Joffroi's sight. I did not withhold the truth of your siring all these years – in a perhaps misguided attempt to keep my son safe from the same man who brought about my father's ruin and death – simply for you to fall foul of him now.

His father had not only set him free. He had all but ordered Dominic to leave.

The throat-tightening, bone-shuddering alternative being that he stand on the scaffold alongside his uncle and the man he had just called father to his face for the first – and perhaps last – time.

And as simply as that was his decision... his choice – that in the end was no choice at all – made. So be it.

Dominic returned to the familiar set of rooms to find them empty. Glancing around in puzzled surprise, he felt some of the inevitable tension that had been holding him taut to the point of snapping drain away, leaving him feeling momentary like a wrung-out wash cloth flapping loose on a line.

Then pinning down his flying thoughts, he straightened his shoulders and was looking about him for some indication of what was toward when he heard the door open quietly behind him.

His heart flaring on a burst of fear and a love there was no longer any need to conceal, he turned, expecting... *hoping* to see his father. Only to drop his gaze in order to meet the soft blue eyes of the Lady Céline de Veraux.

"Grandmère!"

The word left his lips on a jerky breath, followed a moment later, when he realised she was not alone, by the word he had longed for the right to say, but which now barely made it past the invisible noose wrapped so tightly about his throat he thought it must strangle all sound.

"Father!"

"Nic!"

His father's voice was scarcely steadier than his own, his grey eyes as wide as the cloud-covered northern skies, the roil of stormy emotions plain to see.

"God of Light, you came back! Why in Hell's name would you commit such folly unless..."

Something in those grey eyes changed, as if a cloud had covered the sun, the all-too-familiar mask of control dropping once more over those lean features as his father said with a granite-like lack of emotion,

"Unless you have found the words to tell me how much you despise me for what I have done to you. First by carelessly giving you life, then keeping secret from you the truth you were entitled to hear. As if instead of trying to protect the son I... had a duty towards, I was merely ashamed of you."

"Were you?" Dominic demanded harshly.

If only his father had said he loved him instead of merely feeling a duty towards him.

"Ashamed of you? No! Of myself, yes."

Adding with a flash of some unexpected and unguarded emotion,

"Damn it, how could it be otherwise?"

"You were very young, Joscelin," Lady Céline put in. "Scarce sixteen yourself, and you did what you could for Elen."

"How would you know that?" his father asked savagely, rounding ruthlessly on the gentle lady who had given him life. "How *can* you know that?"

"I know because I tended you when you were brought to the Healing House in Vézière injured and close to death. It was obvious that you were much troubled about the girl you had unthinkingly got with child. And I know too because Rowène told me how deeply Elen's fate preyed upon your mind, and how much you *loved* your son – not merely that it was your duty to care for him – and how you feared for his life should Joffroi de Rogé learn of his de Chartreux blood. Nic..."

She turned earnestly to Dominic, warming him with her use of the affectionate diminutive of his given name.

"You *do* believe me?"

"Yes," he said. "If only because I want to so damned much."

He gave a cracked laugh and continued wryly, determined to speak what was in his heart and mind this once.

"A candle-notch on the battlements in the freezing cold, and a conversation with a crumbling skull may have made Ulric regard me as a madman, but it was Lucius de Chartreux who brought me to my senses."

"Sweet God of Mercy! Lucius was there? Or his wraith at least?"

Lady Céline's voice trembled, and Dominic wondered if she would dare the icy battlements herself in the hope of catching one last glimpse of the moon-silvered shade of the man she had clearly loved with all her heart.

Very likely she would, if she were half as stubborn as her son, but he – her grandson – could not permit her to risk herself in such folly.

"No," he said hastily. "I... it is hard to describe how it was... it was as if Lord Lucius stood beside me. Even though the moonlight showed the wall walk empty, I know he was there. I heard no words, just felt his presence. But Lady Rowène's voice, now that *was* real. I could hear her in my head."

He grimaced, looked at his booted feet, then lifted his gaze and said it anyway.

"In my heart, I could feel her near."

He looked straight at his father, a direct challenge, a test as to whether the time truly had come for the truth or whether his father would still lie to him for his own protection.

"She is not really dead, is she? Your sister, Rowène?"

An odd smile touched his father's normally impervious face.

"No, Nic, you are right. She is alive."

Then the unaccustomed gentleness left his father's voice, returning to its normal steel-hard rasp.

"Pray gods I may keep her so. Luc too."

Grey eyes regarded Dominic with a bleak, hard-won dispassion.

"You do realise that if you stay with me, as my son rather than my servant, you risk your life?"

"I am not witless, Father. Of course I know that. But if I am to be hanged as a traitor's spawn, as seems more likely than not, I may just as well earn the death. Now... I know you are planning something, so tell me what I can do to help?"

A full candle-notch later they stood together – four men and one woman – ranged around the bed where Luc de Chartreux lay, burned, bleeding and, even to Dominic's inexperienced eyes, dying.

On being applied to for direction, his father had slipped back into the skin of the coldly-composed Commander of Mithlondia's Guardians he had worn so well and for so long.

Having already gained Prince Linnius' agreement to release the prisoner into his custody – he had not said how he obtained this permission, and neither Dominic nor Lady Céline had wasted breath by asking – and leaving his mother to brew a draught of pain-killing herbs, he had sent Dominic to the guardians' barracks to find one Rafe of Oakenleigh, with the request that he meet his commander at the entrance to the palace dungeons, while he himself had sought out his former Second.

What those three men had been done there in the darkness below the brightly-lit palace had been savage and bloody, resulting in two of Black Joffroi's men being killed outright, and two others injured beyond recovery, setting the way free for Lord Joscelin, his sword-brothers and his son to bear away the battered body of the man who presently lay, still and barely breathing, in his half-brother's bed.

Having prepared her potion, Lady Céline was now weeping silently as she attempted to dribble a few drops of the draught between Luc's raw lips, while the men watched her ministrations in a tense, tight-lipped, grey-faced silence.

Dominic himself had been violently sick, though he was recovered enough now to stand unobtrusively at the foot of the bed, forcing himself to breathe in the thick, rank air that stank of blood and vomit and every other substance a body under duress could yield.

If the older men – soldiers all three of them, and accustomed to the grim sights of the battlefield – could withstand it without flinching, he was determined to do no less, despite his lack of years and experience.

Luc de Chartreux was his uncle, after all... though the gods knew at present he looked like nothing more than a badly-butchered carcass, and the only resemblance he bore to the brother who stood staring down at him with the blank eyes of a stone statue was his blood-matted, white-threaded midnight-dark hair and the glimpse of grey glittering between half-closed, salt-clogged lashes.

When they had first brought him in, wrapped loosely in Gabriel de Marillec's mantle for the duration of his journey from dungeon to his half-brother's quarters, the damage done to him had not been immediately visible to prying eyes, only his companions knowing that beneath the soft mantle the man they carried was clothed only in blood and bodily fluids.

This state being revealed when they gently laid him upon the hastily stripped-down bed, Lady Céline had – after her first soft, quickly suppressed cry of distress – taken competent charge, cleaning and binding the terrible wounds as best she could, the men working with blade, teeth and brute force to rapidly reduce the discarded sheet to suitable pads and strips of linen, Dominic helping as and where he could.

Nothing, however, could erase the memory from his mind of the shattered bones... the raw, torn and blistered flesh.

Though Luc had been awake and aware when they had taken him from the dungeon, the journey and Lady Céline's ministrations appeared to have achieved what torture could not, and now he lay on the soft bed, barely breathing, his blackened and bruised eyes almost closed, tears seeping between his matted lashes to run past his skewed, broken nose, and down over the burned flesh of his cheeks to be lost in the heavy growth of dark beard,

And all the while, fresh bright blood blossomed.

Not only on his bindings but also the sheet upon which he was lying and the light blanket they had covered him with against the chill that pervaded the bedchamber despite the valiant warmth of the two braziers that had been placed as close to the bed as possible without risking setting the heavy blue hangings on fire.

Now, having done all that could be done to make Luc comfortable, the three men were regarding each other in silent dismay, each soundlessly asking that which Dominic himself was wondering – how even a strong, healthy man, as it was obvious his uncle Luc had been, could survive such indescribably vicious treatment.

"What are his chances?" Dominic heard his father ask, his voice low and grim.

"There is no more that I can do to help him," Lady Céline replied, her voice barely audible. "In all truth, Joscelin, I do not think anyone can save him, except possibly..."

She broke off, frowning over her shoulder.

"What is that noise? Who comes here at such a time? Pray gods it is not Joffroi de Rogé, for I will not be responsible for the consequences! Or... could it be that *you* sent for someone, Joscelin?"

The faint sound of raised voices penetrated the strained silence that had fallen over the bedchamber, disturbed only by the raw, uneven sawing as the breath passed in and out of Luc de Chartreux's shattered chest.

"No, it was not Josce!"

The harsh voice was so far removed from the light, liquid accents Dominic was accustomed to, he almost did not connect that rough rasp to Gabriel de Marillec.

"It was me, Madame. And if I am right, this may be Luc's only hope of healing. If I am wrong, then Hell will seem a pleasant place after this."

And Dominic, catching a glimpse of de Marillec's face as he stalked past, could not repress a shudder at the sight of the wraith-white countenance in which his eyes blazed a clear yellow, bright as citrine and ringed in darkness that was at least as black and bleak as the outer reaches of Hell itself.

Almost as one, they turned and followed de Marillec, listening in bemusement as he tersely assured the guard on the door that everything was in order, then ushered the newcomers into the main room.

Yet even as Dominic stood gaping at the sight of Adèle de Marillec and the slightly-built youth leaning on her far from sturdy frame, he heard an oath and a gasp from behind him and felt himself thrust rudely aside as Rafe of Oakenleigh pushed past him with a grated exclamation.

"Jacques!"

"Rafe!"

Dominic recovered his balance in time to see the pale-faced, sapling-thin outlaw turn towards the big, fair-haired guardian striding across the chamber towards him, the anxiety and pain in the younger man's grey eyes washed away in a blaze of relief and what, even to Dominic's jaundiced gaze, was unmistakably love.

Whatever else Jacques had intended to say, it died in his throat as Rafe – in utter disregard of the presence of his commanding officer, his sword-brother and the two noblewomen – wrapped the unresisting youth in his arms and silenced him with a deeply carnal kiss. To which Jacques responded by pressing himself even closer against the bigger man and twining his fingers in the short strands of barley-pale hair.

At that, Dominic very nearly threw up for the third time that evening but something made him clamp his jaw shut tight against the nausea roiling in his belly, while that same instinct that he was missing something important made him glance around at his companions to see how *they* were reacting to this appalling scene.

Astonishingly Lady Céline was blinking tears from her eyes, and if Gabriel de Marillec was regarding the pair with a somewhat sour half smile, Lady Adèle seemed frankly stunned.

Only Dominic's father – save for the very faintest of sardonic gleams in his grey eyes – appeared completely unmoved by the scene playing out in front of him.

Which proved rather more conclusively than Dominic cared for, that the younger of his father's outlawed half-brothers was far too closely involved with a man who not only wore the guardians' mark on his arm but was a man whom his father called friend.

Catching his father's eye, Dominic sent him a mute plea, and with a nod and an ominous clearing of his throat, Mithlondia's High Commander said coldly,

"If you two have quite finished treating my quarters as a brothel – again! – perhaps you might like to remember that your kinsman lies dying in the next room!"

Rafe looked up, his expression dazed and distant.

Then, as his mind once more returned to his surroundings he dropped his arms, allowing Jacques to take one stumbling step backward.

Yet even as Rafe reached out an instinctive hand to steady his lover, his irate dark blue gaze was skimming over the man who had rebuked him so cuttingly before settling with scorching rage on the slender form of the former Second.

Seeing himself the focus of the bigger man's fury, Gabriel de Marillec threw up his hands in the manner of a man warding off a blow, saying with quick apology,

"Forgive me, Rafe, I should have told you..."

"Too bloody right, you should. As for you..."

He rounded on Jacques, giving him a rough shake.

"What in the dark depths of fucking hell do you think you are doing here in the palace? If it is not bad enough that Luc..."

"For gods'sake, Rafe," Jacques snapped, pulling himself free. "It was for Luc's sake that I came to Lamortaine."

"And you think Joffroi would not hesitate to do to *you* what he has already done to Luc," Ranulf snarled back. "Then where would Val and Lissie be?"

"Hell'sdeath, Josce!"

De Marillec raised his voice sufficiently to be heard over the argument raging in the midst of them.

"Can you not exert your authority over these two? Luc's life is more important than a lover's quarrel."

His glittering eyes narrowed as he caught Dominic's disgusted gaze.

"And I think perhaps it is time someone had a word with the lad here. Explain..."

"Explain?" Dominic bit out, too angry now to guard his tongue. "I am not a child. I can see what dark desires bind those two. And I do not need *you* – you of all men, Messire de Marillec! – to explain the kind of intimacies men engage in between themselves!"

"That is just as well since I have no intention of explaining them. And regardless of your opinion of me, Dominic Fitzjoscelin, you *will* come with me and you *will* listen," de Marillec informed him in the suddenly crisp tone that had once commanded half an army. "*Now!*"

And gripping Dominic hard above the elbow, the slender, disgraced nobleman effortlessly pushed him through the door into the antechamber, tossing a few more words over his shoulder as he did so.

"Since it is obvious that he knows part of the truth, Josce, he may as well hear the rest of it. And, Jacques, for pity's sake, see what you can do for Luc. I cannot bear..."

He broke off as he caught Jacques' compassionate grey gaze.

"Well, you know it anyway, I have no secrets from you. Do what you can, I will be back shortly."

With Gabriel's abrupt departure on his mission of truth – or perhaps seeking temporary reprieve from a scene that affected him too sorely – those left behind exchanged a single, bleak glance and then stepped aside to allow Rowène to follow Joscelin into the chamber where their brother lay, bruised, burned and barely breathing in the blue-curtained bed.

With the hectic flush that had been the visible residue of her stormy embrace with Ranulf having fled at the first glimpse of Luc's tortured body, Rowène' face was now as grey as the soiled snow in the courtyard outside as she struggled against the twin enemies of her own weakness and her brother's pain, the true depth of which she now realised he had somehow managed to keep from her.

She had sensed his suffering, yes. How could it be otherwise when they were linked by their mother's blood? But that he should have come this close to death without her knowing...

"There is no more I can do to aid him," the Eldest was saying, her gentle voice seeming to come from some vast distance, when in fact the healer had come quietly into the room and was now standing beside her.

"It is, as Messire Gabriel said, in your hands now."

Taking a deep breath, Rowène lowered her hand to rest on her brother's bandaged chest, wherein the cage of cracked ribs and mutilated flesh his heart still contrived against all odds to beat.

Eyes closed, she stood in soul-sick silence, exploring the full, harrowing extent of her brother's injuries for what seemed an eternity to her, let alone the others whom she sensed were waiting for her to speak... praying that when she did, she would tell them that she could indeed do the impossible and save her brother's life.

She was still standing thus when she heard Gabriel and Nic came quietly back into the room, and glanced up in time to see Gabriel nodding once to Josce and Rafe to tell them all was well. As if anything in this morass of pain and heart-break could be well!

As for Nic, he was staring at her, grey eyes wide and flooded with disbelief. Then, as he lowered his eyes to his dying uncle, any and all light was abruptly snuffed out.

Yet still Rowène remained silent, unmoving, until finally, when the tension in the room would have shattered if another moment had gone by in silence, she stirred, swaying slightly on her feet.

"Here!"

Ranulf's voice was rough in her ear as he set down the stool he had snatched up, close by the head of the bed.

"Sit down before you fall down. For all Lady Adèle's unstinting care, it is obvious that you are in pain, and weak as a kitten."

"Do not fuss, Rafe," Rowène murmured in answer to the faintly reminiscent smile that had momentarily softened his hard mouth at the word 'kitten'.

Then, as she lowered herself carefully onto the stool,

"I am fine."

It was, of course, a mistake to make any such spurious claim, and she could see from the flare of temper in his eyes that he was about to snap some sort of acerbic response.

Before he could do so, however, Gabriel demanded tersely,

"Well, Ro?"

"It is worse, much worse than I believed, but there is the merest breath of a chance..."

Barely able to breathe herself, Rowène forced herself to meet the aching anxiety in his pleading amber-gold eyes, as she continued for his hearing alone,

One chance, Ré. One only. And perhaps it is not even a chance. Merely the wraith of a hope that may prove real... if moonlit dreams do indeed bear true message.

Damn it, no, Ro!

Gabriel's voice was sharp in her head, unheard by anyone else.

You, better than anyone, know I cannot take the torture of any more bloody dreams... cannot sift the truth or lies from any more mystical messages. Only madness lies along that path! For you, as well as for me!

Then, evidently catching the suspicion darkening the glance Ranulf shot from one to the other, he added harshly, out loud for all to hear,

"Hell'sdeath, Ro! If you have nothing better to offer than false hope, I would I had not brought you here."

"Gabriel, dear, I would have come anyway," she said with a weary sigh, even as she looked around at the others, her kin.

"I do believe there is a chance for Luc. But I cannot do it alone. And even if Luc's life can be saved, I do not think it will be achieved without some sacrifice on the part of those of us who take what Gabriel, perhaps rightly, calls the path of madness."

"If you know any way of saving Luc's life, then show us what to do," Joscelin put in before Gabriel could reply. "Whatever the cost, I for one am willing to pay it."

"I did not say I would not pay the price," Gabriel interjected huskily, his eyes a blazing fire of gold and amber flames. "I will, gladly! Even to my wretched, worthless life!"

Joscelin shot him a silencing glare and continued flatly,

"Whatever you mean to do, Ro, it must be done now. We will get no second chance. Even if Luc could survive another day, Linnius would only agree to release him into my custody for this one night. By the first watch of tomorrow morning he must be taken under guard to the great hall. Linnius also stipulated that both Gabriel and I be part of that guard. Public proof of our loyalty to the crown," he finished drily.

Rowène gave him a look but only said with a frown,

"The great hall? Not the Counsel Chamber?"

"No, the great hall. Linnius – or rather Joffroi de Rogé – wants as many people as possible to witness Luc's trial and sentencing, thus dragging the de Chartreux name so deep into the mire that there will be no chance of it ever being held in honour again."

"So, even if it is possible to save Luc's life," Rowène said slowly. "It is only a false trial and a traitor's death that awaits him?"

"I am afraid so," Joscelin admitted grimly. "But the longer he lives, the greater the likelihood that I can think of a way to get him clear of the palace."

"Watched as closely as you are, what odds do you give me on that, Josce? No, do not answer, I will not gamble with Luc's life, not as he is now. If you cannot come up with a viable plan by morning..."

She hesitated, but it had to be said.

"Then for Luc's sake I see no other way forwards than to brew a lethal potion and drip it down his throat, drop by drop until he can take no more. And I do not think it would take many drops the state he is in!"

"No, it would not," the Eldest confirmed quietly. "And while I do not judge you for that resolve, dear one, you will neither brew nor administer such a deadly draught. Luc is your brother and I will not permit you to darken your soul with fratricide."

"And you do not love him too?" Rowène retorted, turning her head to look up at the woman who had once been her father's mistress and was now the respected leader of the healers of Vézière.

"And what about the gods you serve, Mother? The Gods of Light and Mercy?"

"This *is* a mercy that I would bring to Luc," Lady Céline replied.

"We all know that he cannot live long as he is. Nor would I myself do anything to save him for the traitor's noose. Because yes, I do love him. Almost as deeply as I love Joscelin, because Luc is his father's son too. I loved Lucius more than honour, more than life itself. As long as he lived I could not leave him, in spirit at least, and when he died, I thought to take my own life too so that I could be with him in that golden realm beyond the sunset. But his children still lived and so I lived for them, loving the children that witch Ariène bore him as surely I did my own son.

"I do not think I have failed with that love too badly... save perhaps for Juliène," she finished, her passionate words fading into sadness.

"Since you have made mention of Ju," Rowène said, somewhat reluctantly. "If we are to save Luc and bring him to freedom rather than the scaffold, I will need her help as well as..."

"No!"

Ranulf's voice came from above and behind her, flat and hard with anger.

"It is too dangerous, Ro! Surely you cannot have forgotten what happened the last time you crossed her path, here in this very palace? How she repaid you when you risked yourself to save her life and her equally worthless honour?"

"It is not something I am like to forget, not when we..."

She slid a wary glance at Joscelin's grim face and hurried on.

"When matters ended as they did. But this is different, Rafe. This time it is Luc who needs her help and whatever Ju has become, whatever she thinks of me, I would swear she loves him still. Enough perhaps to slip the icy shackles the Winter Lady has locked around her heart and join with those she would normally throw to the wolves without a second thought."

"*Perhaps* does not sound a particularly firm foundation on which to place our trust or Luc's life," Joscelin commented, his cool, dispassionate tones those of the High Commander of Mithlondia rather than their kinsman.

"It is the best I can offer," Rowène said bluntly. "I *cannot* do this without Ju. That said," she continued wryly. "It were probably best if I were not the one to ask for her assistance. Bearing in mind how we parted, she is scarce likely to listen to any plea of mine."

"Certainly not if what you have told me of the circumstances of that last meeting still holds any sway over her actions," Lady Céline commented a trifle tartly, her exasperated blue gaze encompassing both Rowène and Ranulf, neither of whom bothered to contradict her assessment, and with a faint sigh, she continued,

"Very well, *I* will talk to Juliène. As far as she is aware I have no allegiance save to the cause of healing and the gods I serve."

The Eldest looked again at Luc's broken body, shuddered as though she felt his agony in her own bones and continued,

"I will go and seek her now, though where she may be is more than I can say. I do not remember seeing either her or the princess in the great feast hall earlier."

"In that case, likely they are both in the royal apartments," Ranulf offered grudgingly. "Linette often takes her meal there of an evening, preferring Lilia's company to that of the noise and press of folk in the feast hall. But even if Juliène is there also, and will listen to you, Eldest," he continued grimly. "I still do not like the thought of trusting someone who knows so little of loyalty. After all, what is to prevent that treacherous bitch from immediately betraying all of us to her mother or Joffroi?"

"Nothing save her love for Luc," Rowène murmured, leaning wearily back on the stool, so that her head and shoulders were resting against Ranulf's legs.

"I do not like it myself but unfortunately it is a chance we must take. As for Luc... the gods know he is in no state to care either way. But we must find Ju before we can go any further."

"I... I know where Juliène will be," came a trembling voice.

Looking up, Rowène saw that Adèle – whom she had thought to have left for her own chamber long since – was standing at the foot of the bed, her horror-filled blue eyes travelling from Luc to Gabriel and back again, her pale lips barely moving as she said,

"I can take you to her, Eldest."

This offer running contrary to her own plans, Rowène directed her gaze across the bed at the man presently standing alongside one of her brothers as he stared down bleakly at the other. After a moment's concentration she saw him start and look up to meet her eyes.

Holding her breath, she watched as amber yielded gradually to gold behind the mask of his bronze lashes, and finally after long moments of silent argument he grimaced, conceding defeat, and said,

"No, *I* will take you, Eldest, if Adèle will but tell me where I may find Madame de Lyeyne."

"Why should I not go?" Adèle demanded, rounding fiercely on her lord-by-binding. "Do you not trust me to do even this much for your lov... for *him*?"

"We *do* trust you, Adèle," Rowène intervened hastily.

490

She darted another fleeting glance at Gabriel's taut, bleached countenance, then returned her attention to her friend.

"But I need you to do something for me that Gabriel cannot. Will you not hear me out, Adèle?"

She gestured to the main chamber and after a moment's hesitation Adèle followed her out, not noticeably mollified by Rowène's words.

"Well?" Adèle enquired gracelessly when they were out of earshot of the others. "What is it you want me to do that is so important? Or did you just want to get me away from Gabriel lest I say anything else to him you think I should not?"

"What lies between you and Gabriel is your own concern, and if you choose to speak of it before others... then that too is your affair. As to the favour I would ask of you... it is such that, yes, I would prefer it to remain between the two of us. For the time being at least."

Adèle looked momentarily disconcerted, then nodded,

"Go on."

"You told me that when you left Kaerellios, Queen Xandra gave you a box of rare Kardolandian remedies? Powdered roots, seeds and the like?"

Adèle nodded, the suspicion in her blue eyes growing rather than dissipating.

"I need something from that box," Rowène said, trying to keep any hint of her own contradictory emotions out of her voice. "If, that is, what I seek is there at all."

"If it means so much to you, and it is there, you may have it," Adèle replied. "Though I still do not see why you need me. Here is the key, you know where I keep the box. More than that, you know what you are looking for."

"Unfortunately," Rowène gave her friend the smallest of rueful smiles. "And much though I hate to admit it, I have used all my stock of strength just walking down here, and even that I could not have managed without your aid. And so I put my trust in you, that you will find and bring me what I need, as swiftly as you can."

"Oh, very well," Adèle agreed on a defeated sigh. "But you will have to tell me exactly what it is that I am to look for."

"If it is there, you will recognise it easily enough," Rowène said, and proceeded to describe that which she sought, watching as an appalled comprehension abruptly returned the horror to her friend's eyes.

"Oh, Ro, are you sure?" Adèle whispered.

"That I am doing the right thing?"

Rowène hesitated, her gaze going to the open door through which she could just glimpse the bed wherein lay her brother's broken body.

"No, I am far from sure. But in the end, if Juliène does not come or refuses her aid, there will be but one path for Luc to walk through this darkness."

Adèle having slipped away on her errand, and Gabriel and the Eldest departing on theirs, Rowène went back to sit by her brother's bed, her thoughts turning without volition and very little hope towards her sister, almost able to see her as she sat in the concealing shadows beyond the flicker of red-gold flames dancing on the hearth in the Hall of Fire.

"I will *not* weep," Juliène told herself as she sat stiffly on her stool, back rigidly straight, trembling fingers clenched tightly in the lap of her green velvet gown.

"It is *not* my fault. *None* of what has happened is my doing. Not here. Not in Kaerellios."

Throughout every one of those five long years she had been away, she had wanted only to be back in Mithlondia – preferably in Vézière, if she were to take honesty to its unaccustomed limit – and not a day had gone by when she had not thought of Luc or Guyard de Martine.

And now... when she found herself once more within the intrigue-ridden environs of the Palace of Princes, she wished contrariwise that she was five thousand leagues away again.

For if she had not returned, the only man she truly loved would still be free.

And the man she dared not love would be safe from her scheming. *Goddess, if only...*

But then she realised she was back where she had started.

Trying to justify her actions.

Pretending she felt no guilt for her brother's peril.

Or that she bore no blame for Luc's situation.

He was a man after all, capable of making his own decisions and taking responsibility for their outcome.

Even so, she could not forget the part she had played – a part she could not even claim she had played unwittingly, for if she had only thought far enough ahead she would have seen the inevitability of it all – in setting the trap into which her beloved brother had so recklessly walked.

Her only excuse was that when it all started, four years ago, she could never have envisaged Luc becoming involved...

As it was, having already spent the better part of a year in Kaerellios, Juliène found herself restless and discontented, and more than ready to take ship north again.

The entertainments and amusements that had seemed so exciting when she had been a girl growing up at the royal Kardolandian court held no interest for her as a woman-grown, and for all the hedonistic freedom to take a lover when and where she chose, only one man now entered her thoughts.

For much as she may have wished otherwise, she could not deny that she had been shaken to her soul by the farewell kiss Guyard de Martine had given her that night at Vézière!

She had asked him to kiss her as if he meant it... and if heat and passion were any indication he had done just that!

And she, who had intended to remain in command of herself and her heart... she who had grown to hate being touched in any way by a man... had succumbed within mere moments of his warm mouth meeting hers.

Forgetting completely that her aim was to enchant him, enslave him, and finally break him.

Forgetting too what had gone before, and that which must come after. Sending all else into oblivion.

Until all she could remember was that she was Juliène and he was Guyard... and that for those precious, wonderful moments they were as one.

Then he had drawn back, and she, made wary by her mindless yielding to his kiss, had seized the opportunity to escape, to journey south where she might spend her days amidst the exotic flowers and cool marble halls of the Kardolandian palace, and forget Guyard de Martine had been anything more than a dream.

Except that she had not forgotten. *Could not* forget.

Goddess help her, until she had felt his arms about her and tasted his kiss, she had thought herself dead to passion, and indeed if it had been only that, she thought she could have withstood him.

It had been the unexpected tenderness underlying the passion that had broken through her defences to cup her heart with gentle hands.

Nor had it helped quell her turmoil when Queen Xandra, on discovering that Juliène had some acquaintance with the former Mithlondian slave she rather annoyingly alluded to as her golden harper, had seemed to take a perverse delight in seeking Juliène out in order to share in explicit detail every memory of the man who had shared her bed, soothed her cares away with his music and brought her such poignant pleasure, until the moment when the queen had reluctantly had to uphold her oath to Juliène's sister and set her lover free.

All Juliène could do in response was grit her teeth and wish that she too could be free of the palace that had been her home for ten years, the palace she had left so unwillingly thirteen years before and to which she had so willingly fled in the hopes of forgetting the man who was *her* harper, whatever false notions the Kardolandian queen might harbour.

Unfortunately for Juliène's wishes, Princess Linette seemed perfectly content to remain in Kaerellios and until she or Kaslander decided otherwise, Juliène knew she was stuck, like a moon-moth caught within the deadly embrace of the mortiana lily.

Thus Juliène had begun to work, subtly at first, to convince Linette that it was time to bring her visit to an end, and when the gentle persuasion of words failed, she had reluctantly been forced to employ other methods.

Nothing truly dangerous to Linette or little princess Lilia – or so she told herself – just enough to give Linette a feeling of disquiet about living in the Kardolandian palace... a growing anxiety about the safety of her child.

Yet still they remained, and the days, and months, and years continued to pass, until Juliène began to lose all sense of how long they had been gone from Mithlondia.

Guyard de Martine's face began to fade from her mind, until all she could remember was the colour of his eyes – the gentle blue of a hazy Mithlondian summer sky – and his hair – a dark wheat gold streaked with moonlight – and the tender passionate warmth of his mouth on hers, for which she could find no fitting comparison but yet held the memory close with a fierce determination.

Until, eventually, that memory too began to fade.

Reality was the Kardolandian sky arching over her head, the hot, hard, iridescent blue of the far south, where wheat was an unknown word.

And whilst there was moonlight in plenty, the waters of her scrying bowl remained frustratingly blank, the blackness broken only by the pinprick light of far distant stars.

Only the near soundless whisper of his voice and the occasional ripple of notes from his harp echoed sometimes in her restless dreams.

Little enough, yet it was all she had, and she clung to these imperfect reflections of her heart with a tenacity she had not known was in her until all else was gone.

Including the hope that they would ever return to Mithlondia where, she told herself, she had unfinished business with Guyard de Martine.

Perhaps it was because she was distracted by thoughts of Guyard and the only kiss they had ever shared that it took her so long to realise that it was not, and never had been, Linette who was keeping the Mithlondians there in Kardolandia.

It was Kaslander.

And he had in his leash not some mere imp of mischief but the daemon of death himself.

For while Juliène had taken some degree of care not to endanger Linette or Lilia, Kaslander knew no such scruples, to the point where Juliène had actually been relieved to see Ranulf de Rogé's grim, weather-worn visage the day he strode without warning into the royal palace in Kaerellios.

Having clasped Gabriel de Marillec's arm, and bowed to the ladies, he had given Kaslander one straight, savage look of warning from those exceptionally dark blue eyes before taking up guard duty on the princesses, his orders and authority coming direct from the High Commander of Mithlondia himself.

All well and good.

If only that the same ship which had carried Ranulf to Kaerellios had not also brought Juliène a letter from her mother.

A letter that contained certain very specific instructions regarding the man who was not only Second of Mithlondia's Guardians but also the heir to the lordship of Marillec and – by repute if nothing else – a man whose personal predilections would fit in very well at the Kardolandian court.

Up until then Juliène had generally managed to ignore Gabriel de Marillec's presence. That said, she could not help but be aware that he had to all intents and purposes refrained from taking advantage of the situation, either for the casual slaking of his desires or a more formal affair, remaining celibate and therefore faithful.

Though whether he kept faith with the woman who wore his binding band or her brother, Juliène had no way of knowing.

In truth, she had not cared. It was no affair of hers.

Until the order came from her mother that made it her business.

An order that Juliène, to whom Gabriel de Marillec's honour meant less than nothing, had not hesitated to obey, finding a suitable tool almost immediately in the person of the slave, Sukash.

It had taken little in either coin or cunning to persuade Sukash that his best chance of a coupling with the man he so obviously desired lay in following her advice, and so Juliène set herself to study the pattern of de Marillec's days and nights, and armed with that knowledge, had arranged that little scene on the white sands at dawn, though she left the actual seduction to Sukash.

As it was, Juliène did not care either way whether de Marillec indulged himself with the slave or not. All that mattered was that Adèle should believe her lord-by-binding guilty of a physical intimacy that – with the testimony she would be obliged to give – would see him hanged once he set foot again on Mithlondian soil...

Except that when they did finally return to Mithlondia and the Guardians' Second had been duly arrested, tried and sentenced to hang in Lamortaine's place of execution, Juliène was suddenly confronted with a truth she should have known all along.

That through her jealous dislike of Gabriel de Marillec, she had blindly baited the trap that had now taken her beloved brother!

Of course Luc should have had more sense than to fall into such a trap but still...

No! That was a pointless trail of thought.

For regardless of blame, Luc *would* be arraigned before the High Counsel on a charge of treason.

A trial to which every high-ranking nobleman in Mithlondia had been summoned to attend.

Nevertheless, it had taken several weeks, given the severity of the winter weather and the dangerous travelling conditions to achieve this goal, but finally the last of them had arrived in Lamortaine this very day and the Counsel was complete.

And, goddess help her, Luc's trial set for the morrow.

So now Juliène found herself seated in the Hall of Fire, wrapped about in her own bitter thoughts, with little inclination to wonder much about anything that did not immediately touch on her brother's perilous situation – and the role she herself had played in bringing it about!

Thus, when the door opened some while later and a plainly-clad man made his way into the dimly-lit chamber, firelight glimmering gold on the head he bent in a respectful bow, she could only stare at him in utter shock.

And crawling fear.

For if her mother knew that Guyard de Martine was in Lamortaine...

Oh, gods, how much worse can this day get!

Apparently unaware of Juliène's presence, he took a seat on a stool some little distance from the fire about which the ladies were gathered, and only after he had settled his harp against his shoulder and plucked the first notes of a tune Juliène had never forgotten, did he look up to meet her yearning, disbelieving, ultimately despairing gaze – and it was immediately obvious from the subdued sympathy in his eyes that he was aware both of her brother's imprisonment, and what his likely fate would be.

Goddess help me! Give me the strength not to betray myself!

Of how deep was her longing to feel Guyard's strong arms close around her as he drew her to rest against his broad shoulder... to feel his lips skim her hair as he murmured words of reassurance in her ear... even as she ackowledged that there was no possible way that *anyone* could save her brother from the executioner's noose and knives.

If only Luc had not been so blindly *stupid* as to come to Lamortaine...

And all for the sake of a man he had not seen for five years. A man who had quite possibly betrayed him several times over in another's arms.

Not that she would take out her anger and rage at her brother on Guyard.

Could not even if she had wanted to since she did not dare speak to him, nor even look at him for more than a half dozen heartbeats at a time.

Ah, but how she longed to go to him, to...

Abruptly the tightening thread of her thoughts was broken as the door opened and she looked up to see a man and a woman standing outlined against the torch-lit passage outside.

A small, serene woman of middle years in grey robes and a white headrail.

The Eldest of the Sisters of Mercy of Vézière.

And a slender man with fire-bronzed hair.

The very man, damn him to death and eternal torment, for whose sake her brother had ended up in chains!

At the same time as that sudden, incredulous identification of Gabriel de Marillec shattered ice inside her skull, Juliène's pent-up anger burst from her like water crashing over a high cliff onto the black rocks below, and she threw herself at the man, fingers crooking first into talons, then clenching into fists with which she beat against his unresisting form until strong hands pulled her away and folded her into an embrace that was as much restraint as sympathy.

"Hush, Juli, hush. He is hurting as much as you are."

It was the voice she had so longed to hear, the arms she had needed to feel about her.

Yet nothing Guyard could say or do would change her brother's fate, or Gabriel de Marillec's part in it.

Even so, she allowed herself to relax into the comfort of his embrace and it was only after she had soaked his shirt with her tears, weeping out five years of frustration and five weeks of fear, that she returned to some sense of where she was... and forced herself to step back out of his arms.

"Are you feeling better now, Juliène?" she heard Princess Linette say in a voice of concern.

And then in a more distant tone,

"I thank you for your timely intervention, Master Finch, and for your patience with Lady Juliène. I fear she is sadly upset at present by her brother's... situation."

"Understandably so, your highness," Guyard agreed softly, as he retreated soundlessly back into the shadows.

Standing there, suddenly alone, Juliène was still aware of his presence, the small spark of warmth in her heart telling her that if she needed him – really needed him – he would come to her without hesitation.

Therefore, she *must not* need him, she told herself, repeating it over and over until she could command her voice sufficiently to say,

"I ask your pardon, your highness. I do not know what came over me."

"I think perhaps you should ask pardon of Messire de Marillec also," Linette said pointedly.

"There is no need," de Marillec put in swiftly, and long before Juliène had managed to bring herself to speak any such words. "If it were not for me, her brother would not be..."

He stopped abruptly, the words choking in his throat,

"And I would not be here now... to beg a boon of you, your highness. And of *her*."

"Indeed, Messire?" Linette asked when Juliène – her tongue knotted by outrage and indignation – would not. "What is this favour?"

"To beg your permission to take Madame de Lyeyne to her brother."

He turned his feral amber gaze back towards Juliène, some message in it that she refused to read.

His voice even harder and flatter than his eyes, he added nastily when she disdained to speak to him,

"That is, Madame, if you would see your brother before tomorrow's trial and its inevitable ending on a blood-soaked scaffold!"

"Luc! Goddess, I must go to him."

The words broke from her, unable to remain silent any longer in the face of the ghastly image drawn so vividly by de Marillec's suddenly brutal voice, and turning her back on the hateful man, she looked pleadingly at the princess.

"By your leave, your highness?"

"Of course you must go to him," Linette assured her. "Return to your duties when..."

She faltered, before continuing with barely a tremor in her tone,

"When you are able."

"Thank you, your highness."

And without looking directly at de Marillec.

"Where is he, Messire?"

"I will take you to him."

"You..."

Juliène paused, her contemptuous gaze fixed on the man standing before her, long hair lank and loose, devoid now of the spark of flame she thought she had glimpsed earlier, his face pale where it was not bruised yellow or purple.

Gone was the fine-boned beauty of the man she had seen on that white beach lapped by the lapis waters of the southern sea, and yet she remembered all too vividly what he had been meant to do there... and with the recollection of how he had in all probability betrayed her brother, even though it had been at her own connivance, her distaste and anger arose anew.

"You think I would go anywhere with the vile, disgusting degenerate you have proved yourself to be?"

De Marillec shrugged what she knew to be deceptively slender shoulders, his fine sword-steel strength hidden beneath a dirty leather jerkin and stinking, blood-stained linen.

"Not willingly perhaps," he drawled in answer to her accusation.

Expressive light brown brows, devoid of all charcoal colouring, lifted as he continued with languid irony,

"But like it or not, Madame, you will not get to see Luc without me. Though if it makes you feel any easier, the Eldest will accompany you and protect you from any possible contamination by my dissolute person on the way there. And once we reach the place where your brother is, I am sure that my Lady Adèle – who, if I am honest, views me with much the same distaste as you yourself do – will be only too happy to perform a similar service."

To Rowène's unspoken relief, Adèle had not wasted time searching through the medicine chest but had simply brought the whole box down to Joscelin's quarters instead, though even then it had taken Rowène several moments of poking, with equal parts urgency and reluctance, through the myriad cedar-lined compartments before she found that which she was seeking.

That achieved she stood, staring down at the three scarlet seeds, vivid and bright against the skin of her palm as tiny pin-pricks of blood, while Adèle watched her from the other side of the brazier, her blue eyes troubled as if only now wondering whether her tacit connivance in Rowène's actions would destroy her lord-by-binding as surely as the man he loved.

Unable to meet her friend's accusing gaze for more than a few heartbeats, Rowène closed her eyes, conjuring up the image of her brother as he had appeared the last time she had seen him before today.

That day of spring sunshine, apple blossom breeze, primrose-starred grass and bright, bird-song skies when he had unexpectedly appeared in Lasceynes, come to visit his sister and sisters' children before the start of the campaigning season.

Clear and vital against the darkness of her closed lids, she saw him again, tall and lean and laughing. The harsh lines that duty, responsibility and the life of a hunted outlaw had carved upon his face erased by a rarely expressed joy in living as he and Val raced their mounts through the walnut groves below the castle.

Later yet Rowène had seen his grey eyes warm with love and pride as he praised the progress Lissie had made in the herbal she was doggedly writing and illustrating in her still unformed hand.

Whatever other losses and betrayals Luc had suffered, Rowène knew that he held her daughter and Juliène's son close to his heart, as dear to him – perhaps even dearer – than any children of his own body would have been. She knew too that Luc would do anything, not only to ensure their continuing freedom, but also that their innocence remained intact and untainted.

Anything. Even to giving up his own life.

Which was, she realised, exactly what he had done.

She knew of instinct – the bond that linked her by blood, mind, heart and soul to her brother – that once Luc had accepted that there would be no escape, no reprieve from the end awaiting him and that ultimately his body or his will would fail, he had made his peace with the gods and had then concentrated on holding out as long as he could, finally yielding to the pressure of unimaginable pain only when Joscelin had been brought to his cell and would know what he said.

According to Josce, Luc had allowed Joffroi de Rogé's torturers the illusion that they had broken their prisoner and dragged from him the answers to all the questions their master had asked, including the names of the other outlaws who had once followed Luc and the whereabouts of their former hideouts in Lasceynes Forest. None of which information was like to do much harm now.

But Luc had also – after a long look begging forgiveness from Joscelin – acknowledged that he knew Josce to be his father's son, albeit pretending to a contempt and hatred for his half-brother so venomous that even Joscelin had been half-convinced of its veracity.

Caring for nothing then beyond earning the death that would put him beyond all pain, Luc had gone on to confess to any and all of the crimes of which he stood accused – including theft, highway robbery, murder, and sodomy – some of which he was in truth guilty of, and finally the one that he was not. The one that would take him to the scaffold. Treason against the crown.

Triumphant as de Rogé had been at his seeming victory, he had nonetheless had to admit defeat when it came to discovering the location of Luc's sisters' children. For that was the one piece of information that Luc had refused to yield up.

Lissie and Val were dead, he had insisted, at the hands of de Rogé's hell-hounds, and according to Josce nothing that had been done to him had been able to make him retract that statement.

All of which had brought Luc to his present position, broken and bleeding and on the very border of death. A death he would either go to tomorrow by royal command, in further ignominy and pain or – if Juliène did not come, as appeared increasingly likely given the length of time Gabriel and Lady Céline had been gone – tonight with Rowène's sorrowing assistance.

She looked again at the seeds of the mortiana lily, scarlet as blood, glanced once more at the closed door through which she had given up hope that her sister would ever walk, then back towards the open door of the bedchamber, where she could just glimpse the bed upon which Luc lay, closely watched over by Joscelin and Ranulf.

Then with an almost silent sigh, and under Adèle's horrified gaze, she tilted her hand.

Rather than slipping easily into the black potion below, however, the seeds seemed to cling to the skin of her sweating palm, and even as Rowène gave a muffled curse of despair and reached out with her free hand to dislodge the deadly seeds, the sound of a latch lifting made her glance over her shoulder to see first Gabriel, then the Eldest hasten through the doorway, another figure clinging to the concealing shadows behind.

"Ju! You came!"

Rowène spoke before she thought and saw the indistinct form stiffen and jerk forwards, green eyes wide in a face even paler than usual, scorn hardening her gaze as she looked her sister up and down, surveying her masculine clothing with contempt.

A derision that only deepened in the moment when Juliène recognised that the linen shirt and the mulberry and blue tunic Rowène was wearing could only belong to Gabriel de Marillec, though the garments were considerably cleaner than anything the man himself was wearing.

"*You!* And *him!* I should have guessed!"

"Yes, me," Rowène said shortly in response to her sister's excoriating exclamation, ignoring the second part of the unsavoury implication.

She took a step away from the brazier, and with the deadly seeds suddenly vanished from sight, wiped her burning hand on a fold of her borrowed tunic.

"Surely you did not expect me to stay away when Luc is *this close...*"

She held up her thumb and forefinger, barely a whisper of air between them.

"To death."

Thus bluntly reminded of the reason for her presence, Juliène flinched and demanded shakily,

"I want to see him. You... you just keep out of my sight."

Rowène sighed, shrugged, and stepped back, catching Lady Céline's eye as she did so.

"Very well, I will leave it to the Eldest to show you where Luc lies."

"This way, my lady," the older woman murmured.

And with another look of flashing scorn split raggedly between Gabriel and Rowène, Juliène followed her grey-robed guide towards the bedchamber, Gabriel treading silently afterwards, his bruised face set hard with purpose, leaving Rowène to glance sideways at Adèle to see how well she was bearing the strain of her lord's actions – and it was abundantly clear that the strain was severe indeed.

Yet even as Rowène started to walk towards her friend, hoping to offer the gods only knew what by way of comfort, she jolted to a halt as she heard her sister cry out in shock and horror and a heart-wrenching pain.

"Oh, gods, Luc! What have they done to you?"

Without volition, Rowène limped the few steps to the bedchamber door, entering to find her sister clinging to the nearest bedpost, her gaze fixed on the broken body beneath the crimson-stained sheet.

The next moment Rowène saw Ju reach out one trembling hand towards the fingers that lay atop the sheet, roughly splinted and bandaged in bloody linen, only to withdraw without touching her brother, instead bringing her hands up to cover her mouth as if to hold back the tide of nausea that had already overwhelmed the rest of them on seeing the state to which Luc had been reduced.

Tears filling her eyes and spilling down her blanched cheeks, Juliène turned to glare around at the grim faces surrounding the bed.

"How could you do this to him? You are all culpable! All of you!"

The furious green gaze sought out Rowène first, as she had known it must do.

"You! You let *him...*"

Splintered emerald shot through the candlelit shadows to land on Joscelin's stony countenance.

"Do this! And *him!*"

The bright, jewel-hard glance flicked out like a lash towards Gabriel's lividly-scarred but otherwise wraith-pale face.

"And *him!*"

She turned on the big, fair-haired figure maintaining a silent, narrow-eyed guard at the far side of the bed, arms folded across his broad chest, seemingly the least moved of them all by the tirade of poisonous accusation engulfing every corner of the chamber.

Trembling hands fisted in the flowing green velvet skirts of her gown, Juliène turned her attention back to Joscelin, stalking around the bed until she stood right in front of him, head tilted back so as to be able to direct her venom straight up into his set face.

"You miserable, base-born cur! How cold and heartless are you that you could torture him so cruelly! Your own blood! Your *brother!* Or was that the reason? For revenge! Because he is our father's only legitimate and much beloved son? Whereas you can never be more than Lucius de Chartreux's chance-got and unacknowledged *bastard!*"

"And you!"

She returned her attention to Ranulf, glaring across the bed at him when Joscelin gave her no answer beyond an icily impenetrable stare down the length of his long de Chartreux nose.

"*You* stood by and let this happen. Why? Is it that you were jealous of Luc because he has taken your place in Val's life? Because he is your son's father in all but name!"

Ranulf regarded his son's mother for a moment in silence, his dark blue eyes so black with anger that for a suffocating heartbeat Rowène thought he would try to strangle her sister, only releasing her hard-held breath when she saw that he remained rigidly under control, his only response a low, snarled,

"Speak for yourself, you twisted bitch!"

Couched in the Rogé dialect as it was, the exact translation clearly passed Juliène by, though the tone was enough to make her pause and stare at her former lover in suspicion. Unfortunately, it was not sufficient to halt her venomous round of accusation as finally she came to a halt before Gabriel's slender figure.

"And you," she hissed. "You did this to him. To the man you were supposed to love! Why? Out of shame because you had betrayed him in another's bed? Another's body?"

Beneath the ragged red scar and the purple-green bruising surrounding it, Gabriel's face was as white and bloodless as Luc's, his amber eyes so deeply steeped in pain Rowène could feel it in her own flesh.

But even as she stepped forwards in an attempt to shield him from Juliène's vicious attack, another voice made itself heard.

Rough, halting, barely audible it caused them all to turn with varying degrees of hope and incredulity towards the figure in the bed.

"Ju... no... it was not... like that..."

"Luc! Oh, Luc! Goddess be thanked, you can hear me, you are with me still."

With which, Juliène flung herself onto her knees beside the bed, sobbing wildly, her hands reaching out for her brother's, though she did not dare take hold of them until slowly, awkwardly, the splinted fingers moved to cover hers.

"Ju... sweeting... do not... weep. Listen... to me..."

Something in that grey thread of a voice must have penetrated her hysteria for she raised her head from the coverlet, revealing a blotched and swollen face so utterly unlike her normal lily-cool beauty that none seeing it could doubt the sincerity of her love for her brother.

"What is it, Luc? Tell me. You want me to avenge you? Visit on these miserable curs the pain they have dealt out to you. I swear to you that I will see them suffer a thousand-fold..."

"No, Ju!"

Momentarily there was steel in his tone.

"What?"

She looked at him, bewilderment in the luminous, leaf-green eyes, tears sparkling in the candlelight like raindrops in the sun.

"But surely..?"

"No..." Luc reiterated breathlessly. "None of this... is... their fault. Not Josce... not Rafe... not... Ré."

Juliène shook her head.

"I do not believe you. De Veraux must have given the order. And de Marillec is his Second, whilst *he*..."

She glared across the bed at Ranulf.

"He is their loyal lap-dog, servicing their whims, following their commands."

Luc moved his head infinitesimally against the pillow, the lank tangled rat tails of ragged black hair dragging across the white linen.

"It was... not them."

"I do not believe you," Juliène repeated.

"Believe it," Rowène snapped, her small stock of patience with her sister systematically shredded by every baseless accusation she had thrown at them.

"Gods above, Ju! Do you have so little faith in Luc's word that you would question it now? I thought you loved him. Certainly you have trusted him to raise your son all these years."

"I do love him!" Juliène cried, green eyes glaring again. "I just..."

Then turning her back on Rowène.

"So if not them, then who did do this to you? Luc, only tell me and I will believe it. I swear it!"

"Who else but... Joffroi de Rogé," came the agonised gasp. "And he will do... as much again... to Val... to your son... if he can..."

"No, no, no."

Juliène collapsed against the bed, sobbing in disbelief, until slowly – as she came to accept that Luc spoke the truth – disbelief changed to fear, and finally grief when she looked up to see why her brother had said no more and realised that his eyes were closed, his breathing shallower and far more ragged than it had been when she had first entered the room.

"Oh, gods! Goddess! He is not..."

"No, child."

Lady Céline spoke with a gentle compassion Rowène knew herself incapable of offering her sister. Just as she would never be able to forgive Ju for what she had said to Joscelin or Ranulf or Gabriel.

"He is not gone from us," the Eldest continued softly. "Though I fear it will not be long. Until then, you may stay and keep watch over him, if you wish it."

"And if you can hold your vicious tongue," Ranulf growled, in Mithlondian this time. "Otherwise I swear I will throw you out myself, whatever our respected healer says."

Juliène threw a look of loathing at her son's father and pushed to her feet. Then, glancing back at the barely-moving figure of her brother, said flatly,

"No, this cannot be. I will not lose him now."

With that she reached out and grabbed hold of Rowène's arm, sharp nails digging into her skin through the rough linen of her shirtsleeve.

"Do something, Ro!" she demanded. "You are a healer. You have the power of the Faennari. You can save him!"

Rowène wrenched her arm free and jerked her head towards the door to the main living chamber.

"Come with me. I am not having this conversation here, Ju."

A dozen heartbeats later Rowène stood facing her sister over the banked heat of the brazier.

Picking up the singed rag, she wrapped it about her hand and carefully dislodging the small pot from the glowing embers, placed it on the nearby table.

"What is that?" Juliène asked, regarding the steaming surface of the dark liquid with distaste. "And why have you brought me here?"

"That black draught holds freedom from pain for Luc. And what I have to say to you should be kept between us two, we who are of the blood of the Faennari."

"Then you *can* save him?"

Suddenly the green eyes were burning with a wild hope, all the old animosity for her sister abandoned.

"No, I can not," Rowène said stonily.

"But you said..."

"I told you once before that I cannot restore life once the daemons of death have taken a grip, and that still holds true. Luc is already in their embrace whether you want to admit it or not. All I, or any other mortal healer, can do is make his passing easier."

"Then what was the point of bringing me out here?" Juliène exclaimed petulantly. "Or did you just want to prevent me from sharing Luc's last precious moments of life? Because I accused your brutish lover and your filthy bastard brother of treachery? Because I made that wretched worm, de Marillec, face up to the truth about himself?"

"How can you think that I would deny you what comfort you can gain from being with Luc at this time," Rowène sighed. "None of us would. Not even after your little spat of poison earlier. Believe me, Josce and Rafe and R... Gabriel expect nothing else from you."

"Then why am I out here with you, and not in there with Luc?"

"Forget your own wishes for a moment, Ju, and listen to me. *I* cannot give Luc back his life but there is a chance that he can be saved. By one whose powers of healing are far greater than anything I could ever aspire to."

"You mean..."

"Yes, the goddess whose fey blood legend has it that we share. And for that I need your help..."

"You have it, Ro. Anything. Just tell me."

And for the first time since seeing the state to which Luc had been reduced, Rowène dared to feel something that was akin to hope...

"So this is the path you mean to take?"

The serene voice came from behind her.

"I wondered if it would come to this."

Glancing over her shoulder, Rowène saw Lady Céline standing just inside the doorway, and behind her, all the others who had followed the grey-robed healer from the bedchamber.

"Tell me, what must we do, child?"

"No," Gabriel snapped before Rowène had a chance to say the words herself. "You cannot involve yourself in this, Eldest."

His gaze swept his companions, his eyes turning from warm amber to glowing citrine as he spoke.

"Nor can any of you. Believe me that way lies madness and death. I have seen it in my dreams."

Then he looked at Rowène, visibly bracing himself before adding,

"But *I* can take that path. And I will. If the goddess demands a life in place of his, I will gladly give her mine, since if it were not for me, Luc would not be here now, on the brink of death."

"We all failed him," Joscelin put in harshly.

His bleak grey gaze settled momentarily on his adder-tongued half-sister.

"We are all guilty. Juliène was right in that, however much Luc may deny it."

"Enough self-recrimination," Rowène put in sharply. "Yes, we failed him. And he... I hate to say it, but Luc knew the risks, and still took them. For a cause he thought worthwhile."

She did not look at Gabriel.

She did not need to, attuned as they were.

"But if we are to do this, we must do it now. Gabriel is right though, it is never less than dangerous to have dealings with the deities who rule the realms of earth and sky, life and death..."

"Hush, Ro, we know the dangers," Joscelin put in. "You do not rid yourself of us so easily."

"Then you are determined to stay? All of you?"

A ripple of nods and a low murmur of masculine agreement from her kinsmen confirming their decision, she glanced once more at Gabriel before turning to Lady Céline and Adèle.

"You should go now, both of you."

"Go?" Adèle repeated blankly as her blue gaze briefly sought out the slight form of her lord before returning to Rowène.

"Are you speaking for yourself, Ro, or for my lord – oh yes, I saw the look that passed between you, I know you can hear each other's thoughts – so perhaps it is not you but rather he who orders my departure. Well, Gabriel? Do you wish me to go?"

"It is not my decision," he replied tonelessly. "But if it was... well, it is as Ro says, you should not be involved in this."

"Because Luc is your..."

"No," he interrupted, his voice and manner strained almost to breaking. "Not because of what is between him and me, but rather because it is madness for you to involve yourself in a desperate venture such as this. Not when you share neither Luc's blood nor that of the Faennari."

"And you are telling me *you* do?" Adèle demanded in disbelief.

In reply, Gabriel held up his right hand, palm outwards.

In the chancy candlelight it was impossible to see the faded white scar of a decades-old blood-oath but the implication was obvious enough to cause Adèle to lose what little colour anger had flagged in her cheeks.

Flinching, she glanced down at her own palm and the mark of the binding oath she had sworn with the man who had, in his youth, sworn a different oath with another...

And with this realisation her chin came up, her blue eyes no longer the soft, beckoning blue of a summer sky but hard and flat as a sheet of winter water.

"Then since you and I swore a blood-oath I must also share your lover's blood. So I will stay and, if I can, help save his life..."

She took a ragged breath.

"For *you*, my lord."

She swallowed before continuing unsteadily,

"But if he lives beyond tomorrow's dawn, and Joscelin finds a way to get him away from the palace... then I would ask you to give me a child! If you do that... then I will release you from the terms of our binding and you may go to him with my blessing."

"And I too shall stay, though I put no conditions on my help," Lady Céline put in.

Her normally quiet voice resounded clearly in the stunned silence that followed Adèle's extraordinary statement, and firm enough that even had Gabriel recovered sufficiently from his shock to argue further he would not have done so.

Then, turning to hold Rowène's eyes, almost daring her to object, Joscelin's mother added softly,

"Luc is my son, by love if not by blood. I could not save his father, but if there is any chance at all that I can help to save Lucius' son, I will not turn away."

She glanced once, with rueful apology, at Joscelin, her true son, but he only shrugged as if expecting no less and said curtly,

"You may as well let her stay, Ro. You only waste breath and time trying to make her leave."

He looked then at Adèle, flushed as her lord was pale, and trembling with emotion.

"If you do truly wish to help Luc, Madame, you may stay too."

His voice roughened to a deep rasp.

"But the gods help you if you mean him harm."

Apparently satisfied by her silence that he had made his point, Joscelin turned back to Rowène.

"What do you need us to do, Ro?"

"First, before we even set foot on this path I need to know whether you have thought of a way to get Luc out of the palace without incurring Linnius' wrath or the High Counsel's suspicion?"

"I have."

Not so much as a flicker of uncertainty showed in Joscelin's grey eyes or crossed his hard face as he gave her this assurance and Rowène could do no other than take him at his word.

"Very well then, but I must warn you all that what we are about to do carries no guarantee of success, no surety that some if not all of us will not be walking the sunset path alongside Luc. I want you to understand that, and that each and every one of you is free to leave now, before it is too late to turn back."

One last time she turned to look them all in the eye, one by one, gauging their readiness, their determination, their willingness to sacrifice some part of themselves.

Josce and Gabriel she had no doubts about, or Ranulf either, but Dominic was so young and besides he barely knew his uncle.

As for Adèle, she had a far simpler test to pass – the sincerity of her desire to help a man she had no cause to love – but somewhat to Rowène's surprise, the blue eyes met her grimly questioning gaze without flinching, though the soft voice was less sure.

"N... now w... what?" Adèle asked, somewhat shakily.

"Now," Rowène replied. "We do what we must to save Luc's life."

She took a deep breath.

"And because of who he is, we must reach out beyond the waiting daemons, beyond the silent gods who have no power over the darkness of the night, to call down the healer of souls, the silver lady of the stars, none other than the Moon Goddess of the Faennari herself."

Verse 4

Mourning Veils About The Moon

The notion of calling down a goddess sounded terrifying but commenced in an almost disappointingly ordinary manner.

Or so Adèle thought as she watched Rowène rummaging through her half-brother's small clutter of possessions, apparently searching for the silver goblet that Prince Marcus had presented Joscelin with all those years ago when he had been promoted to the position of Second of the Guardians, an action that had probably been the prince's last formal pronouncement before his death.

Whilst Rowène was pursuing her quest – accompanied by caustic reminiscences regarding the time she had spent at court, much of it in her half-brother's quarters – Dominic had been despatched to fill a bucket with snow, and then, the goblet eventually being unearthed, Joscelin somewhat sheepishly undertook to polish all trace of tarnish from the neglected vessel, finally revealing the exquisite engraving beneath.

This task being completed to her satisfaction, Rowène cleared a space amidst the rolls of parchment and other rubbish on her half-brother's writing table and set the goblet down, the polished surface shining almost as bright a silver as the moon outside, the winged horse of Mithlondia seeming about to take flight in the flickering glow of the candle flames.

Unable to make any further progress until Dominic came back, Rowène had returned to the bedroom where the Eldest was keeping watch in her stead, leaving Adèle to stare pensively at the goblet and Juliène to pace restlessly up and down the main chamber, clearly impatient for the boy's return.

Nor did she hesitate to turn all her pent-up ire on the lad when Dominic finally appeared, white crystals clinging to the shoulders and folds of his cloak, dark hair gleaming with melted snow, cheeks nipped red by the icy cold.

"Where have you been, you wretched boy?" Juliène demanded crossly.

"Do you think we have all night to wait on a mere servant's pleasure?"

"Pardon, my lady," the lad replied with a look of baffled dislike. "The snow in the courtyard was filthy to say the least of it, having been trampled, pissed and shat on by several score men and horses over the past few days. Jacques... Lady Rowène, I should say..."

Here the poor boy's cheeks burned even redder than warranted by his foray into the chilly outdoors – or his descent into vulgarity in a noblewoman's presence, for which little lapse Adèle freely forgave him since it clearly annoyed Juliène as much as his respectful attitude towards her disreputable sister.

"Lady Rowène requested only the purest, most pristine clean snow," Dominic continued his explanation in a flat, unfriendly tone. "And so I went out into the gardens where it has been untouched since the last snowfall."

Juliène turned away with a scornful huff, just as Rowène came to thank the lad with a warm smile, brushing a hand over the sleeve of his tunic as she did so, and exclaiming as she realised he was soaked through. At which point Dominic rather ruefully admitted he had misjudged the depth of snow and had fallen headlong into it.

Seeing his involuntary shiver, the Eldest took swift charge, urging him to go and change out of his wet clothes while she set some wine to mull against his return.

By the time this remedy against a potential chill had been administered, Rowène had melted the snow over the other brazier and was carefully decanting the pure liquid thus obtained into the silver goblet.

Then, with everyone gathered once more in the bedchamber, arranged in some specific order seemingly known only to Rowène, she directed Dominic to open the windows and Rafe to douse the candles, leaving them enclosed in a darkness lit only by the slanting rays of the midwinter moon.

"Now what, Ro?" Joscelin asked quietly, his deep voice breaking the tense silence that now bound them all in the silver-edged shadows.

"A brother's blood, if you will give it."

His eyes seemed to narrow for the briefest of heartbeats at his half-sister's reply but there was no hesitation in the hand that dropped to the hilt of the dagger sheathed at his belt.

Pressing the lethally sharp point of the blade to the calloused forefinger of his left hand, he waited until a droplet of blood welled up, black in the moonlight.

"Is this what you need, Ro?"

"It is. Three drops, no more, no less. Here..."

As Rowène made to carry the goblet of water to Joscelin, the Eldest reached out to take it from her.

"Let me do this, dear one."

Reluctantly allowing the older woman her way, Rowène watched as Joscelin let three dark droplets fall into the water, then turned to the man standing silent and grimly watchful at her side, murmuring,

"Now you, Rafe."

The guardian having performed this task without word or fuss, Rowène next turned her compelling grey gaze on the lad standing wide-eyed by the open window, the frozen lake glittering under the moonlight at his back.

"And you too, Dominic. That is, if you do not mind."

"This... this will help my uncle?" the lad asked unsteadily, causing Adèle to start slightly at the implication of his speech.

"I hope so. If that which I saw in my dreams holds true."

While no-one else voiced the question – Joscelin and Rafe evidently trusting Rowène without the need for explanation – Adèle knew that it must be in all their minds, as it was in hers.

A curiosity Rowène now satisfied.

"Three times three, the blood of Luc's mortal kin... Josce, Rafe, and you, Nic."

Even as Joscelin's son held out a hand for his father's blade, Rowène was turning slightly, seeking out and holding Gabriel's feral stare as she continued softly,

"And three times three, the blood of the Luc's fey kin. That is Ju, and me... and *you*, Gabriel."

"Goddess, no! This cannot be!"

While Adèle certainly heard Juliène's startled hiss of horrified comprehension it was, gods knew, nothing to the feeling she herself was experiencing as her frantic gaze sought out her lord-by-binding, her lips soundlessly spinning his name,

"Gabriel!"

She could not see him in the gathering darkness.

He was indistinguishable, a shifting, silent, silver-grey shadow, nebulous, untouchable, no more than illusion.

Just as the once solid floor of Joscelin's quarters seemed now to be without foundation, shattering beneath her, a thousand wickedly sharp segments of jagged stone opening about the abyss into which she felt herself tumbling... helpless to save herself from the realisation that the man she had lived alongside for the past four years was as much a stranger to her now as he had been on the day she had first sworn the binding oath with him five years before.

She had not known him then.

She wondered if she ever would?

Then abruptly, as if by some power outside herself, the flagstones were firm beneath her feet again, and she found she could see again, faces and forms once more clear in the wash of moonlight.

Glancing around, she caught Rowène's eye on her, saw the faint frown drawing the dark copper brows together, moonlight catching in the tousled curls as she cocked her head, waking a hint of the same glint that Adèle had occasionally seen in Gabriel's hair, despite the care he had taken to hide it from everyone. Including her.

And she, gods help her, she had let him!

Dear God of Light, how did I not see it before?

The truth had been there before her every day that she and Gabriel had been together.

In his changeable citrine-gold eyes.

In the flicker of bronze-red fire amidst the light brown of hair and brows and lashes... of stubble and chest hair... and that other...

"Damn it all, Adèle! You told me you knew what he was!"

Rowène's terse rebuke cut through her hysteria, honed with an exasperated edge that rubbed Adèle's already sore heart raw.

"I thought I did!" Adèle snapped. "Quite clearly, I was wrong!"

Her gaze turned back towards her lord-by-binding for the briefest of broken heartbeats.

"Indeed I must congratulate you, my lord, on deceiving me – along with the rest of the realm – so well as to your true nature. And to think I did my utmost to save you from the vultures of the High Counsel, out of a mistaken loyalty to the truth that I thought was between us!"

Gabriel flinched at the implied accusation but before he could protest or explain – always supposing he had even intended to –

Juliène's voice, brittle as parchment-thin ice, reminded Adèle that others beside herself might have an interest in Gabriel's secrets.

"Goddess, Ro! Are you trying to tell us that *he* is of the blood of the Faennari? And that you would treat him as our equal? Are you mad?"

"I am not going to debate this with you, Ju," Rowène retorted sharply. "You will just have to take my word for it. And next time you see Gabriel in the full light of day, actually look at the man – with an open mind rather than this unseemly contempt the Winter Lady has bred in you. Look him in the eye, look into his soul, and then tell me that I am wrong."

"I think on balance I would rather take your not-always-reliable word that he is what you say he is," Juliène replied with an unrepentant sneer. "A cursed half-thing, neither mortal nor fey. Rather than look the... man, did you call him... in the eye. Such an action would require me to come within at least six feet of the filthy, cowardly cur and nothing on this earth would induce me to do that after this night."

"Believe me, Madame, the feeling is entirely mutual," Gabriel cut in, his light voice uncharacteristically crisp. "But if I am willing to tolerate your treacherous company, perhaps you can contrive to ally yourself with me. For if I am a cursed half-fey, so are you. And if you still have difficulty in accepting my blood, just remind yourself for whose sake we are joined in this uneasy alliance."

And in case Juliène had missed the point, Rafe chose that moment to add impatiently,

"Just take the bloody knife, Juliène, and stop arguing! Or do you refuse to spill three drops of your precious blood to save Luc's life?"

"Just as long as no-one expects me to do likewise for *her*," Juliène snarled, snatching the knife from the soldier and glaring over the bloodstained blade at her sister.

"Or *him!*"

Green eyes glittering bright and hard as frosted emeralds in the silver light, she cast one last look of scathing contempt and burning hatred at Gabriel, causing Adèle to shiver anew.

It was only then that the anger and pain she had felt, following the revelation of this last secret her lord-by-binding had been concealing from her, began almost imperceptibly to refine into some other, far less readily recognisable, emotion.

That had been then.

Now, uncounted aeons later, Adèle still shivered, this time with cold rather than fear, huddled in the unlit darkness of the bedchamber, unnoticed – or more likely ignored – by the others in the room, all of whom shared either a bond of blood or affection with Luc de Chartreux, whereas she most definitely could make claim to neither.

She had come here initially for Rowène's sake and had remained, yielding to the sense of horrified pity that had assailed her when she had first glimpsed the state of the man in the bed. For no decent man – and for all her dislike she could not deny de Chartreux that accolade – should have to endure what had been done to him.

And having stayed, she could not deny that it had hurt to have her presence looked upon with indifference by the man whose binding band she wore, as heavy and cold now as when she had first put it on, though in the intervening years she had almost ceased to notice its weight as she and Gabriel had managed to make some sort of life together.

Now, however, the oath they had sworn that autumn day nearly five and a half years ago was once more set at naught.

By her own doing just as much as his, she reflected unhappily, as she gave in and began to chafe her arms, goose-fleshed beneath the sensible layers of linen and wool, shivering again as the snow-sharp breath of the midwinter night flirted boldly about the hem of her gown, and whispered insidiously across her cheek, curling like a cold hand about her throat, burning like an icy blade as loneliness stabbed deep into her heart.

She should, she supposed, be accustomed by now to being the outsider, and in these increasingly awkward circumstances should be more than content to be shunned, shut out, set aside... at least until she could come to terms with what she had just learned.

Not only about herself, but Gabriel as well.

And found that the mere voicing of his given name in her mind was sufficient cause to make her cringe, the shudder rippling through her utterly unrelated to the snow-laden chill that had long-since penetrated to every corner of this freezing cold crypt of a chamber.

God of Light! What have I done?

Even now she could not quite believe the demand she had made – heedless of the others in the room, not all of whom she accounted friend – that Gabriel give her a child! And then, if that were not humiliation enough, she had gone on to tell him that if he did that, she would set him free to be with his lover!

Truly she must have taken leave of her senses.

Yet even worse than that piece of reckless self-betrayal was the discovery that Gabriel, the man she thought she had known – the man who had become her friend, if never her lover... unless he came reluctantly to her bed now as the price of his freedom – in the end she had not known him at all.

I know what he is.

Foolishly, she had said those words to Rowène scant days before, believing them to be true.

Yet now, tonight, she had finally realised how wrong – how blindly, stupidly, wilfully wrong – she had been!

The bitter truth was that she had known *nothing* of Gabriel's darker secret.

The secret Rowène obviously did know.

Had, in all probability, always known.

The secret that threatened Gabriel's sanity rather than merely his life.

A truth, she now realised, she should have seen long since.

If only she had not been so blinkered by the open secret of his love for Luc de Chartreux, then surely she would have been able to see Gabriel de Marillec for who – and what – he really was.

The same man she had seen – really seen for the first time tonight – only after the candles had been blown out, leaving them here, in a darkness lit only by the light of the midwinter moon, tense and waiting for...

Well, Rowène and her sister might have some notion as to how a goddess would respond to their pleas. Adèle herself could make no such claim.

Indeed, she was not even sure she believed in the existence of this mythical deity, and the power she supposedly held within her shining hands.

That way lies madness.

So Gabriel had warned them, the grim words no more than the simple truth, gods help them all.

For who knew who, out of all of them, would be blessed enough to see the sun rise on another day.

She had thought at times over the past few days that perhaps she did not care much whether she lived or died but now, dear God of Mercy, how she longed for light, and warmth.

For life.

For primroses in the spring, harebells in the summer.

For blue skies and green meadows, for streams sparkling in the autumn sunlight, children laughing as they splashed in the shallows, fair-haired and free.

Lissie and Val, she told herself. Yet in her heart she knew it was not her friend's children she yearned to watch at play.

She wanted – had wanted for so many barren years during which she had lied both to herself and her lord – a child of her own. Girl or boy, it mattered not. As long as he or she was not cursed at birth, as the man who would provide the seed that gave them life had been...

She shivered again, momentarily drawing a glinting glance from her lord-by-binding, almost as if he had sensed the direction of her thoughts, and unable to meet his burning gaze, bright as golden flame, she looked quickly away.

Whether he had finally cast off the cloak he had, for the most part, kept wrapped about his inner self, or whether their quest to call down the silver Goddess of the Faennari had lit him from the inside, she thought he had never seemed so distant and untouchable.

As distant and untouchable as the glittering stars themselves.

Gabriel Aurélien de Marillec.

The man she had never fully known until this night.

And, God of Light, *how* she wished this seemingly interminable night were over... one way or the other.

How many candle notches, Adèle wondered, had burned down since Juliène had arrived in a whirl of green velvet, tears and acrimonious accusations? That had been some time after the first watch of evening and it was now close to midnight. Or so she judged, casting another glance out of the open window at the star-scattered sky, wherein the full moon – myth, or in truth the manifestation of a forbidden deity – shone in shimmering silver splendour, as remote and indifferent to mortal pain as it had ever been.

Not even aware that she was shivering again, Adèle started as, unseen and unheard, a man came up beside her, draping a bergamot-scented mantle about her inadequately-covered shoulders.

Gabriel.

Even as his name rose unbidden to her lips, the sight of the bitter twist to his finely-shaped mouth strangled all sound before she could speak.

"You are still my lady, Adèle," he murmured. "And I have not yet foresworn my duty to care for you."

Duty, she repeated on a silent sigh.

Ah well, if that was all there was between them, then it would undoubtedly be his *duty* to get her with child if his lover lived.

And if de Chartreux died?

She sighed again, thinking it very likely that Gabriel would find some way of accompanying him on his journey beyond the sunset. Or wherever it was that those of the blood of the Faennari went once the daemons of death had finished weaving their dark shrouds.

Whereas she would take a completely different path when her time came.

Struck by the loneliness of that thought, she cast a frowning glance towards the silver-edged shadows masking the far side of the bed where she knew Rowène had taken up position.

It was only then that Adèle realised that, in spite of the borrowed shirt, breeches and boots, she had no trouble thinking of the other woman as Rowène rather than Jacques. Almost as if whatever powers of enchantment her fey friend usually wielded were fully engaged in maintaining her brother's frail grip on life rather than her own protective disguise.

Indeed, when seen in the last flicker of candlelight, Rowène had been holding her brother's bandaged fingers within her own as she half sat upon the bed, leaning against the supporting strength of the guardian, Rafe of Oakenleigh.

Remembering that now, it seemed most blatantly obvious to Adèle that there was some intimacy well beyond friendship between those two, though how that might have been forged she had no notion, given their respective stations and allegiances.

It also occurred to Adèle to wonder whether the brutish, base-born guardian and the high-born, half-fey healer might not be making the most of the opportunities life sent them, knowing that they too must be separated in death.

Just as she and Gabriel would be, even more so than they were in life.

And death, she concluded, would come sooner rather than later at this rate since they were all like to freeze into corpses before morning!

Teeth chattering, she shivered violently as a whirl of wintry wind whipped across the floor to insinuate itself beneath the hem of her gown, adding another layer of ice to her feet in their soft leather slippers, her legs despite her woollen stockings mere frozen lumps of goose-pimpled flesh.

She doubted she would ever be warm again, and indeed could only wonder at the stoical indifference demonstrated by her companions.

As it was, if it were not for the fact that she could hear the rasping breaths of the dying man, still faintly audible over Juliène's eerie singing, she might have supposed de Chartreux to have succumbed to the lethal cold already.

Yet surely he could not last much longer in such bleak and bitter conditions?

Gods, please gods, give him the strength to survive.

And by the heedless depth of her anxiety did Adèle judge just how desperately she was willing him not to die.

Whether because if he did, Gabriel would scarcely feel obliged to fulfill her expectations – the thought of how he might accomplish this making her tremble with something other than cold...

"Do be still, Adèle!"

Juliène's irritated hiss momentarily replaced her unintelligible song.

"Or else leave with my goodwill. Goddess knows this calling is difficult enough, even aided by those who perceive the starlight within the shadows, let alone with those blind mortals who do not for an audience! And while the bond of blood does give some strength to our plea, *you* have nothing..."

"Ju!"

The weary voice came from the other side of the bed, half rebuke, half plea.

"Oh, have it your own way, Ro. You always do."

Juliène's snap at her sister contained neither grace nor kindness.

"But be it on your head if we fail!"

The banked anger in her tone was easily sufficient to scorch her sister and still have heat left over with which to singe Adèle.

"As for you, stay if you must. Just do not distract me again."

"I know this is hard for you, my dear."

The Eldest's voice came from close beside Adèle, the merest whisper of sound against her ear as the high, clear, utterly unearthly song began again.

"But endure if you can. Whatever is going to happen, it will be soon."

Pray gods the Eldest is right, this waiting is killing me.

That said, the long waiting silence was beginning to tell on everyone – though with the possible exception of young Dominic it would seem that they could all manage to conceal their bodily discomfort and bitter disappointment rather better than Adèle was contriving to do.

Of course, Adèle thought, Joscelin, Gabriel and Rafe were all soldiers, accustomed to holding themselves silent and still, while the Eldest's commitment to those in her care would enable her to watch over the sick – Adele would not allow herself to think the word *dying* – man for as long as it was needful...

"Look, something's happening to the moon!"

Dominic's voice, sharp and febrile with excitement or fear, disturbed the frozen forms gathered about the bed.

Turning slowly, barely able to move, but welcoming the excuse to make the attempt, Adèle saw that the lad was now leaning out of the open window, the better to see whatever it was he had noticed.

Then as she looked beyond him, she found herself sucking in an involuntary breath that sent ice crystals shattering through her frozen core as she realised what had caught his attention.

In contrast to the glittering clarity of the stars, the moon's brightness was dimming as a shadow began to slip slowly but inexorably across the shining silver circle.

"What is it?" Dominic asked, his low murmur a mingling of confusion, doubt and dawning awe. "The wind has dropped, and there are no clouds to be blown even if there were. It's like those dark veils the ladies wear, almost as if..."

He shook his head, unable to finish his thought.

"As if the goddess is already mourning the loss of one of her sons," the Eldest said quietly.

Mourning veils the moon...

Like the scarce-heard music of a harper's song, the words whispered through Adèle's mind but she did not – could not – speak them aloud.

Not when Gabriel was staring out of the window, hands braced on the frost-sparkling sill, his gaze directed across the glimmering frozen waters of the lake towards the now almost completely concealed moon, his face seen in the last shimmer of starlight revealing far too openly his heart-sick despair, and the soul-deep fear that the man he loved was already lost.

In the next breath the dark veils fell full across the face of the moon and the only light remaining came from the flickering silver sparks of the far distant stars, each the soul of a loved one long since gone beyond the sunset into the endless darkness, and where another shining flame must soon be lit.

"No! Gods, no!"

Gabriel's voice broke on that scarce-heard protest, and Adèle instinctively braced herself for the long-drawn wolf howl of desolated loss that would surely follow.

There was only silence, however.

And while Adèle was grateful to be spared this further humiliation she could not ignore the flashing knife-blade of jealousy that stabbed through her as she sensed the way that Rowène – the woman she had called friend – reached out to touch Gabriel's heart and mind, giving balm to his hurt in a way that was only possible because they shared the same fey bond of blood.

A bond to which Adele would always be the outsider, even though it was she who wore Gabriel's binding band and bore his name.

Almost as if drawn down by the desolate misery of her thoughts shrouds of darkness were suffusing the chamber, wrapping them all about so that they seemed to be swathed in the thickest of mourning veils, until the only thing anchoring Adele to any sense of place or self were the rasping breaths of the dying man.

Then, between one laboured breath and the next she realised that the darkness was lifting, and heard what was surely the most unexpected of sounds – a child's laugh of joyous delight – and felt a wave of fear and wonder and disbelief run through her like the ripple of moonlight riding the cresting waves of some far-off shore.

Hardly daring to move, caution warring with curiosity in her mind, Adèle glanced back at the window to find her view was no longer impeded by her lord's taut shoulders.

Blinking in disbelief, she saw what looked like a young girl, clad in the simplest of white, knee-length tunics playing some gentle game out on the frozen lake with, of all things, a pretty mist-grey kitten.

The child's wild, startlingly silver halo of hair was woven through with white star-flowers, and her small, dancing feet were *bare*.

Yet even as Adele started forward in helpless protest, the child caught the cat up, bestowed a kiss upon its furry forehead before setting it on its tiny feet.

Then having seemingly finished the game the child began to walk across the ice, as sure-footed as if treading a flower-filled meadow, towards the window that gave onto the darkened bedchamber, a white wraith-owl swooping past her shoulder to disappear into the night with a haunting cry.

With every pace they drew closer, both child and cat seemed to change infinitesimally, until the girl standing beside the wide-eyed, speechless young man keeping watch just inside the window's shadow seemed of an age with him.

No longer a carefree child but a young woman of grace and beauty, clad in a shimmering white gown that left uncovered her dainty feet, the silken fall of her waist-length hair adorned by a formal circlet of the same star flowers that had previously been scattered through her untamed tresses.

Granting the awestruck Dominic a smile over her shoulder as she glided effortlessly past him, the apparition advanced towards Adèle, the slender, graceful form changing shape once more, the belly beneath the pale draperies now as rounded as the full moon itself.

So that the lady, her silver-gilt hair now braided around her queenly head, who passed so close to Adèle appeared older, though no less radiant in her fecund fertility.

Did the forbidden Goddess of the Faennari – for Adèle could no longer doubt the evidence of her eyes – thus mock her desire to bear a child of her own? And not just any man's child, but one sired by the half-fey man whose binding band had once felt like a shackle about her wrist, but now felt as light as starshine.

To her awe and astonishment and dawning hope, Adèle saw the vision shake her head, and heard words take form in her mind in a voice like the muted murmur of a distant waterfall mingled with the delicate chiming of tiny silver bells,

Not mockery. A foretelling.

And heard herself reply,

Ah, Lady, can this be true? That Luc will live, and Gabriel come to me? If only for as long as it takes him to get me with child!

Alas, the goddess gifted her no further speech, pausing not in her gliding passage, the light of her footsteps a silvery sheen on the flag-stoned floor, until she stood tall and shining, an otherworldly beauty unveiled in a nimbus of light, all her wondrous power and might momentarily revealed to mortal eyes.

Stunned herself, Adele was scarcely surprised to see Joscelin, Gabriel, Rafe and Rowène sink down on bended knee, one after the other, heads bowed in homage, at the same time shielding their eyes from the silver light welling from that enchanted form, the flawless face filled now with a sternness of purpose, a gravity tempered by compassion.

Lastly the goddess turned towards Juliène, the only one of those gathered in that chamber who seemed to tremble with fear as well as the reverence that held them all.

After a long moment, during which the goddess held her eyes in silent conversation, Juliène bowed her head in acquiescence to the immortal being, whose face Adèle could now see held some slight but significant resemblance not only to Juliène and her mother but also – and far more disturbingly – to the fine-boned beauty still visible beneath the scars and bruising presently marring the face of Adèle's lord-by-binding.

Finally the shining figure – now almost too bright for any mortal eyes to bear – seemed to turn the brilliant perception of her gaze upon them all, one by on.

It was a moment that held no time and no touch at all of earthly reality. A moment of silent communication, of question asked and sacrifice offered.

Adèle knew what she herself had promised but what, she wondered, would the others yield of themselves to preserve Luc de Chartreux's life?

What would Joscelin give up for his half-brother?

Or Gabriel for the man he loved?

What would Luc's sisters sacrifice for his sake?

And would anything be asked of Rafe or Dominic or the Eldest, who when all was said and done were little more than bystanders?

Her curiosity was cut short abruptly, unanswered, as the goddess turned towards the grey-robed Sister of Mercy.

One slender graceful hand extended in imperious demand, she stood, wondrous beyond words, slender as a white birch, her robes the softly shimmering gossamer of moonlight on mist, her pure, inviolable beauty crowned with a diadem of crystal and pearl, beneath which her shining silver hair flowed down to mingle with her swirling draperies, her eyes reflecting the light of a thousand stars.

An aureole of radiant light revealed the Goddess of the Faennari at the full, brilliant flowering of her power.

Receiving the goblet from the Eldest, the mere act of enclosing the vessel in her almost translucent hands caused the liquid within to glow with a light as clear and ethereal as that of moonlight itself.

With a movement as gentle as that of a gossamer silk scarf lifting on a midsummer breeze, the goddess removed one of the flowers from her hair, and when Gabriel – perhaps in answer to some silent command only he could hear – took Luc into his arms, easing him upright so that he was leaning against his shoulder, the goddess dipped the flower into the liquid and brushed it across the dying man's raw, cracked lips.

Once, twice, thrice.

Then dipped and brushed again.

Once, twice, thrice.

Again... and again... and again...

Until finally all the moon-drenched draught was gone.

Emerging from her bone-cramping trance, Adèle discovered that dawn was now lighting the sky beyond the window, turning the snow-encrusted surface of the icy lake to the hue of the palest blush rose.

Slowly, very slowly, she turned her gaze towards the bed.

But instead of the glowing goddess of the previous night's vigil she saw only a bent, haggard old crone in a ragged robe.

Straightening wearily from the bed, the old woman stumbled with all the stiffness of ancient bones, reaching out to clutch at the softly-wrinkled hand of the Eldest of the Sisters of Mercy.

And for an endless heartbeat they stood together, fingers entwined. Mortal woman and immortal goddess, grey-clad healers both.

Then the fey creature that had been sitting neatly at the foot of the bed, keeping silent watch with an unblinking blue stare, yawned and stretched.

Stepping on delicate white paws that barely seemed to dent the heavy cover, the cat sprang with an almost soundless *prrp* into its mistress' arms, its small soft nose nuzzling the hollow, sagging cheek.

The scarce-seen flicker of a smile lit mist-grey eyes to clear silver, even as the hag-like creature seemed to shrink in on itself, its inner glow diminishing as the ephemeral form it lit faded into shadow before their gaze...

Until, between one disbelieving breath and the next, even that last remaining wisp of a wraith was gone.

And the only indication that a deity had ever descended to walk amongst mere mortals was a small mist-pale cat, curled up, nose under tail.

Asleep on Luc de Chartreux's unmoving breast.

Verse 5

The Death of All Hope

Becoming aware of an indefinable shift in the air, Juliène stirred, lifting her head from the hard wooden bed post against which she must have fallen asleep, and winced as pain shot through her stiff neck and frozen limbs.

For one bleak, utterly blank moment she could not think where she was.

Nor even *why* she should be half kneeling, half lying in cramped discomfort on a cold stone floor, surrounded by the stench of stale male sweat and blood-soaked bedding.

Not only that, there appeared to be a window open somewhere behind her, letting in both the icy breath of frost to further chill her limbs and, as she saw as she prised open her swollen eyelids, the faintest hint of a glimmering golden dawn, the silence surrounding her softened only by the softly soothing purr of a contented cat.

Perhaps Amber and Jade had slipped into her chamber again...

But no, she knew that could not be right. This was not her chamber. Nor was this huge bed, with its heavy cover and faded curtains embroidered discreetly with tiny silver swans, one she had ever seen before. It could only, she realised, with appalled certainty, belong to one man. Though what in gods' name she was doing in Joscelin de Veraux's private quarters...

At that, everything came flooding into her mind with all the tumultuous force of a white waterfall in winter... the truce born of desperation with those she hated, in the hope of saving the life of the brother she loved...

Luc!

Pushing to her feet, grasping at bed post and curtains to help haul herself up, she focussed her frantic gaze on the face of the man lying beneath the royal blue covers.

Her brother had always been a handsome man but now her breath caught at the eldritch beauty that limned his lean features with the faintest sheen of ephemeral silver.

Beneath the livid marks of torture he looked at peace, dark lashes resting against forever pale cheeks.

And as that terrible truth slowly seeped through Juliène's frozen mind, a silent moan of despair and disbelief rose into an equally silent howl of misery and unending pain.

She wanted to rail against the deities, the Gods of Light and Mercy, but how could she when it was her own goddess who had taken the sacrifice she had offered, weighed it and found it wanting.

Even so, one last frail, fragile hope made her reach out to touch him.

Luc lay cold and still beneath her questing fingers, the only warmth left in his body the place where the small, fey creature lay curled up, quietly purring, above the heart that would never beat again.

Wanting, *needing* to take out her pain and grief on someone... anyone... she turned on the person who had brought her here... promised her hope... and then utterly failed to fulfill that promise, damn her!

Except her sister, when Juliène found her, was lying almost as pale and motionless as Luc himself, cradled against her lover's chest, the face Ranulf bent close to hers very nearly the same colour as the streaks of grey in his short, barley-blond hair and beard.

"Is she dead?" Juliène demanded harshly, not caring if she was, only that in dying Rowène had baulked her of a target for her vituperation.

"No," Ranulf replied, his voice hoarse, barely above a raw whisper. "Thank the gods."

He glanced briefly at the bed, his dark blue eyes unreadable, then back at her.

"I am sorry, Ju."

It said much that he called her by the affectionate diminutive of her given name.

It also served to twist the knife already carving her heart apart.

"I do not want your pity," she snapped. "I just want my brother back! Luc, oh gods, Luc!"

And knowing she could no longer hurt him with her touch, she reached out to take his hand, pressing his poor broken fingers against her cold cheek... her trembling lips...

Until finally, tenderly, she laid his hand – faintly warm from her farewell kiss – back to rest against his breast.

Her sight blurred by the tears she refused to let fall, she took one last look at this brother whom she had loved so dearly.

The brother for whom she would have tried to fight free of her mother's web.

The brother for whom she had yielded up the only thing that was truly hers to give away.

All in bitter vain, since Luc had died anyway, slipping away from her in the star-lit silence of that mid-winter's night.

She should have known this would be the outcome, Juliène thought bleakly.

A punishment on them all for daring to challenge the daemons of death, the end foretold even in the moment the deities had set their dark veils of mourning about the moon.

What further punishment awaited her when she eventually faced the Winter Lady she neither knew nor cared.

Luc was gone and nothing would bring him back.

She had been mad to think otherwise.

What she had seen...

What she *thought* she had seen in the silvered shadows of this chamber had been no more than enchanted illusion.

A grief-induced dream.

A dangerous deception to twist the mind and shatter a hope that should never have been given credence in the first place.

Wanting only to flee this place of desolation and death, she took one unsteady step away from the bed, then another, reluctantly tearing herself away from her brother's body even though she knew his soul was long-since flown, his wraith even now walking the paths beyond the sunset...

No, no, that was wrong!

It was dawn lighting the sky, and in the dim chill of the unseen sun she cast her cold eyes over the others in the room, her companions in this failed endeavour, as they began to stir and stumble to their feet, and felt nothing for any of them save a distant, corrosive hatred.

Simply because they were here and alive.

Unwanted witnesses to her failure and bitter, bitter loss.

What did *they* know of her sacrifice? Her sorrow?

She wanted nothing of any of them.

Not courteous words of condolence.

Not the compassion she saw in the Eldest's blue eyes as she slowly stood up, assisted by the black-haired young man wearing the green and silver livery of Juliène's despised half-brother.

And, if she were not mistaken, Rowène's favourite brother.

Goddess! Why could he not have been taken in Luc's place? Why should he not be walking the paths of darkness instead of Luc?

Damn him! Damn him!

A movement catching her eye, she looked around to see the man she had just cursed lurch to his feet and, after a single glance at the figure in the bed, turn away to slump down onto the window seat. There to bury his head in his hands, calloused fingers clenching in his hair, loosening the narrow braids, where surely the streaks of silver were more thickly threaded than they had been the night before?

If that were so, Juliène was fiercely glad of it.

Perhaps, she conceded, de Veraux did feel some guilt at his half-brother's death but what, she questioned in seething resentment, had he been prepared to offer of himself to save Luc's life?

What had Rowène?

What had de Marillec?

Whatever it was, it had not been enough!

And because of their lack, Luc was dead!

Damn them all to the darkest depths of the outermost edge of eternity, forever to be chained in a hell of loneliness and pain!

It was with such vengeful thoughts suffusing her mind like a malignant mist, that something between a sniff and a subdued sob made her glance sharply over her shoulder, to find Adèle de Marillec wiping tears from her pale cheeks.

What right did that whimpering wretch have to cry, Juliène demanded silently, a renewed rage edging her sorrow. Adèle had never known Luc, save as a rival for the love and loyalty she had clearly been foolish enough to expect to be bestowed on her by the man whose binding band she wore.

So if not in grief, then perhaps she wept for the child de Marillec would *never* give her now, Luc's death having broken the bargain Adèle had been so brazen as to try and force on her lord-by-binding yesterday evening, when they had all had hope that this venture might have some other, sweeter, end.

As for de Marillec himself, he was standing at the far end of the bed, his face in shadow.

The long hair lying loose and tangled over his bowed shoulders showed a dull, lank, light brown, with not even the faintest flicker of the bronze fire Juliène thought she had glimpsed by last night's candlelight, the expression of stunned disbelief on his bruised and stubbled face serving to soothe a momentary balm over her own grief-ravaged heart.

She was *glad* he was hurting.

For Gabriel de Marillec was the one who, more than anyone else in this room, was responsible for bringing her brother to this state, where the daemons of death had brought the only healing possible to his broken body.

Damn him! Damn him! Damn him!

And on that thought she turned and walked towards the door.

She was done here.

Let her cursed sister, her twice-cursed bastard brother, and Luc's thrice-cursed lover prepare his body for what must come. She wanted no part in it.

"A moment, Madame!"

De Veraux's voice behind her was surprisingly level, albeit the firm tone betrayed a raw undertone of emotion she did not wish to acknowledge, even as he continued,

"Nic!"

"Yes, Father?"

"Escort Lady Juliène back to her chamber or wherever else she may wish to go."

She started to protest that she needed no escort, let alone that of her bastard half-brother's bastard spawn...

Then shrugged a spiritless acceptance.

What did it matter? She wanted only to get away.

To some quiet place where she could weep the tears she would not – could not – allow herself to shed.

Not yet.

Not in front of them.

Never in front of them!

Farewell, Luc, best and most beloved of brothers. May the goddess keep you safe, whichever path your feet now walk upon.

She was almost out of the chamber when she heard de Veraux's voice, crisper now as if he were regaining something of his normal impervious control, and although it was clear that his words were not directed at her, she could not help listening, especially when she heard her sister's name.

"Here, Rafe! Let me take Ro. The gods know you look half dead on your feet, man."

"No, *I* will look after her," Ranulf replied, a fierce possessiveness in his hoarse voice. "You see to *him*."

Whether by that Ranulf meant her brother or his distraught lover, Juliène did not care.

She did not care about anything any more.

Moving on swift, barely steady feet she made for the outer door, one last unwilling look over her shoulder revealing the sight of Ranulf brushing a tender kiss across the pale brow of the limp figure in his arms, the look on his face one she had never, ever seen directed towards herself.

Goddess, how she yearned for someone to love and hold and comfort *her*!

It was many broken, countless moments later, that she walked wearily through the door to the Hall of Fire and found that in one respect at least the goddess had not failed her.

For unexpectedly, and against all odds, Guyard was there.

Waiting for her.

As he had waited all through that long, lonely night, not knowing – or so he told her later – if she would return but unable to leave lest she did and, needing him, find him gone.

Only then, with the warm comfort of his strong arms about her, did she finally allow herself the miserable relief of release as she sobbed and howled and railed out her grief and rage and endless sense of loneliness.

Not only at the loss of her brother, but also, selfishly, for herself as well.

For once he saw her in the full light of day... saw what she had become... not even Guyard, her gentle harper, would want her now.

Verse 6

Honour Guard

With every corner of the bedchamber rapidly filling with the crystalline, snow-white light of the merciless mid-winter's morning, there was no concealing the pale stillness of the body lying in the blue-curtained bed.

Certainly not from the three men presently gathered around it, an honour guard to keep the corpse watch for their sword-brother.

And on the floor beneath the window lay what appeared to be a young lad curled up in a nest of fur-lined cloaks – sleeping soundly, or simply unconscious – his curly chestnut hair lit to fiery red, the tangled strands bright against the folds of mulberry, royal blue and forest green tucked close about him.

As if only just noticing how far the advancing light had swept the night's shadows from the room, the tallest of the men half-turned from the bed to frown at his sleeping sister with a grey-granite gaze scarcely less grim than that with which he had been regarding his brother's body.

"Should she not be waking soon?" he demanded abruptly.

Receiving no reply from his companions other than an uneasy shrug from the big, fair-haired guardian at the foot of the bed, Joscelin glanced sharply at the slender man standing across from him, his head bowed, long hair falling forwards to shadow his face.

"De Marillec!"

"What?!"

His former Second's head jerked up, responding to the terse tone of command as much as his name.

"I said, should she not be waking soon?" Joscelin repeated.

"Why are you asking me?" Gabriel demanded hoarsely. "I am as blind as you in this matter."

"Hardly," Joscelin gritted. "You are half-fey. So is she. And whilst Adèle may have been speaking out of jealous pique last night, she was right about you and Ro, you do share..."

"*Jealous?* Adèle? Of me? You must be..."

"Shut up, the pair of you!" Ranulf snarled over his shoulder.

"I think she is coming around, and the last thing she needs is to wake to find the two of you at each other's throats."

Whilst Joscelin and Gabriel were still facing each other like fighting cocks, Ranulf was down on his knees, one calloused hand reaching out to smooth the tangled strands of hair away from her creased brow and salt-stained cheeks, and as Rowène opened her eyes the things she had been hearing – and seeing as if looking down on them from the starlit heights – began to come together to make at least a modicum of sense.

"Rafe? Oh, Rafe!"

She gave him a smile, unguarded for once and fit to rival the rose-gold dawn for beauty and light.

"Ro! Thank the gods."

A grimace flickered across his bearded face, unseen by the woman now enclosed in his arms, her head nestled into the hollow of his shoulder.

"Or perhaps I should say, thank the goddess!"

"Both the gods and the goddess, I think," Rowène murmured.

Content for the moment, she turned her head so that her cheek rested against the warmth of his skin, revealed where his partially unlaced shirt had slipped awry, taking in the scent of him, her breath sighing through the soft hair on his chest, gentle as a sea breeze over summer-gold gorse.

Then, as she heard the sound of booted footsteps, she peered over Ranulf's shoulder to catch sight of the two men who had been keeping watch, one on either side of the bed, the taller of the pair now walking towards her.

Becoming painfully aware of the frown with which he was regarding both her and the man in whose strong arms she had momentarily forgotten everything, including her purpose here, she felt a flush of belated embarrassment rise to her face.

"Oh, dear! Josce."

Staggering to her feet with Ranulf's help, she went to slip her arms about her brother's waist.

He resisted for a moment only before relenting, yielding to his own need, resting his cheek against her hair as she laid her head against his chest, drawing strength from the satisfyingly steady sound of his heartbeat, even as she felt him take comfort from her closeness.

Finally, and only when she sensed some of the coiled tension leave his lean frame, did she pull away, turning towards the last man, who remained unmoving beside the bed, as if he could not bear to leave for even a moment the man who had been everything to him.

"Gabriel?"

He glanced up briefly from his study of her brother's still body, responding unsmilingly to the underlying question in her greeting.

"I am all right, Ro."

Then, still holding her with his enigmatic amber stare, added in the same emotionless tone,

"You called me Ré last night, if you remember?"

He dropped his gaze to the man in the bed.

"It is short for Aurélien, you know, though no-one save Luc has ever called me by that name. Nor have I wanted them to."

Then even as she started to apologise he surprised her with a swift, wry half-smile that despite everything momentarily rendered his bruised and battered face startlingly handsome again.

"I do not mind. You have earned the right to that familiarity."

His eyes took in the two other men.

"As have you. What we went through together last night..."

He shook his head, looked down at Luc, then back to Rowène, his eyes seen in the dawn light more gold now than amber, the stubble on his jaw and upper lip glinting with the same flicker of witch-fire flame as could be seen in her own shoulder-length curls, and which would be clearly visible in Gabriel's longer hair if he did not deliberately keep it lank and lifeless.

Well? It was a wordless plea. *Am I wrong?*

About Luc? She replied in the same manner, mind to mind, and stepping forwards briefly touched her fingers to the cool skin of Luc's cheek, before easing her hand beneath the warm body of the sleeping cat, causing Mist to twitch and stir before settling once more into purring repose.

Barely daring to breathe in this moment of truth, Rowène closed her eyes, feeling the soft weight of the cat's living warmth, and below her palm...

Letting out her breath in the longest of ragged sighs, she opened her eyes, and meeting Gabriel's golden gaze, spoke for all to hear,

"You are not wrong, Ré. Luc is *alive*."

"Gods... *goddess* be thanked! And you are sure, Ro?"

Joscelin's voice broke into her own silent prayer of thanks to the Silver Lady of the Stars.

"Yes, quite sure," she answered him with a smile that combined amusement, relief, love and sheer joy with the sudden urge to burst into tears.

"Come, Josce! Feel for yourself if you do not believe me. Only try not to disturb Mist as you do it."

"Mist?"

Joscelin approached his brother and his small furry companion with a respectful care.

"Is this by any chance the same cat I thought I saw with you when you were here caring for Rafe after his flogging?"

"One and the same," Rowène agreed. "She also kept me company when your mother and I were nursing your grandsire. She has always come to me in time of greatest need, and last night she accompanied the most powerful healer of them all. And now the Lady has left her beloved companion here to help keep Luc anchored to this life, even as he sleeps in the semblance of death."

Helpless now to keep back her tears, she watched as Joscelin slid one sword-calloused hand carefully beneath the cat, provoking the creature to open both luminous blue eyes, make one swipe of her rough-edged tongue over Joscelin's thumb, before settling into a more comfortable position, nose under tail.

Joscelin allowed his hand to rest on the linen-wrapped wreckage of his brother's chest for a score of heartbeats, perhaps counting those faint but perceptible beats in his head, then obviously satisfied that Rowène had spoken the truth and that Luc truly had survived the night, slid his fingers free again.

Seeing Ranulf watching the proceedings with a frown knitting his brows – perceptibly more grey than fair in the clear morning light – Joscelin cocked his head in enquiry.

"What is wrong, Rafe? Is this not the end we strove so hard to achieve? For which, gods know, we each gave up some part of ourselves. Do you count the cost too high now that we know Luc has survived?"

"No, it is not that, Josce. What we did... what I promised... I would do again without hesitation. It is just... have you taken any thought at all to what happens now?"

Ranulf turned to his other sword-brother.

"Gabr..."

Then corrected himself as the younger man smiled and raised light brown-bronze brows.

"Ré?"

And lastly to Rowène herself.

"Ro?"

She shook her head.

"No, I am afraid I took thought only to getting this far. I trusted Josce for the rest of it."

She was looking at him now, with a frown to match Ranulf's, as her brother failed to give her the immediate assurance she sought.

"Josce? You told me you had an idea as to how we would get Luc out of the palace. Are you telling me now that you do not? Oh gods, Josce, I *trusted* you! With our brother's *life*!"

"I *do* have a plan," Joscelin said curtly, his words falling like ragged stones into the suddenly accusing silence. "Whether it works or not is a different matter."

A grimace deepened the grey shadows on his dark-stubbled face as he concluded on a harsh exhalation,

"In all truth, I was hoping to think of a better one, but since I have not... well, we will just have to pray that the deities – all three of them – continue to look kindly on our endeavours in this matter."

"*This* is your plan?! Gods help us, Josce, this is utter bloody madness!"

With Ranulf not mincing his words, it was left to Rowène to say,

"Could we not do as Gabriel did when he got Edwy out of the palace all those years ago?"

They were seated on and around Joscelin's writing table, eating the warm rolls filled with fried bacon that Dominic had brought back from the kitchens on his return from escorting Juliène to the Hall of Fire, and Rowène's words emerged in a combination of incoherence and flying crumbs.

"I do not believe such a ploy would work a second time," Joscelin pointed out relatively mildly, before adding grimly,

"Besides which, it will do Luc no good at all if I act in direct defiance of Linnius' orders."

"Even so..." Ranulf started.

"Josce's plan does have the advantage of putting us all in the public eye," Gabriel cut in, his voice thoughtful. "Where we can be seen as not aiding and abetting the escape of a traitor from justice. Indeed, it might just be brash and bold enough to deceive everyone, friend and enemy alike, as to the truth we need to hide."

"I can see that, and for the most part I do not doubt we would succeed," Ranulf agreed. "Except where it comes to Joffroi."

His last words held a warning none of them could afford to ignore.

"If I know my bloody, black-hearted brother at all – and I damn well should after all this time..."

For the briefest moment his dark blue eyes locked with Gabriel's suddenly slitted gaze.

"Joffroi will not take anything that Josce puts before him without question. Or without dragging his tame witch in to verify his doubts. So that even if we did manage to deceive Joffroi in the first instance, Ariène – more than you, Ré, or Ro – has the sight, the senses, the power of the Faennari. And she has honed her skills over the years until they are keener than anything either of you can match, and she will surely see through our deception in a heartbeat. Or do you think I am wrong?"

"No," Gabriel agreed grimly. "Nevertheless, it is a risk we must take."

He was staring at the bread and bacon in his hand but clearly seeing something very different in his mind. Then, absently licking the trail of fat dripping down his long fingers and beneath the binding band encircling his narrow wrist, looked up to say,

"The goddess helped us last night, and by her grace she will continue to do so. After all, why save Luc... why leave Mist here to help guard and heal him... only to abandon him to the wolves and vultures with the coming of dawn?"

"And there you have it," Ranulf retorted. "Last night was *her* time, when she was at her most powerful, perceptible even to mortals like me who have no fey blood and precious little belief even in the gods, let alone the... what did you call her, Ro? The Silver Lady of the Stars. Yet I did see her, did believe in her. But now..."

He gestured towards the window, beyond which the sun's light was skating across the frozen lake, laying down lines of clear crisp white-gold, the sky above a deep and profound blue in which a myriad of secrets could be concealed.

"Perhaps she *is* still there, still watching from afar, but *I* see no stars, no moon, not even the palest trace of her presence, and that being so, surely she has no strength to aid us now?"

"You may be right," Rowène conceded. "I cannot see her either. Nevertheless, it is as Gabriel said, she *has* left us Mist. Why would she do that if she did not wish us to succeed. Added to which, we are not entirely helpless, the four of us together. We still have our wits and the..."

She was going to say *courage* but Ranulf cut in, putting it with the bluntness she had come to expect of him,

"And the balls to face down Joffroi and his witch in a public contest of sheer bloody-mindedness?"

He grinned suddenly, answering his own question, dark blue eyes beginning to brighten with the light of battle.

"Well, perhaps we do at that."

"So, we are all agreed?" Joscelin said, swallowing the last of his bread, washing it down with a mouthful of the weak ale Dominic had served them with, waiting until they had all in turn given their assent.

"Right, now we make our preparations, and make them well."

He raised his voice slightly,

"Nic, fetch warm water and plenty of it, after which I have another errand for you. Ro, see to Luc if you will, ready him as if for his bier. Gabriel and I need to shave, and Rafe..."

"I will go and fetch the rest of my gear, and mail and a helm for Gabriel as well. I will not be long."

With that, Ranulf followed Dominic from the chamber, leaving Gabriel staring pensively after him.

"I confess I did wonder... but in all these years he has never actually confirmed it. Not that I ever asked him outright. The gods know, I think I did not want it to be true..."

Rowène stared at him in turn, noting with some concern the flicker of citrine in his otherwise dispassionate amber gaze.

"You wondered? Rafe, you mean?"

"Yes, he said it himself. He is Black Joffroi's brother. Not some mere by-blow either but, unless I am very much mistaken, his only legitimate brother."

Something that was not a smile twitched the corners of his firm mouth, the stubble about his lips snatching fire from the dawn light.

"He may not have told you about it, Ro, but my first meeting with Ranulf de Rogé was *not* a propitious one. I have never forgotten it. Or him. So that, even before today, I was almost sure…"

"Yes, Rafe is Ranulf," Rowène agreed. "And if it is any consolation, Ré, my first meeting with him, at Chartre back in '94, was not a happy one either."

Gabriel gave a small snort of almost amusement.

"No, I do not suppose it was. We have all of us come a long way since then, but I am glad he has finally trusted me with the truth."

Some thought flickered far back behind the surface amber of his eyes.

"And of course, he is the rightful lord of Valenne, is he not? No wonder Joffroi would see him dead."

"Rafe is as much lord of Valenne as you are the rightful lord of Marillec," Rowène murmured, before adding with some deliberation,

"Speaking of which, will you keep the terms of that somewhat… ah… unusual bargain Adèle proposed last night?"

Effectively brought back from the dark abyss of memory or vision he had begun to slip into, Gabriel said nothing in reply, but at least his eyes were once more clear amber rather than clouding into fey gold.

It was left to Joscelin to break the tension, saying tersely,

"For pity's sake, keep out of it, Ro! The fulfilment or otherwise of any such bargain is between Gabriel and his lady. And only then if we manage to get Luc safe away from the palace, and restored to full health. Now, if you want to make yourself useful while we are waiting for Nic to return with the water, you can find a comb, and order and braid my hair for me."

"Mine too, if you will, once it is clean," Gabriel said, the wry half-smile he sent her giving absolution for her interference in his private affairs.

Then looking across at Joscelin, included his friend and sword-brother in their conversation.

"The gods know we have much to accomplish, and little enough time in which to achieve it if we are to be done before the palace begins to stir in earnest."

"Oh, and when we have done all that needs doing, you can put aside whatever thought you might have of dismissing me to safety as you did with your mother and Adèle," Rowène said.

Looking fiercely from Joscelin to Gabriel, she finished flatly,
"Where Luc and Mist go, for better or worse, so do I."

A distant if sufficiently thunderous noise to impact on her somnolent senses roused Adèle from the thick fog of sleep into which she had fallen the moment she had collapsed onto her bed.

Forcing open her sticky lashes and finally identifying the jumble of sound as someone's fist against the outer door, interspersed with a piping voice calling her name in an increasingly agitated pitch, she stumbled from the bed she only vaguely remembered tumbling into – she glanced at the light-filled sky beyond the green glass window panes – no more than a single candle-notch ago.

And before that... oh gods!

Sheer as a physical pain, stabbing through her mind and twisting into a knot in her belly, came memory...

Of the events of the night before.

Of the stillness that had overtaken her lord-by-binding as he looked down at the unmoving figure of the man in Joscelin de Veraux's bed.

Of the blank look in Gabriel's amber eyes as he ordered her away with dawn's first light.

Unable to think of anything to say to him, she had obeyed, and accompanied by the Eldest, had made her way back to these two miserable rooms, knowing even then that Gabriel would never come to her there, never share any part of himself with her.

She had had but one chance.

And with Luc de Chartreux's death she had lost all hope of ever conceiving Gabriel's child.

Or gaining any happiness for either of them.

And finally to give Gabriel his freedom...

The pounding was now a solid roll of sound, loud enough to overpower her ill-formed thoughts and send them into scattered flight even as she jerked open the door.

"Lady Adèle! Thank the gods, I thought I should have to get one of the guards to break down the door! Come, lady, you are needed."

The form of address – officially she was *Mistress* Adèle in the wake of her lord's disgrace – as much as the boy's royal blue livery told Adèle that this was one of Linette's pages. The princess having steadfastly refused to accept the state to which Adèle had been reduced through her continuing loyalty to the man whose binding band she wore.

"Princess Linette? Does she send for me?" Adèle asked now, her mind a vast void of dull stupidity.

"Yes, my lady, and without delay."

The child – he could not have been more than eight summers old – tried to look suitably stern.

"Just let me get dressed," she replied, amusement at his expression waking somewhere in the distance beyond the heavy weariness that persisted in fogging her wits.

The boy stared back at her, eyes wide.

"Er... my lady..."

She looked down at herself, at the crumpled, stained gown that had seen her through her vigil last night and which she had lacked the will to remove when she had stumbled to her bed.

"Ah! Give me a quarter candle-notch to change my gown and make myself fit to attend her highness. Go. Tell the princess I will be with her shortly."

"Very well, my lady."

The boy made her a jaunty bow and was away, his sprightly step pointing up the contrast with her own tired shuffle.

Why?

Numbly she asked herself the question as she worked wearily through the actions that would make her ready to face an existence that no longer held her lord's lover.

Why must Linette choose today of all days to require my attendance?

The water in the ewer was, of course, freezing cold.

As was the chamber itself, ice frosting into flowers on the inside of the window glass.

Nevertheless, she gritted her teeth and washed – very quickly!

Shivering at the chill, her fingers fumbling and clumsy, she donned a clean shift, her one pair of silk stockings, and a cream wool under-gown, then finally dragged on the only remaining robe she possessed suitable for attendance on the princess.

A simply-cut dress that, given her lack of servants, she could lace herself into, the material a shade of worn gold that reminded Adèle almost unbearably of the fey colour of her lord's eyes as she had last seen them in the light of this morning's dawn.

Adèle arrived, a little later than she had said, at the princess' apartments to find Rhys leaning on his spear outside the door, looking almost as desperately tired as she felt herself to be.

Of course, she thought, Rhys must have been keeping guard all night, presumably standing in for the guardian who had spent the night in his commander's quarters, watching over a dying man, and would certainly be in no fit state to resume his duties without some hours' sleep.

Her attempt at a smile going decidedly awry as memories from the previous night surged once more into the forefront of her mind, Adèle managed to stumble through the standard morning greeting and was about to walk past Rhys when the door opened and a tall, black-haired young man she recognised came out.

Shocked into full wakefulness, she could only stare while he, burdened as he was with the bundle in his arms, could do no more than incline his head at the sight of her, before striding away with an easy grace that Adèle could not help but envy.

His clear grey eyes may have held more than a hint of strain, but even so it was plain that Dominic Fitzjoscelin was far less affected by the night's vigil than she.

Then again, he – unlike Rafe or Rhys – had youth on his side, while she felt herself to be at least a thousand years old right now.

Her mind a dull blur of fatigue, curiosity flickered briefly as whatever the young man was carrying slipped in his arms, and she caught the sheen of pale blue silk before he grappled the trailing edge of cloth, tucking it firmly back within its dark wrapping.

The next moment he turned a corner of the passageway and was gone.

"My lady? Are you all right?"

Brought out of her puzzled confusion by the tired roughness in Rhys' voice, she blinked and said,

"Thank you, yes, I will go in now."

And reminding herself why she was here.

"I must not keep the princess waiting any longer."

Adèle entered the royal apartments in a state of weary wariness as to what she might find.

Linette, she knew, had a deep affection – Adèle would not call it more, even though it was – for Joscelin de Veraux and would no doubt be fretting herself as to how he was coping with his half-brother's imprisonment and trial.

Except there would be no trial now, Adèle realised, with Luc already dead. So perhaps it was for the best, after all.

For Joscelin at least...

"Ah, Adèle, there you are."

The princess came hastening across the chamber towards her, pausing when she drew close enough to clearly see Adèle's face.

"Oh my dear, what has happened? You look..."

"As if I had lived through a nightmare?"

"Certainly as if you had not slept at all last night," Linette said quietly. "I suppose it is this terrible situation with Messire de Chartreux? How is your..."

She hesitated, visibly wincing, and discarded her question.

Adèle answered it anyway.

"Gabriel is as you might expect." She grimaced. "Broken."

Linette could find nothing to say to this. Indeed there was nothing to say.

That did not stop the princess from taking hold of her hands, pressing them gently.

"Perhaps when your lord gets over the loss of his..."

She cast a look over her shoulder towards the little girl seated on a rug in front of the fire flickering brightly in the huge stone hearth.

"Over the loss of his foster-brother, he will remember the woman who has stood by him through all of this."

"Or perhaps he will simply follow his lover..." Adèle was too weary and far too heart-sore to be tactful. "Into death."

Besides, she thought, Lilia was not listening to dull, grown-up conversation. She was too absorbed in her attempts to lure a yawning Jade and a dozing Amber into chasing the length of braided wool she was trailing before them.

It was such a *normal* scene, she thought. So far removed from the moonlight and shadows of the night, the mystery, the awe, the sheer impossibility of what Adèle had witnessed, and that was even now fading into the realm of dreams and harp songs...

Linette's gasp of shock brought her abruptly back to herself.

"His *lover*! You are telling me, after all we went through at his trial to prove your lord's innocence, that Gabriel de Marillec and Luc de Chartreux were indeed lovers in the Kardolandian manner?"

"Lovers?"

Adèle considered the question, as if at a distant remove. Then shook her head.

"No, perhaps not in that sense. Or at least not for many years. But that Gabriel loved him to the exclusion of all others... yes, he did. There is no doubt in my mind about that. Which is why, even if he does not wilfully follow Luc beyond the sunset, he will never have anything left to give to me, least of all that which I most wish for."

"A child?"

Adèle smiled ruefully as she returned her friend's sympathetic gaze.

"I can hardly deny it."

She looked again at Lilia, playing under Lady Isabelle's watchful, yet indulgent, eye.

"But something even beyond that. Something I will never win."

Then shaking herself out of her morbid misery, and pointedly turning the conversation away from herself,

"What do you need me to do for you, your highness?"

"Merely give me your company when I go down to the great hall later this morning," Linette answered with an attempt at calm.

"Having seen the outcome of one mockery of a trial precipitated by Joffroi de Rogé's malfeasance and Lady Ariène's intrigues," the princess continued. "I intend to make sure that Linnius does not yield to their manipulations again. One so-called traitor's head above our gates is more than enough, and I would not see Luc de Chartreux suffer his father's fate. Whatever he was to your lord, he was still Joscelin's brother. *Ah!*"

She flushed guiltily.

"Do not worry, Linette. I already knew that they were brothers," Adèle said drily.

Besides," she added, somewhat bleakly. "I do not think it matters now what happens to Luc."

It was the closest she could come to admitting that she knew Luc de Chartreux to be dead already, and it provoked Linette, her flush fading into pallor, into giving her a sharp look.

"Perhaps not, but the man I met on the Vézière highway all those years ago... the man who brought up his sisters' illegitimate children as his own... the man who has fought these past few years at Joscelin's side to keep our northern lands free from the Atarkarnan barbarians, and that in spite of being hunted all the while like a ravening wolf... that man deserves better than to be brutally dismembered and put on display for the likes of Joffroi de Rogé to spit upon. So what justice... what honour... I can give him, I will."

Then when Adèle said nothing, Linette regarded her even more closely,

"Would you truly wish such a terrible fate on him? Can you watch without a qualm as they quarter his body while he is yet alive, spike his head above the palace gate? Forsake all sense of pity or mercy... simply because he took your lord from you?"

"No. And he did not take Gabriel from me."

Gabriel has always been his.

Arriving outside the great hall alongside the princess, Adèle was aware of the subdued susurration of movement, of whispered words of excitement, a sense of eager anticipation emanating from every person in that quivering crowd.

The one exception it had to be said – apart from Adèle herself and Linette – being Prince Linnius.

Surrounded by the richly-clad lords of the High Counsel, he was standing in strained silence, attired in formal if sombre splendour, the silver circlet of Mithlondia upon his head.

Adèle saw a frown cross his pale brow as she and Linette approached. The next moment he leaned closer to Joffroi de Rogé to ask a question, the answer he received making him shrug in irritable acquiescence, before returning his attention to the closed doors before him, the two guards on either side standing stock-still and emotionless as the marble statues adorning the Kardolandian king's halls.

Brave men, Adèle thought, to risk their prince's ire by the very immobility of their presence.

Then one of the men moved, light glinting off a nobleman's heavy gold signet as his hand lifted to pull the helm from his head, shaking free long black hair, braided warrior fashion and thickly threaded with silver.

Even as Adèle heard Linette gasp, her own gaze was swinging towards the other soldier clad in shimmering mail, releasing her breath in a hiss of relief as she realised that, though slender enough, he was far too tall to be Gabriel.

Thank the gods for small mercies!

Recovering herself with an effort and wondering very much what was toward, Adèle watched in a daze as Joscelin de Veraux dropped gracefully onto one knee.

Just as if he had not spent the greater part of the night on his feet.

Or that the last time he had bent his knee it had not been to honour a goddess whose very name was anathema to the men before him.

As it was, he did not give the most noble lords of the High Counsel so much as a single glance.

When he did lift his head at Linnius' terse command, his cool, unyielding gaze was directed straight at his prince.

"Sire."

His voice, as ever, betrayed no hint of emotion.

How does he do it, Adèle wondered. Is he not in the least bit fearful or worried?

Knowing what she did, she was prey to both anxiety and fear.

As, she suspected, was Linette, innocent though she was in any complicity in Joscelin's actions.

But now, finally, the prince was speaking again.

"What do you here, Messire de Veraux?"

It did not seem a good omen to Adèle that Linnius had chosen formality over familiarity in addressing the man he thought to be his half-brother.

Nor that he was permitting Joffroi de Rogé to murmur only the gods knew what evil in his ear.

Then, deliberately denying Joscelin the chance to respond to his question, the prince continued coldly,

"You gave me your word last night that you would have the traitor de Chartreux here to stand trial this morning, and now I find you apparently barring my way and that of your fellow Counsellors."

"Rather I have been waiting for you, Sire, and indeed I have kept my word. As you will see."

A small, scarce-seen gesture of his hand had the other man setting aside his spear in order to push open the heavy double doors of the great hall.

"Enter, Sire, and see for yourself what has been done in your name to a man no court has ever tried, let alone convicted of treason."

With some premonition of what Joscelin meant to do, Adèle reached out to grab Linette's hand.

"Your highness, you must not see this. Must not involve yourself in this."

"Must not?" Linette tugged her hand free. "Why not?"

She did not give Adèle any chance to explain herself further, but walked forwards, forcing the noblemen to fall back, bowing, until she stood at her brother's side.

Linnius' frown grew more pronounced but he only said,

"What do you here, Linette? The trial of a traitor is no place for a woman."

"I came, as you did, to see justice done," she replied firmly.

Then in a softer tone, her hand coming to rest on her brother's heavily-embroidered sleeve,

"Let Joscelin rise, Linn. It is not fitting to keep him on his knees so long. Surely you, of all people, do not doubt his loyalty?"

"Loyalty to whom, I wonder?" Linnius retorted, not quite as quietly, and whatever Linette saw in his eyes was sufficient to make her drop her hand and step back.

She did not give up though.

"Please, Linnius."

"Oh, very well."

The prince glanced around, at the crowd of common folk – kept back by a fence of levelled spears, held in the hands of soldiers bearing the winged horse on their breasts – then at the faces of his counsellors and courtiers, finally turning an ugly look on the man still kneeling before the doors of the great hall.

"On your feet, de Veraux. I came to see justice done upon Luc de Chartreux. And you will stand before me, where I can see you, when I pronounce judgement. Pray gods I do not account you as guilty as he in his treason."

Words to give any man a moment's qualm, Adèle thought.

Except Joscelin gave no sign of any such unease.

He stood, perhaps a little stiffly and was definitely favouring his right knee when, after waiting for Linnius to come level with him, he stepped into place at his prince's side.

His grey gaze skimmed over Adèle to rest briefly on Linette's face, a flicker of some emotion – warning? regret? – briefly revealed in his eyes, like a breeze-blown cloud reflected in clear water.

Then he shook his head, the movement barely perceptible, and facing forwards once more, walked into the hall where he took the place that the three men standing in formal array around the silk-covered trestle had clearly left for him.

Given her prior knowledge of Luc de Chartreux's demise, and that he had been in no state to *stand* at his trial in any case, Adèle was perhaps not as startled as most of those who crowded – nobles and common folk alike – into the hall after the prince had entered.

That said, even *she* had not expected *this*!

In the exact centre of the hall, lit by the clear winter's light falling through the high windows, the air about heavy with the scent of lavender from the huge bunches of the purple herb hung from the unlit torch brackets around the walls, stood a bier upon which lay the still body of a man.

This was no ordinary bed of the dead though. Standing to the height of a tall man's waist, the bier was draped in softly shimmering silk, pale gold covering the top half beneath Luc's head and upper body, pale blue across the bottom where his feet rested.

Oh, gods! Adèle gave a silent moan. *The de Chartreux colours.*

Then, suddenly remembering Dominic's tightly-clasped, slippery bundle, she slid a glance at Linette's pale, set face.

Gods have mercy! The princess had known, after all, and had clearly chosen to help Joscelin honour his half-brother in this most dangerous manner.

Swallowing against a useless rage and regret, Adèle forced herself closer to the bier and the corpse thereon.

No, she reminded herself, this is not just *any* corpse!

This is Luc de Chartreux.

My lord's lover, foster-brother and for years his only friend.

And knew she must face the naked truth of that, at least this once.

And *naked* it was, she realised in horrified disbelief when she directed her unwilling gaze back towards the bier and the body of the man lying there in full public view, decency preserved only by a hand's-width of folded cloth-of-silver laid across his loins and reaching down to the floor on either side of the bier with perfect precision.

God of Light, give me the strength to endure this without disgracing either myself or my lord!

She had known from the heavy bandaging about Luc de Chartreux's body last night, and the blood on the bed linens, that he must have been tortured beyond all bearing. But to have it laid bare...

With an effort Adèle strangled the half-hysterical thought before it could be born.

For far more indecent, far more shocking, than mere nakedness, was the undeniable truth that almost every bone in her rival's body that could be broken had been. With brutal precision.

Moreover, every inch of his skin was marred by underlying bruises in shades ranging from black to yellow, overlain by the scars of hot iron and razor-sharp blade, some of these marks coming very close to the edge of that strip of folded cloth, so that she could not help but wonder what other agonising atrocities had been inflicted that Luc's kin had chosen not to reveal in public.

It being perfectly plain to Adèle that everything that had been done here on his behalf had been undertaken quite deliberately, and with great care.

Most obviously, Luc's dark, frost-flecked hair had been washed free of blood and vomit, and combed smoothly over his shoulders.

His eyes were closed, though not covered as was customary with silver nobles, his long dark lashes being allowed to rest on his ravaged cheeks as if he were merely sleeping.

Nor were his hands clasped together at his breast over the hilt of a long-sword as she had unconsciously expected, in imitation of the stone effigies to be found in every castle crypt. Instead his hands were left to lie by his side, leaving his breast with its terrible wounds exposed for all to see.

Except she could *not* see clearly, and closed her eyes in a vain attempt to clear the silvery mist that persisted in obscuring her vision. Surely she was not weeping? For Luc de Chartreux!

She blinked, determined not to yield in public to tears for this man she did not even like, whose death it felt hypocritical to mourn.

No, she would leave it to Gabriel to...

Gabriel!

Her head snapped up and around, knowing suddenly that he must be here, very close by. That he would never have left the ravaged corpse of his dead lover to be gaped at or argued over by all and sundry. Would never have left Joscelin, his only friend now living, when his sword-brother had most need of his support.

And indeed, there he was, her lord-by-binding, head held high, his cheeks shaved clean of stubble, his long hair neatly ordered, its natural colour revealed as a gleaming light brown lit to bronze by the pale winter sun. He was standing spear-straight and spear-slender, at the bottom right-hand corner of the bier...

Only then did she realise that if Gabriel was there, so would the others concerned in last night's endeavour be also.

Already dreading what she might see, she looked past Gabriel, to the big, blond-bearded guardian at the top left-hand corner – yes, that would be Rafe – and finally dared to slide a sideways glance at the last corner, where could be seen, shorter than the other three mailed figures, slenderer even than Gabriel, a form that could only belong to Luc's sister, Rowène.

Damn them all! Adele thought, almost angrily. Why must they... why must *she*... put herself into danger in such reckless fashion? If Rowène were to be recognised...

"What in the name of all the daemons in Hell is going on here!"

Joffroi's de Rogé's rumbling growl jerked Adèle out of her state of sick dismay as he pushed past her to confront Joscelin.

"Is this how you keep your word, de Veraux? By deliberately setting out to make a mockery of m... of your prince and the High Counsel of Mithlondia – of which you are yet a member, I would remind you! – in such impudent fashion? By treating this traitor as if he were worthy of the honour due to one of your peers?"

A savage grin revealed de Rogé's teeth, still white and sharp.

"I think, my Lord High Commander, you will find you have gone one insolent step too far this time."

"If anyone is making a mockery of Mithlondian justice," Joscelin retorted icily. "And assuredly somebody *is*, it is not me. Luc de Chartreux was never formally arraigned, never tried, never sentenced. According to Mithlondian law, he died an innocent man."

"He confessed to all the crimes of which he stood accused," de Rogé spat back, florid colour flushing his fleshy, broad-boned face. "You were there. And you witnessed it all, every word, so do not try and deny it now."

"Any man would have yielded under the extremes of pain you and your one-eyed torturer meted out," Joscelin snapped.

Then blatantly dismissing his enemy, turned his attention towards Linnius.

"Step forwards, Sire, and see what has been done in your name, and without..."

Joscelin glared back at Joffroi de Rogé, his mouth flattening into a thin, white line of hard-held fury.

"Without any valid written authority!"

Already pale, the prince did indeed take a step closer to the bier, what little colour he had left in his cheeks draining away, one unsteady hand coming up to cover his mouth, and if he was not sick over his shoes, there were others in the hall who were not so fortunate.

More than one lady had to be led away, Adèle saw, as she struggled to control the upheaval in her own stomach, but it was only as she was watching Marguerite de Vitré exit on her lord's arm, that her eye was caught by the dark-haired noblewoman in green velvet standing just inside the hall doors.

And while she could muster little liking for the other woman, their short-lived friendship long-since turned sour, pity made her capture and hold that tear-filled gaze.

Please, do not come any closer. Do not torment yourself further.

Did Juliène read her thoughts? Or merely give in to the emotion ravaging her slender body.

Whatever the cause, Adèle felt pity replaced by relief – if only briefly – as Juliène slipped quietly away again, accompanied by a broad-shouldered, fair-haired man that Adèle had little difficulty in recognising, despite his humble harper's garb, as her own beloved cousin.

Good Gods above!

Once more Adèle found herself close to grinding her teeth.

First Rowène acting in such thoughtless folly!

And now Guy, whom she had always considered a sensible man!

Except, as he had just conclusively proved, he had no sense at all where Juliène de Lyeyne was concerned.

What in the name of all the gods was he doing here, in the palace? In the great hall! Between – however briefly – the same four walls as his murderous half-brother.

Indeed, if Joffroi de Rogé had not been so enraged with Joscelin that he had no time or thought for anyone else, he would surely have seen and recognised Guy, and then there would have been more than one corpse in the hall, of that Adèle was certain.

As it was, de Rogé was still engaged in snarling abuse and blood-chilling accusations, which Adèle was thankful to see appeared to slide harmlessly off the shield of Joscelin's cold disdain, whilst Prince Linnius stared helplessly from his Chief Counsellor to the High Commander of his army, and all around them the formerly subdued murmurings grew ever louder as noblemen – most vociferously Hervé de Lyeyne – and common folk alike began to argue the rights and wrongs of the matter.

Meanwhile, and almost unnoticed, the ebb and flow of the crowd had gradually pushed the soldiers of the palace guard forwards until the bier was completely encircled, the collective curiosity of the onlookers held at bay only by the four mailed figures at each corner, a slight enough barrier in all truth, but one that continued to preserve a small space of stillness around Luc de Chartreux's body.

Only the gods knew how long the shameful uproar would have continued, if it had not been abruptly silenced with the appearance of a graceful figure clothed all in white, the sinuous silk cloth a-shimmer with crystal droplets and silver thread, the only touch of colour about her being her jewel-green eyes and the complicated coronet of dark fire-red braids wound about her imperious head, the perfection of her pure, polished marble beauty untouched by any mortal emotion, and as she glided through the crowd, all fell back at her approach as sharply as if slashed by ice-tipped stinging nettles.

In the frozen silence that now frosted every corner of the hall, every pair of eyes was fixed on the Lady Ariène de Rogé as she approached the bier upon which lay the broken body of her first-born son, a fluid curtsey before the prince releasing the lock on his tongue long enough for Linnius to croak,

"Madame, forgive the unseemly manner of this gathering, but I have to tell you that your son..."

"Is dead," she finished, her voice silken smooth, sweet as honey, and far steadier than the prince's.

"I knew it already, Sire. It is a day, I must confess, I have long awaited. Mithlondia's very air is cleaner for his death."

Linnius flinched.

Nor was he the only one to shudder at the chill of her words.

The ice-green gaze went beyond the prince to what Adèle could not help but think of as the honour guard about the bier.

"I suppose," Lady Ariène pronounced with delicately frosted scorn. "It is only fitting that a traitor's spawn be surrounded by similar gutter-spewed scum."

Her gaze flitted lightly between the two men closest to her, finally settling with a particularly unpleasant expression on the shorter, slighter of the two.

"And in de Marillec's case, *unnatural, degenerate* gutter-scum."

Adèle swallowed an upsurge of bile.

Gabriel, however, merely tilted his head in acknowledgement of the jibe, a feral light glittering in eyes half hidden by narrowed lashes, otherwise watching expressionlessly as that head, with its crown of fire, turned again towards the man standing at his side, his helm held under his arm.

"And here," Lady Ariène continued as she looked Joscelin up and down, from bare head to spurred heels. "We surely have the lord of all such gutter dregs! Well, de Veraux, nothing to say? Has discretion finally overtaken your paltry attempts at guile? Has the – in common parlance – cat got your tongue?"

Cat?

Adèle shivered, remembering the little creature of mist and moonlight she thought she had seen the night before. Surely Lady Ariène did not... could not know... what they had tried to do?

The tiniest flicker of wariness showed in Joscelin's clear, level gaze before his hard mouth lifted in a tight-lipped smile and with the rough edge of some rarely-heard emotion in his voice, he said,

"If it is scum we are to speak of, Madame, who here is closer to the gutter? I have no doubt you would say Gabriel and Luc... both of them men with the courage to openly give their love and loyalty to another man. To each other. Or perhaps you would say it is me? After all, I am a bastard, born in love outside the bounds of the binding oath, an abomination in your sight. Even so..."

His voice lowered and hardened still further.

"I would far rather be that. Far rather that Gabriel be as he is. Luc as he was. Than the sort of latrine slime you have been spreading your legs for these past dozen years!"

Even as Joffroi de Rogé reacted with predictable fury to this insult, Gabriel stepped forwards, his voice ringing clear above his enemy's spluttering rage as he flicked his long, slender fingers in a gesture of disdain at Linnius' Chief Counsellor.

"See this, Josce! This is the sort of shit-scum that gives sodomites like me and bastards like you a bad name."

He turned the honed edge of his tongue directly on the older man.

"Because you, de Rogé, are worse than scum. An animal... no, for they kill only to survive. Whereas you, you get your prick up by inflicting pain for pleasure! And rend your own kin to satisfy your lust for blood, and your witch-woman's insatiable craving for power."

Adèle found she was clasping Linette's hand hard.

As tightly as the princess was grasping hers.

Both of them thinking the same thing.

Oh gods, why are they doing this?

Neither Joscelin nor Gabriel was stupid.

Neither of them was lacking in self-control.

Yes, they must both be upset, distraught at Luc's death.

And yet what they were doing now went beyond the grief at the death of a brother, a lover.

It was almost as if they were deliberately baiting de Rogé and his lady... holding all their attention on them and away from...

Away from who?

From Luc? But he was dead, beyond all mortal wrangling.

So then... Ah! Rowène!

With that realisation the knot of some emotion darker than fear tightened about Adèle's heart.

For while it was all very well for Joscelin to put his life in danger for his sister, what was Rowène to Gabriel that he would risk himself to such an extent?

Could it be that she, despite her denials...

Then the unworthy thought was lost as de Rogé lunged forwards, spluttering still, spittle flying from his lips, his eyes bulging red in the shiny folds of his purpling face.

"You filthy, buggering..."

What had she missed? Oh gods, what had Gabriel said now to put their enemy into such an ungovernable rage?

"Lying whoreson..."

"It is hardly a lie," Gabriel's shockingly harsh tones ground over the other man's gross fury. "To say that you left your only legitimate brother in the forest to die! Left him bound and helpless but alive, knowing that his eyes would be pecked out by carrion birds, his flesh torn from his bones by scavenging wolves."

Joscelin's voice by contrast was coldly formal and effectively dragged de Rogé's attention around to him like a charging boar forced to change direction.

"Nor is it a lie to say that you sent your illegitimate half-brother to a different living death. By my reckoning, that makes you a fratricide twice over, Messire."

"And a parricide too mostly likely," Gabriel put in sharply.

For a dozen heartbeats there was only a shocked silence throughout the vast hall.

De Rogé stood where he had stopped, a foot from Gabriel, frozen white where formerly he had been flushed. And when he spoke all menace had been wrung from his voice, all threat gone from fists which now fell back to dangle, open and lax, by his side.

"It was de Chartreux's hand that took my father's life," he said hoarsely.

"And you became Lord of Rogé just as you stepped into manhood. How very convenient for you that the spear Lucius de Chartreux carried that day, and with which by all accounts he barely grazed your father, should have put such a fatal poison in his blood."

Gabriel's voice could have cut ice.

As could Joscelin's as he took up the attack,

"Tell me, Messire, did you make the acquaintance of the woman who now wears your binding band before or after your father's death?"

For a moment the dark eyes were blank, all defences down. Then,

"I should be very careful were I you, de Veraux, before you start throwing around accusations like that! Bearing in mind the bloodlines of the traitor you escorted to the scaffold and the one who lies dead behind you. *You* are closer to committing such heinous crimes than I. And perhaps it is time that the prince should be told the truth of that," he finished in a distinctly threatening tone.

Uncowed, Joscelin merely lifted his narrow dark brows and said coolly,

"You are too late, Messire."

Just as Linnius pushed forwards to demand, somewhat hotly,

"What should I know? And if it is something you already knew, Messire de Rogé, why have you not thought to tell me, your prince, before this moment?"

"Pardon, Sire, I have only just become aware myself that this base wretch you have graced with your favour is in truth..."

"Lucius de Chartreux's bastard."

Joscelin's clear, cool voice rang over the disdainful rumble, the ripples of his claim running through the crowded hall to lap against the enclosing walls, washing the rising murmurs into silence again.

And then in a quieter tone that reached no farther than those immediately around him, Joscelin continued flatly,

"As I said, you are too late, Messire. I told the prince last night when I went to beg him to release my half-brother into my custody."

"That you might the easier help him to escape, I suppose?"

"No!"

That was Linnius, finally recovered sufficiently from his state of impotent shock, to intervene, trying shakily to hold to the formalities.

"Jos... Messire de Veraux freely told me the truth of his paternity, and asked my permission to get a healer in to tend his half-brother, He also..."

"Well, if he did manage to find a healer willing to tend a self-confessed traitor, it did not do any good did it?" de Rogé dared to cut in, his confidence clearly returning.

"Or perhaps," he continued. "There was no healer, and that was merely one more lie in a lifetime of concealing the truth about his birth from you and the Counsel, and in reality the bastard simply smothered de Chartreux in order to save his *brother...*"

There was a sneer on the last word, the same corrosive contempt colouring the rest of his leading sentence.

"From the same well-earned death as their treacherous father went to. That he himself should go to, Sire. By law."

"No," the prince protested. "Joscelin has proved his loyalty time and again."

Then with one of his mercurial shifts in thought and temper.

"But is it true, de Veraux? What Joffroi says. You gave me your word that you would not let de Chartreux escape today's trial and yet, clearly there will be no trial now."

The prince turned a troubled look on the man he had grown up thinking of as his half-brother.

It was not Joscelin who answered him, instead regarding the prince with a tight-lipped look at having his word questioned.

"Sire, if I may beg leave to speak?"

Linnius blinked in confusion at the small, grey-clad Sister of Mercy who had slipped through the crowd of courtiers to dip a curtsey before him and now stood, hands lightly clasped, cornflower-blue eyes calm, face serene.

"You are..."

"I am the Eldest of the Sisters of Mercy of Vézière, Sire. I came to court in attendance on Lord Nicholas and, with his permission, spent last night at the bedside of a dying man."

Her head, with its neat headrail of white linen, turned to look sadly at the bier.

"This man, Sire. I washed and bound his wounds..."

"And fed him a lethal potion to stop his heart?" Lady Ariène suggested as she stepped forwards to face the woman who had once been Céline de Veraux, her green eyes mocking, her voice icy smooth, her insinuation obvious.

"As you have done before to other men of nobler birth."

"No, he was too far gone to swallow," the Eldest replied, a hint of something that was neither serene nor calm in the gaze she flicked towards her old enemy.

"I merely made him as comfortable as was possible. As his mother should have done, had she cared for him at all!"

Returning her attention to the prince, the Eldest said quietly,

"I stayed by my patient's side until all life was gone, Sire, and I tell you now he could never have lived with wounds like that. There was no need for Lord Joscelin hasten his end. Nor did he."

"And you would be prepared to swear an oath before the gods to that effect?" the prince demanded, clearly trying to regain some control over the situation.

"Certainly, Sire, for it is the truth."

Linnius glanced around, as if wondering what to do next, his gaze moving jerkily from Joscelin to Joffroi de Rogé, then around the hall at the forest of faces watching him.

He swallowed audibly.

"It... er... it seems there is nothing more to be said. It merely remains to... er... remove the..."

He slid a glance between Joscelin and Gabriel, towards the still figure on the bier, shuddered and tried again to complete his sentence.

559

"Remove the..."

"The stinking corpse of a filthy traitor, Sire," de Rogé put in harshly. "Drag it to the scaffold where the executioner awaits. De Chartreux has escaped the trial, Sire, but he can still be executed in due form."

"He is dead!" Joscelin bit out, his voice edged with anger. "Let him lie, as he is, wherever the prince deems fit."

"The palace crypt, no doubt?" de Rogé sneered.

"No, I do not expect that. He was an outlaw after all, but even if it is a pauper's pit, I will accept it."

"And that would suit you, would it not?" de Rogé retorted, his dark eyes narrowing in suspicion and derision. "Which is reason enough not to do it. Dead or not, I say we make sure this traitor cannot rise again. Quarter the cur, Sire, and stick his head above the main gate alongside his father's."

Even as Adèle frowned in distaste at the thought, she realised she was again missing something and bent a closer look at Joscelin and Gabriel.

For all their surface control, it seemed to her that both men were strung taut almost to the point of shattering. Though *why* was another matter. Whatever their feelings for the man, Luc *was* dead and beyond any further torment or indignity de Rogé might propose.

"Sire, is there really any need for such extreme measures?"

Joscelin's voice was level once more, appealing to what Adèle had always considered Linnius' under-developed sense of reason.

"Luc de Chartreux is no threat to the throne. He never has been, but even if you believe him guilty, surely it is better to let him lie in some unmarked grave and be forgotten."

"On the contrary, Sire, you must show the realm that you are a strong ruler, that you will not have the laws of this land – just laws made by your Counsel – set at naught. Show your people that you will not tolerate traitors, even in death. Messire de Veraux should know better than to suggest it. I understand why you would not wish to doubt his loyalty! Yet I cannot help feeling that, bearing in mind his blood ties to the de Chartreux, one his father, the other his brother, his loyalty to you should not be taken for granted."

Clearly torn, the prince glanced from his Chief Counsellor to his High Commander, the doubt in his eyes seeping back into his voice.

"Joscelin?"

"I am as loyal to you, Sire, and the royal house of Mithlondia as I have ever been. I have served and protected you and Princess Linette for more than half my lifetime, putting your lives before my own, without asking for anything in return. In your service, I have shed my blood on a score of battlefields, leaving my own lands in the hands of a steward. I have not been home to Veraux in years, either to sit in judgement or show my people that their lord does indeed care for their welfare. Can your Chief Counsellor make any such claim?"

His contemptuous, ice-grey gaze flicked towards de Rogé.

"Correct me if I am wrong, Messire, but have you ever been within sniffing distance of a battlefield? I do not mean one of your petty little raids along the Larkenlye, resulting in torched hovels, raped women, tortured men, orphaned children. I am talking about life and bloody death along the northern border, on the blood-soaked sands of the Malvraine coast. As I recall, you were accustomed to send your younger brother to do your fighting for you, while you remained snug in the Counsel Chamber, acquiring lands by dubious means, and amassing more wealth in your coffers than any other man in Mithlondia, including your prince."

Adèle thought for a moment that de Rogé was going to lose his slipping grip over his temper, and wondered if Joscelin had deliberately taunted him to such an end, but after a few moments of tight-jawed tension, he managed to say through clenched teeth,

"Chartreux and Valenne fell to my hand quite lawfully, and if you argue otherwise you impugn Prince Linnius' honour as well as mine own."

He gave a sneering smile when Joscelin − wisely, Adèle felt, considering he had risked himself and Gabriel enough already − did not reply to that accusation, and seeing this, de Rogé turned towards the prince, determined it seemed to prove himself blameless of any charge.

"You may not remember my brother Ranulf, but I can assure you, Sire, he was a wild youth, much given to drunkenness and debauchery of all sorts, who grew up in spite of my best efforts into a greedy, discontented man. Forsaking his oath of fielty, he turned on me, stealing both money and my ward, the Lady Juliène de Chartreux, first dishonouring, then abandoning her. Not content with that, he then laid false claim to the lordship of Valenne that should lawfully have come to me as the eldest son. In consequence of which he died the death all thieves merit. I make no apology for it, Sire. As for de Chartreux..."

A tip of his head indicated the figure on the bier.

"He too should be brought to justice, Sire. And since he has escaped facing it in full, may I suggest an... extension to the usual punishment, to someone who can – and will – feel it in his stead."

Linnius frowned uncertainly, his confusion mirrored on the faces of those around him.

"I do not understand you, Messire. And if you mean to have Joscelin stand in his place, think again. He may not be my father's son as I have thought for so long, but he is still my kin, my cousin."

"What? How?"

"Ah, you did not know that did you, Messire?"

Linnius looked childishly pleased at knowing something his Chief Counsellor did not.

"His grandsire was also my grandsire."

Adèle watched de Rogé work it out.

"Prince Raymund?"

She herself was beyond surprise, beyond interest in Joscelin's genealogy.

"So he is the bastard of a royal bastard," Lady Ariène murmured somewhat mockingly. "What a charming heritage. Still, as long as he is loyal to you, Sire, you need not fear he will pit his royal blood against yours. And if he does, no doubt my lord will put him in his place, as surely as he has already done to your bastard kinsman's treacherous father and brother."

Linnius stopped smiling and snapped,

"We have been through all this, Madame. Joscelin is loyal and I will have no word said against him. As for his half-brother, just tell me plainly what you propose, Messire?"

"Simply this, Sire. Once the executioner has struck off his head, rather than cutting off de Chartreux's prick and sticking it in his mouth as I was originally going to suggest, why not give it to de Marillec instead. He can have its like cast in bronze and use it to pleasure hi..."

"For gods'sake, de Rogé, keep that foul tongue of yours still!"

Almost before Adèle could blink, Joscelin was at the other man's throat, literally choking him into gagging silence, as he snarled in his ear,

"Not all the women here are whores or life-draining leeches like your accursed witch. The princess..."

"Enough!"

For once Linnius' voice was assured and firm as he addressed the close-locked noblemen.

"Unhand him, Joscelin! As for you, Messire de Rogé, you go too far. As Joscelin says, my sister is present. And other ladies of my court."

"My apologies, Sire... your highness," de Rogé said hoarsely, shrugging himself free of Joscelin's grip and bowing to Linette. "I forgot myself in my desire to see justice done."

"Forgot too," Linette put in swiftly, her blue eyes filled with distaste as she looked into Joffroi de Rogé's bloodshot eyes. "The gently lady who bears me company today. Whatever her lord is, she is surely innocent and does not deserve to hear you smear further filth over the name she has no choice but to bear."

She turned to Linnius, her hand on his arm, her voice softer now.

"This public wrangling brings no credit to any of us. Discuss to what end you will consign Messire de Chartreux's body in the Counsel Chamber if you wish, but ultimately the decision is yours and should be made when you are quiet and at peace with yourself and the gods."

"Yes," Linnius grasped gratefully at the period of grace she had offered him. "That is what I must do."

He hesitated, uncertain again.

"But what about the... the body. I cannot give it into Joscelin's charge, not after the things Joffroi has been saying, and I cannot leave it here. And what about them?"

He nodded towards the townsfolk crowding into the hall.

"Let the people see what they have come to see," Linette replied. "To try and conceal what has happened here today will only give rise to worse rumour. As for Joscelin, I am sure he can be trusted both to keep order and obey your wishes in this matter. He barely knew his brother in life, let him have this time to make his farewells."

Clearly relieved at his sister's suggestion, the prince made a short speech to the effect that he was retiring to consider the matter but that any who wished to do so might step forward to view the body.

He would, he further declared, pronounce final judgement in the Star Chamber at noon the following day, word of which would be cried throughout the town so that all would know the outcome.

With that Linnius swept from the hall, counsellors and courtiers at his heels.

Linette lingered a heartbeat longer, then gestured to Adèle to accompany her back to her apartments.

Discreet as the princess had been, Adèle had nevertheless seen the look that passed between her and Joscelin – a look that held worry and reassurance and love.

Once she would have envied them their understanding, pitied them perhaps.

Now, however, she had other things – other problems – to worry about.

Not least the slender, bare-headed man standing at Joscelin's right hand, his face as white as the clean shift she had so quickly donned this morning, and considerably whiter than his own unlaundered linen.

When the last gawking townsman had left the hall, when the last grim-faced noblemen – Robert de Vitré, Justin de Lacey and Nicholas de Vézière, the latter attended by the Eldest – had followed them, Joscelin signed to Dominic that he should shut the great doors, and then unable to hold his weariness at bay any longer, slumped down onto his knees beside the bier.

"Thank the gods that is over."

"For now," Gabriel murmured, dropping down beside him, his arm briefly about his friend's shoulders, before twisting to look behind him.

"Will you not come and sit with us, Ro?"

"Give me a moment..."

Considerably longer than a moment passed before she stumbled from her place at the top corner of the bier, to collapse with a jingling of ring-mail, leaning back to back with Ranulf who had already eased down onto the floor with all the grace of an old man.

"Damnation, but I am tired," he groaned, pulling off his helm and yanking off his mail glove, the better to rub his fingers over his face.

"'Ware the peep holes," Rowène cautioned them all, suddenly remembering. "There is one on the west side of the hall, and probably more I do not know about."

"Hell can take any watchers tonight," Gabriel muttered, pulling her to rest with her head in his lap. "Sleep, Ro, you have earned it."

And in answer to the expression he saw darkening Ranulf's face as the other man turned to glare at him,

"Back off, Rafe. Better that any watchers there may be should see her in my arms than yours. Unless, of course, you have a sudden yearning for a reputation as unsavoury as mine?"

"We have got this far," Joscelin intervened quietly. "By acting together, each looking out for his sword-brother, or..."

He nodded at Rowène with a wisp of a smile as he continued,

"Or sister. Let us not quarrel now. If anyone is watching us, all they will see are four soldiers who having been on duty all day, have it in mind to stand down from their corpse watch now there is no-one here to be impressed by it. Even Gabriel and I, it will be thought, have limits to which we can mourn."

He raised his voice, addressing the young man leaning against the wall by the door.

"Nic, be a good lad and go find us some food and a jug of wine. I for one am not too tired that I can ignore any longer the demands of my belly. Oh, and make sure that it is Ulric on duty outside the hall. If I am to sleep tonight, I want to do so with some assurance that I will wake up in the morning without my throat being slit."

"Never mind food, I just need not to be standing upright, even if only for a candle-notch," Rowène groaned. "I never knew mail could be so heavy, or the weight sink right down to my feet. I respect you, my sword-brothers..."

She smiled at the three men.

"More now than ever. I am sure my ankles must be as swollen as they were when I was two seasons gone with... when I was carrying Lissie."

She caught the haunted look in Ranulf's dark blue eyes, knew he was remembering the child he had seeded in her womb, the child she had not managed to carry two months, let alone two seasons.

The next moment he had turned his head, so that all she saw was the splintering of candlelight against his weathered cheek.

"I remember that," Joscelin said with a wry grin, his sleet-grey eyes softened by a rare teasing laughter. "Your belly was so great, your gowns stretched so tight I cannot fathom how they did not split at the seams, and you waddled like a duck when you walked."

"Adèle wants a child," Gabriel said abruptly, killing the mirth dead, and his eyes when Rowène shifted against his leg to look up at him were a dull, desolate shade of shadowed amber. "And I gave my word to the Lady of the Stars that I would fulfil my side of that bargain."

Ranulf opened his mouth to say something and then, at a look from Joscelin, shut it again, leaving it to Rowène to say gently,

"It will be all right, Ré. Luc would not begrudge you giving Adèle a child."

"No, I know he would not. He said as much to me before I took the binding oath with her."

He sent a glinting glance at Ranulf.

"And as I told Adèle on our binding night, I have lain with as many women as men so any crude advice you may have in mind to offer you can keep to yourself."

"I was merely going to say," Ranulf remarked, mildly for him. "That it is not performing the deed that is the difficult part..."

"Even for such as I?"

"Tie a bloody knot in your tongue, de Marillec," Ranulf growled. "You are not so different from me, for all you are half-fey and Luc's lover. I was going to say it is what comes afterwards... keeping your woman and child safe through childbirth, then through the years of your son or daughter's childhood and youth, until he or she is grown. That, my friend, is the truly difficult part."

"You lost a child?" Gabriel asked, quietly enough that Ranulf could ignore him if he wanted to.

"Two. One, a boy I never wanted, gods forgive me. He died at birth. The other, a girl-child..."

He did not look at Rowène but she could feel his pain.

"The gods damn me for the circumstances of her conception, but even so I wanted her, even knowing her life would mean my death. But she never lived to be born. As for the son I do have, I rarely see him and have had scant hand in his rearing after the first year, save providing coin for his keep. If ever I were to sire another child, which considering my state of perpetual bloody celibacy..."

He grinned mirthlessly at Joscelin, his expression softening to wry acceptance as he momentarily met Rowène's gaze, before once again addressing Gabriel.

"Is as unlikely as my regaining the lordship of Valenne. But if I did, then I would want a different life for him, or her. To be a father in truth."

"And so you take it upon yourself to question what sort of father I would make to Adèle's child?" Gabriel asked. "Bearing in mind what I am – disinherited, disgraced and a half-fey sodomite to boot."

Ranulf shrugged.

"It is no affair of mine. But if you are any sort of man, you need to be asking yourself that question before you risk conception. Your seed. Your child. Your responsibility. And consider very carefully the terms of the bargain you struck with the woman who wears your binding band. A child for your freedom, if I remember aright. How much of a father will you be if you abandon her the moment you have spilled your seed, leaving her to carry and bring up your child alone?"

"Damn you, de Rogé!"

Gabriel's voice was deadly quiet, the cold slither of a blade coming free from its sheath.

"Damn you to Hell if you think I have not already sent myself half-mad thinking of that."

Then his head dropped, his hair a soft fall of sunlit bronze, and so long it brushed against Rowène's cheek, making her start.

"Did you know, Ro, that I tried to kill your lover the first time I saw him," Gabriel remarked.

His voice was still quiet, holding the reflection of distant memories, his eyes flickering gold within the shadows thrown by his hair.

"Years ago now, when he still went by his family name. It was understandable then, you will admit. But now.. now he is my sword-brother, my friend so help me..."

"And still you would like to take your blade to me," Ranulf finished with a grin. "There is always the practice yard tomorrow. If we live that long. I confess I did not like the look in Joffroi's eye earlier. We are marked men, now even more than before."

"There is that," Gabriel replied, straightening up again. "Unfortunately, Rafe, whether I beat you or not..."

"And you more than likely would."

"It still will not take the sting of truth from your words."

"Let us just see what tomorrow brings," Rowène suggested with another yawn. "All depends on Linnius' decision. Whether he listens to Joffroi's bloody counsel or the more reasonable voices of those few of his Counsel who just want the whole matter dealt with discreetly, and then forgotten."

"Linette will try and persuade him too," Joscelin reminded them. "Linnius is fond of her and may well allow himself to be influenced by what she says, as he was earlier today."

"We can but hope," Rowène sighed, though the sound was pessimistic even to her own ears.

None of the three men bothered with a reply, Joscelin and Ranulf merely exchanging a grim look. And while she could no longer see the expression on Gabriel's face, she felt the twitch of muscle in the leg her cheek was resting upon.

They ate the cold meats, cheese and bread that Dominic provided, washed down with spiced Marillec wine which only Joscelin seemed able to swallow with any ease.

Gabriel downed his share with a bitter expression and Ranulf with a grimace, while Rowène was simply too weary to notice what she was drinking, though usually she could not stomach the stuff.

With the waning of the pale winter daylight, and the onset of night, she stumbled to her feet to check on Luc again, reassured to find his heart beating steadily beneath Mist's curled body, the little cat visible to her eye if no-one else's.

It did seem to her though that the fey creature's pearl-grey fur was glowing ever brighter in the river of silver moon beams now falling through the high windows to illuminate the bier in a shining, shimmering circle of light that, together with Mist's watchful presence, would surely serve to hold the daemons of darkness at bay for another night.

At least Rowène hoped that was what it meant, for none of them could stay awake another night, though they might contrive some sort of guard rota between the five of them.

That, however, was something to be discussed with the others, not a decision she must take alone.

For now she contented herself with tenderly tucking the heavy coverlet that Dominic had brought, along with the food, more securely around her brother's body.

Luc was cold – gods' knew, they all were, there being no fire lit in the great hearth tonight for obvious reasons – but she doubted her brother felt the chill.

Luc was far from his tortured body, walking in the goddess' healing light.

Perhaps beneath white thorn trees where cuckoos called in eternal spring or strolling beside the sparkling stream that ran through the star-flowered meadows beyond the moon.

If Linnius' judgement went against him tomorrow, his soul would remain there forever.

If, however, the prince decided on a pauper's grave, then they must think of a way to get her brother's body out of the palace, to somewhere he might eventually heal in peace...

"How is he?"

Gabriel's almost soundless question, half a breath, half a thought voiced as he came to stand at her side, pulled her back from her prayers, her plans.

"Still with us," she murmured, wary as ever of the spy-holes high in the walls of the hall.

"The goddess has stopped his wounds from bleeding, started his bones to healing, and now she has sent him to wander the starlit paths of darkness, but do not fear, Ré, Mist will keep him tethered to this life, this place."

She cocked her head suddenly, curiosity pushing through her weariness to ask silently,

Can you see her? Mist, I mean?

And heard the smile in Gabriel's voice, though no-one else would.

Oh, yes. As clearly as I see you.

The affectionate amusement abruptly left his voice.

As clearly as I see what is to be. I wish to the gods I did not.

PART IV

SPRING

1208

Verse 1

Winter Eternal

It was Spring.

A beautiful, brilliant, gloriously vibrant spring.

Vital with colour and vigorous new growth in every shade of green there ever was.

A time when birds sang amidst the unfurling leaves, the good-wives of Lamortaine threw wide their shutters, swept the dirt and dreariness of the past season through their open doors, and set washing to flap gaily out upon the drying grounds beside the lake, the reflected blue of the water now dotted by a myriad of puff-ball ducklings and seven fluffy grey cygnets.

Out in the fields beyond the town walls, men sweated with oxen and plough to prepare the way for the spring-sown crops – barley, oats, peas and beans – grateful for the fresh breeze as they worked.

Everywhere weariness and gloom were replaced by chatter and laughter, fostering the hope that this coming year would be a better one – in every way – than the one that had, all of a sudden, melted away under the beneficent barrage of the bright spring sun.

Even the palace passageways seemed less shadowy, the servants who hastened along them more cheerful, the courtiers who graced the tapestried halls marginally less inclined to gripe and snipe at each other.

Only one woman did not smile at the coming of spring.

Nor could blossoming flowers and melodious birdsong melt the ice about her heart.

For with the cruel death of her beloved brother, Juliène de Lyeyne felt that her soul had been shackled in everlasting winter.

This particular morning in late spring, Juliène found herself sitting on the window seat in her chamber, gazing in desultory fashion out over the delicate greenery of the palace gardens towards the lake.

Looking but not seeing, all her thoughts being turned inward, remembering Luc and the far-off – and far happier – days of her childhood when her brother had been with her, his laughter warm, his grey eyes kind.

Yet by the time she had left her childhood behind and returned, already a woman, to Chartre, Luc had become little more than a shadow at the edge of her life.

And now he was not even that.

Just a stiff-limbed corpse on a bed of pale blue and gold silk, his soul long since flown beyond the stars...

"Lady Juliena? M'lady?"

Recalled by the sound of her name, she looked around to see her tire-maid moving about the chamber, pulling gowns from the clothing chest, shaking them, laying them on the bed, patiently trying to capture her mistress' wandering attention, to redirect her thoughts towards what she would wear today.

In truth, Juliène did not care what she wore, and was perfectly willing to leave it to Siflaed to decide. The girl seemed to have developed sufficient instinct not to suggest anything too gaudy in colour, nor anything bearing the glittering embroidery her mistress had once delighted in.

Indeed, if the decision had been left solely to Juliène she would have continued to dress in the plain dark green gown she had been wearing the day she had gone to the great hall of the palace and found her brother lying upon his silk-hung bier.

The day her life, as she had known it, had come to an end.

It might have come quite literally to an end too, if it had not been for Guyard abandoning his own duties to his lord and discreetly keeping her company for the rest of that seemingly endless day.

At the least, she thought, she would have lost her mind.

At the worst, she would have taken the small glass vial with its marking of scarlet thread from its secret hiding place at the bottom of her clothing chest, and drained it to the last drop.

She had not done so – had reluctantly given her word to Guy that she would not, even after he had returned to Vézière and could no longer prevent her from following her brother into death – and in the succeeding days she had made a discovery that would have startled her had she been capable of feeling any such emotion.

She was, it would appear, no longer frightened of her mother, either for herself or for her son.

Oh, her mother still made constant threats against Val, but not even these could serve to rouse Juliène from her apathy, since she had concluded that if the Winter Lady truly knew where Val was living she would have had Joffroi move against him long ago, either to capture or kill him outright.

Since neither of these eventualities had come to pass, obviously wherever Rowène had hidden him – and Juliène had to assume that with Luc's death her sister had taken over guardianship of the boy – Val was safe enough and likely to remain so.

Juliène had made no attempt to discover her son's whereabouts.

Not only because she would not, but also because she could not. Her ability to see people and places in the waters of her scrying bowl had always been haphazard and since the night she had come face to face with her goddess, it had deserted her completely.

If only she could say the same of her lord-by-binding!

Following the painful lesson he had learned at Guyard's ungentle hands five years before, Hervé had not laid a violent finger on her, either in or out of the bed he still shared with her when he could find nowhere better.

Unfortunately, that situation had recently and shockingly been changed by the sudden death, just after midwinter, of Hervé's only legitimate son.

Of course, Herluin had been ailing already – Juliène suspected he had contracted some sort of pox, since he had been even more indiscriminate in his whoring than his father, if such were possible – and weakened as he had been, he proved to be easy prey when the winter hag swept through the court.

Not that Herluin had been the only one to die that winter, from cold, starvation, or the kiss of the winter hag, and those men who formed the corpse watch – soldiers on punishment detail, petty criminals, and most notably the Guardians' former Second, Gabriel de Marillec – had been kept busy.

Collecting the dead from street corners and palace apartments alike, they had piled the corpses of the high-born in the palace crypt, those of the common folk in a stone shed just outside the town walls from whence they would be removed, either to be buried or burned on a massive pyre as soon as spring should melt the snow, thaw the ground and firewood would no longer be measured by its weight in silver.

It had been a bitter winter for everyone, the harshest in living memory, the daemons of death collecting a far greater tally than usual.

Juliène cared only that her brother had been one of that number, though it had not been the cold that had killed him, but rather his own recklessness.

She had thought nothing could touch her frozen heart in the days following Luc's passing, only to discover the flaw in her reasoning with Herluin's death. For Hervé, with a barely sane resolve to thwart his younger brother Léon's ambitions to become the next lord of Lyeyne, had returned to their binding bed with the determined and deliberate intent to sire another son.

Initially as indifferent to that as she was to everything else in her life, Juliène had made no attempt to stop him, simply lying beneath his weight as he grunted and cursed and fumbled, all through the long dark of winter, her body trembling under the violent force of his thrusts, her mind drifting to a place far away...

To the green-dappled light of a wood in late spring, where the song of the nearby steam mingled merrily with that of the birds in the branches above a grassy bank covered with tiny white and purple flowers. It was nowhere she had ever been in life, but perhaps in death she would find it again, and the man with whom she shared that verdant bed. Ah, Guyard...

Until with dawn seeping through the shuttered window, she would return from that enchanted place to find Hervé gone or fallen into a snoring slumber, and be dimly relieved that it was over for another night.

Thrice the moon had waxed and waned since Hervé had returned to her bed, and thick-skulled though he was, he could not have failed to take note of her woman's flow.

Each time she bled he had demanded to know why she was not breeding. And each time she had told him, with a calm that bordered on recklessness, that it was not possible for her to conceive another child. That he himself had taken away any chance of life burgeoning in her womb with his vicious attack on her six years before.

The first time he had been furious, and had taken his belt to her.

The second time his anger had been far worse, the broad leather strap being replaced by a thin birch whip.

The third time had nearly been fatal.

It had not been so bad to start with, though frightening enough with Hervé raging violently about the room, breaking whatever could be broken, while Juliène had simply stood still in the centre of it all, watching him, until her silent withdrawal had finally caught his attention.

He had turned on her then, putting his big, black-furred hands around her slender white throat, and with his dark piggy eyes boring into hers, had threatened to strangle her and throw her body out of the window, as he had done to 'that other stupid bitch' who had previously worn his binding band.

So Guyard had been right.

That had been her only thought as the gold-petalled shadows of long-gone roses had mercifully closed in around her.

Hervé had murdered that unfortunate woman, and now he was about to murder her.

With her last few heartbeats she had focused her thoughts not on the brother she would soon be meeting again, but on the man she would be leaving behind, calling to mind Guyard's gentle blue eyes, his firm, warm mouth... before remembering that she had lost him, lost his strength and kindness, lost all chance of binding him to her when she had lost her beauty.

It seemed the final straw, proving she had nothing left to lose, and in that moment she had opened her eyes, laughing scornfully into Hervé's face, daring him to do as he had threatened.

For long, uncounted, steadily darkening heartbeats, she had felt his thick fingers tightening...

Until it finally lodged in the slow-moving cogs of what passed with him for a mind that this was what she wanted.

That she had no fear of the daemons of death... that she would even welcome his setting her feet on the path along which Luc had already walked.

So that, just as she felt the cold, but not ungentle, hands of the gathering daemons and saw the starlit darkness of eternity deepening behind them, Hervé had thrown her from him with a frustrated oath.

He had stamped from the chamber, leaving her with a bruised throat and aching heart, and had barely spoken to her since that day. Nor had he come within two yards of her again, either in private or under the eyes of the court.

Hervé, she knew, would never touch her again.

She should be relieved at that outcome. Yet she felt nothing, unless it were a distant regret that Guyard would never know, since even though he would no longer want her physically, still he would be glad that she was safe from Hervé's brutality...

"Shall I brush your hair, my lady?"

Her tire-maid's eminently practical question served to remind her that she was not alone and that another day lay empty before her.

Did she want the girl to brush her hair, to prepare her to face another day at court? Did she even care? She thought that very likely she did not.

Her only answer therefore was a desultory shrug that Siflaed, perforce grown bolder and more knowledgeable in her mistress' ways over the past season, evidently chose to interpret as permission. Taking up the comb from amongst the neglected pots of scented unguents and untouched vials of perfume, she drew it carefully through Juliène's long hair.

Not carefully enough it would seem, if the subdued gasp was any indication, and while Juliène did not particularly care about anything, she felt bound to make some remark when the maid's subdued sniffing threatened to turn to tears.

Even so there was no perceptible emotion in her voice as she said, "What is the matter, Siflaed?"

"Oh, m'lady, your beautiful hair. No matter what I does wi' it, it jus' carries on breakin'. 'Tis fallin' out so fast, I'm afeared ye'll... ye'll..."

"Soon have none left?" Juliène finished when the maid apparently could not bring herself to express the enormity of the calamity in words.

By contrast, Juliène regarded the handful of brittle black strands Siflaed had pulled from between the comb's teeth with a distant indifference.

"Oh, m'lady, it did use t'be so soft an' shiny, like a blackbird's wing in the sunlight..."

"And now it feels as coarse as a horse's mane, what little there is of it. Sad, yes, but if I am not troubled, Siflaed, you need hardly weep over it. And it really does not matter. If it comes to that, I can always wear a full head rail like the Sisters of Mercy do."

The girl was not listening though.

"Oh, no, ye couldn't do that, m'lady. 'Twouldn't be fittin'. But mayhap if I wash yer hair in a mixture of herbs an' honey? That might gi'e it some strength an' shine again. Nex' time we go ter Vézière, I'll ask the Eldest what she thinks. Or mebbe even that Sister Fayla what helped heal ye that time."

"As you wish," Juliène replied with a shrug, her tone no more than tepid, even mention of her wretched sister no longer able to arouse any anger – any emotion at all – in her.

Evidently distressed by this lack of interest, Siflaed continued earnestly, her Lyeyne dialect thickening her words,

"I'm sure th'Eldest'ud be able t'help ye, m'lady."

"Possibly she could," Juliène replied.

She managed the merest lilt of the lips, something that was meant to be a smile for the Lyeyné serving woman who had put up with her all these years, only the goddess knew why, since Juliène would be the first to admit she had not been an endearing mistress.

"But as I am not likely to be visiting Vézière any time soon, if ever again, you must reconcile yourself. It may be a long time indeed before you see any of the Grey Sisters again."

"But... but..." The maid stared at her, a slow blush rising in her cheeks. "But what about..."

She hesitated again, glancing at the closed door to the passageway, and lowered her voice to no more than a nearly soundless whisper.

"What about that Master Finch? I thought ye went ter Vézière ter see *him*. 'Cos ye... *liked* him."

"Master Finch? Oh, you mean Lord Nicholas' household harper?"

Juliène raised her brows in an effort to appear imperiously indifferent, more to protect Guyard's anonimity than her own unredeemable reputation.

"I admit the man is certainly more skilled with a harp than many who make such claim, but that is all there is to it. Whatever you may be imagining, Siflaed, you would be better to put it from your mind."

"An' he likes ye too, m'lady," her tire-maid continued stubbornly, refusing to be put down. "I seen how he looks at ye."

Goddess!

When had the girl grown from a shrinking, fearful creature into this outspoken companion who cared what happened to her self-centred mistress?

"An' why else would he ha' looked arter ye when..."

The brown eyes dropped suddenly but not before Juliène had caught a glimpse of tears.

"When Lord Joffroi did them terrible, awful things t' yer brother." Juliène swallowed.

"I did not know you had seen my brother."

"Aye, I did, m'lady. I'd come lookin' fer ye, 'cos ye'd not slept in yer bed all that night, an' I were worried 'bout ye. Then I remembered that yer brother were due t' stand trial that day, so I went down t' the hall t' see if I could find ye. An' there ye were, jus' comin' out. I could see as ye was upset, an' I tried t' get t' ye, but then I seen as how Master Finch was wi' ye, an' I knew ye'd be safe wi' him whate'er happened. Jus' like I knew somethin' bad had happened in the hall an' though I didn't want t' go, I got swept along o' ev'ryone else, an' then I seen him. Yer brother, m'lady, all laid out on his silken bed."

There were tears on her cheeks now, not just in her eyes.

"I'm right sorry, m'lady, 'bout what they done t' him. He didn't deserve that, no how. He were a good man, an' Lord Joffroi should ne'er ha' had him tortured like that, 'specially when he didn't ha' the prince's auth... auth... ority." She stumbled over the formal term. "Anyhow that's what Lord Joscelin said, I heard him meself. An' that yer brother died 'an innocent man, 'cording t' Mithlondian law."

She repeated the words firmly, her softly accented voice carrying a disconcerting echo of Joscelin de Veraux's crisp, cultured tones.

"But he is still *dead*," Juliène said numbly. "Nothing can bring my brother back to me. Nothing can give Luc his life back. Let him laugh or... or love again."

"I know that's so, m'lady, but at least he's got his good name... the family name that is, back ag'in."

Siflaed's voice cut through Juliène's vague thoughts, turning the hidden darkness uppermost, like soil against the plough share, revealing her vengeful hope concerning the depth of pain Gabriel de Marillec must have suffered that day, and might indeed still be crippled by...

Then, when she realised what Siflaed had said, she demanded with a frown,

"What in gods' name do you mean, girl? How can the de Chartreux name be cleared by any of this? Luc was to be tried as a traitor and a s...s..."

Her voice descended into a sibilant whisper, unable to utter the pertinent word, instead concluding in a brittle tone,

"And, gods forgive him, as Gabriel de Marillec's lover."

"Aye, but he *weren't*, m'lady. Tried, that is! As a traitor. As fer t'other... Well, I don't care 'bout that, e'en if 'twere true, though like enough 'tweren't!"

There was a distinct note of defiance in Siflaed's voice.

"'Tis like Lord Joscelin said..."

The maid coughed at the recollection of whatever it was that Joscelin de Veraux had said, and looked momentarily embarrassed.

"Is't true that he's yer brother too, m'lady? Wrong side o' the blanket like?"

"Yes, it is true," Juliène murmured, even the realisation that this secret was now common knowledge failing to incite her usual ire, other than to wish once again that her bastard half-brother had been the one to die instead of Luc.

"But I really do not wish to talk about it, Siflaed. Just tell me what he – Lord Joscelin, that is – said."

"'Tis like I said afore, m'lady. An' if one bit's true, like enough t'other part is too. An' 'tis not jus' Lord Joscelin as is sayin' it. 'Tis the same where'er you go. In the streets, in the palace kitchens, in the guardians' barracks as like as not. *Ev'ryone's* sayin' it, m'lady."

"Saying *what?*"

"That yer brother was *innocent*," Siflaed reiterated patiently.

"O' ev'rythin'. An' that mebbe yer father was too. That 'twere all Lord Joffroi's lies, 'cos he wanted... beg pardon, m'lady... yer lady-mother t' wife. As well as the wealth from yer father's lands t' keep her in silks an' them green an' white gems her likes so much. They's also sayin' as how he murdered his own brother an' the old lord o' Valenne jus' 'cos he couldn't stand fer his brother t' be *Lord* Ranulf, wi' a place on the High Counsel, same as him. An' now folk're startin' t' remember how his half-brother jus' disappeared. Ye knows, m'lady, Sir Guy. Him what helped Millie an' me, an' played the harp so..."

"Never mind that," Juliène interrupted almost sharply, yielding to the unexpectedly urgent need to take Siflaed's mind away from the subject of Guyard de Martine before the girl could make the – to her, obvious – connection between him and Master Finch.

"People have been talking about Lord Joffroi like that for years," she pointed out dismissively.

"Aye, folks gossip all th' time," Siflaed agreed equably.

"But now they *means* it. Yer brother's bein' hailed as a hero. Ye know, like one o' them fellows in the old songs what braved fire-drakes in the mountains or sailed the far seas in search of gold an' gems, all fer honour an' love of a fair maid. Not that he did that, o' course, what wi' bein' outlawed an' Lord Gabriel an' all, but still 'tis said yer brother an' his men looked arter honest folk an' protected them ag'in' Lord Joffroy an' his Black Hunt. That bein' so, m'lady, I reckon folk'll be singin' songs 'bout yer brother soon, don't ye?"

Evidently seeing the bleak look on Juliène's face, Siflaed sighed heavily.

"I knows ye wants yer brother back, m'lady, an' that ye'd tear him from the icy grip o' the daemons o' death wi' yer bare hands if ye could. But ye can't. What's done is done, an' if he loved ye half as much as ye loved him, I reckon he wouldn't want t' see ye give up all chance o' happiness in yer own life. Why don't ye go to Véz..."

"No! I am not going to Vézière! And I never want to hear you speak of that place – or Master Finch – ever again."

Somewhat later – a candle-notch, or two, or half a lifetime, Juliène had no sense of passing time – she was once again sitting in the window embrasure, her thin linen night-shift now replaced by a woollen gown in an indigo blue so dark it was almost black.

Her hands were empty of any embroidery, her eyes blind to the beauty of the sunlit palace gardens, and even the smartish rap at the outer door was not sufficient to snare her attention until Siflaed cleared her throat and said questioningly,

"M'lady?"

Juliène glanced around to see that the tire-maid had put down the worn green gown she was mending and was looking to her mistress for direction.

"Oh, very well, see who it is," Juliène sighed, hoping with something that was almost an emotion, that it was neither her mother nor Hervé.

It was not. Rather the face that appeared in the opening was round, freckled, beardless and distinctly impudent.

"'Tis young Alain, one of Princess Linette's pages, m'lady," Siflaed informed her, quite unnecessarily since Juliène could see the lad's royal blue livery for herself.

At the same time she suffered a small pang of desolation as it struck her quite unexpectedly that this lad must be about Val's age... or a little younger, or perhaps older... the pain in her breast sharpening as she realised that she had lost track of the passing years, and that she might never see such an expression on Val's face as this child wore. An expression that seemed natural to boys of a certain age, and which served to remind her yet again how much she had missed of her son's growing years.

She had given him up when he had been just over a year old, and her only glimpse of him since then had been that chance meeting on the highway just south of Vézière. He had been about six then, if her hasty reckoning of the passing seasons was correct, and his face had still held the last sweetly innocent remnant of his baby curves...

"M'lady, will ye go?"

She pulled her thoughts back from that long gone spring day to the encroaching shadows of her chamber.

"Hmm... did you say something, Siflaed?"

"Aye, m'lady, I was sayin' that the princess is askin' fer ye t' attend her this mornin'."

"Oh?"

Juliène considered this request – or summons – with a sense of distant surprise, Linette – perhaps understandably – having shown no particular desire for her company of late.

"Very well then. I am ready."

Several heartbeats later, however, she was still in her chamber, frowning distractedly at Siflaed who was fussing over her gown, making sure her hair was tucked tidily into the plain snood she had hastily donned, muttering suggestions about jewellery into her ear...

"No, nothing, Siflaed," she said, rather more sharply than she had intended. "I need neither gold about my neck nor pearls in my ears. If the princess does not like how I look, she can send me away again."

In truth, she hoped that Linette would.

"So, Alain, how old are you?"

She put the question somewhat tentatively to the page as he walked jauntily beside her through the winding passages towards the royal apartments.

"Eight, my lady, nearly nine."

Val would be twelve... no, thirteen this coming summer.

On the cusp between boyhood and youth already.

What, she wondered, did he look like now?

Were the soft rounded cheeks of childhood already refining into a man's lineaments?

Was his hair still barley-pale like his accursed father's? Or had it darkened over the years to something approaching her own colouring?

Did his eyes still glimmer jewel-green like beryls in the spring sunlight? Or had they faded into the clear, pale de Chartreux grey of his uncle and grandsire?

And finally, would she even recognise him if she ever saw him again?

Not, of course, that such an eventuality seemed at all likely to arise, since Rowène would have hidden him far away by now.

As to where...

It came to Juliène that, given her sister's affinity with their bastard half-brother, Rowène might well have sent Val to Veraux.

Certainly that particular province was far enough from court gossip that if Val *was* there, living under his absent uncle's protection, his identity would be of little interest to the goat-herders, farmers and foresters who struggled to wrest a living from the steep slopes and rugged foothills of the Guardian Mountains.

Torn between love for her son and scorn for her despised half-brother, Juliène put in a prayer to the gods, and her own goddess, that if Val were indeed living in that far-off fief Joscelin de Veraux would keep her son safe.

And if he did not, he would find himself answering to her!

Startled from her vengeful thoughts, she recoiled abruptly as first one cat, then another, shot past her in a blur of fur, streaking through the narrow gap between her skirts and the wall, heading for the open door at the base of the long stairway, with something lean and brown and barking, in hot pursuit.

Thrown even further off balance, she stumbled, gasped, teetered...

And then as if from nowhere felt long, hard fingers close briefly about her arm to steady her.

Pausing a heart-stuttering moment to catch her breath as well as her balance, she leant on the second steel-strong arm that appeared amidst the swirling dust-motes, letting her heartbeat settle, dimly aware that the first hand had gone.

There came the sound of booted feet lightly descending the stairs... the ferocious snarling turned suddenly into a startled yelp... and then silence.

In that silence she looked up, meaning to offer belated thanks to her rescuer... only to leave the words unsaid as the dim light revealed a pair of cool grey eyes set beneath narrow dark brows in a treacherously familiar face.

Luc! Oh goddess! Luc, he looks so much like you. Why can he not <u>be</u> *you?*

With the clawing pain of loss ripping through her heart afresh, she pulled away so violently she almost fell again, only to have the bastard move swiftly to save her a second time.

"Damn you, de Veraux, take your hands off me! Just because you have chosen to publicly humiliate me by claiming to be my father's by-blow does not mean I will ever permit you a brother's familiarity."

"I beg your pardon, Madame. I would have thought the humiliation attendant upon any such claim would be mine. As it is, neither of us would have done other for any woman encumbered by her skirts."

There was no venom in her half-brother's level voice, merely ice, clear and cutting enough to make her blink as he continued,

"Next time, however, I will let you tumble to the foot of the stairs unhindered. If the gods are smiling, you may even break your neck and spare us both the lash of your unwarranted displeasure."

Us? Both?

There it was again, that reference to his companion. But then she had known already that it must have been two different men who had helped her.

And if de Veraux had supplied the arm upon which she had been leaning, whose had been the hand that had caught her so firmly in that first moment of falling?

As if in answer to her unspoken question, another man came running easily up the stairs towards them, the sunlight at his back throwing his face into shadow, though both his slender form and light, urbane voice were instantly recognisable.

"There, Josce! That should keep your little princess and her pets safe. At least from Kaslander's bloody vicious beast. And you have your sister safe, I see."

"Have a care, Gabriel," de Veraux remarked coolly. "Be advised by me. Mind your tongue and keep your distance from the lady. I myself have already caused Madame de Lyeyne considerable disgust, simply by existing. Who knows what pointless offence she may take from your own proximity."

For a moment Juliène almost apologised for her rudeness, before remembering who and what he was. What de Marillec was.

And that for all their protestations of love and loyalty, Luc had died. Because these two men had, in their separate ways, both betrayed him.

Determined to rid herself of their distasteful company, she looked around for the page. The child, however, had apparently taken one look at the two noblemen and chosen to leave her to their mocking mercy.

"It would appear that we are to be your escort from here, Madame," de Veraux said blandly, evidently seeing and interpreting her look.

"And how would you know where I am bound?" she demanded, finding she did still possess the ability to summon disdain from the unplumbed depths of her indifference.

"Because we are, for now, summoned to the same place," came the cool response. "Believe me, I do not like it any better than you do, but where the princess commands, I at least obey."

It was on the tip of Juliène's tongue to make some snide comment, only to find she lacked the will to maintain the necessary emotion, and instead said with the merest trace of bitterness,

"As do I, Messires. As do I."

In her previous existence – before Luc's death – if anyone had told her she would one day be strolling the palace passageways in seeming amity with Joscelin de Veraux and Gabriel de Marillec, she would have laughed with utter scorn.

Now, she simply accepted it.

That is not to say she liked it, nor was she prepared to treat either man with anything approaching courtesy.

Nonetheless, she lacked the will to do other than tolerate their presence, and so they made their way in a silence broken only by the whisper of her woollen hem along the stone floor, a soft counterpoint to the solid sound of the men's booted feet, albeit neither of them was wearing the spurs their high rank entitled them to – regardless of how little Juliène felt either of them deserved such a designation.

Thankfully for her battered senses, it did not take them long to reach Princess Linette's chambers, and after a brief knock, de Veraux pushed the door wide, nodding a wordless command to the bodyguard he found standing just inside the room.

Juliène cast one look at the guardian – fleeting but still sufficient to note the broad, mailed shoulders, the short fair hair paling to grey – just as she heard the princess say,

"Come in, gentlemen, I appreciate your swift response to my message. Juliène, it seems an age since I saw you last but I appreciate you coming now."

Just as if she had had a choice, Juliène thought, though perhaps the princess was merely being polite. In any event, she supposed she could do no less than reciprocate.

"Your highness, I am glad to be here."

She sank down into a full court curtsey, aware that the two men on either side of her were likewise both bowing deeply.

"No, no... no formality," Linette cried, advancing on them with a smile as bright as the spring sunshine welling through the open windows. "Not here, in my private chambers."

"So what *did* you need us for, Linette?" De Veraux queried. "The lad you sent made it sound quite urgent, yet all seems calm enough here."

His keen eyes were travelling around the room as he spoke, seeming to linger a moment longer than necessary – or at least so Juliène thought, since the child was clearly not in any danger of falling – on the little princess kneeling on the window seat, peering anxiously out of the open window, Lady Isabelle standing close by, holding tightly to the back of the child's prettily-embroidered blue dress.

"I sent for you, Josce, because I wish to travel to Vézière," the princess said with an uncharacteristically merry smile. "Now and without delay, it being such a lovely day. I need you to arrange an escort, a litter, horses, shelter, provisions... oh, everything that such a journey implies, and I have forgotten."

The princess was laughing, clearly happy.

Juliène, however, felt only a dull dismay. She could see well enough where this was going.

"As Adèle will be accompanying me," Linette continued. "I thought..."

This clearly to de Marillec.

"That you might wish to be part of the escort, Messire."

"If you and my lady wish it, I am at your service."

He bowed briefly but formally in Adèle's direction, she returning her estranged lord's courtesy with a confused nod and a blush, leaving Linette to turn all the charm in her royal blue gaze onto Juliène.

"And I want you to come too, Juliène. It has been a sad winter for you, I know, but it is spring now and perhaps a short, easy journey through the countryside to visit the Grey Sisters is just the thing to heal your spirits, if only a little. So will you come? I will not press you if you truly do not want to leave... Lamortaine." *Leave Luc's grave.*

For one bright blazing moment, when it seemed all her imprisoned emotions were about to break free of the icy shackles Luc's death had locked about them, Juliène almost said 'no'.

Then all the fire went out of her heart and she merely said flatly,

"As you say, your highness, it will do me good."

After all, despite her earlier words to Siflaed, what did it really matter whether she was in Lamortaine or Vézière?

Yes, Guyard would be in Vézière, but the odds of her seeing, let alone speaking to him, were slim indeed for he would be busy about Lord Nicholas' affairs, and even if he were not, his own good sense would surely prevent him from turning up at the Healing House simply because the inevitable gossip would report her presence there.

"You will not regret it," Linette was saying, her glowing smile fit to rival the beauty of a sunburst glimpsed through a swaying cloud of apple blossom.

Juliène merely curtseyed, and said,

"Give me leave to go and set my maid to packing."

"Of course. Tell her we will be gone a se'ennight at least. No need to pack anything fancy or formal. I do not intend to put Messire Nicholas to the trouble of entertaining us. But hurry, make haste, I do not wish to wait one moment more than necessary before setting out."

Four days later they rode through the open gates of Vézière's Healing House to the accompaniment of the bronze bells chiming in the fresh, flower-scented breeze.

Thus Juliène found herself back in the place where she had so vehemently denied, both to herself and her maid, that she ever wished to be again.

The journey – largely, Juliène was forced to admit, due to Joscelin de Veraux's meticulous planning and Siflaed's care for her mistress' comfort – had been relatively easy and even pleasant, travelling through the sweetly greening countryside, the spring sunshine warm, the weather doubly mild after the appalling bitterness of the winter just gone, the gentle air fragrant with growing grass and newly-turned soil.

Even so, with the unabated raw ache in Juliène's heart rendering her unfit to share her companions' gaiety, she had kept as much to herself as the princess allowed. Yet in spite of her determined state of solitary apathy, she could not help but make certain observations – some cynical, some merely surprising – about the men and women in whose company she so reluctantly travelled, as well as the man they had left behind in the Palace of Princes.

Indeed it would be difficult to forget the stale-drunk accusations and violent threats Kaslander had thrown about on the day of their departure. Malicious words that, for all no-one alluded to them openly, proved impossible to entirely leave behind.

Their effect could be seen in the barely perceptible stir of emotion in de Veraux's grey eyes when little Princess Lilia tugged on his tunic hem to be picked up or called him 'Uncle' Joscelin.

Seen also in the wary discretion Gabriel de Marillec employed in his dealings with the woman who wore his binding band but who was – if Kaslander was correct, and Juliène was certain he was, in this instance at least – carrying some other man's child.

Seen too in the faint, but perceptible, distance Linette kept between herself and the man everyone in the realm must now know to be her cousin rather than her half-brother, though it was plain that there was a deep affection and trust between them still.

On Linette's part at least. As for de Veraux, he was never more than coolly courteous towards the princess – or at least as far as Juliène could see. What happened out of the public eye was possibly another matter.

As for little Lilia, she appeared to meet the tedium of the four-day journey with a cloudless joy, alternately between travelling in the litter with her mother, and riding in turn before each of the three men who had in their various ways guarded her since her birth, and continued to do so now. Not least from the father who clearly hated her and would hurt her in any way he could, though the child should be safe enough in the Grey Sisters' enclave, Juliène concluded.

As for her own personal feelings, having finally arrived at the Healing House, Juliène found herself in a state of some ambivalence.

On the one hand she was glad to have the journey done – that never-forgotten flight half way across the realm in company with Ranulf, Ancalion, Gwynhere and an infant Val having left her with an unwavering dislike of travel of any description.

On the other hand, she knew she would be as out of place amongst the healing sisterhood as a sour apple in a basket of sweet plums. Her discontent made much worse by a dread of seeing Guyard again.

Goddess! Would she ever live down the embarrassment of their last meeting when she had first wept in his arms, then *begged* him to make love to her, driven by the need to feel alive in defiance of the black truth of Luc's death.

And he had refused.

Oh, he had done it kindly enough – she could not imagine Guyard ever being less than a gentle man – but whatever he said, she knew he had refused because he had not desired her.

How could he when her face had been blotched and ugly with semi-hysterical tears?

Nor would he want her now, when she was simply ugly...

A sudden soft ripple of grey and white, like a wave caressing a pebbly shore, made her look up to see the Eldest of the healers, flanked by Sisters Winfreda and Aldith, approaching the royal party where they waited just outside the gates.

Naturally enough, the Eldest went first to greet Linette and Adèle, asking after their health, a knowing gleam in her blue eyes, before turning to make much of the little princess and her pets, finally smiling a discreet, if undeserved, welcome at de Veraux, de Marillec and the bare-headed bodyguard.

This welcome was hardly universal, however, and with the other soldiers of the escort already dismissed to find lodging up at the castle, the presence of the remaining three men, now standing unobtrusively beside their mounts, was sufficient to summon Sister Winfreda's look of tight-pursed displeasure.

Not so Sister Aldith, whose round face expressed only unalloyed pleasure at being requested by the Eldest to assist the men in tending to the assorted riding horses and pack animals.

Only then did the Eldest turn towards Juliène, the slightest hint of stiffness in her manner, the faintest suggestion of dismay in her eyes, though none was allowed to disturb the serenity of her tone.

"Welcome, Lady Juliène. May the gods grant you peace in this place, and help to heal the soreness of grief from your heart."

"I thank you for your good wishes, Eldest," she managed with the closest she could come to courtesy. "But I fear that such a feat is beyond any power, mortal or divine."

The healer who had stood at Luc's bedside a scant season ago and watched him die – in spite of the vaunted skills of Juliène's wretched sister, and the acceptance by their goddess of each and every secret sacrifice made to her – held her accusing gaze for another few heartbeats.

"I am sorry, Juliène. For everything," the Eldest said quietly.

The next moment she had turned to lead the princess and her companions towards the simple rooms set aside for visitors, urging them all to settle in and be at ease, adding that supper would be served in the refectory at sun-down or, if the princess so desired, in her own chamber.

The demands of friendship and courtesy being satisfied, the Eldest excused herself without once looking at Juliène again.

Linette having decided against the appearance of arrogance that eating in her own chamber might give, they had all – with the exception of the three men who must have taken themselves off to eat at one of the taverns in the town – shared the simple yet tasty and well-cooked supper of rabbit stew, herb-flavoured dumplings, nutty bread and goat's cheese, served to the Grey Sisters in the large, well-lit refectory.

There was even a plate of Sister Gilda's honey cakes for Lilia, and a dish of milk and raw rabbit scraps for Amber and Jade, who had been almost as pleased as Juliène herself to reach journey's end.

Nonetheless, and in spite of her relief at no longer having to eat from a bowl balanced on her knees beside a smoky camp fire, under the constant assault of a contingent of midges, Juliène merely picked at her own food.

The gods knew she had eaten rabbit stew aplenty whilst travelling in Ranulf's grim company from Marillec to Valéntien, the memory of that journey making her doubly relieved that he was nowhere to be seen this evening.

While they had managed by some twist of misfortune to make a child together, they could rarely achieve more than a strained tolerance for each other's company.

He disliked her, and in return she felt nothing but contempt for him. Even more so since she had discovered that he had chosen to give himself – or at least his body, she did not believe he possessed a heart, along with his own peculiar sense of loyalty – to her deceitful cat of a sister.

As for Rowène herself, Juliène had already taken the precaution of surveying every face around the table, in particular those encircled by the full white linen wimple of the healers.

Though as she had not forgotten her sister's uncanny ability to appear as a beardless youth when she chose, neither had Juliène neglected to inspect those others who crowded into the refectory – beggars, travellers, servants of the house, and those strangers who came seeking cures, advice, or simply a meal from the Grey Sisters.

Rowène, however, was not to be seen in any of her guises, strengthening Juliène's notion that her sister must be hiding out in Veraux with Val and her own misbegotten brat.

Thank the goddess for that small grace! Long may she continue to be absent from my sight!

As far as Juliène was concerned, her sister had betrayed her more times than she could count.

First, Rowène had taken her lover, then her son, then her chance of another child. Not content with that, her sister had undoubtedly tried to set Guyard against her. And finally, after giving her cause to hope that with the goddess' intervention all would be well with Luc, Rowène had let their brother die.

Luc! Oh, Luc!

Unable to control the sudden surge of despair that overwhelmed her once more, Juliène rose from the table and, nearly blind with tears, fumbled her way from the refectory, almost falling over the little princess where she sat on the floor, playing with her pets and heedlessly sharing her plate of honey cakes with a pair of ill-clad beggar brats!

Ignoring the startled hiss from one of the cats, and the curious glances she was collecting from those seated closest to her, Juliène caught her balance, aided by the unexpected intervention of the taller of the beggar children – both of whom had leapt to their feet as she stumbled into their midst, the one throwing out a supporting hand, the other clasping the little princess protectively in her arms.

Pulling free, Juliène reached the refectory door and flinging it open, fled into the night as swiftly as her confining skirts would allow.

She half expected the Eldest or Siflaed to follow her, the former to offer hollow words of solace, the latter to flutter and fuss about her. To her deep relief she made it back to her chamber alone.

Goddess knew it was not *their* soothing she needed, or secretly yearned for.

Curling herself into a ball upon the narrow bed she allowed herself once more to weep for everything she had lost. And not just her brother, or her beauty. For this time there were no strong arms to hold her, no gentle voice to murmur comforting words, no warm mouth to feather soft kisses over her hair.

She was alone.

And nothing could change that desolate truth.

Not only had she lost Luc, a truth she had no choice but to learn to live with.

She had lost Guyard too.

And it was this last loss she now found so difficult to accept.

Rising unrefreshed from a restless night's sleep, Juliène left Linette and Adèle in close consultation with the Eldest – both young women sharing the same underlying shimmer of secret joy they had worn ever since that morning Juliène had been summoned to the royal apartments.

Wearily waving away Siflaed's anxious attendance, Juliène set off on an ambling and aimless meander through the enclave's grounds, ending up some time later in the midst of a neatly ordered plot of earth with herbs sprouting fresh and fragrant growth, the neatly turned rows of soil ready for planting with peas and beans, lettuce and radishes. Or possibly carrots and cabbages, leeks and turnips.

She pulled a face, admitting her ignorance.

It did not matter. Vegetables held no interest for her.

Nothing did.

Leaving the kitchen garden behind, she detoured around some scratching chickens, a strutting cockerel, and the malodorous midden heap, and found herself in the orchard.

Indifferent as she was to her surroundings in general, she found her grey thoughts lightening a little, charmed despite herself by the prettiness of the soft pink and white billow of blossom adorning the apple, pear and plum trees, in which unseen birds sang merrily.

Everything felt so alive around her, she could not help but allow some of spring's enchantment to seep into her own sluggish blood.

Taking a little more care for her path now, she avoided the bee skeps in the near corner of the garth, and keeping a cautious distance from the beady-eyed nanny goat and the loudly-honking geese who had been left to range free through the enclave's grounds, she drifted deeper into the scented tangle of flowering trees, belatedly wary of the ruinous effects of damp grass, not to mention goat and goose droppings, on her leather slippers and skirt hems.

Somewhere, not too far away, she could hear children's voices, and came to a hesitant halt, listening until she distinguished Lilia's high-pitched voice from those most probably belonging – here she sniffed disdainfully, wondering at Linette's laxity – to the same pair of beggar brats from the refectory the evening before.

For a moment, prompted by some reluctant sense of duty to Linette, Juliène actually considered going to look, before concluding that the child sounded happy enough.

Moreover, even in the relative safety of the healers' enclave, it was a surety that one or other of the royal bodyguards would be lurking somewhere close by, de Marillec making up for his lack of the brawn Ranulf displayed such a surfeit of by his swift deftness with a blade of any description.

With a flicker of a grimace at the thought of the two men she disliked so much Juliène turned away from the children's laughter, walking onwards until the only sound disturbing the vivid spring silence was the light hum of bees busy in the blossom above her head.

It was, she thought, almost pleasant to be alone, with no care for herself or anyone else...

Until, coming to a short wall covered with honeysuckle and rambling roses, green of leaf and heavy with tight-furled flower buds, she heard a voice she knew.

A voice she *did* care about.

Swaying slightly, she came to a halt, the better to listen, finding herself almost sick from the surge of contrary emotions sweeping through her.

Dread. Yearning. Disbelief.

And finally – when she eventually managed to make some sense of what she was hearing – a raging tide of fury.

"She should be told," the first voice was saying.

The voice she had last heard whispering words of comfort as his big warm hands gently stroked her back.

"You do not know – *cannot* know – how terrible this has all been for her."

"And I suppose *you* bloody do!"

This other voice she knew too, and while the faint trace of an accent was the same as that of the first speaker, the tone was a shade deeper, harsh with impatience, and the language employed far coarser as he continued,

"For gods'sake, Guy! She's a fucking manipulative *whore!* Always has been, always will be, and..."

"For pity's sake, Ran! Do you think she had a *choice!*"

"Of course she had a choice, and if you are too blinded by her enchantments to admit that she's got your bollocks twisted between her lily-white fingers..."

"Watch your tongue, Ranulf..."

"Why? Because I am telling the truth and you do not like it?"

"No, because she deserves better than your crude dismissal after all she has been through. But then you have never shown the slightest compassion or respect for any woman, have you? The gods know you have had more women than I have seen sunrises and you treat them all like whores, even R..."

"Do not bloody say it, Guy!"

"Then keep a civil tongue in your head when you speak of J... of my... of this particular lady."

Finally a lighter, undoubtedly feminine voice that Juliène had no difficulty whatsoever in recognising as her sister's! Though how... or why... And if Ro was here, then where...

Shaking off her shock, Juliène came to realise that while her sister did not appear to be speaking directly to either of the quarrelling men, she was definitely talking about them, with an affectionate humour distinctly tinged with exasperation.

"Gods above! You have known them longer than I have, Edwy. Were they always like this?"

"Aye, right enough," replied a rough voice presumably belonging to the unknown Edwy. Siflaed's Edwy, perhaps? Carrying the same Rogé accent as the other two men, though it was far more pronounced than that of either of Lord Jacques' sons, it seemed likely that he was indeed Edwy of Rogérinac.

"Stand together 'gainst all comers they would, but t'otherwise 'twere like flint against steel, sparks flyin' 'twixt the pair o' 'em all the time, 'specially when there were a woman involved. Eh, Ran?"

"Bugger off, brother!" Ranulf riposted caustically.

Causing Juliène to blink and wonder whether he used the term literally? It was entirely possible, given Lord Jacques' reputation.

"As it is," Ranulf had continued without pause. "I am damned if I know what you are doing here anyway. Apart from amusing yourself at our bloody expense!"

"Aye, well, I've waited long enough for the chance," the other man retorted. "An' since my arse is still sore from two days in the saddle, an' for once my charges have other eyes ter watch o'er them, I might just as well be here as there. Though hell knows I'd get more sense out o' *them* than ye two. The las' time I seen the pair o' ye bicker this badly was the day..."

"Oh, enough, gentlemen, enough!" Rowène's voice intervened, apparently addressing all three men impartially. "We all have better things to be doing than indulging in family quarrels!"

There was a small silence, then her sister's voice came again, careful, diffident, no longer amused.

"Look, Guy, I know Ranulf could have put it better, but some part of what he said does have the merit of being true, in that whatever Juliène means by you, assuredly it will be to serve her own ends. Sooner or later she *will* bring you down."

"No," Guyard said flatly. "In this you are wrong. All of you! Whatever any of you say, you have no proof, merely your opinion, and I highly doubt it is impartial..."

"You are right." Rowène again. "It is not. But then neither is yours. Listen to yourself, Guy, and tell me she has not bewitched you, well and truly."

"She has never tried." Guyard's reply still sounded stubborn. "Why in gods' name would she? I am nothing to her. Nor, before you say it, has she has ever betrayed me. And believe me, she has had every opportunity to do so."

"And I suppose it does not trouble you that she once tried to have your brother arrested and dishonourably discharged from the guardians?"

"Oh, be fair, Rowène! Your sister can scarcely be blamed for her antipathy towards my brother, considering how badly Ranulf treated her in the past..."

"Aye, Guy, the past," the other man, Edwy, interjected. "So let it stay in the past where it belongs. Whate'er he did or didn't do back then is not at issue here. As for what is... well, why d'ye not jus' ask the man hisself what he would have us do."

"Edwy, the voice of pragmatic reason, as always," Ranulf remarked, more than a little ironically, Juliène thought.

"Come on then, if we are to do this, best we do it now before some mischance takes the whole bloody matter out of our hands, and all our care and planning slides straight into Hell's icy pit, taking us all along with it."

There was a moment's silence as if they were looking at each other, perhaps seeking some sort of conclusion to their argument, and then, apparently having reached it, Ranulf said tersely,

"I don't like it but then it is not my decision. I just hope you do not come to regret it."

A pause.

A subdued murmur.

Then Ranulf's voice again, hard and brutally clear.

"No, *you* can bloody well do it, Guy. After all, you are the one who wanted to tell that treacherous little witch the truth in the first place."

"Tell me *what?*" Juliène demanded.

Storming around the end of the wall, she found herself in a small, sheltered square of garden. Refusing to look directly at Guyard, she served the other two men and her treacherous sister with a look of excoriating scorn that would, she hoped, serve to hide the unwarranted hurt welling in her heart.

"Assuming, of course..."

Her voice was like the crack of falling icicles in the ensuing silence.

"That *I* am the treacherous little witch in question."

Verse 2

Precious Beyond Price

"Ju?!"

The woman clad in healer's grey was staring at Juliène as if she had seen a wraith, her face as white as her headrail, her eyes a darker shade of grey, holding all the warmth of the wind-whipped eastern seas, or of lightning flashing across a frozen lake.

Three men were ranged at Rowène's back, two of whom Juliène had known by their voices alone. Guyard, Ranulf... and the other must be the one they called Edwy.

Brown of hair and hazel-eyed, whether he did in truth share the blood of the two fair-haired, blue-eyed sons of Jacques de Rogé – and there was perhaps a shadow of similarity in the broad cheekbones of each weathered face – there was no mistaking the bond of brotherhood that held them together against the intruder.

Her.

"Where in the fucking frozen depths of hell did *you* spring from?" Ranulf queried unpleasantly.

His dark blue eyes narrowing in suspicion, he flicked a glance behind her, his hand dropping to the hilt of the long knife sheathed at his side.

A tilt of the greying-fair head sent Edwy striding with swift, silent steps towards the archway through which Juliène had just entered.

"And how much did you hear?" Rowène demanded, her level grey gaze hostile in the extreme.

Just as if it were she, Juliène, who was in the wrong, and not they who were conspiring to keep the truth – whatever it might be – from her.

"Enough to know that Guyard has something to tell me that none of you wanted him to," she said accusingly.

"Too bloody right," Ranulf growled, just as Guyard pushed aside his restraining hand.

"We have just been through all this, and as you said, it is not your decision to make, Ran."

He was close enough now that Juliène could see the grave expression in his light blue eyes, and her heart seized in her breast.

"What is it, Guyard? Tell me quickly. It is not Val, is it? Oh Goddess, tell me nothing has happened to my son."

"Val?" He sounded surprised. "No, this has nothing to do with Val."

"Then what?"

In response, Guyard half turned and stepped back so that Juliène could see what the men's bulk had previously concealed from her.

Her sister, now crouched in the grass before an old man seated on a bench in the sunshine beneath a flowering almond tree, his hands clasped in hers, the drifting, breeze-borne petals no whiter than the hair flowing about his blanket-wrapped shoulders.

Suddenly the man looked up, straight at Juliène, and in the moment after his fathomless grey eyes met hers all she could see was a great darkness, edged by the misty silver radiance of a mid-winter moon, and then... nothing.

When the great, terrible, empty nothingness finally resolved itself into the more simple darkness of her closed lids, Juliène did not immediately open her eyes, content for the moment to remain as she was, knowing without the need to look in whose warm, comforting embrace she lay.

She knew those strong arms, knew the very scent of the man, knew in the hidden depths of her heart that he, of all men, would never let her down.

Herself... she was not so sure of!

Had she truly seen what she thought she had seen?

Or had it been merely a trick – and a cruel trick at that – of spring sunlight filtering through white flowers?

It could not possibly be true.

She knew it could not.

But for as long as she kept her eyes closed, she could hold onto the heart-breaking hope that it might be.

It was only when she became aware of the building tension in the hard body against which she rested, and realised that he knew that she was back with him, that she steeled herself to set aside her folly.

And then in the full knowledge that her dream was about to be shattered into a thousand crystalline shards, she finally allowed her lashes to flutter open.

To look into eyes as soft a shade as the sky behind his fair head, albeit the clear blue was clouded with concern.

Seeing this she could not resist raising a hand to touch his lightly bearded cheek as she murmured his name.

"Guyard."

He permitted the familiarity, a slight flush caressing his cheekbones as he murmured,

"Are you all right now?"

"Yes. Or at least I think so. I do not usually swoon away like some hapless, love-lorn maiden."

"It must have been the shock, for which I am truly sorry."

"*You* have nothing to apologise for. It is me. I... I think I must be going mad. I thought I saw my brother. Luc. Not his wraith, but himself. A living man... though..."

Her voice trembled a little.

"His hair was as white as a wraith's would be."

"Juli," Guyard started gently.

Before allowing another voice, hoarse and alarmingly weak but still recognisable as that of her beloved brother, to take over,

"Come, see... feel for yourself, little sister."

"Luc? Oh, Luc!"

Delight and disbelief ran simultaneously through her limbs, the one giving her strength, the other immediately sapping it away again.

Unable to stand, Juliène simply flung herself towards her brother, landing beside him in a tangle of uncooperative limbs, crushed grass and twisted velvet.

Wrapping her arms about his booted legs, she laid her cheek against the reassuring reality of warm flesh over hard bone, and wept with incoherent joy.

"Gently, Juliène, gently. Luc is still far from regaining his former strength and robust health."

Catching a glimpse of a grey robe, Juliène turned to snarl at her sister, only realising at the last moment that the soft voice belonged to a completely different healer.

"But he will?" she said instead.

Less in question than fierce demand, as if by her own strength of need she could make it so.

"Gods willing," the Eldest replied.

She must have seen the way Juliène's gaze was scouring the small, sheltered garden for she added with barely a pause,

"Ah! If you are looking for Rowène, she and Rafe and Edwy have other duties to which they must attend just now."

I would wager a prince's ransom on that, Juliène thought acidly. *Thus taking the coward's way out of any confrontation. At least Guyard is still here.*

"However, you may remain with Luc, if you wish, for a little while..."

"What the Eldest means," Luc finished the healer's caution in the same heartbreaking dry wisp of his former firm voice.

"Is that you can stay with me until I fall asleep again. I am afraid it does not take much to weary me these days, Ju, but with the good care lavished on me by our own sister and the Eldest, I have no doubt I will one day be the man I once was.

"Well... almost," he finished, more than a little wryly, an odd faraway look that Juliène could not interpret creeping in to shadow the sunlit clarity of his eyes.

Then evidently recalling himself with an effort,

"Come, Ju, come sit here beside me."

Taking her hand in his blessedly mended fingers he scanned her face, feature by feature, even as her own eyes were desperately roaming over her brother's face, almost as if she feared he would disappear if she took her gaze from him for so much as a heartbeat.

"I am sorry no-one saw fit to tell you sooner that I had survived my encounter with Mithlondian justice," Luc said quietly.

"And I thank you for all you did for me on that midwinter night... all you gave up for me. I do not remember much about it but I know it could not have been as easy as the others have tried to persuade me it was. No-one deals with the deities without paying some sort of price."

"I would have done anything to give you that chance of life," she replied in a fierce whisper.

"Paid any price asked of me."

Then lowering her voice still further so that Guyard, who had withdrawn a little but was watching her with tender compassion writ plain upon his face, would not hear her.

"And losing my beauty is not so terrible if it means our mother can no longer use me in the furtherance of her schemes, either to manipulate weak men or break strong ones."

Despite his frail appearance her brother's eyes were keen and clear, the glance he angled between her and Guyard telling her that he knew perfectly well to whom the last part of her speech alluded.

He said nothing further though, merely closing his fingers more firmly around hers in a wordless gesture of love and support that meant so much to her. For if Luc approved of her... feelings for Guyard – and she was not sure what they were herself – then all would be well.

For her, if not her duplicitous sister.

In punishment for Rowène's lies, Juliène was determined to put paid to any similar acceptance Luc might be considering of their sister's ongoing – and blatantly obvious – liaison with Guyard's half-brother.

As for Luc's own relationship with Gabriel de Marillec...

Sighing, she resolved to show a little less hostility to the man in future, difficult though it would undoubtedly be.

Remembering how close she – they – had come to losing Luc to the star-lit shadows of eternity, she forced back the bitter bile that decades of jealousy had left bubbling in her belly, telling herself that surely she could manage to share her brother with de Marillec for whatever span of time they had won for him.

Unless...

She snatched at the sudden, startling thought and examined it carefully from all sides.

Unless de Marillec's share in their combined sacrifice that mid-winter's night had been to *give up* all claim on Luc's affections... and if that were indeed so, then perhaps – just perhaps – de Marillec had decided instead to uphold the terms of his binding oath, distasteful though that act must have been for all concerned.

With the worm of malice once more winding its way through her mind, its cold poison insidiously seeping through the momentary warmth of her heart, to surround her soul in a web of fine-spun ice, Juliène allowed herself to consider whether it was possible that the child Adèle was carrying had in truth sprung, not from some casual coupling with a nameless lover as it was commonly supposed, but from her lawful lord-by-binding's seed.

Incredible as it seemed, that child – if a boy, and born within the time stipulated by the High Counsel – would be from birth the legitimate master of Marillec's wine-rich wealth.

Thus ensuring that his mother would be secure in her position, during his minority at least.

Ah! Now *that* was a reason Juliène could understand.

It was the most compelling – indeed the only – reason she could think of for Adèle de Marillec to accept into her bed and her body a man who had been condemned in public court as another man's lover, self-interest evidently proving a far stronger incentive than her inevitable disgust at such a coupling.

As for de Marillec himself, Juliène could *almost* bring herself to pity him *if* this had indeed been his sacrifice to the Moon Goddess. The price he had agreed to pay to give the man he loved a second chance at life.

Luc would be free to live his life as he chose.

Gabriel de Marillec, however, would still be disgraced, disinherited and dependent on first his wife's, then his son's, charity to put clothes on his back and food in his mouth, since he could hardly earn more than a few marks a week doing the filthy tasks no other guardian would willingly perform, and which was all the employment the High Counsel would permit his Commander to offer him.

Did Luc know about his lover's reconciliation with the woman who wore his binding band? If not, she was determined that he would never learn of it from her.

Suddenly anxious lest his close encounter with the wraith-lands had heightened her brother's latent fey perceptions, she said hastily and almost at random as she reached out to touch a long strand of the snowflake-white hair brushing soft against her arm,

"What happened to your hair?"

"Ah, Ju! No-one treads as far as I did along the path to eternity and then turns back to the land of the living without paying some sort of toll. And it was little enough, compared to what you or Ro or Ga... or any of the others have given up for me."

Ah! So he did know – or suspect – what his lover had done. Nevertheless, she would not be the one to bring it into the open. Instead she said,

"Oh? So what did Rowène give up then?"

He cocked his head, considering her for several long heartbeats.

"That you must ask her yourself, Ju. Though I doubt she will tell you, given the strain you have put on the bond that once existed between you."

603

Then before she could protest that not all of that tension had been of her making, he asked gently,

"But tell me how you have fared these past few seasons. Not well, I think. The gods know you look as if the lightest of summer breezes would carry you away."

"I have not cared enough to eat," Juliène admitted. "Indeed, if it had not been for Siflaed – my maid, that is – forever nagging at me, I do not think I would have bothered at all. Now, of course..."

She smiled a little tremulously.

"Now I think I could eat a whole basket of Sister Gilda's honey cakes."

"And de Lyeyne? I do not ask whether a boor like him treats you well, since such a thing is beyond his capacity. It would be enough to know that he does not take his fists to you, or has hurt you in any other way?"

"Not... not since Guyard visited a little of his own violence on him."

The reassurance sat heavily in her belly, compounded by her omission of the nauseating frequency with which Hervé had forced himself on her since Herluin's death, and her near strangulation at his hands.

But then, Juliène did not want Luc's first action once he had regained his strength to result in putting himself at risk of execution again, this time by punishing de Lyeyne for his past brutality towards her. And even if it continued after she returned to court, she was determined that she could – and would – endure it in silence rather than put her beloved brother in danger once more.

"Forget Hervé," she said quickly. "I would not soil this lovely morning with thought of him. Tell me instead how you escaped from the palace."

Not only because she was hoping to divert his attention but also because she truly wanted to know.

Wanted particularly to hear what part her whore of a sister and their bastard half-brother had played, whilst she herself had been deliberately excluded!

She did not care so much about the others.

Ranulf, obviously, had been motivated by his desire to get under her sister's skirts, and as for de Marillec, Juliène would have expected him to aid Luc in any way he could. It was, perhaps, his only saving grace.

That left Guyard and the Eldest, and while they had clearly become involved at some point in the proceedings, Juliène bore them no rancour. It was plain from the conversation she had overhead earlier that Guyard had wanted her to be told of Luc's escape, and the Eldest's cooperation was essential if Luc were to remain within the walls of the Healing House until he had fully recovered.

Slowly, the pauses between his words becoming longer as he wearied, Luc told her what had happened.

Some of which he remembered seeing through the moon-shot shadows as he lay semi-conscious in his half-brother's bed, and the rest...

The rest he had glimpsed through the gilded veils of the setting sun as he lingered beside the stone bridge that spanned the river at the parting of the paths to the wraith-lands, looking back to bid what he had thought to be his final farewell to those he loved.

While Juliène did not pretend to understand even half of his mysterious allusions, she made no demur, attributing his present whimsy to a reaction against the stark experience of his near death.

He must have seen her look of bemusement though.

"Never mind that now," he said, the slight smile on his pale lips reflected in his rain-grey eyes. "You will see it all in your own time, and I pray that time is many happy years hence. As for how I got from the palace to here..."

He paused, frowning slightly.

"It all started, I suppose, with the honour guard Joscelin and Gabriel, Rafe and Rowène kept about my bier in the great hall. You knew about that?"

She nodded stiffly.

"I saw it."

"Well then, as Ro tells the tale, after seeing the lengths that Joscelin was prepared to go for me, Linette went to Linnius to plead on my behalf. For once, the prince yielded to his sister's subtler persuasions rather than the bloody demands of his chief counsellor, and as you already know, declared that my body should be thrown into a pauper's pit, responsibility for that action being given over to Joscelin, thank the gods. If it had been de Rogé, I would not be here now."

"No. He was not pleased by being passed over, as he saw it, like that."

An understatement.

Well did Juliène remember her mother's icy rage and Joffroi's goblet-smashing fury at that decision, though she had thought little of it at the time, the lord of Rogé, Chartreux and Valenne being prone to violence in word and deed whenever the prince showed his hated rival any favour, no matter how small.

"So how did de Veraux get you out of the palace?"

"If I tell you, it is to go no further, Ju," Luc said warningly. "I know you do not care for our half-brother but more lives than Joscelin's are at stake here. Betray him and you betray everyone else involved. Including Guy de Martine."

The threat slipped silken-soft from her brother's lips, binding her as surely as an iron shackle.

"I will not say anything to anyone," she said sharply. "No matter who connived in your escape."

Then it came to her.

"Ah! It was Messire Nicholas, of course!"

"Yes. Clearly it troubled his conscience that the son of his old *friend...*"

There was more than a thread of irony woven through her brother's words.

"Should be tossed so ignominiously into a pit of quick-lime – as soon as it became possible to dig one, of course – along with a score of nameless, maggot-ridden miscreants. So he went to Joscelin and suggested it might be more fitting were my corpse to be laid to rest somewhere out on the open moors. In secret, of course. A suitable substitute body being found..."

He did not say it but Juliène understood well enough that with de Marillec in charge of the corpse-collecting parties and savage winter still holding the land tight in its icy jaws, there would have been no shortage of bodies in the poorer quarters of Lamortaine.

"And that body being duly disposed of, all that was left to do was for Josce and Guy to bundle me up in a blanket, and stow me and my little friend there..."

He nodded up at the small grey cat lying stretched out along the branch above him, pale blue eyes wide open and oddly watchful.

"In the carriage in which Messire Nicholas had travelled down to Lamortaine."

Luc said no more.

Nevertheless Juliène could imagine the rest with an almost unnatural clarity.

How Lord Nicholas, accompanied by his harper, the Eldest of the Grey Sisters, and the long-nosed, chestnut-haired youth whom palace gossip had reported as being, for a short time at least, Gabriel de Marillec's catamite, had returned to Vézière, bearing Luc's still outwardly lifeless body here to the Healing House, where gradually he had come back to himself, cared for in this secluded corner of the enclave by 'Sister Fayla'.

"As soon as I am well enough to travel, I will leave," Luc concluded. "Though I fear that will not be a day too soon for Sister Winfreda."

Despite his rueful tone, there was a frown between his brows, the starkness of those slender, slashing lines made even more striking by comparison with the silvery fall of hair that framed his frighteningly pale face.

"I must..."

"You must not go before you are ready," Juliène said hastily, terrified anew that her brother might venture back into the wild before he was fully recovered. And even then, what would he do, how would he live?

Then seeing that he was still frowning,

"What is it, Luc? Tell me, and let me help you."

"I am worried about Rowène," he said. "With things as they are, she cannot continue as she has done these past dozen years, either as Jacques de Chartreux or Brother Justinian. Even her position here, as Sister Fayla..."

Rowène would not survive?

Juliène ground her teeth, knotted her fingers together and strove not to scream out her frustration.

Let her wretched sister survive as she had always done, bewitching everyone she met into believing her by turns a humble, virtuous healer or an ill-kempt, harmless youth.

Better by far if Luc worried about himself!

Then it came to Juliène what he meant, and she nearly laughed aloud as she realised exactly what her sweet, lying sister had sacrificed to save their brother, leaving Rowène in effect helpless – powerless either to heal or enchant – so that from now on she would have to fend for herself as any ordinary mortal woman would.

If all else failed, Juliène thought, a small smile of vindictive amusement tugging at her mouth, Rowène could always go and warm Ranulf's bed in exchange for his protection, and see how *she* liked the bitter and uncomfortable reality of being a soldier's leman.

She had more sense than to suggest such a thing to Luc though.

Particularly not now when his face was almost as white as his hair, and what had previously been a mere hint of strain and weariness had now deepened into dark lines of shadow about his mouth and eyes. Trying to keep her underlying worry at bay, she said,

"You are tired, Luc. Will you not rest now?"

"Yes, forgive me, Ju. I think I must. But we can speak again later, if you like. It is so long since we have had the chance to talk."

"Like? Of course I would like! I want to spend as much time as I can with you whilst I am here."

"And how long will you be here, Ju?"

She shrugged.

"However long Linette wishes to stay. She and A..."

She bit her tongue, inwardly chastising herself for her stupidity.

"She is here to consult with the Sisters about... well, about..."

"About the child she carries," Luc finished for her. His brows lifting, he said levelly,

"I am neither blind, nor deaf, Ju. Certainly I am no naive innocent where women are concerned, having two very wilful if much loved sisters."

Juliène nodded, flushing slightly, and knotted her fingers again.

Holding her brother's coolly considering look, she tightened her grip until she could feel every bone stark and brittle beneath her flesh.

"Madame de Marillec is with child too, is she not?"

Then when Juliène said nothing in answer to that question that sounded more like a statement, Luc gave her another wry smile.

"It is all right, Ju. You are betraying no secrets. Gabriel told me last night."

"Did he tell you who..."

No, she couldn't ask such an unforgivably intrusive question. Not of Luc.

A flicker of something showed beyond the surface calm of his ashen face. Nevertheless, his voice was as steady as his eyes as he said,

"He did."

And? Is it his child?

Luc said nothing more, however, and she was not going to push him to put it into words. Which did not prevent him from giving her a wintry smile as if he sensed something of her thoughts.

"It is not what you think, Ju."

It is not? So who in gods' name did Adèle yield up her precious chastity to, if not her lord-by-binding?

Casting about for an alternative, Juliène recalled how the woman who wore Gabriel de Marillec's binding band had always had a blush and a smile for his commanding officer, though perhaps not so much of late.

Nor had she ever seen any evidence, in public at least, that de Veraux lusted after his former Second's lady. Even so...

Could it be, Juliène wondered, that her ice-cold bastard of a half-brother had a somewhat more promiscuous nature than she had formerly given him credit for. She assumed, as a matter of course, that he visited the courtesans of the Crimson Rose with some regularity, but if her present conjectures were correct, he was also warming the beds of not one but two high-born noblewomen, with possibly dangerous and certainly far-reaching consequences.

Not that she cared. Joscelin de Veraux might share her de Chartreux blood, he would never be her brother. He was merely the unacknowledged son of her father's mistress!

As if the very thought of Céline de Veraux had called her up, Juliène became aware that the Eldest had returned to the sheltered garden, Guyard turning to speak to her, and Luc having fallen into an abstracted silence, Juliène was able to hear something of their low-toned conversation.

"Guy," she heard the Eldest say. "I am a little... concerned about Juliène."

"Why, when she is so happy?"

"That is just it," the healer continued gravely. "I fear that her very obvious happiness will give our enemies cause to wonder at this sudden change in her. We have taken so much trouble to keep Luc's presence here – his very life – safe from that witch who gave birth to him and who would like nothing more than to see his head on a spike alongside his father's."

"Juliène would never betray Luc," Guyard protested, warming her with his defence. "She loves him too much."

Before adding very quietly, very evenly,

"Perhaps the only person she does truly love."

"I agree that she would not betray Luc wittingly," the Eldest agreed briskly. "But now, in her first boundless burst of happiness... better I think if you take her somewhere quiet, somewhere she can... release her overflowing joy where no malicious eyes can see her and report back to Joffroi or Ariène."

"Yes, but take her where?" Guyard queried. "I can hardly walk with her through the town and expect it not to be noted by Joffroi's spies."

"Ask Sister Aldith for the loan of a pair of horses, there are enough in the stables at present and Joscelin will not mind. You could ride along the north road a little ways towards the moors. Few folk use that track nowadays, and it has the added advantage that since it starts just beyond our gates you need not go into the town at all."

"Even so, should someone see her riding with me, there *will be* gossip... with the further damage to her reputation that will entail. No, Eldest, I will do nothing to put her at risk from any abuse de Lyeyne may feel like inflicting on her."

"Neither would I, Guy. Not when I know what Hervé is capable of... The same violent disregard for women that runs in every male of the de Lyeyne line. His father was just the same, gods know, making my poor sister's life a misery. But that is neither here nor there. We must take thought for Juliène's safety now."

"That is what I am trying to do, and being seen with a lowly harper..."

"Come now, you are far more than that, Guy. The steward of Vézière in all but name. Everyone knows it though Lord Nicholas will not make the appointment public, lest it wake suspicion in the murky depths of your half-brother's mind. As to Juliène, let us be honest, Guy, she hardly bears the appearance of a rich noblewoman in that drab rag of a gown. If anyone should see her, I think it more likely she will be taken for a merchant's wife, perhaps even the mysterious Mistress Nell with whom your name has been linked on at least one occasion in the past."

"Good gods above! That was years ago! Besides which, how did *you* come to hear about that unseemly escapade?"

"My dear Guy," the Eldest sounded amused. "Sister Gilda loves to gossip almost as much as your fellow musician, Maury. And while your daughter and nephew call me 'Grandmère' I am not in my dotage yet."

It was at this point that Juliène decided it might be best to remind them that she was still there, Luc having fallen into a doze even as she had shamelessly listened to the conversation in which she figured as the chief topic.

Easing her fingers free from her brother's light clasp, she rose carefully to her feet and once certain that Luc would not slip sideways off the bench without the support of her shoulder, walked over to Guyard and the Eldest.

"He is sleeping," she informed the healer, low-voiced, with an anxious look over her shoulder.

"It is all part of the healing," replied the Eldest – Juliène would not think of her as Céline de Veraux, *could not* without remembering what the woman had once been to Lucius de Chartreux. "I will sit with Luc for a while in your place, and entrust you instead to Master Finch's escort. I have spoken with the princess, and since she does not require your attendance you are free to amuse yourself as you wish for the remainder of the day."

"Even to keeping company with a mere harper?" Juliène enquired, the innocence of her expression underlined, to her own amazement, with just the slightest hint of mischief.

Goddess! When was the last time she had felt like teasing anybody?

But today was different. Today her brother had been returned to her.

"I do not think the princess would begrudge you the freedom of a ride on such a lovely day in the company of a man she respects," the Eldest was saying serenely. "A man *I* trust to keep you safe."

"And what do you say, Master Finch? Can you spare the time from your duties to take me riding over the moors?" Juliène asked him archly, wanting his company more than she dared tell him, hence her slightly acerbic tone.

In reply, he offered his arm with a half bow and a smile that warmed her to her soul.

"I am at your service, my lady. Always."

Juliène laid her hand on his arm with a tremulous smile, and with one last look back at Luc, allowed Guyard to lead her into the orchard, where they were immediately concealed from any watching eyes by the fragrant canopy of pink and white petals.

Only then did the events of the morning sweep in to overwhelm her in a wave of sweet-tasting wonder.

The indisputable fact that her brother was alive.

That the sun was shining. That it was spring.

That *she* was alive.

Lifting her hand from Guyard's wrist, she flung both arms around his neck in giddy delight, and as if sensing her gesture had sprung from joyful exuberance rather than calculated seduction, he closed his own arms around her and, joining in with her laughter, swung her around as if she were an innocent child rather than a woman in her thirtieth decade.

After a dizzying few moments, he set her down gently, keeping his arms about her while she laughed up into his grinning face, his eyes between dark gold lashes showing a mix of amusement, bemusement and carefree mirth, bright as the sun dazzle dancing along the lilting blue waters of Chartreux Bay.

"I think the Eldest was right," he murmured, still smiling as he looked down into her eyes. "It is better that you get away from here for a while. So will you come with me? Trust yourself to me?"

To her surprise, he must have remembered her dislike of horses from the time he had served as her sister's groom, as well as the castle harper in Chartre, for he added wryly before she could reply,

"Even if we must ride?"

"So long as you take me up before you," she suggested, still in a manner of mischief rather than any more malicious motive. "I shall mind neither mode of transport nor destination."

She feared for a moment that he would say it was not fitting, then he seemed to toss aside all concern regarding propriety, taking her teasing words in the spirit they had been offered, so that when they came to the enclave's stables he shook his head at Sister Aldith's offer of assistance and set about readying just one mount – the unremarkable bay gelding she recognised as belonging to his brother.

Lifting her effortlessly to the saddle, Guyard swung up behind her, settling her back against him as he took the reins in one hand, his other arm lying snug about her waist, keeping her safe.

Guiding the horse with knees and voice, he took them out through the open gates.

"Where do we go?" she asked as he turned away from the town.

"There is a place I go sometimes when I feel the need to be quiet and reflect," he replied. "I think... I hope you will like it."

"It is not up on the moors, is it?" she asked. "Despite what I said earlier, I must confess that I do not enjoy the openness, the wildness of such empty places. I am a creature of court and castle, Guyard. I like the comfort of ordered gardens and the security of sturdy walls about me, and better yet a roof over my head."

I shall leave it to my sister to play the peasant slut, and let herself be tumbled in the grass to service the lusts of her brutish soldier. I am better than that!

"I cannot offer you a roof," Guyard was saying apologetically. "Nor sturdy walls. But if, when we get to my quiet place, you decide you are not comfortable, we will simply go somewhere else, somewhere you may be at ease."

She was at ease already, Juliène thought dreamily. An odd conclusion, given that she was far from the comforts of court or castle, but true for all that.

Above her, the sun shone like a new-minted gold crown in a sky of shimmering blue silk, sewn here and there with puffy pearlescent clouds, and all around her the land was quilted in rich browns and greens of every jewelled shade from jade to beryl to emerald, embossed and embroidered with flowers of white and pink, purple and blue, and brilliant blazing yellow.

And strangely she felt herself to be a part of it all, wearing as she did a diadem of such glorious joy as must restore her lost beauty, granting her a power so great that nothing could destroy this moment of pure happiness.

"Thank you, Guyard," she murmured, moving her head slightly against his chest, breathing deeply the scent of skin, sweat and spring flowers, of warm horse and worn leather.

"For what?" he murmured back, keeping the animal moving beneath them to an ambling walk.

"For believing in me. When your brother and my sister did not. I heard enough to know that you were arguing with them on my behalf."

"I am sure, in time, they would..."

"No, Guyard, they would not."

"Maybe not," he conceded. "But Luc always meant for you to know. I thought of sending a message to the palace but had no assurance you would receive it if I did. It was just fortunate that the princess chose to come to Vézière now."

"And to think I nearly refused to come. I should have had more faith in the goddess. And in you."

She turned her smile into his chest again, revelling in his warmth, his scent, the soft tickle of hair curling through the loose lacing of his shirt.

"Oh, Guyard, I am so happy, I feel I could sing a song sweeter than ever mermaid sang to mortal man... dance as lightly as a thousand butterflies over a field of flowers. I could never have remained within the walls of the Healing House without giving myself... giving the truth about Luc away. The Eldest was right about that. I only hope you do not mind that she asked you to accompany me? Am I taking you away from your duty to Messire Nicholas?"

"I told you, do not worry about that. I am where I want to be. Where I have wanted to be for... so many years now."

Feeling his arm tighten briefly around her waist, she relaxed back against him, allowing the rhythmic sway of the horse beneath her, the easy strength of the man who held her, to bind her about with the silken strands of happiness.

If only she could remain like this, with him, forever.

Unfortunately, all she had – all *they* had – was this one day.

And not even a full day at that.

All too soon she would have to go back.

To Vézière. And, in time, to Lamortaine...

"Oh, gods! What will happen when I return to court?" she asked, terror rising suddenly to shatter her happiness. "No-one, let alone my mother or Joffroi, must ever suspect that Luc does not lie in some pauper's pit, or that he left Lamortaine with your lord's connivance, and your active assistance. Goddess help me, I must do nothing to betray either you or Luc."

"You will not give either of us away," Guyard replied.

His voice was as firm as the muscles in the arm around her, or the spread thighs beneath her, and which she could not help but be aware of, anxiety notwithstanding or the reassurance of his belief in her.

"You gave up so much, Juli, love Luc too dearly to betray him by some carelessness now."

And in that moment she believed him.

Not only in the truth of his words, but that whatever she felt for Guyard de Martine was true too.

A gift from the goddess.

Quite simply, something that was meant to be.

So that when he brought her eventually to a small, sheltered clearing where a little stream ran sparkling and clear, singing its own merry song in sweet harmony with the birds in the nearby trees, and lifted her down to set her feet upon a mossy bank starred with tiny white strawberry flowers and edged all about with violets, she felt scarcely a flicker of surprise.

Looking about her at this enchanted place she had thought existed only in her dreams, she drew in a deep breath of that heady air, almost as if she were a crystal goblet, filling herself to the brim with the scent of green moss, rich earth and sunlit leaves, and for the second time that day she said,

"Oh, Guyard, I am so very happy."

His arms came around her without any hesitation at all, and as she leaned back against him she did not need to see his face to hear the smile in his voice as he murmured in her ear,

"Because your brother is alive."

"Yes, but more than that. *I* feel alive, for the first time in... forever perhaps. I am alive, and you are alive, and we are here in this beautiful place. Together."

She turned in his arms and pulled back a little, the encircling embrace of his arms loosening to accommodate her.

She did not seek her freedom, however, only sufficient space to lift a hand to cup his softly-bearded cheek, then rising on her toes, she laid her lips against his. He kissed her back, gently, warmly... yet without the unfettered passion she longed for, causing her to draw back, pain stabbing deep into the heart she had forgotten to protect.

"What is it, Guyard? Do you no longer... desire me? Now that I have... lost my beauty."

Self-conscious now as she had not been for the past season, she touched her dull, lifeless hair, the dry skin of her cheek, that had once been as smooth and soft as the inner petals of a snow-lily.

She did not regret giving up her beauty to save her brother's life, but still...

"I honour what you did for Luc," Guyard said quietly. "What you sacrificed for him. And to me, nothing has changed, you are still as beautiful as before. No, even more radiant, since it is a beauty that lights your very soul rather than some superficial gilded enchantment of the Faennari."

"Pretty words," Juliène said, her tone sounding brittle rather than lightly amused as she had intended. "A harper's flummery no less. If you did not want me in Lamortaine that mid-winter's night, you are scarce like to find me desirable now."

He laughed, not entirely with amusement.

"The gods know, if you do not, that I have desired you since the first moment I saw you, in your mother's solar in Chartre castle. Desired you – wanted you – as I have never desired or wanted a woman before or since."

She felt a flash of triumph that she had so overwhelmingly eclipsed her sister in this at least – and, to a lesser degree, Queen Xandra of Kardolandia – only at the last moment obeying some little-used sense of discretion to conceal her victory, lest it destroy this most fragile of moments.

"From the top of your head..." Guyard's voice was steady and sincere, his eyes revealing the first flickers of a banked blue fire.

"Every single silken strand of your beautiful hair, soft as starlight, dark as midnight, woven through with silver ribbons. To the tips of your toes, delicate and dainty as the tiniest pink sea-shell in all the Star Isles. You wore a narrow circlet of twisted silver about your left ankle, and it rang like a tiny silver bell when you moved.

"In my dreams I have kissed your lovely feet, tasted your honeysuckle-sweet lips, caressed every inch of your petal-soft skin a thousand times. Given you in return the chance to taste all the joy and delights your body should feel... until I have sent myself half out of my mind with desire for you... with the need just to be close to you, even if I could never be with you as only a lover can."

"Then why will you not touch me now if you feel... like that?"

"Because I would not have you kiss me – *lie with me* if, gods forbid, it should go that far, as I fear it would if once I started to kiss you – out of some misplaced sense of gratitude, which in all honesty is all I can expect you to feel for me."

"Oh, Guyard. Please believe me, this is not about gratitude, nor mere affection, though I do feel both for you."

"It is revenge then? Because of Ran? And Rowène."

For a heartbeat she was silenced.

Then, with a gesture that took in their perfect solitude, she said simply,

"Can you see anyone here save us two?"

She saw his gaze go beyond her, rising to pensively study what little he could see of the afternoon sky, and reading the doubt in his eyes, she seized his hand.

"It is still daylight, Guyard. The Faennari have no power over you – over either of us – here."

She waited until he met her eyes, and then said again, more softly,

"This time is for us. For you and me. I know my own mind and what is in my heart."

She hesitated but in the end it was so easy to say,

"I love you, Guyard."

He looked at her, clearly taken aback by her declaration, doubt plain to see in eyes that were as clear a blue as that of the sky above them, and out of a desperate need to convince him, she added with all the sincerity she had in her.

"And *because* I love you I will let it be your choice as to how we use these few fleeting moments we have together, precious beyond price as they are to me."

"To me too," he said softly.

At last he closed his arms around her, drawing her against him as she had wanted him to do, taking her mouth with his own... and then taking all that she could give him... returning her love with a heart-breaking, soul-shaking intensity.

He was warmth and gentleness, generosity and passion, awakening and answering all those same feelings and sensations in her, heightening her pleasure until she was so lost to it that she was barely aware of raking her nails down his damp back, causing his eyes to darken still further and his kiss – his every movement – to deepen almost beyond bearing.

And when finally he lost himself inside her...

All she saw was *his* face

All she felt was *his* most welcome weight stilled between her thighs as the sweet warmth of his living seed filled her lifeless womb.

All she heard was *his* laboured breathing, slowly settling, as the separate scents of spring violets and honeysuckle and the combined scent of their love-making wrapped them about in an invisible mantle of contentment and peace.

For that one pure moment it had been love between them.

Juliène and Guyard.

With no thought of anyone else – mother, sister, former lover – intruding to spoil that rare, wonderful, precious moment when they had been as one... body, heart and soul.

It was late afternoon, the sunset banners already beginning to fly across a lavender sky, when they returned to the Healing House, Juliène once more riding before Guyard, his arms about her rather more closely than he had held her on the way out.

Until, as they drew nearer to the town, he seemed to retreat a little, both physically and emotionally from her.

While this could not help but cause her a small spasm of hurt, she refused to allow her doubts to destroy the rare feeling of contentment, and the even rarer sensation of peaceful well-being that had followed their love-making.

It did, nonetheless, put her a little on edge, leaving her raw and aching for their all too transitory happiness.

Then, as she rode into the healers' enclave, she saw the one person guaranteed to revive all the old jealousies and resentments, her fury rushing back to lay waste to her fragile sense of happiness.

Rowène – clad in the healer's pale grey robe that was all that remained to her now – was crossing the yard and though she could scarcely have missed Juliène's arrival with Guyard, she paid no heed, instead continuing on her way towards the orchard, hand in hand with a giggling Lilia, swinging the little princess in the age-old game of childhood, with the cheerful assistance of one of the beggar brats from the night before.

A beggar brat who, having lost or discarded the coif she had been wearing in the refectory, was now revealed as having hair the colour of sun-shot gold silk!

A darkness beginning to gather about her heart and shadow the edges of her vision, Juliène turned in Guyard's arms, and on seeing him bestow an openly loving smile on the laughing, golden-haired girl, reigned in her rising emotions enough to say tightly,

"Who is she, Guyard? That beggar child?"

He did not reply immediately, and she wondered in growing disgruntlement if he had even heard her question. Goddess! Had he forgotten her presence, and what they had done together, so quickly?

Still without a word, he allowed her to slide to the ground – though it felt neither firm nor solid, her legs were trembling so badly – and then, kicking his feet free of the stirrups, dropped down himself.

Only then did he give her a quick, almost diffident glance as he said,

"Here is someone I would like you to meet, Juli."

The beggar girl, her beauty and grace rising above the rags of her kingfisher-blue gown like a swan from a lake, had already turned towards the sound of his voice, as a flower seeks out the sun, and with a word to her companions, left them to stand, smiling, in front of Guyard.

Juliène did not need to see her soft summer blue eyes – the same shade as those of the man beside her – or to hear Guyard's introduction to know who she must be.

"Juli, this is my daughter, Alysiène. Lissie, this is the Lady Juliène de Lyeyne. Your mother's sister," he added, and Juliène wondered if there was the slightest edge of warning to his tone.

The child – although she was scarcely a child any longer – gave her a clear-eyed stare, before remembering her manners and making the briefest of reluctant curtseys.

"Lady de Lyeyne."

A moment later she added with the blunt directness of the child she had clearly not quite outgrown,

"Are you Val's mama then?"

"Yes, I am," Juliène replied tersely, discarding the more conventional expression of happiness at this meeting. "Is..."

She swallowed.

"Is he here?"

Lissie glanced at her father for direction, then tilted her head almost imperceptibly, the rays of the setting sun weaving flickers of fire through her wheat-fair braids.

"He's somewhere hereabouts. I don't know where exactly. He went off earlier with Edwy and Rafe. Swords," she added, expanding her explanation at Juliène's impatient look.

"Gra... the Eldest won't have them practising inside the walls, you see. She says it upsets the Sisters. Well..."

The girl scrunched up her faintly freckled, undeniably long de Chartreux nose and said fairly,

"Sister Winfreda, at least."

"And what about your mother? Does it upset her too?" Juliène asked slyly. "Or is she quite happy to watch Rafe – you did say Rafe, did you not – display his prowess with a sword?"

She did not think Lissie understood her lewd allusion enough to be shocked by it. Or to question Juliène's emphasis on the presence of the man the child seemed not to know to be her uncle. She was certainly shocked by something though.

"My... my mother is dead," she said uncertainly. "Is... is she not, Papa?"

"Then who is that standing behind you?" Juliène asked, just as Guyard begged, quick and low,

"Do not meddle in this, Juli. Please."

"Meddle? Surely your daughter should know the truth about her wh... her mother?"

"Not now, Juliène!" he said, rather more forcefully.

She sensed his gaze lift beyond her to assess the audience they had begun to acquire – Linette, Lilia, the child's nurse, the Eldest, and a couple of the Grey Sisters who went hastily about their business at a commanding glance from the senior healer.

"No, tell me now," Lissie demanded, not in the least politely.

Her lip was trembling and her face had gone as pale as the late afternoon clouds drifting over the apricot sky.

"Papa?"

She glanced from her father to the woman who had come up quietly to stand beside her.

"Sister Fayla? What does Lady Juliène mean? You cannot be my mama."

"Lissie..."

It was said softly, lovingly, a plea for understanding.

"Yes, Lissie, I am."

"But why did you not tell me before? And why..." Her frowning gaze went from her mother to her father and back again.

"Why do you not live with Papa up at the castle? Or... or wear his binding band?"

620

"Because..." Rowène started to say.

"Because there is already a woman who wears my binding band," Guyard intervened flatly. "And Sister Fayla..."

Juliène saw Lissie's eyes flash blue fire at her father and she practically shouted the next words at him.

"She is a healer, Papa! Sworn to the gods!"

Another thought seemed to occur to her.

"Did you already have a wife when you... when you and Sister Fayla... you know..."

She flushed, her fair skin flaring from pale rose to pained scarlet, and waved her hand in wordless accusation when the specific phrase failed her.

Fucked, Juliène would have said, borrowing from Ranulf's crude vocabulary, for coarse as the word undoubtedly was, she could not bear to think that it might have been love that Guyard had felt when he had lain with her sister.

His voice heavy with regret he was saying,

"Yes, Lissie, I am sorry to say I did break my binding vows for your mother's sake."

Glancing at him, Juliène saw that beneath the normal healthy burnish of sun and wind he was almost as white as his daughter as he continued,

"But in my defence, Lissie, I had long been estranged from the Lady Mathilde, my... wife. And your mother was *not* Sister Fayla when I... when we... Back then. She was..."

Keenly aware of their unwanted audience, now expanded to include Luc, Gabriel de Marillec, Adèle, Siflaed and Joscelin de Veraux, Guyard lowered his voice.

"She was the Lady Rowène de Chartreux, and..."

He hesitated, as if wishing there were some way out of damning himself further.

"And *what?*" Lissie demanded hotly.

"And a prisoner. A hostage for her people, to prevent further bloodshed."

"A prisoner?" Her voice was high with horror. "*Yours?*"

"No. My broth... my half-brother's. He was – is – a nobleman. One of the high lords of Mithlondia. I was his steward, and responsible for your mother's safety while she was under our roof. In spite of the circumstances we became... friends, Lissie."

"But still..."

The girl was obviously fighting to understand how such a thing could have happened.

"So you did not love her? Woo her? As a harper courts his lady's favour in the songs? It was just..."

She waved her hand again, tears beginning to shimmer in her eyes.

"Lissie, dearling, it *was* love..."

"Then why are you not together? Why are you with *her*?"

That scornful blue glare was directed in turn at Guyard, Juliène, and finally her mother, scorching all three of them without mercy.

"And why are *you* with Rafe, Sister Fayla? I saw you with him last night, you know. Out in the orchard. Kissing! Letting him... *touch* you!"

The girl sounded as if she might be sick then and there, and despite her own somewhat precarious position as the instigator of this little reunion, Juliène could not help the flush of malicious satisfaction at seeing her sister blanch with guilt and horror that her young daughter had witnessed whatever intimacies she and her lover had been sharing under the spring stars.

"I thought he was some sort of kin to you," Lissie continued shakily. "Not your... your..."

"Paramour?" Juliène suggested silkily when Lissie failed to find a word to suit, adding with spurious compassion,

"Child, whatever happened last night between your mother and that particular soldier, I very much doubt it was her fault. I know Rafe of old, and he is a man who has an insatiable itch for the pleasures to be found with a woman. He does not care who the woman is – noblewoman, tavern slut or healer – so long as he gets what he wants."

"For pity's sake, Juliène, stop this. Stop this now!"

Guyard's voice was harsh with a deep-seated anger, vibrating like his own harp strings.

"She is a child, she does not need to hear you saying such things about her mother. Thank the gods her cousin is not here to hear you reviling his father."

Then, as something caught his eye,

"Edwy! What are you doing here? And what in hell have you done with Val? Gods forbid, he should be dragged into this mess too!"

Juliène would have ignored the man now glowering at her save that – with her ears attuned to the one name that could bring her malice to a halt, stopping her as no mere appeal to her better nature could – she needed desperately to know the answer to the question Guyard had put to him.

The whereabouts of her son, whose name she now repeated in a dazed whisper,

"Val? He is here?"

"Yes, sister, he is," Rowène answered grimly, having exchanged a quick, flickering glance with the man, Edwy. "So I suggest you mind your viper's tongue before you do any more damage to innocent souls."

Then lowering her voice until it was almost inaudible, Rowène dared to rest her hand on her daughter's shoulder in what was surely a doomed attempt to comfort the child, who was shaking with hurt and bewilderment, all her joyful innocence shattered by her parents' deception.

"Lissie, sweetheart..."

The girl ducked out from under the tentative touch, considered and rejected the comfort her father was silently offering, and looking wildly around for refuge saw her uncle standing at the very edge of the scene, the man who must have been the closest thing she had had to a constant in her life.

Despite her need, she stopped short of hurling herself into his arms, since it must have been obvious even to her young eyes that it was only by the force of his own will and the braced strength of his companion's shoulder that her kinsman remained upright at all.

As for said companion, Juliène guessed from the look of arrested attention in Lissie's eyes that the child had sensed that Gabriel de Marillec was more than just a friend to her uncle.

Equally clearly, she accepted the situation for what it was, and in spite of her own distress, bestowed upon him a swift, sweet smile, then as Luc put out a hand to draw her into a shaky embrace, she shook her head.

"Look... look after him, my lord," she instructed de Marillec in a voice that still trembled with tears.

And to Luc in a broken whisper,

"I love you, uncle. You know I do. I just wish you had told me before *she* did."

"I am sorry, Lissie..."

Ignoring his hoarse attempt at an apology, she shook her head, and turning, flung herself into the Eldest's comforting arms, the sobs she had held back until now finally breaking free.

"Oh, Grandmère... I just want my..."

"Mama?" the Eldest murmured, as she hugged the girl who was almost as tall as she was, against her.

"No, not her. Not Sister Fayla! What is *she* to me? I... I want my Uncle Jacques! He... he is more to me than *she* could ever be!"

She blinked salt-clogged eyelashes, then turned to glare over her shoulder at the woman she knew only as Sister Fayla.

"Where is he?" she demanded unsteadily. "Jacques is your brother too, isn't he? So why isn't he here now? Why?"

Her words were submerged in another choked sob.

"I want Ja... Jacques."

The child was close to hysteria now, her whole body shaking in the Eldest's tenderly protective embrace, her distraught accusations only slightly muffled by the healer's thick woollen robes.

"Where is he, Grandmère? Has Sister Fayla sent him away somewhere? Just like she always used to do, whenever she came to see Uncle Luc or..."

"Or you, child?" the healer prompted gently.

"*Me?*"

There was a startled note to Lissie's question, as if she were suddenly considering the possibility that her mother might actually have been visiting her, rather than Luc. Or perhaps she was simply on the brink of grasping the truth as to why she had never seen her Uncle Jacques and Sister Fayla in the same place at the same time.

Juliène had already opened her mouth, delighted with this unexpected opportunity to denounce her sister's final lie, when she felt Guyard's hand close firmly around her arm.

"No, not a word!"

The low voice grating in her ear was uncharacteristically harsh.

"You have caused enough grief for one day. This damnable mess is for Rowène and me to sort out. Since, gods forgive me, I am not guiltless in causing my daughter's unhappiness. We should have told her – and Val – the truth long ago."

"The truth?" A grim, if youthful voice, spoke suddenly from behind them. "Well, let's hear it then!"

Startled, Juliène broke away from Guyard's grip to see that the tall beggar brat from the refectory – how could she not have recognised him before? – was now standing between her and Rowène, fists clenched, a look of fury twisting his young face into lines it was never meant to wear.

Impatiently shaking away the long strands of flax-fair hair that clung to his flushed face, he stalked up to Juliène, his eyes hard and hot.

"Is it true? What you said earlier!"

"Is what true?" she asked warily, wishing she had not allowed the malice that had nearly consumed her heart to overcome the more recent feelings of peace and belonging that Guyard had awoken in her.

Goddess! This is my son!

This tall, skinny lad with bleached barley hair, whose accusing green gaze was on a level with hers, so that it was like seeing her own eyes reflected in a mirror, though his face was pure de Rogé.

"What you said about Rafe and... and Sister Fayla?"

For all his voice had not yet broken, it came out as something approaching a growl.

She broke the lock of their eyes with an effort, and glancing over his shoulder saw that Ranulf had now come up – shirtless and sweating – to stand beside Rowène, completing the circle.

And something, some sharp stab of jealousy, some moment of malevolent madness, made her laugh lightly and say in glib reply to her son's question,

"Is what true? That your father treats Lissie's mama as his personal whore? Of course it is. Ask him yourself if you do not believe me. He is right there. The man who fourteen years ago sacked Chartre castle, raped three women, one of them a maidservant, and then the two daughters of the house, and in so doing got you on me. There he is! The man who gave you life. Ranulf Jacques de Rogé!"

"*He...*"

Val glanced over his shoulder, fair brows snapping together in a frown that was the mirror of his sire's, before glaring back at Juliène, seemingly indifferent to the fact that she was his mother.

"You are saying that *he* is my father? And that his name is not even Rafe? That he is a *de Rogé*? Black Joffroi's filthy full-blood brother?"

"Yes."

Something flared in the green eyes at her flat reply.

Turning on his bare heel, Val stalked up to the man who had fathered him. And with not the slightest warning of his intention, spat straight into Ranulf's face.

Spat a further stream of furious invective in a dialect Juliène could not understand, though the sense of it was plain enough.

Then before anyone could do or say anything to stop him, snatched up the bay's trailing reins and flinging himself into the saddle, rode full tilt out through the gates, heading up the grass-grown emptiness of the north road into the wild, desolate lands beyond.

"Bugger it all to Hell! Ran, you stay here an' try an' sort out this shit-storm yon poison-viper's made! I'll go after the lad," Edwy shouted over his shoulder at his brother as he ran for the stable.

He emerged less than a dozen heartbeats later, mounted on the bare back of Joscelin de Veraux's fleet-footed grey stallion.

Then he was gone, leaving Ranulf shocked, stunned and white as the crumpled shirt still clenched in his fist.

Not that anyone else was in much better state, and only when Edwy was out of sight and earshot did Juliène begin to realise what she had done, and by that time Rowène's furious voice was ringing in her ears.

"Gods above, Ju, what daemon possesses you that you must say and do these terrible things? Or does it give you pleasure to cause such pain and misery to those who share your blood but not your allegiance to the Winter Lady?"

Juliène wrenched her head around, her eyes and mind still filled with the vision of her fleeing son, to see her sister standing, pale and shaking, before her, a living wraith in shades of grey and white.

"As if you are guiltless in all this," she snapped, trying to shield herself from the truth of those pointed accusations, trying to turn the blame onto her sister.

"It is you who have lied to your daughter... my son, all these years! Whatever pain and distress they are now suffering can be laid squarely on *your* shoulders, Ro, not mine."

"What truth I kept from them was for their own protection."

"Oh, really? And tossing up your skirts for my son's father... what was that?"

"Aside from being none of your bloody business?"

Rowène was even closer now, almost nose to nose with Juliène who tried desperately not to recoil from the icy ferocity in her sister's eyes.

"One thing I will tell you, Ju. Whatever is between Ranulf and I – and yes there is something, I am not going to deny it – was forged by something deeper than lust, stronger than self-interest. Whereas your deliberate seduction of my daughter's father was simply a means to an end! And do not try and tell me you have not been lying together!"

Rowène's voice bit like the frost-sharp edge of a winter's wind,

"You have moss in your hair, and stains on your..."

Abruptly, her sister seemed to remember the presence of the Eldest, the princess and her own weeping daughter and forebore to offer further blatant words of proof, though Juliène was all too aware of the burn of Guyard's short beard, the marks left by his mouth, the very scent of him that had soaked into her skin.

She felt suddenly naked, as if everyone must see what they had done together on that mossy bank by the singing stream, and so struck back as hard as she could.

"So what if I *did* lie with him?" she hissed. "*You* have no claim on him, after all."

"No, I have no claim on him as a lover," Rowène conceded, without giving ground at all. "But he is still my daughter's father. Still my kinsman. Still a man for whom I feel a deep affection. A good and honourable man who does not deserve to couple with a heartless, treacherous whore in the mistaken belief that she is a woman who has a fondness for him."

"I d..."

Her sister's grey eyes were like shards of ice.

"Do not *dare* to tell me you care for him. Not when I know you for the soulless witch who has sworn to break him."

For a moment Juliène could not speak, caught on the brink of a chasm, torn between what had once been the truth and what she knew to be the truth now.

She could not, however, afford to allow her sister to put that same doubt into Guyard's mind and so she forced a scornful laugh.

"Do you think me so lack-wit that I cannot see what you are doing? And I will not have it! You are trying to distract attention from your own shameful behaviour by turning Guyard against me, and it will not work. I love him and he loves me. He will not believe your lies!"

627

"I should not be so sure of that, were I you," Rowène snapped back. "Or have you forgotten what you said to me the night Guy got us all away from Vézière and the Black Hunt? The night you first became aware that he had returned to Mithlondia. Now let me see if I can remember your exact words... ah, yes..."

She closed those icy grey eyes and when she spoke again, it was as if Juliène's own voice was coming from her sister's mouth.

"Now I know where he is. And from this night onwards, Guyard de Martine is mine! And I am going to break him."

Then she opened her eyes and spoke with her natural intonation.

"Do you deny saying those exact words, Ju?"

"Of course I do, more especially as you have left out the part you played in..."

"Of course you do," Rowène parodied, over-riding her feeble attempt at defence. "Deny it to me all you will, but look your lover in the eyes, if you can, and tell *him* that you never set out to break him at the Winter Lady's command."

"I..."

"Do it, Ju!"

"Is it true, Juli? Is it as Rowène says?"

Though Guyard's voice was still gentle, she could hear the depth of doubt... of hurt... beneath.

She wanted to deny it, to keep his faith in her intact, to keep the memory of their time together untarnished.

Yet she found she could not lie to him.

Not when he held her eyes with his own.

"Yes, then! If you must know, my mother did order me to seduce you, body and soul. But that is not why I lay with you today, I swear it, Guyard. Please say that you believe me."

"Surely you are not going to try and convince us it was love?" Rowène interjected scornfully.

"You would not believe me if I said it was!"

Juliène snarled the swift aside at her sister before turning back to Guyard, holding his gaze, willing to spill every last drop of blood from her heart if it would prove her sincerity.

"I love you, Guyard. I told you that as we lay together by the stream."

She glanced around and, raising her voice, spoke for all to hear, not just him.

"And I tell you now, before these witnesses. I love you."

Ignoring the sardonic look in her sister's eyes, she lowered her voice again, speaking with a quiet intensity, determined to make Guyard believe her.

"Whatever I have said or done today, it was never meant to hurt you. Please, Guyard, you were there with me, *in* me. You must have been able to feel how close we were, to know that my feelings for you were true. *Are* true."

She was almost weeping now.

"Guyard, you must believe me."

"I do not know if I can," he said at last. "Believe me, I want to, Juli, but..."

He shook his head violently.

"No, I cannot think of this now. I have to see to Lissie."

"What?"

Juliène stared up at him, confused.

"What about her?"

"Did you not even see her go? You must be the only person here who did not. She is upset, distressed. Obviously. It is scarcely surprising. Discovering the mother she thought was dead is very much alive. Learning that her father has been fornicating indiscriminately and unlawfully with her mother's sister. No, it does not make pretty listening, does it, Juliène? Not even to us, grown men and women who have seen something of life. Certainly not to a sheltered girl of thirteen summers. But whatever else I have done, I am still Lissie's father, and so I – or rather Ro and I together – must go and see what we may do to ease our daughter's pain and confusion."

He started to say something else, but Rowène was at his side now, and Juliène could tell that his mind and heart were bound up with the need to alleviate his daughter's distress, whilst the woman he had merely tumbled – *indiscriminately and unlawfully* – by a woodland stream was already forgotten.

Or perhaps not quite.

"The gods know," he sighed. "I am as much to blame as anyone for making this mess."

And with a faint shrug at what he clearly perceived to be his own folly, he bent forwards with a murmured,

"Farewell, Juli. I... will not see you again."

Brushing a kinsman's kiss across her forehead, he turned to stride away in the direction of the orchard, Rowène at his side, abandoning Juliène in the midst of a semi-circle of closed, contemptuous, condemnatory faces.

Even Luc, standing in the shadows and leaning heavily on Gabriel de Marillec's arm, was regarding her without a trace of compassion colouring his ashen countenance. Not even the slightest flicker of sympathy to soften the stern expression in his bleak grey gaze.

Goddess! What have I done?

Now – when it was far, far too late – she remembered her words to Guyard back by the stream, just before they had made love.

Precious beyond price.

That was how she had described their coming together today.

Yet before the sun had even set on the self-same day, she had destroyed that, oh so, fragile union.

She had thought her life unbearable when she had lost Luc and Guyard a season ago.

To lose them both again, and this time as a result of her own ungovernable vindictiveness and venom, was a far more bitter price to pay.

Unable to stand the weight of eyes upon her, Juliène turned and fled, the chiming of the bronze bells outside the Healing House ringing mockingly in her ears.

Verse 3

A Cold Wind from the North

Almost exactly a se'ennight after that vicious and divisive confrontation in the yard of Vézière's Healing House, the royal party prepared to return to Lamortaine, much to Sister Winfreda's ill-concealed delight.

By that time both Joscelin's and Ranulf's mounts had returned to the Healing House, discovered early one morning when Sister Aldith had opened the gates, Rye's reins looped about a branch of the spindleberry tree, the grey stallion peaceably cropping the grass close by.

There had, however, been no sign of either Edwy or Val.

Careful inspection confirming that there was no trace of blood on the bay's harness or any other sign of foul play, Rowène had to assume – for the sake of her own peace of mind as well as Ranulf's – that both his brother and son were safe and unharmed in body, though she had little doubt that Val was still hurting in other ways.

Left with no alternative, Rowène had carried the bitter tidings to Ranulf that while his horse had returned, his son had clearly chosen not to.

A harsh fact he accepted in a grim, stony-faced silence before turning away, and not long afterwards Rowène had heard the rhythmic thud of axe on wood coming from the direction of the orchard as he set about replenishing the Grey Sisters' log pile.

That had been three days ago and now, with the sun barely above the rounded, gold-rimmed mound of High Peak rising out of the misty line of hills rolling away towards the eastern sea, the royal party was making ready to leave.

The riding horses had been saddled, the litter made ready, and as Joscelin and Ranulf busied themselves making the final checks that all was secure and the ladies' comfort assured, the jingle of bridle bits and stirrup irons announced the arrival of the soldiers of the escort party, and it was to the accompaniment of these ordinary sounds that the princess and her companions completed their farewells to the

Eldest, and those of her healers who had gathered to see them off, Sister Winfreda and her sour countenance being conspicuously – and thankfully – absent.

Elsewhere, and having already made their own brief but difficult valedictions, two figures – a slender, mailed soldier and a tall, grey-robed healer of a height with her companion – stood together, just beyond the open gateway, their low-voiced conversation masked by the tinkling of the bronze bells in the spindleberry tree.

"You are worried about Val, aren't you?" Gabriel murmured. "Understandably, when you love him as if he were your own."

"I am worried about a lot of things," Rowène admitted ruefully. "Yourself included, Ré."

"Me?"

He considered her for a moment, his eyes a clear, heart-warming amber.

"You need not worry about me, Ro. Luc will recover, and Adèle and I have managed to come to... an understanding. She is content enough with the situation, and for my part I will do my best to be a good father to her child when it is born. But Val..."

His gaze returned to the moors she was once more studying so pensively.

"Has Edwy with him to keep him from doing anything too stupid," she concluded his half-formed thought, more in hope than assurance.

"And just what stupid things did you have in mind, Ro?"

She shrugged irritably.

"How would I know? I have never been a thirteen-year old boy who has just learned that the man he has looked up to and tried to emulate since he met him seven years ago is not only his father but a de Rogé to boot. In other words a reiver, a whoremonger, and everything else rotten that goes with that name."

"Only in your sister's prejudiced eyes," Gabriel said flatly. "Edwy will set him right – after all, he has known his brother far longer and much better than Juliène could ever hope to do. He will keep Val safe, and bring him back to you when the lad is ready to face you – and Ranulf – again."

He hesitated, then asked,

"And Lissie? How is she coping with all this, poor child?"

Rowène grimaced.

"Still not talking. At least not to me, or to her father."

There was very little Gabriel could say to that, and thankfully he did not try.

Nevertheless she felt, and appreciated, his silent sympathy, his expressive gaze telling her just how deeply he felt for her misery.

Then a heartbeat later, and completely without warning, she saw his eyes go blank and a ripple of tension cross his face, twisting it into a hard mask of tight-drawn lines.

"Gabriel? What is it?"

He shivered convulsively.

"Do you not feel it, Rowène?"

Even his voice was no longer his own, no longer light and incisive but dull, devoid of emotion, dead.

"A bitter wind blowing down from the north, bearing the crows of war on its wings?"

She stared at him for a moment, then lifted her face into the soft breeze, fragrant with the scent of apple blossom and lilac.

Contrary to his words, it was as balmy a day in late spring as it could possibly be.

Dreading what she would see, she looked into his eyes, the warm amber clouding... then clearing... before crystallising into citrine even as she reached out to him.

Knowing how Gabriel both hated and feared falling prey to these 'fits' of foresight in public – when the full truth of his fey heritage, the unwanted inheritance he had hidden for so many years behind the mask of an effete courtier, would be made plain to any who saw him – she laid a gently restraining hand on his arm, hoping her touch might serve to keep his wits from wandering off down some dark, thorny path where she could no longer follow him.

Pitching her voice carefully low, she spoke his name – the only name that might possibly reach him.

"Ré!"

Nothing.

He still stood, quivering almost imperceptibly under her fingers, his gaze straining northwards.

Her anxiety stalling the breath in her throat, she glanced warily around. For all it was early yet, this *was* a public place and people were beginning to move about. Country folk heading in for the weekly market were trundling past them, townsfolk nearby were opening shutters, sweeping steps, gathering to gossip in the narrow street...

Worse still, she and Gabriel were already attracting attention.

The sight of a healer with her hand clasped about the arm of a healthy – and startlingly handsome – soldier... well, it was hardly surprising they would be the recipient of curious stares and raised eyebrows.

Glancing frantically behind her she caught sight of Sister Aldith in the yard, crooning her farewells to the horses, and assumed Joscelin and Ranulf must likewise be busy amongst the restless animals.

Until she realised that while Joscelin was unobtrusively occupied in watching the princess and therefore remained unaware of the potential for disaster, Ranulf had stilled, his hand resting against Rye's gleaming neck, and in the heartbeat when his eyes met hers something changed in his face, his suddenly narrowed gaze moving from her to Gabriel's stiff figure and then back again.

It was plain that he could tell that something was amiss, no doubt recognising the warning signs.

Frowning, he dropped his hand and made to walk towards them but Rowène shook her head.

Not yet! I can manage.

At least she hoped she could bring Gabriel back without garnering any further unwanted attention.

Tightening her fingers, she tried again.

"Ré, please! Come back."

And with a shudder and a gasp, he did, staggering slightly as he wrenched himself out of the shrouding darkness only he could see into the sunlight of the spring morning, all within a half-dozen heartbeats.

She had been afraid he might collapse, as he had done on that other occasion she had witnessed this fey transition here in Vézière, and had known she would not have the strength to keep him on his feet.

This time – thank the gods – he recovered more quickly, holding his stance upright with a palpable effort, long bronze-tipped lashes sweeping down to hide eyes that yet held a hint of glittering gold.

Then as his sharp ears caught the sound of hoof beats approaching down the road from the north, his head came up again, his eyes the feral amber of a mountain cat.

Half relieved, half even more worried than before, Rowène followed the direction of his gaze.

God of Light, let it be Edwy and Val. God of Mercy, give Ranulf the chance to make some peace with his son before he must leave for Lamortaine. For who knows when his duty will allow him to return. Let Val...

But there was no time for more as just then the horsemen emerged from the pollarded green of the poplar copse, cantering easily down the grass-grown track that ran to the south of the town, and Rowène could see immediately that none of the figures was that of Valéri de Chartreux or Edwy of Rogérinac.

It was indeed a much larger party than the beloved pair she had hoped to see. A dozen or so men riding fiery war-horses, and while she could not make out faces clearly, half of them appeared to be dressed in the rough, practical garb worn by the guardians appointed to range along the Atarkarnan border, while the remainder of the group were clad after the manner of those who lived to the north of the Tarkan River, their weathered faces below caps of fur almost obscured by long, black, braided beards.

Perhaps not surprisingly, the strange warriors also appeared to be armed to the teeth, although...

She squinted, trying to see decipher what it was they carried across their saddles. It looked like...

"That's Beric," Ranulf's voice spoke suddenly from behind her, making her start. "What in bloody hell is he doing this far south?"

"I rather think the question you should be asking," Gabriel said grimly. "Is not what is he doing here but why he is accompanied by the barbarian chieftain and his bodyguard? That *is* Attan, is it not, Rafe?"

As Ranulf swore harshly in acknowledgement, Rowène turned once more to Gabriel.

"Is this what you meant?" she asked urgently, her gaze fixed on his still tense face. "When you spoke of a cold wind from the north?"

He did not reply for a long moment, merely stood watching the horsemen come ever closer, his hand dropping to the hilt of the sword he had belted back on this morning in preparation for departure.

"Is that what I said?"

He gave her a sidelong glance.

"When I was... wandering, weak and witless?"

He muttered an ugly oath concerning his blood-lines that made Rowène, largely inured though she was to coarse language, wince.

Seeing this, a shadow darkened his eyes but before he could apologise, she reached out to grip the leather jerkin he wore over his mail and pulled him around to face her, saying fiercely,

"You are *not* weak, Ré. Gods know, I would have gone mad long since if I had been cursed with that particular blood-gift of the Faennari."

"I hoped... believed that I had lost it," he said bleakly. "Along with..."

Luc.

But she did not say it. There was no need. They each knew what the other had given up.

"Hell knows it would be no loss!" Gabriel groaned. "And I would have given it away gladly. It seems, however, that I am not to be rid of this curse so easily."

Then, straightening his mailed shoulders as if to settle more evenly the heavy weight of his invisible burden, he said stonily,

"Ah, look! Beric has seen us, and is coming this way. Quick, before he gets here, tell me again what I said. The exact words, Ro."

"Very well. You said, *Do you not feel it, Rowène? A bitter wind blowing down from the north, bearing the crows of war on its wings.* And that was all before I managed to pull you back. Perhaps I should not have done so?"

He shuddered, and even as Rowène felt the illusory touch of crimson-stained snowflakes chilling her own cheek, he shook his head and said in a low voice,

"No, I thank the gods you did bring me back before I could drown in the outer darkness of eternity. One day... oh gods, Ro, I fear that one day I will not be able to return."

He swallowed and made a clear effort to control himself, his voice coming more steadily,

"As to the words themselves, I just wish I had some idea what they may mean."

"In other words, just another bloody cryptic foretelling of doom and gloom," Ranulf cut in sardonically. "Hell's frozen depths, de Marillec! Can you not see something more cheerful for a change?"

For a moment Rowène thought Gabriel would snap at the gibe.

Instead, and with a shrug of those shoulders that always seemed too slender for the weight of mail he so effortlessly carried – his 'gift' being another matter entirely – he said wryly,

"I am what I am, de Rogé. And not so very different to you in many ways."

Then he grinned, much to Rowène's surprise, and punching Ranulf lightly on his mailed arm, the one that carried the guardians' mark, he added,

"For like me, Rafe, if you had chosen hearth and home over the likelihood of floggings and blood-soaked battlefields, you would never have had that bloody mark pricked into your skin."

With an answering grin Ranulf returned the gesture with a force that rocked the lighter man on his heels, and started to say,

"Speak for yourself, you half-fey ar..."

Cutting himself short with a flicker of a midnight blue glance in Rowène's direction, he continued with barely a pause,

"Come on, Ré, we had better go and alert Josce. Since whether this be truce or treachery on the barbarians' part, he is the poor bastard who will have to deal with it."

"Not alone though, Rafe," Gabriel muttered.

And turning, found Joscelin already at his side, eyes narrowed in icy appraisal of the approaching horsemen.

"No," Ranulf agreed drily as he fell in on the other side of his sword-brother. "Never alone."

"Bloody, damned fools, the pair of you," Joscelin concluded crisply.

Verse 4

The Sealing of an Unlikely Alliance

"No! Absolutely not!"

In a rare loss of temper, Joscelin de Veraux smashed his clenched fist down on the polished wood, hard enough to make pitchers, goblets, and not a few of the men seated around the table jump – including the blind nobleman hosting this hastily assembled, and far from ordinary, meeting of the Mithlondian High Counsel.

"This is an iniquitous demand, and I will not..."

"Will not what?" Joffroi de Rogé demanded brusquely.

Coming to his feet, his black-clad bulk looming menacingly on the opposite side of the table, his disdainful dark eyes locked onto Joscelin's furious grey gaze as he continued unchecked,

"Come on, de Veraux! Tell us all on what pathetic grounds you dare to oppose a clause that, once formalised, will cement the alliance between Mithlondia and Atarkarna? Daemons balls! I cannot believe that even *you* would see that fledgling friendship founder merely because you do not care for one of the conditions? Just because your whore of a mother chose to get you by spreading her lovely white legs for Prince Raymund's unacknowledged bastard, that does not give you the right to dictate to this Counsel, or..."

"Messire de Rogé! Please! Surely there is no need to be quite so deliberately offensive?"

Nicholas de Vézière's voice held as much strain as it did shock, his thin hands moving helplessly under the palpable threat of violence that pervaded every corner of the makeshift Counsel Chamber.

As if sensing the tension fairly vibrating in the stuffy air, the huge hound lying on the floor beside his master's chair lurched to his feet with a warning growl, lips lifting back from viciously pointed teeth which it gave every appearance of wanting to use.

Even as Joffroi de Rogé took an instinctive step backwards, de Vézière's hand unerringly came to rest upon the great golden head, soothing the beast with a low-voiced murmur before addressing his next remark to the whole chamber.

"Surely, Messires, we are here to discuss an alliance with the Atarkarnans which will benefit both our realms, rather than to foment quarrels between ourselves or call into question the honour of a noblewoman long since gone from our lives."

"Unless of course de Rogé is still carrying a grudge because he wanted to shag the slut himself," an unidentifiable voice muttered, not quite quietly enough, into the ear of the nobleman seated next to him at the far end of the long table.

Predictably, Joscelin felt his shoulders tighten at this further public insult to his mother but what was more suprising was the way Joffroi de Rogé's head snapped around.

Pausing only long enough to send a swift glare in the direction of the malefactor, he returned his attention to Joscelin, leaning even further across the table towards him and lowering his voice to a malevolent hiss,

"Or could it be, de Veraux, that you have a personal interest in the matter under discussion?"

Before Joscelin could open his mouth to utter any of the completely unacceptable retorts crashing around inside his head, a drawling voice from the far side of the room said lazily,

"Well, I for one consider it a great honour for the brat. Let us hope she has the wit to represent Mithlondia's interests in this matter and that she finally proves herself good for something."

A second violent explosion of searingly volatile anger nearly made Joscelin's head shatter asunder, and only the gods knew what he might have said to Kaslander if he could have delivered the words presently choking in his throat like logs jamming a swollen river.

Fortunately, Nicholas de Vézière spoke first, his voice a bridge of forced calm amidst the storm of contention that had just broken as he addressed Prince Kaslander.

"I think we would all agree that the child is overly young to bear the burden of such a weighty responsibility, your highness. That being so, perhaps it would be only courteous at this point to consult with the child's mother before this discussion goes any further. She may well feel some hesitation in allowing her daughter to be used in such a manner."

"For the greater good of the realm," someone – Joscelin could not see who – put in pompously. "Surely in such circumstances she can hardly refuse her consent?"

"Especially when she has another brat on the way," Kaslander threw in callously. "So even if she never sees the girl again after the treaty is signed, she can hardly complain. Though I have no doubt she will try and influence the decision of this Counsel with her tears."

"Just like every other wretched snivelling woman I've ever come across," Hervé de Lyeyne agreed, adding with a sneer, "And after all, what else is a girl-child useful for, if not to gain land or gold through the binding-bed..."

"She is only six bloody years old!" Joscelin snarled.

And catching sight from the corner of his eye of the sly leer twisting his vile kinsman's dissipated countenance, took a step towards him, fists clenched.

"You disgusting, maggot-riddled piece of perversion, if you so much as *look* at her..."

He was stopped by Justin de Lacey who risked bodily violence on his own account by stepping solidly in front of him.

"He is all that, and more, de Veraux," the older man muttered. "And if necessary I will kill him myself, but do you really want to get yourself thrown out of this Counsel for the sake of that filthy-minded, arse-licking cur. How will you help the child then?"

Joscelin shook his head, struggling to regain control, knowing that de Lacey was right.

"Daemon's balls, de Veraux!" Joffroi de Rogé's voice ground out behind him, harsh, impatient. "Anyone would think it was *your* daughter we were planning to send off into the northern wilds, never to be seen again."

"Besides which," Linnius spoke up for the first time. "Any prospective binding between the child and whatever barbarian warrior Chief Attan nominates is years ahead of us. For now she is simply a hostage for our good faith."

A disgruntled expression settled over the prince's pallid face.

"*I* am the one who is expected to take the binding oath – and to bed – a barbarian woman by the end of this summer."

"Not just any barbarian woman, your highness," Robert de Vitré pointed out. "But Chief Attan's only daughter who, to judge by the look in his eyes when he speaks of her, is very dear to him."

"Whilst *I* have yet to even see the woman," Linnius muttered, the merest edge of a whine to his protest. "She could be ugly as a wild boar for all I know, with the temperament to match."

"Sire, I beg you not to imply as much to her father," de Vitré said, striving to maintain a tactful tone in spite of the aghast expression in his eyes.

"And if by some damnable chance he does, it is to be hoped that since the Atarkarnans speak little of our tongue, Chief Attan would not understand such a flagrant insult," de Lacey murmured for Joscelin's ears alone.

"A word of warning – he understands more than most people think," Joscelin muttered back.

"Just as well then that a few of your men have, in turn, managed to learn something of the barbarian speech during their years on the border," de Lacey commented. "Though the gods alone know how they managed it."

"By risking their necks, not to mention their balls, each time they went over the border," Joscelin replied grimly, forcing himself to stay.

When all he really wanted to do was put himself squarely in the middle of the argument raging around the prince's seat as to the best way to seal what was, at present, the shakiest of alliances.

"Excuse me, de Lacey."

"No, you are better off keeping out of it," his companion said firmly. "If you lose your temper again, you will only have them asking why, and I think you would not wish to make what is already a bad situation for the child and her mother completely untenable."

The embers of his barely banked fury effectively doused by de Lacey's words, Joscelin glanced at his sometime ally, only to find the other man's hazel gaze sweeping the chamber, then when no-one appeared to be taking any notice of them, added even more drily,

"I may occasionally question your good sense, de Veraux, but never your courage, or that of your sword-brothers."

Joscelin felt his brows rise.

"Indeed? How so?"

"How so, indeed? Do you know, I truly thought de Rogé might fall down dead of apoplexy when you first brought that Valennais... remind me, what name does he go by?"

"Rafe. Rafe of Oakenleigh," Joscelin replied, more than a little warily.

"Yes, that was the name. How could I have forgot?"

Joscelin eyed the older man narrowly, not believing for a moment that he had forgotten.

De Lacey gave him a lupine grin.

"Well, when you brought *Rafe of Oakenleigh* into this business, I admit I did wonder what you were about. Bearing in mind the previous time the man came into de Rogé's line of sight. To put it bluntly, I do not believe our respected Chief Counsellor is any less murderously disposed now towards the man who so closely resembles his dead brother as he was on that first occasion. Or, come to that, that bloody reckless fool, de Marillec, indispensable though they have both proved to be as interpreters between the Atarkarnans and ourselves."

"Indeed, Rafe and Gabriel are marked men whether we succeed or fail," Joscelin said tersely, allowing himself to be led away from the argument currently raging around Prince Linnius.

"They always have been," de Lacey remarked. "How could it be otherwise? At least this way..."

"Messires!"

Linnius' faintly querulous tones somehow managed to rise above the conflicting advice of his counsellors.

"I have decided that in all honour I cannot proceed further until I have spoken to my sister. As Messire de Vézière has pointed out, Lilia is her only child..."

"Until she drops the whelp currently swelling her belly," Kaslander put in with a coarse laugh.

"The child who may be Mithlondia's heir," de Vitré reminded him with a frown of distaste at the Kardolandian prince.

Then turned hastily back to Linnius.

"At least until after you and the Lady Atarellen are bound, and blessed with children of your own."

"Why in hell's foul breath we must be cursed with that poxy Kardolandian whoremonger in our counsels," de Lacey muttered bitingly under his breath. "I shall never understand."

"On the contrary, de Lacey, you understand perfectly well," Joscelin replied coolly, and with only a hint of acid in the look he aimed over de Lacey's shoulder at the man he despised so much.

His temper once more under control with the realisation that Linette would at least be consulted, rather than commanded regarding her daughter's fate, he continued ironically,

"Gabriel de Marillec's seat was vacant and needed to be filled by someone de Rogé could count on, if not to actively support him, at least to participate with the minimum of interest in the governance of a realm Kaslander has never, thank the gods, adopted as his..."

"Joscelin!"

Recognising the imperious voice of his prince, he turned to face Linnius, reasonably confident that his face was once more its usual expressionless mask.

"Sire?"

"Send one of your men down to the Healing House to escort my sister up here."

And then evidently anticipating Joscelin's reply,

"No, I need you to stay here and finish going through the rest of Attan's demands."

"But..."

"If I may be permitted to offer a suggestion, Sire," Nicholas de Vézière intervened before Joscelin could point out that the three men he most trusted were all out on the moors with Chief Attan and his guard.

"Rather than take any of Messire de Veraux's guardians from their duties..."

The blind gaze came unerringly to rest on Joscelin.

"You will find my steward waiting outside this room, Messire de Veraux. Send him down to the Healing House in your stead. I assure you he can be trusted in every respect."

"I wonder how the negotiations are going?" Princess Linette mused, her gaze lifting from the little gown she was sewing to the castle on the hill above, its towers just visible between the leaves of the apple trees in whose dappled shade she and her closest companion were seated.

Adèle looked up too, but unlike her friend, her eyes were not directed towards the high walls with their bright banners flickering in the summer sunlight but had strayed inexorably towards the ever rising heights of the nearby moors, the heather just beginning to spread a purple haze across the dull green of late summer.

"I wonder how my lord is managing with the Atarkarnan chief and his men," she muttered. "I think they were planning a stag hunt for today. Pray gods he returns safely."

"And what do *you* think, Sister Fayla?"

The princess' well-aimed question caused the grey-clad figure, presently walking in as unobtrusive a manner as possible past the seated women, to come to an abrupt and reluctant halt.

Rowène had been on her way to see how Luc was faring this morning and far from wishing to intrude on the conversation – having chosen to avoid both Linette and Adèle in the wake of the disastrous revelations they had witnessed on their previous visit – had hoped to be overlooked as merely one more healer going about her business.

Unfortunately, when directly addressed by royalty, she could scarcely disobey or cling to anonimity, and so pausing only long enough to grimace at the blameless blue sky, she turned and bowed her head.

"Your highness, may I be of service somehow?"

"Oh, do stop pretending we were not once all friends," Linette snapped. "Or that you are not Joscelin's sister, Lissie's mother, Rafe's mi..."

"Kinswoman!" Rowène interjected harshly and in defiance of all protocol. "I have *never* been his mistress. Never shared his bed."

Of course that did not take account of the two times he had been in *her* bed, neither of which bore mentioning, although for vastly different reasons.

Seemingly untroubled by Rowène's breach of etiquette, Linette merely tilted her head in consideration of her words.

"Indeed? I must have misunderstood the substance of what Juliène was saying that day. Perhaps one day, you will be so kind as to explain to me how a common soldier comes to be kin to the Lord of Chartreux's daughter. If as you say, that is all he is to you?"

Rowène bit her lip and muttered a curse under her breath, all the time praying that Linette had indeed missed the revelation that Rafe was in truth Ranulf de Rogé.

For she was very sure that if the princess did ever realise it, not only would she be horrified but would have him thrown out of the guardians at the very least. And at the worst brought to trial for crimes he had long since expiated.

"He has Valennais blood," Rowène said eventually. "As do I. That makes us kin."

"Very well, if you tell me that is all my bodyguard is to you," the princess replied. "I must take your word for it."

"Rafe has never been my lover. He never will be," Rowène reiterated grimly through gritted teeth.

Linette eyed her closely.

"But you would like him to be? No, you need not answer that, I know what you would say, that it is impossible for far too many reasons, and it is of course your own affair. Now, what I really want to hear is what you think about the ongoing negotiations with Chief Attan. I have no doubt that Joscelin and Gabriel tell you things they would never dream of mentioning to Adèle or I."

Rowène hesitated, thankful that the inquisition over her feelings for Ranulf appeared to be over for the moment, but while she could hardly pretend ignorance of the current situation, she did not in truth think she knew much more than Linette at this stage in the proceedings. So it was with no little wariness that she said,

"I have every faith in Joscelin, your highness. And Chief Attan is so desperate for Mithlondian aid against the Eastern Empire, I cannot think he would make any wildly unacceptable demands."

She glanced at Adèle, aware that their old friendship was still overshadowed by the other woman's envy of the fey bond that existed between Rowène and Adèle's lord-by-binding.

Not wanting to stir the embers of Adèle's jealousy any further, however, she avoided the use of either of Gabriel's given names.

"As for your lord-by-binding, you need not worry yourself, Adèle. He can hold his own, whatever the situation, whether it be..."

Then, as she unexpectedly caught sight of Lissie and Lilia a little way away playing some game with Lyra and Mist, she abandoned all thought of Gabriel, her hand coming up to grip the lichened trunk of the apple tree in whose shadow she stood, partially concealed from the children.

"And I am sure *you* would know," Adèle's voice was both sharp and bitter.

So much for her attempt not to upset her friend! She took a moment to put a curb on her temper, then turned back and said with strained patience,

"Do not snipe, Adèle. It is not good, either for you or the child you carry. Please, I beg you, do not set your son against his father before he has even been born."

Adèle set her hand protectively against the silk-covered bulge, her blue eyes hard and unforgiving.

"How do you know I am carrying a son? Did my lord 'see' it and tell you? When he has not even told me? But then *Gabriel...*"

Her voice shook as she spoke his name.

"Is still closer to you and your wretched brother than he ever will be to me."

"He is *your* lord-by-binding," Rowène said pointedly. "And unless you drive him to break his word, he will not see or speak to Luc ever again."

"But he loves him still," Adèle cried. "You know he does."

"Of course he does!"

Belatedly Rowène tried to gentle her tone, seeing how upset Adèle was, and fearing she would pass on her distress to the babe she carried.

"Listen to me, Adèle. You cannot expect your lord to simply to put aside, as if it had never been, the trust and affection he and my brother have shared through a score of years. Gabriel has given you what you wanted – the child you asked of him last mid-winter's night. Is that not enough for you?"

"No! I thought it would be but... it is not," Adèle admitted.

"None of us have what we most long for," the princess sighed, unexpectedly rejoining the tense conversation. "All we can do is make the best of what we do have."

As if unaware of Rowène's keenly observant gaze, Linette's white fingers dropped to caress the rounded curve of her own unborn babe, the blue eyes that rested on the nearby children holding more than a hint of fear, the same fear that was in her voice as she whispered,

"At the least, Adèle, you know that your lord would never repudiate or harm your child in any way, as I fear Kaslander means to do to mine, despite the fact that I have willingly had his own carelessly-begotten offspring fostered in my own household."

"No, Gabriel would never disown any child I bore. If only because for so many years he hoped some other man might be persuaded to plant the seed," Adèle replied with a laugh that held much pain and little humour. "And thus save my lord the irksome duty of doing so himself."

"If he hoped for any such thing," Rowène said tartly. "It was only because he wished to save your child from inheriting his own fey blood. For gods'sake, Adèle, do not make his life, or that of his son, any more difficult and dangerous than it already is!"

In the somewhat shocked silence that fell between them, Rowène reflected that of the two women who had come to Vézière's Healing

House to wait out the weeks until the birth of their babes, she could sympathise with Linette's fears a good deal better than Adèle's megrims. Nonetheless, she had given her word to the Eldest to aid them both – in so far as her own curtailed powers allowed – and losing her temper with Adèle would certainly not help.

She was just about to make another attempt to soothe her friend's tiresome – and, in her opinion, only remotely reasonable – complaints when the warning cackle of the enclave's flock of geese made her look beyond her companions, to see Guy come striding past the gaggle of aggressive birds, his soft leather boots a certain measure of protection against the sharply pecking beaks.

Pausing on the buttercup-gilded grass before the princess, he bowed low before them all, the sunlight reflecting up from the flowers to glimmer on his fair head, the dark wheat-gold strands now paling into silver – very much, Rowène realised with a jolt of awareness at how rapidly the seasons were passing, as Ranulf's was doing.

And she was struck again, as she had been years before, when she had seen them that day standing together in a doorway in Chartre castle, one in the sunlight, the other in the shadow, discovering that she could still be disconcerted, not only by how closely the two brothers resembled each other – perhaps more so now than at any other time in the intervening years – but how different was the way in which she loved them both.

"Your highness, Lady Adèle, Sister Fayla."

His voice was pleasant, his phrasing formal as it always was when addressing his princess, his kinswoman or his daughter's mother in public.

Yet something about the guarded expression in his light blue eyes brought Rowène to a state of alertness.

"Good day to you, Master Finch."

The princess sounded pleased to see him, not least, Rowène did not doubt, because his arrival had brought an effective end to the argument between her and Adèle.

"Have you come with your harp to entertain us?" Linette continued.

He spread his hands in an apologetic gesture.

"Forgive me, your highness, not today."

"Then what?"

"Lord Joscelin sent me to escort you up to the castle. Apparently the Counsellors wish to... discuss some matter concerning the alliance they are attempting to make with the Atarkarnans."

"And what is this matter?"

He hesitated again, clearly uncomfortable, the arrival of the two girls saving him the necessity of having to prevaricate further.

"Good day, Master Finch."

Lilia greeted him with a happy smile, the gentle-mannered harper having become something of a favourite of hers whilst she had been staying at the Healing House.

"Look who I have found, Master Finch!"

Lovingly, the child stroked the small grey and white cat cradled in her arms, nuzzling the soft fur, before looking up to say,

"She belongs to the old man who is living at the end of the orchard until he gets well again. He said I could play with her for a while, and that her name is Mist, but I am going to call her Pearl, because she is the same colour as the one Uncle Joscelin gave to Mama."

Biting her lip, Rowène glanced at Linette to see her slender, shaking fingers rise to clutch the single pearl that hung on a silver chain about her neck. She was sure Guy had seen the movement too, though all he said as he dropped onto his haunches in front of the little princess was,

"Pearl is a very pretty name for a very pretty kitty."

As the shadow of his own daughter fell across him, Guy straightened to his full height, his hand making an involuntary movement as if to touch her hair – she had lost her cap again, together with the binding about her plaits, so that her hair tumbled over her shoulders, sunlight shot through with fire – then, with a heavy sigh, allowed his hand to drop back to his side.

"Good day, Lissie," he said quietly.

The regretful line of his firm mouth eased into a smile as his gaze dropped to survey the normally untouchable cat draped about her neck in boneless abandon, albeit the slitted yellow gaze still held a feral glitter not unlike the look Rowène had more than occasionally glimpsed in Gabriel de Marillec's eyes.

"It looks as if you have made a friend of Lyra, Lissie," he remarked softly. "Quite a feat, if all I have heard about that cat is true."

Innocuous as his words had been, they brought no response, the silence lengthening uncomfortably as his daughter continued to look up at him, unidentifiable thoughts skimming like clouds behind her clear blue gaze, until Rowène truly dreaded what the child might say when – or if – she did open her mouth.

Even now, a full season after that terrible day, Lissie had still not reconciled herself to the truths her parents had withheld from her.

Finally she seemed to make up her mind and said,

"Master Finch."

Master Finch, not Papa.

Her tone was colourless, a mere acknowledgement of his presence, her curtsey correct. She did not wish him a good day, or make any reply to his attempt to break through the tangle of briars that had sprung up between them.

And if Rowène could see the heartbreak in his eyes – gods knew, he was in no state to hide it – so must the others.

Even Lissie, had she not armoured herself so thoroughly against her parents' hurt. And why should she not when she was hurting too, and it was they who had caused her distress?

"Yes, well..."

Linette cleared her throat, breaking the awkward silence.

Averting her eyes from the painful confrontation between the harper and the child he so clearly loved, she addressed her own little daughter.

"Lilia, poppet, I have to go up to the castle this morning."

"Can I come too?"

"Not today, sweetheart."

"Oh."

The little girl strove to master her disappointment.

"Will you see Uncle Joscelin? Can you ask him if he will come and see us later? I want to show him Pearl."

"If I see him, I will ask him," Linette promised. "Although I cannot promise that he will be able to come down and see y... see Pearl today. Or even tomorrow. You know how busy he is at the moment, with the Counsel and the Atarkarnan chief.."

At this, Lilia pulled a very unprincess-like face.

"I know, Mama. The Eldest explained it all to me. Lots of talking and things to sign. But *I* think Uncle Joscelin would rather be out on the moors with Messire Gabriel and Rafe, and those strange men with their funny furry hats and cloaks. Do they not get very hot wearing all that fur in this weather?"

The child sounded entirely serious, and Rowène could not help but smile, until she heard Linette say,

"I expect your... Uncle Joscelin would rather be out on the moors too." Wincing as the princess stumbled audibly over the appellation.

"Unfortunately," Linette continued, recovering herself. "His duty keeps him in the castle with the rest of the High Counsel."

The princess managed a smile of sorts as she brushed a swift caress over her daughter's soft cheek, running her fingers through the rioting raven-dark curls.

"Which is where I must go now. You stay here with Lissie and the kitties. Be good for Lady Adèle and Sister Fayla. I will be back soon."

Over the dark head, Linette's eyes met Rowène's frowning gaze, the anxiety she would not permit to enter her voice or worry her daughter, plain to see in the clouded sky blue depths.

Look after her, that look said. *Whatever happens.*

"Always," Rowène said aloud.

Briefly, she met Guy's bleak gaze and added to herself,

Though only the gods know why Linette would trust me to care for her child when she must be only too well aware of the mess I have made of bringing up my own daughter.

"Forgive me, your highness, but if you are ready," Guy said, breaking the silent thread of Rowène's thought. "Prince Linnius and his Counsellors are waiting."

Linette did not return to the Healing House until very much later that day, by which time the gilded shadows of a perfect summer's evening were already sweeping down to enfold the peaceful enclave in darkness.

Meeting the princess at the gate, just before it closed, one look at Linette's face was sufficient to subdue any illusion Rowène might have harboured that the terms the Counsel wished to discuss with her had been in any way acceptable.

The sharp clatter of iron-shod hooves against the stone cobbles of the lower streets made Rowène glance beyond the partially shut gate to see Chief Attan and his bodyguard ride past, accompanied by the three guardians assigned to keep him company during his time in Mithlondia, the sight serving to point up how brittle such a peace truly was and how easily shattered by the political alliances struck by heartless men.

Yet even while she accepted that her duty lay with the princess, Rowène could not help but strain her ears and eyes to catch any break in the bay's steps, any sign that Ranulf meant to pause at the Healing House.

After all, Gabriel came punctiliously every morning just after dawn to enquire of the Eldest regarding Adèle's welfare.

Ranulf, however, had not been next or nigh the place and what little Gabriel could tell Rowène regarding his sword-brother's state of mind had not been reassuring.

Nor was it likely to have been improved by the only tidings Rowène had been able to pass on – that far from coming back to Vézière, Val had returned to Justin de Lacey's stronghold, where it seemed he intended to remain until such time as Luc should be recovered enough to move on, at which point Val meant to join him, wherever that may be.

It was Edwy who had ridden over from Lasceynes to inform Rowène that the boy was safe, and he had only with the greatest reluctance added the final stick to the pyre of her hope that Val would eventually come around to accepting the situation, by telling her that the boy had declared his intention to have nothing further to do with the man who was his father. Ever.

That being so, it did not take Rowène's lost ability to touch Ranulf's thoughts to know that he must be bleeding inside.

She also knew that with the Atarkarnans' arrival and Princess Linette's confinement within the walls of the Healing House, he had transferred from the royal bodyguard to Joscelin's personal retinue, where his duties as escort and translator to Chief Attan kept him occupied from before dawn to past midnight.

None of which had prevented her from wandering amongst the stark shadows of the fruiting apple trees in the failing hope that the man she loved might yet sense her own pain and come to her in the soft silence between midnight and dawn, her wistful thoughts borne away on the white wings of the wraith owls as they swooped past, so close that their wingtips might brush a tear from her cheek – if, that is, she had allowed herself to weep – their presence a testament to how close her heart was to breaking at the continued absence of the man she loved.

Tonight, however, for the first time since Ranulf had come to Vézière she did not walk in the orchard.

Tonight she knew she must remain with Linette, to try and bring her some small measure of comfort.

If comfort there could be, bearing in mind the terms of this latest treaty agreed between Mithlondia and Atarkarna.

Old enemies forced by circumstance to make common cause against a new and far mightier enemy.

An alliance of two comparatively tiny realms against the endless might of the Eastern Empire, the treaty signed this very day here in Vézière, the formalities to be concluded with the binding of Prince Linnius to Chief Attan's daughter Atarellen at the height of the Midsummer Feasting in Lamortaine.

A treaty bound in blood.

It would, as the princess herself said, have been beyond belief for trust and friendship to spring up immediately between two such disparate peoples, based on words alone.

Unfortunately for Linette there was one final condition to be fulfilled, one last barrier against treachery.

The act that would set the living seal on this unlikely alliance.

In return for Atarellen putting aside her life of freedom on the wild northern plains – and quite possibly a man she loved – in order to make her home within the stone walls of the Palace of Princes in Lamortaine, her father had demanded that some lady of similar standing must put her own life and happiness into Atarkarnan hands.

And young as she was, there was only one bearer of royal Mithlondian blood that would satisfy Chief Attan's pride.

Little Princess Lilia.

The grey-eyed daughter that Linette adored, and Joscelin could never openly acknowledge as his own.

Verse 5

"I Will Beg If I Have To"

Midsummer's Day 1208 came far, far too swiftly. And not only for Linette, Joscelin and Lilia.

Atarellen, who had once considered herself no more than an ordinary woman of the White Eagle tribe of the Atarkarnan people, looked about her in dread, gazing at the myriad unfamiliar faces surrounding her, as suffocatingly close as the cloth-covered walls, in preference to looking at the pallid-faced young man to whom she must now give her body and her loyalty if she wanted his army's strength to defend the grassy plains where she had been born and grown up, riding on the wind, swimming in icy streams agleam with spawning salmon, watching the bear cubs fishing for those same salmon, listening for the far, high cry of the snow eagle as it circled the distant forested peaks.

Linette, standing close by, wept in silent agony in anticipation of the moment she must bid farewell to her little daughter forever, even the lively kicking of the babe beneath the hand resting on her belly proving to be no comfort.

Joscelin, from his position at one side of the hall, fought to keep his eyes away from Linette and Lilia, where they stood flanked by Gabriel and Adèle, and his expression from betraying his utter sense of helplessness and unabated fury, only slowly becoming aware that Atarellen's father had moved to stand close enough to him that their shoulders touched.

The Atarkarnan chief, clad in all his barbarian finery of bear fur and raw amber, and still smelling strongly of horse and goat, held his silence for a dozen heartbeats, the look in his black eyes holding something of Joscelin's own pain.

"I... fear," the older man muttered, his Mithlondian thick and guttural. "You fear also?"

"For our realms, our freedom, our people?" Joscelin murmured back. "I would be a fool if I did not. The Eastern Empire can so easily ride over us all."

"Not that. We fight together. We *win*."

The bushy, charcoal-black brows were knit in the effort of comprehension and conversation in a language not his own, though he had clearly made good use of his time with the soldiers of his escort over the past few weeks. Then the bearded chin, the long plaits decorated with amber and gold, lifted to indicate Atarellen.

"I fear for daughter of my blood."

The black gaze snapped back towards Joscelin.

"You fear for daughter of *your* blood. This makes us same."

Joscelin could feel himself going white but had the sense not to deny the Atarkarnan's statement.

"We speak after binding," Attan said brusquely. "Come to tall tower when moon rides high. Bring warrior you call... Rafe."

Accordingly after the binding oaths had been sworn, the celebratory feast held, the wine of reluctant friendship drunk, the bedding ceremony witnessed, and Mithlondian nobles and Atarkarnan barbarians alike had fallen asleep in varied states of inebriation, more or less in their own beds or blankets, Joscelin made his way to the top of the highest tower in the royal palace, Ranulf at his back.

Neither of them had taken more than a token swallow of the mead and wine that had flowed so freely for most of the day, Joscelin out of a fear he might vomit it up, Ranulf because he had been on duty throughout it all. Even so, for a moment when they heard what Attan had to say, they had both wondered whether it was them or the Atarkarnan who was drunk

"*What* did he say?" Joscelin demanded, shaking his head as if that would settle his thoughts into a semblance of sense, then as Ranulf opened his mouth to question Attan in his own tongue, added quickly,

"No, do not bother, I heard him the first time. I just think I... failed to understand him properly."

The Atarkarnan looked at them in turn, and in spite of Joscelin's words, repeated what he clearly thought to be a clever offer.

"*You* fear for Lily-child, perhaps right, perhaps not. *My* people no let warrior come with child to guard. So send harper. Finch is name. Look like *him*," he concluded, stabbing a finger at Ranulf.

Then he shrugged into the resulting silence, his tone indicating that the matter should have been settled by now.

"Send harper. Make sense to me."

"Send the harper?" Ranulf echoed as he turned to Joscelin, struggling to control his tone, his words coming fast enough that the Atarkarnan chief would likely not follow them.

"Damn it all, man! You cannot seriously be thinking of sending Guy with the child? Yes, he was taught how to handle himself in a fight, just as I was taught the rudiments of playing the harp when we were children. I understand you want Lilia to be safe, the gods know I do, and that the Atarkarnans will only allow one person to attend her but there must be some other..."

An implacable growl rumbled over Ranulf's protest.

"Harper. Or nothing. Ride north with dawn. Get harper on way."

With that Attan turned and ducking through the low door, disappeared into the torch-lit stairwell, the big bear-like shadow marking his descent on the circular walls.

Only when it had finally been swallowed by the deeper shadows beyond the flickering fiery glow did the two men turn to face each other in the thin remnant of light shed by the paling midsummer moon.

Even then there was silence between them, both men considering the implications of what had been said – and not said.

Eventually Joscelin forced himself to speak the words out loud.

"Rafe, I will beg if I have to. On my knees if that is what it takes. You must know what she means to me."

He made to move but Ranulf grabbed his arm, holding him upright, anger razoring his tongue.

"For gods'sake, Josce! Do not dare go down on your fucking knees to me! Yes, I do bloody know what Lilia means to you. What Val means to me. Or Lissie to Guy. But that does not mean that he... that I... Oh, bloody fucking hell, Josce!"

"Just ask him, Rafe. If he agrees..."

"If he agrees, we are still faced with the problem of Attan."

"It was Attan who suggested it in the first place," Joscelin reminded him.

"Not what you are asking of Guy and me, he didn't," Ranulf said darkly.

"Are you saying you will not even consider it?"

Joscelin's voice was like the cracking of ice.

Then abruptly the frost of anger left his face, though his eyes

655

remained as bleak as Hell's cold caverns.

"No, you are right, Rafe, it was a mad idea. I will not send either of you to your death in some barbarian fire pit."

"So who will you send to guard Lilia?" Ranulf asked drily. "It must be someone she knows and trusts, and that narrows the choice considerably. Her nurse? The poor woman would not last a week in the barbarian encampments. And do not even think of suggesting Rowène. I have no doubt she would go without hesitation, simply because you are her brother and she loves you, and Lilia, but I will not be party to putting her into such danger."

"So where does that leave us? Where does it leave Lilia, damn it!"

"We go with Attan's suggestion," Ranulf said flatly. "It is all we can do. If I leave now I can reach Vézière half a day ahead of you, with time to speak to Guy and..."

He stopped.

"And Rowène," Joscelin finished for him.

"Yes, she deserves to be told the truth at the outset, rather than leave her to discover it, as she surely would. And if war with the Eastern Empire is coming..."

"That too is a certainty!"

"That being so, I must see her before I go... bid her farewell properly."

Joscelin gave him a cynical look.

"Just try not to get her with child, Rafe."

The faint grey light of oncoming dawn was more than sufficient for Joscelin to see the dangerous look in his sword-brother's dark blue eyes.

"In the circumstances, Josce, that is a fucking poor jest."

"In the circumstances," Joscelin replied stonily. "It is the last thing I would find amusing."

Ranulf gave a curt laugh.

"As it happens, neither would I."

Then after another moment, and more to himself than his companion,

"Not that I am likely to get the opportunity to do anything that would result in such unwanted consequences, not if Sister Winfreda has anything to say in the matter. But all I really want, damn it, is the chance to talk to her."

"All I am asking is to talk to Sister Fayla! Is that so unreasonable a request?"

The voice belonging to an unseen man came only faintly to Rowène through the open window of the Eldest's chamber, causing her to drop the cloth she had just squeezed out back into the bowl of cool water.

"From a man like ye?"

That was Sister Winfreda's voice, high and crackling with contempt.

"A soldier, a ravisher of innocents, a man who has already abandoned one misbegotten child if not more, a..."

"Of that litany of bloody lies, only *one* of those things is true of me," came the grating reply.

Then in a completely different tone,

"Please, Sister Winfreda, I must speak with Fayla. Just for a quarter candle-notch, it does not even have to be alone..."

"Certainly 'twould not be alone," the woman huffed with indignant dislike, and Rowène could imagine her drawing her scrawny frame even more upright. "But 'twill not be at all. Now, be gone. Ye're not welcome here, now nor never."

"Then let me speak with the Eldest..."

"No! The Eldest is laid up with the summer sickness an' is in no condition to see anyone, least of all..."

"Yes, yes, least of all a man like me!"

The sardonic masculine voice sliced through Sister Winfreda's high-pitched refusal, sharp as his own sword blade and as dry as the desert wind blowing over the Kardolandian sands.

As dry as poor Sister Héloise's cracked lips which now moved, making painful, soundless words.

Retrieving the cloth, striving to remain calm, Rowène wrung it out again and dabbed it over the Eldest's burning face.

"Do not try to talk, Mama-Louise," she murmured softly. "All will be well. Here, take a sip of water."

Her attention torn between the sick woman and the half-heard voice of the man she had feared she would never see again, she raised the Eldest high enough to take a sip from the beaker of honey water.

"Go to him, child."

"What?"

The frail voice had sounded stronger, the words clear enough, yet still Rowène dared not believe what she was hearing.

"Go to him," the Eldest repeated. "Tell Sister Winfreda you have... my permission... to speak to... him... He would not come... were it not... urgent."

"But I cannot just leave you..."

"Any of the others can... care for me... until your return."

A hot hand came up as if to brush the doubt from Rowène's face.

"Go, child! Before it is too late! And he is gone for good."

Unfortunately by the time Rowène had managed to find one of the other healers to tend to the Eldest in her absence and had made her breathless way to the entry there was no sign of Ranulf, only Sister Winfreda looking smugly pleased with herself.

"He's gone," she remarked, with quite unnecessary relish on seeing Rowène. "If ye're looking for that godless brute of a soldier, that is."

"Then I will go after him," Rowène snapped, taking a step towards the open gates. "I have the Eldest's permission to speak with him."

"But the Eldest is ill, not in her right mind," Sister Winfreda spoke loudly enough that anyone else – healer, servant, visitor, there was always someone within earshot – could hear.

"And until she is well again, 'tis I, as the senior healer after her, who makes the decisions. And 'tis I who says that ye, as a Sister of Mercy o' Vézière, shall have no speech wi' this man at all. For yer own sake an' for the honour of our order, which ye have already brought into disrepute more than once already."

Rowène fought not to wince as that shaft hit home, to find some argument that might persuade the intractable woman before her to change her narrow-set mind.

"Or..." Sister Winfreda gave her a predatory smile. "If ye chose to put off the grey robes of the Sisterhood, chose to become a common woman of the town..."

"A whore in other words," Rowène said bluntly. "Why not just say what you mean, Sister Winfreda?"

"If the colour fits, then wear it!" the older woman retorted, anger mottling her face almost as crimson as Mistress Cherry's best gown.

"But know this, if ye walk out through those gates, if ye seek out that man for speech or *anything else...*"

The sneer that twisted her thin lips said quite blatantly what her words merely implied.

"Then ye do not walk back through those same gates. Not for any

cause. If he gives ye the pox, ye can die in the street. If he gets ye wi'
child, then ye can have it under a hedgerow."

All of which Rowène would have risked, if there had not also been
Lissie and Luc to consider.

If Sister Héloise did not recover from the summer sickness, then it
was inevitable that Sister Winfreda would become the next Eldest,
and not only would she keep her word as regards Rowène, she would
have Lissie and Luc thrown out as well. Lissie might go to Lasceynes,
but Luc was still in no condition to travel any distance.

"Decide," Sister Winfreda demanded harshly. "Whether ye be
healer or whore!"

"I am a healer," Rowène said quietly, bowing her head lest the
older woman take note of the defiance in her eyes and keep watch
over her so closely she would not be able to put into action the idea
that had passed through the encroaching darkness of her mind with
all the swift, shining brilliance of a shooting star.

Meanwhile, Ranulf was riding slowly up the cobbled street towards
Vézière's market square, reins loose on the gelding's neck, leaving
Rye to pick his own way.

Even though he had failed to see Rowène, his duty must still take
him to the castle and a conversation with his brother that promised to
be anything but easy.

And while he had ceased being angry with Joscelin even before he
had left the palace, accepting that what his kinsman had asked of
him was, in all practicality, the only way forward if Lilia were to be
kept safe, Ranulf did not anticipate that Guy would see it in the same
light.

Or at least, not straight away. And time was something they had
very little of.

Because of that lack, he had ridden Rye far harder than he would
normally have done, needing to reach Vézière with enough time to
take his farewell of Rowène and persuade Guy to fall in with the
Atarkarnan chief's suggestion.

Now, having failed dismally to get word – alone or otherwise –
with Rowène, all that was left to him was to seek out his brother.
However long that took, considering as the man might not even be in
Vézière. Then again, he now had the time he might have spent with
Rowène to find and talk to Guy.

As to how long that might be, Ranulf estimated that Attan and his party would be no more than a couple of leagues behind him and, with evening slowly gilding the distant rise of moor and sky, he guessed that they would make camp for the night, and be within sight of Vézière's walls no later than mid-morning of the following day, which gave Ranulf the evening to convince his brother that Joscelin's plan could actually work and – what would be more important to Guy – that it was the right, if not the only viable, way forward.

Yet even as Ranulf tried to plan out what he would say to his brother, he realised that he had not *quite* given up all hope of seeing Rowène, even wondering briefly whether Guy would help him if he asked... before dismissing the notion out of hand.

Indeed he would be lucky if his brother would even speak to him after the debacle of the previous spring, which would make talking him into agreeing to Joscelin's request somewhat more difficult than taking down a fully-armed Atarkarnan warrior bare-handed.

Except, he reminded himself wryly, from now on the Atarkarnans were no longer the enemy.

Soon they would be fighting shoulder to shoulder against the uncounted strength of the Eastern Empire, an aggressor they had never anticipated the need to face, and about which they knew very little, save that its armies had conquered, and now held dominion, over all the vast lands that lay beyond the edge of Mithlondian maps, from the uncharted territory to the north and east of Atarkarna as far south as the Spice Isles, possibly even encroaching into Kardolandian waters eventually.

Against such a force, they could muster the wild and not particularly disciplined Atarkarnan horsemen, their own small cavalry wing, the men who formed the band of border rangers, the very small company of guardians based in Lamortaine, and the men-at-arms who owed allegiance first to the Mithlondian noblemen they served.

All thanks to bloody Joffroi's long-running and persistent campaign to undermine Joscelin's position, Mithlondia no longer had a standing army and Ranulf saw little point in hiding from the truth that it would take the intervention of the gods to save them from annihilation.

Nor would he conceal it from Guy, though he thought his brother perfectly capable of reading the situation for himself.

Whether an unarmed harper travelling north as companion to little Princess Lilia, or a soldier sent to defend the coasts and borders of Mithlondia or Atarkarna, there seemed little hope of a happy ending for either of them.

Which made it all the more imperative that he see Rowène and make his farewells in person.

There was so much he wanted to say to her.

More than that, he wanted – as he had always wanted, since that very first moment of meeting on the Chartre road, his need only growing stronger with the passing years – to feel her nestling in his arms, her heart beating against his own, to smell the roses in her hair, to taste the warmth and sweetness of her mouth...

And perhaps there was a way! To talk, if nothing else...

Lacking any definite direction from his rider, Rye had come to a halt at the edge of the market square, dropping his head to snuffle at something he evidently considered edible in the gutter, and as Ranulf gathered his thoughts and the reins together, his eyes fell on the house at the far end of the market square.

A house where he had never been particularly welcome in the past, although the silver in his purse might go some way towards smoothing his entry now.

Not into some whore's bed but towards something that held far more allure for him – the long, downwards sloping garth that ended in a high wall, on the other side of which lay the orchard belonging to the Sisters of Mercy.

And if Jacques could safely scale that wall and survive the drop on the other side, surely he could do no less.

Decision made, he nudged Rye with his heels, guiding the animal not towards the castle as it clearly expected, but through the nearly empty square towards the brothel.

Dropping down from the saddle, he beckoned to one of the local urchins to hold his horse whilst he went inside to negotiate the terms of his visit, only to recoil slightly as he turned towards the door and found himself chest to the abundantly-displayed breasts of one of the women of the house.

"Ah! Mistress... er..."

He sorted rapidly through the names of the three women and his mostly unpleasant memories of previous visits.

"Mistress Birch. Good day to you."

The tight smile on the whore's reddened lips matched the narrowed eyes and the tart tone of her voice, if not the words she uttered.

"A-hah! Jus' the man I were lookin' fer. Welcome, good sir, ter the House o' the Crowing Cockerel."

"Me?" Ranulf could not prevent the dubious note seeping into his voice.

As if his question had put the same doubt into the woman's mind, he saw the unfriendly gaze drop from his face to study him even more carefully from boots to bare head before the dark eyes returned to his face again.

Owing to the informal nature of his errand, he was wearing plain, dark blue breeches, an unbleached linen shirt that had seen better days, loosely laced because of the summer's heat, his only visible weapon being a dagger sheathed at his hip – discounting the one in his boot – while his sword, mail and the rest of his guardians' gear were bundled into a pack secured to Rye's saddle.

So to someone who did not know him well, he might be mistaken for...

There! He saw it again – the flicker of doubt in Mistress Birch's hooded eyes.

"Show me your arm!" she demanded.

Knowing what she was asking he did not bother to argue but simply shoved the loosely rolled shirt sleeve even further up his left arm to reveal the mark pricked into the skin just below his shoulder, watching as relief warred with reluctance on the whore's hard features.

"Come on in," she said, stepping back to allow his entry. "There's someone here as 'ud like ter see a big lad like ye. Is wantin' it somethin' desperate, ye might say."

The words were enticing. The tone was not.

He did not move.

"Let us be clear on one thing, Mistress Birch. I did not come here seeking paid company. Nor to make trouble for you. I need a favour, that is all."

His hand dropped to his purse, his next words sardonic,

"Naturally, I do not expect you to accommodate me out of good will, but I can pay whatever price you consider reasonable."

"So what's this favour then?"

"That you forget you have seen me, and let me walk straight through your house and out into the garden."

"Ye've an urgent need ter use the privy p'raps?"

She eyed the silver coins glinting in his hand, before looking up at him mockingly.

"'Tis an uncommon high price ter pay fer a piss, I'm thinkin'."

Ranulf regarded her with exasperation.

"I am sure you know bloody well I did not come here to use your privy. Now, will you let me through or not?"

"Aye, I reckon I will at that. Five half-nobles'll buy ye stablin' fer yer horse, an' a room wi' a bed an' a woman fer the whole night."

"As I have already told you, I do not want a room, a bed or a woman," he began.

"Do ye not?" she asked, looking back at him over her bare shoulder as she led the way through the lower chamber, her charcoal-lined eyes wide and dark as peat pools.

"I remember ye tellin' me once ye didn't want a man neither, so I'm wonderin' what it is ye *do* want, me fine fella. An' will ye know it, if 'tis set afore ye?"

Having offered this somewhat obscure remark, Mistress Birch paused at the foot of the narrow wooden staircase he had ascended once before and gestured him upwards.

"Ye'll not want ter be goin' ter... the privy 'til it's full dark. Nor yet linger down here, I'm thinkin'. Best fer us both if ye go upstairs ter wait. Las' door on the left, the room's empty. "

She had a point, he conceded silently, even if he could not help but suspect she was amusing herself at his expense.

"Very well."

He hardened his tone.

"But understand me well, Mistress Birch, I neither want nor need company whilst I am waiting."

"As ye will," the woman agreed.

Then with a sly smile,

"Since ye want neither man nor wench, I'll take it that ye're practised enough in dealin' wi' yer needs by yerself."

She tilted her head as professional interest replaced whatever it was that had briefly set that spark of suppressed laughter dancing in her dark eyes.

"Though if ye should change yer mind, I might be minded ter assist ye another time."

She raised her brows, and smiled at him knowingly.

"For a price, o' course."

He shook his head, not bothering with a retort, and made his way slowly up the creaking stairs to the room Mistress Birch had indicated.

He was still trying to calculate how long it would be until sunset, and how much longer after that it would be sensible to wait before he made his move, not to mention whether he would break his neck going over the wall in the starlit darkness... when he pushed open the unlocked door and found that the damned woman had lied to him after all about the absence of female companionship to while away the last golden hours until it was time for him to leave.

Verse 6

One Night to Last an Eternity

"Gods! Ro!"

Save for that one soft exclamation as he hastily shut the door behind him, Ranulf found himself standing speechless, staring in utter disbelief at the woman before him.

Of all the ways he had expected the day to end, *this* had never come into the reckoning.

Yes, he had hoped to see her, alone if possible, though he would have taken the hindrance of another's presence if that had been the only way in which he could speak to her.

But to find her here! Now! Like this!

Desperately he tried to reconcile the woman he had last seen clad in the healer's subdued garb of grey robe and white headrail with this fey apparition in a crimson gown, bare shoulders only partially concealed by her long waving hair.

And whilst it was true that her hair was not as long as when he had first set eyes on her fourteen years ago, still it was longer than that of the outlaw lad who had roamed the forests and fells. It tumbled loose and vibrant, catching sparks from the last light of the setting sun so that each strand flickered like witch-fire, evoking disquieting echoes of that far-off dawn in Chartre.

Then she spoke, just one word, her voice as soft as a wraith owl's wings, so that he only belatedly realised the name she had just called him by.

His own name, given to him by his father at his birth, not the one he had assumed after he had broken his oath of allegiance to his older brother.

He had been Rafe for so long now, the only people who called him by his true given name – and that only on rare occasions – being Josce and Gabriel, Guy and Edwy, and Rowène herself, and though he knew in his mind it had not been so long, it seemed an eternity since he had last heard his name on her lips.

Ranulf.

Struggling to ground himself in reality, he managed to say,

"What in hell's dark depths are you doing here, Ro? And dressed like that for f... for pity's sake."

"Hoping to see you."

She smiled a little uncertainly and he had to forcibly stop himself from striding over and taking her in his arms, reassuring her with hands and mouth, with words and kisses. But that way, gods knew, would lead all too swiftly to other, greater intimacies from which there would be no returning. For either of them.

"As for Mistress Cherry's best gown," she smoothed a nervous hand down the cheap silk. "I thought it better not to take the chance of being seen about a brothel wearing my own robes and thus risking bringing further disrepute to the Grey Sisters."

"But why are you here at all, damn it?"

"I overheard you talking to Sister Winfreda and came to the gateway as soon as I could but you were already gone and she would not let me go after you. So I climbed the orchard wall and asked the girls..."

Girls, she called them, Ranulf thought in helpless amusement. As if they were her friends, rather than three hard-faced harlots whom circumstance had made a lifetime older than her.

"I asked the girls for their help. Willow got me through the public room and upstairs unseen, Cherry helped me with the gown, and Birch said she would go and find you. Which clearly she did," she concluded with a smile that glimmered like sunlit rain in her beautiful grey eyes. "Because here you are."

"Here I am," he agreed, still not quite able to believe that the gods would grant him such undeserved grace.

Then remembering those five half-nobles that had greased the wheels of the gods' will, added caustically,

"And how much did they charge *you* for such service?"

"Nothing."

"Nothing?" he repeated incredulously, and watched as the slender shoulders rose in a shrug.

"Perhaps because I have been of assistance to them in the past, when they have had no choice but to come down to the Healing House."

What she did not say, what Ranulf knew instinctively of her, was that she of all the Sisters of Mercy in Vézière, and likely the whole realm, would not have treated them as scum because of their profession but simply as women who had need of her healing skills.

Now they had helped her in return, and being as it had brought them together he could hardly quibble about the five half-nobles Mistress Birch had charged him. Not when he would have given every coin in his purse for this chance.

"So?"

Her voice brought him out of his musing.

"What brings *you* to Vézière, Rafe? And what was it you needed to speak to me so desperately about?"

"What? Oh, yes, that!"

Hurriedly, distractedly, wishing she would call him by his own name again, he gave her the gist of his commission from Joscelin.

His mind, however, was not truly engaged with the dangers and difficulties that lay ahead.

Not when his heart – and, to be crudely honest, the heat and heaviness in his groin – were dragging him back into the past.

To that morning in Chartre castle. To that room filled with golden light, and the red-haired girl in the crimson gown.

Then even as he stood, lost between the present and the past, the years between slid away and she spoke straight into his thoughts.

"Ranulf. What do you want?"

They were the same words she had spoken that long ago morning, though the tone was entirely different. Not frightened and angry, but – gods help him – soft, seductive and sensually inviting.

What *did* he want?

"You!" he blurted. "Only you. Always."

"And if tonight is all we have? As it seems it may well be, until we meet again in Gabriel's bloody meadows under a crimson sky?"

Understanding what she did not say aloud, he could not help the grimace that twisted his mouth into the thin, cruel, hard lines of the man he had been that long-ago morning. Ranulf de Rogé at his worst.

"Tonight *is* all we have, damn it!"

Then, with an effort, he sloughed off the wolf skin of that man and said with all the gentleness he could find in his scarred soul,

"So let me... let us make the most of it so that we... so that *you* will have something good to remember of me when we are parted – as we will be, given the different paths we are bound to walk, both in life and the eternity beyond."

His fingers dropped to brush the hilt of the knife at his belt.

"I would I could swear myself to you formally, in blood, before witnesses... but I will be damned before I ask you to break the laws of this land more than you will do by lying with me..."

He paused, suddenly unsure.

"You will... let me love you as I want to? As I should have done that morning in Chartre?"

"Gods, yes!"

She laughed, a little shakily.

"You know I have no enchantment in me anymore. What you see before you... this is what I am, who I am. *Your* woman, Ranulf. Always. And as such I mean to share that bed with you, at least until the dawn sets our feet on those separate paths, and our very different fates."

A flicker of pain flashed across her face at the thought of that final parting, then with a visible effort she banished all thought of what must be and walked towards him, stopping barely a hand's width away from him, her grey eyes clear, considering, glimmering a little, like mist in the moonlight.

"So you remember that morning at Chartre?" she asked.

"How could I forget," he replied, an edge of darkness to his tone. "Even if I wanted to? My soul is damned because of it. And rightly so."

"Perhaps," she said. "And yet... do you suppose it is possible that we could... not live that day again – there can be no going back, no changing what you did – but perhaps we could make a new set of memories to overlay the old ones?"

"I am willing to try, if you are," he murmured, lifting his hand to touch her hair, combing his calloused fingers through the skeins of fiery silk.

At the same time, she slid her hands up his chest with agonising slowness, resting a moment over the place where his heart beat with thunderous rapidity, before allowing her fingers to continue their tantalising journey... pausing briefly, cool against the pulse thrumming in his neck, then eased upwards again, rasping softly over his lightly bearded jaw and the prickly stubble of his upper lip, finally tracing the outline of his mouth.

"This is different," she said with a smile as his lips pressed a tender kiss against her thumb. "You were clean-shaven then, save for the odd bit of stubble you had missed in your hung-over haste."

She ran her fingers gently through his shoulder-length flax and silver hair.

"And I confess I will miss the length of this brushing against my breast when you... come over me as you did then. You... do remember how it was... between us that morning?"

He gave her a slightly startled look.

"I told you, Ro. I have forgotten nothing of that morning, nothing that has *ever* been between us. But do you truly want me to... take you as I did then?"

"Yes," she said. "Exactly as you did that dawn. The difference is that this time I want you as much as you want me. As much as I wanted you that night in the Palace of Princes, when circumstance denied us completion. This time there is nothing to stop us. The room is ours without fear of interruption for as long as we need it."

A shadow flitted so quickly behind her eyes he was not even sure he had seen it.

"Well, at least until dawn's first light," she amended. "That is... if you want me to stay that long?"

"Oh, gods, Ro. I would you could stay for ever!"

His arms went around her, drawing her close, holding her so tightly he feared he must be hurting her. As he had hurt her fourteen years ago – though gods know that had never been his intention.

Now, thankfully, she gave no sign of the fear and revulsion she had felt for him then.

If anything, she strained against him even more closely and when he bent his head to take her mouth with his, she did indeed welcome him with a heat and passion that was as fierce as her icy rebuttal had been fourteen years ago.

He had no awareness of how long he remained lost in that kiss, drunk on long-denied desire and much more recently admitted love, breaking apart only when it became necessary to breathe, by which time he was aroused beyond consideration of anything save the need to give himself to the woman in his arms, in whatever manner she wanted to take him.

Distant but still vivid memories of that morning in Chartre castle had him catching her up in his arms – tenderly this time – and carrying her to the bed, where he carefully set her down on the edge and then, despite her earlier words and the urging of his own rampant body, he found himself hesitating.

"I meant it, Ranulf," she said softly, holding his gaze. "I want this. I want you."

Rolling slightly, she presented him with the angle of her back that he might loosen the tight lacing that held her borrowed gown moulded to her every curve as if it had been made for her alone... and when his unsteady fingers had finally completed the task, she allowed the silk to slip completely from her shoulders, revealing soft white breasts budded with dusk-rose nipples.

"Oh gods," he swore again.

He had seen her naked before, of course.

That morning of sun-gilded mist in Chartre, and then again by moonlight and torchlight in that cramped chamber in the Palace of Princes.

The first occasion had been spawned of brutal, drugged lust on his part, loathing on hers, ending in shame and pain and blood-stained sheets.

The second had been little better, started in scrambling haste, no more than a ruse between friends, meant to confuse their enemies, yet resulting in dishonour for her and the chance of death for him had not her brother kept rather more control over his temper than Ranulf himself had wielded over his desire.

This time, thank the gods, was as different as summer starlight is from the black storms of winter.

Here was no violence, no haste, no deceit.

Only sweet enticement leading to a freely given love.

Almost diffidently, he stepped between the legs she had already spread the better to accommodate him, reassured when she reached out to stroke the hard line of his cock confined within his breeches.

Then as her searching fingers plucked open the laces to ensure the freedom it so urgently craved, he gently slid the crimson skirts of her gown up until she lay revealed before him, her skin impossibly white against the rough dark wool cloth that covered his own thighs.

He saw her bite her lip, obviously remembering... or, gods willing, replacing her memories with ones he hoped would bring her joy rather than pain. Even so...

"Are you sure?" he asked again.

"I am sure."

And so saying, she reached out to caress his aching length. Even as his own fingers sought not only to prepare, but also to pleasure her, as some counter to the discomfort he did not see how he could avoid inflicting on her, unaccustomed as he knew her to be to the crude invasion of a man's engorged prick.

Gods!

He groaned and gritted his teeth, fearing he would lose control.

She was so warm, so wet, so wonderfully welcoming against his caressing fingers.

Everything he had dreamed of and spent himself to, night after lonely night, seeking ever to hold in his mind those few precious heartbeats when she had allowed him to put himself inside her when he lay beneath her that night in the Palace of Princes.

Hell knew, the tight-wrapped fingers of his sword hand had been no substitute for what he truly wanted but it had been all he had if he were to keep faith with her.

And he had done, until now...

Now, he was truly there in that honeyed place.

Gods! He could scarcely believe it!

Not even when he felt her close about his straining cock.

Not even when he looked down into her eyes and saw nothing but love for him in the clear depths. The same love that he felt for her...

Heart of my heart, soul of my soul!

The same love, unspoken though it was, that made him determined to give her the tender, loving and passionate pleasure she deserved. It was also, as he well knew, his responsibility *not* to...

But there all coherent thought failed him as he gave himself to her.

After all those long years of wanting and waiting, the fire that had blazed between them had been fierce beyond measure, incandescent passion immolating all chance of thought or care.

So that afterwards, even as they lay content beyond words to be at last naked and in each other's arms, Ranulf felt every stab from the rough-sharpened daggers of black contrition and self-contempt... and all the while the sweat of the most loving and complete coupling he had ever experienced cooled on his body... along with the seed he had only partially spilled where he should have made damned sure it had all bloody well been spent.

"I'm sor..."

"No, do not say it."

She turned swiftly, lithe as a seal, to put her fingers against his lips.

He kissed them gently, then regretfully pushed them aside, determined to say what must be said.

"If my carelessness has resulted in a child..."

"Then I would not have it any different."

Her gaze was level, loving, accepting of the consequences.

"Nevertheless, next time you will allow me the lover's right to exercise both care and control, to give as well as receive pleasure."

"Oh, so there is to be a next time? Perhaps as it was that night in the palace?"

"If you wish. I want only to give you pleasure."

"And would you find it pleasurable," Rowène enquired with a flicker of mischief in her smile, her fingers moving in a deliberate downwards caress. "Now?"

"Since now is all we may have, then yes, let me love you as many times as I can manage – though given that I am no longer a lust-driven youth, that may not be saying much – and then only if *you* wish it. The last thing I want to do is hurt you in any way."

"You have not. You will not. And, since you still doubt it, you *did* give me pleasure, Ranulf. Much pleasure, my dearest love."

Could he believe her assurances? He wanted to... and yet there was still something in her eyes.

"What is it, sweetheart?"

She was silent a moment, then released a soft sigh that stirred the damp hairs of his chest.

"It is obviously still troubling you... that we are here... like this."

Her gesture took in the sparse furniture almost filling the small bedchamber, the gaudy bed hangings, the straw-stuffed pillow, the coarse linen sheets.

"Of course it does. Damn it all, Ro! I want to claim you publicly as the woman who wears my binding band, who holds my heart, who is the other half of my soul. Not to take you like this, knowing full-well what gossip will say if it ever comes to light. A common soldier and a healer, fu... fornicating in a brothel no less."

"Forget the gossips. We have already faced the backlash of that particular scene at Lamortaine, and survived."

She regarded him in thoughtful consideration as her fingers absently played with the hair on his chest, and he waited patiently for the result of her deliberations, simply content to lie with her in his arms, and at last she said,

"I know you want more for us than a tawdry-seeming tumble so..."

She leaned over him, deftly lifting the knife from the belt he had laid across the stool when he had finally shed his clothes, and held it out to him, hilt first.

"No law-breaking, no witnesses, just you and me, Ranulf and Rowène. A simple oath of love and fielty."

She looked suddenly uncertain.

"If you are sure you want to bind yourself to me only."

"Gods, Ro, do you doubt me still? Since that dream meeting in the rose arbour... you remember that?"

"I remember that. I wept, even though I still thought I hated you, because I thought I would never see you again."

"I wonder you wanted to, the bastard I was then. But that is not what I wanted to say. What I want you to know is that I have had no other in my bed since that night. And since that morning in Chartre there has never been another to hold my heart. That is some thirteen or fourteen years by my reckoning, so believe me, Ro, I am not going to change now, no matter how many years it may be before we can be together again. If we ever are. Yet still I will know that you are mine and I am yours. And I shall take that memory with me to lighten the darkness of what will be a bloody long eternity without you."

Warm lips tasting of honeyed mead stopped his words, stirring him into passion once more, but all the while below the heat he was aware of the unspoken desperation that edged their apparent acceptance of the situation.

If tonight was all they had, then he was resolved to make the most of it, storing up memories to last him for the eternity they would have apart.

More than that, something – perhaps a whisper from the goddess he had promised to serve, or the gut instinct of a man who had been around Gabriel de Marillec too bloody long – told him that he would not see Rowène again.

Afterwards, he drew her drowsy body closer against him, until all he could smell was her, all he could feel was her, and with her murmured *I love you*, the only words he wanted to hear, he finally allowed his eyes to close and yielded his weary, sated body to sleep.

Verse 7

The Grey Light of Dawn

Ranulf woke to find himself alone in the back bedchamber of Vézière's brothel, and the silver-grey light of a summer's dawn lifting the darkness outside the unshuttered window.

It was no more than he had expected. Or deserved.

I never even told her I loved her, not in so many words!

He had shown her, he thought, but that was not quite the same as saying to her – as she had said to him – *I love you.*

So even though he would have wished to see her safely back over the wall and through the orchard, he could understand why Rowène had gone without waking him, leaving the bed they had shared before the sky had even begun to brighten into blue.

She had, after all, already risked much by coming to him the night before. Risked far more, he knew, than merely Sister Winfreda's wrath, and that was perilous enough.

Cursing at the thought of what else she risked, he ran a hand over the place where she had lain so close beside him all night.

The crumpled sheets still held the faintest trace of her warmth, her soft rose scent... he kicked the upper layer back, grimacing as he studied the damp stains smeared across the linen upon which they had lain.

Goddess, keep her safe. And gods, let her not find herself carrying my child. Let her not suffer for my carelessness. Not again!

Closing his eyes, he imagined himself back at the Swanfleet Bridge, sky the colour of copper reflected in the gilded water flowing beneath his feet, watching as Rowène de Chartreux rode away from him, his black cloak wrapped about her, giving her what scant protection he could from the shame he had put upon her.

And on her shoulder she had worn the silver thorn and falcon brooch of their shared Valennais blood-lines – though neither of them had known of the kinship at the time. He had made her promise to send the brooch back to him if she found herself carrying his child.

Except she had not sent for him, he reminded himself grimly.

He had a feeling that she would not have done so even if she had carried the babe to term.

And this time?

He had to face the hard truth that he might never know.

But, damn it, he wanted – *needed* – to know. He would speak to her again, make her understand that this time she *must* tell him.

Hell curse this light, surely it was not too late!

There must still be a chance that he could catch her if he got off his arse and stopped this bloody pointless mithering!

With the hope that she might not yet be gone from him, he scrambled across the bed and, heedless of his nakedness, leaned out of the window, his gaze scouring the length of the brothel's narrow garth, past the ordered rows of vegetables, to the woodpile, the ramshackle shed that did duty as a privy, and the high wall beyond.

"Bloody pissing hell!"

Save for the merry chirping of blackbird and thrush, all was quiet and still, the sparkling dawn dew holding only one set of footprints leading down through the garden and ending at the wall, upon the top of which sat the sentinel silhouette of Lyra, slitted golden eyes intently watching a flirting flock of tiny finches.

Finches... Finch... Guy... Josce!

"Shit!"

Rowène was gone, he could see that for himself.

And not a single fucking thing he could do about it!

He accepted that, though hell knew with bloody bad grace.

But as to the other part of his errand here...

He swore as he snatched up the clothes he had dropped anyhow on the floor, and again as other pressures made themselves felt, and then a third time on discovering no chamber pot under the bed, and in sheer bloody defiance of Mistress Birch, Sister Winfreda, the town busybodies, and his life to come, returned to the open window to relieve both his ruffled feelings and his full bladder.

Finally dressed, he went to collect his daggers from the stool, meaning to restore them to boot and belt, only to frown as the glint of some other metal caught his eye.

Bending closer, he found himself squinting at something that had not been there the night before.

Something circular and flat and silver, about the size across of his clenched fist.

Something he had not seen since a frosty winter's morning thirteen and a half years ago.

Slowly he picked up the cloak pin, rubbing his thumb absently over the pattern of thorn flowers encircling a falcon, wings outstretched in flight.

It was, as he well knew, the insignia of the lords of Valenne.

Rowène had kept it safe through all those years, he realised.

So why had she chosen to give it back to him now?

Not a question he could answer, even had he the time to ponder such matters.

He dropped the brooch into his purse and buckled his belt, feeling somewhat naked without the familiar weight of his sword at his hip, and was just turning away, his mind already grappling with the problem of finding and convincing Guy, in the short span of time he had left, to fall in with Joscelin's plan when he found himself pausing...

Casting one last glance at the bed he had shared for one brief night with the woman to whom he had given his heart, and quite possibly a child he would never see and she could surely not want, regardless of what she had told him.

Your seed, your child, your responsibility.

He froze, frowning.

Where had he heard those words before?

Then he remembered.

He himself had spoken them to Gabriel de Marillec, and he could almost hear the other man's light, bitingly acerbic tone as he flung his own words back to him,

How much of a father will you be if you abandon her the moment you have spilled your seed, leaving her to carry and bring up your child alone?

Damning himself to the outermost reaches of icy hell for yet again proving to be the most feckless sort of bastard ever born, Ranulf was already turning towards the door when a flicker of fire caught his eye, and bending back over the bed he saw in the brighter light of morning what the grey half-light of dawn had hidden from him.

Snagged on the rough pillow, a single fiery strand of hair the length of his forearm.

Working quickly, but with great care nonetheless, he twisted it around the third finger of his left hand where the gold signet ring of

676

the lords of Valenne would have been, had not Joffroi stolen it from their grandsire's finger.

This new ring of living bronze was a makeshift arrangement at best but one he judged would hold until he could secure it more firmly.

He cast another glance out of the window, gauging from the strengthening clarity of the light just how little time he had left to find his brother before Attan's arrival, though he guessed that Joscelin would delay the Atarkarnan chief as long as possible, not only to give Ranulf time to complete his errands but also to stave off the moment when Joscelin must bid farewell to his daughter.

Ranulf knew all about that sort of pain. Knew too the pain of *not* being able to say farewell... of knowing he was hated by the son he had tried to do his best by since the boy's birth.

Then again, perhaps he did deserve Val's contempt, his violent rejection, the vile name his son had called him.

His hand lifted as if to brush the memory of spittle from his cheek.

And with another savage oath, he turned his back on the bed and the babe he might have made there.

Letting himself out of the chamber, Ranulf made his way along the narrow passageway, down the creaking staircase and through the main chamber of the brothel, seeing no-one except a pale-faced, heavy-eyed servant girl who came in through the front door carrying a bucket of water she had evidently lugged from the well in the square.

She had paused, apparently to brush a lank hank of hair from her sweating face, but on hearing his approach, took one look at his face and hastened to step out of his way.

From somewhere he managed to drag a reassuring smile and the courtesy of a word of thanks, which the startled girl repaid with a slyly speculative smile of her own. Remembering where he was, and in consideration of the fact that she would most likely be the one sent to clean up after him, Ranulf held his temper in check and instead folded a silver half-noble into her surprised hand.

"For your trouble," he murmured.

Stepping past her through the open door, took a deep breath of the clean morning air... and then fell into a fit of coughing as he almost choked on it.

Or rather at the disgusted look on the face of the man standing squarely in front of him, arms folded across his broad chest.

The very man he most wanted to see.

In the very last place he wanted to be seen by him.

"*Shit!* Guy! What in bloody damnation are *you* doing here?"

Guy regarded him for several long moments of intense silence, his brother's expression neither pleased nor pleasant.

Finally, after a quick glance around the square, already busy with townsfolk about their daily tasks, he spoke, his voice level and quiet.

"What am *I* doing here, Ran? What else would I be doing outside a brothel except waiting for you, brother. I see age has not changed your habits. Does *she* know, I wonder, that you are whoring behind her b..."

"Hold your tongue, curse you!"

Despite being strongly tempted to follow that snarled command by informing his brother that he knew nothing of his habits now, Ranulf forced his temper back under control and merely said, with the sardonic smile he knew would irritate Guy to hell and back,

"I must make the most of civilised advantages whilst I have them. As for my feelings and fielty – or lack – for the woman who..."

He fought not to claim her for his own if only this once.

"Let us just say, I have as little desire to discuss her with you, brother, as you would your own feelings towards her bitch of a sister."

He saw Guy's fists clench, and smiled inwardly at the ease with which he could still bait his brother. Then brushing past him, made his way into the small stable next to the brothel and busied himself with getting Rye tacked up, all the time aware of his brother's grimly disapproving gaze.

Aware too that this was no place to discuss Joscelin's proposition, particularly not with the mood Guy was in. In fairness though, at least the man had not walked away as soon as he had said his piece.

"So how did you know I was here?" Ranulf asked as he led the gelding out into the square where a big flame-chestnut stallion was lipping geraniums under an urchin's worshipful guard.

"This is a small town, Ran," Guy retorted as he reached for the reins, flipping a bronze mark at the child.

"Have you been living so long in the halls of kings and princes that you have forgotten how swiftly and accurately rumour flies with the breeze beneath its wings? It is heady stuff indeed when a fair-haired man who carries himself with all the arrogance of a royal guardian – one moreover who bears sufficient likeness to Nicholas de Vézière's household harper to be his close kin, if not his twin – rides into the town..."

"And even more gossip-worthy when both men ride out together," Ranulf muttered, pulling himself into the saddle with a weary groan.

"A hard night, brother?" Guy commented, distaste underlying his uncharacteristically harsh humour.

A hard night, and a bitter dawn.

Ranulf kept his thoughts to himself, however, saying only,

"Something like that, Guy."

Then, belatedly observing the familiar instrument bag slung over his brother's shoulder, and the other packs secured behind his saddle, added,

"You are bound on some errand for Messire Nicholas?"

"I was." He seemed to read something in Ranulf's face. "But it can wait a while."

"Then ride with me a little way, brother? There is something I must speak with you about. Something that cannot wait."

Thankfully, much of the tension eased between them as they rode out of the town together, the sweetness of the summer's morning restoring some small sense of the closeness they had enjoyed in their younger years...

Years spent riding together over Rogé's High Moors, hunting the red deer that had kept them alive through the long winters, driving off the wolf packs that had threatened the villagers of their domain from Mallowleigh in the north down to Rogérinac itself, birding in the Salt Marshes of Tawne in the autumn when the wild geese were in flight. Swimming in the coldly shimmering grey-green waters off Black Rock Cove, sometimes with Edwy, sometimes just the pair of them, returning to the castle shivering and laughing – and when they had been very young and Lady Rosalynde still alive, more often than not bringing with them some treasure of water-polished pebble or shining shell to show her.

Then there had been the more contentious times, their childhood behind them, set abruptly aside with Lady Rosalynde's death, followed by their father's whilst they were still young men not quite settled into their skins.

They had continued to ride together, but on vastly differing errands, Ranulf slumped in his saddle, heavy-eyed, with the stale sweat and perfume stench of the Sarillac brothel still on him, Guy riding silently at his side, disapproval written in the very straightness of his shoulders, every rigid bone in his back.

He, of course, had come from seeing Hilde, their old nurse, and the pretty, scheming Mathilde. While Edwy, riding some paces behind them, had been there to guard their backs, and as far as Ranulf could recall, neither he nor Guy had made issue of where, or with whom, the young garrison soldier had spent the night.

Now, finding himself riding again alongside Guy, Ranulf found himself looking over his shoulder more than once for the man they had not known at the time to be their half-brother.

But of course Edwy was in Lasceynes now, doing a kinsman's duty by Ranulf's son, and hopefully keeping the boy out of too much trouble.

How long that would last, Ranulf did not care to consider too closely. Or what would happen once Luc was well enough to leave the Healing House.

He rather suspected that Luc would rejoin Beric's band of border rangers, taking Val and Edwy with him. Into the heart of the battle against the Eastern Empire.

"So what is this word you would say to me?"

Guy spoke suddenly into the silence that had held between them since they had mounted up outside the brothel.

Taking a deep breath, Ranulf drew rein and dismounted, and after a moment his brother followed suit, heavy dark blond brows knitting together.

"Well, Ran? Spit it out!"

And so Ranulf told him what Joscelin wanted of them, voice flat, eyes free of the emotion seething in his breast.

Guy heard him out without attempting to interrupt, the frown deepening even more, his mouth hardening into that stubborn line Ranulf knew well.

He was quite expecting him to say 'no' and was already ordering his counter-arguments when Guy said coldly,

"Very well."

"What?"

"You heard me, Ran. I do not like it. But then neither do I have any expectation that either of us will live long enough to regret it. Messire Nicholas will need to be told though. I cannot just ride out and leave him to discover my betrayal of the trust he has placed in me."

"No, of course not."

Ranulf wiped unnaturally damp palms against his leg, glanced across at his brother's attire, so similar to his own in cloth and style. Loose linen shirt, close-fitting breeches, soft leather boots. Even their hair was of a similar length, Guy's perhaps a slightly darker shade of fair than this own, wheat rather than flax.

The only material difference between them was the sword once more sheathed at his side, and the harp in its bag at his brother's back.

"De Vézière will be told," Ranulf promised.

Guy eyed him for a moment – the blue far cooler than that of the summer sky glimpsed through the dancing poplar leaves – then, apparently satisfied, shrugged broad shoulders.

"So be it. We may as well get on with it then."

Except, with their preparations made, swiftly and with little fuss or speech, and ready once more to mount up, Guy managed to surprise him a second time, taking Ranulf's tentatively outstretched arm and pulling him in close.

"May the gods guard you, brother, and bring you safe through this latest tangle of thorns you have seen fit to ensnare us both in."

"It was Joscelin's bloody idea, not mine," Ranulf muttered.

Then loosening his own grasp, added somewhat grimly,

"As it is, I think the gods will need to be watching over you more than me. Fare you well, brother. I have the feeling that next time we meet, it will be to fulfil the bloody terms of the prophecy that nearly broke Gabriel de Marillec's mind the year you returned to Mithlondia, and which has haunted us all since."

"I do not know how much faith I would put in the foretellings of the fey or half-fey," Guy retorted.

"And you a harper," Ranulf mocked. "Tell me, have you never seen a mermaid combing out her hair in a golden dawn? Nor watched a wild-rose moon rise in the midsummer sky?"

"Yes, to the second," Guy snorted. "And no, to the first. I only have your word about that, remember."

He cocked his head, evidently considering the situation, before concluding drily,

"As it is, you make none so ill a bard yourself, Ran. When you put your mind to it."

It was a little before mid-morning when the two men emerged from the small green-leaved copse, riding together until they reached the parting of their ways, taking their final farewell of each other with no more than half a dozen words exchanged between them, and a brief, if heartfelt clasp of solidly-muscled arms.

The horses moving apart, the harper on the chestnut stallion cantering back towards the walled town and the castle rising from the crest of the hill, where he went first to speak to Lord Nicholas, and then up onto the wall-walk of the battlements to await the arrival of Chief Attan and little Princess Lilia, his harp slung at his back.

Meanwhile, the soldier, now clad in full mail, despite the summer heat, his royal blue mantle flung back from his shoulders to reveal the winged horse emblazoned on his tunic, was riding south along the highway towards Lamortaine.

He paused once, before he passed out of sight of Vézière, turning in the saddle to look back up at the castle walls, his eyes narrowed against the sun in an attempt to discern the man he knew would be standing there.

He raised his hand once, then set the bay gelding into motion again, riding with grim determination to take his place at Joscelin de Veraux's side.

Part V

Summer

1209

Verse 1

The Land of the Seven Tribes

"Hola, Harper!"

The big, fair-haired man thus hailed rose easily to his feet and stood atop the small grassy knoll, waiting while the chief of all the Atarkarnan tribes slid down from the bare back of his magnificent stallion and made his way up through the long, waving spears of abundant grass that spring had seen greening up all across the wide plains, though they were now turning pale with the approach of midsummer.

"They told me you would be here," Chief Attan said as he came to a halt beside the harper, looking with interest at the younger man's clean-shaven face.

"No warrior amongst us would be seen dead like that," he commented as he stroked his own long beard, the black braids adorned with numerous amber beads and glinting with gold.

"To us it is a sign of our manhood."

"Ah, but then I am not a warrior of the seven tribes," the other man replied in Atarkarnan, a language he had perforce become fluent in over the changing course of the past four seasons.

"I am merely a humble Mithlondian harper. In the eyes of your warriors, scarcely even a man at all."

"*I* would not make that mistake," Attan said flatly. "I have seen you fight. Besides, and strange as it seems to our eyes, your beardless state does not ill become you. At least if what I hear is true that certain of my people would willingly share your blankets, though you yourself have chosen to lie with neither man nor woman of the White Eagle tribe."

Black eyes glinted an amused question but the harper declined to be drawn, and Attan continued reflectively,

"As to your other skills, you will have a chance to prove them, if you wish, when the seven tribes meet – those of us not on the embattled borders of our two lands – when we welcome Daerthanis, the Goddess of Summer with trials of speed and strength."

Thick blond brows lifted.

"I shall look forward to it," he said, with a courtesy that held more wariness than warmth.

"It will, of necessity, be a muted celebration compared to former years," Attan went on. "But we must not fail to give Daerthanis her due, else the horses will not come into foal and the deer will desert the grasslands for the hills. It is also the time for the making of new life between the young men and women of the tribe, and there will be food and dancing for all those not otherwise celebrating."

Attan paused, and then said musingly,

"The Lily-child will enjoy the dancing, I think. And perhaps you will play for us? A gift to Daerthanis, who protects you both."

A fleeting grimace crossed the harper's face.

"If you wish it, though I fear my skills are not sufficient to please any deity. I am out of practise."

A look of sly amusement glimmered for a moment in the Atarkarnan's black eyes.

"If you say so, Harper, who am I to argue? And yet I have heard you play for the little princess of your people."

"Cradle songs, children's rhymes, no more," the harper murmured, his manner deprecating. "Nothing compared to the great sagas of your own people as I have heard them declaimed around the fires of the long winter."

Attan nodded at the compliment, but then went on with something of a challenge in his tone,

"Even so, I believe I have heard you call forth from the strings of your harp something that is not a cradle song. It is true that my learning of your tongue is not as good as yours of mine, yet I think you sing of a woman. A woman... of the sea? A *mermaid*? Have I remembered the word aright?"

He finished on a question, striving to hold the harper's gaze, which was now as distant as the sky, shading from dark cobalt to palest blue where it touched the eastern horizon.

"Aye, a fey woman of the sea, with eyes as grey as the waves breaking on black rocks," the harper murmured absently, evidently leagues away, perhaps standing on that same far shore, his gaze seeking out the woman he spoke of with some hidden emotion.

"Your woman?" Attan asked softly. Then receiving no reply other than a flicker of pain around the harper's mouth, continued,

"The Lily-child has such eyes also, sea-grey eyes you would say. Making her kin perhaps to that other. So where is she, Harper?"

"Who?"

"Lily, of course. We are too far from the shore for either of us to catch a glimpse of your strange sea-woman. It is, however, even stranger to see you without the child or her companion."

"She is not far away," the harper replied, a shade grimly as he returned his attention to the Atarkarnan chief. "And well within my sight and hearing. I may be lacking something of skill with the harp but I have no intention of failing in my duty towards the child in any way. Her happiness, safety and well-being are my *only* concern."

He held Attan's eyes.

"And since you were the one who suggested that I accompany the princess, I do not think you can take me to task for holding to that duty now."

"Nor do I," the Atarkarnan replied equably. "I know these past seasons have not turned easily for you, and it took much courage on your part to venture so far from your own land. It has taken my people a long time to accept your presence in my camp. Longer indeed than I had expected or perhaps I should not have suggested bringing the child. Life among the seven tribes is very different from the one you would have led, if I had not interfered. And definitely harder than you would have chosen for your sword-brother's child."

The harper gave the Atarkarnan a narrow look at his allusion to Joscelin, a look the older man met with a placidity that sat oddly on his sharply-lined, wind-weathered features.

"I like the child," Attan said gruffly. "And I respect your sword-brother. Believe me or not as you choose but I mean neither of them ill, Lily least of all. I hope she has not found it too difficult to accept our way of living?"

"Far from it," the harper assured the other man.

He grinned suddenly, some of the grim watchfulness leaving his face.

"See for yourself, Chief Attan."

He gestured to the other side of the knoll, towards the small spring-fed pool where half a dozen dark-haired children in deer-skin tunics were splashing and laughing in the clear shallows. Eye colour being indistinguishable at that distance, it was only Lilia's wild mane of curls that set her apart from her straight-haired companions.

That, and the small mist-grey cat chasing invisible moonbeams through the wind-rippled grass nearby.

"Walk with me," the Atarkarnan chief said, a smile likewise lightening his own harsh features. "Let us see what mischief your little princess makes today."

Genial as the tone was, it was clearly a command, and besides, the harper let neither woman nor man – chief or not – of the seven tribes approach his young charge without his knowledge and consent.

Walking in a surprisingly amicable silence down the grassy slope towards the children, the harper was startled when Attan said brusquely,

"I heard what you did for the people of my tribe this spring when I was away with the warriors. And I thank you."

The harper's hand dropped without volition to his belt, only to lift again with the recollection that the only knife he was permitted to carry was the small eating knife he had honed to razor sharpness, and which he had used only that morning to remove the new-grown prickle of straw-gold stubble from his jaw, under the interested gaze of the child and the distinctly disinterested one of the yawning feline curled up in her lap.

"I defended my princess, that is all," he answered after a moment of silent consideration.

"And in so doing, you also defended the women and children of my tribe," Attan corrected. "Alongside those youths too young to fight, and those who are too stubborn to stand shield to shield with your people. You shed your blood..."

He gestured at the long scabbing cut running the length of the harper's forearm.

"You risked your life – in more ways than one, as both you and I know – for those same elders of my tribe who even now will not permit you to carry anything other than that small blade or a hunting bow."

"It served me well enough that day," he shrugged. "Besides, a harper hardly needs a weapon. That *is* why you told Joscelin to send me, is it not?"

"And my trust has been repaid," Attan said, gruff again. "But I can see you do not want to talk about it, and so we will not."

The harper shook his head, sending long fair strands flying upon the grass-scented breeze.

"There is no point."

Apparently agreeing with him, Attan said nothing more.

Nevertheless, the subject, once laid out in the cool summer sunlight, could not be so easily banished to the depths of the harper's mind – a dark and lonely place he had guarded with grim, unrelenting care for the past four slowly-changing seasons.

Even as he had understood and yielded to Joscelin de Veraux's reasoning, he had still resented the command that had sent him to the wild, wind-swept grasslands of Atarkarna, unarmed and treated by the tribes' people as little better than a nursemaid to a foreign brat and her cat.

Bad enough, he considered, that he had been taken from his proper place, a position where he could put his skills to their best use. But what in the name of all the gods did he know about caring for *any* child? Let alone a princess! A girl-child of six summers!

Not to mention that bloody damned fey cat!

At least, he thought, with a flicker of wayward humour, Pearl had proved entirely capable of looking after herself, though at the time the creature had joined the party, he had not thought so, and indeed would cheerfully have treated Luc de Chartreux to the savage edge of his tongue had the outlaw given him the opportunity.

Luc, however, having suggested to Lilia that she take the wretched animal with her for company – his kinsman obviously having a poor opinion of his own use as companion – had kept well out of the way of that tearful departure.

That said, and his own misgivings aside, the little cat had proved its worth even before the walls of the Healing House were out of sight.

Pearl, for so Lilia called her pet – for a reason the harper refused to allow himself to reflect upon with any great frequency – had proved a far less tiresome traveller than anyone would have supposed, spending the days curled up in a willow basket strapped to the saddle of the sturdy spotted moorland pony provided for the little princess to ride.

Albeit, as the child's resilience and equestrian ability were limited, she spent the greater part of each day riding before the harper on Flame, the big chestnut stallion proving more than capable of bearing her additional weight without showing any strain.

By night the child slept curled up in a nest of blankets, Pearl snuggled in her arms beneath the covers, the small grey furry head whisker-to-cheek with the little girl.

Not that Lilia did not miss her mama and her mother's friends, talking often of Lady Isabelle and Lady Adèle to the only person in the party who could understand her Mithlondian speech.

She chattered too about her 'Uncle' Joscelin – a term that never failed to cause the harper to grimace inwardly – as well as the royal bodyguards, Rafe and Gabriel, with whom she had been on friendly terms since the time when they had been with her in Kaerellios, trusted companions who had steadfastly kept her from harm and provided a rare point of stability in what had been – and still was – a relatively rootless mode of living.

Thought of roots and branches, trees and seedlings, however, only made it all the more obvious to the harper that the one person she never mentioned was Prince Kaslander, the man she – along with the rest of the realm – believed to be her father.

Clearly, Lilia was as terrified of that cursed Kardolandian swine as she had always been, and only too pleased to be anywhere that he was not, eagerly embracing the rigours of travel in her desire to get away. But then, the harper reflected, she had spent much of her short life travelling strange lands and hearing foreign tongues all around.

And as a consequence of having grown up with both Kardolandian and Mithlondian at her command, it did not take Lilia long to pick up words and phrases – most of which the harper would have preferred her neither to have assimilated nor questioned him about – in the common language used by the seven tribes of Atarkarna.

Why, he wondered ruefully, on being asked to explain something Lilia had heard but thankfully not understood, did children always seek out the least acceptable words in any new language.

As it stood, neither Princess Linette nor Joscelin were going to be pleased with him when – *if*, he corrected himself dourly – their daughter was ever returned to her rightful place in the Mithlondian court, and with a full command of the coarser aspects of the Atarkarnan language fluent upon her tongue.

The undisputed truth that in his own far-off youth in that crumbling castle on the cliffs, he and his brother had conducted similar exchanges with Edwy, exchanging crude descriptions of various bodily functions from high Mithlondian to the earthier Rogé dialect and back again was, he considered grimly, neither here nor there. They had been boys, two of them bastards by birth, the other a bastard by practise.

Lilia on the other hand was not only a girl, but a royal princess. Not that she looked the part now, but even back in Kaerellios and Lamortaine, clad in silks and velvets of her high estate, her mother had treated her as a beloved child first, a princess very much second. And while she had been taught by her mother to be courteous to all, whether noble, servant or guardian, Linette had also tried to ensure that her daughter learned to laugh and to play.

At least as far as was possible when Kaslander hated the child more and more with every year that went by, the callous cruelty of his actions, the vicious cut of his tongue, and the swiftness of his hand to strike without cause, all combining to smother Lilia's natural ebullience and sweet vivacity.

In a way, the harper reflected, Attan had done Lilia a favour by taking her away from the court, away from Kaslander, possibly even to the extent of saving her life.

Certainly Lilia appeared to be far happier living the rough, nomadic life of the tribes than she had been during the last year she had spent at court, until the time Linette had removed to the Healing House in Vézière to await the birth of her second child.

A child Kaslander could not possibly have sired, though he had so far said nothing in public to disclaim responsibility – to the best of his knowledge, anyway, Chief Attan being his only source of tidings concerning the events unfolding in the lands south of the Long River or east of the Painted Gorge.

Attan was also one of the few of the tribe who treated the Mithlondian as a normal man.

Even now, three seasons after coming to the plains, the harper still found himself regarded with rude mockery by the greater part of the tribes' people. The exception being those few who eyed him with a flagrant and entirely physical interest.

He would have much preferred simple indifference, since repulsing such blatant offers as came his way – though he tried his damnedest not to cause offence by his refusal – was not always well received and Lilia's situation, indeed the whole bloody delicate balancing act Joscelin had initiated, was fragile enough without his putting any further strain upon it.

Called upon to exercise tact, a skill he had never mastered, he had initially responded to all suggestions of intimacy – verbal or otherwise – with the information that he had a woman back in Mithlondia.

Since that merely produced a blank look that said more clearly than words, *So? She is not here, I am,* he had taken to stating with a bluntness that left no margin for incomprehension that he was in no need of any body to roll with in the grass beneath the sun, or share his blanket under the stars.

At which point, black lashes would momentarily hide black eyes, sharp teeth bite soft lips, to be followed by the almost inevitable reply,

When you do have need, seek me out, and if I have not found another by then, we will lie down together beneath the sun or stars, and take our pleasure.

He had not even come close to considering the redemption of such promises.

Or at least he had.

Once.

But it had not been for any need of his own – though the gods knew he had needs.

Rather it had been for Lilia's sake...

It had been the start of winter, icy winds howling across the plains, the tribes moving towards the forested hills where they would take shelter against the coming snow, and find good hunting amongst the herds of huge-horned elk.

The cold had been intense, with an icy edge that flayed the skin inside his nose with every in-drawn breath and made his eyes water with raw pain.

It was the sort of cold the tribes' people had the experience to deal with, whereas he and Lilia were damnably ill-equipped to face it. Even the worst Mithlondian winter could not compare to the onslaught that they had, at that time, felt the merest leading edge of, and the harper now understood why Attan was so proud and possessive of his great bearskin mantle, it being not only the symbol of authority amongst his people but also, more prosaically, because it kept him warm in the bone-biting misery of an Atarkarnan winter.

Reduced to watching impotently as the child in his care huddled shivering over the wind-whipped flames of the fire he kept burning outside their goat-hide shelter, Pearl held close beneath her chin with hands that turned first red and then blue with cold, he had pushed aside his own pride and gone to the sharp-tongued old woman who had, however reluctantly, helped them when they had first settled with Attan's tribe, meaning to ask again for her advice, or better yet some practical assistance.

The old woman – the Bone Lady, Lilia called her, and he himself knew no other – had not been in her own tent nearby. Instead the relative warmth had been occupied by a much younger woman, her daughter's daughter, he thought, though kinship amongst the tribe was vague, everyone seeming kin in some degree to everyone else.

Of far more importance was the knowledge that Namari was one of the women whose offer of intimacy he had declined – more than once – over the past two seasons.

Now, however, she smiled at him in sly satisfaction, making it plain enough, in both words and gestures – lest he should have trouble comprehending the nature of the bargain she offered – that if he wanted warmer clothing for the child he would have to earn it.

Then and there.

His own personal reluctance aside, Lilia's situation was desperate, and not knowing when, or indeed if, the old woman would return, he knew he had no choice but to accept the distasteful arrangement.

Gods knew, he had done worse things than whoring himself. And if that was what it took, the use of his body in exchange for Namari's help, then that, damn it, was what he would do.

Even though the last thing he wanted was to betray the woman he loved, he had to believe that she would understand the choice before him when it was her own brother's child who was in his care, and when she must know him well enough to realise that he would do whatever was necessary to uphold the oath he had made to Joscelin.

His reluctant hand was at the lacing of his breeches and Namari already spread out on the bed-place, watching him with a lustful intensity that all but made him puke, when the door flap was lifted, and on a howl of icy wind the old woman hobbled into the tent, her sharp black eyes taking in the situation in the brief moment of silence that greeted her unexpected arrival.

Clearly Namari had been irritated by the interruption.

His only thought had been,

Thank you, gods, thank you.

It had taken the old woman no more than a few swift, hissing sentences to dismiss the younger one, though not before Namari had embarked on a torrent of sulky recrimination, and when this had no perceptible effect, the younger woman had stamped out of the tent in a temper – reminding him that women were much the same throughout the five realms!

Left alone with Lilia's Bone Lady, he had turned to find her gripping the smooth-worn antler head of her staff, and regarding him suspiciously.

Hastily he had told her what had brought him to her tent, and the bargain he offered. To haul and chop firewood, and hunt for fresh meat, in return for which he requested furs to clothe the child in his charge and keep her warm at night. Services the Bone Lady accepted with a toothless smile, sending him first to bring Lilia to her tent, then out into the snowy forest to fulfill his side of the bargain.

It had been warm work wielding the heavy wood axe, even with the frozen wind swirling through the snow-weighted pine boughs, and he had finally discarded his jerkin and rolled his shirt sleeves to the elbow. He did not, however, remove his shirt, preferring the discomfort of sweat-soaked linen clinging with icy clamminess to his skin rather than the possibility of baring his upper body to any watching eyes, not least Namari's avid gaze, furious with him as she must be following her humiliation.

Nor was she the only outright enemy he had made amongst the tribes' people, Talmarth son of Talmon being the most vociferously aggressive, though for what reason the harper had not yet fathomed.

Talmarth and Namari aside, the distrust that had greeted his arrival had gradually dissolved over the winter months into indifference, Finch the Harper proving himself to be no more than a harmless and – to them – not even particularly proficient singer of songs. A maker of music that was utterly foreign to their ears, accustomed as they were to their own thrumming drums and plaintive pipes, thin and high as the north wind that blew across their wide, open lands.

As the winter progressed, he took a grim, almost paternal, pride in his charge as Lilia continued to adjust to the primitive way of life, though it was vastly different from anything she had known before.

For his own part, he managed his daily tasks so as to keep her as far as was possible within his sight, whether playing with the other children or crouched at the Bone Lady's knee, as the old woman instructed her in the ways of the tribe, wearing always the soft white fur of the snow fox that had been his gift to her, and against which the little cat draped about the child's neck proved almost impossible to see.

So much so that he often found himself staring into those oddly translucent pale blue eyes, wondering whether it was only Lilia and himself to whom the small fey creature chose to make itself visible, and on those occasions when he had no choice but to leave Lilia unguarded whilst he was off hunting game, he found himself considering also just what power the mist-pale cat might wield if it chose.

In all likelihood, he concluded somewhat ruefully, the cat made a far more effective protector for the little princess than he himself did, unarmed as he was.

Unarmed, that is, until after much discussion with their chief, the elders finally allowed him the use of a bow for hunting purposes, and whilst his proficiency with the weapon would never be on a par with Edwy's, it improved swiftly enough when he had an old woman and a child depending on him to put meat in their bellies through the long chill of winter.

Then, almost without warning the iron grip of ice and blast of frost-white winds had melted into the tender caress of spring, tiny blush-pink fountains of flowers budding on formerly barren branches, followed swiftly by soft tufts of the sweetest green leaves he had ever seen as colour swept through the dark pine-clad slopes of the rising mountains and the hard winter blue of the sky warmed in the wake of the departing army of snow-grey clouds.

Vanquished, winter retreated.

Leaving ice dripping from rock and tree, snow melt trickling into rivers that ran swift and noisy down onto the plains, the roaring, tumbling waters closely followed by the warriors of the tribe who having caught the scent of renewed war on the wind, left the women and children with the youths and gaffers to live their wandering lives in peace as they had always done.

Except that spring – the spring of 1209, as the Mithlondians reckoned it – was different from all those countless others that had gone before, most especially for the people of the White Eagle tribe who, aware though they were of the war with the Eastern Empire, they had as yet no notion that those who still followed the horse herds through the heart of their land might find themselves in danger of losing both their freedom and their lives.

Thus, when the larch lit their green candles across the higher lands, the people of the White Eagle moved down from the hills of the north and drifted east across the grasslands towards the Painted Gorge as they had done every spring in tribal memory, the only difference being that this time they were accompanied by the Mithlondian harper and his princess.

And while the harper was uneasily aware that they were travelling into the disputed borderlands, even he had no notion that the peace of that sweet spring was about to turn quite so bloody.

That is until one morning, whilst out foraging for food on the birch-clad slopes that dropped into the twisting gorge of painted rocks, he heard the sound of horses coming from the valley floor beneath him, the soft thunder of hooves overlaid by the harsh ring of metal against stone, the jingle of bridle bits and something else that made him drop into cover.

For these were sounds he had not heard since he had come to the land of the seven tribes, their horses having no need to be shod or bridled with iron. Nor did their warriors wear mail shirts.

Glancing down from his rocky concealment he had felt the first worm of fear coiling through his belly, for the valley this troop of Eastern soldiers was riding along opened onto the plain close to where the tribe were camped.

The very place, gods damn it, where he had left Lilia happily stringing wooden beads and small, soft, spotted partridge feathers into a necklace under the Bone Lady's gummily-smiling supervision.

Common sense and experience stopped the release of the arrow that instinct had already had him nocking to the bowstring, drawn back to his ear without him even being aware of his actions.

Yes, he could strike one soldier down, perhaps two, before the rest of them raised the alert, sending out scouts, inevitably bringing danger down on the camp, the existence of which the Easterners were – if the gods were kind – as yet unaware of.

Taking a few precious moments to study the riders passing beneath him, he saw that not all of them were soldiers in fish-mail armour, faces hard and alert below pointed conical helms, armed with long spears and curved swords, strange-shaped shields slung from horned saddles.

Three of the men were different, wearing no mail, their saddles hung about with picks and shovels, sacks and odd instruments the harper had never seen before and could make no guess now as to their purpose, save they did not seem like the equipment of war.

Still frowning, he watched as one of the men called out to the soldier riding at the head of the party, and as the cavalcade drew rein, scrambled in ungainly fashion from his mount and with his long robe held out of the way, began to clamber amongst the loose boulders lying about the valley's floor until he could inspect the bands of coloured rock that made up the base of the almost sheer wall.

Definitely not a soldier, the harper thought, regarding the other man's inexplicable excitement as trembling hands produced a tiny pick from the folds of his striped robe and the Easterner began to chip delicately away at the rock... and then, suddenly, the harper had the answer – or at least an answer in part – to the question that had always nagged at him.

Why it was that the Eastern Empire should have chosen to invade a land that held no apparent worth save to the tribes who roamed its wide grassy plains, concerned only with their horses and their own insular way of life.

Such an answer, of course, did nothing to explain why the Golden Emperor of the East had decided to add tiny Mithlondia to his vast, sprawling domains, but that was a puzzle that must wait for another day, and a more devious mind than his.

He had enough to worry about.

Lilia, and every other member of the White Eagle tribe who were going about their peaceable affairs in the encampment at the western end of the rocky valley, were in danger did the scouting party ride much further.

He eyed the stone engineers dubiously, but even if their taste for bloodshed in the pursuit of their glittering goal was limited, the accompanying soldiers were scarcely likely to have the same sense of restraint. Either to relieve the sheer boredom of their obviously tedious escort duty, or a simple desire to annihilate any witnesses to their discovery, they *would* destroy anyone they found living within a day's ride of this place. And the unsuspecting tribes' people were camped little more than half a league away.

The soldiers had horses, the harper merely had the use of his legs.

Still, they were as yet engrossed in their discovery and he had time, he hoped, to get back to the encampment ahead of them.

He made it.

Just.

Leaving him little time to persuade the elders of the danger, much less convince those others who had spent the past three seasons mocking him as less than a man, that he knew a damned sight more than they did about the harsh realities of bloody warfare.

His own preparations made, he found himself recalling the grim castle high above the black rocks and leaping grey-white waves, the gorse-covered cliffs and the occasions when he and his two half-brothers had found themselves ranged together against the rest of the local lads in whatever scuffles and disagreements had broken out between them.

It was odd how even then Edwy had aligned himself with Jacques de Rogé's younger sons, neither Guy nor Ranulf knowing he shared their blood, whilst Joffroi had held himself aloof, scowling not so much at their brawling but at the close friendship they had shared.

A closeness that, in the wind-whispered silence as he waited for the attack even then thundering down on them, he missed as he had not done in years.

Missed with an almost physical ache of loss, the imperturbable steadiness of Edwy at his left shoulder. Missed too, with an even deeper pain, the presence at his right hand of the brother who had once been the other half of himself.

Then, with the enemy just beyond bow shot, he put aside all thought of his brothers, settled himself into position, took a deep breath, and having picked his target... waited a moment... quiet, alert, his gut a knot of tension, his hands as steady as his stance... then exhaled long and slow... and let fly his first arrow.

He loosed two more and then the Eastern soldiers were sweeping down upon on the camp, their long spears and vicious, curved swords giving no quarter to anyone, whether woman, child, beardless youth or white-haired elder.

It had been a nasty, bitty, brutal little battle.

It had left the encampment a ruin of black ash, burned skin, charred wood and smoking tents.

It had sullied the clean air of the plains with the stench of shit, and left pools of thick crimson blood on the hoof-trampled earth, the sweet new grass crushed below the crumpled bodies of old men, untried youths, and women who had proved just as fierce, if not fiercer, in defending their children from these faceless soldiers who sought to take what was not theirs in the name of a man they would probably never see.

In the end the tribes' people had held their own, though the harper could not understand how they had defeated the better armed, better trained violence of the invaders, except through weight of numbers and sheer bloody determination to defend their own.

The fighting done, the man who called himself Finch stood at the edge of what remained of the encampment, breathing heavily and listening to the cries of the gathering carrion birds as blood dripped from his ripped forearm, the sword he had wrenched from the slackened grip of an Eastern soldier now abandoned, whilst behind him women moved amongst the wounded, not yet daring to weep for the fallen or believe that they were safe.

Nor were they, the harper told them bluntly when the elders gathered again amidst the ruins of their camp.

Those soldiers who had survived the debacle would be riding as if all the daemons in Hell were at their heels, heading for the valley of the painted rocks, taking their defeat and their miners with them.

But they would return.

Swiftly, and in numbers the folk of the White Eagle tribe could not hope to stand against.

That being so, they needed to be leagues away by dawn.

A truth the elders had accepted without argument, even though it came from the mouth of the Mithlondian harper...

And now, here was Attan, the chief not only of the White Eagle people but of all the seven tribes of Atarkarna, seeking out that same Mithlondian harper in order to thank him.

Would Attan's gratitude be sufficient to allow his hostages to return to Mithlondia?

Gods, let it be so.

Verse 2

Tidings from Mithlondia

"Rafe?"

"Your highness?"

The level reply had come after the merest heartbeat of hesitation.

The child's response immediate and pettish,

"Don't call me that! I don't like it!"

The man kneeling, bare-chested beside the small mirror of clear water, again halted his hand as he went to draw the sharpened blade across his jaw, this time laying down the knife in order to reach behind him for his shirt.

Decently clad once more, he retrieved the blade and made to return to his task... and then sat back on his heels with a harsh exhalation.

"And I, your highness, would very much prefer that you not call me Rafe."

"Why not? It *is* your name."

"Whereas your name is Elanor Lysette de Mortaine, and you *are* a princess of Mithlondia whether you like it or not."

He made his point with a wary glance around to see who else might be up with the dawn's first frail light, besides himself, his princess and the small, grey cat draped about her neck, the fey creature presently regarding him with a disconcerting pale blue stare.

"No, I'm not," the child insisted with an unprincess-like pout. "I'm just Lily here."

"And I'm Finch the Harper," he said, reminding himself as much as her.

Ranulf... Rafe... Finch...

Even *he* forgot who he was sometimes!

"I may be a child but I am *not* stupid," Lilia informed him over the rough rasp of bristle as he ran a hand over his jaw to discern how much of the pale stubble he had missed.

"Merely indiscreet," he muttered.

She scowled at him, the straight line of her narrow black brows over those glittering grey eyes rendering her relationship to Joscelin de Veraux indisputable to anyone who knew the man as well as Ranulf himself did.

"I don't know what that means," she told him, putting her little chin in the air with an attempt at dignity.

Then negated it somewhat by bending down to pull off the feathery heads of the flowering grasses that brushed against her knees, and said crossly,

"I made sure there was no-one around to hear. If anyone is indis...whatever you said, it is *you*."

She poked a small, grubby, grass-stained finger towards him and he hastily put the knife beyond her reach, before realising she was aiming for his left arm.

Not where the ragged line of the healing scar still showed a raw sore red against the sun-browned skin and glinting gold hair of his forearm, but at the place higher up, where his loosely-rolled linen sleeve concealed the unmistakable mark of the Mithlondian guardians.

"You don't really want any of Chief Attan's people to see that, do you?"

"No," he admitted. "And yes, I was bl... da... stupidly careless just now, your highness."

"I know what you were going to say," she remarked gleefully. "I know how to say it in Atarkarnan too."

"I am sure you do, but you will kindly *not* do so."

"Because I am a princess?"

"Quite."

"Whereas you are just one of Uncle Joscelin's soldiers."

The clear grey eyes regarded him, head with its tangle of black curls on one side as she said,

"You *are* Rafe, aren't you? I know you are. I remember when Mama and me were living in the king's palace in Kaerellios, you used to carry me on your back and pretend you were a sea-dragon and I was a star-fish."

"Perhaps," he replied patiently. "But for as long as we remain in Atarkarna, I am Finch the Harper."

Then, his gaze sharpening under frowning brows.

"Lilia, how long have you known?"

"That you are not the real Finch, you mean? Oh, forever," she said blithely.

Then she wrinkled her nose and, with rather more honesty, admitted,

"Well, almost from the first day, but Pearl told me it was a secret, and that I was not to say anything to anyone."

He eyed the cat's bland, unblinking expression with some suspicion but merely grunted under his breath, before saying sardonically,

"So what happened this morning?"

"I forgot," the child whispered, raven dark lashes feathering down to hide her remorseful tears. "And I should not have done."

Even as the cat reached out to touch a sympathetic paw to the softly flushed cheek, Ranulf heard himself say rather more gently than before,

"As you said, Lilia, I was far more careless than you, with much less excuse. Besides, I have a feeling the truth will come out soon enough now, especially if I have to take part in these cursed trials of skill and strength Chief Attan speaks of."

"And will you? Take part, I mean."

"Not if I can help it. I am too old for such antics. Though I admit," he grinned suddenly. "I would like to test Flame's speed against that of Chief Attan's horse."

"Is Flame yours then?" Lilia asked. "Surely when I saw you last with Uncle Joscelin you were riding a different horse. A brown one."

She thought for a moment, then her eyes lit up again, sparkling like the sunlit waters of Taneth-Rath Tarn.

"Rye! That was his name. Sister Aldith told me. So Flame... does he belong to the real Finch?"

Ranulf nodded, uneasily wondering what else she might have learned from Sister Aldith or the other healers.

Children, he had discovered, had a nasty habit of overhearing that which one least wished them to.

Take that afternoon at Vézière, the last time he had seen his son, the day Val had spat upon him, rejected him...

"So who is he?"

Lilia's curious voice broke through his unpleasant memories.

"Who? Val?" he murmured, his thoughts still far away.

Wondering what if anything he could have done differently, that his son might not now hate him quite so rigorously.

"Val?" Lilia sounded puzzled. "The fair-haired boy from the Healing House, d'you mean? Lissie's foster-brother? No, not him. I know who *he* is."

She cocked her head again and then spoke with devastating simplicity,

"He's your son."

Ranulf winced and shut his eyes.

"Not any more, Lilia. By his own choice, I would add."

He swallowed.

"But if not Val, who were you talking about?"

"Master Finch, of course. The real one. I've seen him too, you know. He used to come down to the Healing House in Vézière to play for Mama and me. He plays much better than you do," she continued critically.

"Though I like that song you sing about the mermaid," she added hastily, clearly not wanting to hurt his feelings.

She need not have worried, Ranulf thought, touched despite himself.

He had no feelings left *to* hurt. Val had trampled his paternal pride into the dust, and he did not dare think of Rowène or dwell on his memories of their last meeting lest he drive himself mad with worry and wanting.

"Master Finch *does* look a lot like you," Lilia was saying. "If I did not know you were you, I would think you were him. Or he was you."

Seeing this was not a conversation he was going to regain control of, Ranulf shrugged and yielded.

"He is my brother, if you must know, and as you said, a much better harper than I am ever like to be."

Guy was also undoubtedly the better man, though in the end Rowène had chosen *him*, Ranulf Jacques de Rogé, despite the filthy reputation of his name and the black temper that could still, on occasion, reduce him to the ravening wolf he had once been.

"So if you are here, being him, where is he?" Lilia asked, her curiosity clearly still unsatisfied. "Is he somewhere being you? With Uncle Joscelin perhaps?"

"As you say, your highness. He is where I would have been, had not your... had not my Commander and Chief Attan between them decided otherwise."

"And once we go home," his little princess said thoughtfully. "He will be Finch and you will be Rafe again?"

"Gods willing, Lilia."

He reached for his abandoned knife.

"And now, I beg you, let me finish what I was doing or else the day will be upon us and neither of us ready. Your hair needs combing, and perhaps to show honour to their goddess, you should wear the white deerskin dress the Bone Lady made for you?"

"And the amber necklace Chief Attan gave me?" she asked, and when he nodded, continued sunnily,

"And then you can braid my hair for me. I still have the ribbons Mama gave me when I..."

Her lip quivered and he saw that her grey eyes were glittering now with tears not sunlight.

She was silent for a long moment, her fingers stroking Pearl's soft fur, and he wondered whether anything he could say would be of the slightest comfort to her.

Probably not, he reflected grimly, considering how poor a parent he had proved to be as far as his only surviving child was concerned. Swords, not words, were all he was proficient in the use of.

"Your highness..."

"I don't want to be a princess," she muttered in sudden tearful defiance. "And I don't want to go home!"

"Lilia..."

"And I don't *ever* want to see my father again. I hate him! And he hates me. And Mama. *And* the baby. So maybe Mama should come here and live with us. She could bring Lady Adèle to look after the baby, and Lord Gabriel to look after her. And I would want Uncle Joscelin to come as well, because he likes Mama and she likes him. And then we could all be happy together."

Not knowing what to say to any of that, he kept his mouth firmly shut.

She peeped at him through wet lashes.

"And perhaps Sister Fayla could come too, and then *you* would be happy and not have so many nightmares."

Bloody hell and damnation!

So she *had* heard the gossip that must have been whispered within the walls of the Healing House. Not to mention whatever he might have shouted out in his sleep!

"Sister Fayla is a healer, that is her calling in life," he said with forced calm. "She cannot leave the Healing House, even if she wished to be with me. And I, whether harper or soldier, am definitely not welcome there. You must just accept, as I have had to do, that her path and mine will not cross again."

The child looked sideways at the cat for a moment, perhaps indulging in some silent conversation of her own, the animal purring so loudly even Ranulf could hear it. Then at last she announced solemnly,

"That's not what Pearl says."

"Is it not? But then, Pearl, for all she is very special, *is* only a cat."

Restraining himself from any pithier comment, Ranulf determinedly reapplied the blade to his jaw and thankfully Lilia found nothing else to say about anything.

At least until he had finished shaving and they were walking back towards the encampment.

She had been running ahead of him, chasing Pearl through the waving strands of knee-high grass, when she paused and looked back a trifle guiltily.

"Oh, I almost forgot, Chief Attan's back and says he wants to talk to you."

In the face of the warning grunt from one of the warriors standing outside the chief's newly erected tent, Ranulf came to an abrupt halt and, pushing aside his impatience and nebulous misgivings, put as bland an expression on his face as he could muster as he stated his errand.

Given leave to enter, he ducked inside, bowing his head in a gesture of genuine respect and speaking the other man's tongue out of courtesy, said steadily,

"Chief Attan. You sent for me? Forgive my tardiness, Lilia had trouble finding me."

The chief of the seven tribes merely waved a leather flask at him.

"No matter. Mare's milk?"

"Not this early in the morning," Ranulf declined with a faint grin.

The name, he reflected, was deceptive, for not only was the 'milk' capable of searing all sense of feeling from the lips, tongue and throat of anyone unaccustomed to drinking it, it also tasted like rank goat piss. Well, at least in his – blunt, if unstated – opinion.

"I would rather not have a headache before the celebrations have even started," he concluded wryly.

"You are competing?" Attan asked, pouring himself a beaker, then filling another from a different container.

"Merely water," he murmured in some amusement in answer to Ranulf's wary look, before asking again,

"So, Harper, do you take part?"

"I had not thought to do so."

"Not even to uphold the honour of your own people amongst mine?" Attan queried. "Of course, I do not suggest you engage in any of the wrestling matches."

For a moment his dark eyes flicked to Ranulf's left sleeve. Then with a grin.

"Everyone in the camp knows of your unwillingness to be seen without your garments. Most consider you unnaturally modest, but then you are Mithlondian, and a harper. Some of the elders, however, or at least since the spring, have begun to wonder whether you might not be hiding something..."

He gestured at the healing slash on Ranulf's arm.

"More scars like that perchance?"

Ranulf felt his gut tighten but said only,

"Certainly my shoulders bear the scars of more than one flogging."

Attan's black eyes widened a little. Whatever he had expected, it had not been this response to his mild mockery.

"Ah! You have a talent for seeking out trouble, I think?"

"Something like that," Ranulf agreed with a shrug of those same whip-scarred shoulders, the fleeting thought of Joscelin and Gabriel, his closest friends regardless of the floggings they had both ordered, serving to steady him for whatever Attan might throw out next in this small battle of words.

He would rather have a sword, but as with the fight in the spring, he would take what he could get. Nor did he truly think that Attan was his enemy, though there were others who were, most notably...

"Talmarth, of course," Attan interrupted his thoughts. "Would have it that you must be malformed in your manly parts since you have guarded them so closely since your arrival."

Ranulf merely grimaced and said somewhat sourly,

"I assure you there is as little wrong with my... manly parts as those of any man of the tribe, including Talmarth son of Talmon."

"I did not think there was."

Attan grinned over the rim of the beaker as he raised it towards his mouth.

"But then I am not Talmarth. Nor am I a woman who would count it a coup to bear a child with hair touched to summer gold by Daerthanis or eyes the colour of the evening sky."

Ranulf flushed uncomfortably and in an attempt to turn the conversation away from himself and a little more in the direction he wished it to take, said abruptly,

"But tell me, how is the Lady Atarellen faring? Did you hear any tidings of her when you were in the south?"

"Better than that," Attan said, some at least of the harsh lines of his face softening. "I saw her, Harper, and she was well."

He sounded relieved, if perplexed.

"For all she has spent the white months trapped within the high stone walls of your prince's palace, she seemed content. She has found companionship with your princess, and your prince worships her."

Ranulf blinked at that, never having supposed Linnius had it in him to lavish any strong emotion on anyone.

That Linette had stood Atarellen's friend he found less incomprehensible, for the gentle woman he had come to know during his years in the royal bodyguard would never have held the loss of her daughter against the stranger who had as little choice as Lilia in the bargain made by ruthless men with their lives.

"And the babe?" Ranulf asked politely, continuing to steer the conversation.

"Will be born soon," Attan replied. "Atarellen says it will be a boy, a prince to unite our peoples. If he is born under the sun of Daerthanis, my people will take that as a sign that all is well, and then... Then, Harper, it is my hope that I may be able to persuade the chieftains and elders of the seven tribes that you and the Lily-child may return to your own land."

"What?"

Ranulf snapped his slightly wandering attention back to the Atarkarnan chief.

"What did you say?"

"I said, with the treaty secured by the birth of Atarellen's child, if it *is* a son, you and Lily may soon be able to go back to Mithlondia."

Gods!

He caught his breath but his fast-running thoughts were beyond his control.

Was it possible that it could be this simple? This soon?

It was true he had planned to ask Attan to release them but it had been at best a flawed hope, the daemons who haunted his dreams having convinced him that Lilia would grow to womanhood among the tribes, while his sword-hand lost its strength and skill, and his prick withered into impotency, both he and Lilia forgetting and forgotten even by their kin.

Now, however, if Attan's words proved true, Ranulf would be able to restore Lilia to her mother, and he himself take up his old place alongside Joscelin and Gabriel.

Once more he would wield a sword instead of a harp. Perhaps even secure the opportunity to make peace with his son. And more than that...

He stared down at the year-old scar across the palm of his left hand... the symbol of something he had refused to allow himself to think about until now... when it seemed at last that perhaps he and Rowène might have the chance to be together.

If, that is, she did not mind the stigma of being thought no more than his leman when in truth the oath they had sworn to each other, the blood they had mingled, made her the other half of his soul.

It was, all of a sudden, a bloody heady hope.

One to celebrate in mare's milk and the wildness of an Atarkarnan horse race.

Yet even as he reached for the flask, the coldly, pragmatic part of his mind came to the fore, forcing him to rein in his galloping thoughts, to ride cautiously forward when hope bade him start packing immediately upon his return to his tent.

Everything, he reminded himself firmly, depended on Atarellen producing a living son.

That truth taking precedence over the possibility of returning both to the fighting and to Rowène – the former setting sparks of anticipation in his blood, the latter igniting a slow burn of longing in his groin – he forced himself to say calmly,

"I take it Lady Atarellen means to remove to the House of the Grey Sisters in Vézière, if she had not done so already?"

"She has not," Attan replied. "Nor does she mean to."

"What..."

Ranulf could feel cold fingers beginning to claw at his breastbone, and he strove to keep his voice level.

"What do you mean?"

Attan gave him a sharpening look.

"Do not think I have forgotten what you said when I first asked you what would happen should Atarellen became with child. I did speak of this Grey House to her, but your prince would not hear of it. He wishes my daughter to remain by his side, to have the best care his court can provide. Is that so wrong, Harper, that he cannot bear to be parted from her?"

"Better to be parted from her until after the child is born," Ranulf said grimly, the fire in his blood and loins abruptly doused, replaced by the sick feeling of helplessness starting to crawl through his gut.

"Rather than lose both her and the child to the incompetence of those same bumbling court physicians who fourteen years ago failed to discern what truly ailed Linnius' father, Prince Marcus, and in so doing condemned an innocent man to a traitor's death for his murder."

He could see that the Atarkarnan chief had not understood every word of his bitter speech but before he could try again, Attan blinked, and picking up on the one part of Ranulf's protest he appeared to comprehend, said,

"No, no, your prince has more sense than to give my precious daughter into the hands of some fumbling old man. He has entrusted her to the care of a noble lady, one as skilled in childbirth as she is beautiful. You will surely know of her. Her name, I think is... Arienne?"

"Daemons below!"

Ranulf swore and swallowed bile, striving to hold off the darkness gathering like a winter's storm just at the edge of his sight.

"Tell me, Chief Attan, tell me that Linnius has not been fool enough to give your daughter into the hands of that bloody-handed witch-whore."

The Atarkarnan chief frowned at him.

"I do not know all these words, but your voice tells me you do not like this lady."

"No," Ranulf ground his teeth. "I do not."

"Yet she is your Chief Counsellor's woman. Surely she can be trusted."

Slowly and clearly, Ranulf told him the truth.

"She can be trusted to serve her own ends. And to kill whoever stands in her way. Whether it be the high-born nobleman with whom she first swore the binding oath. Or the man whose binding band she now wears. If it suits her plans to betray him, she will. And if it serves her to see your daughter and the new-born heir to the Mithlondian throne dead... Then it will be so! And in such a way as no stain of guilt will soil her own soft, white hands."

Attan looked shaken, though still not entirely convinced that Ranulf was not simply making up the whole sordid, unbelievable tale.

"How do you know this, Harper? No-one within the stone walls of your prince's palace has spoken to me of such things."

No-one? What in hell's damned dark depths has been happening in Mithlondia in my absence?

"What about Joscelin de Veraux?" he demanded. "Or the man who was his Second? You must have spoken of this to them?"

"The High Commander of your guardians? No, when we speak, it is of battles or the Lily-child. He, and this other you speak of – this is the one who paints his face like a woman when he is at your court? Who walks like a mountain cat when he is not, and has eyes like sunlight on amber..."

"Yes, him!" Ranulf snorted rudely. "Bloody Gabriel de Marillec."

He watched as Attan fingered the glowing beads strung along the black braids of his beard.

"I think that neither of these men know that Atarellen is with child," he said eventually. "Nor, as I said, would I speak of it with them, only how best to hold the Eastern Empire's army at bay."

"In that case," Ranulf said crisply. "You will just have to take my word for it, that while the Lady Ariène de Rogé is as beautiful a woman as you are ever likely to see in all the five realms, she possesses neither heart nor soul, and is twice as venomous as a red-fanged Atarkarnan viper."

The older man considered him closely.

"Deadly indeed. Yet even if what you say is true, she would not, surely, hurt a child? She, who is a mother herself."

"Yes, she is a mother," Ranulf agreed bleakly. "If you can so call a woman who has spent the past fourteen years trying to destroy the children of her first binding, all for the sake of the son born of her second mating.

"A woman," he continued in grinding tones. "Who strangled or smothered at birth – I know not which, the result was the same – the child her lord's younger brother got on a common serving wench. Believe me, Chief Attan, an insignificant *bâtard...*"

Here he lapsed into Mithlondian, there being no direct translation into Atarkarnan, for to the people of the seven tribes a child was simply a child. One who would grow up to serve Daerthanis, follow the horse herds, and renew the people.

"*Bâtard*. I do not know this word," Attan said curiously. "But odd as it seems to me, I can hear from your voice that it has some unpleasant meaning among your people."

"It means worthless, fatherless, of no account. Such a one could never have been a threat to Ariène's ambitions for her own son. Yet she had that nameless babe killed anyway. The child's mother too."

His voice turned dark and dour at the memory.

"And I was left to bury them both."

The black eyes blinked again in understanding.

"Ah! Did you love them?"

"No. But I would have justice for them. Nor would I see your own daughter suffer a like fate. So, I beg you, Chief Attan, go back to Lamortaine, find the Lady Atarellen and take her to the Grey Sisters at Vézière before it is too late. If anyone can keep your daughter and her unborn child safe from Lady Ariène's evil, it is the Eldest there."

Then, as Attan remained silent, perhaps still doubting, his dark eyes a swirl of shadow and troubled thought, Ranulf pushed his left sleeve up to his shoulder, and laid the sword-calloused fingers of his right hand across the black mark pricked into his skin, although not before he had given the Atarkarnan chief more than enough moments to observe the winged horse of Mithlondia as it rippled across the muscles of his upper arm.

"You know this mark, I believe?"

Attan nodded, no trace of surprise on his face at seeing what Ranulf had so carefully kept hidden until now.

"It is the mark borne by the warriors of your people. Men whose words and deeds I have come over the years to... respect."

"Then listen well, Chief Attan. I see in your eyes that you do not believe me when I speak of the danger to your daughter. But I swear on this mark, the guardians' mark, that what I have told you is the truth. Every word of it. And if I am a liar in the sight of your gods and mine, may this mark be burned from my flesh and my name cast into dishonour forever."

"I believe you, Rafe of the Guardians," Attan said gruffly.

For the first and perhaps the only time admitting what both men had known since before Ranulf had ridden north, a harp at his back instead of a sword at his side.

"Forgive me."

Chief Attan spoke into the lengthening silence that had followed Ranulf's revelation, his words formal, his tone reflective.

"It is not doubt of your words that has trapped my tongue into silence."

"What then?"

"These Grey Sisters... do you remember talking to me of the one you call Fayla?"

"I remember," Ranulf said tightly.

Gods help him, he had not been able to stop himself speaking, however obliquely, of Rowène, and if his loose tongue had now caused danger or misfortune to come to her...

"It seemed to me that you would wish to hear tidings of her," Attan was saying. "So as I was riding past this Vézière, this *town* – is that the word? – where the houses climb about the hill, I halted there, at the place of healing, to ask after her for you."

"You did?"

Ranulf swallowed at this unlooked for kindness from the man who was technically his captor.

"And?"

Attan hesitated, and Ranulf had the oddest sense that the darkness, which had begun to recede beyond the deerskin walls and roof of the tent, was seeping back inside. Wisps of black mist, gathering, deepening, surrounding him, suffocating him...

"She was gone," Attan said, his voice and person already lost in the swirling black shadows.

"Gods, no..."

Ranulf could barely draw breath, his chest heaving with the effort, his voice no more than a low, strained rasp. He felt as if he were back in The Pit again, abandoned to the icy darkness below Valéntien castle, unable to see, unable to move, unable to reach out through his dreams to the woman he had loved even then.

"When I went to the Grey House," the distant voice was saying. "I spoke with an old woman who told me she was their chief... their Eldest. I did not like her. A woman with the body of a stick, sour of face and breath."

"Sister Winfreda," Ranulf muttered. "But what of Sister..."

He struggled to remember by what name Joscelin's mother had been known, and gave up in favour of merely staying on his feet. Besides, the name would mean nothing to Attan anyway.

"What... what of Sister Fayla?" he managed to say.

Damn it all, what had happened to her in his absence?

The only woman he had ever truly loved.

The woman, his conscience reminded him sharply, that he should bloody well have had the strength of will *not* to fucking sleep with!

And if she had been cast out of that place because he had carelessly left her pregnant with his child...

Gods, please gods, no!

The thought that this past year she might have been in desperate need of him, his protection, and he not there for her...

Very, very dimly he became aware that he was on his knees, drenched in icy sweat, bile filling his mouth...

Before he could be sick however, he felt Attan's rough hands on his shoulders, shaking him, repeating words that only slowly began to make sense.

"What weakness saps your blood, man? Your woman left the Grey House of her own will. So said the Sour Stick. Another of the healers went with her. The Sister who was head healer before her."

Thank the gods, Ranulf thought fervently, still on his knees.

At least wherever Rowène had gone, Joscelin's mother had gone with her.

Not that it absolved him of all guilt, or soothed his worst fears, but...

"Where did they go?" he heard himself asking.

"The Sour Stick did not say, but the Smiling Sister who cares for the animals..."

"Sister Aldith," Ranulf supplied without thinking.

He still could not think calmly. Could only strive to hold his blackest fears at bay.

"Yes, that was the name, I think. All your Mithlondian names are strange on my tongue. She told me that both Sister Herluva and

Sister Fayla had left the Grey House to seek out the battle-lines, in order to care for the wounded of both your people and mine."

"Truly?"

Ranulf staggered to his feet and snatching up Attan's abandoned beaker, tossed the contents down his throat, coughing violently as the raw, potent brew burned its way down to his belly, clearing the black mist from his head and steadying his reeling wits.

"Truly," the Atarkarnan chief assured him. "Now, tie your sleeve so that the mark on your arm is concealed again, collect the Lily-child and your harp from your tent, and come and watch the first contests with me. I must chose a champion to represent the White Eagle people when all the tribes gather to celebrate the rise of Daerthanis. Or at least," he finished grimly. "Those amongst us who are not fighting in her name alongside your own people."

"And the Lady Atarellen?" Ranulf reminded the other man harshly. "Will you just leave her to her fate while you celebrate?"

For while Ranulf could allow himself to believe that Rowène was in all likelihood safe somewhere – or as safe as the healers' tent of an army camp can be – he had no such faith that Attan's daughter was similarly situated. And as it seemed that his own and Lilia's release depended firstly on Atarellen giving birth to a son, and then on them both surviving the dangers of childbirth, he had a vested interest in the outcome.

Attan gave him a black look, but merely said,

"I must take today and the next to be with my people. It is expected of me and will be seen of a sign of dishonour to our goddess if I do not. Also I must rest. I am not, Daerthanis knows, as young as you."

Ranulf snorted. He was hardly young himself.

Then older man's face hardened with determination.

"But with the dawn three days hence I will ride back to your land, and bring my daughter to a place where she will be safe from this witch you speak of."

"The Healing House..." Ranulf started to say, then remembered Sister Winfreda, and stopped.

"And there you have it," Attan said. "With your woman gone... no, do not deny it, I have seen the truth in your eyes. This woman you *do* love! But with Sister Fayla no longer at the Grey House, tell me, who am I to entrust my daughter to?"

Ranulf shook his head, trying to think. With Joscelin's mother and Rowène both gone from Vézière...

"Go to Lamortaine," he said abruptly. "And speak with Princess Linette. She will help you."

"Even though it is her son my daughter's babe will supplant?"

"Linette will not care for that," Ranulf assured him. "Indeed I think she will be very well pleased when her... son, did you say... is no longer in line to inherit the Mithlondian throne."

"Yes, Marcus, they tell me he is called, after his grandsire. And you will tell the Lily-child she has a brother?" Attan paused and then added blandly, "I have not seen the babe myself so I cannot tell you if he has the same beautiful eyes as his sister."

Ranulf gave the Atarkarnan chief a brief, sharp glance but refrained from expressing his heartfelt hope that the boy had inherited *none* of his father's distinctive features. Instead he simply nodded and said,

"Yes, I will tell her."

"But not, I think, that she may soon be back with her mother and the new brother?"

"No. I will say nothing until all is certain and settled. I see no good purpose in giving her a hope that may fail, leaving her unhappier than she was before."

Not that Lilia appeared in the least bit unhappy at this particular moment, Ranulf reflected some time later in the day.

Although the great gathering to celebrate the golden ascendancy of Daerthanis, Goddess of Summer, over the lands of the seven tribes of Atarkarna, had not yet started in earnest Lilia had taken his advice and was currently gracing these preliminary games and contests attired in her best raiment, and clearly on her best behaviour.

She was sitting on the grass beside the turf seat from which Chief Attan was watching the proceedings, Ranulf lounging at her side, his harp – or rather his brother's harp – still in its bag nearby.

He only hoped that in turn Guy was taking as good care of his sword. His bleak gaze lifting briefly to the distant horizon, he felt a fleeting flicker of his old resentment as he wondered whether the leather-wrapped hilt of his sword felt in any way familiar to his brother's hand, and whether it answered Guy's will any better than his brother's harp did for him.

Always supposing, he reminded himself grimly, that he and Josce between them had not already sent Guy to his death.

An excited clapping of hands and a breathless question from the child at his side reminded him why Joscelin had asked – why both he and Guy had agreed – to enact such a reckless and barely sustainable exchange of names and roles.

It also made him remember, as he looked down on the wrestling matches, horse racing and the other tests of an Atarkarnan warrior's skill taking place, the midsummer celebrations at Rogérinac after his mother had died but while his father was yet alive.

How he and Guy and Edwy had matched themselves against the rest of the competitors from castle and village under their father's keen gaze.

How in the evening the three of them would celebrate their victories in wrestling, archery or horsemanship with stolen, heady, peat-dark beer, all the while ignoring their elder brother's black scowls.

How, looking back, the remembered glint in Guthlaf's surprisingly tolerant gaze told Ranulf that the garrison commander had known perfectly well of the shared blood that bound him and Guy and Edwy, there being little about Lord Jacques' life that escaped his most loyal retainer's eye.

Ranulf also realised something else as he watched the half-naked youths pitting themselves against each other, sweat gleaming on pale northern skin under a sun whose power here was attributed to the Goddess Daerthanis rather than the Mithlondian God of Light, and listened to the encouragement and applause of fierce, laughing women and hot-blooded men, shouting foreign words in a foreign tongue.

In spite of the many outward differences between the people of Mithlondia and Atarkarna, there was much that was the same.

Whether such similarities would be enough to bind them together should their fragile alliance be placed under any further strain – such as the discovery that Ranulf was not the harmless harper he purported to be or, worse still, that some ill should overtake Atarellen and her unborn child – was another matter, for another day.

For now... he touched one calloused fingertip gently to the ring of fiery bronze about his signet finger... for now, he would simply keep his own secret hope warm in his breast.

Verse 3

As the Flame Runs Swift

"She is dead, may you burn in the dark fire! Your daughter is *dead*!"

The raw, ravaged, grief-enraged voice ripped through the fragrant darkness of the starlit summer night and made the man standing just within the blacker shadow cast by the goat-hide tent freeze where he stood, straining to hear the shattering words over the trickling patter of water.

What a bloody damned inconvenient time to take a piss.

"And it is all your fault!"

The angry voice rose to a shout and cracked into shards of pain.

"If you had just let me take her to my own tent as I wanted – as *she* wanted – she would be alive now. Laughing into the wind, riding free across the grassy plains of our people, crooning cradle songs to our children. Instead she lies cold as stone, *buried* in stone, her soul trapped forever in cold, unforgiving *stone*."

"And the child?" That was Attan, his voice hoarse, his throat sounding too tight for the words.

As, suddenly, was Ranulf's.

Swearing to – or rather at – himself in vitriolic silence, he hurriedly flicked the last droplets from his prick, tucked it away and righted his clothing, trying all the while to ignore the sensation of an ice-slick rope closing about his neck.

He had been half-roused from sleep by a soft paw batting across his cheek, but had ignored the silent demand for attention until, without warning, the cat had tired of the gentle approach and unsheathed its claws into his shoulder.

Whereupon he had bitten off an oath, belatedly looking to see whether his curtailed curse had woken the child curled in her nest of blankets on the other side of the tent, thus adding another word or three to her ever-growing vocabulary of undesirable phrases.

Thankfully Lilia was still asleep and rolling first to his knees, then to his feet, Ranulf had found the cat waiting at the open door flap, its pale blue eyes shining uncannily in the moonlight.

Unsure what the animal was trying to get him to do, but aware suddenly of a need of his own, he stepped carefully around the creature and made his way quietly around the back of the tent, his bare feet silent on the grass, his wits sliding back into drink-sodden sleep, even as he began to water the grass – the inevitable consequence of his joining Attan in the celebrations following the choosing of a champion for the White Eagle tribe.

Only belatedly realising that the cat was still with him, still watching him...

And all at once the warrior's whispered warning that he would normally have heeded long before now – an evening of drinking mare's milk being a piss-poor excuse – brought him to full wakefulness, but by then it was too late to stop what he had already started.

Cursing himself for a feckless fool in disregarding the cat's unusual behaviour, he was already straining eyes and ears for whatever danger the cat had sensed when the angry voice had sliced through the shadows from less than a dozen yards away.

"Dead!"

The voice he knew he should recognise was still snarling, apparently in answer to an inaudible question Attan had asked,

"No, the child is dead too. Not that I care anything for that, the weakling seed of a weakling man. But Atarellen, the Star of Silver Water, *she* was my life. And now those who failed her, those who yet live, they must be made to suffer in her stead."

"Surely, you are not suggesting..." The older man's voice was thick with tears and a terrible, black hopelessness.

"Yes!"

The savage hiss hung on the night air.

"Send the girl-child you took in exchange for Atarellen to join your daughter in her long sleep."

"Atarellen would not want that."

Though shaking, Attan's voice appeared to have regained a modicum of purpose.

"But *I* do," came the bitter voice. "And I have the strength of our people behind me to enforce it. If you want to keep your place as chief of this tribe, let alone chief of all the seven tribes, you will rip Mithlondia's royal flower from the branch. And feed the gelden, that cokenay, that half-man harper who came with her to the dark fires!"

"No! I cannot, and will not, destroy the Lily-child. As for the man you so blindly miscall, if it were not for him you would not have a people to be chieftain of. For that is your aim in all this, is it not, Talmarth son of Talmon?"

Hell and bloody damnation, that's who the bastard is. Bloody Talmarth, of course.

"And what if it is, old man?"

Talmarth was now openly taunting the man whose position he sought to take, his grief – if he had ever truly felt it – a thing of the past, no more than a means to an end.

"It was you, not I, who made alliance with our enemies beyond the Long River. You who called for our warriors to spill our blood for them, to die for them, to lie cold in earth that is not warmed by Daerthanis' light."

"Yes, I did," Attan agreed.

He sounded steadier now, Ranulf thought.

"And there are many who answered my call freely, seeing the need. As you, Talmarth, did not! And I will continue to lead those who are yet prepared to follow me. To save our freedom, our own land, for our own people. From a far greater enemy than Mithlondia has ever been."

He paused, drew in a hard breath.

"You still do not see it, do you, Talmarth? Indeed, it took me much thinking, and in the end it was the Mithlondian harper who made *me* see exactly what it is that the man they call the Golden Emperor of the East wants from our land. Gold, Talmarth! That yellow stuff that, while it is of little value to us, is everything to this man who calls himself Emperor. And I fear he will kill or enslave every man, woman and child of our people to get it."

Attan's voice took on a steely edge.

"Whether you like it or not, Talmarth, we *need* the warriors of Mithlondia as our allies, and I tell you, killing the harper and the child will only set those same warriors at our throats again, and this time their hunger for our destruction will be savage as that of starving wolves in the long cold white of winter."

"Winter? What is this word? You even begin to speak like them!" Talmarth scoffed. "But they will have no time to turn on us. For without our support they will go down under the blades of the Emperor's warriors who are as uncounted as stars in the night sky."

"I warn you, Talmarth," Attan's voice was shaking again. "I know these Mithlondians and the blood oaths that bind them better than you. If you cause harm to come to the child or the harper, there are two in particular of those who wear the winged horse mark pricked into their skin who will not rest until they have twisted a sword through your entrails and watched you bleed to death in the reek of your own cowardly filth."

The vibration of this defiant warning was still thrumming in the still summer air when Ranulf heard a sound he recognised immediately, followed by a grunt that held as much shock as pain, then a thud as of a falling body, and finally the taut voice of Talmarth son of Talmon.

"Not if I put my blade in their bowels first."

Then jeeringly,

"They too will know the taste of defeat and dishonour. As you do now, old man. Think of it as you choke in your *own* reek."

The next moment Ranulf heard Talmarth leave the tent, with no attempt at secrecy, and certainly no challenge from the men who should have been standing guard at the tent's entrance.

He hesitated a moment, torn between his duty to Lilia and his need to find out how desperately Attan had been wounded.

Scooping up the little cat, and refraining from thinking too much about what he was doing, Ranulf looked into the palely gleaming eyes and said firmly,

"Go and wake the child. I will not be long."

Ducking back into his own tent with Attan's dying whisper reinforcing his gut decision, Ranulf found the little princess sitting up in her nest of blankets, the cat cradled in her arms, her face a blur of white in the sparse moonlight.

"What is it, Rafe? What has happened? Pearl told me I must be ready. Ready for what?"

"Listen, Lilia," he said in a quick, low voice. "We do not have much time. Get dressed, pack up only what you need and that I can carry easily."

She looked at him in startled surprise, and then whispered,

"Are we going home?"

He nodded, the icy noose still tight about his throat, his nostrils yet filled with the stench in Attan's tent.

"I know you said you did not want to go home. But it will be all right. I promise."

He had worried a little that the child might delay matters with further questions but she turned away at once, pulling on the plainer of her knee-length tunics and her deerskin boots, grabbing her cloak, then sitting down to sort through their meagre possessions.

With the cool calm she could only have inherited from her father, she grabbed a full water-skin, and wrapped the rounds of flat bread remaining from their supper, together with some cold meat and hard cheese in her sleeping shift, and placed the bundle in the bag Ranulf had laid on the ground between them.

Moving swiftly, he found his own boots and added two tightly rolled blankets to the pack, then slung his brother's harp over his shoulder, together with his mantle, securing it with the silver thorn and falcon pin, finally dropping his hand to check that the amber-hilted dagger he had taken from Attan, after delivering the mercy stroke the dying chieftain had begged of him, was still thrust through the belt at his side, and said quietly,

"Are you ready, Lilia?"

She nodded, eyes wide with excitement and apprehension.

"Then let us go. And pray that the Moon Goddess of the Faennari guides our steps."

And confounds all those who will be hunting us!

Though this thought he did not share with the child.

His last action before leaving the goat-hide tent that had been their home for the past four seasons was to snatch up the small hunting bow and quiver of arrows. How much use it was likely to be was questionable, but he would take all the advantage he could get this far north in Atarkarna, with several hundred leagues of open grassland to traverse.

Territory that would once more be hostile to a Mithlondian soldier and the royal princess in his care.

Slipping silently into the night, Ranulf found that part at least of his hurried prayer to the goddess had been answered.

The clear moonlight had been replaced by a drifting mist that must have crept up from the nearby lake, and now glimmered and shimmered with a fey pearlescent light that allowed the fugitives to see where they were going yet not, he hoped, be seen themselves as they made their way through the sleeping encampment, and over the grassy knoll where just that very morning Lilia had sat at Attan's feet, cheering the young men of the tribe.

A low whistle brought Guy's chestnut stallion stepping out of the mist, and having taken the trouble to seek out and saddle the animal before returning to the tent, all that remained to be done was for Ranulf to secure the blankets and pack, and then lift Lilia up to sit on the big horse. Looking down at him, she whispered,

"But how will Pearl manage without her basket?"

As if in answer the little cat crouched and leapt... landing on Ranulf's shoulder, claws curling first into the wool of his mantle, then penetrating the linen of his shirt, to finally embed themselves in the skin of his shoulder.

Wincing slightly he said,

"I think we must just trust that Pearl will be able to cling to her perch without mishap."

The state of his shoulder was another matter, and one that he did not intend to draw the child's attention to.

"After all," he added wryly as the child continued to regard him dubiously. "She *is* a very special cat, we both know that."

Lilia nodded, looking marginally less worried and wriggled into a more comfortable position, clutching the horn of the saddle in one hand and a hank of the stallion's flowing mane in the other.

Moving carefully – doubtful himself despite his reassuring words to the child concerning the cat's ability to balance and cling on at the pace they must travel at – Ranulf took hold of the reins, put his boot in the stirrup and swung up into the saddle behind Lilia, Attan's last words echoing in his head,

"Take the Lily-child and go! As the flame runs swift with summer fire through the grasslands, so must you. Now set me free... and may Daerthanis ride with you and bring you both safe to your own."

Travelling only by moonlight, resting during that time when the summer sun ruled the Atarkarnan sky, it took them five nerve-racking nights to cross the flat, grassy leagues between the encampment and the sinuous, shining strip of treacherous water that marked the boundary between Atarkarna and Mithlondia, and although there had been no sign of pursuit during that time Ranulf slackened neither the pace nor his sense of wary watchfulness.

On the fifth, and what he sincerely hoped would be their final night of flight, he had woken the weary child just as the sun was setting in a last defiant blaze of golden glory, and put her in the saddle. Then walking beside the dust-coated stallion, he had set off with cautious determination, eyes narrowed for any sign of the swift-flowing Tarkan river, the last barrier to Lilia's safety and one he intended to cross in daylight if possible.

Just as Ranulf thought he sighted the smudged line of dark green trees against the darker hills of Mithlondia that he recognised from previous scouting missions as marking the river, and therefore the border between the two realms, he caught the faint but growing sound of hoof beats on the gilded evening air, and knew the hunters had caught up with them at last.

He said nothing to Lilia but the frightened look she threw at him as he mounted up behind her, and urged the stallion from walk to canter to gallop, was indication enough that she had sensed his sudden tension and understood what it meant. Pray gods she had not also heard the ragged sound of hunting dogs baying their pursuit.

Aware though he was that Flame was suffering too from the endless flight across the plains, Ranulf dared not slacken their pace, reviewing their position as best he could with the thunder of the stallion's hooves loud in his ears.

The northern night – formerly their friend – was now closing in around them with a swiftness that still took Ranulf by surprise, the flat, featureless grasslands dissolving into dimpsy shadows that could as easily hold unseen dangers as prove havens of refuge.

A fleeting glance over his shoulder revealed nothing but encroaching darkness behind, yet he had no doubt that the slightest mishap would bring down on them a pack of Atarkarnan warriors, all set on revenge for the death of their chief's daughter, and quite probably Attan himself if Talmarth had named the Mithlondian harper as his killer.

And why would the true culprit not have put the blame on an innocent stranger – particularly one he already bore a grudge against – rather than telling the elders the truth, if he thought he could get away with it?

Still travelling at the swiftest pace Flame could maintain, they had accomplished a little over half the distance to the river when the stallion suddenly stumbled over some unseen obstacle. Lilia cried out in shock and almost fell, saved only by the steely grip of Ranulf's encircling arm. Nevertheless, the incident proved just how damnably close to disaster they really were.

Muttering encouragement to both child and animal, Ranulf held them all together, his gaze flicking towards the dark ridge of the eastern hills, behind which a growing radiance told him the moon would soon be rising, then risked another glance over his shoulder, cursing as he sensed how little distance now separated the hunters from the hunted.

Close enough that he could hear their voices, fierce with the lust of the chase and the desire for bloody vengeance. Not that Ranulf had ever deluded himself that Talmarth would be any more inclined to mercy now as when he had first flung the tidings of Atarellen's death in her grieving father's face.

Forget Talmarth, Ranulf told himself. *Just concentrate on reaching the river.*

Flame was labouring now, Ranulf could feel it, the stallion's steps less even, his pace faltering, whilst the Atarkarnan warriors, damn them to Hell, were gaining steadily.

Was that the river ahead of them?

He narrowed his eyes in an attempt to see into the misleading shadows. A furlong perhaps... it might just as well be a thousand!

The yells of the tribesmen were plain now, even over the rolling rumble of their horses' hooves, and an arrow whistled past Ranulf's shoulder, causing him to curse even more viciously, uncaring now whether the child might hear, caring only that some half-wit barbarian shit-scum might have struck Lilia with his filthy poisoned arrow.

Another arrow shot out of the shadows, close enough to make Lilia scream, and Pearl to dig her claws deeper into Ranulf's shoulder, the sudden, raking pain making him swear even more profanely.

Linette really was not going to be pleased with him if Lilia ever repeated *that* to her mother!

Gods of Light and Mercy, Silver Lady of the Stars, I beg you, give her that chance...

He felt Flame stumble yet again, fearing for a moment that the stallion was hit, and knowing that even if he was not, the gallant animal had reached the end of his endurance.

Under no circumstances would the beast reach the river carrying them both but, he reasoned, the big horse would scarcely notice the weight of one small, skinny, seven-year old girl.

On that thought Ranulf tightened the reins and drew the sweating stallion to a halt, sliding down almost before the weary animal had come to an unsteady stop.

"What..." Lilia began.

Ranulf did not give her chance to continue.

Pulling his mantle from his pack, he made sure it was pinned securely on her thin shoulder with his silver brooch.

Then winding the reins about her trembling hands, he said curtly,

"Here, take these, and for gods'sake, Lilia, hold on! Cross the river, if you can manage it, and whatever else you do, *do not look back!*"

He slapped a hand against the stallion's rump and leapt back as the chestnut gathered himself for one final burst of speed, hoping that he had not sent the child to her death by drowning in the fast-flowing, rock-strewn river. Ranulf spared perhaps five heartbeats to watch her go, the night lightening perceptibly around them.

Praying that the stallion would not let his small rider fall... that Lilia would keep both her nerve and her balance... that Pearl would...

Damn it all, he still had the bloody cat!

He had meant to send Pearl with Lilia, having the odd notion that the Moon Goddess would not allow any harm to come to the child as long as the fey creature was with her.

Acutely conscious now of the slight weight of the cat beside his left ear, he turned his head, blinking a little at the strain of focusing on the pale blue eyes so close to his own.

"Go," he commanded softly, wondering yet again if he had run moon-mad to expect the animal to understand him. "Go with Lilia. Keep her safe."

Pearl considered him for a moment, then lightly touched her nose to his face in gentle benediction and leapt in a graceful arc from his shoulder to the ground, disappearing like a wisp of grey mist into the long grass.

A quick glance into the distant darkness assuring him that thus far Lilia was safe, he turned his back on the rising moon, standing his ground as the massed horsemen bore down on him in an earth-shaking wave of thunderous noise and heavy hooves, flying manes and shouts of execration.

"Hold!"

Regardless of the shouted order or Ranulf's threatening stance, bow in hand, arrow nocked and ready to let fly, the Atarkarnan horsemen could simply have ridden around – or indeed *over* – him.

Surprise, however, or possibly the iron note of command, made them draw rein, coming to a dust-churning halt, surrounding Ranulf in a rearing, snorting, trampling circle.

At a signal from Talmarth – yes, he could see the bastard clearly now – the tips of several long spears were levelled at his throat and a similar number of arrows aimed at his heart, their fletching showing black in the growing silverish light, but still unmistakable to one who had lost comrades to their poison in the past.

His grim sense of satisfaction that none of the tribesmen had pursued the fleeing child was short-lived, however, as Talmarth whistled a command to the dogs to pick up the scent.

Running past him, noses to the ground, they disappeared into the silvery shadows... only to come fleeing back almost immediately, tails between their legs, whining and whimpering, one at least showing a bloody slash across its muzzle.

A fey, feline yowl rose into the night, causing Ranulf to grin, even as every hair on his body lifted.

"The goddess keep you both," he murmured to the darkness, then turned back to face his death.

Verse 4

A Harper No More

Having accepted his own death as inevitable, it was with a great deal of arrogance and no small amount of contempt that Ranulf lowered the bow, even as he angled his head so as to look Talmarth straight in the eye.

"I know what you did, you stinking piece of shit!"

He spoke in slow, careful Atarkarnan in order that none of the tribesmen might be in any doubt as to what he was saying.

Then, dropping the bow at his feet, he drew Attan's knife from his belt, the amber hilt growing warm in his hand, almost like a friend's clasp, his stance an open invitation to Talmarth to take him on.

Having not the slightest illusion as to how any such bout would end, he was grimly determined to make his mark on the treacherous cur before him, not only for his own pride's sake and to give Lilia time to escape, but also to avenge the Atarkarnan chief he had learned to respect.

Talmarth, perceiving that he was at no further risk of an arrow through his throat and realising he could only lose credence if he did not accept the implicit challenge, slid down from his mount – or to be more accurate, the horse belonging to the man he had murdered – and drew his sword – short and broad but still with a far longer reach than Ranulf's knife.

"Talk all you like, Harper!" he sneered.

His black eyes glittering with satisfaction, and apparently still unaware that the man he thus taunted was anything other than what he had seemed for the past four seasons, Talmarth finished scornfully,

"None of my companions will believe anything a gutless gelden has to say."

"Probably not, if their minds are all as hobbled as yours."

Ranulf too could sneer.

"Then again, they would have to be deaf and blind as well as witless not to realise what a treacherous snake you really are. Ah! So you can recognise the truth when you hea... *Hell!*"

He almost didn't manage to parry the other man's sudden lunge, nearly losing his grip on the knife hilt as the slender blade clashed and slid with a harsh metallic chime against the heavier length of Talmarth's sword.

"When you hear it!" Ranulf finished tightly, eyes narrowing as the other man declined to press his undoubted advantage.

So that was the game? Shit!

With another silent curse for the resulting numbness in his fingers, he gave Talmarth an insolently defiant smile and said with deliberate provocation,

"A child could make a swifter end to such an unequal contest."

"But then I do not seek to make a swift end," Talmarth hissed. "Oh no, Harper, it is the dark fires for you! You, the man... nay, not even a man, a worm, a cokenay... a filthy spy who killed the chief of the seven tribes by stealth and deception! You do not deserve a merciful death. Rather, I shall watch as you writhe in the torment of the sacred flames. And your screams as your skin crackles and burns will be as music to me, sweeter than any note you can pluck from your cursed Mithlondian harp."

"The sacred fire, eh? Not a blade in the belly?" Ranulf mocked in return, refusing to let his mind acknowledge the possibility of such a terrifying fate. "As you did for Attan? Cur and traitor that *you* are."

The next moment, however, all ideas of taunting Talmarth into giving him a clean death shattered... and then coalesced into complete shock as he heard the sound of galloping horses coming up behind him.

Damn it! Not more of the bastards!

Whoever it was, their arrival was greeted by a spatter of startled shouts and much wild gesticulation from the Atarkarnans before him, and unable to resist the temptation, he glanced over his shoulder.

In time to see a small group of shadowy horsemen settle into a semi-circle behind him.

While behind them the bright moon of midsummer's eve rose above the eastern hills, golden and glorious, illuminating the land with a radiance so bright that the shadows of the five huge horses and their unidentified riders stretched dark across the ground until they touched and merged with his own.

The newcomers did not speak, might just as easily have been wraiths as mortal men upon their earth-bound steeds.

Until finally the uneasy silence was broken by a jingling chink, as the closest horse flung up his head, stamped an impatient hoof and blew with noisy familiarity down Ranulf's neck.

A wry smile lifted one side of his mouth, and with a wary look at the staring Atarkarnan warriors, he risked a second, slightly less fleeting glance at the silent shadows beyond his shoulder.

With the moon behind them, all he caught was the brief impression of mailed bodies – two broad, two lean, one deceptively slender – their bare heads limned in golden radiance against the dark sky, each a separate aureole of colour. Brown, bronze, midnight-black, waterfall-white and wheat-fair... and in that moment his heart knew them all, these five men who now held his back.

With his narrowed gaze once more fixed on the restless tribesmen, Ranulf spoke into the odd fey silence that had fallen over them all, asking aloud the question that most troubled him at this precise moment,

"Lilia?"

"Safe," came the reply from behind him, in the cool tone he would have known anywhere. "Thanks to you, Rafe."

No, thanks to the Goddess who rules the night!

"Indeed, when we left her," commented a different, lightly ironic voice. "She was regaling Beric, Jarec and the rest of your old company with what I am sure will prove to be a wildly exaggerated tale of your exploits."

Ranulf grinned to himself, and tucking the dagger back into his belt set to work on the lacing at his wrists.

Knowing that Lilia was safe, that he could not be surrounded or die from a blade in the back, he was determined to earn some small amount of justice for Attan.

Evidently chary of the newcomers, puzzled by Ranulf's actions and annoyed by the quick exchange of words in a language he did not understand, Talmarth edged closer, spitting out an aggressive demand.

Ranulf, still busy working at the cuffs of his sleeves, ignored it until that same level voice behind him asked,

"What does he say, Rafe?"

One knot free, his fingers busy with the other, Ranulf replied with a twitch of a sardonic smile,

"Shorn of any non-existent courtesy, it means 'who the fuck are you'?"

"As I thought," came the unruffled response. "And who the fuck is *he*?"

"Talmarth, son of Talmon, an ambitious whelp who has much in common with Joffroi, did he but know it. He is untrustworthy, treacherous and has no qualms whatsoever about murdering either his own chief or a defenceless child."

"*My* child, I assume?" Joscelin's voice was suddenly harder, colder, and utterly lethal. And not waiting for Ranulf's confirmation,

"Just as well Lilia was not as defenceless as he thought then. Do you want to take him, or shall I?"

"No, I will do it!"

Even as Ranulf spoke, he finally worked the last knot free and then ripped the shirt over his head, ignoring the babble of exclamation that immediately broke out amongst the Atarkarnans on perceiving the distinctive markings, clear in the moonlight, black wings beating against the paler skin of his arm as for one enchanted moment the horse seemed about to take flight into the night.

"Very well, Rafe, he is yours. But first," Joscelin continued with soft menace. "Let me answer that spineless stoat's question. I want him to know exactly who he is taking on here."

Then raising his voice to address the would-be chief of the seven tribes, he said in a clear, frost-crisp voice that effortlessly commanded attention,

"You! Talmarth, son of Talmon!"

Evidently recognising his name and the tone, despite the barrier of a foreign tongue, the Atarkarnan had little choice but to demand an explanation of the only man there who spoke both languages.

"You, Harper, or whatever you are! Tell me what he said."

"You asked, did you not, who he and his companions were," Ranulf reminded him blandly. "Well, he is about to tell you. And I suggest you listen well."

Yet when Joscelin spoke, Ranulf did not – could not, damn it – immediately translate the words, simple though they were.

"We are his brothers and sword-brothers," Joscelin said. "Bound until death."

Patiently waiting until Ranulf had managed to swallow the tightness in his throat and turn the words into the language of the seven tribes, causing Talmarth to raise his sword in white-knuckled defiance, Joscelin added with wintry warning,

"Which means that if you cut him down, unarmed as he is, you will still have the five of us to face."

"Not unarmed for long," came a different voice, accompanied by the ice-edged slither of steel against scabbard ring. "Here, Ran!"

Reacting instinctively to his brother's voice, Ranulf turned, catching the flash and glitter as moonlight danced along the flying blade in the heartbeat before the familiar hilt came to rest in his outstretched hand.

With his own sword in his hand, he dropped into a fighting stance and said loudly enough for the scowling Talmarth and his companions to hear,

"Now we will settle this, you bloody murdering traitor!"

When Talmarth failed to take up his invitation – perhaps the prospect of taking on six battle-ready Mithlondian warriors, rather than one unarmed harper being odds not to his liking – Ranulf cocked his head, regarding the rest of the Atarkarnan horsemen.

"Do your friends know what you are, Talmarth? And would they still follow you if they knew that the man to whom you swore an oath of loyalty lies dead because you put your blade in his belly?"

"No, it was you!" Talmarth shouted over the sudden outbreak of mutterings amongst the men behind him.

"Do not listen to him, my friends! Did he not run, like the coward he is? And see that dagger at his belt? That is the proof of his guilt. Stolen from the man he killed."

With his left hand Ranulf lifted the knife so that all could see it, the amber hilt glowing gold in the gilded light of the luminous midsummer moon.

"Yes, this is Attan's knife."

Ranulf's uncompromising statement was met by a creak of stressed wood as one of the tribesmen drew back the bow he carried.

To be answered by a low growl of warning, the glint of the throwing knife that appeared in Edwy's hand apparently needing no translation whatsoever.

"Yes, I took it," Ranulf continued, holding Talmarth's furious eyes. "At Attan's command. And only after I had done as he demanded and given him the clean death that you denied him when you put your sword in his gut and left him to die a slow, stinking death. A death that, if there is any justice amongst the gods, you yourself will suffer before this night is much older."

"It is a lie!"

Talmarth was still shouting, half turned towards his uneasy companions, the better to appeal to their loyalty.

"You cannot believe a word he says. This man who has spoken falsely to us for every day he has lived among us, saying he was no more than a harper, a maker of music, a singer of songs..."

"A half-man," Ranulf interrupted. "A gelden. A cokenay. Is that not what you thought me, Talmarth? Even after I gave my blood for the people of the White Eagle."

He tilted his left arm so that moonlight ran with rippling clarity along the scar on his forearm, even as his narrowed gaze flicked from one man to another amongst the angry Atarkarnans, picking out faces he recognised.

"You, Ekta. I fought at your side that day on the plain beside the valley of the painted rocks. And you, Takmin, did you not come to me after the Easterners were defeated to thank me for saving your woman and child from their spears? And you..."

"Yes, yes," Talmarth interrupted with a snarl. "We should all have seen you for what you were that day. And if you fought, it was only to save your own filthy life."

"And that of the child in my care," Ranulf agreed, adding grimly. "An innocent child who you would have seen dead if I had not taken her and fled – yes, I admit I ran, but only as far as the river. I always intended to return and seek you out, once I knew Lilia was safe."

"She should be dead," Talmarth hissed in a bitter, barely audible whisper, almost lost as he slashed forwards in savage attack. "As Atarellen is dead."

Parrying the blow, Ranulf raised his voice above the clash of steel.

"Why do you not speak louder, Talmarth. Or do your companions, those who would see you chief of the White Eagle tribe, not know that to claim that place you would willingly *kill an innocent child.*"

He ground out the accusing words, his normally light voice grating harsh as granite shards as he side-stepped the wild slash of his opponent's blade.

"A blood-price was due," Talmarth spat out. "A life for a life. And your precious little Mithlondian princess should have paid it!"

Taking ground with every vicious stab and slash, he continued,

"But Attan was weak, blinded by his folly. I am not. And I *will* be chief of the seven tribes, whatever the poison of your lies."

His breathing coming faster and harder, Ranulf struggled to defend himself against the younger man's punitive attack, the flicker of a caustic thought running through his mind,

Fucking hell, I am out of practise. That's what comes of spending a year as a bloody harper.

The next moment, he saw a chance and took it, only to have his blade deflected before it could draw blood, and catching his breath, he settled to wait for the next opening, answering and denying Talmarth's ambition with grim determination,

"Not if the gods..."

He deflected the glittering point aiming for his heart and took another step back, continuing,

"Decree that I am the one..."

He saw the gap and drove his blade towards it.

Only to have Talmarth close the momentary weakness in his own defence and crash through his own.

"Ah! Shit!"

The icy steel point of Talmarth's blade slid along the barely-healed scar on his forearm, opening it up like a bloody peach, even the lightning flash of shearing agony not sufficient to curb his pain-twisted grin as behind him he heard Guy swear in profane consternation, his instinctive movement to go to his brother's assistance halted by Joscelin's curt command for stillness.

With an effort, Ranulf shut out the men at his back, and riding the sudden scarlet burst of teeth-gritting agony, caught Talmarth's triumphant gaze and – determined to finish it before pain and loss of blood finished him – said as steadily as his uneven breathing allowed,

"Not if the gods decree... that I am the one..."

With the whole weight of his body behind his thrust, he put his sword through the other man, in the exact same manner as Talmarth had done to the man for whom Ranulf sought justice.

Viciously twisting the blade, Ranulf watched as the Atarkarnan staggered back, his scream borne away on the summer breeze, the sword falling from his slackened grasp, his hands instinctively clutching at the ragged ruin of his belly, and the blade still buried deep therein.

With no trace of pity in either voice or face, Ranulf said as coldly as his lack of breath allowed,

"Now who is the one..."

Talmarth, his mouth a raw, red maw agape with pain and shock, slowly crumpled to his knees on the black, blood-splattered silver of the moonlit grass, unheeding of anything other than his impending death, as Ranulf finished flatly, finally ripping his blade free,

"*Who is speaking the truth!*"

Lilia was asleep in her father's arms, and Ranulf was once more riding the weary Flame, his sword-brothers close around him, and the men of the ranger company riding a cautious but probably unnecessary rear-guard behind them.

Light-headed after five nights of forced flight, his gut cramping with hunger, his forearm a blaze of fire, Ranulf finally broke the silence that had held between them as they rode through the moonlight towards the Mithlondian army encampment deep in the eastern hills.

"How did you know where to find us?" he asked, of no-one in particular.

"For once," Gabriel's voice drifted over to him – light, incisive, wryly amused. "I saw something useful in my dreams."

The next question, though of far greater import, Ranulf nearly did not ask at all, dreading the answer even as he said,

"Is it true that Rowène is with the army? Attan told me she had left the Grey Sisters' House in Vézière to bring her healing skills to the battle lines."

A heartbeat of silence.

Startled? Constrained?

Or something far worse?

Yet if he *had* left her to carry his child, surely neither Josce nor Luc would have gone to the trouble of seeking him out, let alone declared their intention of standing by him "to the death". And since none of the five men had flung his feckless disregard in his face, his carelessness that night at Vézière could not have resulted in a child.

Thank the gods. The goddess. Every deity of every known realm.

Now all he needed to know was that Rowène was safe.

"For gods'sake, Josce! Stop bloody torturing me and answer the fucking question. Is she with you or not?"

"Yes, Ro is with the army," Joscelin sighed.

Adding with a faint, uncharacteristic note of bemusement,

"Along with a number of other Mithlondian noblewomen. To whit her sister, my mother, Linette and Adèle... oh, and Mistress Gwynhere as well. They have all left home and hearth to travel in the army's tail and tend the wounded."

A moment's pause, and then Luc spoke for the first time that night, his tone exceedingly dry,

"I have no doubt that Ro will be relieved by your return, more or less undamaged, Rafe. She has been worrying herself sick about you. Not without cause, if that arm is any indication."

"Speaking of which," Joscelin added crisply. "You had better have her take a look at it as soon as we get back to camp."

The long, gaping gash in Ranulf's forearm had already been washed and roughly bound, and though his arm now lay in a sling against his chest, it ached like hell, the pain pulsing black and blood-red with every jolting step his tired mount took towards the Mithlondian encampment.

"Aye."

Edwy's ghoulish voice seemed to come at Ranulf from some great distance, though he knew the man rode right next to him, close enough to catch him if he fell, which seemed at that moment a distinct possibility.

"I reckon Lady Rowena'll have plenty of chance to practise her sewing skills afore she's done wi' ye, brother."

"And only the gods know when either you, or Guy, are going to be fit to fight," Joscelin muttered grimly.

Guy is wounded, and still rode out here after me? Hell knows what I've done to deserve his loyalty.

But it was Gabriel who had the last flippant word on the subject,

"Who would ever have guessed it was so dangerous being a harper."

"Not... a harper," Ranulf managed to say.

Or at least he thought he did... he was beginning to lose all sense of himself, his companions and the bright, moonlit hills through which they rode.

A harper, no more. Just... just Rowène's man now. If she will still have me.

PART VI

MIDSUMMER'S DAY

1209

The Last Verse

Sunrise

The woman kneeling on the bank of the small, serene stream leaned forwards to splash water onto her pale, drawn face, less in the pursuit of cleanliness and more in the hope of waking herself sufficiently to get through another day of blood and screams and shattered bodies.

Drying her face and hands on the ragged skirts of a robe that might once have been pale grey, she sat back on her heels to comb and rebraid her long hair, staring a little pensively into the growing light of this Midsummer's Day, watching as the mirroring waters reflected the sky's changing colours, first copper, then bronze, finally spreading a silken banner of pure, valiant gold.

The preceding days had all run into one long crimson blur, the night before a bottomless chasm of darkness and fear, yet now, just for a few moments before the battle horns were blown again, all was quiet and peaceful, the sounds of the morning, simple and ordinary.

Birds twittering in the nearby trees, a flight of ducks landing on the water with a serried splash, a shining, lissome sparkle of movement as a family of otters rolled about in playful fashion.

If only such peace would last. It could not, of course, but...

Sensing that she was no longer alone, she abandoned wishful thoughts and rose quickly to her feet, turning to see her brothers and sister walking through what had once been a flower-filled meadow, before the grass had been trampled by the constant tread of booted feet going to and from the river, and cropped by the half dozen horses belonging to the most senior ranking officers of the Mithlondian army.

"My mother said we would most likely find you here," Joscelin said without preamble.

He looked drawn and sounded tired. Bloodshot grey eyes glanced keenly around the meadow.

"And for all this is within our own defensive line, you really should not come here without a guard, Ro. Where in damnation is that rogue, Beowulf? All these years he has scarce left your side, and now..."

"I asked him to remain with Rafe and Guy," Rowène cut in gently. "I brought Aelric instead and while you may not see him, I have no doubt that he is somewhere close by."

"She has you there," Luc cut in, the swift grin he flashed at his brother momentarily free from strain. "You will not find a better scout than Aelric in all of five realms."

Joscelin merely snorted, declining to engage in an argument he knew he could not win, and said,

"And speaking of our two harpers, how are they this morning, Ro?"

Rowène grimaced.

"Well, for a start Guy did himself no favours by spending half of yesterday and most of the night riding up hill and down dale."

"You should never have allowed him to go," Juliène interjected waspishly, her accusing glare divided equally between Joscelin and her sister. "Least of all for such a cause!"

"He went for *his* brother and *our* brother's daughter. What better cause is that!" Rowène snapped.

She was still far from reconciled to her sister's presence in the Mithlondian camp, even knowing that Juliène had left her life of comfort, her lord-by-binding and all hope of future respectability to be at Guy's side.

"And if you had seen Linette's face when Lilia was restored to her, Ju, you would not be sniping now," she added sharply.

Juliène gave her a cynical look but Joscelin smiled, the expression softening the carved granite lines of his lean face.

"I, for one, will never forget it. Indeed, I will go farther, Ro."

He held her eyes, so she could be in no doubt of his sincerity.

"I did not think I would ever have cause to say this but I can forgive Rafe anything for having brought Lilia home safely, when both her mother and I thought she was lost to us forever. Indeed, I think in her first happiness Linette would have kissed him, even knowing that he is, or rather was, Ranulf de Rogé."

"She knows?" Rowène asked in bemusement.

"She has known, or at least suspected, for a long time now," Joscelin confirmed. "And might well have admitted it publicly in her first rush of gratitude, had he not nearly fallen like a sack of stones at her feet."

Juliène gave a scornful little laugh and said mockingly,

"He fainted? No hero of harp song there!"

740

"He *had* lost a lot of blood," Rowène pointed out, still striving for patience. "And from what Lilia has been able to tell us, they had been hunted the length of Atarkarna and what little food they carried or foraged, Rafe gave most, if not all, to her. So just perhaps, Ju, he had cause to collapse."

"Maybe so," Juliène conceded grudgingly, almost at the same time as Joscelin repeated,

"So how is he this morning?"

"Still sleeping the poppy-sleep when I left the healer's tent."

"So he has not yet seen you, sister-mine?" Juliène queried. "Unless he recovered his wits while you were plying your trade?"

Rowène gave her a flat look that held not an ounce of sisterly affection.

"He roused a little, but no, to answer your question, I do not think he knew it was me. It is enough that I will see him when he wakes. If, that is, he wants to see me."

She glanced uncertainly at Joscelin.

"You did say last night that he was asking for me?"

Her brother nodded,

"Briefly. He had heard from Attan that you were with the army and he wanted to know if it was true, and I agreed that it was."

"And that is *all* he said? All *you* said?"

"Yes."

Then evidently catching the fleeting frown that drew her dark copper brows together, he added grimly,

"I was just too damned glad to get him back in one piece to speak of... anything else. And as for him... well you said it yourself, Ro, he was barely aware of what was happening around him, half out of his head with pain..."

"Oh, do not make excuses for him, Josce!"

She glanced down at the fading scar across her palm, and the flash of temper faded from her face.

"What is done is done, for good or ill, and this is not the time to be worrying about hurts of the heart."

"No, not when I have something truly important to say," Luc said brusquely.

Tearing his narrowed gaze from the glory of the sunrise, he turned to survey his brother and sisters.

"Something I need the three of you, my closest kin, to hear."

He took a deep breath, pushed a breeze-blown strand of frost-silver hair away out of his eyes, and set out his thoughts in a quiet, emotionless voice.

"The whole realm must know by now that the woman who was born Ariène de Miriél-Lavalle has succeeded in betraying her second lord-by-binding just as thoroughly as she did her first.

"What only a handful of people know is that following evidence given yesterday morning by Joffroi de Rogé, Prince Linnius and the High Counsel have signed a document absolving our father of all possible complicity in Prince Marcus' murder, thus removing the taint of high treason from the de Chartreux name.

"Even more astonishingly, since Joffroi has never been known for his generosity of spirit, and must be feeling like a boar at bay after being so openly betrayed, not only by our mother but by his son as well, Joffroi is now set on restoring Chartre and the lands thereabouts to his one-time rival's rightful heirs."

An odd look drifted like a dark shadow behind Luc's clear grey eyes and Rowène thought she knew what he was about to say.

Finally, after a long moment of silence, he continued with cool formality,

"Being as I will never take the binding oath or sire a child of my own body, I want it known that on my death the lordship will pass to Juliène's son, Valéri de Chartreux, on condition that he shares the revenues and governance of the fief with his foster-sister, Alysiène de Chartreux.

"With battle upon us, there is no time to have the relevant deed drawn up but I want the three of you to swear to uphold my will, because whether we eventually win or lose this war, this is the end of our lives as we have known them. Nothing can be as it was again."

"That sounds like something Gabriel might say," Rowène murmured. "Have you... spoken with him at all, Luc?"

"No, I gave my word that I would not seek him out for any cause," Luc replied bleakly. "And I have kept that oath in all ways."

"And he has not spoken to you?" Rowène asked. "You were in each other's company for most of last night, Luc. Surely it would have done no harm in such..."

"No!" Luc cut mercilessly across her sympathy. "We rode together for one purpose only, a purpose that touched us both nearly. Not for any more... intimate dealings."

He took a hard breath. Visibly forced aside his pain.

"We had no speech together save in the presence of the others who rode with us. I would not expect any other from Gabriel, nor selfishly ask him to break his word, shatter his own honour. He is Adèle's lord-by-binding, the father of her son, and I am his friend, no more."

But you still love him still!

She did not say the words out loud, however.

There was no need.

With the sun rising higher with every heartbeat, bringing increasing sounds of movement from the horse lines and tents, they parted with hand clasps and hugs to go their separate ways.

Joscelin and Luc to ready themselves and their men for the inevitable fighting.

Rowène returning to the healing tent.

Juliène disappearing only the gods knew where.

Behind them the horses continued to graze the meadow and as the day advanced so the last tattered shreds of dawn's bright banner faded from the water, leaving it cool and grey in the early morning light.

Mid-morning

Ranulf was aware that he was awake.

Or at least he thought he was awake.

He knew there was some pressing reason why he should wake further, and yet all he could do was lie there and listen to the sound of voices arguing somewhere nearby.

Two voices.

One clearly that of a young woman. Light and lilting, suffused with a sweet gravity.

The other had deepened since he had last heard it, and it was possible he would not have recognised it at all had the girl not exclaimed,

"Val! You came! I... I was not sure you would."

"I came to see *your* father, Lissie. Not that midden-rat who calls himself *mine*."

"He *is* your father, Val. And I know he would do anything to heal the breach between you..."

"And you know that how, Mistress Long-Nose? Have you been poking around in the debauched darkness of his mind, even as you have been weaving your healing enchantments over his arm? Surely there are better ways to use your power? Better men to save? Your own father, for one!"

"Papa is healing..."

"Or he was before he insisted on riding out on yesterday's mad caper," Val's harsh voice over-rode his cousin's gentler tones, but all Ranulf could think was,

Damn it all to Hell! Why is Val..? Gods above! Why is Lissie here? They should both be safe in Lasceynes...

And then it hit him. What he should have realised last night if he had been thinking at all.

Edwy had been riding beside him, and like a fool, he had been so glad of his brother's presence – that both Edwy and Guy had cared enough to come after him – that he had not taken the thought any further.

Fool!

He should have known that if Edwy were here in Atarkarna's eastern hills, so would Val be too.

As for Lissie... Joscelin had told him that Gwynny was working with the healers, and it seemed likely that she had come here as companion to Guy's daughter.

Even so, something struck him as odd about that conclusion... something he could not quite grasp... and he gave up trying as the disconnected and discordant notes plucked from the strings of a harp sawed across his senses.

"Stop that, Val!" Lissie said sharply. "If you want to do something useful, go and fetch some more water, or wood, or..."

"Or I can fight! That would be useful!" came the belligerent retort.

"Oh, Val! You know Uncle Joscelin says you are too young."

"He also said he needs every man, so therefore he needs me."

"Mama needs you more. I am begging you, Val, do not do anything rash that will get yourself killed. I know it is hard. I know you and Wulf want to fight alongside the soldiers but truly, you are needed here."

"Well, I am not staying here if you are going to expect me to help *him*!" Val retorted, and Ranulf was in no doubt as to which 'him' he had in mind. "Damn it, Lissie, why doesn't he wake up?"

"He should do so soon, Mama said. Then you can tell him you love him and..."

"Love!" Val practically spat the word. "I hate him! Ranulf bloody *Jacques* de Rogé!"

There was such a biting emphasis on the second of his given names that Ranulf nearly managed to break through the bonds binding him in the darkness... unable to move, to speak, even to open his eyes.

"Val, please," Lissie pleaded softly. "I know you do not mean it."

"Much you know, Mistress Soft-heart!" came the sneering reply.

Then on a burst of pain,

"Gods, Lissie, why could not your father be my father also? Rather than the hell-spawned *skraka* who sired me."

"Please do not do this, Val. Not when I know how sorry you are for having spat at him that day at Vézière and calling him..."

"Don't *you* say it!"

"Why? Because you are ashamed of using such a word to your own father?"

"No. Because it is too filthy a term for you to know, let alone use."

"But it is all right for you to do so, Val?"

"Why shouldn't I? He deserved it then," came the vaguely sullen response. "And he deserves it still. You know he does!"

"Uncle Joscelin..."

"Uncle Joscelin feels himself under an obligation. If it were not for Lilia..."

A pause that sat as heavily on Ranulf's breast as a granite boulder, before Val finished stonily,

"Better that the man I will never call Father had died back there on the Atarkarnan plain. At least I would have had one honourable deed to remember him by..."

Then their voices faded altogether, and with his heart a dull ache in his chest and lightning streaks stabbing painfully into the dense darkness behind his eyes, Ranulf felt his gut twist into the most hellish knot and knew he was going to be sick, though gods knew he had nothing other than bitter bile in his belly to retch up.

With a violent effort, and uncaring whether his son was still there to witness his final humiliation, he rolled onto his good arm and heaved helplessly onto the ground beside the rough bracken mattress.

Gods! What had he ever done that his son, *his only living child*, should hate him this much!

Val! The child he had loved for all the fourteen years of his life.

In spite of the circumstances of his conception.

In spite of Ranulf's outright dislike of the woman who had borne him.

The son he had carried in his arms the length of Mithlondia and for whom he had done everything it was possible for a man to do for his child during the first year of his life.

The son for whose sake he had tried so hard to slough off the skin of the ravening wolf his blood-lines and upbringing had for so long made him, to become instead the man his mother would have wanted him to be.

The son who had once proudly declared in Ranulf's hearing that he was going to be a soldier like his father – Val, blithely unaware that the man he knew then as Rafe of Oakenleigh was in truth the same man who had sired him – was now wishing him dead!

He retched again, coughed and spat.

Perhaps he should have let Talmarth kill him after all.

Although there was always today's battle, and with his shield arm out of commission he would be an easy target for an Easterner's sword...

"He did not mean it, Ran!"

A calm, damnably familiar, voice spoke over his head, and Ranulf opened his stinging eyes to a blurry slit, to find that his brother had wakened and having shuffled over from his own pallet was now holding Ranulf's long hair out of the unlovely puddle of watery yellow bile slicking the trampled grass beside his bed.

"It bloody well sounded as if he meant it," Ranulf said hoarsely.

He spat out the last burning remnant of vomit that was fouling his mouth, and shrugging off his brother's careful hands, started to get to his feet... only to drop down onto the rough bed and drag the mantle that was doing duty as a blanket back over his lower body as he recognised the dark-haired woman walking gracefully towards him.

Having finally managed to extricate himself from Princess Linette's tearful thanks, accepted the bowl of boiled oatmeal and honey Adèle de Marillec had brought him, and found enough of his clothes that he could decently abandon his makeshift blanket, Ranulf slipped out of the healer's tent with the excuse that he needed the privy.

What he really needed was to find Rowène.

He had expected to see her working alongside Linette and Adèle amongst the wounded in the healing tent but when this turned out not to be so, he concluded that she must be resting, Guy having – somewhat reluctantly, Ranulf thought – informed him that she had been awake for most of the night, first stitching his arm, then watching over him, only leaving his side when dawn began to lighten the sky and, as far as his brother knew, she had not returned since.

Leaving the long tent filled with the competing scents of crushed grass, sweating bodies, healing herbs, bloody bandages, and broken men, Ranulf looked first towards the sun, blazing bright and merciless in a brazen blue canopy, judging it to be mid-morning at least.

There was only the faintest of breezes to stir the dust-gold air, yet still sufficient to carry the harsh sounds of the battle-storm raging beyond the boundaries of the camp, and bitterly cursing the man responsible for his temporary uselessness, he resolved to discover where the women had put his sword, then beg or borrow a mail shirt, find wherever Jarec had hobbled Rye, and then... He took a deep breath. *Then* he would see whether he could be of any use to Joscelin on the battlefield.

First, however, he had an errand that could wait no longer.

He *had* to find Rowène.

Glancing with growing impatience around the neat circles of the busy encampment, he eventually spotted Gwynny coming out of a nearby tent, carrying a bundle of dirty linen, and taking a guess that he would find Rowène there, walked quickly in that direction.

Hearing movement within, he hesitated for a moment outside – *Gods! What if she does not want to see me?* – then cleared his throat and said,

"It is Rafe. May I come in?"

A pause, then Beowulf's voice, the rough growl overlaid with the heavy Rogé accent he had never lost,

"Aye, come ye in."

The grizzled Mallowleigh man lifted the door flap and stood aside, adding in a low grumble,

"An' about bloody time too, m'lord."

Ranulf started to say something, the intended riposte to the uncomplimentary honorific turning into a strangled exclamation as his gaze fell upon the golden-haired girl standing a mere yard away, crooning to the babe in her arms.

Looking up as his startlement leached into horrified silence, Lissie smiled and, as if his presence was entirely normal and indeed expected, said quite calmly,

"Oh, Uncle Rafe, there you are."

Then when he failed to answer, she added somewhat anxiously,

"Are you feeling... better, Uncle?"

No, Ranulf thought, staring at his brother's daughter with a very grim expression indeed. *I am not bloody feeling better. And if it is Val who is responsible for that babe I am going to beat the hell out of him.*

Evidently seeing, and correctly interpreting the look of absolute fury flushing across his otherwise bloodless face, she laughed a little, perhaps in nervousness, and said,

"It is not what you think, Uncle Rafe! Jacques is not mine. He is *yours*."

Mine!

For a dozen heartbeats he stood stunned, wondering if he had been hit over the head by a mace.

Certainly he had not seen that blow coming.

"Mine?"

He repeated it numbly, staring at the babe as if he had never seen one before, much less sired three... no, four... though only one of them had ever drawn breath until now. Val! Gods! No wonder his son hated him.

And now, according to Lissie, he had another son.

Would this one – *Jacques*, Lissie had called him, obviously named in his father's unavoidable, and for all they knew, permanent absence – grow to hate him too? He could hardly blame him if he did!

Gods forgive him, he had never intended to give life to a child that night at Vézière – and it could only have happened then!

But he had. The proof was before him. Lissie would not lie.

And knowing what he had done, he could not now turn his back, walk out, shrug off his responsibilities.

Nor – no matter how much Val might wish it – could he recklessly throw his life away on the battlefield. Of course, the odds were high that he would still die there anyway, but until then...

Inwardly expecting rejection he held out his good arm. And filthy and foul though he was, Lissie – gods bless her for the trust she showed in him, a trust he had done damned little to earn – made no demur about placing the blanket-wrapped bundle into his embrace.

Looking down into the chubby, contented face beneath the glimmering cap of fine fair hair, he could have wept under the tidal wave of conflicting emotion that swept over him.

Guilt.

Love.

Joy.

Pain.

Until, with only one thought left in his dazed mind, Ranulf looked up to find Lissie watching him with a soft smile of amusement, and in a tone only marginally less grim than the lingering expression in the bodyguard's brown eyes, he demanded,

"If my son is here, Lissie, with you, then where in all this damnable hell of my own making is your – *his* – mother?"

Afternoon

Once again Rowène was down by the river, this time trying to convince herself that now was the right time to tell Ranulf that they had a son.

She feared, from certain things he had said that last night at Vézière, that he would be neither pleased nor proud, and in consequence was uncertain whether he would want to honour the oath they had sworn and bound in blood, let alone acknowledge little Jacques as the child born of that informal binding.

If not, she would not press him, but rather care for her son herself, bringing him up as she had Lissie and Val, though hopefully she had learned from her mistakes and would keep no secrets from Jacques.

She had, however, made her brothers, and Gabriel, and Ranulf's brothers too, swear not to tell him about the child until she had had a chance to do so herself. And she must do it soon, before he found out from camp gossip.

At the same time she would remind him of what she had told him as they lay together in that moonlit chamber at Vézière.

That any child conceived, and born, of that coupling would be cherished – by her at least. And by her brothers too, given enough time for them to forget the circumstances of his conception.

Indeed, it would seem from Joscelin's words this morning that he already had, although when she had first arrived in the Mithlondian camp and confessed why she had found it necessary to leave the Healing House, his initial reaction had been to retreat into an icy cavern of frozen fury.

Luc had merely sighed and told their brother to let her stay.

To which Joscelin had retorted coldly that he had had no thought of turning their sister away, but that he would be hard pressed not take his fists or a blade to Ranulf did he stand before him at that moment.

Fortunately by the time he did, a year had gone by, and Joscelin's rage had burned to ash in the flames of fear for his own daughter, and the war was going badly enough that he needed Ranulf's fighting skills on his side rather than turned against him.

There was no telling how long Josce would hold his tongue however, now that they were all in the same small area... and always supposing that her brother survived today's fighting.

God of Mercy, she prayed, well aware of her selfishness. *Keep all those I love safe, and bring them back to me!*

The peace and quiet that had suffused the dew-wet meadow at dawn was long gone, replaced by the distant roar and rumble from the battle raging in the wide valley beyond the wooded hills to the northeast, and with the knowledge that the wounded would be brought in soon, and the opportunity to speak privately with Ranulf was shrinking with every swift-passing moment, Rowène rose to her feet in a mood of steely determination.

Only to step back in shock, barely catching herself before she stumbled into the river.

"What are *you* doing here?"

"I note you do not ask *who* I am?" the dark-haired youth replied.

"Hardly!" she snorted. "I can see very well who you are. You are," she finished without compliment. "Very much like your father in looks. Does he know you are here, by any chance?"

"No. I am here at my..." He smiled a little, making green lights glint in the deep brown of his eyes. "At *our* mother's request."

"And what does *she* want?" Rowène enquired, tendering not the slightest pretence of politeness to this half-brother she had rarely seen, even in the days before their mother had betrayed his father and left to ally her eldritch enchantments with the military might of the Emperor of the East.

"To speak with you. I am here to get you through the lines."

"No," she said baldly. "I will go nowhere with a treacherous whelp like you. Least of all to see *her.*"

"I think you will find," he said in the silky soft voice he must have learned at their mother's knee. "That you have no choice..."

His dark eyes openly mocking, he assessed her tattered grey robes and the man's shirt and breeches she wore beneath, before finishing with derisive emphasis,

"*Sister.*"

"Of course I have a choice," she retorted coldly.

Her heart, however, was fluttering with fear as she glanced around the grassy meadow.

While Joscelin's grey stallion, Gabriel's spotted gelding and Luc's black mare were of course gone, Flame and Rye remained and if she could reach either of them...

"Unfortunately for you, sister..."

Raoul hissed the words between his teeth as he reached out to grip her arm with the blunt and brutal force he had surely inherited from his father.

"I cannot allow you to do that. And I have enough men, ready and willing to stop you in any way they have to, should you get away from me."

She caught the shadow of movement in the grass beyond the two remaining horses at the same time as half a dozen soldiers in the unfamiliar mail of the Eastern Emperor's army stepped into view close beside her.

Without wasting time wondering how she could possibly have missed seeing them before, she opened her mouth to scream for Aelric to run for his own life.

All that emerged was a choked gasp as her half-brother's clenched fist struck her on the temple, and she felt herself falling into darkness. And this time neither Gabriel nor Ranulf were there to catch her.

"Where am I?"

"Do not worry, you are unharmed and quite safe," came the reply that told her nothing at all.

Dropping her gaze from the softly-billowing silken canopy over her head, Rowène stared in disbelief at the young man – youth really – who was standing nervously by the door flap of a tent that far exceeded in sheer opulent luxury anything she had ever encountered before, even in Kardolandia.

"I suppose I must take your word for that," she said in disgust, before shutting her eyes again, resting her aching head back on one of the many downy cushions upon which she was lying, just as a voice she recognised with a clear sense of disbelief, said caustically above her,

"Unharmed, you say? Safe! Gods above, Raoul! Why would you think we are such fools as to believe such arrant drivel. Or am I just imagining that the bruise on our sister's brow is the size of your fist?"

"Ju!"

Startled, Rowène opened her eyes again, blinking to bring the dark-haired woman sitting beside her into focus.

"You are here too?"

"Of course she is here," their half-brother snapped, his hold on his temper evidently as fragile as his father's – or his uncle's, for that matter. "She is as much my mother's daughter as you are."

Then turning to answer Juliène's scornful question, a hint of appeal creeping into his tone,

"I am your brother, why would I lie to you?"

"Our brother through the woman who has built her life on lies and treachery!" Rowène replied before her sister could speak. "A whore who would now wear an Empress' diadem. As for your de Rogé blood..."

"Do not speak against my father," Raoul snarled, red flaring across his broad cheekbones. "He has suffered as much as anyone from our mother's duplicity. And as for *my* being a de Rogé, I hardly think either of you is in a position to take umbrage. After all, if gossip is true, you – my sisters – have already damned yourselves to public shame by whoring with my de Rogé uncles! From all accounts, your lives and theirs have been inextricably entwined since before my birth, and you will just have to trust that I am telling you the truth now."

"I would as soon trust a poison-fang viper," Rowène retorted.

Feeling at a distinct disadvantage sprawled on the cushions, she struggled into a sitting position, even the pulsing ache above her eye not sufficient to distract from her surprise when Juliène put out a hand to help her, then retained that same steadying hold about her waist. Resisting the temptation to lean on her sister's shoulder, she saw Raoul cast a hasty, harried look around their golden silk prison.

"Listen to me," he said urgently. "Whatever you do, if you want to get out of here alive, do not dri..."

"Ah, here you all are!"

The satin-smooth, snowflake-soft voice had all three of them twitching where they sat or stood, their eyes flying towards the doorway where their mother had so silently appeared.

Gowned in cloth of silver sewn with seed pearls, beryls about her neck and wrists, her long hair blazing like the flames of dark fire, she was, gods help them, as beautiful as winter, and as deadly as ever.

Apparently perfectly at ease in the tense silence that followed her arrival, she regarded her gathered offspring for a dozen frozen heartbeats, the chilling smile curving her mouth momentarily melting into something warmer as she looked at Raoul.

"My handsome son, my..."

The ice-green eyes darted in delicate disgust towards Rowène – bruised and dishevelled, as she knew herself to be – thence to Juliène, resting there with a measure of approval.

"My one beautiful daughter..."

The cool, considering gaze returned to Rowène.

"And the one who has always looked, and behaved, more like a guttersnipe than one of the Faennari."

"If I offend you so much, Madame, I wonder that you had me brought here at all," Rowène replied, as steadily as she could for the erratic beating of her heart. "Certainly I would not have accepted your invitation did that misbegotten creature there give me no choice in the matter."

"And what then would you call that misbegotten creature you yourself gave birth to some three turnings of the moon ago? *His* father, I believe, is a de Rogé? The same man who sired your sister's son? Brother to the man who fathered your daughter? Well?"

Rowène remained silent, refusing to give her mother the satisfaction of confirming the shameful truth of her words.

"Goddess!" the ice-sharp voice snapped. "I cannot understand how I could give birth to two such worthless sluts, not to mention your even more worthless brother."

"Do not insult us by naming Raoul our brother," Rowène flashed back, for the merest lightning moment gaining the upper hand in the conversation.

"I did not..."

A flame of fury flared in those green eyes, then was doused to an icy chill as the Winter Lady said acidly,

"I was talking about that vile degenerate, that..."

"Luc? Is that who you mean? Now there is a man I am proud to call brother!" Rowène declared, recklessly interrupting the spate of venom.

"As am I."

Juliène's voice was shaky but determined, bolstered by the strength of her love for their brother.

And for the first time in a long time Rowène felt the old closeness with her sister, for she knew how much courage it had taken for Ju to defy their mother for Luc's sake.

The Winter Lady's reaction to this defiance was barely perceptible but it was there, the briefest hint of a frown deepening the faint lines that age and malice had finally begun to shade across their mother's seemingly eternal beauty.

"Then you are both fools!" she snapped. "And as unnatural as your accursed brother."

"That being so, I ask again why you had us brought here, Madame?" Rowène demanded.

"I *asked* you to come here, my daughters, to give you one last chance to join me in victory. The chance I first offered you fifteen years ago when you returned to Chartre from Kardolandia. Do you not see that we have come full circle?" Green eyes flickered with chilly contempt. "Or rather, I can see from the stupidly obdurate look on your faces that you do not appreciate my generosity."

"As little as I appreciated it fifteen years ago, Madame, when your scheming brought about my father's death as a traitor and much other unnecessary slaughter besides," Rowène replied. "But you are right in one matter. We *have* come full circle. For my father is now vindicated, his innocence of all wrong-doing publicly proclaimed and my brother restored to the title and lands that are rightfully his! Ah! I see you did not know of that! Perhaps, Madame, your powers are beginning to fail you in your old age!"

"I will *never* be old! For I have the power of the Faennari in my blood. I shall be acclaimed as consort to the Emperor of the East, and in time all the lands and people from Atarkarna in the north to Kardolandia in the south will make obeisance before me."

The words came as a sibilant hiss, and for a moment fury and an unacknowledged fear combined to render the lovely Lady Ariène both ugly and old.

"Not if the Emperor could see you now, the hag-ridden witch you truly are," Rowène retorted boldly, her trembling fingers hidden in the folds of her robe, to be unexpectedly discovered and taken in her sister's equally unsteady clasp.

Hands joined, united again with her twin at last, she waited for the raging ice-storm behind her mother's flashing eyes to break upon their heads.

Finally, just as she thought her shaking legs must give way, she saw her mother bring the lightning fire under control, smoothing the lines from her face with a palpable effort, until she was once more untouchable in all her fey beauty.

"The Emperor will see only that which I wish him to see," the Winter Lady said coldly. "As for you, my daughters, the moment of choice is upon you."

She turned to look at her son.

"Raoul, it is time! Bring the cups!"

He was back within moments, bearing a silver tray on which reposed three identical silver goblets studded with gems of green and white and carnelians as red as fire.

Rowène tightened her grip on Juliène's fingers, took a deep breath in an attempt to steady her fear, and said,

"What is this, Madame?"

"It is simple enough, child. So simple even you can understand it. Here are three cups. Three choices. Three chances. I do not tell you which is which, but here you may drink of victory... of life.... or death."

"And if we choose to drink from none of them?" Juliène whispered.

"Then I will choose for you, and pour it down your throat. I have only to call and men loyal to me will fill this tent, men who will have no qualms at forcing you to drink. Or yield in other ways."

Then, when neither Rowène nor her sister made reply, their mother laughed, the sound reminiscent of icicles sparkling in the winter sun, and said,

"Very well, perhaps I can find something that will help you make up your minds. Raoul, my scrying bowl!."

And when this had been set on the tray, with the goblets arranged around it, she continued commandingly,

"Come, Juliène, come closer and look into the water. Oh, and do not worry if you knock the goblets over and spill their contents. I have more than enough to refill them, until in the end you *will* choose, and you *will* drink."

Shaking visibly, Juliène approached the silver bowl, only to start back with a cry of horror.

"Oh, gods!"

She fell to her knees, sobbing wildly into her hands.

"No, please, no!"

With a wary glance at the marble-faced woman in the shimmering gown, Rowène knelt beside her sister, wrapping her arms around the shaking shoulders.

"What is it, Ju? What did you see?"

"Guyard! Surrounded by soldiers of the empire. In the very heart of the Mithlondian camp. Fighting to save Lissie and the other women in the healing tent from rape and death. Wounded as he is, he cannot last long! Oh, Ro, I cannot bear it."

"Ju, are you sure this is a true seeing, not just some fell trick? The sun is still high..."

"Oh, no, it is true enough," the Winter Lady assured them. "The moon waters cannot lie, even now, such is the strength of my power. So now, Juliène, what will you do? You once told me you would do anything to save Guyard de Martine's miserable life. And that was *before* you had shamed yourself by leaving your lawful lord to live as de Martine's leman. So what will you do to save his life *now*?"

"What... what can I do?" Juliène gasped. "He is outnumbered, wounded..."

"I can call off those who now surround him. If..."

"If what?"

"If you drink from the cup of life."

"What?" Juliène looked up in confusion. "You do not want my life for his?"

"What good would it do me if you were dead?" her mother mocked. "I want your power, feeble though it is, to join with mine. Of course, it also means that once you have yielded to me, you will be wholly in my power, but you will be alive. And even though you will never, ever see him again, you will know that your lover lives also."

"Very well."

Juliène lurched to her feet, hatred in her eyes, a rare determination hardening her bloodless face as commanded,

"Give me the cup."

"No, Ju! There has to be another way."

"No, Ro, there is not! I must do this. For Guyard. Surely you can understand that. Would you do otherwise if it were Ranulf's life in such peril?"

Rowène shook her head, her throat too tight to speak.

With tears in her eyes but determined to honour her sister's decision, she stood silently watching as Juliène raised the goblet her mother handed her to her lips, and drained it to the dregs. Shuddering, she wiped her mouth on her sleeve, the first sign of inelegance Rowène had ever seen in her dainty, beautiful sister, and demanded thickly,

"Now call off your curs."

The Winter Lady merely smiled and beckoned them both to watch as, at some unseen sign, a sword sliced through the water to shear through armour, linen, flesh and bone to impale the living heart of Guyard de Martine.

"*No! Goddess, no!*"

Such was the raw, piercing pain in the eldritch screech that flew from Juliène's white lips as to cause every man within hearing – Easterner, Atarkarnan or Mithlondian – to pause and shudder.

She was on her knees now, her sobbing wails so terrible to hear that Raoul clapped his hands over his ears, while Rowène simply stared in shock from her distraught sister to the wavering image in the scrying bowl, the crumpled body all but obscured by the drifting swirls of crimson now staining the water blood red.

She could not believe that Guy, her kinsman, her daughter's father, was... dead.

"No! Goddess, no!"

She found herself raggedly repeating her sister's plea, all the while aware that she too would have to make a choice. And soon.

"Calm yourself, Juliène!"

The Winter Lady's command was like the crack of ice.

"You have made your choice. Now you must live with it."

"Must I?"

Juliène raised a face ravaged with grief and hatred.

"But no, Madame, you are wrong! I *do* have one other choice left to me. And nothing you say or do can stop me from taking it."

With that, she brought her hand out of her purse, something clenched between her fingers.

Rowène caught the merest glimpse of glass and a thin red thread, before Juliène ripped it free with trembling fingers and raised the vial to her lips.

"I have carried this for a long time, Mother. Since the day you sent Guyard from me the first time. Now I put it to a far better use than any you intended."

"Stop her, Raoul!"

But even as he moved to obey their mother's command, stepping with appalled reluctance towards his kneeling sister, Rowène rose to her feet to block his path.

"No," she said fiercely. "This is her choice."

"Thank you, Ro," came her sister's brittle whisper.

A heartbeat later Rowène heard a horrifying choking sound, and although she would much rather not have looked, she forced herself to turn around, in time to see Juliène slump down onto the soft rug, eyes fluttering closed, the empty vial falling from her fingers.

She did not think Ju was dead, but clearly there was nothing that could stop that final end. All she could do was kneel and take her sister in her arms until she was gone.

Uncounted heartbeats later, Rowène took a deep breath and rose stiffly to her feet. Lifting her chin, she put all her grief-fuelled defiance into her eyes as she faced the woman she and her sister had called, with more truth than they had known, the Winter Lady.

"And what, Madame, do you intend to show me to force me to bow to your evil will?"

"How about your lover and your son?"

Not wanting to, but unable to forgo the chance of seeing Ranulf and Jacques one last time, she set her face to betray as little emotion as possible, and stepped up to the bowl, seeing the water clear again.

And then... there was something else there, just beneath the surface, the images small, distant but perfect in every detail.

For long, endless, heart-breaking moments she watched Ranulf as he wandered through the sunlit meadow, his long light hair loose upon his shoulders, lifting on the summer breeze, then falling back to brush with thistledown softness against the baby held in the crook of his good arm.

And as he gazed down upon their son the look of tender adoration in those dark blue eyes – a look she had never thought to see – gave her the courage to take the next step.

Because, like Ju, she would do anything to keep those whom she loved safe.

Even knowing she could not trust the Winter Lady to keep her side of any bargain, she had to take the chance... any chance... that Ranulf might live to see their son grow to manhood.

"So which cup is mine?" she asked flatly, gesturing at the two remaining goblets flanking the scrying bowl.

"This one," the Winter Lady said, smiling. "The cup of death. Your death that they may live."

"A fair enough bargain," Rowène agreed. "And may the Goddess curse you to everlasting darkness if you do not keep your word."

Taking the goblet, she did not give herself time to think, but drained the bitter liquid, even as it made her belly revolt with its insidious cold. Striving not to retch, she held herself upright and refused to drop her gaze from the Winter Lady's amused appraisal.

"It is a slow poison," her mother informed her. "But there is nothing in five realms that will stop it from doing its work."

Then turning away as if her dying daughters were no longer of any interest to her, she reached for the one remaining goblet.

The cup of victory.

With a soft smile that for once held no shadow of ice but spoke only of love, she looked at her last-born son.

"For us, Raoul! May the Goddess bring us victory, swift and sure."

Raoul muttered something under his breath, his dark brown eyes unreadable as he watched his mother for endless moments. Until with the glitter of triumph lending her green gaze the brilliance of moon-shot crystal she placed the empty goblet back onto the tray.

"There, it is done! Come, my son."

She held one white hand out towards him, only to have him take a step back, his face pale.

"No."

"What do you mean, no? This is..."

She broke off, her beringed fingers rising to clutch at her throat, her eyes widening... darkening... as she stared in disbelief at the youth.

"What... what have you done?"

And when he did not answer, merely returned her horrified look with hatred clear to see in his narrowed, green-flecked eyes, she gave vent to a terrible moan.

"I loved you, Raoul! The only one of my children I truly loved. Everything I did... it was for you."

"No! You never loved me. You smothered me. And whatever you did, it was for your own glory. You were the one who wanted to be consort to an Emperor, to wield power beyond belief. And for that you destroyed *their* father..."

He gestured wildly at Juliène's crumpled body and Rowène's frozen one.

"You destroyed their father, *and* mine, and have done your best to do likewise by my half-brother, who is a decent man. And now you have killed my sisters, and sent assassins after their children, *my kin*, leaving me cold and empty and alone. As I have always been."

"And as you always will be," she sneered, swaying but venomous to the end. "What will you do now? Matricide!"

"I am what you have made me," he scowled, his black de Rogé brows meshing over dark eyes that yet held a hint of fey green.

"As to what I may become, whatever that is, for good or ill, you, Madame, will not be here to see it."

"Do not think my power will end just because I am gone from your sight? Fool! By the time this day is done there will be none left of the cursed de Chartreux blood-line! Those assassins you spoke of? Even now they are seeking out your sisters' children. At my order. But it is in *your* name that they will kill them, so that the name of Raoul de Rogé will be reviled throughout Mithlondia, just as your father's has been all these years."

Raoul looked even more shaken by this barb but managed one last flash of bravado.

"Even so, Madame, I will take my chance. My Uncle Ranulf managed to rise above the vile reputation he earned in his youth. So will I. Or die trying. And in the spirit of that, I am taking my sisters back to the Mithlondian lines. That they may at least be with those they love at the end. And then... then, Madame, I am going to find my father."

He took a deep, unsteady breath.

"As for you, Madame, I curse you to shrivel and rot into a toothless, powerless, mumbling old hag, condemned to the outermost reaches of Hell for all eternity."

With that he knelt and taking Juliène's limp, slender form into his arms, struggled to his feet with a grunt – he was only a lad after all, not yet grown into the broad-shouldered strength of his father and uncles – and walked towards the doorway without once looking back.

Rowène, stumbling slightly on already numbing feet, *did* look back. And shuddered.

It was as if Raoul's curse had already come into effect.

As if even the Moon Goddess whom Ariène had professed to serve, had turned away from her, taking away the powers of enchantment the Winter Lady had wielded for so long.

So that what lay crumpled on the floor no longer resembled in any way the bewitchingly beautiful Faennari she had seemed for so long.

Instead, all that could be seen was the cursed, wrinkled, soulless hag she was in truth.

Sunset

Only in the last ribbons of sunlight at the end of that Midsummer's Day did Rowène find the man she had been searching for.

He was lying within the shadow of the solitary oak tree – the reason she had not seen him immediately, her eyes being dazzled by the bright banners of gold and bronze and blood-crimson drowning in the nearby river, set there by the light of the setting sun.

He was surrounded by the bodies of those he had fought, and slain. Black-garbed imperial assassins, whose corpses Beowulf and Edwy were now unceremoniously dragging away. And while it was clear that most of the Eastern men had perished by means of the bloody sword now lying just beyond reach of Ranulf's outstretched hand, two at least of the crumpled corpses had the black-fletched, poison-tipped arrows of Atarkarna sunk deep in their purpling flesh.

Hard though Ranulf had fought, one of the Easterners must have broken through his weakened guard – his injured shield arm now little more than a bloody mess – to inflict a series of devastating wounds before making his escape, leaving Ranulf to lie where he had fallen.

Sinking down onto the blood-soaked grass, Rowène lifted his head onto her lap, combing her fingers through his hair, touching trembling fingertips to cheeks that yet held the faintest remnant of warmth beneath the pale gold shadow of stubble.

He was alive, but barely, his bloody lips forming her name as she bent to kiss them, salt tears mingling with the taste of iron in her mouth.

Yet even as he turned his head as if to look up at her, she knew he could not see her, his dark blue eyes slashed across, bloody and blind.

"I knew... when I said farewell to you that morning at Vézière that I would never... see you again," he whispered, his voice barely distinguishable from the dry rattle of the evening breeze through the reeds along the river bank.

"But you can hear me, Ranulf? And feel me? Please say you can feel me here with you."

His lips twitched in a smile reduced by pain to a mere grimace.

"I can feel you, beloved. And smell the roses in your hair."

Incredibly, she felt his free hand – the one she was not clasping so tightly – the hand she had thought useless and crippled, fumbling for the confining folds of her headrail. Sensing his need and the determination that drove him to reach through his pain, she ripped away the linen cloth, tore the bindings from her braids and shook her hair down so that the long waving strands brushed against his searching hand, the blood-wet fingers tightening around the dark fiery locks he would never see again, drawing them closer to his face.

Her hair, she was sure, stank of death, not roses, but Ranulf seemed content.

"Look after our son when I am gone," he said. "And remember always that I loved you, my beautiful sea-fey. As I will continue to love you through all the countless reaches of eternity that we must be apart."

"Oh, gods! Ranulf, wait! I..."

She heard the rattling breath she had learned to dread... felt him sigh and still... even as she finished brokenly,

"I love you, heart of my heart... Always."

How long she wept – softly, but from the very depths of her shattered soul – she did not know. It felt like forever. But forever was yet to come...

At last she looked up, to see the tear-blurred shapes of Edwy and Beowulf straightening from laying two new burdens, these clad in leather and Mithlondian blue, on the ground within the long shadow of the oak tree. Scrubbing at her tears, she recognised the two Chartreux lads that the Rogé men had brought so tenderly to lie alongside their fallen companions as Aelric and Jarec of Anjélais.

God of Mercy, they are both so young. Certainly, too young to die.

She bowed her head again, her tears washing some of the blood from the hand she still clasped between her own. Until something, some quality in the silence around her, made her look up again to see a familiar spear-slender figure walking slowly towards her, his long light brown hair flickering with bronze fire in the dusk-gold light, his glittering eyes meeting hers over the lifeless body he carried in his arms.

The body of the man who, she knew without the need for words, had stepped between certain death and the man he loved.

So now, with the fighting done for the day and dusk falling all around them, they were gathering together, one last time, both the living and the slain, blessed by the gods with the last light of the dying sun, caressed by the goddess with the first rising radiance of the Midsummer night's moon.

Here lay Aelric and Jarec, Juliène and Guy, Ranulf, and Luc beside him.

And then there were the living.

Gabriel, golden eyes blank with grief as he knelt at the side of the man who had been part of his life almost as long as he could remember, and whom he had loved as foster-brother, friend and simply the man himself.

Adèle, standing as close to Gabriel as she dared, looking as always as if she wished to touch him, to hold him, to remind him that she loved him too, but unwilling to disturb the darkness that held him to the exclusion of all else, taking instead what small comfort she could from the child in her arms, Gabriel's son Aurélien.

Nearby, Gwynny stood weeping quietly for those she had loved and lost this grim day, as she had already lost so many from her life, Anne her friend, Ancalion her brother, Hilarion the man she had loved. Thank the gods she still had the children to make her life worth living, else Rowène feared for her sanity.

Then there was Lady Céline, still clad in healer's grey, standing close beside Linette. The princess had baby Marc held against her shoulder, while Lilia had pressed herself against the tall form of her half-brother, her tear-streaked face hidden in the folds of his filthy tunic until suddenly Dominic bent and caught her up in his arms, holding her so that she need not see the distressing scene, one hand tentatively smoothing her tumbled curls, offering what comfort he could.

And finally, Joscelin. Dropping down from his horse to stumble into the circle gathered around his fallen kin, his guarded grey eyes for once expressing his every emotion.

Kneeling in turn by the bodies of his sister... his kinsman... the two young men who had given their lives under his command... his sword-brother... and finally his brother. Taking his own farewell of them with touch or kiss. Then rising to his feet he returned to his own small family, almost absently reaching out to draw Linette into the curve of his mailed arm.

Seeing his shattered grey gaze finally settle on her, Rowène managed a smile for him, her one surviving brother, knowing that if he guessed at the icy progress of the poison through her body he would be beside her immediately, his arms about her, desperately trying to hold the numbing chill at bay with the warmth of his own body.

While she yearned for his strength, she knew his place now was with the mother of his children. And so she smiled her love for him, knowing in her heart that long life – and happiness, she hoped – lay before him, regardless of whatever battles – whether against the Easterners, the Atarkarnans or their own High Counsel – remained to be fought.

As it was, she had no idea how this day's fighting had gone, whether they had won, or lost, or merely brought their enemies to a standstill...

Then, out of the evening mist that had begun to rise from the nearby river to enfold them all, stepped the figure of the last man Rowène would have expected to see so close to the Mithlondian camp. A man she assumed from the golden crown encircling his tall helm, and the jewelled pommel to his great sword, to be the Emperor of all the East.

Even more surprisingly, he came to a halt at Joscelin's side, moonlight glinting off the narrow silver fillet he held in his hand.

This he handed to Joscelin with a brief inclination of his head that spoke of respect if nothing else, followed by a sweeping open-handed gesture in the direction of the battleground and then another from the circlet to Joscelin himself, who looked about as disconcerted as Rowène had ever seen him, whilst the Emperor simply faded back into the shadows now fluttering like dark banners at the edges of her sight as if he had never been there at all.

Except Joscelin was still holding the royal circlet of the rulers of Mithlondian in his hands.

Linnius must have been discovered dead upon the field, she guessed, the realm now left without a ruler or a legitimate heir... those few who yet carried the royal blood of Mithlondia all to be found within that grassy meadow. Neither choice would bring anything other than turmoil and division within the High Counsel but there was no other way forward, and Rowène saw the moment when her dazed brother came to that same conclusion.

Even as she watched, Joscelin's face hardened into its normal unreadable mask, and just for a moment she thought he was going to throw the circlet into the shadow-streaked river. A lifetime of duty and self-control coming to his aid, he turned instead to Linette and placed the silver circlet gently upon her startled brow, before dropping down on one knee before her to kiss her hand and, as Lord of Veraux and High Commander of her armies, formally swear allegiance to the Princess of Mithlondia.

It was enough to make Rowène weep, had she not already wept all the tears that were in her at the knowledge that Ranulf was truly gone from her.

Fifteen years. That was all the time they had been granted, from first meeting to final farewell, their few fleeting moments together shining like silver roses, solitary moments plucked from the hands of the gods, their love beginning and ending on the barbs of cruel, blood-tipped thorns.

If only she could have been sure Ranulf had heard her when she told him she loved him, before he had taken those first steps along the sunset path. A path along which she could not follow him, not when the rising moon was already laying down its light across the darkening river.

That was the road she must take, and sensing how very few moments were left to her Rowène glanced up at the three she most grieved to leave behind.

Lissie, her beautiful daughter, valiantly trying to smile her love through the silent tears that slipped down her face to fall onto baby Jacques' sleeping head.

Goddess! She was so young to be left with the care of her little brother – the son Rowène had known for so short a time, yet loved so much – but Gwynhere – loving, loyal Gwynny – would help her, Rowène was sure.

As would Val... perhaps. Even now, when he was standing so close to Lissie that their shoulders were touching, he still managed to hold himself aloof from the child in her arms, the baby who was brother to them both.

Val looked adrift, alone, but above all else, angry. Though whether at his father or himself, Rowène could not tell. All she knew was that she could do no more for him, this boy she had loved as her own son.

The task of healing, if he were to be healed at all and become the man he was supposed to be, lay with Lissie.

For it was clear now – clear as moonlight itself – that it was Val and Lissie who were the harper and healer of Gabriel's foretelling.

Whether Lissie would be able to heal her cousin, to overcome his anger, and the animosity he displayed for the baby brother they had in common, was another matter. And if she did succeed, it would be a long and hard healing, for the boy had his father's black temper, his feelings made even more fierce by his own sense of guilt.

He had, gods knew, tried to talk to Ranulf, to apologise, to tell him that he loved him, kneeling there in the blood-splattered grass, the Atarkarnan hunting bow discarded by his side, the blood-slick fingers of his father's sword hand gripped hard between his own.

But it was too late, as Rowène knew only too well, the warmth of Ranulf's skin offering the merest illusion of life, the wreck of his shield hand clasped in fingers that were themselves beginning to lose all sensation as the Winter Lady's fell poison slid like shards of ice through her blood, numbing every limb on its journey to her heart, and when it reached there...

Or perhaps it already had.

As from the farthest reaches of the starlit sky, she heard Val's grief-ravaged voice, half-speaking, half-singing, the softly plucked notes of the harp in his hand a poignant accompaniment to his words.

What was it that he was singing?

Something about the rain falling upon his face?

Yet there were no clouds in the clear teal-green evening sky, so perhaps it was not the cool grey rain reminiscent of her brother's eyes of which he sang, but rather the tears sparkling like moonlit crystal on Lissie's pale cheeks, on Joscelin's dark lashes, in Gabriel's amber eyes, in Val's own shattered glass-green gaze.

From somewhere closer, perhaps even as close as her heart, she sensed that Gabriel was speaking, all lightness gone from his voice, buried beneath his raw agony.

The same words, more or less, that he had spoken that night at Vézière as he lay in Luc's arms under the rising light of another midsummer moon.

"Thus comes the day when the sun sets over a field of blood, and the Moon Goddess walks on silver feet amongst the living and the slain. When a harper and a healer stand together within her light.

And with the healing done and the last harp song sung... *now* is it finished."

Dimly she realised that she was still holding Ranulf's cooling fingers between her own, unable to let go, even knowing that he had already gone from her.

As Luc had already gone far beyond Gabriel's reach, half-fey though he was.

"Ré!"

One word to tell him that she felt, and shared, his pain.

Whilst he, of all her friends and kinsmen, would be the only one able to see what was happening behind her own outwardly normal appearance.

Indeed he was looking at her now with an intensity he rarely showed anyone voluntarily, his citrine-yellow eyes shadowed by thick bronze lashes, glittering with tears.

"Do not worry about me," he murmured. "I always knew this day would come. But I wish to the stars that I had been wrong about the rest of it."

He reached out with his free hand and ran long, unsteady fingers through Luc's blood-matted, moon-silvered hair in silent benediction, then looked across at the other still bodies, the silence of the encroaching night broken only by the long, mournful call of a wraith owl.

"Though in the end," he said softly. "It was not quite right. That foretelling. This is not the end for *them*."

His gaze flicked around the circle of kneeling figures.

"For Josce and Linette, Lilia and Marc, for Lissie and Val and little Jacques – the song *will* go on."

"And for you and Adèle too," Rowène reminded him, and saw him smile, more than a little wryly, but at least it was a smile. "For Aurélien, and any who come after him."

"At least one more," he said, gold and citrine and amber all swirling together in the depths of his distant gaze. "A girl, I think."

He blinked and allowed himself to smile at her again.

"We will call her Rowena."

She managed to return his smile, then feeling her strength beginning at last to fail her, slipping away like the sea-bound tide across the glistening grey pebbles of Black Rock Cove, she struggled to finish what she wanted – needed – to say.

"Ré, please... tell Josce, and Lissie and Val, that I love them."

"I will," he promised. "Jacques too when he is old enough to understand. And I give you my word I will watch over them all as far as they will let me, although..."

His finely-shaped lips lifted in rueful amusement.

"Although I have the feeling that Val will not make it easy for me."

"No, I do not suppose he will," she agreed softly. "He is too much his father's son for that."

Goddess help her, she could scarcely see any of them now through the swirling, silver-shot mist, and it was only Gabriel's golden gaze that was tethering her there, holding the poison at bay.

She swallowed icy shards that pierced her throat, and through the pain tried to smile for him one last time.

"I know you wish you had not been right about any of it, especially Luc, but for him, for Guy and Ju, Rafe and I... the last harp song, *our song*, has indeed been sung. And this is... oh, gods, Ré, this is..."

She stopped, unable to go on, as the goddess reached out with gentle, guiding hands.

Just as Gabriel gathered her into his arms.

"I know, Ro, I know. But Luc is waiting for you beyond the mist. Go now with our love to light your way."

"Ré!"

She could see him no longer.

Only through the mist, shimmering silver, glimmering gold, all the radiant colours of the rainbow bridging the endless emptiness between the mortal lands and the star-bright meadows of night, she *felt* the warmth of his lips, sweet as dew-soaked clover, as he whispered a brother's kiss across her brow, and his voice, soft as midsummer rain, was the last thing she heard.

"Until we meet again, in the meadows beyond the moon."

But for her and Ranulf, there would be no second chance.

For them, this was the thorniest of all truths.

This was, and for ever would be...

Farewell

EPILOGUE

THE MEADOWS BEYOND THE MOON

The mist had lifted whilst she had been sleeping, and as she awoke, Rowène looked around with a curiosity bordering on disbelief.

Before her the meadow was empty, even the horses no longer grazed amongst the buttercups and cuckoo flowers, the shadow of the oak tree lying long across the untrammelled grass, while the small, shallow stream had widened and deepened into a serene river, now spanned by a bridge of mellow yellow stone that had definitely not been there when she had fallen asleep in Gabriel de Marillec's arms.

Apparently the bridge marked a parting of the ways, one path crossing the bridge and heading west into the heart of a sunset more dazzlingly glorious than any she had ever seen before, while the other path followed the river on the near side, leading eastwards towards the rising moon.

And this path... this was the way that she must travel.

Knowing this, knowing too that Ranulf had gone on before her, taking the other way that led across the bridge, she could not help but look for him further along that sunset path.

He was nowhere in sight but she could see two young men she did know, ambling along the path, Aelric with his arm slung companionably around his brother's shoulder, amiably arguing some point or other with Jarec, and in spite of her disappointment that it was not the man she longed to see, one last time, she smiled at seeing the brothers reunited.

As if sensing her gaze, they turned and waved, before continuing on their way together.

As would Ranulf and Guy be together too, she assured herself. Somewhere beyond that strangely familiar bridge where she lingered, able to look beyond but not to pass over.

Far away in the distance rose a great cliff of cloud, whereon stood a many towered castle, apricot and peach and amber, lit from behind by a wondrous gloriole, its gossamer windows looking out onto golden forests of misty trees and the glimmering waves of a sun-gilded sea.

There would be found Lord Gilles and his three sons, Ancalion, Hilarion and Jacques, united at last. Her father too, and Lucien, perhaps strolling the wall walks or riding the sea shore.

And there, in some beautiful, wild garden of lavender and chamomile and thyme, hung all about with honeysuckle and roses, the Lady Rosalynde herself would be working. Grandmère Anne would like that garden, Rowène mused, and perhaps Guy's mother, Lady Alys, walked there too, as she waited for her son. Even now, did they lift their heads, one dark, one fair, as they heard the footsteps of their sons, and Rowène could not help but wonder whether the gentle, dark-haired lady she had occasionally seen in her dreams would be proud of the men those two boys whom she had loved so much had grown into.

Rowène hoped so, for it had been a long, hard path that Ranulf had walked since his mother's death.

With a sigh she brought gaze back to the river, where seven white swans glided with exquisite grace along the dark blue water.

Water that was the same colour as Ranulf de Rogé's eyes.

He should, she thought wistfully, be waiting for her here. Leaning against the bridge, booted feet crossed at the ankle, arms folded across his chest, his shoulder-length pale hair ruffled by the evening breeze and lit by the sunset light to pure gold.

Except – and it hurt her heart more than she cared to admit – he was not there, and there would be no final farewell for them.

Nevertheless, she whispered it anyway,

Farewell, Beloved. I will see you amongst the stars.

For surely the shining souls of all those others who had already crossed that golden bridge must soon reveal themselves in the dusk-blue depths of the eternal reaches of the midnight sky?

In the meantime there was no point in lingering any longer there at the parting of the ways. So with one last look, she yielded to the force drawing her along the river bank towards the silver moon, the white swans sailing silently down the river beside her.

She had expected to walk into darkness as soon as she left the bridge and the sunset path behind, but though the brilliance of that last sunburst had receded into dusk and she was now headed towards a range of shadowy hills shrouded in the more sombre hues of night, there was still colour a-plenty to delight the eye if not lift her sorrow.

Here a flash of red and green revealed a woodpecker... there a fan of blue and green showed her a peacock's vibrant plumage, while bright butterflies of orange and yellow fluttered in delicate dance all around her.

The evening sky was alive with birds... soaring, diving, darting, fluttering. Swallows, finches, linnets, jays... wagtails doing their bobbing dance on the path before her.... blackbirds and thrushes competing to sing the sweetest song.

And everywhere there were flowers. Lupins and lavender, tall hollyhocks and tiny violets, gillyflowers, roses, mallow, marigolds, and so many, many more, weaving a seemingly endless carpet of colour and scent.

It was only much later – how much later, she did not know, time having no measure in this place, wherever and whatever it was – she noticed the colours about her were fading into the quieter shades of cream, meadowsweet and elderflower, the paler gold of primroses, the soft white froth of ladies lace.

The animals too were becoming more muted in hue.

She saw a small spotted deer cross the path with a white flash of tail... glimpsed a brown hedgehog busy snuffling amongst the fallen leaves of an oak tree... a tawny owl perched just above her in the branches of a silvery beech.

At some point in her journey the path turned away from the stream, meandering instead through endless fields of ripe, rustling barley the colour of her beloved's hair, patched here and there with swatches of blood-red poppies.

Not wishing to be reminded of the way Ranulf's hair had been matted and splattered with his own lifeblood, she was not sad when the pathway left the fields, bringing her to a long avenue of giant linden trees, so tall their topmost leaves seemed able to caress the arching blue of the sky above.

Taking a breath, she entered the gently whispering shadows, the dappled light beneath the great branches weaving a lazy serenity, undisturbed by the hypnotic humming of bees busy among the delicate golden flowers. Flowers that gradually become paler and paler... until at the farthest end of the avenue the petals no longer glimmered of gold but rather of silver, the woodbells in the grass at the feet of the mighty trees spreading a haze of white, not blue.

Finally emerging into the open meadow beyond the linden avenue, she found herself surrounded by the moonlit darkness she had always expected to find at the end of this path, night descending softly all around her, the stars in their familiar formations lighting the lavender sky above.

Looking up, she found her father's star, though not alas the two she truly sought.

Still, obscurely comforted by the thought that she was not alone she returned her gaze to the pathway and found that she was no longer alone in truth, having in the interim acquired a companion.

A most welcome companion indeed... in the form of a small, very familiar, pale grey cat who slipped soundlessly out of the shadowy dew-silvered grass to keep her company.

Mist!

Kneeling, she gently rubbed the little cat behind its ears, smiling at the resultant purr of pleasure as the animal butted her hand in affectionate greeting.

At last though she rose to her feet and set off again, Mist stepping daintily beside her, so close that her tail occasionally brushed against Rowène's knee. And with company, the journey seemed suddenly easier, though no less long.

Until, finally, just as Rowène was beginning to wonder if she must wander forever, she came to a place she half thought she should recognise.

A meadow where blue and silver butterflies flitted lightly between star flowers and moon daisies, plants which she had never before seen growing in the same place now flourishing together in wild abundance beneath thorn trees taller than any she had ever seen... save once, long ago, in a half-remembered, half-forgotten dream.

That odd sense of homecoming growing upon her, she glanced up at the clusters of fragrant thorn blossoms, the branches bearing them being twined all about with vines of white roses and the palest of golden honeysuckle, whilst even farther above her head unseen larks sang in that odd silvery-blue sky.

And just as in her dream, a cuckoo was calling from the oak trees now gradually emerging from the gossamer mist that still veiled the more distant view, and she knew not only where she was... but that she had finally arrived where she was meant to be.

For this was the place where harp song met myth... the eternal meadows beyond the moon, realm of the Moon Goddess and the fabled Faennari.

Taking a deep breath, Rowène took a step forwards, and then another, walking slowly towards the stream and the single, solitary oak tree she could see there, forerunner of others still half wreathed in drifting shrouds of moon-silvered mist.

Only to stumble to a dazed stop at the sight of the man who walked silently out of the mist to stand before her.

A man with long, raven-dark hair and laughing grey eyes.

A man who was, to her further bewilderment, carrying a child in his arms.

A man who looked like her brother and who, she was utterly relieved to hear, sounded like her brother when he spoke.

"Ro, what took you so long?"

"Luc?!"

"Why so surprised? My blood is the same as yours, after all, and besides Ré told you I would be waiting, did he not?"

"Yes, but..."

She did not seem able to get past that singularly doubting word, and evidently seeing her glance first over her shoulder, back along the path she had just travelled, then all around her, he added,

"No, Ré is not here. He will be along when it is his time, and as you should know, that time is not yet. But I sensed that you would be here soon and so I kept watch for you. And look who I found whilst I was waiting... or rather, I should say, she found me."

She heard, but paid little heed to Luc's words, her wondering gaze unable to concentrate on anything save the change that had taken place in her brother's appearance since she had last seen him.

His long hair, restored once more to a shining midnight-black, save for the glimmer of starlight at his temples, framed a lean face that was unlined and luminously handsome. Moreover, he was smiling at her confusion in gentle amusement as if this was the most natural meeting.

Which, she supposed it was, save for...

She tilted her head, staring at the little girl waiting quietly in his arms.

"You said... she found you? Are you saying that you... have a child? That she is yours?"

Her repeated astonishment was, she realised, more than a little unflattering.

Luc seemed to take no offence, instead throwing his head back and laughing out loud, carefree as she had not seen him in years.

"Hardly," he said. "With hair like that!"

And even in the misty half-light, she could see that the child – she seemed about two years old – had hair that more closely resembled moon-bleached barley in colour than a raven's glossy plumage.

"Goddess! Is she..."

She stopped, unable to contemplate the possibility, her gaze flickering upwards towards the stars, seeking the one that had been there for the past fifteen years but which was now missing.

"Ah! You see it now," Luc said lightly, the laughter in his grey eyes dimming somewhat as he added, "Yes, this is child you never told me about. And I can guess why."

But before she could say anything in protest or explanation, his tone softened again as he looked down at the little girl in his arms,

"She tells me her name is Fleur, and she has been waiting for her mama for a long time now."

Instinctively holding out her arms for the child – for Fleur – Rowène could not help but notice that even in this fey realm, Luc still seemed disinclined to give Ranulf any credit for paternal feelings.

Then she saw that her brother was smiling again.

In truth, grinning would not be too outrageous a description of his knowing expression.

"What?" she asked, refusing to allow irritation to darken her bitter-sweet joy in finally holding the child she had lost so long ago.

"It is not just Fleur who has been waiting for you," Luc informed her with a quirk of his narrow, level brows.

"Ju? She is here?"

Still intent on the little girl in her arms, it was the most absent of questions, answering herself in a similarly distracted fashion.

"Well, so she would be, she left before I did."

"Of course Ju is here," Luc agreed, still grinning. "And not alone as you can see."

He waved a casual hand towards the oak trees.

And when Rowène spared a single, swift, disinterested glance in that direction, she saw that there were indeed several shadowy forms standing in the subdued starlight with her sister.

Dividing a vague smile between Luc and Juliène, Rowène returned her bemused attention to Fleur, who having spotted the little cat was now wriggling to get down.

Still not quite believing the gift she had been given, Rowène dared not take her eyes off Fleur as the little girl knelt beside the translucent animal, one tiny hand stroking the soft fur, neither child nor cat seeming quite real, both of them glowing like pearls in the misty moonlight.

As it was, with her hair sliding over her shoulders like a waterfall of silver light and her eyes of dark mysterious amethyst, Fleur seemed every bit as insubstantial as the reflected shimmer of starshine in a mountain pool, as dainty and delicate as the starflower of her name.

"Do not worry, Ro."

Evidently sensing her sudden, and perfectly reasonable fear, Luc's deep voice, still rippling with amusement, sounded behind her.

"I must admit I thought as you do at first, but I can assure you, she will not vanish. She – or rather her soul – is as real as you or I."

"Thank the goddess," she murmured.

For Fleur.

And for giving me something of Ranulf to keep close to my heart through the long ages of eternity.

Not just the child, Rowène.

Against all expectation the answering voice spoke in her head.

Except... Goddess!

That had not been her brother's low voice. Nor even Gabriel's.

Just as familiar, of course.

Just as beloved. If not more so.

But impossible all the same.

Light as honed steel, holding the faintest edge of something that brought back a myriad memories.

Of moonlight and Marillec wine...

The scent of chamomile...

The touch of rough linen and tender hands, and a thousand other things...

Surely it could not be... not *here!*

She turned, heartsick with fear that she had been mistaken, the victim of some cruel illusion...

"No jest," the man now facing her assured her, a wry smile in his dark blue eyes.

Eyes she had last seen bloodied and blinded, now blessedly whole again, the long hair tumbling over his shoulders as pale a shade of silver-fair as his daughter's, gleaming faintly in the fey light.

He *looked* like the man she loved and had thought lost to her forever, and yet... not entirely.

For while this was indeed the reflection of Ranulf de Rogé as she had first seen him, the sardonic glint in his eyes had been replaced by a rueful amusement, the hard line of his mouth softened into tenderness.

How...

"By the unlooked-for grace of the goddess," he answered her unspoken question aloud. "As to why..."

He glanced around, then shrugged.

"Perhaps she simply has a soft heart for damned, mismatched lovers."

Something in his voice... some fleeting, flashing thought, like a goldfinch taking flight... made her peer again, with rather more attention this time, into the shadows of the moonlit meadow now opening out behind his shoulder, and was rewarded by the sight of Juliène's dark head very close to Guy's fair one... before dismissing both her sister and Ranulf's brother from her thoughts.

Time enough!

For now she was concerned with only one man, and she brought her gaze back quickly, more than half expecting him to have slipped back into the mists of memory and wishful thinking.

Only to find him still there and reassuringly solid, despite the starlight shimmering all about him.

"Well, here I am, in a place I never, ever thought to be," he said, something of her own disbelief edging his voice. "And here I will stay..."

Uncharacteristically he hesitated, a heart-shaking uncertainty slipping into his eyes and voice.

"If... if you will have me, Rowène?"

"Surely you need not ask that?" she replied, as with tears of happiness rising to her eyes, she finally dared to accept that he was truly there, and that they would be together with the child they had made and lost, right back at the very beginning of their tale.

"I thought you knew by now," she added softly. "I *love* you, Ranulf."

"As I love you, Rowène. Heart of my heart. Always."

With no further words needed – questions, explanations, they could all wait – she returned his smile, and walking into his open arms lifted her mouth for his kiss.

With the scent of chamomile surrounding her once more, she made two discoveries.

First, that he tasted as he had done that misty morning at Chartre.

Of Marillec wine.

Blackberries and honey, tart and sweet, the heady strength guarding a subtle tenderness at its heart.

Not seeing the gentleness in either wine or man, she had hated them both.

Now...

Now, when she loved him, she thought she could drink the wine of his kisses forever...

And in all Truth,
here in the Meadows beyond the Moon,
Forever was what they had.

22249086R00440

Printed in Great Britain
by Amazon